D1438797

THE OXFORD LIBRARY OF
SHORT NOVELS

THE
OXFORD LIBRARY OF
Short Novels

Chosen and Introduced by
JOHN WAIN

Volume III
Mann to McCullers

GUILD PUBLISHING LONDON
1990

This edition published 1990 by
Guild Publishing
by arrangement with Oxford University Press

Introduction and selection © John Wain 1990

CN 2127

Set by Selectmove Limited
Printed in Great Britain by
Richard Clay Ltd, Bungay, Suffolk

Contents

Acknowledgements

Albert Camus, *L'Étranger*, © 1942, Éditions Gallimard. This translation copyright © 1946. Reprinted by permission of Hamish Hamilton Ltd.

Anton Chekhov, *My Life*, from *The Oxford Chekhov*, Vol. 8, *Stories 1895–1897*, translated and edited by Ronald Hingley, © Ronald Hingley 1965, reprinted by permission of Oxford University Press.

Colette, *Chéri*, translated by R. Stenhouse, reprinted by permission of Martin Secker & Warburg Ltd.

Carson McCullers, *The Member of the Wedding*, reprinted by permission of Barrie & Jenkins Ltd.

Thomas Mann, *Death in Venice*, translated by T. H. Lowe-Porter, reprinted by permission of Martin Secker & Warburg Ltd.

Thomas Mann

DEATH IN VENICE

1912

THOMAS MANN (1875–1955) came of a prosperous, ultra-respect-able family in Lübeck, and worked in a bank before becoming first a writer of short stories and then of novels. This background is evident in his choice of themes during the earlier phase of his work; *Buddenbrookes* (1901) chronicles the decline of a respected Lübeck family through four generations, and *Tonio Kruger* and *Tristan* both dramatize the tension between the values of the bourgeois and those of the artist. *Death in Venice* brings into even sharper focus the incompatibility of a life devoted to imaginative creativity with the solid virtues of respectable society.

Thomas Mann supported the action of the German Government in going to war in 1914 (thus causing a lifelong rift with his novelist brother Heinrich, who was a dedicated pacifist) but very little that happened subsequently in Germany met with his approval. He was in sympathy with the efforts of the Weimar Republic to set up a liberal democracy, but when this collapsed into the Nazi regime in 1933, Mann, who happened at the time of Hitler's seizure of power to be in Switzerland, did not return home, and in 1936 publicly dissociated himself from the Nazis in a statement issued through a Zürich newspaper and given wide international publicity. Since by that time he was a world celebrity and the holder of the Nobel prize for literature (1929), the rebuke to Hitler was as severe as could have been administered by one individual; the official response was to deprive Mann of his German identity. He accepted the offer of Czech nationality but, fortunately in view of what was going to happen, did not make his home there; from 1941 to 1952 he lived in California and thereafter in Switzerland.

Mann's many famous novels include *The Magic Mountain*, 1927; the trilogy *Joseph and his Brethren*, 1933–43; *Lotte in Weimar*, 1939, an historical reproduction of an episode in the life of Goethe; and *Dr Faustus*, 1947. Towards the end of his life he took up the picaresque novel form, a loosely connected string of episodes usually featuring a hero who is a *picaro*, someone on the fringe of society, and with this as his instrument returned to his early theme of the opposition of the artist and society in *Confessions of Felix Krull, Confidence Man* (1954), in which the artist-figure is projected as an actual trickster who lives by keeping his fellow citizens thoroughly deceived.

DEATH IN VENICE

GUSTAVE ASCHENBACH—or von Aschenbach, as he had
been known officially since his fiftieth birthday—had set out
alone from his house in Prince Regent Street, Munich, for
an extended walk. It was a spring afternoon in that year of
grace 19—, when Europe sat upon the anxious seat beneath
a menace that hung over its head for months. Aschenbach
had sought the open soon after tea. He was overwrought
by a morning of hard, nerve-taxing work, work which had
not ceased to exact his uttermost in the way of sustained
concentration, conscientiousness, and tact; and after the noon
meal found himself powerless to check the onward sweep of the
productive mechanism within him, that *motus animi continuus* in
which, according to Cicero, eloquence resides. He had sought
but not found relaxation in sleep—though the wear and tear
upon his system had come to make a daily nap more and
more imperative—and now undertook a walk, in the hope
that air and exercise might send him back refreshed to a good
evening's work.

May had begun, and after weeks of cold and wet a mock
summer had set in. The English Gardens, though in tenderest
leaf, felt as sultry as in August and were full of vehicles
and pedestrians near the city. But towards Aumeister the
paths were solitary and still, and Aschenbach strolled thither,
stopping awhile to watch the lively crowds in the restaurant
garden with its fringe of carriages and cabs. Thence he took his
homeward way outside the park and across the sunset fields. By
the time he reached the North Cemetery, however, he felt tired,
and a storm was brewing above Föhring; so he waited at the
stopping-place for a train to carry him back to the city.

He found the neighbourhood quite empty. Not a wagon in
sight, either on the paved Ungererstrasse, with its gleaming
tram-lines stretching off towards Schwabing, nor on the
Föhring highway. Nothing stirred behind the hedge in the
stonemason's yard, where crosses, monuments, and commem-
orative tablets made a supernumerary and untenanted graveyard opposite the real one. The mortuary chapel, a structure
in Byzantine style, stood facing it, silent in the gleam of the

ebbing day. Its façade was adorned with Greek crosses and tinted hieratic designs, and displayed a symmetrically arranged selection of scriptural texts in gilded letters, all of them with a bearing upon the future life, such as: 'They are entering into the House of the Lord' and 'May the Light Everlasting shine upon them.' Aschenbach beguiled some minutes of his waiting with reading these formulas and letting his mind's eye lose itself in their mystical meaning. He was brought back to reality by the sight of a man standing in the portico, above the two apocalyptic beasts that guarded the staircase, and something not quite usual in this man's appearance gave his thoughts a fresh turn.

Whether he had come out of the hall through the bronze doors or mounted unnoticed from outside, it was impossible to tell. Aschenbach casually inclined to the first idea. He was of medium height, thin, beardless, and strikingly snub-nosed; he belonged to the red-haired type and possessed its milky, freckled skin. He was obviously not Bavarian; and the broad, straight-brimmed straw hat he had on even made him look distinctly exotic. True, he had the indigenous rucksack buckled on his back, wore a belted suit of yellowish woollen stuff, apparently frieze, and carried a grey mackintosh cape across his left forearm, which was propped against his waist. In his right hand, slantwise to the ground, he held an iron-shod stick, and braced himself against its crook, with his legs crossed. His chin was up, so that the Adam's apple looked very bald in the lean neck rising from the loose shirt: and he stood there sharply peering up into space out of colourless, red-lashed eyes, while two pronounced perpendicular furrows showed on his forehead in curious contrast to his little turned-up nose. Perhaps his heightened and heightening position helped out the impression Aschenbach received. At any rate, standing there as though at survey, the man had a bold and domineering, even a ruthless, air, and his lips completed the picture by seeming to curl back, either by reason of some deformity or else because he grimaced, being blinded by the sun in his face; they laid bare the long, white, glistening teeth to the gums.

Aschenbach's gaze, though unawares, had very likely been inquisitive and tactless; for he became suddenly conscious that the stranger was returning it, and indeed so directly, with such hostility, such plain intent to force the withdrawal of the other's eyes, that Aschenbach felt an unpleasant twinge, and turning his back, began to walk along the hedge, hastily resolving to give the man no further heed. He had forgotten him the next minute. Yet whether the pilgrim air the stranger wore kindled his fantasy or whether some other physical or psychical influence came in play, he could not tell; but he felt the most surprising consciousness of a widening of inward barriers, a kind of vaulting unrest, a youthfully ardent thirst for distant scenes—a feeling so lively and so new, or at least so long ago outgrown and forgot, that he stood there rooted to the spot, his eyes on the ground and his hands clasped behind him, exploring these sentiments of his, their bearing and scope.

True, what he felt was no more than a longing to travel; yet coming upon him with such suddenness and passion as to resemble a seizure, almost a hallucination. Desire projected itself visually: his fancy, not quite yet lulled since morning, imaged the marvels and terrors of the manifold earth. He saw. He beheld a landscape, a tropical marshland, beneath a reeking sky, steaming, monstrous, rank—a kind of primeval wilderness-world of islands, morasses, and alluvial channels. Hairy palm-trunks rose near and far out of lush brakes of fern, out of bottoms of crass vegetation, fat, swollen, thick with incredible bloom. There were trees, mis-shapen as a dream, that dropped their naked roots straight through the air into the ground or into water that was stagnant and shadowy and glassy-green, where mammoth milk-white blossoms floated, and strange high-shouldered birds with curious bills stood gazing sidewise without sound or stir. Among the knotted joints of a bamboo thicket the eyes of a crouching tiger gleamed—and he felt his heart throb with terror, yet with a longing inexplicable. Then the vision vanished. Aschenbach, shaking his head, took up his march once more along the hedge of the stonemason's yard.

He had, at least ever since he commanded means to get about the world at will, regarded travel as a necessary evil, to be endured now and again willy-nilly for the sake of one's health. Too busy with the tasks imposed upon him by his own ego and the European soul, too laden with the care and duty to create, too preoccupied to be an amateur of the gay outer world, he had been content to know as much of the earth's surface as he could without stirring far outside his own sphere—had, indeed, never even been tempted to leave Europe. Now more than ever, since his life was on the wane, since he could no longer brush aside as fanciful his artist fear of not having done, of not being finished before the works ran down, he had confined himself to close range, had hardly stepped outside the charming city which he had made his home and the rude country house he had built in the mountains, whither he went to spend the rainy summers.

And so the new impulse which thus late and suddenly swept over him was speedily made to conform to the pattern of self-discipline he had followed from his youth up. He had meant to bring his work, for which he lived, to a certain point before leaving for the country, and the thought of a leisurely ramble across the globe, which should take him away from his desk for months, was too fantastic and upsetting to be seriously entertained. Yet the source of the unexpected contagion was known to him only too well. This yearning for new and distant scenes, this craving for freedom, release, forgetfulness—they were, he admitted to himself, an impulse towards flight, flight from the spot which was the daily theatre of a rigid, cold, and passionate service. That service he loved, had even almost come to love the enervating daily struggle between a proud, tenacious, well-tried will and this growing fatigue, which no one must suspect, nor the finished product betray by any faintest sign that his inspiration could ever flag or miss fire. On the other hand, it seemed the part of common sense not to span the bow too far, not to suppress summarily a need that so unequivocally asserted itself. He thought of his work, and the place where yesterday and again to-day he had been forced to lay it down, since it would not yield either to patient effort or a swift *coup de main*. Again and again he had tried to break or untie the knot—only to retire at last from the attack with a shiver of repugnance. Yet the difficulty was actually not a great one; what sapped his strength was distaste for the task, betrayed by a fastidiousness he could no longer satisfy. In his youth, indeed, the nature and inmost essence of the literary gift had been, to him, this very scrupulosity; for it he had bridled and tempered his sensibilities, knowing full well that feeling is prone to be content with easy gains and blithe half-perfection. So now, perhaps, feeling, thus tyrannized, avenged itself by leaving him, refusing from now on to carry and wing his art and taking away with it all the ecstasy he had known in form and expression. Not that he was doing bad work. So much, at least, the years had brought him, that at any moment he might feel tranquilly assured of mastery. But he got no joy of it—not though a nation paid it homage. To him it seemed his work had ceased to be marked by that fiery play of fancy which is the product of joy, and more, and more potently, than any intrinsic content, forms in turn the joy of the receiving world. He dreaded the summer in the country, alone with the maid who prepared his food and the man who served him; dreaded to see the familiar mountain peaks and walls that would shut him up again with his heavy discontent. What he needed was a break, an interim existence, a means of passing time, other air and a new stock of blood, to make the summer tolerable and productive. Good, then, he would go a journey. Not far—not all the way to the tigers. A night in a *wagon-lit*, three or four weeks of lotus-eating at some one of the gay world's playgrounds in the lovely south. . . .

So ran his thoughts, while the clang of the electric tram drew nearer down the Ungererstrasse; and as he mounted the platform he decided to devote the evening to a study of maps and railway guides. Once in, he bethought him to look back after the man in the straw hat, the companion of this brief interval which had after all been so fruitful. But he was not in his former place, nor in the tram itself, nor yet at the next stop; in short, his whereabouts remained a mystery.

Gustave Aschenbach was born at L——, a country town in the province of Silesia. He was the son of an upper official in the judicature, and his forebears had all been officers, judges, departmental functionaries—men who lived their strict, decent, sparing lives in the service of king and state. Only once before had a livelier mentality—in the quality of a clergyman—turned up among them; but swifter, more perceptive blood had in the generation before the poet's flowed into the stock from the mother's side, she being the daughter of a Bohemian musical conductor. It was from her he had the foreign traits that betrayed themselves in his appearance. The union of dry, conscientious officialdom and ardent, obscure impulse, produced an artist—and this particular artist: author of the lucid and vigorous prose epic on the life of Frederick the Great; careful, tireless weaver of the richly patterned tapestry entitled *Maia*, a novel that gathers up the threads of many human destinies in the warp of a single idea; creator of that powerful narrative *The Abject*, which taught a whole grateful generation that a man can still be capable of moral resolution even after he has plumbed the depths of knowledge; and lastly—to complete the tale of works of his mature period—the writer of that impassioned discourse on the theme of Mind and Art whose ordered force and antithetic eloquence led serious critics to rank it with Schiller's *Simple and Sentimental Poetry*.

Aschenbach's whole soul, from the very beginning, was bent on fame—and thus, while not precisely precocious, yet thanks to the unmistakable trenchancy of his personal accent he was early ripe and ready for a career. Almost before he was out of high school he had a name. Ten years later he had learned to sit at his desk and sustain and live up to his growing reputation, to write gracious and pregnant phrases in letters that must needs be brief, for many claims press upon the solid and successful man. At forty, worn down by the strains and stresses of his actual task, he had to deal with a daily post heavy with tributes from his own and foreign countries.

Remote on one hand from the banal, on the other from the eccentric, his genius was calculated to win at once the adhesion of the general public and the admiration, both sympathetic and stimulating, of the connoisseur. From childhood up he was pushed on every side to achievement, and achievement of no ordinary kind; and so his young days never knew the sweet idleness and blithe *laissez aller* that belong to youth. A nice observer once said of him in company—it was at the time when he fell ill in Vienna in his thirty-fifth year: 'You see, Aschenbach has always lived like this'—here the speaker closed the fingers of his left hand to a fist—'never like this'—and he let his open hand hang relaxed from the back of his chair. It was apt. And this attitude was the more morally valiant in that Aschenbach was not by nature robust—he was only called to the constant tension of his career, not actually born to it.

By medical advice he had been kept from school and educated at home. He had grown up solitary, without comradeship; yet had early been driven to see that he belonged to those whose talent is not so much out of the common as is the physical basis on which talent relies for its fulfilment. It is a seed that gives early of its fruit, whose powers seldom reach a ripe old age. But his favourite motto was 'Hold fast'; indeed, in his novel on the life of Frederick the Great he envisaged nothing else than the apotheosis of the old hero's word of command, '*Durchhalten,*' which seemed to him the epitome of fortitude under suffering. Besides, he deeply desired to live to a good old age, for it was his conviction that only the artist to whom it has been granted to be fruitful on all stages of our human scene can be truly great, or universal, or worthy of honour.

Bearing the burden of his genius, then, upon such slender shoulders and resolved to go so far, he had the more need of discipline—and discipline, fortunately, was his native inheritance from the father's side. At forty, at fifty, he was still living as he had commenced to live in the years when others are prone to waste and revel, dream high thoughts and postpone fulfilment. He began his day with a cold shower over chest and back; then, setting a pair of tall wax candles in silver holders at the head of his manuscript, he sacrificed to art, in two or three hours of almost religious fervour, the powers he had assembled in sleep. Outsiders might be pardoned for believing that his *Maia* world and the epic amplitude revealed by the life of Frederick were a manifestation of great power working under high pressure, that they came forth, as it were, all in one breath. It was the more triumph for his morale; for the truth was that they were heaped up to greatness in layer after layer, in long days of work, out of hundreds and hundreds of single inspirations; they owed their excellence, both of mass and detail, to one thing and one alone: that their creator could hold out for years under the strain of the same piece of work, with an endurance and a tenacity of purpose like that which had conquered his native province of Silesia, devoting to actual composition none but his best and freshest hours.

For an intellectual product of any value to exert an immediate influence which shall also be deep and lasting, it must rest on an inner harmony, yes, an affinity, between the personal destiny of its author and that of his contemporaries in general. Men do not know why they award fame to one work of art rather than another. Without being in the faintest connoisseurs, they think to justify the warmth of their commendations by discovering in it a hundred virtues, whereas the real ground of their applause is inexplicable—it is sympathy. Aschenbach had once given direct expression—though in an unobtrusive place—to the idea that almost everything conspicuously great is great in despite: has come into being in defiance of affliction and pain, poverty, destitution, bodily weakness, vice, passion, and a thousand other obstructions. And that was more than observation—it was the fruit of experience, it was precisely the formula of his life and fame, it was the key to his work. What wonder, then, if it was also the fixed character, the outward gesture, of his most individual figures?

The new type of hero favoured by Aschenbach, and recurring many times in his works, had early been analysed by a shrewd critic: 'The conception of an intellectual and virginal manliness, which clenches its teeth and stands in modest defiance of the swords and spears that pierce its side.' That was beautiful, it was *spirituel*, it was exact, despite the suggestion of too great passivity it held. Forbearance in the face of fate, beauty constant under torture, are not merely passive. They are a positive achievement, an explicit triumph; and the figure of Sebastian is the most beautiful symbol, if not of art as a whole, yet certainly of the art we speak of here. Within that world of Aschenbach's creation were exhibited many phases of this theme: there was the aristocratic self-command that is eaten out within and for as long as it can conceals its biologic decline from the eyes of the world; the sere and ugly outside, hiding the embers of smouldering fire—and having power to fan them to so pure a flame as to challenge supremacy in the domain of beauty itself; the pallid languors of the flesh, contrasted with the fiery ardours of the spirit within, which can fling a whole proud people down at the foot of the Cross, at the feet of its own sheer self-abnegation; the gracious bearing preserved in the stern, stark service of form; the unreal, precarious existence of the born intrigant with its swiftly enervating alternation of schemes and desires—all these human fates and many more of their like one read in Aschenbach's pages, and reading them might doubt the existence of any other kind of heroism than the heroism born of weakness. And, after all, what kind could be truer to the spirit of the times? Gustave Aschenbach was the poet-spokesman of all those who labour at the edge of exhaustion; of the overburdened, of those who are already worn out but still hold themselves upright; of all our modern moralizers of accomplishment, with stunted growth and scanty resources, who yet contrive by skilful husbanding and prodigious spasms of will to produce, at least for a while, the effect of greatness. There are many such, they are the heroes of the age. And in Aschenbach's pages they saw themselves; he justified, he exalted them, he sang their praise—and they, they were grateful, they heralded his fame.

He had been young and crude with the times and by them badly counselled. He had taken false steps, blundered, exposed himself, offended in speech and writing against tact and good sense. But he had attained to honour, and honour, he used to say, is the natural goal towards which every considerable talent presses with whip and spur. Yes, one might put it that his whole career had been one conscious and overweening ascent to honour, which left in the rear all the misgivings or self-derogation which might have hampered him.

What pleases the public is lively and vivid delineation which makes no demands on the intellect; but passionate and absolutist youth can only be enthralled by a problem. And Aschenbach was as absolute, as problematist, as any youth of them all. He had done homage to intellect, had overworked the soil of knowledge and ground up her seed-corn; had turned his back on the 'mysteries', called genius itself in question, held up art to scorn—yes, even while his faithful following revelled in the characters he created, he, the young artist, was taking away the breath of the twenty-year-olds with his cynic utterances on the nature of art and the artist life.

But it seems that a noble and active mind blunts itself against nothing so quickly as the sharp and bitter irritant of knowledge. And certain it is that the youth's constancy of purpose, no matter how painfully conscientious, was shallow beside the mature resolution of the master of his craft, who made a right-about-face, turned his back on the realm of

knowledge, and passed it by with averted face, lest it lame
his will or power of action, paralyse his feelings or his passions,
deprive any of these of their conviction or utility. How else
interpret the oft-cited story of *The Abject* than as a rebuke
to the excesses of a psychology-ridden age, embodied in the
delineation of the weak and silly fool who manages to lead fate
by the nose; driving his wife, out of sheer innate pusillanimity,
into the arms of a beardless youth, and making this disaster an
excuse for trifling away the rest of his life?

With rage the author here rejects the rejected, casts out
the outcast—and the measure of his fury is the measure of
his condemnation of all moral shilly-shallying. Explicitly he
renounces sympathy with the abyss, explicitly he refutes the
flabby humanitarianism of the phrase: '*Tout comprendre c'est tout
pardonner.*' What was here unfolding, or rather was already in
full bloom, was the 'miracle of regained detachment', which
a little later became the theme of one of the author's
dialogues, dwelt upon not without a certain oracular emphasis.
Strange sequence of thought! Was it perhaps an intellectual
consequence of this rebirth, this new austerity, that from now
on his style showed an almost exaggerated sense of beauty,
a lofty purity, symmetry, and simplicity, which gave his
productions a stamp of the classic, of conscious and deliberate
mastery? And yet: this moral fibre, surviving the hampering
and disintegrating effect of knowledge, does it not result in its
turn in a dangerous simplification, in a tendency to equate the
world and the human soul, and thus to strengthen the hold of
the evil, the forbidden, and the ethically impossible? And has
not form two aspects? Is it not moral and immoral at once;
moral in so far as it is the expression and result of discipline,
immoral—yes, actually hostile to morality—in that of its very
essence it is indifferent to good and evil, and deliberately
concerned to make the moral world stoop beneath its proud
and undivided sceptre?

Be that as it may. Development is destiny; and why should
a career attended by applause and adulation of the masses
necessarily take the same course as one which does not share
the glamour and the obligations of fame? Only the incorrigible
bohemian smiles or scoffs when a man of transcendent gifts
outgrows his carefree prentice stage, recognizes his own worth

and forces the world to recognize it too and pay it homage, though he puts on a courtly bearing to hide his bitter struggles and his loneliness. Again, the play of a developing talent must give its possessor joy, if of a wilful, defiant kind. With time, an official note, something almost expository, crept into Gustave Aschenbach's method. His later style gave up the old sheer audacities, the fresh and subtle nuances—it became fixed and exemplary, conservative, formal, even formulated. Like Louis XIV—or as tradition has it of him—Aschenbach, as he went on in years, banished from his style every common word. It was at this time that the school authorities adopted selections from his works into their text-books. And he found it only fitting—and had not thought but to accept—when a German prince signalized his accession to the throne by conferring upon the poet-author of the life of Frederick the Great on his fiftieth birthday the letters-patent of nobility.

He had roved about for a few years, trying this place and that as a place of residence, before choosing, as he soon did, the city of Munich for his permanent home. And there he lived, enjoying among his fellow-citizens the honour which is in rare cases the reward of intellectual eminence. He married young, the daughter of a university family; but after a brief term of wedded happiness his wife had died. A daughter, already married, remained to him. A son he never had.

Gustave von Aschenbach was somewhat below middle height, dark and smooth-shaven, with a head that looked rather too large for his almost delicate figure. He wore his hair brushed back; it was thin at the parting, bushy and grey on the temples, framing a lofty, rugged, knotty brow—if one may so characterize it. The nose-piece of his rimless gold spectacles cut into the base of his thick, aristocratically hooked nose. The mouth was large, often lax, often suddenly narrow and tense; the cheeks lean and furrowed, the pronounced chin slightly cleft. The vicissitudes of fate, it seemed, must have passed over his head, for he held it, plaintively, rather on one side; yet it was art, not the stern discipline of an active career, that had taken over the office of modelling these features. Behind this brow were born the flashing thrust and parry of the dialogue between Frederick and Voltaire on the theme of war; these eyes, weary and sunken, gazing through their glasses, had

beheld the blood-stained inferno of the hospitals in the Seven
Years War. Yes, personally speaking too, art heightens life.
She gives deeper joy, she consumes more swiftly. She engraves
adventures of the spirit and the mind in the faces of her
votaries; let them lead outwardly a life of the most cloistered
calm, she will in the end produce in them a fastidiousness,
and over-refinement, a nervous fever and exhaustion, such as a
career of extravagant passions and pleasures can hardly show.

Eager though he was to be off, Aschenbach was kept in Munich
by affairs both literary and practical for some two weeks after
that walk of his. But at length he ordered his country home
put ready against his return within the next few weeks, and
on a day between the middle and the end of May took the
evening train for Trieste, where he stopped only twenty-four
hours, embarking for Pola the next morning but one.

What he sought was a fresh scene, without associations,
which should yet be not too out-of-the-way; and accordingly he
chose an island in the Adriatic, not far off the Istrian coast. It
had been well known some years, for its splendidly rugged cliff
formations on the side next the open sea, and its population,
clad in a bright flutter of rags and speaking an outlandish
tongue. But there was rain and heavy air; the society at the
hotel was provincial Austrian, and limited; besides, it annoyed
him not to be able to get at the sea—he missed the close and
soothing contact which only a gentle sandy slope affords. He
could not feel this was the place he sought; an inner impulse
made him wretched, urging him on he knew not wither; he
racked his brains, he looked up boats, then all at once his
goal stood plain before his eyes. But of course! When one
wanted to arrive overnight at the incomparable, the fabulous,
the like-nothing-else-in-the-world, where was it one went? Why,
obviously; he had intended to go there, what ever was he doing
here? A blunder. He made all haste to correct it, announcing
his departure at once. Ten days after his arrival on the island
a swift motor-boat bore him and his luggage in the misty
dawning back across the water to the naval station, where
he landed only to pass over the landing-stage and on to the
wet decks of a ship lying there with steam up for the passage
to Venice.

It was an ancient hulk belonging to an Italian line, obsolete, dingy, grimed with soot. A dirty hunchbacked sailor, smirkingly polite, conducted him at once belowships to a cavernous, lamplit cabin. There behind a table sat a man with a beard like a goat's; he had his hat on the back of his head, a cigarstump in the corner of his mouth; he reminded Aschenbach of an old-fashioned circus-director. This person put the usual questions and wrote out a ticket to Venice, which he issued to the traveller with many commercial flourishes.

'A ticket for Venice,' he repeated, stretching out his arm to dip the pen into the thick ink in a tilted ink-stand. 'One first-class to Venice! Here you are, *signore mio*.' He made some scrawls on the paper, strewed bluish sand on it out of a box, thereafter letting the sand run off into an earthen vessel, folded the paper with bony yellow fingers, and wrote on the outside. 'An excellent choice,' he rattled on. 'Ah, Venice! What a glorious city! Irresistibly attractive to the cultured man for her past history as well as her present charm.' His copious gesturings and empty phrases gave the odd impression that he feared the traveller might alter his mind. He changed Aschenbach's note, laying the money on the spotted table-cover with the glibness of a croupier. 'A pleasant visit to you, signore,' he said, with a melodramatic bow. 'Delighted to serve you.' Then he beckoned and called out: 'Next' as though a stream of passengers stood waiting to be served, though in point of fact there was not one. Aschenbach returned to the upper deck.

He leaned an arm on the railing and looked at the idlers lounging along the quay to watch the boat go out. Then he turned his attention to his fellow-passengers. Those of the second class, both men and women, were squatted on their bundles of luggage on the forward deck. The first cabin consisted of a group of lively youths, clerks from Pola, evidently, who had made up a pleasure excursion to Italy and were not a little thrilled at the prospect, bustling about and laughing with satisfaction at the stir they made. They leaned over the railings and shouted, with a glib command of epithet, derisory remarks at such of their fellow-clerks as they saw going to business along the quay; and these in turn shook their sticks and shouted as good back again. One of the party,

in a dandified buff suit, a rakish panama with a coloured scarf,
and a red cravat, was loudest of the loud: he outcrowed all the
rest. Aschenbach's eye dwelt on him, and he was shocked to
see that the apparent youth was no youth at all. He was an
old man, beyond a doubt, with wrinkles and crow's-feet round
eyes and mouth; the dull carmine of the cheeks was rouge,
the brown hair a wig. His neck was shrunken and sinewy,
his turned-up moustaches and small imperial were dyed, and
the unbroken double row of yellow teeth he showed when he
laughed were but too obviously a cheapish false set. He wore
a seal ring on each forefinger, but the hands were those of an
old man. Aschenbach was moved to shudder as he watched
the creature and his association with the rest of the group.
Could they not see he was old, that he had no right to wear
the clothes they wore or pretend to be one of them? But they
were used to him, it seemed; they suffered him among them,
they paid back his jokes in kind and the playful pokes in the
ribs he gave them. How could they? Aschenbach put his hand
to his brow, he covered his eyes, for he had slept little, and
they smarted. He felt not quite canny, as though the world
were suffering a dreamlike distortion of perspective which he
might arrest by shutting it all out for a few minutes and then
looking at it afresh. But instead he felt a floating sensation,
and opened his eyes with unreasoning alarm to find that the
ship's dark sluggish bulk was slowly leaving the jetty. Inch by
inch, with the to-and-fro motion of her machinery, the strip of
iridescent dirty water widened, the boat manoeuvred clumsily
and turned her bow to the open sea. Aschenbach moved over
to the starboard side, where the hunchbacked sailor had set
up a deck-chair for him, and a steward in a greasy dress-coat
asked for orders.

The sky was grey, the wind humid. Harbour and island
dropped behind, all sight of land soon vanished in mist. Flakes
of sodden, clammy soot fell upon the still undried deck. Before
the boat was an hour out a canvas had to be spread as a shelter
from the rain.

Wrapped in his cloak, a book in his lap, our traveller
rested; the hours slipped by unawares. It stopped raining, the
canvas was taken down. The horizon was visible right round:
beneath the sombre dome of the sky stretched the vast plain

of empty sea. But immeasurable unarticulated space weakens our power to measure time as well: the time-sense falters and grows dim. Strange, shadowy figures passed and repassed—the elderly coxcomb, the goat-bearded man from the bowels of the ship—with vague gesturings and mutterings through the traveller's mind as he lay. He fell asleep.

At midday he was summoned to luncheon in a corridor-like saloon with the sleeping-cabins giving off it. He ate at the head of the long table; the party of clerks, including the old man, sat with the jolly captain at the other end, where they had been carousing since ten o'clock. The meal was wretched, and soon done. Aschenbach was driven to seek the open and look at the sky—perhaps it would lighten presently above Venice.

He had not dreamed it could be otherwise, for the city had ever given him a brilliant welcome. But sky and sea remained leaden, with spurts of fine, mistlike rain; he reconciled himself to the idea of seeing a different Venice from that he had always approached on the landward side. He stood by the foremast, his gaze on the distance, alert for the first glimpse of the coast. And he thought of the melancholy and susceptible poet who had once seen the towers and turrets of his dreams rise out of these waves; repeated the rhythms born of his awe, his mingled emotions of joy and suffering—and easily susceptible to a prescience already shaped with him, he asked his own sober, weary heart if a new enthusiasm, a new preoccupation, some late adventure of the feelings could still be in store for the idle traveller.

The flat coast showed on the right, the sea was soon populous with fishing-boats. The Lido appeared and was left behind as the ship glided at half speed through the narrow harbour of the same name, coming to a full stop on the lagoon in sight of garish, badly built houses. Here it waited for the boat bringing the sanitary inspector.

An hour passed. One had arrived—and yet not. There was no conceivable haste—yet one felt harried. The youths from Pola were on deck, drawn hither by the martial sound of horns coming across the water from the direction of the Public Gardens. They had drunk a good deal of Asti and were moved to shout and hurrah at the drilling *bersaglieri*. But the young-old man was a truly repulsive sight in the condition to which his company with youth had brought him. He could not carry his wine like them: he was pitiably drunk. He swayed as he stood—watery-eyed, a cigarette between his shaking fingers, keeping upright with difficulty. He could not have taken a step without falling and knew better than to stir, but his spirits were deplorably high. He buttonholed anyone who came within reach, he stuttered, he giggled, he leered, he fatuously shook his beringed old forefinger; his tongue kept seeking the corner of his mouth in a suggestive motion ugly to behold. Aschenbach's brow darkened as he looked, and there came over him once more dazed sense, as though things about him were just slightly losing their ordinary perspective, beginning to show a distortion that might merge into the grotesque. He was prevented from dwelling on the feeling, for now the machinery began to thud again, and the ship took its passage through the Canal di San Marco which had been interrupted so near the goal.

He saw it once more, that landing-place that takes the breath away, that amazing group of incredible structures the Republic set up to meet the awe-struck eye of the approaching seafarer: the airy splendour of the palace and Bridge of Sighs, the columns of lion and saint on the shore, the glory of the projecting flank of the fairy temple, the vista of gateway and clock. Looking, he thought that to come to Venice by the station is like entering a palace by the back door. No one should approach, save by the high seas as he was doing now, this most improbable of cities.

The engines stopped. Gondolas pressed alongside, the landing-stairs were let down, customs officials came on board and did their office, people began to go ashore. Aschenbach ordered a gondola. He meant to take up his abode by the sea and needed to be conveyed with his luggage to the landing-stage of the little steamers that ply between the city and the Lido. They called down his order to the surface of the water where the gondoliers were quarrelling in dialect. Then came another delay while his trunk was worried down the ladder-like stairs. Thus he was forced to endure the importunities of the ghastly young-old man, whose drunken state obscurely urged him to pay the stranger the honour of a formal farewell. 'We wish you a very pleasant sojourn,' he babbled, bowing and scraping. 'Pray keep us

in mind. *Au revoir, excusez et bon jour, votre Excellence.*' He
drooled, he blinked, he licked the corner of his mouth, the
little imperial bristled on his elderly chin. He put the tips
of two fingers to his mouth and said thickly: 'Give her our
love, will you, the p-pretty little dear'—here his upper plate
came away and fell down on the lower one. . . . Aschenbach
escaped. 'Little sweety-sweety-sweet-heart' he heard behind
him, gurgled and stuttered, as he climbed down the rope stair
into the boat.

Is there anyone but must repress a secret thrill, on arriving
in Venice for the first time—or returning thither after long
absence—and stepping into a Venetian gondola? That singular
conveyance, come down unchanged from ballad times, black
as nothing else on earth except a coffin—what pictures it calls
up of lawless, silent adventures in the plashing night; or even
more, what visions of death itself, the bier and solemn rites and
last soundless voyage! And has anyone remarked that the seat
in such a bark, the arm-chair lacquered in coffin-black, and
dully black-upholstered, is the softest, most luxurious, most
relaxing seat in the world? Aschenbach realized it when he had
let himself down at the gondolier's feet, opposite his luggage,
which lay neatly composed on the vessel's beak. The rowers
still gestured fiercely; he heard their harsh, incoherent tones.
But the strange stillness of the water-city seemed to take up
their voices gently, to disembody and scatter them over the
sea. It was warm here in the harbour. The lukewarm air of the
sirocco breathed upon him, he leaned back among his cushions
and gave himself to the yielding element, closing his eyes for
very pleasure in an indolence as unaccustomed as sweet. 'The
trip will be short,' he thought, and wished it might last forever.
They gently swayed away from the boat with its bustle and
clamour of voices.

It grew still and stiller all about. No sound but the splash of
the oars, the hollow slap of the wave against the steep, black,
halbert-shaped beak of the vessel, and one sound more—a
muttering by fits and starts, expressed as it were by the
motion of his arms, from the lips of the gondolier. He was
talking to himself, between his teeth. Aschenbach glanced up
and saw with surprise that the lagoon was widening, his vessel
was headed for the open sea. Evidently it would not do to give

himself up to sweet *far niente*; he must see his wishes carried
out.

'You are to take me to the steamboat landing, you know,'
he said, half turning round towards it. The muttering stopped.
There was no reply.

'Take me to the steamboat landing,' he repeated, and this
time turned quite round and looked up into the face of the
gondolier as he stood there on his little elevated deck, high
against the pale grey sky. The man had an unpleasing, even
brutish face, and wore blue clothes like a sailor's, with a yellow
sash; a shapeless straw hat with the braid torn at the brim
perched rakishly on his head. His facial structure, as well as
the curling blond moustache under the short snub nose, showed
him to be of non-Italian stock. Physically rather undersized, so
that one would not have expected him to be very muscular, he
pulled vigorously at the oar, putting all his body-weight behind
each stroke. Now and then the effort he made curled back his
lips and bared his white teeth to the gums. He spoke in a
decided, almost curt voice, looking out to sea over his fare's
head: 'The signore is going to the Lido.'

Aschenbach answered: 'Yes, I am. But I only took the
gondola to cross over to San Marco. I am using the *vaporetto*
from there.'

'But the signore cannot use the *vaporetto*.'

'And why not?'

'Because the *vaporetto* does not take luggage.'

It was true. Aschenbach remembered it. He made no
answer. But the man's gruff, overbearing manner, so unlike
the usual courtesy of his countrymen towards the stranger,
was intolerable. Aschenbach spoke again: 'That is my own
affair. I may want to give my luggage in deposit. You will
turn round.'

No answer. The oar splashed, the wave struck dull against
the prow. And the muttering began anew, the gondolier talked
to himself, between his teeth.

What should the traveller do? Alone on the water with this
tongue-tied, obstinate, uncanny man, he saw no way of enforcing
his will. And if only he did not excite himself, how pleasantly he
might rest! Had he not wished the voyage might last forever? The
wisest thing—and how much the pleasantest!—was to let matters

take their own course. A spell of indolence was upon him; it came
from the chair he sat in—this low, black-upholstered arm-chair,
so gently rocked at the hands of the despotic boatman in his rear.
The thought passed dreamily through Aschenbach's brain that
perhaps he had fallen into the clutches of a criminal; it had not
power to rouse him to action. More annoying was the simpler
explanation: that the man was only trying to extort money. A
sense of duty, a recollection, as it were, that this ought to be
prevented, made him collect himself to say:

'How much do you ask for the trip?'

And the gondolier, gazing out over his head, replied: 'The
signore will pay.'

There was an established reply to this; Aschenbach made it,
mechanically:

'I will pay nothing whatever if you do not take me where I
want to go.'

'The signore wants to go to the Lido.'

'But not with you.'

'I am a good rower, signore, I will row you well.'

'So much is true,' thought Aschenbach, and again he relaxed.
'That is true, you row me well. Even if you mean to rob me, even
if you hit me in the back with your oar and send me down to the
kingdom of Hades, even then you will have rowed me well.'

But nothing of the sort happened. Instead, they fell in with
company: a boat came alongside and waylaid them, full of
men and women singing to guitar and mandolin. They rowed
persistently bow for bow with the gondola and filled the silence
that had rested on the waters with their lyric love of gain.
Aschenbach tossed money into the hat they held out. The
music stopped at once, they rowed away. And once more the
gondolier's mutter became audible as he talked to himself in fits
and snatches.

Thus they rowed on, rocked by the wash of a steamer returning
city wards. At the landing two municipal officials were walking
up and down with their hands behind their backs and their
faces turned towards the lagoon. Aschenbach was helped on
shore by the old man with a boat-hook who is the permanent
feature of every landing-stage in Venice; and having no small
change to pay the boatman, crossed over into the hotel opposite.
His wants were supplied in the lobby, but when he came back his

possessions were already on a hand-car on the quay, and gondola
and gondolier were gone.

'He ran away, signore,' said the old boatman. 'A bad lot, a
man without a licence. He is the only gondolier without one. The
others telephoned over, and he knew we were on the look-out, so
he made off.'

Aschenbach shrugged.

'The signore has had a ride for nothing,' said the old man, and
held out his hat. Aschenbach dropped some coins. He directed
that his luggage be taken to the Hôtel des Bains and followed
the hand-car through the avenue, that white-blossoming avenue
with taverns, booths, and pensions on either side it, which runs
across the island diagonally to the beach.

He entered the hotel from the garden terrace at the back and
passed through the vestibule and hall into the office. His arrival
was expected, and he was served with courtesy and dispatch. The
manager, a small, soft, dapper man with a black moustache and
a caressing way with him wearing a French frock-coat, himself
took him up in the lift and showed him his room. It was a
pleasant chamber, furnished in cherry-wood, with lofty windows
looking out to sea. It was decorated with strong-scented flowers.
Aschenbach, as soon as he was alone, and while they brought in
his trunk and bags and disposed them in the room, went up to
one of the windows and stood looking out upon the beach in its
afternoon emptiness, and at the sunless sea, now full and sending
long, low waves with rhythmic beat upon the sand.

A solitary, unused to speaking of what he sees and feels, has
mental experiences which are at once more intense and less
articulate that those of a gregarious man. They are sluggish,
yet more wayward, and never without a melancholy tinge.
Sights and impressions which others brush aside with a glance,
a light comment, a smile, occupy him more than their due; they
sink silently in, they take on meaning, they become experience,
emotion, adventure. Solitude gives birth to the original in us, to
beauty unfamiliar and perilous—to poetry. But also, it gives birth
to the opposite: to the perverse, the illicit, the absurd. Thus the
traveller's mind still dwelt with disquiet on the episodes of his
journey hither: on the horrible old fop with his drivel about a
mistress, on the outlaw boatman and his lost tip. They did not
offend his reason, they hardly afforded food for thought; yet they

seemed by their very nature fundamentally strange, and thereby vaguely disquieting. Yet here was the sea; even in the midst of such thoughts he saluted it with his eyes, exulting that Venice was near and accessible. At length he turned round, disposed his personal belongings and made certain arrangements with the chambermaid for his comfort, washed, and was conveyed to the ground floor by the green-uniformed Swiss who ran the lift.

He took tea on the terrace facing the sea and afterwards went down and walked some distance along the shore promenade in the direction of Hôtel Excelsior. When he came back it seemed to be time to change for dinner. He did so, slowly and methodically as his way was, for he was accustomed to work while he dressed; but even so he found himself a little early when he entered the hall, where a large number of guests had collected—strangers to each other and affecting mutual indifference, yet united in expectancy of the meal. He picked up a paper, sat down in a leather arm-chair, and took stock of the company, which compared most favourably with that he had just left.

This was a broad and tolerant atmosphere, of wide horizons. Subdued voices were speaking most of the principal European tongues. That uniform of civilization, the conventional evening dress, gave outward conformity to the varied types. There were long, dry Americans, large-familied Russians, English ladies, German children with French *bonnes*. The Slavic element predominated, it seemed. In Aschenbach's neighbourhood Polish was being spoken.

Round a wicker table next him was gathered a group of young folk in charge of a governess or companion—three young girls, perhaps fifteen to seventeen years old, and a long-haired boy of about fourteen. Aschenbach noticed with astonishment the lad's perfect beauty. His face recalled the noblest moment of Greek sculpture—pale, with a sweet reserve, with clustering honey-coloured ringlets, the brow and nose descending in one line, the winning mouth, the expression of pure and godlike serenity. Yet with all this chaste perfection of form it was of such unique personal charm that the observer thought he had never seen, either in nature or art, anything so utterly happy and consummate. What struck him further was the strange contrast the group afforded, a difference in educational method, so to speak, shown in the way the brother and sisters were clothed and treated. The girls, the eldest of whom was practically grown up, were dressed with an almost disfiguring austerity. All three wore half-length slate-coloured frocks of cloister-like plainness, arbitrarily unbecoming in cut, with white turn-over collars as their only adornment. Every grace of outline was wilfully suppressed; their hair lay smoothly plastered to their heads, giving them a vacant expression, like a nun's. All this could only be by the mother's orders; but there was no trace of the same pedagogic severity in the case of the boy. Tenderness and softness, it was plain, conditioned his existence. No scissors had been put to the lovely hair that (like the Spinnario's) curled about his brows, above his ears, longer still in the neck. He wore an English sailor suit, with quilted sleeves that narrowed round the delicate wrists of his long and slender though still childish hands. And this suit, with its breast-knot, lacings, and embroideries, lent the slight figure something 'rich and strange', a spoilt, exquisite air. The observer saw him in half profile, with one foot in its black patent leather advanced, one elbow resting on the arm of his basket-chair, the cheek nestled into the closed hand in a pose of easy grace, quite unlike the stiff subservient mien which was evidently habitual to his sisters. Was he delicate? His facial tint was ivory-white against the golden darkness of his clustering locks. Or was he simply a pampered darling, the object of a self-willed and partial love? Aschenbach inclined to think the latter. For in almost every artist nature is inborn a wanton and treacherous proneness to side with the beauty that breaks hearts, to single out aristocratic pretensions and pay them homage.

A waiter announced, in English, that dinner was served. Gradually the company dispersed through the glass doors into the dining-room. Late-comers entered from the vestibule or the lifts. Inside, dinner was being served; but the young Poles still sat and waited about their wicker table. Aschenbach felt comfortable in his deep arm-chair, he enjoyed the beauty before his eyes, he waited with them.

The governess, a short, stout, red-faced person, at length gave the signal. With lifted brows she pushed back her chair and made a bow to the tall woman, dressed in palest grey, who now entered the hall. This lady's abundant jewels were pearls, her manner was cool and measured; the fashion of her gown and the arrangement of her lightly powdered hair had the simplicity prescribed in certain circles whose piety and aristocracy are equally marked. She might have been, in Germany, the wife of some high official. But there was something faintly fabulous, after all, in her appearance, though lent it solely by the pearls she wore: they were well-nigh priceless, and consisted of ear-rings and a three-stranded necklace, very long, with gems the size of cherries.

The brother and sisters had risen briskly. They bowed over their mother's hand to kiss it, she turning away from them, with a slight smile on her face, which was carefully preserved but rather sharp-nosed and worn. She addressed a few words in French to the governess, then moved towards the glass door. The children followed, the girls in order of age, then the governess, and last the boy. He chanced to turn before he crossed the threshold, and as there was no one else in the room, his strange, twilit grey eyes met Aschenbach's, as our traveller sat there with the paper on his knee, absorbed in looking after the group.

There was nothing singular, of course, in what he had seen. They had not gone in to dinner before their mother, they had waited, given her a respectful salute, and but observed the right and proper forms on entering the room. Yet they had done all this so expressly, with such self-respecting dignity, discipline, and sense of duty that Aschenbach was impressed. He lingered still a few minutes, then he, too, went into the dining-room, where he was shown to a table far off from the Polish family, as he noted at once, with a stirring of regret.

Tired, yet mentally alert, he beguiled the long, tedious meal with abstract, even with transcendent matters: pondered the mysterious harmony that must come to subsist between the individual human being and the universal law, in order that human beauty may result; passed on to general problems of form and art, and came at length to the conclusion that what seemed to him fresh and happy thoughts were like the flattering inventions of a dream, which the waking sense proves worthless and insubstantial. He spent the evening in the park, that was sweet with the odours of evening—sitting, smoking, wandering about; went to bed betimes, and passed the night in deep, unbroken sleep, visited, however, by varied and lively dreams.

The weather next day was no more promising. A land breeze blew. Beneath a colourless, overcast sky the sea lay sluggish, and

as it were shrunken, so far withdrawn as to leave bare several
rows of long sand-banks. The horizon looked close and prosaic.
When Aschenbach opened his window he thought he smelt the
stagnant odour of the lagoons.

He felt suddenly out of sorts and already began to think of
leaving. Once, years before, after weeks of bright spring weather,
this wind had found him out; it had been so bad as to force him
to flee from the city like a fugitive. And now it seemed beginning
again—the same feverish distaste, the pressure on his temples,
the heavy eyelids. It would be a nuisance to change again; but if
the wind did not turn, this was no place for him. To be on the safe
side, he did not entirely unpack. At nine o'clock he went down to
the buffet, which lay between the hall and the dining-room and
served as breakfast-room.

A solemn stillness reigned here, such as it is the ambition
of all large hotels to achieve. The waiters moved on noiseless
feet. A rattling of tea-things, a whispered word—and no other
sounds. In a corner diagonally to the door, two tables off his
own, Aschenbach saw the Polish girls with their governess. They
sat there very straight, in their stiff blue linen frocks with little
turn-over collars and cuffs, their ash-blond hair newly brushed
flat, their eyelids red from sleep, and handed each other the
marmalade. They had nearly finished their meal. The boy was
not there.

Aschenbach smiled. 'Aha, little Phaeax,' he thought. 'It seems
you are privileged to sleep yourself out.' With sudden gaiety he
quoted:

Oft veränderten Schmuck und warme Bäder und Ruhe.

He took a leisurely breakfast. The porter came up with his
braided cap in his hand, to deliver some letters that had been
sent on. Aschenbach lighted a cigarette and opened a few letters
and thus was still seated to witness the arrival of sluggard.

He entered through the glass doors and walked diagonally
across the room to his sisters at their table. He walked with
extraordinary grace—the carriage of the body, the action of the
knee, the way he set down his foot in its white shoe—it was all so
light, it was at once dainty and proud, it wore an added charm
in the childish shyness which made him twice turn his head as he

crossed the room, made him give a quick glance and then drop his eyes. He took his seat, with a smile and a murmured word in his soft and blurry tongue; and Aschenbach, sitting so that he could see him in profile, was astonished anew, yes, startled, at the godlike beauty of the human being. The lad had on a light sailor suit of blue and white striped cotton, with a red silk breast-knot and a simple white standing collar round the neck—a not very elegant effect—yet above this collar the head was poised like a flower, in incomparable loveliness. It was the head of Eros, with the yellowish bloom of Parian marble, with fine serious brows, and dusky clustering ringlets standing out in soft plenteousness over temples and ears.

'Good, oh, very good indeed!' thought Aschenbach, assuming the patronizing air of the connoisseur to hide, as artists will, their ravishment over a masterpiece. 'Yes,' he went on to himself, 'if it were not that sea and beach were waiting for me, I should sit here as long as you do.' But he went out on that, passing through the hall, beneath the watchful eye of the functionaries, down the steps and directly across the board walk to the section of the beach reserved for the guests of the hotel. The bathing-master, a barefoot old man in linen trousers and sailor blouse, with a straw hat, showed him the cabin that had been rented for him, and Aschenbach had him set up table and chair on the sandy platform before it. Then he dragged the reclining-chair through the pale yellow sand, closer to the sea, sat down, and composed himself.

He delighted, as always, in the scene on the beach, the sight of sophisticated society giving itself over to a simple life at the edge of the element. The shallow grey sea was already gay with children wading, with swimmers, with figures in bright colours lying on the sand-banks with arms behind their heads. Some were rowing in little keelless boats painted red and blue, and laughing when they capsized. A long row of *capanne* ran down the beach, with platforms, where people sat as on verandas, and there was social life, with bustle and with indolent repose; visits were paid, amid much chatter, punctilious morning toilettes hob-nobbed with comfortable and privileged dishabille. On the hard wet sand close to the sea figures in white bath-robes or loose wrappings in garish colours strolled up and down. A mammoth sand-hill had been built up on Aschenbach's right, the work of children, who had stuck it full of tiny flags. Vendors of sea-shells, fruit, and cakes knelt beside their wares spread out on the sand. A row of cabins on the left stood obliquely to the others and to the sea, thus forming the boundary of the enclosure on this side; and on the little veranda in front of one of these a Russian family was encamped; bearded men with strong white teeth, ripe, indolent women, a Fräulein from the Baltic provinces, who sat at an easel painting the sea and tearing her hair in despair; two ugly but good-natured children and an old maidservant in a head-cloth, with the caressing, servile manner of the born dependent. There they sat together in grateful enjoyment of their blessings: constantly shouting at their romping children, who paid not the slightest heed; making jokes in broken Italian to the funny old man who sold them sweetmeats, kissing each other on the cheeks—no jot concerned that their domesticity was overlooked.

'I'll stop,' thought Aschenbach. 'Where could it be better than here?' With his hands clasped in his lap he let his eyes swim in the wideness of the sea, his gaze lose focus, blur, and grow vague in the misty immensity of space. His love of the ocean had profound sources: the hard-worked artist's longing for rest, his yearning to seek refuge from the thronging manifold shapes of his fancy in the bosom of the simple and vast; and another yearning, opposed to his art and perhaps for that very reason a lure, for the unorganized, the immeasurable, the eternal—in short, for nothingness. He whose preoccupation is with excellence longs fervently to find rest in perfection; and is not nothingness a form of perfection? As he sat there dreaming thus, deep, deep into the void, suddenly the margin line of the shore was cut by a human form. He gathered up his gaze and withdrew it from the illimitable, and lo, it was the lovely boy who crossed his vision coming from the left along the sand. He was barefoot, ready for wading, the slender legs uncovered above the knee, and moved slowly, yet with such a proud, light tread as to make it seem he had never worn shoes. He looked towards the diagonal row of cabins; and the sight of the Russian family, leading their lives there in joyous simplicity, distorted his features in a spasm of angry disgust. His brow darkened, his lips curled, one corner of the mouth was drawn down in a harsh line that marred the curve of the cheek, his frown was so heavy that the eyes seemed to sink in as they uttered beneath the black and vicious language of hate. He looked down, looked threateningly back once more; then giving it up with a violent and contemptuous shoulder-shrug, he left his enemies in the rear.

A feeling of delicacy, a qualm, almost like a sense of shame, made Aschenbach turn away as though he had not seen; he felt unwilling to take advantage of having been, by chance, privy to this passionate reaction. But he was in troth both moved and exhilarated—that is to say, he was delighted. This childish exhibition of fanaticism, directed against the good-naturedest simplicity in the world—it gave to the godlike and inexpressive the final human touch. The figure of the half-grown lad, a masterpiece from nature's own hand, had been significant enough when it gratified the eye alone; and now it evoked sympathy as well—the little episode had set it off, lent it a dignity in the onlooker's eyes that was beyond its years.

Aschenbach listened with still averted head to the boy's voice announcing his coming to his companions at the sand-heap. The voice was clear, though a little weak, but they answered, shouting his name—or his nickname—again and again. Aschenbach was not without curiosity to learn it, but could make out nothing more exact than two musical syllables, something like Adgio—or, often still, Adjiu, with a long-drawn-out *u* at the end. He liked the melodious sound, and found it fitting; said it over to himself a few times and turned back with satisfaction to his papers.

Holding his travelling-pad on his knees, he took his fountain-pen and began to answer various items of his correspondence. But presently he felt it too great a pity to turn his back, and the eyes of his mind, for the sake of mere commonplace correspondence, to this scene which was, after all, the most rewarding one he knew. He put aside his papers and swung round to the sea; in no long time, beguiled by the voices of the children at play, he had turned his head and sat resting it against the chair-back, while he gave himself up to contemplating the activities of the exquisite Adgio.

His eye found him at once, the red breast-knot was unmistakable. With some nine or ten companions, boys and girls of his own age and younger, he was busy putting in place an old plank to serve as a bridge across the ditches between the sand-piles. He directed the work by shouting and motioning with his head, and they were all chattering in many tongues— French, Polish, and even some of the Balkan languages. But his was the name oftenest on their lips, he was plainly sought after, wooed, admired. One lad in particular, a Pole like himself, with a name that sounded something like Jaschiu, a sturdy lad with brilliantined black hair, in a belted linen suit, was his particular liegeman and friend. Operations at the sand-pile being ended for the time, they two walked away along the beach, with their arms round each other's waists, and once the lad Jaschiu gave Adgio a kiss.

Aschenbach felt like shaking a finger at him. 'But you, Critobulus,' he thought with a smile, 'you I advise to take a year's leave. That long, at least, you will need for complete recovery.' A vendor came by with strawberries, and Aschenbach made his second breakfast of the great luscious, dead-ripe fruit. It had grown very warm, although the sun had not availed to pierce the heavy layer of mist. His mind felt relaxed, his senses revelled in this vast and soothing communion with the silence of the sea. The grave and serious man found sufficient occupation in speculating what name it could be that sounded like Adgio. And with the help of a few Polish memories he at length fixed on Tadzio, a shortened form of Thaddeus, which sounded, when called, like Tadziu or Adziu.

Tadzio was bathing. Aschenbach had lost sight of him for a moment, then descried him far out in the water, which was shallow a very long way—saw his head, and his arm striking out like an oar. But his watchful family were already on the alert; the mother and governess called from the veranda in front of their bathing-cabin, until the lad's name, with its softened consonants and long-drawn *u*-sound, seemed to possess the beach like a rallying-cry; the cadence had something sweet and wild: 'Tadziu! Tadziu!' He turned and ran back against the water, churning the waves to a foam, his head flung high. The sight of this living figure, virginally pure and austere, with dripping locks, beautiful as a tender young god, emerging from the depths of sea and sky, outrunning the element—it conjured up mythologies, it was like a primeval legend, handed down from the beginning of time, of the birth of form, of the origin of the gods. With closed lids Aschenbach listened to this poesy hymning itself silently within him, and anon he thought it was good to be here and that he would stop awhile.

Afterwards Tadzio lay on the sand and rested from his bathe, wrapped in his white sheet, which he wore drawn underneath the right shoulder, so that his head was cradled on his bare right arm. And even when Aschenbach read, without looking up, he was conscious that the lad was there; that it would cost him but the slightest turn of the head to have the rewarding vision once more in his purview. Indeed, it was almost as though he sat there to guard the youth's repose; occupied, of course, with his own affairs, yet alive to the presence of that noble human creature close at hand. And his heart was stirred, it felt a father's kindness: such an emotion as the possessor of beauty can inspire in one who has offered himself up in spirit to create beauty.

At midday he left the beach, returned to the hotel, and was carried up in the lift to his room. There he lingered a little time before the glass and looked at his own grey hair, his keen and weary face. And he thought of his fame, and how people gazed respectfully at him in the streets, on account of his unerring gift of words and their power to charm. He called up all the worldly successes his genius had reaped, all he could remember, even his patent of nobility. Then went to luncheon down in the dining-room, sat at his little table and ate. Afterwards he mounted again in the lift, and a group of young folk, Tadzio among them, pressed with him into the little compartment. It was the first time Aschenbach had seen him close at hand, not merely in perspective, and could see and take account of the details of his humanity. Someone spoke to the lad, and he, answering, with indescribably lovely smile, stepped out again, as they had come to the first floor, backwards, with his eyes cast down. 'Beauty makes people self-conscious,' Aschenbach thought, and considered within himself imperatively why this should be. He had noted, further, that Tadzio's teeth were imperfect, rather jagged and bluish, without a healthy glaze, and of that peculiar brittle transparency which the teeth of chlorotic people often show. 'He is delicate, he is sickly,' Aschenbach thought. 'He will most likely not live to grow old.' He did not try to account for the pleasure the idea gave him.

In the afternoon he spent two hours in his room, then took the *vaporetto* to Venice, across the foul-smelling lagoon. He got out at San Marco, had his tea in the Piazza, and then, as his custom was, took a walk through the streets. But this walk of his brought about nothing less than a revolution in his mood and an entire change in all his plans.

There was a hateful sultriness in the narrow streets. The air was so heavy that all the manifold smells wafted out of houses, shops, and cook-shops—smells of oil, perfumery, and so forth—hung low, like exhalations, not dissipating. Cigarette smoke seemed to stand in the air, it drifted so slowly away. Today the crowd in these narrow lanes oppressed the stroller instead of diverting him. The longer he walked, the more was he in tortures under that state, which is the product of the sea air and the sirocco and which excites and enervates at once. He perspired painfully. His eyes rebelled, his chest was heavy, he felt feverish, the blood throbbed in his temples. He fled from the huddled, narrow streets of the commercial city, crossed many bridges, and came into the poor quarter of Venice. Beggars waylaid him, the canals sickened him with their evil exhalations. He reached a quiet square, one of those that exist at the city's heart, forsaken of God and man; there he rested awhile on the margin of a fountain, wiped his brow, and admitted to himself that he must be gone.

For the second time, and now quite definitely, the city proved that in certain weathers it could be directly inimical to his health. Nothing but sheer unreasoning obstinacy would linger on, hoping for an unprophesiable change in the wind. A quick decision was in place. He could not go home at this stage, neither summer nor winter quarters would be ready. But Venice had not a monopoly of sea and shore: there were other spots where these were to be had without the evil concomitants of lagoon and fever-breeding vapours. He remembered a little bathing-place not far from Trieste of which he had had a good report. Why not go thither? At once, of course, in order that this second change might be worth the making. He resolved, he rose to his feet and sought the nearest gondola-landing, where he took a boat and was conveyed to San Marco through the gloomy windings of many canals, beneath balconies of delicate marble traceries flanked by carven lions; round slippery corners of wall, past melancholy façades with ancient business shields reflected in the rocking water. It was not too easy to arrive at his destination, for his gondolier, being in league with various lace-makers and glass-blowers, did his best to persuade his fare to pause, look, and be tempted to buy. Thus the charm of this bizarre passage through the heart of Venice, even while it played upon his spirit, yet was sensibly cooled by the predatory commercial spirit of the fallen queen of the seas.

Once back in his hotel, he announced at the office, even before dinner, that circumstances unforeseen obliged him to leave early next morning. The management expressed its regret, it changed his money and receipted his bill. He dined, and spent the luke-warm evening in a rocking-chair on the rear terrace, reading the newspapers. Before he went to bed, he made his luggage ready against the morning.

His sleep was not of the best, for the prospect of another journey made him restless. When he opened his window next morning, the sky was still overcast, but the air seemed fresher—and there and then his rue began. Had he not given notice too soon? Had he not let himself be swayed by a slight and momentary indisposition? If he had only been patient, not lost heart so quickly, tried to adapt himself to the climate, or even waited for a change in the weather before deciding! Then, instead of the hurry and flurry of departure, he would have before him now a morning like yesterday's on the beach. Too late! He must go on wanting what he had wanted yesterday. He dressed and at eight o'clock went down to breakfast.

When he entered the breakfast-room it was empty. Guests came in while he sat waiting for his order to be filled. As he sipped his tea he saw the Polish girls enter with their governess, chaste and morning-fresh, with sleep-reddened eyelids. They crossed the room and sat down at their table in the window. Behind them came the porter, cap in hand, to announce that it was time for him to go. The car was waiting to convey him and other travellers to the Hôtel Excelsior, whence they would go by motor-boat through the company's private canal to the station. Time pressed. But Aschenbach found it did nothing of the sort. There still lacked more than an hour of train-time. He felt irritated at the hotel habit of getting the guests out of the house earlier than necessary; and requested the porter to let him breakfast in peace. The man hesitated and withdrew, only to come back again five minutes later. The car could wait no longer. Good, then it might go, and take his trunk with it, Aschenbach answered with some heat. He would use the public conveyance, in his own time; he begged them to leave the choice of it to him.

The functionary bowed. Aschenbach, pleased to be rid of him, made a leisurely meal, and even had a newspaper of the waiter. When at length he rose, the time was grown very short. And it so happened that at that moment Tadzio came through the glass doors into the room.

To reach his own table he crossed the traveller's path, and modestly cast down his eyes before the grey-haired man of the lofty brows—only to lift them again in that sweet way he had and direct his full soft gaze upon Aschenbach's face. Then he was past. 'For the last time, Tadzio,' thought the elder man. 'It was all too brief!' Quite unusually for him, he shaped a farewell with his lips, he actually uttered it, and added: 'May God bless you!' Then he went out, distributed tips, exchanged farewells with the mild little manager in the frock-coat, and, followed by the porter with his hand-luggage, left the hotel. On foot as he had come, he passed through the white-blossoming avenue, diagonally across the island to the boat-landing. He went on board at once—but the tale of his journey across the lagoon was a tale of woe, a passage through the very valley of regrets.

It was the well-known route: through the lagoon, past San Marco, up the Grand Canal. Aschenbach sat on the circular bench in the bows, with his elbow on the railing, one hand shading his eyes. They passed the Public Gardens, once more the princely charm of the Piazzetta rose up before him and then dropped behind, next came the great row of palaces, the canal curved, and the splendid marble arches of the Rialto came in sight. The traveller gazed—and his bosom was torn. The atmosphere of the city, the faintly rotten scent of swamp and sea, which had driven him to leave—in what deep, tender, almost painful draughts he breathed it in! How was it he had not known, had not thought, how much his heart was set upon it all! What this morning had been slight regret, some little doubt of his own wisdom, turned now to grief, to actual wretchedness, a mental agony so sharp that it repeatedly brought tears to his eyes, while he questioned himself how he could have foreseen it. The hardest part, the part that more than once it seemed he could not bear, was the thought that he should never more see Venice again. Since now for the second time the place had made him ill, since for the second time he had had to flee for his life, he must henceforth regard it as a forbidden spot, to be forever shunned;

senseless to try it again, after he had proved himself unfit. Yes, if he fled it now, he felt that wounded pride must prevent his return to this spot where twice he had made actual bodily surrender. And this conflict between inclination and capacity all at once assumed, in this middle-aged man's mind, immense weight and importance; the physical defeat seemed a shameful thing, to be avoided at whatever cost; and he stood amazed at the ease with which on the day before he had yielded to it.

Meanwhile the steamer neared the station landing; his anguish of irresolution amounted almost to panic. To leave seemed to the sufferer impossible, to remain not less so. Torn thus between two alternatives, he entered the station. It was very late, he had not a moment to lose. Time pressed, it scourged him onward. He hastened to buy his ticket and looked round in the crowd to find the hotel porter. The man appeared and said that the trunk had already gone off. 'Gone already?' 'Yes, it has gone to Como.' 'To Como?' A hasty exchange of words—angry questions from Aschenbach, and puzzled replies from the porter—at length made it clear that the trunk had been put with the wrong luggage even before leaving the hotel, and in company with other trunks was now well on its way in precisely the wrong direction.

Aschenbach found it hard to wear the right expression as he heard this news. A reckless joy, a deep incredible mirthfulness shook him almost as with a spasm. The porter dashed off after the lost trunk, returning very soon, of course, to announce that his efforts were unavailing. Aschenbach said he would not travel without his luggage; that he would go back and wait at the Hôtel des Bains until it turned up. Was the company's motor-boat still outside? The man said yes, it was at the door. With his native eloquence he prevailed upon the ticket-agent to take back the ticket already purchased; he swore that he would wire, that no pains should be spared, that the trunk would be restored in the twinkling of an eye. And the unbelievable thing came to pass; the traveller, twenty minutes after he had reached the station, found himself once more on the Grand Canal on his way back to the Lido.

What a strange adventure indeed, this right-about face of destiny—incredible, humiliating, whimsical as any dream! To be passing again, within the hour, these scenes from which in

profoundest grief he had but now taken leave forever! The little
swift-moving vessel, a furrow of foam at its prow, tacking with
droll agility between steamboats and gondolas, went like a shot to
its goal; and he, its sole passenger, sat hiding the panic and thrills
of a truant schoolboy beneath a mask of forced resignation. His
breast still heaved from time to time with a burst of laughter over
the contretemps. Things could not, he told himself, have fallen
out more luckily. There would be the necessary explanations,
a few astonished faces—then all would be well once more, a
mischance prevented, a grievous error set right; and all he had
thought to have left forever was his own once more, his for as
long as he liked. . . . And did the boat's swift motion deceive
him, or was the wind now coming from the sea?

The waves struck against the tiled sides of the narrow canal.
At Hôtel Excelsior the automobile omnibus awaited the returned
traveller and bore him along by the crisping waves back to the
Hôtel des Bains. The little mustachioed manager in the frock-
coat came down the steps to greet him.

In dulcet tones he deplored the mistake, said how painful it was
to the management and himself; applauded Aschenbach's resolve
to stop on until the errant trunk came back; his former room, alas,
was already taken, but another as good awaited his approval. '*Pas
de chance, monsieur,*' said the Swiss lift-porter, with a smile, as he
conveyed him upstairs. And the fugitive was soon quartered in
another room which in situation and furnishings almost precisely
resembled the first.

He laid out the contents of his hand-bag in their wonted places;
then, tired out, dazed by the whirl of the extraordinary forenoon,
subsided into the arm-chair by the open window. The sea wore a
pale-green cast, the air felt thinner and purer, the beach with its
cabins and boats had more colour, notwithstanding the sky was
still grey. Aschenbach, his hands folded in his lap, looked out.
He felt rejoiced to be back, yet displeased with his vacillating
moods, his ignorance of his own real desires. Thus for nearly an
hour he sat, dreaming, resting, barely thinking. At midday he saw
Tadzio, in his striped sailor suit with red breast-knot, coming up
from the sea, across the barrier and along the board walk to the
hotel. Aschenbach recognized him, even at this height, knew it
was he before he actually saw him, had it in mind to say to
himself: 'Well, Tadzio, so here you are again too!' But the casual

greeting died away before it reached his lips, slain by the truth in his heart. He felt the rapture of his blood, the poignant pleasure, and realized that it was for Tadzio's sake the leavetaking had been so hard.

He sat quite still, unseen at his high post, and looked within himself. His features were lively, he lifted his brows; a smile, alert, inquiring, vivid, widened the mouth. Then he raised his head, and with both hands, hanging limp over the chair-arms, he described a slow motion, palms outward, a lifting and turning movement, as though to indicate a wide embrace. It was a gesture of welcome, a calm and deliberate acceptance of what might come.

Now daily the naked god with cheeks aflame drove his four fire-breathing steeds through heaven's spaces; and with him streamed the strong east wind that fluttered his yellow locks. A sheen, like white satin, lay over all the idly rolling sea's expanse. The sand was burning hot. Awnings of rust-coloured canvas were spanned before the bathing-huts, under the ether's quivering silver-blue; one spent the morning hours within the small, sharp square of shadow they purveyed. But evening too was rarely lovely: balsamic with the breath of flowers and shrubs from the near-by park, while overhead the constellations circled in their spheres, and the murmuring of the night-girded sea swelled softly up and whispered to the soul. Such nights as these contained the joyful promise of a sunlit morrow, brim-full of sweetly ordered idleness, studded thick with countless precious possibilities.

The guest detained here by so happy a mischance was far from finding the return of his luggage a ground for setting out anew. For two days he had suffered slight inconvenience and had to dine in the large salon in his travelling clothes. Then the lost trunk was set down in his room, and he hastened to unpack, filling presses and drawers with his possessions. He meant to stay on—and on; he rejoiced in the prospect of wearing a silk suit for the hot morning hours on the beach and appearing in acceptable evening dress at dinner.

He was quick to fall in with the pleasing monotony of this manner of life, readily enchanted by its mild soft brilliance and ease. And what a spot it is, indeed!—uniting the charms of a luxurious bathing-resort by a southern sea with the immediate nearness of a unique and marvellous city. Aschenbach was not pleasure-loving. Always, wherever and whenever it was the order of the day to be merry, to refrain from labour and make glad the heart, he would soon be conscious of the imperative summons—and especially was this so in his youth—back to the high fatigues, the sacred and fasting service that consumed his days. This spot and this alone had power to beguile him, to relax his resolution, to make him glad. At times—of a forenoon perhaps, as he lay in the shadow of his awning, gazing out dreamily over the blue of the southern sea, or in the mildness of the night, beneath the wide starry sky, ensconced among the cushions of the gondola that bore him Lido-wards after an evening on the Piazza, while the gay lights faded and the melting music of the serenades died away on his ear—he would think of his mountain home, the theatre of his summer labours. There clouds hung low and trailed through the garden, violent storms extinguished the lights of the house at night, and the ravens he fed swung in the tops of the fir trees. And he would feel transported to Elysium, to the ends of the earth, to a spot most carefree for the sons of men, where no snow is, and no winter, no storms or downpours of rain; where Oceanus sends a mild and cooling breath, and days flow on in blissful idleness, without effort or struggle, entirely dedicate to the sun and the feasts of the sun.

Aschenbach saw the boy Tadzio almost constantly. The narrow confines of their world of hotel and beach, the daily round followed by all alike, brought him in close, almost uninterrupted touch with the beautiful lad. He encountered him everywhere—in the salons of the hotel, on the cooling rides to the city and back, among the splendours of the Piazza, and besides all this in many another going and coming as chance vouchsafed. But it was the regular morning hours on the beach which gave him his happiest opportunity to study and admire the lovely apparition. Yes, this immediate happiness, this daily recurring boon at the hand of circumstance, this it was that filled him with content, with joy in life, enriched his stay, and lingered out the row of sunny days that fell into place so pleasantly one behind the other.

He rose early—as early as though he had a panting press of work—and was among the first on the beach, when the sun was still benign and the sea dazzling white in its morning slumber. He gave the watchman a friendly good-morning and chatted with the barefoot, white-haired old man who prepared his place, spread the awning, trundled out the chair and table on to the little platform. Then he settled down; he had three or four hours before the sun reached its height and the fearful climax of its power; three or four hours while the sea went deeper and deeper blue; three or four hours in which to watch Tadzio.

He would see him coming up, on the left, along the margin of the sea; or from behind, between the cabins; or, with a start of joyful surprise, would discover that he himself was late, and Tadzio already down, in the blue and white bathing-suit that was now his only wear on the beach; there and engrossed in his usual activities in the sand, beneath the sun. It was a sweetly idle, trifling, fitful life, of play and rest, of strolling, wading, digging, fishing, swimming, lying on the sand. Often the women sitting on the platform would call out to him in their high voices: 'Tadziu! Tadziu!' and he would come running and waving his arms, eager to tell them what he had found, what caught—shells, seahorses, jelly-fish, and sidewards-running crabs. Aschenbach understood not a word he said; it might be the sheerest commonplace, in his ear it became mingled harmonies. Thus the lad's foreign birth raised his speech to music; a wanton sun showered splendour on him, and the noble distances of the sea formed the background which set off his figure.

Soon the observer knew every line and pose of this form that limned itself so freely against sea and sky; its every loveliness, though conned by heart, yet thrilled him each day afresh; his admiration knew no bounds, the delight of his eye was unending. Once the lad was summoned to speak to a guest who was waiting for his mother at their cabin. He ran up, ran dripping wet out of the sea, tossing his curls, and put out his hand, standing with his weight on one leg, resting the other foot on the toes; as he stood there in a posture of suspense the turn of his body was enchanting, while his features wore a look half shamefaced, half conscious of the duty breeding laid upon him to please. Or he would lie at full length, with his bath-robe around him, one slender young arm resting on the sand, his chin in the hollow of his hand; the lad they called Jaschiu squatting beside him, paying him court. There could be nothing lovelier on earth than the smile and look with which the playmate thus singled out rewarded his humble friend and vassal. Again, he might be at the water's edge, alone, removed from his family, quite close to Aschenbach; standing erect, his hands clasped at the back of his neck, rocking slowly on the balls of his feet, day-dreaming away into blue space, while little waves ran up and bathed his toes. The ringlets of honey-coloured hair clung to his temples and neck, the fine down along the upper vertebrae was yellow in the sunlight; the thin envelope of flesh covering the torso betrayed the delicate outlines of the ribs and the symmetry of the breast-structure. His armpits were still as smooth as a statue's, smooth the glistening hollows behind the knees, where the blue network of veins suggested that the body was formed of some stuff more transparent than mere flesh. What discipline, what precision of thought were expressed by the tense youthful perfection of this form! And yet the pure, strong will which had laboured in darkness and succeeded in bringing this godlike work of art to the light of day—was it not known and familiar to him, the artist? Was not the same force at work in himself when he strove in cold fury to liberate from the marble mass of language the slender forms of his art which he saw with the eye of his mind and would body forth to men as the mirror and image of spiritual beauty?

Mirror and image! His eyes took in the proud bearing of that figure there at the blue water's edge; with an outburst of rapture he told himself that what he saw was beauty's very essence; form as divine thought, the single and pure perfection which resides in the mind, of which an image and likeness, rare and holy, was here raised up for adoration. This was very frenzy—and without a scruple, nay, eagerly, the ageing artist bade it come. His mind was in travail, his whole mental background in a state of flux. Memory flung up in him the primitive thoughts which are youth's inheritance, but which with him had remained latent, never leaping up into a blaze. Has it not been written that the sun beguiles our attention from things of the intellect to fix it on things of the sense? The sun, they say, dazzles; so bewitching reason and memory that the soul for very pleasure forgets its actual state, to cling with doting on the loveliest of all the objects she shines on. Yes, and then it is only through the medium of some corporeal being that it can raise itself again to contemplation of higher things. Amor, in sooth, is like the mathematician who in order to give children a knowledge of pure form must do so in the language of pictures; so, too, the god, in order to make visible the spirit, avails himself of the forms and colours of human youth, gilding it with all imaginable beauty that it may serve memory as a tool, the very sight of which then sets us afire with pain and longing.

Such were the devotee's thoughts, such the power of his emotions. And the sea, so bright with glancing sunbeams, wove in his mind a spell and summoned up a lovely picture: there was the ancient plane-tree outside the walls of Athens, a hallowed, shady spot, fragrant with willow-blossom and adorned with images and votive offerings in honour of the nymphs and Achelous. Clear ran the smooth-pebbled stream at the foot of the spreading tree. Crickets were fiddling. But on the gentle grassy slope, where one could lie yet hold the head erect, and shelter from the scorching heat, two men reclined, an elder with a younger, ugliness paired with beauty and wisdom with grace. Here Socrates held forth to youthful Phaedrus upon the nature of virtue and desire, wooing him with insinuating wit and charming turns of phrase. He told him of the shuddering and unwonted heat that comes upon him whose heart is open, when his eye beholds an image of eternal beauty; spoke of the impious and corrupt, who cannot conceive beauty though they see its image, and are incapable of awe; and of the fear and reverence felt by the noble soul when he beholds a godlike face or a form which is a good image of beauty: how as he gazes he worships the beautiful one and scarcely dares to look upon him, but would offer sacrifice as to an idol or a god, did he not fear to be thought stark mad. 'For beauty, my Phaedrus, beauty alone, is lovely and visible at once. For, mark you, it is the sole aspect of the spiritual which we can perceive through our senses, or bear so to perceive. Else what should become of us, if the divine, if reason and virtue and truth, were to speak to us through the senses? Should we not perish and be consumed by love, as Semele aforetime was by Zeus? So beauty, then, is the beauty-lover's way to the spirit—but only the way, only the means, my little Phaedrus.' . . . And then, sly arch-lover that he was, he said the subtlest thing of all: that the lover was nearer the divine than the beloved; for the god was in the one but not in the other—perhaps the tenderest, most mocking thought that ever was thought, and source of all the guile and secret bliss the lover knows.

Thought that can emerge wholly into feeling, feeling that can merge wholly into thought—these are the artist's highest joy. And our solitary felt in himself at this moment power to command and wield a thought that thrilled with emotion, an emotion as precise and concentrated as thought: namely, that nature herself shivers with ecstasy when the mind bows down in homage before beauty. He felt a sudden desire to write. Eros, indeed, we are told, loves idleness, and for idle hours alone was he created. But in this crisis the violence of our sufferer's seizure was directed almost wholly towards production, its occasion almost a matter of indifference. News had reached him on his travels that a certain problem had been raised, the intellectual world challenged for its opinion on a great and burning question of art and taste. By nature and experience the theme was his own: and he could not resist the temptation to set it off in the glistering foil of his words. He would write, and moreover he would write in Tadzio's presence. This lad should be in a sense his model, his style should follow the lines of this figure that seemed to him divine; he would snatch up this beauty into the realms of the mind, as once the eagle bore the Trojan shepherd aloft. Never had the pride of the word been so sweet to him, never had he known so well that Eros is in the word, as in those perilous and precious hours when he sat at his rude table, within the shade of his awning, his idol full in his view and the music of his voice in his ears, and fashioned his little essay after the model Tadzio's beauty set: that page and a half of choicest prose, so chaste, so lofty, so poignant with feeling, which would shortly be the wonder and admiration of the multitude. Verily it is well for the world that it sees only the beauty of the completed work and not its origins nor the conditions whence it sprang; since knowledge of the artist's inspiration might often but confuse and alarm and so prevent the full effect of its excellence. Strange hours, indeed, these were, and strangely unnerving the labour that filled them! Strangely fruitful intercourse this, between one body and another mind! When Aschenbach put aside his work and left the beach he felt exhausted, he felt broken—conscience reproached him, as it were after a debauch.

Next morning on leaving the hotel he stood at the top of the stairs leading down from the terrace and saw Tadzio in front of him on his way to the beach. The lad had just reached the gate in the railings, and he was alone. Aschenbach felt, quite simply, a wish to overtake him, to address him and have the pleasure of his reply and answering look; to put upon a blithe and friendly footing his relation with this being who all unconsciously had so greatly heightened and quickened his emotions. The lovely youth moved at a loitering pace—he might be easily overtaken; and Aschenbach hastened his own step. He reached him on the board walk that ran behind the bathing-cabins, and all but put out his hand to lay it on shoulder or head, while his lips parted to utter a friendly salutation in French. But—perhaps from the swift pace of his last few steps—he found his heart throbbing unpleasantly fast, while his breath came in such quick pants that he could only have gasped had he tried to speak. He hesitated, sought after self-control, was suddenly panic-stricken lest the boy notice him hanging there behind him and look round. Then he gave up, abandoned his plan, and passed him with bent head and hurried step.

'Too late! Too late!' he thought as he went by. But was it too late? This step he had delayed to take might so easily have put everything in a lighter key, have led to a sane recovery from his folly. But the truth may have been that the ageing man did not want to be cured, that his illusion was far too dear to him. Who shall unriddle the puzzle of the artist nature? Who understands that mingling of discipline and licence in which it stands so deeply rooted? For not to be able to want sobriety is licentious folly. Aschenbach was no longer disposed to self-analysis. He had no taste for it; his self-esteem the attitude of mind proper to his years, his maturity and single-mindedness, disinclined him to look within himself and decide whether it was constraint or puerile sensuality that had prevented him from carrying out his project. He felt confused, he was afraid someone, if only the watchman, might have been observing his behaviour and final surrender—very much he feared being ridiculous. And all the time he was laughing at himself for his serio-comic seizure. 'Quite crestfallen,' he thought. 'I was like the gamecock that lets his wings droop in the battle. That must be the Love-God himself, that makes us hang our heads at sight of beauty and

weighs our proud spirits low as the ground.' Thus he played
with the idea—he embroidered upon it, and was too arrogant
to admit fear of an emotion.

The term he had set for his holiday passed by unheeded;
he had no thought of going home. Ample funds had been
sent him. His sole concern was that the Polish family might
leave and a chance question put to the hotel barber elicited
the information that they had come only very shortly before
himself. The sun browned his face and hands, the invigorating
salty air heightened his emotional energies. Heretofore he had
wont to give out at once, in some new effort, the powers
accumulated by sleep or food or outdoor air; but now the
strength that flowed in upon him with each day of sun and sea
and idleness he let go up in one extravagant gush of emotional
intoxication.

His sleep was fitful; the priceless, equable days were divided
one from the next by brief nights filled with happy unrest.
He went, indeed, early to bed, for at nine o'clock, with the
departure of Tadzio from the scene, the day was over for him.
But in the faint greyness of the morning a tender pang would
go through him as his heart was minded of its adventure; he
could no longer bear his pillow and rising, would wrap himself
against the early chill and sit down by the window to await
the sunrise. Awe of the miracle filled his soul new-risen from
its sleep. Heaven, earth, and its waters yet lay enfolded in the
ghostly, glassy pallor of dawn; one paling star still swam in
the shadowy vast. But there came a breath, a winged word
from far and inaccessible abodes, that Eos was rising from the
side of her spouse, and there was that first sweet reddening
of the farthest strip of sea and sky that manifests creation to
man's sense. She neared, the goddess, ravisher of youth, who
stole away Cleitos and Cephalus and, defying all the envious
Olympians, tasted beautiful Orion's love. At the world's edge
began a strewing of roses, a shining and a blooming ineffably
pure; baby cloudlets hung illuminated, like attendant amoretti,
in the blue and blushful haze; purple effulgence fell upon the
sea, that seemed to heave it forward on its welling waves; from
horizon to zenith went quivering thrusts like golden lances, the
gleam became a glare; without a sound, with godlike violence,
glow and glare and rolling flames streamed upwards, and with

flying hoof-beats the steeds of the sun-god mounted the sky. The lonely watcher sat, the splendour of the god shone on him, he closed his eyes and let the glory kiss his lids. Forgotten feelings, precious pangs of his youth, quenched long since by the stern service that had been his life and now returned so strangely metamorphosed—he recognized them with a puzzled, wondering smile. He mused, he dreamed, his lips slowly shaped a name; still smiling, his face turned seawards and his hands lying folded in his lap, he fell asleep once more as he sat.

But that day, which began so fierily and festally, was not like other days; it was transmuted and gilded with mythical significance. For whence could come the breath, so mild and meaningful, like a whisper from higher spheres, that played about temple and ear? Troops of small feathery white clouds ranged over the sky, like grazing herds of the gods. A stronger wind arose, and Poseidon's horses ran up, arching their manes, among them too the steers of him with the purpled locks, who lowered their horns and bellowed as they came on; while like prancing goats the waves on the farther strand leaped among the craggy rocks. It was a world possessed, peopled by Pan, that closed round the spellbound man, and his doting heart conceived the most delicate fancies. When the sun was going down behind Venice, he would sometimes sit on a bench in the park and watch Tadzio, white-clad, with gay-coloured sash, at play there on the rolled gravel with his ball; and at such times it was not Tadzio whom he saw, but Hyacinthus, doomed to die because two gods were rivals for his love. Ah, yes, he tasted the envious pangs that Zephyr knew when his rival, bow and cithara, oracle and all forgot, played with the beauteous youth; he watched the discus, guided by torturing jealousy, strike the beloved head; paled as he received the broken body in his arms, and saw the flower spring up, watered by that sweet blood and signed for evermore with his lament.

There can be no relation more strange, more critical, than that between two beings who know each other only with their eyes, who meet daily, yes, even hourly, eye each other with a fixed regard, and yet by some whim or freak of convention feel constrained to act like strangers. Uneasiness rules between them, unslaked curiosity, a hysterical desire to give rein to their suppressed impulse to recognize and address each other; even, actually, a sort of strained but mutual regard. For one human being instinctively feels respect and love for another human being so long as he does not know him well enough to judge him; and that he does not, the craving he feels is evidence.

Some sort of relationship and acquaintanceship was perforce set up between Aschenbach and the youthful Tadzio; it was with a thrill of joy the older man perceived that the lad was not entirely unresponsive to all the tender notice lavished on him. For instance, what should move the lovely youth, nowadays when he descended to the beach, always to avoid the board walk behind the bathing-huts and saunter along the sand, passing Aschenbach's tent in front, sometimes so unnecessarily close as almost to graze his table or chair? Could the power of an emotion so beyond his own so draw, so fascinate its innocent object? Daily Aschenbach would wait for Tadzio. Then sometimes, on his approach, he would pretend to be preoccupied and let the charmer pass unregarded by. But sometimes he looked up, and their glances met; when that happened both were profoundly serious. The elder's dignified and cultured mien let nothing appear of his inward state; but in Tadzio's eyes a question lay—he faltered in his step, gazed on the ground, then up again with that ineffably sweet look he had; and when he was past, something in his bearing seemed to say that only good breeding hindered him from turning round.

But once, one evening, it fell out differently. The Polish brother and sisters, with their governess, had missed the evening meal, and Aschenbach had noted the fact with concern. He was restive over their absence, and after dinner walked up and down in front of the hotel, in evening dress and a straw hat; when suddenly he saw the nunlike sisters with their companion appear in the light of the arc-lamps, and four paces behind them Tadzio. Evidently they came from the steamer-landing, having dined for some reason in Venice. It had been chilly on the lagoon, for Tadzio wore a dark-blue reefer-jacket with gilt buttons, and a cap to match. Sun and sea air could not burn his skin, it was the same creamy marble hue as at first—though he did look a little pale, either from the cold or in the bluish moonlight of the arc-lamps. The shapely brows were so delicately drawn, the eyes so deeply dark—lovelier he was than words could say, and as often the thought visited Aschenbach, and brought its own pang, that language could but extol, not reproduce, the beauties of the sense.

The sight of that dear form was unexpected, it had appeared unhoped-for, without giving him time to compose his features. Joy, surprise, and admiration might have painted themselves quite openly upon his face—and just at this second it happened that Tadzio smiled. Smiled at Aschenbach, unabashed and friendly, a speaking, winning, captivating smile, with slowly parting lips. With such a smile it might be that Narcissus bent over the mirroring pool, a smile profound, infatuated, lingering, as he put out his arms to the reflection of his own beauty; the lips just slightly pursed, perhaps half-realizing his own folly in trying to kiss the cold lips of his shadow—with a mingling of coquetry and curiosity and a faint unease, enthralling and enthralled.

Aschenbach received that smile and turned away with it as though entrusted with a fatal gift. So shaken was he that he had to flee from the lighted terrace and front gardens and seek out with hurried steps the darkness of the park at the rear. Reproaches strangely mixed of tenderness and remonstrance burst from him: 'How dare you smile like that! No one is allowed to smile like that!' He flung himself on a bench, his composure gone to the winds, and breathed in the nocturnal fragrance of the garden. He leaned back, with hanging arms, quivering from head to foot, and quite unmanned he whispered the hackneyed phrase of love and longing—impossible in these circumstances, absurd, abject, ridiculous enough, yet sacred too, and not unworthy of honour even here: 'I love you!'

In the fourth week of his stay on the Lido, Gustave von Aschenbach made certain singular observations touching the world about him. He noticed, in the first place, that though the season was approaching its height, yet the number of guests declined and, in particular, that the German tongue had suffered a rout, being scarcely or never heard in the land. At table and on the beach he caught nothing but foreign words. One day at the barber's—where he was now a frequent visitor—he heard something rather startling. The barber mentioned a German family who had just left the Lido after a brief stay, and rattled on in his obsequious way: 'The signore is not leaving—he has no fear of the sickness, has he?' Aschenbach looked at him. 'The sickness?' he repeated. Whereat the prattler fell silent, became very busy all at once, affected not to hear. When Aschenbach persisted he said he really knew nothing at all about it, and tried in a fresh burst of eloquence to drown the embarrassing subject.

That was one forenoon. After luncheon, Aschenbach had himself ferried across to Venice, in a dead calm, under a burning sun; driven by his mania, he was following the Polish young folk, whom he had seen with their companion, taking the way to the landing-stage. He did not find his idol on the Piazza. But as he sat there at tea, at a little round table on the shady side, suddenly he noticed a peculiar odour, which, it seemed to him now, had been in the air for days without his being aware: a sweetish, medicinal smell, associated with wounds and disease and suspect cleanliness. He sniffed and pondered and at length recognized it; finished his tea and left the square at the end facing the cathedral. In the narrow space the stench grew stronger. At the street corners placards were stuck up, in which the city authorities warned the population against the danger of certain infections of the gastric system, prevalent during the heated season; advising them not to eat oysters or other shell-fish and not to use the canal waters. The ordinance showed every sign of minimizing an existing situation. Little groups of people stood about silently in the squares and on the bridges; the traveller moved among them, watched and listened and thought.

He spoke to a shopkeeper lounging at his door among dangling coral necklaces and trinkets of artificial amethyst, and asked him about the disagreeable odour. The man looked at him, heavy-eyed, and hastily pulled himself together. 'Just a formal precaution, signore,' he said, with a gesture. 'A police regulation we have to put up with. The air is sultry—the sirocco is not wholesome, as the signore knows. Just a precautionary measure, you understand—probably unnecessary. . . .' Aschenbach thanked him and passed on. And on the boat that bore him back to the Lido he smelt the germicide again.

On reaching his hotel he sought the table in the lobby and buried himself in the newspapers. The foreign-language sheets had nothing. But in the German papers certain rumours were mentioned, statistics given, then officially denied, then the good faith of the denials called in question. The departure of the German and Austrian contingent was thus made plain. As for other nationals, they knew or suspected nothing—they were still undisturbed. Aschenbach tossed the newspapers back on the table. 'It ought to be kept quiet,' he thought, aroused. 'It should not be talked about.' And he felt in his heart a curious elation at these events impending in the world about him. Passion is like crime: it does not thrive on the established order and the common round; it welcomes every blow dealt the bourgeois structure, every weakening of the social fabric, because therein it feels a sure hope of its own advantage. These things that were going on in the unclean alleys of Venice, under cover of an official hushing-up policy—they gave Aschenbach a dark satisfaction. The city's evil secret mingled with the one in the depths of his heart—and he would have staked all he possessed to keep it, since in his infatuation he cared for nothing but to keep Tadzio here, and owned to himself, not without horror, that he could not exist were the lad to pass from his sight.

He was no longer satisfied to owe his communion with his charmer to chance and the routine of hotel life; he had begun to follow and waylay him. On Sundays, for example, the Polish family never appeared on the beach. Aschenbach guessed they went to mass at San Marco and pursued them thither. He passed from the glare of the Piazza into the golden twilight of the holy place and found him he sought bowed in worship over a prie-dieu. He kept in the background, standing on the fissured mosaic pavement among the devout populace, that knelt and muttered and made the sign of the cross; and the crowded splendour of the oriental temple weighed voluptuously on his sense. A heavily ornate priest intoned and gesticulated before the altar, where little candle-flames flickered helplessly in the reek of incense-breathing smoke; and with that cloying sacrificial smell another seemed to mingle—the odour of the sickened city. But through all the glamour and glitter, Aschenbach saw the exquisite creature

there in front turn his head, seek out and meet his lover's
eye.

The crowd streamed out through the portals into the brilliant
square thick with fluttering doves, and the fond fool stood aside
in the vestibule on the watch. He saw the Polish family leave
the church. The children took ceremonial leave of their mother,
and she turned towards the Piazzetta on her way home, while
his charmer and the cloistered sisters, with their governess,
passed beneath the clock tower into the Merceria. When they
were a few paces on, he followed—he stole behind them on
their walk through the city. When they paused, he did so too;
when they turned round, he fled into inns and courtyards to
let them pass. Once he lost them from view, hunted feverishly
over bridges and in filthy *culs-de-sac*, only to confront them
suddenly in a narrow passage whence there was no escape,
and experience a moment of panic fear. Yet it would be untrue
to say he suffered. Mind and heart were drunk with passion,
his footsteps guided by the daemonic power whose pastime it
is to trample on human reason and dignity.

Tadzio and his sisters at length took a gondola. Aschenbach
hid behind a portico or fountain while they embarked and
directly they pushed off did the same. In a furtive whisper he
told the boatman he would tip him well to follow at a little
distance the other gondola, just rounding a corner, and fairly
sickened at the man's quick, sly grasp and ready acceptance of
the go-between's role.

Leaning back among soft, black cushions he swayed gently in
the wake of the other black-snouted bark, to which the strength
of his passion chained him. Sometimes it passed from his view,
and then he was assailed by an anguish of unrest. But his guide
appeared to have long practice in affairs like these; always, by
dint of short cuts or deft manoeuvres, he contrived to overtake
the coveted sight. The air was heavy and foul, the sun burnt
down through a slate-coloured haze. Water slapped gurgling
against wood and stone. The gondolier's cry, half warning, half
salute, was answered with singular accord from far within the
silence of the labyrinth. They passed little gardens high up the
crumbling wall, hung with clustering white and purple flowers
that sent down an odour of almonds. Moorish lattices showed
shadowy in the gloom. The marble steps of a church descended

into the canal, and on them a beggar squatted, displaying his misery to view, showing the whites of his eyes, holding out his hat for alms. Farther on a dealer in antiquities cringed before his lair, inviting the passer-by to enter and be duped. Yes, this was Venice, this the fair frailty that fawned and that betrayed, half fairy-tale, half snare; the city in whose stagnating air the art of painting once put forth so lusty a growth, and where musicians were moved to accords so weirdly lulling and lascivious. Our adventurer felt his senses wooed by this voluptuousness of sight and sound, tasted his secret knowledge that the city sickened and hid its sickness for love of gain, and bent an ever more unbridled leer on the gondola that glided on before him.

It came at last to this—that his frenzy left him capacity for nothing else but to pursue his flame; to dream of him absent, to lavish, loverlike, endearing terms on his mere shadow. He was alone, he was a foreigner, he was sunk deep in this belated bliss of his—all which enabled him to pass unblushing through experiences well-nigh unbelievable. One night, returning late from Venice, he paused by his beloved's chamber door in the second storey, leaned his head against the panel, and remained there long, in utter drunkenness, powerless to tear himself away, blind to the danger of being caught in so mad an attitude.

And yet there were not wholly lacking moments when he paused and reflected, when in consternation he asked himself what path was this on which he had set his foot. Like most other men of parts and attainments, he had an aristocratic interest in his forbears, and when he achieved a success he liked to think he had gratified them, compelled their admiration and regard. He thought of them now, involved as he was in this illicit adventure, seized of these exotic excesses of feeling; thought of their stern self-command and decent manliness, and gave a melancholy smile. What would they have said? What, indeed, would they have said to his entire life, that varied to the point of degeneracy from theirs? This life in the bonds of art, had not he himself, in the days of his youth and in the very spirit of those bourgeois forefathers, pronounced mocking judgement upon it? And yet, at bottom, it had been so like their own! It had been a service, and he a soldier, like some of them; and art was war—a grilling, exhausting struggle that nowadays wore one out before one could grow old. It had been a life of self-conquest, a life against odds, dour, steadfast, abstinent; he had made it symbolical of the kind of over-strained heroism the time admired, and he was entitled to call it manly, even courageous. He wondered if such a life might not be somehow specially pleasing in the eyes of the god who had him in his power. For Eros had received most countenance among the most valiant nations—yes, were we not told that in their cities prowess made him flourish exceedingly? And many heroes of olden time had willingly borne his yoke, not counting any humiliation such as if it happened by the god's decree; vows, prostrations, self-abasements, these were no source of shame to the lover; rather they reaped him praise and honour.

Thus did the fond man's folly condition his thoughts; thus did he seek to hold his dignity upright in his own eyes. And all the while he kept doggedly on the traces of the disreputable secret the city kept hidden at its heart, just as he kept his own—and all that he learned fed his passion with vague, lawless hopes. He turned over newspapers at cafés, bent on finding a report on the progress of the disease; and in the German sheets, which had ceased to appear on the hotel table, he found a series of contradictory statements. The deaths, it was variously asserted, ran to twenty, to forty, to a hundred or more; yet in the next day's issue the existence of the pestilence was, if not roundly denied, reported as a matter of a few sporadic cases such as might be brought into a seaport town. After that the warnings would break out again, and the protests against the unscrupulous game the authorities were playing. No definite information was to be had.

And yet our solitary felt he had a sort of first claim on a share in the unwholesome secret; he took a fantastic satisfaction in putting leading questions to such persons as were interested to conceal it, and forcing them to explicit untruths by way of denial. One day he attacked the manager, that small, soft-stepping man in the French frock-coat, who was moving about among the guests at luncheon, supervising the service and making himself socially agreeable. He paused at Aschenbach's table to exchange a greeting, and the guest put a question, with a negligent, casual air: 'Why in the world are they forever disinfecting the city of Venice?' 'A police regulation,' the adroit one replied; 'a precautionary measure, intended to protect the health of the public during this unseasonably warm and sultry weather.' 'Very praiseworthy of the police.' Aschenbach gravely responded. After a further exchange of meteorological commonplaces the manager passed on.

It happened that a band of street musicians came to perform in the hotel gardens that evening after dinner. They grouped themselves beneath an iron stanchion supporting an arc-light, two women and two men, and turned their faces, that shone white in the glare, up towards the guests who sat on the hotel terrace enjoying this popular entertainment along with their coffee and iced drinks. The hotel lift-boys, waiters, and office staff stood in the doorway and listened; the Russian family displayed the usual Russian absorption in their enjoyment—they had their chairs put down into the garden to be nearer the singers and sat there in a half-circle with gratitude painted on their features, the old serf in her turban erect behind their chairs.

These strolling players were adepts at mandolin, guitar, harmonica, even compassing a reedy violin. Vocal numbers alternated with instrumental, the younger woman, who had a high, shrill voice, joining in a love-duet with the sweetly falsettoing tenor. The actual head of the company, however, and incontestably its most gifted member, was the other man, who played the guitar. He was a sort of baritone buffo; with no voice to speak of, but possessed of a pantomimic gift and remarkable burlesque *élan*. Often he stepped out of the group and advanced towards the terrace, guitar in hand, and his audience rewarded his sallies with bursts of laughter. The Russians in their parterre seats were beside themselves with delight over this display of southern vivacity; their shouts and screams of applause encouraged him to bolder and bolder flights.

Aschenbach sat near the balustrade, a glass of pomegranate-juice and soda-water sparkling ruby-red before him, with which he now and then moistened his lips. His nerves drank in thirstily the unlovely sounds, the vulgar and sentimental tunes,

for passion paralyses good taste and makes its victim accept
with rapture what a man in his senses would either laugh at
or turn from with disgust. Idly he sat and watched the antics
of the buffoon with his face set in a fixed and painful smile,
while inwardly his whole being was rigid with the intensity
of the regard he bent on Tadzio, leaning over the railing six
paces off.

He lounged there, in the white belted suit he sometimes
wore at dinner, in all his innate, inevitable grace, with his
left arm on the balustrade, his legs crossed, the right hand on
the supporting hip; and looked down on the strolling singers
with an expression that was hardly a smile, but rather a distant
curiosity and polite toleration. Now and then he straightened
himself and with a charming movement of both arms drew
down his white blouse through his leather belt, throwing out
his chest. And sometimes—Aschenbach saw it with triumph,
with horror, and a sense that his reason was tottering—the
lad would cast a glance, that might be slow and cautious, or
might be sudden and swift, as though to take him by surprise,
to the place where his lover sat. Aschenbach did not meet
the glance. An ignoble caution made him keep his eyes in
leash. For in the rear of the terrace sat Tadzio's mother and
governess; and matters had gone so far that he feared to make
himself conspicuous. Several times, on the beach, in the hotel
lobby, on the Piazza, he had seen, with a stealing numbness,
that they called Tadzio away from his neighbourhood. And his
pride revolted at the affront, even while conscience told him it
was deserved.

The performer below presently began a solo, with guitar
accompaniment, a street song in several stanzas, just then the
rage all over Italy. He delivered it in a striking and dramatic
recitative, and his company joined in the refrain. He was a
man of slight build, with a thin, undernourished face; his
shabby felt hat rested on the back of his neck, a great mop
of red hair sticking out in front; and he stood there on the
gravel in advance of his troupe, in an impudent, swaggering
posture, twanging the strings of his instrument and flinging
a witty and rollicking recitative up to the terrace, while the
veins on his forehead swelled with the violence of his effort.
He was scarcely a Venetian type, belonging rather to the

race of Neapolitan jesters, half bully, half comedian, brutal, blustering, an unpleasant customer, and entertaining to the last degree. The words of his song were trivial and silly, but on his lips, accompanied with gestures of head, hands, arms, and body, with leers and winks and the loose play of the tongue in the corner of his mouth, they took on meaning; an equivocal meaning, yet vaguely offensive. He wore a white sports shirt with a suit of ordinary clothes, and a strikingly large and naked-looking Adam's apple rose out of the open collar. From that pale, snub-nosed face it was hard to judge of his age; vice sat on it, it was furrowed with grimacing, and two deep wrinkles of defiance and self-will, almost of desperation, stood oddly between the red brows, above the grinning mobile mouth. But what more than all drew upon him the profound scrutiny of our solitary watcher was that this suspicious figure seemed to carry with it its own suspicious odour. For whenever the refrain occurred and the singer, with waving arms and antic gestures, passed in his grotesque march immediately beneath Aschenbach's seat, a strong smell of carbolic was wafted up to the terrace.

After the song he began to take up money, beginning with the Russian family, who gave liberally, and then mounting the steps to the terrace. But here he became as cringing as he had before been forward. He glided between the tables, bowing and scraping, showing his strong white teeth in a servile smile, though the two deep furrows on the brow were still very marked. His audience looked at the strange creature as he went about collecting his livelihood, and their curiosity was not unmixed with disfavour. They tossed coins with their finger-tips into his hat and took care not to touch it. Let the enjoyment be never so great, a sort of embarrassment always comes when the comedian oversteps the physical distance between himself and respectable people. This man felt it and sought to make his peace by fawning. He came along the railing to Aschenbach, and with him came that smell no one else seemed to notice.

'Listen!' said the solitary, in a low voice, almost mechanically; 'they are disinfecting Venice—why?' The mountebank answered hoarsely: 'Because of the police. Orders, signore. On account of the heat and the sirocco. The sirocco is oppressive. Not good for the health.' He spoke as though surprised that anyone could ask, and with the flat of his hand he demonstrated how oppressive the sirocco was. 'So there is no plague in Venice?' Aschenbach asked the question between his teeth, very low. The man's expressive face fell, he put on a look of comical innocence. 'A plague? What sort of plague? Is the sirocco a plague? Or perhaps our police are a plague! You are making fun of us, signore! A plague! Why should there be? The police make regulations on account of the heat and the weather. . . .' He gestured. 'Quite,' said Aschenbach, once more, soft and low; and dropping an unduly large coin into the man's hat dismissed him with a sign. He bowed very low and left. But he had not reached the steps when two of the hotel servants flung themselves on him and began to whisper, their faces close to his. He shrugged, seemed to be giving assurances, to be swearing he had said nothing. It was not hard to guess the import of his words. They let him go at last and he went back into the garden, where he conferred briefly with his troupe and then stepped forward for a farewell song.

It was one Aschenbach had never to his knowledge heard before, a rowdy air, with words in impossible dialect. It had a laughing-refrain in which the other three artists joined at the top of their lungs. The refrain had neither words nor accompaniment, it was nothing but rhythmical, modulated, natural laughter, which the soloist in particular knew how to render with most deceptive realism. Now that he was farther off his audience, his self-assurance had come back, and this laughter of his rang with a mocking note. He would be overtaken, before he reached the end of the last line of each stanza; he would catch his breath, lay his hand over his mouth, his voice would quaver and his shoulders shake, he would lose power to contain himself longer. Just at the right moment each time, it came whooping, bawling, crashing out of him, with a verisimilitude that never failed to set his audience off in profuse and unpremeditated mirth that seemed to add gusto to his own. He bent his knees, he clapped his thigh, he held his sides, he looked ripe for bursting. He no longer laughed, but yelled, pointing his finger at the company there above as though there could be in all the world nothing so comic as they; until at last they laughed in hotel, terrace, and garden, down to the waiters, lift-boys, and servants—laughed as though possessed.

Aschenbach could no longer rest in his chair, he sat poised for flight. But the combined effect of the laughing, the hospital odour in his nostrils, and the nearness of the beloved was to hold him in a spell; he felt unable to stir. Under cover of the general commotion he looked across at Tadzio and saw that the lovely boy returned his gaze with a seriousness that seemed the copy of his own; the general hilarity, it seemed to say, had no power over him, he kept aloof. The grey-haired man was overpowered, disarmed by this docile, childlike deference; with difficulty he refrained from hiding his face in his hands. Tadzio's habit, too, of drawing himself up and taking a deep sighing breath struck him as being due to an oppression of the chest. 'He is sickly, he will never live to grow up,' he thought once again, with that dispassionate vision to which his madness of desire sometimes so strangely gave way. And compassion struggled with the reckless exultation of his heart.

The players, meanwhile, had finished and gone; their leader bowing and scraping, kissing his hands and adorning his leave-taking with antics that grew madder with the applause they evoked. After all the others were outside, he pretended to run backwards full tilt against a lamp-post and slunk to the gate apparently doubled over with pain. But there he threw off his buffoon's mask, stood erect, with an elastic straightening of his whole figure, ran out his tongue impudently at the guests on the terrace, and vanished in the night. The company dispersed. Tadzio had long since left the balustrade. But he, the lonely man, sat for long, to the waiters' great annoyance, before the dregs of pomegranate-juice in his glass. Time passed, the night went on. Long ago, in his parental home, he had watched the sand filter through an hour-glass—he could still see, as though it stood before him, the fragile, pregnant little toy. Soundless and fine the rust-red streamlet ran through the narrow neck and made, as it declined in the upper cavity, an exquisite little vortex.

The very next afternoon the solitary took another step in pursuit of his fixed policy of baiting the outer world. This time he had all possible success. He went, that is, into the English travel bureau in the Piazza, changed some money at the desk, and posing as the suspicious foreigner, put his fateful question. The clerk was a tweed-clad young Britisher, with his eyes set close together, his hair parted in the middle, and radiating that steady reliability which makes his like so strange a phenomenon in the *gamin*, agile-witted south. He began: 'No ground for alarm, sir. A mere formality. Quite regular in view of the unhealthy climatic conditions.' But then, looking up, he chanced to meet with his own blue eyes the stranger's weary, melancholy gaze, fixed on his face. The Englishman coloured. He continued in a lower voice, rather confused: 'At least, that is the official explanation, which they see fit to stick to. I may tell you there's a bit more to it than that.' And then, in his good, straightforward way, he told the truth.

For the past several years Asiatic cholera had shown a strong tendency to spread. Its source was the hot, moist swamps of the delta of the Ganges, where it bred in the mephitic air of that primeval island-jungle, among whose bamboo thickets the tiger crouches, where life of every sort flourishes in the rankest abundance, and only man avoids the spot. Thence the pestilence had spread throughout Hindustan, ranging with great violence; moved eastwards to China, westward to Afghanistan and Persia; following the great caravan routes, it brought terror to Astrakhan, terror to Moscow. Even while Europe trembled lest the spectre be seen striding westward across country, it was carried by sea from Syrian ports and appeared simultaneously at several points on the Mediterranean littoral; raised its head in Toulon and Malaga, Palermo and Naples, and soon got a firm hold in Calabria and Apulia. Northern Italy had been spared—so far. But in May the horrible vibrios were found on the same day in two bodies: the emaciated, blackened corpses of a bargee and a woman who kept a greengrocer's shop. Both cases were hushed up. But in a week there were ten more—twenty, thirty in different quarters of the town. An Austrian provincial, having come to Venice on a few days' pleasure trip, went home and died with all the symptoms of the plague. Thus was explained the fact that the German-language papers were the first to print the news of the Venetian outbreak. The Venetian authorities published in reply a statement to the effect that the state of the city's health had never been better; at the same time instituting the most necessary precautions. But by that time the food supplies—milk, meat, or vegetables—had probably been contaminated, for death unseen and unacknowledged was devouring and laying waste in the narrow streets, while a brooding, unseasonable heat warmed the waters of the canals and encouraged the spread of the pestilence. Yes, the disease seemed to flourish and wax strong, to redouble its generative powers. Recoveries were rare. Eighty out of every hundred died, and horribly, for the onslaught was of the extremest violence, and not infrequently of the 'dry' type, the most malignant form of the contagion. In this form the victim's body loses power to expel the water secreted by the blood-vessels, it shrivels up, he passes with hoarse cries from convulsion to convulsion, his blood grows thick like pitch and he suffocates in a few hours. He is fortunate indeed, if, as sometimes happens, the disease, after a slight *malaise*, takes the form of a profound unconsciousness, from which the sufferer seldom or never rouses. By the beginning of June the quarantine buildings of the *ospedale civico* had quietly filled up, the two orphan asylums were entirely occupied, and there was a hideously brisk traffic between the *Nuovo Fundamento* and the island of San Michele, where the cemetery was. But the city was not swayed by high-minded motives or regard for international agreements. The authorities were more actuated by fear of being out of pocket, by regard for the new exhibition of paintings just opened in the Public Gardens, or by apprehension of the large losses the hotels and the shops that catered to foreigners would suffer in case of panic and blockade. And the fears of the people supported the persistent official policy of silence and denial. The city's first medical officer, an honest and competent man, had indignantly resigned his office and been privily replaced by a more compliant person. The fact was known; and this corruption in high places played its part, together with the suspense as to where the walking terror might strike next, to demoralize the baser elements in the city and encourage those antisocial forces which shun the light of day. There was intemperance, indecency, increase of crime. Evenings one saw many drunken people, which was unusual. Gangs of men in surly mood made the streets unsafe, theft and assault were said to be frequent, even murder; for in two cases persons supposedly victims of the plague were proved to have been poisoned by their own families. And professional vice was rampant, displaying excesses heretofore unknown and only at home much farther south and in the east.

Such was the substance of the Englishman's tale. 'You would do well,' he concluded, 'to leave to-day instead of tomorrow. The blockade cannot be more than a few days off.'

'Thank you,' said Aschenbach, and left the office.

The Piazza lay in sweltering sunshine. Innocent foreigners sat before the cafés or stood in front of the cathedral, the centre of clouds of doves that, with fluttering wings, tried to shoulder each other away and pick the kernels of maize from the extended hand. Aschenbach strode up and down the spacious flags, feverishly excited, triumphant in possession of the truth at last, but with a sickening taste in his mouth and a fantastic horror at his heart. One decent, expiatory course lay open to him; he considered it. To-night, after dinner, he might approach the lady of the pearls and address her in words which he precisely formulated in his mind: 'Madame, will you permit an entire stranger to serve you with a word of advice and warning which self-interest prevents others from uttering? Go away. Leave here at once, without delay, with Tadzio and your daughters. Venice is in the grip of pestilence.' Then might he lay his hand in farewell upon the head of that instrument of a mocking deity; and thereafter himself flee the accursed morass. But he knew that he was far indeed from any serious desire to take such a step. It would restore him, would give him back himself once more; but he who is beside himself revolts at the idea of self-possession. There crossed his mind the vision of a white building with inscriptions on it, glittering in the sinking sun—he recalled how his mind had dreamed away into their transparent mysticism; recalled the strange pilgrim apparition that had wakened in the ageing man a lust for strange countries and fresh sights. And these memories again brought in their train the thought of returning home, returning to reason, self-mastery, an ordered existence, to the old life of effort. Alas! the bare thought made him wince with a revulsion that was like physical nausea. 'It must be kept quiet,' he whispered fiercely. 'I will not speak!' The knowledge that he shared the city's secret, the city's guilt—it put him beside himself, intoxicated him as a small quantity of wine will a man suffering from brain-fag. His thoughts dwelt upon the image of the desolate and calamitous city, and he was giddy with fugitive, mad, unreasoning hopes and visions of a monstrous sweetness. That tender sentiment he had a moment ago evoked, what was it compared with such images as these? His art, his moral sense, what were they in the balance beside the boons that chaos might confer? He kept silence, he stopped on.

That night he had a fearful dream—if dream be the right word for a mental and physical experience which did indeed befall him in deep sleep, as a thing quite apart and real to his senses, yet without his seeing himself as present in it. Rather its theatre seemed to be his own soul, and the events burst in from outside, violently overcoming the profound resistance of his spirit; passed him through and left him, left the whole cultural structure of a life-time trampled on, ravaged, and destroyed.

The beginning was fear; fear and desire, with a shuddering curiosity. Night reigned, and his senses were on the alert; he heard loud, confused noises from far away, clamour and hubbub. There was a rattling, a crashing, a low dull thunder; shrill halloos and a kind of howl with a long-drawn *u*-sound at the end. And with all these, dominating them all, flute-notes of the cruellest sweetness, deep and cooing, keeping shamelessly on until the listener felt his very entrails bewitched. He heard a voice, naming, though darkly, that which was to come: 'The stranger god!' A glow lighted up the surrounding mist and by it he recognized a mountain scene like that about his country home. From the wooded heights, from among the tree-trunks and crumbling moss-covered rocks, a troop came tumbling and raging down, a whirling rout of men and animals, and overflowed the hillside with flames and human forms, with clamour and the reeling dance. The females stumbled over the long, hairy pelts that dangled from their girdles; with heads flung back they uttered loud hoarse cries and shook their tambourines high in air; brandished naked daggers or torches vomiting trails of sparks. They shrieked, holding their breasts in both hands; coiling snakes with quivering tongues they clutched about their waists. Horned and hairy males, girt about the loins with hides, drooped heads and lifted arms and thighs in unison, as they beat on brazen vessels that gave out

droning thunder, or thumped madly on drums. There were
troops of beardless youths armed with garlanded staves; these
ran after goats and thrust their staves against the creatures'
flanks, then clung to the plunging horns and let themselves
be borne off with triumphant shouts. And one and all the
mad rout yelled that cry, composed of soft consonants with
a long-drawn *u*-sound at the end, so sweet and wild it was
together, and like nothing ever heard before! It would ring
through the air like the bellow of a challenging stag, and be
given back many-tongued; or they would use it to goad each
other on to dance with wild excess of tossing limbs—they never
let it die. But the deep, beguiling notes of the flute wove in and
out and over all. Beguiling too it was to him who struggled
in the grip of these sights and sounds, shamelessly awaiting
the coming feast and the uttermost surrender. He trembled,
he shrank, his will was steadfast to preserve and uphold his
own god against this stranger who was sworn enemy to dignity
and self-control. But the mountain wall took up the noise and
howling and gave it back manifold; it rose high, swelled to a
madness that carried him away. His senses reeled in the steam
of panting bodies, the acrid stench from the goats, the odour
as of stagnant waters—and another, too familiar smell—of
wounds, uncleanness, and disease. His heart throbbed to the
drums, his brain reeled, a blind rage seized him, a whirling
lust, he craved with all his soul to join the ring that formed
about the obscene symbol of the godhead, which they were
unveiling and elevating, monstrous and wooden, while from
full throats they yelled their rallying-cry. Foam dripped from
their lips, they drove each other on with lewd gesturings and
beckoning hands. They laughed, they howled, they thrust their
pointed staves into each other's flesh and licked the blood
as it ran down. But now the dreamer was in them and of
them, the stranger god was his own. Yes, it was he who
was flinging himself upon the animals, who bit and tore and
swallowed smoking gobbets of flesh—while on the trampled
moss there now began the rites in honour of the god, an orgy
of promiscuous embraces—and in his very soul he tasted the
bestial degradation of his fall.

The unhappy man woke from this dream shattered, un-
hinged, powerless in the demon's grip. He no longer avoided

men's eyes nor cared whether he exposed himself to suspicion. And anyhow, people were leaving; many of the bathing-cabins stood empty, there were many vacant places in the dining-room, scarcely any foreigners were seen in the streets. The truth seemed to have leaked out; despite all efforts to the contrary, panic was in the air. But the lady of the pearls stopped on with her family; whether because the rumours had not reached her or because she was too proud and fearless to heed them. Tadzio remained; and it seemed at times to Aschenbach, in his obsessed state, that death and fear together might clear the island of all other souls and leave him there alone with him he coveted. In the long mornings on the beach his heavy gaze would rest, a fixed and reckless stare, upon the lad; towards nightfall, lost to shame, he would follow him through the city's narrow streets where horrid death stalked too, and at such time it seemed to him as though the moral law were fallen in ruins and only the monstrous and perverse held out a hope.

Like any lover, he desired to please; suffered agonies at the thought of failure, and brightened his dress with smart ties and handkerchiefs and other youthful touches. He added jewellery and perfumes and spent hours each day over his toilette, appearing at dinner elaborately arrayed and tensely excited. The presence of the youthful beauty that had bewitched him filled him with disgust of his own ageing body; the sight of his own sharp features and grey hair plunged him in hopeless mortification; he made desperate efforts to recover the appearance and freshness of his youth and began paying frequent visits to the hotel barber. Enveloped in the white sheet, beneath the hands of that garrulous personage, he would lean back in the chair and look at himself in the glass with misgiving.

'Grey,' he said, with a grimace.

'Slightly,' answered the man. 'Entirely due to neglect, to a lack of regard for appearances. Very natural, of course, in men of affairs, but, after all, not very sensible, for it is just such people who ought to be above vulgar prejudice in matters like these. Some folk have very strict ideas about the use of cosmetics; but they never extend them to the teeth, as they logically should. And very disgusted other people would be if they did. No, we are all as old as we feel, but no older, and grey hair can misrepresent a man worse than dyed. You, for instance, signore, have a right to your natural colour. Surely you will permit me to restore what belongs to you?'

'How?' asked Aschenbach.

For answer the oily one washed his client's hair in two waters, one clear and one dark, and lo, it was as black as in the days of his youth. He waved it with the tongs in wide, flat undulations, and stepped back to admire the effect.

'Now if we were just to freshen up the skin a little,' he said.

And with that he went on from one thing to another, his enthusiasm waxing with each new idea. Aschenbach sat there comfortably; he was incapable of objecting to the process—rather as it went forward it roused his hopes. He watched it in the mirror and saw his eyebrows grow more even and arching, the eyes gain in size and brilliance, by dint of a little application below the lids. A delicate carmine glowed on his cheeks where the skin had been so brown and leathery. The dry, anaemic lips grew full, they turned the colour of ripe strawberries, the lines round eyes and mouth were treated with a facial cream and gave place to youthful bloom. It was a young man who looked back at him from the glass—Aschenbach's heart leaped at the sight. The artist in cosmetic at last professed himself satisfied; after the manner of such people, he thanked his client profusely for what he had done himself. 'The merest trifle, the merest, signore,' he said as he added the final touches. ' Now the signore can fall in love as soon as he likes.' Aschenbach went off as in a dream, dazed between joy and fear, in his red neck-tie and broad straw hat with its gay striped band.

A lukewarm storm-wind had come up. It rained a little now and then, the air was heavy and turbid and smelt of decay. Aschenbach, with fevered cheeks beneath the rouge, seemed to hear rushing and flapping sounds in his ears, as though storm-spirits were abroad—unhallowed ocean harpies who follow thoses devoted to destruction, snatch away and defile their viands. For the heat took away his appetite and thus he was haunted with the idea that his food was infected.

One afternoon he pursued his charmer deep into the stricken city's huddled heart. The labyrinthine little streets, squares, canals, and bridges, each one so like the next, at length quite made him lose his bearings. He did not even know the points of the compass; all his care was not to lose sight of the figure after which his eyes thirsted. He slunk under walls, he lurked behind buildings or people's backs; and the sustained tension of his senses and emotions exhausted him more and more, though for a long time he was unconscious of fatigue. Tadzio walked behind the others, he let them pass ahead in the narrow alleys, and as he sauntered slowly after, he would turn his head and assure himself with a glance of his strange, twilit grey eyes that his lover was still following. He saw him—and he did not betray him. The knowledge enraptured Aschenbach. Lured by those eyes, led on the leading-string of his own passion and folly, utterly lovesick, he stole upon the footsteps of his unseemly hope—and at the end found himself cheated. The Polish family crossed a small vaulted bridge, the height of whose archway hid them from his sight, and when he climbed it himself they were nowhere to be seen. He hunted in three directions—straight ahead and on both sides of the narrow, dirty quay—in vain. Worn quite out and unnerved, he had to give over the search.

His head burned, his body was wet with clammy sweat, he was plagued by intolerable thirst. He looked about for refreshment, of whatever sort, and found a little fruit-shop where he bought some strawberries. They were overripe and soft; he ate them as he went. The street he was on opened out into a little square, one of those charmed, forsaken spots he liked; he recognized it as the very one where he had sat weeks ago and conceived his abortive plan of flight. He sank down on the steps of the well and leaned his head against its stone rim. It was quiet here. Grass grew between the stones and rubbish lay about. Tall, weather-beaten houses bordered the square, one of them rather palatial, with vaulted windows, gaping now, and little lion balconies. In the ground floor of another was an apothecary's shop. A waft of carbolic acid was borne on a warm gust of wind.

There he sat, the master: this was he who had found a way to reconcile art and honours; who had written *The Abject*, and in a style of classic purity renounced bohemianism and all its works, all sympathy with the abyss and the troubled depths of the outcast human soul. This was he who had put knowledge underfoot to climb so high; who had outgrown the ironic pose and adjusted himself to the burdens and obligations of fame; whose renown had been officially recognized and his name ennobled, whose style was set for a model in the schools. There he sat. His eyelids were closed, there was only a swift, sidelong glint of the eyeballs now and again, something between a question and a leer; while the rouged and flabby mouth uttered single words of the sentences shaped in his disordered brain by the fantastic logic that governs our dreams.

'For mark you, Phaedrus, beauty alone is both divine and visible; and so it is the sense's way, the artist's way, little Phaedrus, to the spirit. But, now tell me, my dear boy, do you believe that such a man can ever attain wisdom and true manly worth, for whom the path to the spirit must lead through the senses? Or do you rather think—for I leave the point to you—that it is a path of perilous sweetness, a way of transgression, and must surely lead him who walks in it astray? For you know that we poets cannot walk the way of beauty without Eros as our companion and guide. We may be heroic after our fashion, disciplined warriors of our craft, yet are we all like women, for we exult in passion, and love is still our desire—our craving and our shame. And from this you will perceive that we poets can be neither wise nor worthy citizens. We must needs be wanton, must needs rove at large in the realm of feeling. Our magisterial style is all folly and pretence, our honourable repute a farce, the crowd's belief in us is merely laughable. And to teach youth, or the populace, by means of art is a dangerous practice and ought to be forbidden. For what good can an artist be as a teacher, when from his birth up he is headed direct for the pit? We may want to shun it and attain to honour in the world; but however we turn, it draws us still. So, then, since knowledge might destroy us, we will have none of it. For knowledge, Phaedrus, does not make him who possesses it dignified or austere. Knowledge is all-knowing, understanding, forgiving; it takes up no position, sets no store by form. It has compassion with the abyss—it *is* the abyss. So we reject it, firmly, and henceforward our concern shall be with beauty only. And by beauty we mean simplicity, largeness, and renewed severity of discipline; we mean a return to detachment and to form. But detachment, Phaedrus, and preoccupation with form lead to intoxication and desire, they may lead the noblest among us to frightful emotional excesses, which his own stern cult of the beautiful would make him the first to condemn. So they too, they too, lead to the bottomless pit. Yes, they lead us thither, I say, us who are poets—who by our natures are prone not to excellence but to excess. And now, Phaedrus, I will go. Remain here; and only when you can no longer see me, then do you depart also.'

A few days later, Gustave Aschenbach left his hotel rather later than usual in the morning. He was not feeling well and had to struggle against spells of giddiness only half physical in their nature, accompanied by a swiftly mounting dread, a sense of futility and hopelessness—but whether this referred to himself or to the outer world he could not tell. In the lobby he saw a quantity of luggage lying strapped and ready; asked the porter whose it was, and received in answer the name he already knew he should hear—that of the Polish family. The expression of his ravaged features did not change; he only gave that quick lift of the head with which we sometimes receive the uninteresting answer to a casual query. But he put another: 'When?' 'After luncheon,' the man replied. He nodded, and went down to the beach.

It was an unfriendly scene. Little crisping shivers ran all across the wide stretch of shallow water between the shore and the first sand-bank. The whole beach, once so full of colour and life, looked now autumnal, out of season; it was nearly deserted and not even very clean. A camera on a tripod stood at the edge of the water, apparently abandoned; its black cloth snapped in the freshening wind.

Tadzio was there, in front of his cabin, with the three or four playfellows still left him. Aschenbach set up his chair some half-way between the cabins and the water, spread a rug over his knees, and sat looking on. The game this time was unsupervised, the elders being probably busy with the packing, and it looked rather lawless and out-of-hand. Jaschiu, the sturdy lad in the belted suit, with the black, brilliantined hair, became angry at a handful of sand thrown in his eyes;

he challenged Tadzio to a fight, which quickly ended in the downfall of the weaker. And perhaps the coarser nature saw here a chance to avenge himself at last, by one cruel act, for his long weeks of subserviency: the victor would not let the vanquished get up, but remained kneeling on Tadzio's back, pressing Tadzio's face into the sand—for so long a time that it seemed the exhausted lad might even suffocate. He made spasmodic efforts to shake the other off, lay still and then began a feeble twitching. Just as Aschenbach was about to spring indignantly to the rescue, Jaschiu let his victim go. Tadzio, very pale, half sat up, and remained so, leaning on one arm, for several minutes, with darkening eyes and rumpled hair. Then he rose and walked slowly away. The others called him, at first gaily, then imploringly; he would not hear. Jaschiu was evidently overtaken by swift remorse; he followed his friend and tried to make his peace, but Tadzio motioned him back with a jerk of one shoulder and went down to the water's edge. He was barefoot and wore his striped linen suit with the red breast-knot.

There he stayed a little, with bent head, tracing figures in the wet sand with one toe; then stepped into the shallow water, which at its deepest did not wet his knees; waded idly through it and reached the sand-bar. Now he paused again with his face turned seaward; and next began to move slowly leftwards along the narrow strip of sand the sea left bare. He paced there, divided by an expanse of water from the shore, from his mates by his moody pride; a remote and isolated figure with floating locks, out there in sea and wind, against the misty inane. Once more he paused to look: with a sudden recollection, or by an impulse, he turned from the waist up, in an exquisite movement, one hand resting on his hip, and looked over his shoulder at the shore. The watcher sat just as he had sat that time in the lobby of the hotel when first the twilit grey eyes had met his own. He rested his head against the chair-back and followed the movements of the figure out there, then lifted it, as it were in answer to Tadzio's gaze. It sank on his breast, the eyes looked out beneath their lids, while his whole face took on the relaxed and brooding expression of deep slumber. It seemed to him the pale and lovely Summoner out there smiled at him and beckoned; as though with the hand he lifted from his hip, he pointed outward as he hovered on before into an immensity of richest expectation.

Some minutes passed before anyone hastened to the aid of the elderly man sitting there collapsed in his chair. They bore him to his room. And before nightfall a shocked and respectful world received the news of his decease.

Colette

CHÉRI

1920

SIDONIE-GABRIELLE COLETTE (1873–1954) was a woman of outstanding and highly individual talents, with an experience that ranged from a rural childhood in the idyllic countryside of Burgundy, through years of domestic unhappiness in Paris when her first husband, Henri Gauthier-Villars ('Willy'), kept her in a state of subjection verging on slavery, to positions of the highest dignity and respect, the first woman ever to be elected to the *Académie Goncourt* and subsequently its first woman President. In between she had much theatrical experience, both in the Paris music-halls, where she earned a living for six years after separating from Willy, and on the legitimate stage starring in dramatizations of her own works.

Colette's characteristic note is an unflinching realism in confronting the selfishness and sensuality of which the human being is capable, while maintaining a certain stylish flippancy and elegance, a love of life, which seems always to have an optimism at its heart. But perhaps when one has said all that, one has said only that she is a Parisienne, so deeply loved by the French because she has captured something otherwise ungraspable that is the essence of their city.

Chéri was followed by a sequel, *La Fin de Chéri* (1926), which rounds off the tragicomic little story with perfect neatness; but *Chéri* can stand without it, as it did for the first six years of its life.

Rooted in Paris as she was, Colette would occasionally voyage back in imagination to her rural girlhood, when her surroundings were natural and her companions as often animal as human, particularly in *The House of Claudine*, 1922, *Sido*, 1929, and *A Lesson in Love* (*La Naissance du Jour*), 1932.

'GIVE it me, Léa, give me your pearl necklace! Do you hear me, Léa? Give me your pearls!'

No answer came from the huge brass-bedecked wrought-iron bedstead that glimmered in the shadows like a coat of mail.

'Why won't you let me have your necklace? It looks every bit as well on me as on you—even better!'

At the snap of the clasp, ripples spread over the lace-frilled sheets, and from their midst rose two magnificent thin-wristed arms, lifting on high two lovely lazy hands.

'Leave it alone, Chéri! You've been playing long enough with that necklace.'

'It amuses me. . . . Are you frightened I'll steal it?'

He was capering about in front of the sun-drenched rosy-pink curtains—a graceful demon, black against a glowing furnace; but when he pranced back towards the bed, he turned white again from top to toe, in his white silk pyjamas and white Moorish slippers.

'I'm not frightened,' the soft, deep voice answered from the bed. 'But you'll wear out the thread. Those pearls are heavy.'

'They certainly are,' Chéri said with due respect. 'Whoever gave you this lot never meant to make light of you!'

He was standing in front of a pier-glass framed in the space between two windows, gazing at the reflection of a very youthful, very good-looking young man, neither too short nor too tall, hair with the blue sheen of a blackbird's plumage. He unbuttoned his pyjamas, displaying a hard, darkish chest, curved like a shield; and the whites of his dark eyes, his teeth, and the pearls of the necklace gleamed in the over-all rosy glow of the room.

'Take off that necklace!' The female voice was insistent. 'Do you hear what I say?'

The young man, motionless in front of his image, laughed softly to himself: 'Yes, yes, I heard you. I know so well you're terrified I'll make off with it!'

'No, I'm not. But if I did offer it to you, you're quite capable of taking it.'

He ran to the bed and bounded into it. 'You bet I am! I rise above the conventions. Personally, I think it's idiotic for a man to allow a woman to give him a single pearl for a tie-pin, or two for a pair of studs, and then to consider himself beyond the pale if she gives him fifty. . . .'

'Forty-nine.'

'Forty-nine—as if I hadn't counted! I dare you to say they don't look well on me! Or that I'm ugly!'

Léa sat up in bed. 'No, I won't say that. For one thing, because you'd never believe me. But can't you learn to laugh without crinkling up your nose like that? I suppose you won't be happy till you've wrinkles all up the side of your nose!'

He stopped laughing at once, let the skin on his forehead relax, and drew in the fold under his chin like a coquettish old woman. They looked at each other in open hostility—she, leaning on her elbow in a flurry of frills and lace; he, sitting side-saddle on the edge of the bed. He was thinking 'Who's she to talk of any wrinkles I may have one day?' and she 'Why is he so ugly when he laughs?—he who's the very picture of beauty!' She thought for a moment, then finished aloud: 'It's because you look so ill-natured when you're joking. You never laugh except unkindly—*at* people, and that makes you ugly. You're often ugly.'

'That's not true!' Chéri exclaimed crossly.

Anger knitted his eyebrows close above his nose, magnified his eyes, glittering with insolence behind a palisade of lashes, and parted the chaste bow of his disdainful mouth. Léa smiled to see him as she loved him best: rebellious only to become submissive, enchained lightly but powerless to free himself. She put a hand on his young head, which impatiently shook off the yoke. Like someone quieting an animal, she murmured, 'There, there! What is it? What is it, then?'

He fell upon her big beautiful shoulder, nuzzling and butting his way into his favourite resting-place with eyes already shut, seeking his customary long morning sleep in the protection of her arms. But Léa pushed him away. 'None of that now, Chéri! You're having luncheon with our national Harpy, and it's already twenty to twelve!'

'Not really? I'm lunching at the old girl's? You too?'

Lazily Léa settled deeper into the bed.

'Not me, I'm off duty. I'll go for coffee at half-past two or
tea at six, or for a cigarette at a quarter to eight. Don't worry;
she'll always see enough of me. And besides, I've not been
asked.'

Chéri's sulky face lit up with malice.

'I know, I know why! We're going to have high society.
We're going to have the fair Marie-Laure, and that poisonous
child of hers.'

Léa brought her big blue wandering eyes to rest.

'Oh, really! The little girl's charming. Less so than her
mother, but charming. Now take off that necklace, once and
for all.'

'Pity,' Chéri sighed, as he undid the clasp: 'It would look so
well in the trousseau.'

Léa raised herself on her elbow: 'What trousseau?'

'Mine,' Chéri said with ludicrous self-importance. '*My* trousseau, full of *my* jewels, for *my* marriage!'

He bounded in the air, executed a perfect *entrechat-six*,
returned to earth, butted his way through the door-curtains,
and disappeared, shouting: 'My bath, Rose! And quick about
it! I'm lunching at the old girl's!'

'That's that,' Léa thought. 'We'll have a lake in the bathroom
and eight towels floating in it, and razor scrapings in the basin.
If only I had two bathrooms!'

But, as on former occasions, she soon saw that this would
mean getting rid of a wardrobe and lopping off a corner of
her dressing-room, and so concluded, as on former occasions:
'I shall simply have to put up with it till Chéri gets married.'

She lay down again on her back and noticed that Chéri,
undressing the night before, had thrown his socks on the
mantelpiece, his pants on the writing-table, his tie round the
neck of her portrait bust. She could not help smiling at this
hasty masculine disorder, and half closed her large tranquil
eyes. Their blue was as beautiful as ever, and so were the thick
chestnut lashes.

At the age of forty-nine, Léonie Vallon, called Léa de
Lonval, was nearing the end of a successful career as a
richly kept courtesan. She was a good creature, and life
had spared her the more flattering catastrophes and exalted
sufferings. She made a secret of the date of her birth; but

willingly admitted—with a look of voluptuous condescension for Chéri's special benefit—that she was approaching the age when she could indulge in a few creature comforts. She liked order, fine linen, wines in their prime, and carefully planned meals at home. From an idolized young blonde she had become a rich middle-aged *demi-mondaine* without ever attracting any outrageous publicity. Not that she went in for any pretences. Her friends remembered a Four-in-Hand Meet at Auteuil, about 1895, when the sub-editor of *Gil Blas* had addressed her as 'dear artist' and she had answered: 'Artist! Oh come, my good friend, my lovers must have been telling tales. . . .'

Her contemporaries were jealous of her imperturbable good health, and the younger women, whose figures were padded out in front and behind after the fashion of 1912, scoffed at her opulent bust. Young and old alike envied her the possession of Chéri.

'Though, good heavens!' Léa used to say, 'there's no reason why they should. They're welcome to him! I don't keep him on a lead. He goes out by himself.'

But in this she was not altogether speaking the truth, for she was proud of a liaison—sometimes, in her weakness for the truth, referring to it as 'an adoption'—that had lasted six years.

'Trousseau,' Léa said over again. 'Marriage for Chéri! It's not possible, it's not . . . human . . . you can't give an innocent girl to Chéri! Why, it would be throwing a doe to the hounds! People don't know what Chéri is!'

As if telling the beads of a rosary, she ran her fingers over the necklace which Chéri had tossed on the bed. She put it away at night now because, with his passion for fine pearls and his fondness for playing with them in the morning, he would have noticed too often that her throat had thickened and was not nearly so white, with the muscles under its skin growing slack. She fastened the pearls round her neck without getting up, and took a hand-mirror from the bedside-table.

'I look like a gardener's wife,' was her unflattering comment, 'a market-gardener's wife. A market-gardener's wife in Normandy, off to the potato-fields wearing a pearl necklace.

I might as well stick an ostrich feather in my nose—and that's being polite!'

She shrugged her shoulders, severely critical of everything she no longer loved in herself: the vivid complexion, healthy, a little too ruddy—an open-air complexion, well suited to emphasize the pure intensity of her eyes, with their varying shades of blue. Her proud nose still won her approval. 'Marie-Antoinette's nose!' Chéri's mother was in the habit of saying, without ever forgetting to add: 'and in another two years our Léa will have a chin like Louis Seize.' Her mouth, with its even row of teeth, seldom opened in a peal of laughter; but she smiled often, a smile that set off to perfection the lazy flutter of her large eyes—a smile a hundred times lauded, sung, and photographed—a deep, confiding smile one never tired of watching.

As for her body—'Everyone knows,' Léa would say, 'that a well-made body lasts a long time.' She could still afford to show her body, pink and white, endowed with the long legs and straight back of a naiad on an Italian fountain; the dimpled hips, the high-slung breasts, 'would last,' Léa used to say, 'till well after Chéri's wedding.'

She got out of bed, and, slipping into a wrap, went to draw back the long curtains. The noonday sun poured into the gay, rosy, over-decorated room. Its luxury dated: double lace curtains, rose-bud watered silk on the walls, gilded woodwork, and antique furniture upholstered in modern silks. Léa refused to give up either this cosy room or its bed, a massive and indestructible masterpiece of wrought iron and brass, grim to the eye and cruel to the shins.

'Come, come!' Chéri's mother protested, 'it's not as bad as all that. Personally, I like this room. It belongs to a period. It has a style of its own. It suggests La Païva.'

The remembrance of this dig made Léa smile as she pinned up her hair. She hurriedly powdered her face on hearing two doors slam, and the thud of a male foot colliding with some delicate piece of furniture. Chéri came back into the room in shirt and trousers, his ears white with talcum powder. He was in an aggressive mood.

'Where's my tie-pin? What a wretched hole this is! Have they taken to pinching the jewellery?'

'Marcel must have stuck it in his tie to go to the market,' Léa gravely replied.

Chéri, who had little or no sense of humour, was brought up short by the little quip like an ant by a lump of coal. He stopped his angry pacing up and down, and found nothing better to say than: 'Charming! and what about my boots?'

'Your what?'

'The calf, of course!'

Léa smiled up at him from her dressing-table, too affectionately. 'You said it, not I,' she murmured in caressing tones.

'The day when a woman loves me for my brains,' he retorted, 'I shall be done for. Meanwhile I must have my pin and my boots.'

'What for? You don't wear a tie-pin with a lounge suit, and you've got one pair on already.'

Chéri stamped his foot. 'I've had enough of this! There's nobody here to look after me, and I'm sick of it all.'

Léa put down her comb. 'Very well, say goodbye to it all for good!'

He shrugged his shoulders, like a young tough. 'You wouldn't like it if I did!'

'Be off with you! I hate guests who complain of the cooking and leave bits and pieces all over the place and cream-cheese sticking to the mirrors. Go back to your sainted mother, my child, and stay there.'

Unable to meet Léa's gaze, he lowered his eyes, and broke out into schoolboy protests. 'Soon I shan't be allowed to open my mouth! Anyhow, you'll let me have your motor to go to Neuilly?'

'No.'

'Why not?'

'Because I'm going out in it myself at two, and because the chauffeur is having his dinner.'

'Where are you going at two?'

'To say my prayers. But if you need three francs for a taxi . . . Idiot,' she added tenderly. 'At two I'll probably come to your lady mother's for coffee. Does that satisfy you?'

He tossed his head like a young buck. 'You bite my head off, you won't give me anything I ask for; they hide my things away, they—'

'Will you never learn to dress yourself?'

She took the tie from Chéri's hands and tied it for him.

'There! And that frightful purple tie. . . . However, it's just the thing for the fair Marie-Laure and family. . . . And you wanted to wear a pearl on top of all that! You little dago. . . . Why not earrings into the bargain?'

His defences were down. Blissful, languid, irresolute, supine, he surrendered again to a lazy happiness and closed his eyes. . . .

'Nounoune darling . . .' he murmured.

She brushed the hair off his ears, combed a straighter parting in the bluish locks of his black hair, dabbed a little scent on his temples, and gave him a quick kiss, unable to resist the tempting mouth so close to her own.

Chéri opened his eyes, and his lips, then stretched out his hands.

She moved away. 'No. It's a quarter to one! Be off now, and don't let me see you again!'

'Never?'

'Never,' she laughed back at him with uncontrollable tenderness.

Left to herself, she smiled proudly, and a sharp little sigh of defeated desire escaped her as she listened to Chéri's footsteps crossing the courtyard. She saw him open and close the gates, drift away on his winged feet, only to encounter the adoring glances of three shop girls walking along arm-in-arm.

'Lawks! He's too good to be true! Let's touch him to see if he's real!'

But Chéri took it all for granted and did not even turn round.

II

MY bath, Rose! Tell the manicurist she can go, it's far too late now. My blue coat and skirt—the new one—the blue hat with the white under-brim, and the little shoes with the straps . . . No, wait . . .'

Léa, with one leg across the other, rubbed her ankle and shook her head.

'No, the blue kid laced boots. My legs are a little swollen to-day. It's the heat.'

Her elderly maid, butterfly-capped, raised understanding eyes to Léa. 'It's . . . it's the heat,' she repeated obediently, shrugging her shoulders as much as to say: 'We know . . . Nothing lasts for ever. . . .'

With Chéri out of the house, Léa became herself again, very much alive, cheerful, and on the spot. Within an hour, she had been given her bath, followed by a spirit-rub scented with sandal-wood, and was ready dressed, hatted, and shod. While the curling-tongs were heating, she found time to run through the butler's book and send for Émile, the footman, and call his attention to the blue haze on one of the looking-glasses. She ran an experienced eye—rarely taken in—over everything in the room, and lunched in solitary bliss, with a smile for the dry Vouvray and for the June strawberries, served, with their stalks, on a plate of Rubelles enamel as green as a tree-frog after rain. Someone in the past who appreciated good food must have chosen the huge Louis Seize looking-glasses and the English furniture of the same period, for this rectangular dining-room, light, airy sideboards, high pedestalled dumb-waiters, spindly yet strong Sheraton chairs, in a dark wood with delicate swags. The looking-glasses and the massive silver caught the full light of day, with a touch of green reflected from the trees in the Avenue Bugeaud. Léa, as she ate, examined a fork for any suspicion of pink cleaning-powder left in the chasing, and half closed one eye the better to judge the quality of the polish on the dark wood. Standing behind her, the butler watched this performance nervously.

'Marcel!' Léa said, 'for the last week or so, the wax on your floors has been smeary.'

'Does Madame think so?'

'Madame does think so. Add a little turpentine while you're melting it in a double saucepan; it's quite easy to do again. You brought up the Vouvray a little too soon. Close the shutters as soon as you've cleared the table; we're in for a heat-wave.'

'Very good, Madame. Will Monsieur Ch—Monsieur Peloux be dining?'

'Probably. . . . No *crème-surprise* to-night. We'll just have a strawberry water ice. Coffee in the boudoir.'

As she rose from the table, straight and tall, the shape of her legs visible under a dress that moulded her hips, she had ample time to note the 'Madame is beautiful' in the butler's discreet glance, and this did not displease her.

'Beautiful,' Léa whispered on her way up to the boudoir. 'No. . . . No longer. I have now to wear something white near my face, and very pale pink underclothes and tea-gowns. Beautiful! Pish. . . . I hardly need to be that any longer.'

All the same, she allowed herself no siesta in the painted silk boudoir, when she had finished with coffee and the newspapers. And it was with battle written on her face that she gave her chauffeur the order: 'To Madame Peloux's.'

The tree-lined road through the Bois, dry beneath the young, already arid, faded June foliage—the toll-gate— Neuilly— Boulevard d'Inkermann—'How many times have I come this way?' Léa wondered. She began to count, then tired of counting and softened her tread on the gravel outside Madame Peloux's house to overhear any sounds coming from it.

'They're in the garden-room,' she concluded.

She had put on more powder before approaching the house and tightened the fine-mesh, misty blue veil under her chin. Her answer to the manservant's formal request to come through the house was: 'No; I'd rather go round by the garden.'

A real garden—almost a park—completely surrounded the vast white villa, typical of the outer suburbs of Paris. Madame Peloux's villa had been called 'a country residence' in the days when Neuilly was still on the outskirts of Paris. This was apparent from the stables, converted into garages, the other offices with their kennels and wash-houses, not to mention the size of the billiard-room, entrance hall, and dining-room.

'This is a handsome investment of Madame Peloux's,' her female devotees never tired of repeating—the old toadies who, in exchange for a dinner or a glass of brandy, came there to take a hand against her at bezique or poker. And they added: 'But then, where has Madame Peloux not got money invested?'

Walking along in the shade of the acacia trees, between trellised roses and huge clumps of rhododendrons in full blaze, Léa could hear the murmur of voices, and, rising above it, Madame Peloux's shrill nasal trumpet notes and Chéri's dry cackle.

'That child's got an ugly laugh,' she thought. She paused a moment to listen more attentively to a new feminine note; weak, pleasing, quickly drowned by the redoubtable trumpeting. 'That must be the girl,' she said to herself, and a few quick steps brought her to the garden-room with its glass front, from which Madame Peloux burst out with a 'Here comes our beautiful friend!'

A little round barrel of a woman, Madame Peloux—in reality Mademoiselle Peloux—had been a ballet-dancer from her tenth to her sixteenth year. Occasionally Léa would search for some trace in Madame Peloux that might recall the once chubby little fair-haired Eros, or the later dimpled nymph, and found nothing except the big implacable eyes, the delicate aggressive nose, and a still coquettish way of standing with her feet in 'the fifth position,' like the members of the *corps de ballet*.

Chéri, coming to life in the depths of a rocking-chair, kissed Léa's hand with involuntary grace and ruined his gesture by exclaiming: 'Hang it all! you've put on a veil again, and I loathe veils.'

'Will you leave her alone!' Madame Peloux interposed. 'You must never ask a woman why she is wearing a veil. We'll never be able to do anything with him,' she said to Léa affectionately.

Two women had risen to their feet in the golden shade of a straw blind. One, in mauve, rather coldly offered her hand to Léa, who looked her over from head to foot.

'Goodness, how lovely you are, Marie-Laure! you're perfection itself!'

Marie-Laure deigned to smile. She was a red-haired young woman with brown eyes, whose physical presence alone was enough to take your breath away. She drew attention, almost coquettishly, to the other young woman, by saying: 'But would you have recognized my daughter Edmée?'

Léa held out a hand which the girl was reluctant to shake.

'I should have known you, my child, but a schoolgirl alters so quickly, and Marie-Laure alters only to become always more disconcertingly lovely. Are you quite finished with school now?'

'I should hope so, I should hope so,' exclaimed Madame Peloux. 'You can't go on for ever, hiding her under a bushel, such a miracle of grace and charm, and she's nineteen already!'

'Eighteen,' said Marie-Laure sweetly.

'Eighteen, eighteen! . . . Yes of course, eighteen! Léa, you remember? This child was just making her first Communion the year that Chéri ran away from school, surely you remember? Yes, yes, you did, you little good-for-nothing, you ran away and Léa and I were driven nearly out of our wits!'

'I remember perfectly,' Léa said, and she exchanged an imperceptible little nod with Marie-Laure—something corresponding to the '*touché*' of a punctilious fencer.

'You must get her married soon, you must get her married soon!' pursued Madame Peloux, who never failed to repeat a basic truth at least twice. 'We'll all come to the wedding.'

She brandished her little arms in the air, and the young girl glanced at her with ingenuous alarm.

'She's just the daughter for Marie-Laure,' thought Léa, gazing at her more closely. 'She has all her mother's dazzling qualities but in a quieter key: fluffy, ash-brown hair, that looks as if it were powdered; frightened, secretive eyes and a mouth she avoids opening even to speak or smile. . . . Exactly what Marie-Laure needs as a foil—but how she must hate her!'

Madame Peloux insinuated a maternal smile between Léa and the young girl: 'You ought to have seen how well these two young people were getting on together in the garden!'

She pointed to where Chéri stood smoking a cigarette on the other side of the glass partition, his cigarette-holder clenched between his teeth, and his head tilted back to avoid the smoke. The three women looked at the young man who—forehead held at an angle, eyes half shut, feet together, motionless—looked for all the world like a winged figure hovering dreamily in the air. Léa did not fail to observe the expression of fright and subjugation in the girl's eyes, and she took pleasure in making her tremble by touching her on the arm. Edmée quivered from head to foot, withdrew her arm, and whispered almost savagely, 'What?'

'Nothing,' Léa replied, 'I dropped my glove.'

'Come along, Edmée!' Marie-Laure called negligently.

Silent and docile, the girl walked towards Madame Peloux, who flapped her wings: 'Leaving already? Surely not? We must meet again soon, we must meet again soon!'

'It's late,' Marie-Laure said, 'and you'll be expecting any number of people as it's Sunday afternoon. The child is not accustomed to company.'

'Of course not, of course not,' Madame Peloux said tenderly. 'She's had such a sheltered existence . . . such a lonely life!'

Marie-Laure smiled, and Léa gave her a look as much as to say, 'That's one for you!'

'But we'll call again soon.'

'Thursday, Thursday! Léa, you'll come to lunch on Thursday?'

'I'll be here,' Léa answered.

Chéri had rejoined Edmée at the entrance to the room and stood beside her, disdaining all conversation. He had heard Léa's promise, and turned round: 'Splendid, then we can go for a run in the motor.'

'Yes, yes, just the thing for you young people,' Madame Peloux insisted, touched by his proposal. 'Edmée can sit in front next to Chéri, at the wheel, and the rest of us will go at the back. Youth at the helm, youth at the helm! Chéri, my love, will you ask for Marie-Laure's motor?'

Her small stumpy feet kept slipping on the gravel, but she managed to take her two visitors to the corner of the path, where she handed them over to Chéri. On her return, she found that Léa had taken off her hat and was smoking a cigarette.

'Aren't they sweet, those two!' Madame Peloux gasped. 'Don't you think so, Léa?'

'Delicious,' Léa breathed out in the same puff as her cigarette smoke. 'But really, that Marie-Laure!'

'What's Marie-Laure been up to?' asked Chéri, as he rejoined them.

'How lovely she is!'

'Ah! Ah!' Madame Peloux began in formal assent. 'That's true, that's true. She has been really lovely.'

Chéri and Léa caught each other's eye and laughed.

'Has been?' Léa emphasized the past tense. 'But she's the picture of youth. Not a single wrinkle! And she can wear the palest mauve, such a foul colour! I loathe it and it loathes me.'

Madame Peloux raised her big pitiless eyes and thin nose from her brandy-glass.

'The picture of youth, the picture of youth!' yapped Madame Peloux. 'Pardon me, pardon me! Marie-Laure had Edmée in 1895, no . . . '94. She'd just run away with a singing-teacher, leaving Khalil Bey flat, though he'd given her the famous pink diamond which . . . No, no! Wait! . . . That must have been the year before!'

The trumpet notes were shrill and off key. Léa put a hand over her ear, and Chéri declared, with some feeling: 'Everything would be heavenly on an afternoon like this, if only we could be spared my mother's voice!'

She looked at her son with no sign of anger, accustomed to his insolence. Dignified, feet dangling, she settled herself back in a basket chair too high for her short legs. In one hand she warmed her glass of brandy. Léa, rocking herself gently to and fro, glanced occasionally at Chéri, who lay sprawled on a cool cane settee, coat unbuttoned, a cigarette dying between his lips, a lock of hair over one eyebrow. 'He's a handsome young blackguard,' she thought admiringly.

There they remained, peacefully side by side, making no effort to talk or be sociable, happy after their own fashion. Years of close familiarity rendered silence congenial, and Chéri slipped back into his lethargy, Léa into her calm. As the afternoon became hotter, Madame Peloux pulled her narrow skirt up to her knees, displaying her tight little sailor's calves, and Chéri ripped off his tie—reproved by Léa in an audible 'Tch, tch.'

'Oh! leave the child alone,' Madame Peloux protested, as from the depths of a dream. 'It's much too hot! Would you care for a kimono, Léa?'

'No, thank you. I'm perfectly comfortable.'

Their unbuttoned siestas disgusted her. Never once had her young lover caught her untidily dressed, or with her blouse undone, or in her bedroom slippers during the day. 'Naked, if need be,' she would say, 'but squalid, never!'

She picked up her picture paper again, but did not read it. 'These Pelouxs – mother and son alike!' she thought dreamily. 'They've only to sit themselves down at a good meal or in the heart of the countryside and—snap!—the mother whisks off her stays and the son his waistcoat. They behave like publicans out on a holiday, the pair of them.' She cast a vindictive eye on one of the publicans in question, and saw that he had fallen asleep, his eyelashes spread against his pallid cheeks, his mouth closed. His upper lip, lit from below, reflected two silver pinpoints of light at the twin curves of its delicious Cupid's bow, and Léa was forced to admit that he looked far more like a sleeping god than a licensed victualler.

Without moving from her chair, she gently plucked the lighted cigarette from between Chéri's fingers and put it in the ash-tray. The hand of the sleeper relaxed and the tapering fingers, tipped with cruel nails, drooped like wilting flowers: a hand not strictly feminine, yet a trifle prettier than one could have wished; a hand she had kissed a hundred times—not in slavish devotion—but kissed for the pleasure of it, for its scent.

From behind her paper, she glanced at Madame Peloux. Was she asleep too? Léa always liked to remain awake while mother and son dozed, allowing her a quiet hour's self-communing in the dappled sunlight of a broiling afternoon. But Madame Peloux was not asleep. She was sitting bolt upright in her wickerwork chair, like a Buddha staring into space, and sipping her *fine-champagne* with the absorption of an alcoholic baby.

'Why doesn't she go to sleep?' Léa wondered. 'It's Sunday. She's lunched well. She's expecting her sponging old cronies to drop in for her five o'clock tea. By rights she ought to be having a snooze. If she's not snoozing, it's because she's up to some devilment or other.'

They had known each other for twenty-five years. Theirs was the hostile intimacy of light women, enriched and then cast aside by one man, ruined by another: the tetchy affection of rivals stalking one another's first wrinkle or white hair. Theirs was the friendship of two practical women of the world, both adepts at the money game; but one of them a miser, and the other a sybarite. These bonds count. Rather late in their day, a stronger bond had come to link them more closely: Chéri.

Léa could remember Chéri as a little boy—a marvel of beauty with long curls. When quite small he was known as Fred, and had not yet been nicknamed Chéri.

Sometimes forgotten and sometimes adored, Chéri grew up among wan housemaids and tall sardonic men-servants. Although his birth had mysteriously brought wealth to the house, no 'Fräulein', no 'Miss' was ever to be seen at Chéri's side; and his mother had preserved him to the accompaniment of piercing shrieks, from 'these ghouls'.

'Charlotte Peloux, you belong to another age.' The speaker was the moribund, mummified, but indestructible Baron de Berthellemy. 'Charlotte Peloux, in you I salute the only light woman who ever had the courage to bring up her son as the son of a tart! You belong to another age! You never read, you never travel, you make a point of knowing your neighbour's business, and you abandon your child to the tender mercies of the servants. How perfect! How absolutely About! . . . Or, better still, how like a novel by Gustav Droz. . . . And to think that you've never heard of either! . . .'

Chéri had enjoyed the full freedom of a profligate upbringing. When barely able to lisp, he was quick to pick up all the backstairs gossip. He shared in the clandestine suppers of the kitchen. His ablutions varied between milky immersions in his mother's orrisroot baths and scanty cat-licks with the corner of a towel. He suffered from indigestion after a surfeit of sweets, or from pangs of hunger when no one remembered to give him his supper. He was wretchedly bored at every Battle of Flowers, where Charlotte Peloux would exhibit him—half-naked and catching cold—sitting on drenched roses; but it so happened, when he was twelve, that he had a glorious adventure in an illicit gambling-den, when an American woman allowed him to play with a fistful of louis d'or, and called him 'a little masterpiece'. At about the same time, Madame Peloux imposed a tutor on her son—an Abbé, whom she packed off at the end of ten months 'because,' she confessed, 'whenever I caught sight of that black robe trailing along the passages, it made me think I was housing a female relation: and God knows there are few things more depressing than having a poor relation to stay!'

At the age of fourteen, Chéri had a taste of school. He didn't believe in it. He broke prison and ran away. Madame Peloux not only found the energy to incarcerate him a second time, but also, when faced with her son's tears and insults, took to her heels with hands over her ears screaming, 'I can't bear the sight of it! I can't bear the sight of it!' So sincere were her cries that she actually fled from Paris, in the company of a man who was young but far from scrupulous. Two years later she came back, alone. It was the last time she succumbed to an amorous impulse.

She found, on her return, that Chéri had shot up too fast; that his cheeks were hollow and his eyes black-ringed; that he dressed like a stable-lad and spoke with a worse accent than ever. She beat her breast, and snatched him back from the boarding-school. He utterly refused to work; demanded horses, carriages, jewels; insisted on a substantial monthly allowance; and, when his mother began to beat her breast and shriek like a pea-hen, he put a stop to her cries by saying: 'Madame Peloux, ma'am, don't carry on so. My venerable mother, if no one except me drags you down into the gutter, you're likely to die a comfortable death in your downy bed; I don't altogether fancy a trustee for my estate. Your cash is mine. Let me go my own way! Men friends cost next to nothing—a dinner and a bottle of champagne. As for the fair sex, surely, Ma'me Peloux, seeing that I take after you, you can trust me not to treat 'em to more than a trinket—if that!'

He pirouetted about while she shed tears and proclaimed herself the happiest of mothers. When Chéri began buying motor-cars, she trembled once more; but he simply advised her: 'Keep an eye on the petrol, Ma'me Peloux, if you please!' and sold his horses. He was not above checking the two chauffeurs' books. His calculations were quick and accurate, and the figures he jotted down on slips of paper—dashed off rapidly, round and regular—were in marked contrast to his rather slow and childish handwriting.

At seventeen he was like a little old man, always fussing over his expenses: still good-looking—but skinny and short-winded. More than once Madame Peloux ran into him on the cellar steps, coming up from checking the bottles in the racks and bins.

'Would you believe it?' she said to Léa. 'It's too wonderful.'

'Much too wonderful,' Léa answered, 'he'll come to a bad end. Chéri! Show me your tongue!'

He put out his tongue, made a face, and showed other signs of disrespect. Léa took no notice. She was too intimate a friend, a sort of doting godmother, whom he called by her Christian name.

'Is it true,' Léa enquired, 'that you were seen last night at a bar, sitting on old Lili's knees?'

'Her knees!' scoffed Chéri. 'She hasn't had any for ages. They foundered years ago.'

'Isn't it true,' Léa persisted with greater severity, 'that she made you drink gin laced with pepper? You know gin is bad for the breath!'

On one occasion, Chéri, hurt, snapped back at Léa: 'I can't think why you bother me with all these questions. You must have seen what I was up to; you were tucked away in that cubby-hole at the back, with Patron your prize-fighter friend.'

'That's perfectly correct,' Léa answered, unmoved. 'There's nothing of the dissipated schoolboy about Patron. He has other attractions, and a good deal more to recommend him than a perky little face and two black rings round his eyes.'

That week Chéri had been out on the razzle in Montmartre and les Halles, consorting with ladies of the town who called him 'poppet' and 'my pet vice', but he had got no kick out of it: he suffered from migraines and a dry cough. Madame Peloux poured out her heartbreaking woes—'Life is nothing but a series of crosses for us mothers'—to her masseuse, to her stay-maker, Madame Ribot, to old Lili, to the Baron de Berthellemy, and thus passed painlessly from the state of being the happiest-of-parents to that of the martyr-mother.

A night in June, when Madame Peloux and Léa and Chéri were together in the garden-room at Neuilly, was to change the destinies of the young man and the middle-aged woman. Chéri's friends had gone off for the evening—little Baxter, a wholesale wine-merchant, and the Vicomte Desmond, a hanger-on of his, barely of age, difficult and arrogant—and so Chéri had returned to the maternal fold, and habit had drawn Léa there also.

For one more evening, in a whole sequence of such occasions, these two women, each suspicious of the other, found themselves together. They had known each other for twenty years; they shared a past made up of similarly dull evenings; they lacked other friends; and, in their later days, they had become mistrustful, self-indulgent, and cut off from the world, as women are who have lived only for love.

Both were staring in silence at Chéri, who never spoke. Madame Peloux lacked the strength to take her son's health in hand, but hated Léa a little more each time she bent her white neck and glowing cheeks over Chéri's pallid cheek and transparent ear. She would willingly have bled that healthy female neck, already wrinkled by the so-called lines of Venus, in order to give a touch of colour to her slim lily-green son: yet it never occurred to her to take her darling away to the country.

'Chéri, why are you drinking brandy?' Léa scolded.

'Out of politeness to Ma'me Peloux—who would otherwise be drinking alone,' Chéri answered.

'What are you going to do to-morrow?'

'Dunno, and you?'

'I'm off to Normandy.'

'With?'

'That's none of your business.'

'With our friend Spéleïeff?'

'Don't be so stupid. That was over two months ago. You're behind the times. Spéleïeff's in Russia.'

'Chéri, darling, what can you be thinking of?' sighed Madame Peloux. 'Don't you remember going last month to the charming dinner given by Léa to celebrate the end of the affair? Léa, you've never let me have the recipe for those langoustines I enjoyed so much.'

Chéri sat up, his eyes sparkling. 'Yes, yes, langoustines swimming in a creamy sauce! How I'd like some now!'

'You see,' Madame Peloux said reproachfully, 'he's got no appetite to speak of and yet he's asking for langoustines.'

'Shut up!' Chéri snapped. 'Léa, are you off to the shady woods with Patron?'

'Certainly not, my boy. Patron and I are merely friends. I'm going on my own.'

'Nice to be so rich!' Chéri threw out.

'I'll take you with me, if you like: there'll be nothing to do but eat and drink and sleep. . . .'

'Where is this place of yours?' He had risen to his feet and was standing over her.

'You know Honfleur—the Côte de Grâce—don't you? Sit down; you're green in the face. Now as you go down the Côte de Grâce, you know those farm gates where we always say, in passing, your mother and I . . .'

She turned round to where Madame Peloux was sitting. Madame Peloux had disappeared. The discretion with which she had faded away was something so unlike the normal Charlotte Peloux, that they looked at each other and laughed in surprise.

Chéri sat down close to Léa. 'I'm tired,' he said.

'You're ruining your health.'

He drew himself up in his chair, with offended vanity. 'Oh! I'm still in good enough fettle, you know.'

'Good enough! For others perhaps . . . but not . . . not for me, I'd have you know.'

'Too green?'

'The very word I was looking for. So why don't you come down to the country? No nonsense, of course. Ripe strawberries, fresh cream, cakes, grilled spring chicken . . . that's just what you need—and no women.'

He let himself snuggle up to Léa's elbow and shut his eyes.

'No women . . . grand . . . Léa, tell me, you're my pal? You are? Then let's be off. Women indeed! I'm fed up with 'em. Women! I've seen all they've got to show.'

These vulgarities were muttered in a drowsy voice. Léa listened to his soft tone, and felt his warm breath against her ear. He had taken hold of her long string of pearls and was rolling the larger ones between his fingers. She slipped her arm under his head and so accustomed was she to treating the boy in this way that, almost without thinking, she pulled him towards her and rocked him in her arms.

'How comfy I am!' he sighed. 'You're a good pal. I'm so comfy.'

Léa smiled, as though hearing praise she valued intensely. Chéri seemed to be ready to drop off to sleep. She looked very closely at his glistening, almost dewy, eyelashes sunk flat against the cheeks and then at the cheeks themselves, hollowed by his joyless dissipation. His upper lip, shaved that morning, was already bluish, and the pink lampshades lent his mouth an artificial colour.

'No women!' Chéri exclaimed, as though dreaming. 'Then . . . kiss me!'

Taken my surprise, Léa made no movement.

'Kiss me! I tell you!'

He rapped out his order, frowning, and Léa felt embarrassed by the rekindled gleam in his eyes. It was as if someone had switched on the light. She shrugged her shoulders and kissed the forehead so close to her lips. He drew his arms tighter around her neck, and pulled her down towards him.

She shook her head only at the very instant that their lips touched, then she remained absolutely motionless, and held her breath like someone listening. When he released his hold, she broke away from him, rose to her feet, took a deep breath, and put a hand up to tidy her unruffled hair. She turned to him, rather pale and with rueful eyes and said, teasingly: 'That was a bright idea!'

He lay far back in the rocking-chair, speechless, and scrutinized her with a suspicious, questioning gaze, so that she asked: 'What is it?'

'Nothing,' Chéri said. 'I know what I wanted to know.'

She blushed with humiliation, then skilfully defended herself.

'What do you know? That I like your mouth? My poor child, I've kissed uglier. What does that prove? D'you think I'm going to fling myself at your feet and cry "Take me!" You talk as if you've known only nice young girls! D'you imagine I'm going to lose my head because of a kiss?'

She grew calmer while speaking and wished to prove her self-control.

'Listen, child,' she persisted, as she leaned over him, 'd'you think a handsome mouth means anything to me?'

She smiled down at him, completely sure of herself, but unaware that there remained on her face a sort of very faint quiver, an appealing sadness, and that her smile was like a rainbow after a sudden storm.

'I'm perfectly calm. Even if I were to kiss you again, or even if we . . .' She stopped and pouted with scorn. 'No, no, I really can't see you and me doing that.'

'Nor could you see us doing what we did just now,' Chéri said, taking time over his words. 'And yet you don't mind doing it, and not in a hurry, either. So now you're thinking of going further, are you? *I* never suggested such a thing.'

They faced each other like enemies. Léa was afraid to reveal a desire she had not yet had time to develop or to disguise; she resented this child, so suddenly cold and perhaps derisive.

'You're right,' she conceded lightly. 'Let's say no more about it. Shall we say instead that I'm offering to put you out to grass! And the food will be good . . . *my* food, in other words.'

'We'll see,' Chéri answered. 'Shall I bring the Renouhard tourer?'

'Of course; you're not going to leave it behind with Charlotte.'

'I'll pay for the petrol, but you'll feed the chauffeur.'

Léa burst out laughing. 'I'll feed the chauffeur! Ha! Ha! There speaks the son of Madame Peloux! Get along with you! You forget nothing. . . . I'm not usually inquisitive, but I should love to eavesdrop when you're making up to a woman.'

She sank into a chair and fanned herself. A sphinx-moth and a number of long-legged mosquitoes hovered round the lamps; scents of the countryside drifted in from the garden, now that night had fallen. A sudden waft from an acacia burst in upon them, so distinct, so active, that they both turned round, half expecting to see it advancing towards them.

'It's the rose-acacia,' Léa said.

'Yes,' Chéri said. 'But to-night it has sipped a draught of orange-flower water.'

She stared at him, in vague admiration, astonished that he had hit upon such an idea. He was breathing in the scent in helpless rapture, and she turned away, suddenly fearful lest he might call her; but he did call, and she went to him.

She went to kiss him, on an impulse of resentment and selfishness, and half thinking to chastise him. 'Just you wait, my boy. . . . It's all too true that you've a pretty mouth, and, this time, I'm going to take my fill because I want to—and then I'll leave you, I don't care what you may say. Now . . .'

Her kiss was such that they reeled apart, drunk, deaf, breathless, trembling as if they had just been fighting. She stood up again in front of him, but he did not move from the depths of his chair, and she taunted him under her breath, 'Well? . . . Well?' and waited for an insult. Instead, he held out his arms, opened his vague beautiful hands, tilted his head back as if he had been struck, and let her see beneath each eyelash the glint of a shining tear. He babbled indeterminate words—a whole animal chant of desire, in which she could distinguish her name—'darling'—'I want you'—'I'll never leave you'—a song to which she listened, solicitous, leaning over him, as if unwittingly she had hurt him to the quick.

III

WHEN Léa recalled their first summer in Normandy, she would sum it up impartially: 'I've had other naughty little boys through my hands, more amusing than Chéri, more likeable, too, and more intelligent. But all the same, never one to touch him.'

'It's funny,' she confided to the old Baron de Berthellemy, towards the end of the summer of 1906, 'but sometimes I think I'm in bed with a Chinee or an African.'

'Have you ever had a Chinaman or a Negro?'

'Never.'

'Well then?'

'I don't know. I can't explain. It's just an impression.'

The impression had grown upon her slowly, also an astonishment she had not always been able to conceal. Her earliest memories of their idyll were abundantly rich, but only in pictures of delicious food, superb fruit, and the pleasure of taking pains over her country larder. She could still see Chéri—paler in the blazing sunlight—dragging along his exhausted body beneath the lime-tree tunnels in Normandy, or asleep on the sun-warmed paving beside a pond.

Léa used to rouse Chéri from sleep to cram him with strawberries and cream, frothy milk, and corn-fed chicken. With wide, vacant eyes, as though dazed, he would sit at dinner watching the mazy motions of the moths round the bowl of roses, and then look at his wrist-watch to see whether the time had come to go to bed: while Léa, disappointed but unresentful, pondered over the unfulfilled promises of the kiss at Neuilly and good-naturedly bided her time.

'I'll keep him cooped up in this fattening-pen till the end of August, if need be. Then, back in Paris again—ouf!—I'll pack him off to his precious studies.'

She went to bed mercifully early, so that Chéri—after nuzzling against her till he had hollowed out a selfishly comfortable position—might get some sleep. Sometimes, when the lamp was out, she would watch a pool of moonlight shimmering over the polished floor, or listen, through the chorus of rustling aspens and shrilling crickets, unceasing by night or day, to the deep, retriever-like sighs that rose from Chéri's breast.

'Why can't I go to sleep? Is there something wrong with me?' she vaguely wondered. 'It's not this boy's head on my shoulder—I've held heavier. The weather's wonderful. I've ordered him a good plate of porridge for to-morrow. Already his ribs stick out less. Then why can't I go to sleep? Yes, of course, I remember. . . . I'm going to send for Patron, the boxer, to give the boy some training. We've plenty of time between us, Patron and I, to spring a surprise on Madame Peloux.'

She fell asleep, lying stretched out on her back between the cool sheets, the dark head of her naughty little boy resting on her left breast. She fell asleep, to be aroused sometimes—but only just—by a waking desire of Chéri's towards the break of day.

Patron actually arrived after they had been two months in their country retreat, with his suitcase, his small pound-and-a-half dumb-bells, his black tights, his six-ounce gloves, and his leather boxing-boots, laced down to the toe. Patron, with his girlish voice, his long eyelashes, and his splendid tanned skin, as brown as the leather of his luggage—he hardly looked naked when he took off his shirt. And Chéri, by turns peevish, listless, or jealous of Patron's smooth strength, started the slow, oft-repeated movements. They were tiresome, but they did him good.

'One ... sss ... two ... sss ... I can't hear you breathing ... three ... sss ... Don't think I can't see you cheating there with your knee ... sss ...'

An awning of lime foliage filtered the August sunlight. The bare bodies of instructor and pupil were dappled with purple reflections from the thick red carpet spread out upon the gravel. Léa watched the lessons with keen attention. Sometimes during the quarter of an hour's boxing, Chéri, drunk with new-found strength, lost all control and, red-faced with anger, attempted a foul blow. Rock-like, Patron stood up to his swings, and from the height of his Olympian glory let fall oracular words—words of wisdom that packed more weight than his proverbial punch.

'Steady on now! That left eye's wandering a bit! If I hadn't stopped myself in time, it would have had a nasty taste of the stitches on my right glove.'

'I slipped,' Chéri said, enraged.

'It's not a question of balance,' Patron went on, 'it's a question of morale. You'll never make a boxer.'

'My mother won't let me, isn't that a pity?'

'Whether your mother lets you or not, you'll never make a boxer, because you've got a rotten temper. Rotten tempers and boxing don't go together. Aren't I right, Madame Léa?'

Léa smiled, and revelled in the warm sun, sitting still and watching the bouts between these two men, both young and both stripped. In her mind she kept comparing them. 'How handsome Patron is—as solid as a house! And the boy's shaping well. You don't find knees like his running about the streets every day of the week, or I'm no judge. His back, too, is ... will be ... marvellous. Where the devil did Mother Peloux drop her line to fish up a child like that? And the set of his head! quite a statue! But what a little beast he is! When he laughs, you'd swear it's a greyhound snarling!' She felt happy and maternal—bathed in quiet virtue. 'I'd willingly change him for anyone else,' she said to herself, with Chéri naked in the afternoon beside her under the lime-tree bower, or with Chéri naked in the morning on her ermine rug, or Chéri naked in the evening on the edge of the warm fountain. 'Yes, handsome as he is, I'd willingly make a change, if it weren't a question of conscience!'

She confessed her indifference to Patron.

'And yet,' Patron objected, 'the lad's very nicely made. There's muscles on him now such as you don't see on our French lads; his are more like a coloured boy's—though he couldn't look any whiter, I must say. Nice little muscles they are, and not too showy. He'll never have biceps like melons.'

'I should hope not, Patron! But then, you know, I didn't take him on for his boxing!'

'Of course not,' Patron acquiesced, letting his long lashes droop, 'there's—your feelings to be considered.'

He was always embarrassed by Léa's unveiled allusions to sex, and by her smile—the insistence of the smiling eyes she brought to bear on him whenever she spoke of love.

'Of course,' Patron tried another tack, 'if he's not altogether satisfactory . . .'

Léa laughed: 'Altogether! no . . . but I find being disinterested is its own reward. Just as you do, Patron.'

'Oh! me . . .' He waited in fear and hope for the question that did not fail to follow.

'Always the same, Patron? You still won't give way an inch?'

'I won't give way, Madame Léa, and I've just had a letter from Liane by the midday post. She says she's all alone, that I've no good reasons for refusing, and that her two admirers have left her.'

'Well?'

'Well, I don't believe it! I won't give way, because she won't give way. She's ashamed, she says, of a man who works for his living—specially when it pulls him out of bed so early every day for his training—a man who gives boxing lessons and teaches Swedish gymnastics. We've only got to meet, and the row starts all over again. "Anyone'd think," she shouts at me, "that I'm not in a position to support the man I love!" That shows very nice feelings, I don't say it doesn't, but it doesn't fit in with my ideas. Everyone's funny about something. It's just like you said, Madame Léa, it's all a question of conscience.'

They were talking in low tones under the trees: he prudish and half naked; she dressed in white, the colour flaming in her cheeks. They were enjoying the pleasure of a friendly understanding: they shared the same taste for the simple things of life, good health and a sort of plebeian decency. And yet Léa would not have been shocked had Patron received handsome presents from a beautiful and expensive woman like Liane. 'Fair exchange is no robbery.' And she did her best to break down Patron's 'funny feelings' by arguments based on homespun justice. These leisurely conversations always revealed their worship of the same twin deities—love and money, and would drift away from money and love to come back to Chéri and his deplorable upbringing, to his exceptional good looks ('harmless, after all,' as Léa would say) and to his character ('virtually non-existent,' as Léa would say). They had a taste for sharing confidences, and a dislike of new words or ideas, which they satisfied in these long talks. They were often disturbed by the preposterous apparition of Chéri, whom they thought either asleep or motoring down some baking hot road—Chéri, looming into sight, half naked, but equipped with an account book, a stylo behind his ear.

'Look at our Mister Adding-machine,' Patron said admiringly. 'All got up as a clerk in a bank.'

'What can this mean?' Chéri shouted from afar. 'Three hundred and twenty francs for petrol? Somebody must be swilling the stuff! We've been out four times in the last fortnight—and seventy-seven francs for oil!'

'The motor goes to the market every day,' Léa replied. 'And while we're on the subject, it appears your chauffeur had three helpings of the joint for his dinner. Don't you think that's stretching our agreement a bit far? . . . Whenever a bill sticks in your throat, you look just like your mother.'

At a loss for an answer, he stood uncertain for a moment, shifting from one slender foot to the other, poised with winged grace like a young Mercury. This always made Madame Peloux swoon with delight and yelp, 'Me when I was eighteen! Winged feet! winged feet!' He cast about for some insolent retort, his whole face a-quiver, his mouth half open, his forehead jutting forward, in a tense attitude that showed off to advantage the peculiar and diabolic upward twist of his eyebrows.

'Don't bother to think of an answer,' Léa said kindly. 'I know you hate me. Come and kiss me. Handsome devil. Fallen angel. Silly goose. . . .'

He came, calmed by the softness of her voice, yet ruffled by her words. Seeing them together, Patron once again let the truth flower on his guileless lips.

'As far as first-rate bodies go, Monsieur Chéri, you have one all right. But whenever I look at it, Monsieur Chéri, I feel that if I was a woman I'd say to myself: "I'll come back again in ten years' time." '

'You hear, Léa? He says in ten years' time,' Chéri said insinuatingly, pushing away the head of his mistress as she leaned towards him. 'What do you think of that?'

But she did not deign to listen. The young body owed to her its renewed vigour, and she began patting it all over, touching it anywhere and everywhere, on the cheek, on the leg, on the behind, with the irreverent pleasure of a nanny.

'What d'you get out of being spiteful?' Patron then asked.

Chéri allowed a savage, inscrutable gaze to sweep over every inch of the waiting Hercules before he answered. 'I find it comforting. You wouldn't understand.'

In fact, Léa herself understood precious little about Chéri after three months' intimacy. If she still talked to Patron, who now came only on Sundays, or to Berthellemy, who arrived without being invited but left again two hours later, about 'sending Chéri back to his blessed studies', it was because the phrase had become a kind of habit, and as though to excuse herself for having kept him there so long. She kept on setting a limit to his stay, and then exceeding it. She was waiting.

'The weather is so lovely. And then his trip to Paris last week tired him. And, besides, it's better for me to get thoroughly sick of him.'

For the first time in her life she waited in vain for what had never before failed her: complete trust on the part of her young lover, a self-surrender to confessions, candours, endless secrets—those hours in the depths of the night when, in almost filial gratitude, a young man unrestrainedly pours out his tears, his private likes and dislikes on the kindly bosom of a mature and trusted friend.

'They've always told me everything in the past,' she thought, obstinately. 'I've always known just what they were worth—what they were thinking and what they wanted. But this boy, this brat . . . No, that would really be the limit.'

He was now strong, proud of his nineteen years, gay at meals, and impatient in bed; even so he gave away nothing but his body, and remained as mysterious as an odalisque. Tender? Yes, if an involuntary cry or an impulsive hug is an indication of tenderness. But the moment he spoke, he was 'spiteful' again, careful to divulge nothing of his true self.

How often at dawn had Léa held him in her arms, a lover soothed, relaxed, with half-closed lids! Each morning his eyes and his mouth returned to life more beautiful, as though every waking, every embrace, had fashioned them anew! How often, at such moments, had she indulged her desire to master him, her sensual longing to hear his confession, and pressed her forehead against his, whispering, 'Speak. Say something. Tell me . . .'

But no confession came from those curved lips, scarcely anything indeed but sulky or frenzied phrases woven round 'Nounoune'—the name he had given her when a child and the one he now used in the throes of his pleasure, almost like a cry for help.

'Yes, I assure you, he might be a Chinee or an African,' she declared to Anthime de Berthellemy, and added, 'I can't tell you why.' The impression was strong but confused, and she felt lazily incompetent to find words for the feeling that she and Chéri did not speak the same language.

It was the end of September when they returned to Paris. Chéri went straight to Neuilly, the very first evening, to 'spring a surprise' on Madame Peloux. He brandished chairs, cracked nuts with his fist, leaped on to the billiard-table and played cowboy in the garden at the heels of the terrified watch-dogs.

'Ouf!' Léa sighed, as she entered her house in the Avenue Bugeaud, alone. 'How wonderful!—a bed to myself!'

But at ten o'clock the following night she was sipping coffee and trying not to find the evening too long or the dining-room too large, when a nervous cry was forced from her lips. Chéri had suddenly appeared, framed in the doorway—Chéri, wafted on silent, winged feet.

He was not speaking or showing any sign of affection, but just running towards her.

'Are you mad?'

Shrugging his shoulders, disdaining all explanations, just running towards her. Never asking 'Do you love me?', 'Have you already forgotten me?' Running towards her.

A moment later they were lying in the middle of Léa's great brass-encumbered bed. Chéri pretended to be worn out and sleepy. This made it easier to grit his teeth and keep his eyes tight shut, suffering as he was from a furious attack of taciturnity. Yet, through his silence, she was listening as she lay beside him, listening with delight to the distant delicate vibration, to the imprisoned tumult thrumming within a body that sought to conceal its agony, its gratitude, and love.

IV

'WHY didn't your mother tell me this herself at dinner last night?'

'She thought it better it should come from me.'

'No!'

'That's what she said.'

'And you?'

'What about me?'

'Do you think it better?'

Chéri raised uncertain eyes to Léa's. 'Yes.' He appeared to think it over a moment and repeated: 'Yes, far better, in fact.'

In order not to embarrass him, Léa looked away towards the window.

The August morning was dark with warm rain, which fell vertically on the already rusted foliage of the three plane-trees in the garden court.

'It might be autumn,' she said, and sighed.

'What's the matter?' Chéri asked.

She looked at him in astonishment. 'Nothing, I don't like the rain, that's all.'

'Oh! All right, I thought . . .'

'What?'

'I thought something was wrong.'

She could not help giving a frank laugh. 'Wrong with me, because you're getting married? No, listen . . . you're . . . you're so funny.'

She seldom laughed outright, and her merriment vexed Chéri. He shrugged his shoulders and made the usual grimace while lighting a cigarette, jutting out his chin too far and protruding his lower lip.

'You oughtn't to smoke before luncheon,' Léa said.

He made some impertinent retort she did not hear. She was listening to the sound of her own voice and its daily lectures, echoing away down the past five years. 'It's like the endless repetition in opposite looking-glasses,' she thought. Then, with a slight effort, she returned to reality and cheerfulness.

'It's lucky for me that there'll soon be someone else to stop you smoking on an empty stomach.'

'Oh! *she* won't be allowed to have a say in anything,' Chéri declared. 'She's going to be my wife, isn't she? Let her kiss the sacred ground I tread on, and thank her lucky stars for the privilege. And that will be that.'

He exaggerated the thrust of his chin, clenched his teeth on his cigarette-holder, parted his lips, and, as he stood there in his white silk pyjamas, succeeded only in looking like an Asiatic prince grown pale in the impenetrable obscurity of palaces.

Léa drew the folds of her pink dressing-gown closer about her—the pink she called 'indispensable.' She was lazily turning over ideas which she found tiresome, ideas that she decided to hurl, one by one, as missiles against Chéri's assumed composure.

'Well, why are you marrying the child?'

He put both elbows on the table and, unconsciously, assumed the composed features of his mother. 'Well, you see, my dear girl . . .'

'Call me Madame or Léa. I'm neither your housemaid nor a pal of your own age.'

She sat straight up in her armchair and clipped her words without raising her voice. He wanted to answer back. He looked defiantly at the beautiful face, a little pale under its powder, and at the frank blue light of her searching eyes. But he softened, and conceded, in a tone most unusual for him, 'Nounoune, you asked me to explain. . . . It had to come to this in the end. And besides, there are big interests at stake.'

'Whose?'

'Mine,' he said without a smile. 'The girl has a considerable fortune of her own.'

'From her father?'

He rocked himself to and fro, his feet in the air. 'Oh, how do I know? What a question! I suppose so. You'd hardly expect the fair Marie-Laure to draw fifteen hundred thousand out of her own bank account, would you? Fifteen hundred thousand, and some decent family jewels into the bargain.'

'And how much have you?'

'Oh, I've more than that of my own,' he said with pride.

'Then you don't need any more money?'

He shook his smooth head and it caught the light like blue watered silk. 'Need . . . need . . .? You know perfectly well we don't look at money in the same way. It's something on which we never see eye to eye.'

'I'll do you the justice to say that you've spared me any reference to it during the last five years.' She leaned towards him and put her hand on his knee. 'Tell me, child, how much have you put by from your income in these five years?'

He cavorted like a clown, laughed, and rolled at Léa's feet, but she pushed him aside with her toe.

'No, tell me the truth . . . fifty thousand a year, or sixty? Tell me, sixty? Seventy?'

He sat down on the carpet facing away from Léa, and laid his head back on her lap. 'Aren't I worth it, then?'

He stretched out to his full length, turned his head to look up at her, and opened wide his eyes. They looked black, but their true shade, Léa knew, was a dark almost reddish brown. As though to indicate her choice of what was rarest among so much beauty, she put her forefinger on his eyebrows, his eyelids, and the corners of his mouth. At moments this lover, whom she slightly despised, inspired her with a kind of respect by his outward form. 'To be as handsome as that amounts to nobility,' she said to herself.

'Tell me, child, how does this young person feel about you?'

'She loves me. She admires me. She never says a word.'

'And you—how do you behave with her?'

'I don't,' he answered simply.

'Delightful love duets,' Léa said dreamily.

He sat up, crossing his legs tailor fashion.

'You seem to me to be thinking a lot about her,' he said severely. 'Don't you think of yourself at all, in this upheaval?'

She gazed at Chéri with an astonishment that made her look years younger—eyebrows raised and lips half open.

'Yes, you, Léa. You, the victimized heroine. You, the one sympathetic character in all this, since you're being dropped.'

He had become rather pale, and his tough handling of Léa seemed to be hurting him.

Léa smiled. 'But, my darling, I've not the slightest intention of changing my life. Now and then, during the next week, I'll come across a pair of socks, a tie, a handkerchief on my shelves ... and when I say a week ... you know in what excellent order my shelves are kept! Oh, yes, and I'll have the bathroom redone. I've got an idea of putting in encrusted glass. . . .'

She fell silent and assumed an almost greedy look as she traced a vague outline with her finger. Chéri continued to look vindictive.

'You aren't pleased! What do you want, then? Do you expect me to go to Normandy to hide my grief? To pine away? To stop dyeing my hair? To have Madame Peloux rushing to my bedside?' And she imitated Madame Peloux, flapping her arms and trumpeting: ' "The shadow of her former self, the shadow of her former self! The poor unfortunate creature has aged a hundred years, a hundred years!" Is that what you want?'

He had been listening with a smile that died on his lips, and a trembling of the nostrils that might be due to emotion. 'Yes!' he cried.

Léa rested her smooth, bare, heavy arms on Chéri's shoulders.

'My poor boy! But at that rate, I ought to have died four or five times already! To lose a little lover. . . . To exchange one naughty little boy. . . .' She added in lower, lighter tones: 'I've grown used to it!'

'We all know that,' he said harshly. 'I don't give a damn—d'you hear me?—I don't give a single damn that I wasn't your first lover. What I should have liked, or rather what would have been . . . fitting . . . decent . . . is to be your last.' With a twist of his shoulders, he shrugged off her superb arms. 'After all, what I am saying to you now is for your own good.'

'I understand perfectly. You think only of me. I think only of your fiancée. That's all very nice, all very natural. It's clear that we both have hearts of gold.'

She rose, waiting for some outrageous rejoinder. But he said nothing, and it hurt her to see for the first time a look of discouragement on his face.

She bent over and put her hands under his armpits.

'Now then, come along, get your clothes on. I've only to put on my dress, I'm ready underneath, and what in the world is there to do on a day like this except to go to Schwabe and choose a pearl for you? You see, I must give you a wedding present.'

He jumped up, his face aglow: 'Top-hole! A pearl for my shirt-front! A pale pink pearl. I know the very one!'

'Not on your life! A white one, something masculine for pity's sake! Don't tell me, I know which one just as well as you. It'll ruin me, as usual. However, think of the money I'm going to save when you're out of the way!'

Chéri adopted a more reticent attitude. 'Oh, that . . . that depends on my successor.'

Léa turned back at the door of her boudoir and gave him her gayest smile, showing her strong teeth and the fresh blue of her eyes skilfully darkened by bistre.

'Your successor? A couple of francs and a packet of cigarettes! And a glass of cassis on Sunday—that's all the job will be worth! And I'll settle money on your children.'

V

THEY both became extremely gay for the next few weeks. Chéri's official duties as a fiancé separated them for a few hours each day, sometimes for a night or two. 'We mustn't let them lose confidence,' Chéri declared. Léa, kept by Madame Peloux at a safe distance from Neuilly, satisfied her curiosity by plying Chéri with a hundred questions. Whenever he came back to Léa's house, he was full of his own importance and heavy with secrets which he at once divulged. He was like a schoolboy playing truant.

'Oh, my sainted aunt!' he shouted one day, cramming his hat down on Léa's portrait-bust. 'The goings-on at the Peloux Palace Hôtel ever since yesterday!'

She began by scolding him, laughing already in anticipation.

'Take your hat off that, in the first place. And in the second, don't invoke your wretched aunt in my house. Well, what's been happening now?'

'A riot, Nounoune! A riot's broken out among the ladies. Marie-Laure and Ma'me Peloux are scratching each other's eyes out over the marriage settlement!'

'No!'

'Yes! It was a superb sight. (Look out for the olives. . . . I'm going to impersonate Ma'me Peloux as a windmill. . . .) "Separate bank accounts! Separate bank accounts! Why not a trustee? It's a personal insult, a personal insult. You forget that my son has his own fortune! . . . May I inform you, Madame . . ." '

'She called her Madame?'

'She most certainly did. "Let me tell you, Madame, that my son has never had a ha'porth of debts since he came of age and the list of his investments bought since 1910 is worth . . ." is worth this, that, and the other, including the skin off my nose, plus the fat off my bottom. In short, Catherine de Medici in person! But even more artful, of course!'

Léa's blue eyes glistened with tears of merriment. 'Oh, Chéri! you've never been funnier in your life! What about the other? The fair Marie-Laure?'

'Her? Oh! terrible, Nounoune. That woman must have at least a dozen corpses in her wake. Dolled up in jade green, red hair, painted to look eighteen, and the inevitable smile. The trumpetings of my revered Mamma failed to make her bat an eyelid. She held her fire till the assault was over, then she came out with: "It might perhaps be wiser, dear Madame, not to talk too loudly about all the money your son put by in 1910 and the years following. . . ." '

'Bang! Straight between the eyes! . . . Between yours. Where were you while all this was going on?'

'Me? In the large armchair.'

'You were actually in the room?' She stopped laughing, and eating. 'You were there? What did you do?'

'Cracked a joke, of course. Ma'me Peloux had just seized hold of a valuable piece of bric-à-brac, to avenge my honour, when I stopped her without even getting up. "My adored mother, calm yourself. Follow my example, follow that of my charming mother-in-law, who's being as sweet as honey . . . as sweet as sugar." And that's how I managed to arrange that the settlement should apply only to property acquired after marriage.'

'I simply don't understand.'

'The famous sugar plantations that the poor little Prince Ceste left to Marie-Laure by his will. . . .'

'Yes?'

'Forged will! Fury of the Ceste family! Lawsuit pending! Now d'you get it?'

He crowed.

'I get it. But how did you get hold of the story?'

'Ah! I'll tell you! Old Lili has just pounced with her full weight upon the younger of the Ceste boys, who's only seventeen and religious. . . .'

'Old Lili? What a nightmare!'

'And he babbles family secrets in her ear between every kiss. . . .'

'Chéri! I feel sick!'

'And old Lili tipped me off at Mamma's At Home last Sunday. She simply adores me! Besides, she respects me because I've never wanted to go to bed with her. . . .'

'I should hope not!' Léa sighed. 'Yet all the same . . .' She broke off to reflect, and it seemed to Chéri her enthusiasm was flagging.

'Well, you must say it was pretty smart of me, eh?'

He leaned across the table; and the sunshine, playing over the silver and the white table-cloth, lit him up like a row of footlights.

'Yes . . .' 'All the same,' she was thinking, 'that poisonous
Marie-Laure simply treated him like a ponce . . .'

'Is there any cream cheese, Nounoune?'

'Yes . . .' '. . . and he showed no more surprise than if she
had thrown him a flower. . . .'

'Nounoune, will you let me have that address? the address
of the place where you get your cream cheese—for the new
cook I've engaged for October?'

'Are you mad? It's home-made. I *have* a cook, you know.
Think of the *sauce aux moules* and *vol-au-vent!*' '. . . it's true I've
practically kept the boy for the last five years. . . . But all the
same he has an income of three hundred thousand francs a
year. That's the point. Can you be a ponce with three hundred
thousand a year? But why ever not? It doesn't depend on the
amount, but on the man. . . . There are some men I could
have given half a million to, and that wouldn't make them a
ponce. But how about Chéri? After all, I have never actually
given him any money. All the same . . .'

'All the same,' she broke into speech. 'She treated you like
a gigolo!'

'Who did?'

'Marie-Laure!'

He brightened at once, like a child.

'Didn't she? Didn't she just, Nounoune? That's what she
meant, wasn't it?'

'So it seems to me.'

Chéri raised his glass of Château-Chalon, almost the colour
of brandy. 'So here's to Marie-Laure! What a compliment, eh?
And if anyone can still say it of me when I'm your age, I shan't
ask anything better!'

'If that's enough to make you happy . . .'

She listened to him absent-mindedly till the end of
luncheon. Accustomed to her half-silences and her worldly
wisdom, he asked for nothing better than the usual maternal
homilies—'Take the brownest crusts. Don't eat so much new
bread. . . . You've never learnt how to choose a fruit. . . .' All
the time, secretly disgruntled, she was reproaching herself, 'I
must make up my mind what I want! What would I really have
liked him to do? Get up on his hind legs and hiss "Madame,
you have insulted me! Madame, I am not what you take

me for!" I'm responsible, when all's said and done. I've spoon-fed him, I've stuffed him with good things. . . . Who in the world would have thought that one day he'd want to play the paterfamilias? It never occurred to me! Even supposing it had—as Patron would say, "Nature will out." Even supposing Patron had accepted Liane's proposals, his nature would have come out all right if anyone had hinted at the fact in his hearing. But Chéri . . . has Chéri's nature. He's just Chéri. He's—'

'What were you saying, child?' she interrupted her thoughts to ask. 'I wasn't listening.'

'I was saying that never again—never, do you hear me—will anything make me laugh so much as my scene with Marie-Laure!'

—'There you are,' Léa concluded her thoughts, 'it . . . it merely made him laugh.'

Slowly she rose to her feet, as though tired. Chéri put an arm round her waist, but she pushed it away.

'What day is your wedding to be, now I come to think of it?'

'Monday week.'

His candour and detachment terrified her. 'That's fantastic!'

'Why fantastic, Nounoune?'

'You don't look as if you were giving it a thought!'

'I'm not,' he said calmly. 'Everything's been arranged. Ceremony at two o'clock, saving us all the fuss and rush of a wedding breakfast. Instead, a tea-party at Ma'me Peloux's. After that, sleepers, Italy, the Lakes. . . .'

'Are the Lakes back in fashion?'

'They are. There'll be villas, hotels, motor drives, rest-aurants, like Monte Carlo, eh?'

'But the girl! There's always the girl. . . .'

'Of course there's the girl. She's not much, but she's there!'

'And I'm no longer there.'

Chéri had not expected her to say this and showed it. His face became disfigured, and he suddenly turned white about the mouth. He controlled his breath to avoid an audible gasp, and became himself again.

'Nounoune, you'll always be there.'

'Monsieur overwhelms me.'

'There'll always be you, Nounoune ...' and he laughed awkwardly, 'whenever I need you to do something for me.'

She did not answer. She bent to pick up a tortoiseshell comb that had fallen to the floor and pushed it back in her hair, humming to herself. She went on humming a little snatch of a song in front of a looking-glass, pleased with herself, proud of having kept her self-control so easily, covered up so successfully the only emotional moment of their separation, proud of having held back words that must never be said: 'Speak ... beg for what you want, demand it, put your arms round my neck. . . . You have suddenly made me happy. . . .'

VI

MADAME PELOUX must have been talking a great deal and for a long time before Léa appeared. The high colour on her cheeks emphasized the sparkle of her large eyes, which expressed only an indiscreet and inscrutable watchfulness. This Sunday she was wearing a black afternoon dress with a very narrow skirt, and nobody could fail to have observed that her feet were tiny and her stays too tight. She stopped talking, took a little sip from the petal-thin brandy glass warming in her hand, and nodded at Léa in lazy contentment.

'Isn't it a lovely day? Such weather, such weather! Would any one believe we're in the middle of October?'

'Oh, no, never. . . . Most certainly not!' two obsequious voices answered in chorus.

Beside the curving garden path a stream of red salvias wound between the banks of grey-mauve Michaelmas daisies. Golden butterflies flitted as if it were summer and the scent of chrysanthemums, strengthened by the hot sun, was wafted into the garden-room. A yellowing birch-tree trembled in the wind above beds of tea-roses, where the last of the bees still were busy.

'But what's this weather,' yelled Madame Peloux, suddenly waxing lyrical, 'but what's this weather, when compared to what *they* must be having in Italy?'

'Yes, indeed! . . . Just what I was thinking!' the attendant voices echoed.

Léa turned with a frown in their direction. 'If only they would hold their tongues,' she thought.

The Baroness de la Berche and Madame Aldonza were sitting at a card-table, playing piquet. Madame Aldonza, an aged ballerina, with legs eternally swathed in bandages, was distorted with rheumatism, and wore her shiny black wig a little askew. Opposite her, a head or more taller, the Baroness squared her rigid shoulders like a country priest's. Her face was large and had grown alarmingly masculine with age. She was a bristling bush of hair—hair in her ears, tufts in her nostrils and on her lip, and rough hairs between her fingers.

'Baroness, don't forget I made ninety,' Madame Aldonza bleated like a goat.

'Score it, score it, my good friend! All I want is to see everyone happy.'

An endless flow of honied words masked her savage cruelty. Léa looked at her closely as if for the first time, felt disgusted, and turned back to Madame Peloux. 'Charlotte, at least, *looks* human,' she thought.

'What's the matter with you, my Léa? You don't seem your usual self?' Madame Peloux enquired tenderly.

Léa drew up her handsome figure and answered: 'Of course I am, Lolotte dear ... it's so comfortable here in your house, I was merely relaxing,' thinking all the while, 'Careful now ... she's just as cruel as the other,' and she at once assumed an expression of flattering contentment, of dreamy repletion, and accentuated it by sighing, 'I lunched too well. ... I really must get thinner. I shall start a strict diet from to-morrow.'

Madame Peloux flapped her hands and simpered.

'Isn't a broken heart enough to do that?'

'Oh, oh, oh! Ha-ha! Ho-ho!' guffawed Madame Aldonza and the Baroness de la Berche. 'Ha-ha-ha!'

Léa rose to her full height in her autumn dress of sombre green, handsome under her satin hat trimmed with sealskin, youthful among these old ruins over whom she cast a gentle eye. 'Oh, la-la, my dears! Give me a dozen such heart-breaks, if that would help me to lose a couple of pounds!'

'Léa, you're astounding,' the old baroness shot at her in a puff of smoke. 'Madame Léa, think of me, please, when you throw away that hat,' old Madame Aldonza begged. 'Madame Charlotte, you remember your blue one? It lasted me two years. Baroness, when you've quite finished ogling Madame Léa, perhaps you'll be kind enough to deal the cards to me.'

'Very well, my sweet, and may they bring you luck!'

Léa stopped for a moment by the door, then stepped out into the garden. She picked a tea-rose, which shed its petals. She listened to the breeze in the birch, to the trams in the Avenue, to the whistle of the local train. The bench she sat on was warm, and she closed her eyes, letting her shoulders enjoy the warmth of the sun. When she opened her eyes again, she hurriedly turned her head in the direction of the house, feeling positive that she was going to see Chéri standing in the entrance with his shoulder against the doorway.

'What can be the matter with me?' she wondered. Piercing screams of laughter and a little chorus of greeting from indoors brought her, trembling slightly, to her feet. 'Can I be suffering from nerves!'

'Ah, here they are, here they are!' Madame Peloux trumpeted, and the deep bass of the Baroness chimed in 'Here come the happy pair!'

Léa shivered, ran as far as the door and stopped short: there, in front of her, were old Lili and her adolescent lover, Prince Ceste, just arriving.

Perhaps seventy years of age, with the corpulence of a eunuch held in by stays, old Lili was usually referred to as 'passing all bounds', without these 'bounds' being defined. Her round pink painted face was enlivened by a ceaseless girlish gaiety, and her large eyes and small mouth, thin-lipped and shrunken, flirted shamelessly. Old Lili followed the fashion to an outrageous degree. A striking blue-and-white striped skirt held in the lower part of her body, and a little blue jersey gaped over her skinny bosom crinkled like the wattles of a turkey-cock; a silver fox failed to conceal the neck, which was the shape of a flower-pot and the size of a belly. It had engulfed the chin.

'It's terrifying,' Léa thought. She was unable to tear her eyes away from details that were particularly sinister—a white sailor hat, for instance, girlishly perched on the back of a short-cut, strawberry-roan wig; or, again, a pearl necklace visible one moment and the next interred in a deep ravine which once had been termed a '*collier de Vénus*'.

'Léa, Léa, my little chickabiddy!' old Lili exclaimed as she did her best to hasten towards Léa. She walked with difficulty on round swollen feet, tightly swaddled in high-heeled laced boots with paste buckles on the ankle-straps, and was the first to congratulate herself on this performance: 'I waddle like a duckling! it is a special little way I have. Guido, my passion, you remember Madame de Lonval? Don't remember her too well or I'll tear your eyes out. . . .'

A slim youth with Italian features, enormous empty eyes, and a weak receding chin kissed Léa's hand hastily and retired into the shadows without a word. Lili caught him in flight, pulled his head down to her scaly chest, calling the onlookers to witness: 'Do you know what this is, Madame, do you know what this is? This, ladies, is the love of my life!'

'Restrain yourself, Lili!' Madame de la Berche advised in her masculine voice.

'But why? But why?' from Charlotte Peloux.

'For the sake of decency,' said the Baroness.

'Baroness, that's not nice of you! I think they're so sweet. Ah!' she sighed, 'they remind me of my own children.'

'I was thinking of them,' Lili said, with a delighted smile. 'It's our honeymoon too, Guido's and mine. Indeed, we've just come to ask about the other young couple! We want to hear all about them.'

Madame Peloux became stern. 'Lili, you don't expect me to go into details, do you?'

'Oh, yes, yes, I do,' Lili cried, clapping her hands. She tried to skip, but succeeded only in raising her shoulders and hips a little. 'That's always been my besetting sin, and always will be! I adore spicy talk! I'll never be cured of it. That little wretch there knows how I adore it.'

The silent youth, called to bear witness, did not open his mouth. The black pupils of his eyes moved up and down against the whites, like frantic insects. Léa watched him, rooted to the spot.

'Madame Charlotte told us all about the wedding ceremony,' bleated Madame Aldonza. 'The young Madame Peloux was a dream in her wreath of orange blossom!'

'A madonna! A madonna!' Madame Peloux corrected at
the top of her voice, with a burst of religious fervour. 'Never,
never, has anyone looked so divine. My son was in heaven! In
heaven, I tell you! . . . What a pair they made, what a pair!'

'You hear that, my passion? Orange blossom!' Lili murmured. 'And tell me, Charlotte, what about our mother-in-
law, Marie-Laure?'

Madame Peloux's pitiless eyes sparkled: 'Oh, her! Out of
place, absolutely out of place. In tight-fitting black, like an eel
wriggling out of the water—you could see everything, breasts,
stomach—everything!'

'By Jove!' muttered the Baroness de la Berche with military
gusto.

'And that look of contempt she has for everybody, that look
of having a dose of cyanide up her sleeve and half a pint of
chloroform inside her handbag! As I said, out of place—that
exactly describes her. She behaved as if she could only spare
us five minutes of her precious time—she'd hardly brushed
the kiss off her lips, before she said, "Au revoir, Edmée, au
revoir, Fred," and off she flew.'

Old Lili was breathing hard, sitting on the edge of her chair,
her little grandmotherly mouth, with its puckered corners,
hanging half open. 'And who gave the usual advice?' she
threw out.

'What advice?'

'The little talk—oh, my passion, hold my hand while I say
it!—instruction for the young bride. Who gave her that?'

Charlotte Peloux took offence and stared at her. 'Things
may well have been done in that way when you were young,
but the practice has fallen into disuse.'

The sprightly old girl plumped her fists on her thighs:
'Disuse? Disuse or not, how would you know anything about
it, my poor Charlotte? There's so little marrying in your
family!'

'Ha-ha-ha!' the two toadies imprudently guffawed.

But a single glance from Madame Peloux made them
tremble. 'Peace, peace, my little angels! You're each enjoying
your paradise on earth, so what more do you want?' The
Baroness stretched out a strong arm, like a policeman keeping
order, between the purple faces of Lili and Madame Peloux.

But Charlotte scented battle like a war-horse. 'If you're looking for trouble, Lili, you don't have to look further than me! Because of your age, I must treat you with respect, and if it weren't for that . . .'

Lili shook with laughter from chin to thigh. 'If it weren't for that, you'd get married yourself just to give me the lie? I know—it's not so hard to get married! Why, I'd marry Guido like a shot, if only he were of age!'

'Not possible!' gasped Charlotte, so taken aback that she forgot her anger.

'But, of course . . . Princess Ceste, my dear! *la piccola principessa! Piccola principessa*, that's what my little Prince always calls me!'

She nipped hold of her skirt, and, in turning, displayed a gold curb-chain where her ankle ought to have been. 'Only,' she continued mysteriously, 'his father . . .'

By now out of breath, she made a sign to the silent young man, who took up the tale in a low rapid voice as if he were reciting his piece: 'My father, the Duke of Parese, threatens to put me in a convent if I marry Lili.'

'In a convent!' Charlotte Peloux squealed. 'A man in a convent!'

'A man in a convent!' neighed Madame de la Berche in her deep bass, 'Egad! if that isn't exciting!'

'They're barbarians,' Aldonza lamented, joining her misshapen hands together.

Léa rose so abruptly that she upset a glass.

'It's uncoloured glass,' Madame Peloux observed with satisfaction. 'You'll bring good luck to my young couple. Where are you running off to? Is your house on fire?'

Léa managed to squeeze out a sly little laugh: 'On fire? In a sense, perhaps. Ssh! no questions! It's a secret.'

'What? Already? It's not possible!' Charlotte Peloux cheeped enviously. 'I was just saying to myself that you looked as if . . .'

'Yes, yes! You must tell us! Tell us everything,' yapped the three old women.

Lili's quilted fists, old Aldonza's deformed stumps, Charlotte Peloux's hard fingers had seized upon her wrist, her sleeve, her gold-mesh bag. She snatched her arm away from all these claws and succeeded in laughing again, teasingly: 'No, it's far too early in the day, it would spoil everything! It's my secret.' And she rushed away to the hall.

But the door opened in front of her and a desiccated old fellow, a sort of playful mummy, took her into his arms: 'Léa, lovely creature, a kiss for your little Berthellemy, or he won't let you pass!'

She gave a cry of fright and impatience, struck off the gloved bones retarding her progress, and fled.

Neither in the avenues of Neuilly, nor on the roads through the Bois, turning to blue in the fast-falling twilight, did she allow herself a moment's reflection. She shivered slightly and pulled up the windows of the motor-car. She felt restored by the sight of her clean house, the comfort of her pink bedroom and boudoir, overcrowded with furniture and flowers.

'Quick, Rose, light the fire in my room!'

'But, Madame, the pipes are already at their winter temperature. Madame should not have gone out with only a fur round her neck. The evenings are treacherous.'

'A hot-water bottle in my bed at once, and for dinner a cup of thick chocolate beaten up with the yolk of an egg, some toast, and a bunch of grapes. . . . Hurry, dear, I'm freezing. I caught cold in that junk-shop at Neuilly. . . .'

Once under the sheets, she clenched her teeth to stop them chattering. The warmth of the bed eased her stiffened muscles, but still she did not altogether relax, and she went through the chauffeur's expense book till the chocolate arrived. This she drank at once, frothy and scalding. She chose her *chasselas* grapes one by one, the long greenish-amber bunch dangling by its stem against the light.

Then she turned out the bedside lamp, settled herself in her favourite position, flat on her back, and gave way.

'What can be the matter with me?'

She succumbed again to anxiety and started to shiver. She was obsessed by the vision of an empty doorway, with clumps of red salvia on either side. 'I can't be well,' she thought, 'one doesn't get into a state like this over a door!' Again she saw the three old women, Lili's neck, and the beige rug that Madame Aldonza had trailed about with her for the past twenty years. 'Which of them am I going to look like in ten years' time?'

Though she did not feel alarmed at this prospect, her anxiety increased still further. She let her mind wander from one incident of her past life to another, from this scene to that, trying to rid her thoughts of the empty doorway framed by red salvia. She was growing restless in her bed and trembled slightly. Suddenly she jumped as though shot, racked by a pain so deep that at first she thought it must be physical, a pain that twisted her lips and dragged from them, in a raucous sob, a single name: 'Chéri!'

Tears followed, beyond all control at first. As soon as she had regained her self-control, she sat up, wiped her face, and turned on the lamp again. 'Ah! That's what it is! Now I understand!'

She took a thermometer from the drawer of her bedside table and put it under her arm. 'My temperature's normal, so it's nothing physical. I see. I'm just unhappy. Something must be done about it.'

She drank some water, got out of bed, bathed her inflamed eyes, put on a little powder, poked the fire, and went back to bed. She was on her guard, full of mistrust for an enemy she had never known: grief. She had just said goodbye to thirty years of easy living: years spent pleasantly, intent often on love, sometimes on money. This had left her, at almost fifty, still young and defenceless.

She made fun of herself, ceased to feel her grief, and smiled. 'I think I was out of my mind just now. There's nothing wrong with me any longer.'

But a movement of her left arm, which bent automatically to hold and shelter a sleeping head, brought back all her agony, and she sat up with a jump. 'Well, this *is* going to be fun!' she said out loud and sternly.

She looked at the clock and saw that it was barely eleven. Overhead passed the slippered tread of the elderly Rose, on her way up the stairs to the attic floor. Then there was silence. Léa resisted the impulse to call out for help to this deferential old body. 'Don't give the servants anything to gossip about. We musn't have that.'

She left her bed again, wrapped herself up warm in a quilted silk dressing-gown and toasted her feet. Then she half opened her window and listened for she knew not what. A moist and milder wind had brought clouds in its wake and the lingering leaves in the neighbouring Bois sighed with every gust. Léa shut the window again, picked up a newspaper, and looked at the date—'October the twenty-sixth. Exactly a month since Chéri was married?' She never said 'Since Edmée was married.'

Following Chéri's example, she did not yet count his young wraith of a wife as really alive. Chestnut-brown eyes, ashy hair which was very lovely with the vestige of a crimp in it—all the rest melted away in her memory like the contours of a face seen in a dream.

'At this very moment, of course, they'll be in each other's arms in Italy. And . . . and I don't mind that in the least.'

She was not boasting. The picture of the young couple she had called up, the familiar attitude it evoked—even Chéri's face, as he lay exhausted for a minute, with the white line of light between his tired eyelids—aroused in her neither curiosity nor jealousy. On the other hand, an animal convulsion again racked her body, bending her double, as her eye fell on a nick in the pearl-grey wainscot—the mark of some brutality of Chéri's. 'The lovely hand which here has left its trace, has turned away from me for ever,' she said. 'How grandly I'm talking! Soon grief will be turning me into a poet!'

She walked about, she sat down, she went to bed again and waited for daylight. At eight o'clock Rose found her writing at her desk, and this upset the old lady's-maid.

'Is Madame not well?'

'So-so, Rose. Age, you know. . . . Doctor Vidal thinks I ought to have a change of air. Will you come with me? It promises to be a cold winter here in Paris. We'll go south to the sun, and eat meals cooked in oil.'

'Whereabouts will that be?'

'You want to know too much. Simply have my trunks brought down, and give my fur rugs a good beating.'

'Madame will be taking the motor-car?'

'I think so. I'm sure of it, in fact. I'll need all my creature comforts now, Rose. Just think of it, this time I'm going all on my own. It's going to be a pleasure trip.'

During the next five days Léa rushed all over Paris; wrote, telegraphed, and received telegrams and answers from the south. And she said goodbye to Paris, leaving behind a short letter addressed to Madame Peloux which she started no less than three times:

My dear Charlotte,

You'll forgive me if I go away without saying goodbye to you, and keep my little secret to myself. I'm making a perfect fool of myself . . . and why not? It's a short life, let's make it a gay one.

I send you an affectionate kiss. Remember me to the child when he comes back.

Your incorrigible

Léa.

PS—Don't trouble to come and interview my butler or concierge; no member of my household knows anything at all about it.

VII

'DO you know, my adored treasure, I don't think you're looking very well.'

'It's the night in the train,' Chéri answered shortly.

Madame Peloux did not dare to say just what she thought. She found her son changed. 'He's . . . yes, he's sinister!' she decided; and she ended by exclaiming enthusiastically, 'It's Italy!'

'If you like,' Chéri conceded.

Mother and son had just finished breakfasting together, and Chéri had condescended to praise with an oath his cup of 'housemaid's coffee', made with creamy milk, well sugared, slowly reheated, with buttered toast crumbled into it and browned till it formed a succulent crust.

He felt cold in his white woollen pyjamas and was clasping his knees to his chest. Charlotte Peloux, anxious to look pretty for her son, had put on a brand-new marigold négligée, and a boudoir-cap fitting tight across the forehead. This made her face stand out, bare and macabre.

Finding her son's eye fixed upon her, she simpered: 'You

see, I've adopted the grandmother style. Very soon, I'll powder my hair. Do you like this cap? Rather eighteenth century, don't you think? Dubarry or Pompadour? How do I look in it?'

'Like an old convict,' Chéri said witheringly. 'Next time you must run up a warning signal.'

She groaned, then shrieked with laughter: 'Ha-ha-ha. You've a sharp tongue in your head and no mistake!'

But he did not laugh. He was staring out at the lawn powdered with snow after last night's fall. His nervous state was visible only in the spasmodic twitching of his jaw muscles. Madame Peloux was intimidated. She, too, was silent. The faint tinkle of a bell sounded.

'That's Edmée, ringing for her breakfast,' said Madame Peloux.

Chéri did not answer. 'What's wrong with the heating? It's freezing in here!' he said a moment later.

'It's Italy!' Madame Peloux repeated lyrically. 'You come back here, your eyes and your heart full of the warm sun of the south, and find you've landed at the Pole—at the North Pole. There hasn't been a flower on the dahlias for the last week. But don't worry, my precious! Your love-nest will soon be finished. If the architect hadn't gone down with paratyphoid, it would be ready for you now. I warned him. If I told him once, I told him twenty times: "Monsieur Savaron . . ." '

Chéri, who was standing by the window, turned round sharply. 'What was the date on that letter?'

Madame Peloux opened her large child-like eyes: 'What letter?'

'The letter from Léa you showed me.'

'She put no date on it, my love; but I got it the night before my last Sunday At-home in October.'

'I see. And you don't know who it is?'

'Who what is, my paragon?'

'Whoever it was she went away with, of course.'

Malice clothed Madame Peloux's stark features. 'No. Would you believe it, nobody has an idea! Old Lili is in Sicily, and none of my set has a clue! A mystery, an enthralling mystery! However, you know me, I've managed to pick up a few scraps here and there . . .'

Chéri's dark eyes expanded: 'What's the tattle?'

'It seems it's a young man . . .' Madame Peloux whispered. 'A young man not . . . not particularly desirable, if you know what I mean . . . very well made, of course!' She was lying, careful to insinuate the worst.

Chéri shrugged his shoulders.

'Well made, did you say? Don't make me laugh! My poor Léa! I can see him from here—a hefty little fellow from Patron's training-quarters—black hairs on his wrists and clammy hands. . . . Well, I'm going back to bed now; you make me tired.'

Trailing his bedroom slippers, he went back to his room, dawdling in the long corridors and on the spacious landings of the house he seemed to be discovering for the first time. He ran into a pot-bellied wardrobe, and was amazed. 'Damned if I knew that thing was there. . . . Oh, yes, I vaguely remember. . . . And who the devil's this chap?' He was addressing an enlarged photograph, in a deep black frame, hanging funereally near a piece of coloured pottery, equally unfamiliar to Chéri.

Madame Peloux had been installed in this house for the last twenty-five years, and had kept every unfortunate result of her bad taste and acquisitiveness. 'Your house looks like the nest of a magpie that's gone batty,' was old Lili's reproachful comment. She herself had a hearty appetite for modern pictures, and still more for modern painters. To this Madame Peloux had replied: 'I believe in letting well alone.'

If the muddy green paint—'The green of hospital corridors,' Léa called it—flaked off in one of the passages, Madame Peloux would have it repainted a similar muddy green; or if the maroon velvet on a *chaise-longue* needed replacing, she was careful to choose the same maroon velvet.

Chéri paused by the open door of a dressing-room. Embedded in the maroon marble-topped wash-stand were jug and basin of plain white with a monogram, and over the two electric-light fittings were lily-shaped bead shades. Chéri shuddered as though caught in a violent draught—'Good God, how hideous, what an old junk-shop!'

He hurried away. At the end of the passage, he came upon

a window edged with small pieces of red and yellow stained glass. 'That's the last straw!' he said grumpily.

He turned to the left and roughly opened a door—the door of his nursery—without knocking. A little cry came from the bed where Edmée was just finishing her breakfast. Chéri closed the door and stared at his wife without going any closer.

'Good morning,' she said with a smile. 'You do look surprised to see me here!'

She lay bathed in a steady blue light reflected from the snow outside. Her crimped ashy chestnut hair was down, but barely covered her prettily curved shoulders. With her pink-and-white cheeks matching her nightgown, and her rosy lips paler than usual from fatigue, she looked like a light-toned picture, not quite finished and rather misty.

'Aren't you going to say good morning to me, Fred?' she insisted.

He sat down close beside his wife and took her in his arms. She fell back gently, dragging him with her. Chéri propped himself on his elbow to look down more closely at her. She was so young that even when tired she still looked fresh. He seemed astonished by the smoothness of her fully rounded lower eyelids, and by the silvery softness of her cheeks.

'How old are you?' he asked suddenly.

Edmée opened her eyes, which she had closed voluptuously. Chéri stared at the brown of their pupils and at her small square teeth.

'Oh, come! I shall be nineteen on the fifth of January, and do try and remember it.'

He drew his arm away roughly and the young woman slipped into the hollow of the bed like a discarded scarf.

'Nineteen, it's prodigious! Do you know that I'm over twenty-five?'

'But of course I know that, Fred. . . .'

He picked up a pale tortoiseshell mirror from the bed-table and gazed at himself. 'Twenty-five years old!'

Twenty-five years of age and a face of white marble that seemed indestructible. Twenty-five, but at the outer corners of the eye and beneath it—delicately plagiarizing the classical design of the eyelid—were two lines, visible only in full light, two incisions traced by the lightest, the most relentless, of fingers.

He put back the mirror: 'You're younger than I am. That shocks me.'

'Not me!'

She had answered in a biting voice, full of hidden meaning. He took no notice.

'Do you know why my eyes are beautiful?' he asked in all seriousness.

'No,' Edmée said. 'Perhaps because I love them?'

'Stuff!' Chéri said, shrugging his shoulders. 'It's because they're shaped like a sole.'

'Like what?'

'Like a sole.'

He sat down near her to give a demonstration.

'Look—here—the corner next the nose is the head of the sole. And then—the upper curve, that's the back of the sole; whereas the lower line runs perfectly straight and that's its belly. And the other corner that tapers up to my temples, that's the sole's tail.'

'Oh?'

'Yes, but if I had an eye shaped like a flounder, that's to say, with the lower part as much curved as the top, then I should look silly. See? You've passed your matric., did you know that?'

'No, I must admit . . .'

She broke off, feeling guilty, because he had spoken sententiously and with exaggerated passion, like some one with a mania. 'There are moments when he looks like a savage,' she thought, 'like a man from the jungle. Yet he knows nothing about plants or animals, and sometimes he doesn't seem even to know about human beings.'

Sitting close beside her, Chéri put one arm round her shoulders and with his free hand began to finger the small, evenly matched, very round and very beautiful, pearls of her necklace. Intoxicated by the scent which Chéri used too much of, she began to droop like a rose in an overheated room.

'Fred! Come back to sleep! We're both tired. . . .'

He seemed not to have heard. He was staring at the pearls with obsessed anxiety.

'Fred?'

He shivered, leaped to his feet, furiously tore off his pyjamas and jumped naked into bed, seeking the place to rest his head on a shoulder where the delicate collar-bone was still youthfully sharp. The whole of Edmée's body obeyed his will as she opened her arms to him. Chéri closed his eyes and never moved. She took care to remain awake, a little smothered under his weight, and thinking him asleep. But almost at once he turned over away from her with a sudden pitch, imitating the groans of someone fast asleep, and rolled himself up in the sheet at the other side of the bed.

'He always does that,' Edmée noted.

All through the winter, she was to awaken in this square room with its four windows. Bad weather delayed the completion of the new house in the Avenue Henri-Martin—bad weather, and Chéri's whims. He wanted a black bathroom, a Chinese drawing-room, a basement fitted up with a swimming pool and gymnasium. To the architect's objections he would answer: 'I don't give a damn. I pay, I want the work done. To hell with the cost.' But every now and again he would cast a ruthless eye over an estimate and proclaim 'You can't bamboozle young Peloux.' Indeed, he held forth on standardization, fibro-cement, and coloured stucco with unexpected glibness and a memory for exact figures that compelled the contractor's respect.

Rarely did he consult his young wife, although he paraded his authority for her benefit and took pains, when occasion arose, to cover his deficiencies by giving curt commands. She was to find that he possessed an instinctive eye for colour, but had only contempt for beauty of shape and period differences.

'You simply clutter up your head with all that stuff and nonsense, what's your name, yes, you, Edmée. An idea for the smoking-room? All right, here's one: Blue for the walls—a ferocious blue. The carpet purple—a purple that plays second fiddle to the blue of the walls. Against that you needn't be afraid of using as much black as you like and a splash of gold in the furniture and ornaments.'

'Yes, you're right, Fred. But it will be rather drastic with all those strong colours. It's going to look rather charmless without a lighter note somewhere . . . a white vase or a statue.'

'Nonsense,' he interrupted rather sharply. 'The white vase you want will be me—me, start naked. And we mustn't forget a cushion or some thingumabob in pumpkin-red for when I'm running about stark naked in the smoking-room.'

Secretly attracted and at the same time disgusted, she cherished these fanciful ideas for turning their future home into a sort of disreputable palace, a temple to the greater glory of her husband. She offered little resistance, just gently requested 'some little corner' for a small and precious set of furniture upholstered with needlework on a white ground—a present from Marie-Laure.

This gentleness masked a determination that was young yet far from inexperienced; it stood her in good stead during the four months of camping out in her mother-in-law's house. It enabled her to evade, throughout these four months, the enemy stalking her, the traps laid daily to destroy her equanimity, her still susceptible gaiety, and her tact. Charlotte Peloux, over-excited at the proximity of so tender a victim, was inclined to lose her head and squander her barbs, using her claws indiscriminately.

'Keep calm, Madame Peloux,' Chéri would throw out from time to time. 'What bones will there be left for you to pick next winter if I don't stop you now?'

Edmée raised frightened, grateful eyes to her husband, and did her best not to think too much, not to look too much, at Madame Peloux. One evening Charlotte, almost heedlessly, three times tossed across the chrysanthemum table-piece Léa's name instead of Edmée's.

Chéri lowered his satanic eyebrows: 'Madame Peloux, I believe your memory is giving way. Perhaps a rest cure is indicated?'

Charlotte Peloux held her tongue for a whole week, but Edmée never dared to ask her husband: 'Did you get angry on my behalf? Was it me you were defending? Or was it that other woman, the one before me?'

Life as a child and then as a girl had taught her patience, hope, silence; and given her a prisoner's proficiency in

handling these virtues as weapons. The fair Marie-Laure
had never scolded her daughter: she had merely punished
her. Never a hard word, never a tender one. Utter loneliness,
then a boarding-school, then again loneliness in the holidays
and frequent relegations to a bedroom. Finally, the threat of
marriage—any marriage—from the moment that the eye of
a too beautiful mother had discerned in the daughter the
dawn of a rival beauty, shy, timid, looking a victim of tyranny,
and all the more touching for that. In comparison with this
inhuman gold-and-ivory mother, Charlotte Peloux and her
spontaneous malice seemed a bed of roses.

'Are you frightened of my respected parent?' Chéri asked
her one evening.

Edmée smiled and pouted to show her indifference: 'Frightened? No. You aren't frightened when a door slams, though
it may make you jump. It's a snake creeping under it that's
frightening.'

'A terrific snake, Marie-Laure, isn't she?'

'Terrific.'

He waited for confidences that did not come and put a
brotherly arm round his wife's slender shoulders: 'We're sort
of orphans, you and I, aren't we?'

'Yes, we're orphans, and we're so sweet!'

She clung to him. They were alone in the big sitting-room,
for Madame Peloux was upstairs concocting, as Chéri put it,
her poisons for the following day. The night was cold and
the window panes reflected the lamplight and furnishings
like a pond. Edmée felt warm and protected, safe in the
arms of this unknown man. She lifted her head and gave a
cry of alarm. He was staring up at the chandelier above them
with a look of desperation on his magnificent features, and
two tears hung glistening between the lids of his half-closed
eyes.

'Chéri, Chéri, what's the matter with you?' On the spur
of the moment she had called him by the too endearing
nickname she had never meant to pronounce. He answered
its appeal in bewilderment and turned his eyes down to look
at her.

'Chéri, oh God! I'm frightened. What's wrong with you?'

He pushed her away a little, and held her facing him.

'Oh! Oh! You poor child, you poor little thing! What are you frightened of?'

He gazed at her with his eyes of velvet, wide-open, peaceful, inscrutable, all the more handsome for his tears. Edmée was about to beg him not to speak, when he said, 'How silly we are! It's the idea that we're orphans. It's idiotic. It's so true.'

He resumed his air of comic self-importance, and she drew a breath of relief, knowing that he would say no more. He began switching off all the lights with his usual care, and then turned to Edmée with a vanity that was either very simple or very deceitful: 'Well, why shouldn't I have a heart like everybody else?'

VIII

'WHAT are you doing there?'

He had called out to her almost in a whisper, yet the sound of Chéri's voice struck Edmée so forcibly that she swayed forward as if he had pushed her. She was standing beside a big open writing-desk and she spread her hands over the papers scattered in front of her.

'I'm tidying up . . .' she said in a dazed voice. She lifted a hand and it remained poised in mid-air as though benumbed. Then she appeared to wake up, and stopped lying.

'It's like this Fred. You told me that when we came to move house you'd hate to be bothered over what you'd want to take with you, all the things in this room . . . the furniture. I honestly wanted to tidy, to sort things. Then the poison, temptation came . . . evil thoughts . . . one evil thought. . . . I implore your forgiveness. I've touched things that don't belong to me. . . .'

She trembled bravely and waited.

He stood with his forehead jutting forward, his hands clenched in a threatening attitude; but he did not seem to see his wife. His eyes were strangely veiled, and ever after she was to retain the impression of having spoken with a man whose eyes were deathly pale.

'Ah, yes,' he said at length. 'You were looking . . . you were looking for love-letters.' She did not deny it. 'You were hunting for my love-letters.'

He laughed his awkward, constrained laugh.

Edmée felt hurt, and blushed. 'Of course you must think me a fool. As if you were the kind of man not to lock them away in a safe place or burn them! And then, anyhow, they're none of my business. I've only got what I deserved. You won't hold it too much against me, Fred?'

Her pleading had cost her a certain effort, and she tried deliberately to make herself look appealing, pouting her lips a little and keeping the upper half of her face shadowed by her fluffy hair. But Chéri did not relax his attitude, and she noticed for the first time that the unblemished skin of his cheeks had taken on the transparence of a white rose in winter, and that their oval contour had shrunk.

'Love-letters,' he repeated. 'That's howlingly funny.'

He took a step forward, seized a fistful of papers and scattered them: post-cards, restaurant bills, tradespeople's announcements, telegrams from chorus girls met one night and never seen again, *pneumatiques* of four or five lines from sponging friends; and several close-written pages slashed with the sabre-like script of Madame Peloux.

Chéri turned round again to his wife: 'I have no love-letters.'

'Oh!' she protested. 'Why do you want—'

'I have none,' he interrupted; 'you can never understand. I've never noticed it myself until now. I can't have any love-letters because—' He checked himself. 'But wait, wait. . . . Yes, there was one occasion, I remember, when I didn't want to go to La Bourboule, and it . . . Wait, wait.'

He began pulling out drawers and feverishly tossing papers to the floor.

'That's too bad! What can I have done with it? I could have sworn it was in the upper left-hand . . . No. . . .'

He slammed back the empty drawers and glowered at Edmée.

'You found nothing? You didn't take a letter which began "But what do you expect, I'm not in the least bored. There's nothing better than to be separated one week in every month," and then went on to something else. I don't remember what, something about honeysuckle climbing high enough to look in at the window.'

He broke off, simply because his memory refused to come to his aid, and he was left gesticulating in his impatience.

Slim and recalcitrant, Edmée did not quail before him. She took refuge in caustic irritability. 'No, no, I *took* nothing. Since when have I been capable of *taking* things? But if this letter is so very precious to you, how is it you've left it lying about? I've no need to enquire whether it was one of Léa's?'

He winced, but not quite in the manner Edmée had expected. The ghost of a smile hovered over his handsome, unresponsive features; and, with his head on one side, an expectant look in his eyes, and the delicious bow of his mouth taut-stretched, he might well have been listening to the echo of a name.

The full force of Edmée's young and ill-disciplined emotions burst forth in a series of sobs and tears, and her fingers writhed and twisted as if ready to scratch. 'Go away! I hate you! You've never loved me. I might not so much as exist, for all the notice you take of me! You hurt me, you despise me, you're insulting, you're, you're . . . You think only of that old woman! It's not natural, it's degenerate, it's . . . You don't love me! Why, oh why, did you ever marry me? . . . You're . . . you're . . .'

She was tossing her head like an animal caught by the neck, and as she leaned back to take a deep breath, because she was suffocating, the light fell on her string of small, milky, evenly matched pearls. Chéri stared in stupefaction at the uncontrolled movements of the lovely throat, at the hands clasped together in appeal, and above all at the tears, her tears. . . . He had never seen such a torrent of tears. For who had ever wept in front of him, or wept because of him? No one. Madame Peloux? 'But,' he thought, 'Madame Peloux's tear's don't count.' Léa? No. Searching his memory, he appealed to a pair of honest blue eyes; but they had sparkled with pleasure only, or malice, or a rather mocking tenderness. Such floods of tears poured down the cheeks of this writhing young woman. What could be done about all these tears? He did not know. All the same, he stretched out an arm, and as Edmée drew back, fearing some brutality perhaps, he placed his beautiful, gentle, scented hand on her head and patted her ruffled hair. He did his best to copy the tone and speech of a voice whose power he knew so well: 'There, there. . . . What's it all about? What's the matter, then? There . . . there. . . .'

Edmée collapsed suddenly, fell back huddled in a heap on a settee, and broke out into frenzied and passionate sobbing that sounded like yells of laughter or howls of joy. As she lay doubled up, her graceful body heaved and rocked with grief, jealousy, fury, and an unsuspected servility. And yet, like a wrestler in the heat of a struggle, or a swimmer in the hollow of a wave, she felt bathed in some strange new atmosphere, both natural and harsh.

She had a good long cry, and recovered by slow degrees, with periods of calm shaken by great shudders and gasps for breath. Chéri sat down by her side and continued to stroke her hair. The crisis of his own emotion was over, and he felt bored. He ran his eyes over Edmée as she lay sideways upon the unyielding settee. This straggling body, with its rucked-up frock and trailing scarf, added to the disorder of the room; and this displeased him.

Soft as was his sigh of boredom, she heard it and sat up. 'Yes,' she said, 'I'm more than you can stand. . . . Oh! it would be better to . . .'

He interrupted her, fearing a torrent of words: 'It's not that. It's simply that I don't know what you want.'

'What I want? How d'you mean, what I . . .'

She lifted her face, still wet with tears.

'Now listen to me.' He took her hands.

She tried to free herself. 'No, no, I know that tone of voice. You're going to treat me to another of those nonsensical outbursts. When you put on that tone of voice and face, I know you're going to prove that your eye is shaped like a striped super-mullet, or that your mouth looks like the figure three on its side. No, no, I can't stand that!'

Her recriminations were childish, and Chéri relaxed, feeling that after all they were both very young. He pressed her warm hands between his own.

'But you must listen to me! . . . Good God! I'd like to know what you've got to reproach me with! Do I ever go out in the evenings without you? No! Do I often leave you on your own during the day? Do I carry on a secret correspondence?

'I don't know—I don't think so—'

He turned her this way and that like a doll.

'Do I have a separate room? Don't I make love to you well?'

She hesitated, smiling with exquisite suspicion. 'Do you call that love, Fred?'

'There are other words for it, but you wouldn't appreciate them.'

'What you call love . . . isn't it possible that it may be, really, a . . . kind . . . of alibi?' She hastened to add, 'I'm merely generalizing, Fred, of course . . . I said "*may* be," in certain cases. . . .'

He dropped Edmée's hands. 'That,' he said coldly, 'is putting your foot right in it.'

'Why?' she asked in a feeble voice.

He whistled, chin in air, as he moved back a step or two. Then he advanced upon his wife, looking her up and down as if she were a stranger. To instil fear a fierce animal has no need to leap. Edmée noticed that his nostrils were dilating and that the tip of his nose was white.

'Ugh!' he breathed, looking at his wife. He shrugged his shoulders, turned, and walked away. At the end of the room he turned round and came back again. 'Ugh!' he repeated. 'Look what's talking!'

'What are you saying?'

'Look what's talking, and what it says. Upon my word, it actually has the cheek to . . .'

She jumped up in a rage, 'Fred,' she said, 'don't dare to speak to me again in that tone! What do you take me for?'

'For a woman who knows exactly how to put her foot in it, as I've just had the honour of informing you.'

He touched her on the shoulder with a rigid forefinger, and this hurt her as much as if he had inflicted a serious bruise. 'You've matriculated; isn't there somewhere some kind of a proverb which says, "Never play with knives or daggers" or whatever it may be?'

'Cold steel,' she answered automatically.

'That's right. Well, my child, you must never play with cold steel. That's to say, you must never be wounding about a man's . . . a man's favours, if I may so express it. You

were wounding about the gifts, about the favours, I bestow
on you.'

'You . . . you talk like a cocotte,' she gasped.

She blushed, and her strength and self-control deserted
her. She hated him for remaining cool and collected, for
keeping his superiority: its whole secret lay in the carriage
of his head, the sureness of his stance, the poise of his arms
and shoulders.

The hard forefinger once more pressed into Edmée's
shoulder.

'Excuse me, excuse me . . . It'll probably come as a great
surprise when I state that, on the contrary, it's you who
have the mentality of a tart. When it comes to judging such
matters, there's no greater authority than young Peloux. I'm
a connoisseur of "cocottes", as you call them. I know them
inside out. A "cocotte" is a lady who generally manages to
receive more than she gives. Do you hear what I say?'

What she heard above all was that he was now addressing
her like a stray acquaintance.

'Nineteen years old, white skin, hair that smells of vanilla;
and then, in bed, closed eyes and limp arms. That's all very
pretty, but is there anything unusual about it? Do you really
think it so very unusual?'

She had started at each word, and each sting had goaded
her towards the duel of female *versus* male.

'It may be very unusual,' she said in a steady voice, 'how
could *you* know?'

He did not answer, and she hastened to take advantage
of a hit. 'Personally, I saw much handsomer men than you
when we were in Italy. The streets were full of them. My
nineteen years are worth those of any other girl of my age,
just as one good-looking man is as good as the next. Don't
worry, everything can be arranged. Nowadays, marriage is
not an important undertaking. Instead of allowing silly scenes
to make us bitter . . .'

He put a stop to what she had to say by an almost pitying
shake of the head.

'My poor kid, it's not so simple as that.'

'Why not? There's such a thing as quick divorce, if one's
ready to pay.'

She spoke in the peremptory manner of a runaway school-girl, and it was pathetic. She had pushed back the hair off her forehead, and her anxious, intelligent eyes were made to look all the darker by the soft contours of her cheeks now fringed with hair: the eyes of an unhappy woman, eyes mature and definitive in a still undeveloped face.

'That wouldn't help at all,' Chéri said.

'Because?'

'Because . . .' He leaned forward with his eyelashes tapered into pointed wings, shut his eyes and opened them again as if he had just swallowed a bitter pill. 'Because you love me.'

She noticed that he had resumed the more familiar form of addressing her, and above all the fuller, rather choked tones of their happiest hours. In her heart of hearts she acquiesced: 'It's true, I love him. At the moment, there's no remedy.'

The dinner bell sounded in the garden—a bell which was too small, dating from before Madame Peloux's time, a sad clear bell reminiscent of a country orphanage. Edmée shivered. 'Oh, I don't like that bell. . . .'

'No?' said Chéri absent-mindedly.

'In our house, dinner will be announced. There'll be no bell. There'll be no boarding-house habits in our home—you'll see.'

She spoke these words without turning round, while walking down the hospital-green corridor, and so did not see, behind her, either the fierce attention Chéri paid to her last words, or his silent laughter.

IX

HE was walking along with a light step, stimulated by the rathe spring, perceptible in the moist gusty wind and the exciting earthy smells of squares and private gardens. Every now and again a fleeting glimpse in a glass would remind him that he was wearing a becoming felt hat, pulled down over the right eye, a loose-fitting spring coat, large light-coloured gloves, and a terra-cotta tie. The eyes of women followed his progress with silent homage, the more candid among them bestowing that passing stupefaction which can be neither feigned nor hidden. But Chéri never looked at women in the street. He had just come from his house in the Avenue Henri-Martin, having left various orders with the upholsterers: orders contradicting one another, but thrown out in a tone of authority.

On reaching the end of the Avenue, he took a deep breath of the good spring scents carried up from the Bois on the heavy moist wing of the west wind, and then hurried on his way to the Porte Dauphine. Within a few minutes he had reached the lower end of the Avenue Bugeaud, and there he stopped. For the first time in six months his feet were treading the familiar road. He unbuttoned his coat.

'I've been walking too fast,' he said to himself. He started off again, then paused and, this time, trained his eyes on one particular spot: fifty yards or so down the road—bareheaded, shammy-leather in hand, Ernest the concierge—Léa's concierge—was 'doing' the brasswork of the railings in front of Léa's house. Chéri began to hum, realized from the sound of his voice that he never did hum, and stopped.

'How are things, Ernest? Hard at work as usual?'

The concierge brightened respectfully.

'Monsieur Peloux! It's a pleasure to see Monsieur again. Monsieur has not changed at all.'

'Neither have you, Ernest. Madame is well, I hope?'

He turned his head away to gaze up at the closed shutters on the first floor.

'I expect so, Monsieur, all we've had has been a few postcards.'

'Where from? Was it Biarritz?'

'I don't think so, Monsieur.'

'Where is Madame?'

'It wouldn't be easy for me to tell you, Monsieur. We forward all letters addressed to Madame—and there's none to speak of—to Madame's solicitor.'

Chéri pulled out his note-case, and cocked an eye at Ernest.

'Oh, Monsieur Peloux, money between you and me? Don't think of it. A thousand francs won't make a man tell what he doesn't know. But if Monsieur would like the address of Madame's solicitor?'

'No thanks, there's no point. And when does she return?'

Ernest threw up his hands: 'That's another question that's beyond me. Maybe to-morrow, maybe in a month's time. . . . I keep everything in readiness, just the same. You have to watch out where Madame is concerned. If you said to me now, "There she comes round the corner of the Avenue," I shouldn't be surprised.'

Chéri turned round and looked towards the corner of the Avenue.

'That's all Monsieur Peloux wants? Monsieur just happened to be walking by? It's a lovely day. . . .'

'Nothing else, thank you, Ernest. Goodbye, Ernest.'

'Always at Monsieur's service.'

Chéri walked up as far as the Place Victor-Hugo, swinging his cane as he went. Twice he stumbled and almost fell, like people who imagine their progress is being followed by hostile eyes. On reaching the balustraded entrance to the Métro, he leaned over the ramp to peer down into the pink-and-black recesses of the Underground, and felt utterly exhausted. When he straightened his back, he saw that the lamps had been lighted in the square and that the blue of dusk coloured everything around him.

'No, it can't be true. I'm ill.'

He had plumbed the depths of cavernous memories and his return to the living world was painful. The right words came to him at last. 'Pull yourself together, Peloux, for God's sake! Are you losing your head, my boy? Don't you know it's time to go back home?'

This last word recalled a sight that one hour had sufficed to banish from his mind: a large square room—his own nursery; an anxious young woman standing by the window; and Charlotte Peloux, subdued by a Martini.

'Oh, no,' he said aloud. 'Not that! That's all over.'

He signalled to a taxi with his raised stick.

'To the . . . er . . . to the Restaurant du Dragon Bleu.'

Chéri crossed the grill-room to the sound of violins in the glare of the atrocious electric light, and this had a tonic effect. He shook the hand of a maître d'hôtel who recognized him. Before him rose the stooping figure of a tall young man. Chéri gave an affectionate gasp. 'Desmond, the very man I wanted to see! Howdydo?'

They were shown to a table decorated with pink carnations. A small hand and a towering aigrette beckoned towards Chéri from a neighbouring table.

'It's La Loupiote,' Vicomte Desmond warned him.

Chéri had no recollection of La Loupiote, but he smiled towards the towering aigrette and, without getting up, touched the small hand with a paper fan lying on his table. Then he put on his most solemn 'conquering hero' look, and swept his eyes over an unknown couple. The woman had forgotten to eat since he had sat down in her vicinity.

'The man with her looks a regular cuckold, doesn't he?'

He had leaned over to whisper into his friend's ear, and his eyes shone with pleasure as if with rising tears.

'What do you drink, now you're married?' Desmond asked, 'Camomile tea?'

'Pommery,' Chéri said.

'And before the Pommery?'

'Pommery, before and after.' And, dilating his nostrils, he sniffed as he remembered some sparkling, rose-scented old champagne of 1889 that Léa kept for him alone.

He ordered a meal that a shopgirl out on the spree might choose—cold fish *au porto*, a roast bird, and a piping hot soufflé which concealed in its innards a red ice, sharp on the tongue.

'Hello!' La Loupiote shouted, waving a pink carnation at Chéri.

'Hello,' Chéri answered, raising his glass.

The chimes of an English wall-clock struck eight. 'Blast!' Chéri grumbled, 'Desmond, go and make a telephone call for me.'

Desmond's pale eyes were hungry for revelations to come.

'Go and ask for Wagram 17–08, tell them to put you through to my mother, and say we're dining together.'

'And supposing young Madame Peloux comes to the telephone?'

'Say the same thing. I'm not tied to her apron-strings. I've got her well trained.'

He ate and drank a lot, taking the greatest care to appear

serious and blasé; but his pleasure was enhanced by the least sound of laughter, the clink of glasses, or the strains of a syrupy valse. The steely blue of the highly glazed woodwork reminded him of the Riviera, at the hour when the too blue sea grows dark around the blurred reflection of the noonday sun. He forgot that very handsome young men ought to pretend indifference; he began to scrutinize the dark girl opposite, so that she trembled all over under his expert gaze.

'What about Léa?' Desmond asked suddenly.

Chéri did not jump: he was thinking of Léa. 'Léa? She's in the South.'

'Is all over between you?'

Chéri put his thumb in the armhole of his waistcoat.

'Well, of course, what d'you expect? We parted in proper style, the best of friends. It couldn't last a lifetime. What a charming, intelligent woman, old man! But then, you know her yourself! Broadminded ... most remarkable. My dear fellow, I confess that if it hadn't been for the question of age ... But there *was* the question of age, and you agree—'

'Of course,' Desmond interrupted.

This young man with lack-lustre eyes, though he knew just how to perform the wearing and difficult duties of a parasite, had just yielded to curiosity and blamed himself for such rashness. Chéri, circumspect and at the same time highly elated, never stopped talking about Léa. He made all the right remarks, showed all the sound sense of a married man. He spoke in praise of marriage, while giving Léa's virtues their due. He extolled the submissive sweetness of his young wife, and thus found occasion to criticize Léa's independence of character. 'Oh, the old devil, she had her own ideas about everything, I can tell you!'

He went a step further in his confidences, speaking of Léa with severity, and even impertinence. He was sheltering behind idiotic words, prompted by the suspicions of a deceived lover, and at the same time enjoying the subtle pleasure of being able to speak of her without danger. A little more, and he would have sullied her name, while his heart was rejoicing in his own memories of her: sullied the soft sweet name which he had been unable to mention freely during the last six months, and the whole gracious vision he had of Léa, leaning over him with her two or three irreparable wrinkles, and her beauty, now lost to him, but—alas—ever present.

About eleven o'clock they rose to go, chilled by the emptiness of the almost deserted restaurant. However, at the next table, La Loupiote was busy writing letters and had called for telegraph forms. She raised her white, inoffensive, sheep-like head as the two friends passed by. 'Well, aren't you even going to say good evening?'

'Good evening,' Chéri condescended to say.

La Loupiote drew her friend's attention to Chéri's good looks.

'Would you believe it! And to think that he's got such pots of money. Some people have everything!'

But when Chéri merely offered her an open cigarette-case, she became vituperative. 'They have everything, except the knowledge of how to make proper use of it. Go back home to your mother, dearie!'

'Look here,' Chéri said to Desmond when they were outside in the narrow street, 'Look here, I was about to ask you, Desmond . . . Wait till we get away from this beastly crowd. . . .'

The soft damp evening air had kept people lingering in the streets, but the theatre-goers from the Rue Caumartin onwards had not yet packed the Boulevard. Chéri took his friend by the arm: 'Look here, Desmond . . . I wanted you to make another telephone call.'

Desmond stopped, 'Again?'

'You'll ask for Wagram—'

'17–08.'

'You're marvellous . . . Say that I've been taken ill in your flat. Where are you living?'

'Hôtel Morris.'

'Splendid—and that I won't be back till morning, and that you're making me some mint tea. Go on, old man. Here, you can give this to the telephone-girl, or else keep it yourself. But come back quickly. I'll be sitting waiting for you outside Weber's.'

The tall young man, arrogant and serviceable, went off crumpling the franc-notes in his pocket, without permitting himself a comment. When Desmond rejoined him, Chéri was slouched over an untouched orangeade in which he appeared to be reading his fortune.

'Desmond . . . Who answered you?'

'A lady,' the laconic messenger replied.

'Which?'

'Dunno.'

'What did she say?'

'That it was all right.'

'In what tone of voice?'

'Same as I'm speaking to you in.'

'Oh, good. Thanks.'

'It was Edmée,' thought Chéri.

They were walking towards the Place de la Concorde and Chéri linked arms with Desmond. He did not dare to admit that he was feeling dog-tired.

'Where do you want to go?' Desmond asked.

'Well, old man,' Chéri sighed in gratitude, 'to the Morris; and as soon as we can. I'm fagged out.'

Desmond forgot to be impassive. 'What? It can't be true. To the Morris? What d'you want to do? No nonsense! D'you want to . . .'

'To go to bed,' Chéri answered. And he closed his eyes as though on the point of dropping off, then opened them again. 'Sleep, I want to sleep, got it?'

He gripped his friend's arm too hard.

'Let's go there, then,' Desmond said.

Within ten minutes they were at the Morris. The sky-blue and white bedroom and the imitation Empire furniture of the sitting-room smiled at Chéri like old friends. He took a bath, borrowed one of Desmond's silk night-shirts which was too tight for him, got into bed, and, wedged between two huge soft pillows, sank into dreamless bliss, into the dark depths of a sleep that protected him from all attacks.

X

HE began to count the shameful days as they went by. 'Sixteen . . . seventeen . . . When three weeks are up, I'll go back to Neuilly.' He did not go back. Though he saw the situation quite clearly, he no longer had the strength to cure it. At

night, and in the morning sometimes, he flattered himself
that he would get over his cowardice within an hour or two.
'No strength left? . . . Please, please, I beg of you . . . Not yet
strength enough. But it's coming back. What's the betting I'll
be in the Boulevard d'Inkermann dining-room at the stroke
of twelve? One, two . . .' The stroke of twelve found him in the
bath, or else driving his motor, with Desmond at his side.

At every meal-time he felt optimistic for a moment about
his marriage. This feeling was as regular as a recurrent fever.
As he sat down facing Desmond at their bachelor table, the
ghost of Edmée would appear, and plunge him into silent
thoughts of his young wife's inconceivable deference. 'Really,
that young thing's too sweet! Did you ever see such a dream
of a wife? Never a word, never a complaint! I'll treat her to
one of those bracelets when I get back. . . . Upbringing, that's
what does it! Give me Marie-Laure every time for bringing up
a daughter!' But one day in the grill-room at the Morris, abject
terror was written on his face when he caught sight of a green
dress with a chinchilla collar just like one of Edmée's dresses.

Desmond found life wonderful and was getting a little
fat. He reserved his arrogance for moments when Chéri—
encouraged by him to pay a visit to some 'Prodigious English
girl, riddled with vice,' or to some 'Indian potentate in his
opium palace'—refused point-blank or else consented with
unconcealed scorn. Desmond had long since despaired of
understanding Chéri's ways; but Chéri was paying—and
better than during the best of their bachelor days together.
They ran across the blonde La Loupiote a second time,
when they visited a friend of hers, a woman who boasted
such an ordinary name that nobody ever remembered it;
'What's-her-name . . . you know perfectly well . . . that pal
of La Loupiote's.'

The Pal smoked opium, and gave it to others. The instant
you came into her modest, ground-floor flat, you smelt
escaping gas and stale drugs. She won the hearts of her
guests by a tearful cordiality and by a constant incitement
to self-pity—both objectionable traits. She treated Desmond,
when he paid her a visit, as 'a great big desperately lonesome
boy,' . . . and Chéri as 'a beauty who has got everything and
it only makes him more miserable.' Chéri never touched

the pipe; he looked at the small box of cocaine with the repugnance of a cat about to be dosed, and spent most of the night with his back against the cushioned dado, sitting up on a straw mat between Desmond, who went to sleep, and the Pal, who never stopped smoking. For most of the night he breathed in the fumes that satisfy all hunger and thirst, but his self-control and distrust persisted. He appeared to be perfectly happy, except that he stared now and then, with pained and questioning intensity, at the Pal's withered throat—a skinny, far too red throat, round which shimmered a string of false pearls.

Once, he stretched out a hand and with the tip of his fingers touched the henna-tinted hair on the nape of her neck. He judged the weight of the big light hollow pearls with his hand, then snatched it back with the nervous shiver of someone who catches his finger-nail on a piece of frayed silk. Not long after, he got up and went.

'Aren't you sick to death of all this,' Desmond asked Chéri, 'sick of these poky holes where we eat and drink and never have any girls? Sick of this hotel with the doors always slamming? Sick of the night-clubs where we go in the evenings, and of dashing in that fast car of yours from Paris to Rouen, Paris to Compiègne, Paris to Ville d'Avray? . . . Why not the Riviera for a change? The season down there isn't December and January, it's March, April, or—'

'No,' said Chéri.

'Then what?'

'Then nothing.'

Chéri affected to become amiable and put on what Léa used to call 'his air of worldly superiority'.

'Dear old boy . . . you don't seem to appreciate the beauty of Paris at this time of the year. . . . This . . . er . . . indecisive season, this spring that doesn't seem willing to smile, the softness of the light . . . as opposed to the commonplace Riviera. . . . No, don't you see, I like it here.'

Desmond all but lost his lackey patience. 'Yes, and besides, it may be that the young Peloux's divorce will . . .'

Chéri's sensitive nostrils blenched. 'If you've arranged to

touch a commission from some lawyer friend, you can drop the idea at once. There'll be no such thing as "young Peloux's divorce".'

'My dear fellow! . . .' Desmond protested, doing his best to look hurt, 'You have a very curious way of behaving to a man who has been a friend since your childhood, and who has always . . .'

Chéri was not listening. Instead, he pushed towards Desmond's face a pointed chin and a mouth pursed like a miser's. For the first time in his life he had heard a stranger disposing of his possessions.

He began to reflect. Young Peloux's divorce? Many nights and days had he spent in thinking over these words till they had come to spell liberty, a sort of second boyhood, perhaps something even better. But Desmond's voice, with its affected nasal twang, had just called up the image he had been looking for: Edmée, resolute in her little hat with its long motoring veil, moving out of the house at Neuilly on her way to an unknown house to join an unknown man. 'Of course, that would settle everything,' and his Bohemian side was delighted. At the same time a surprisingly timorous Chéri jibbed, 'That's not the sort of way one behaves!' The image became focused in sharper colour and movement. Chéri could hear the heavy musical note of the iron gate swinging to, and could see beyond it fingers wearing a grey pearl and a white diamond. 'Farewell,' the small hand said.

Chéri jumped up, pushing back his seat. 'Those are mine, all of them! the woman, the house, the rings . . . they all belong to me!'

He had not spoken out loud, but his features expressed such savage violence that Desmond thought his last hour of prosperity had struck. Chéri spoke to him pityingly but without kindness.

'Poor pussy-cat, did I scare you? What it is to be descended from the Crusaders! Come along, and I'll buy you pants as fine as my shirts, and shirts as fine as your pants. Desmond, is to-day the seventeenth?'

'Yes, why?'

'The seventeenth of March. In other words, spring. Desmond, people who think themselves smart, I mean those in the height of fashion, women or men—can they afford to wait any longer before buying their spring wardrobes?'

'Hardly—'

'The seventeenth, Desmond! Come along at once; everything's all right. We're going to buy a huge bracelet for my wife, an enormous cigarette-holder for Madame Peloux, and a tiny tie-pin for you.'

On more than one such occasion he had felt an overwhelming presentiment that Léa was on the point of returning; that she was already back in her house; that the first-floor shutters had been opened, allowing a glimpse of the flowered pink net curtains across the windows, the lace of the full-length curtains at each side, and the glint of the looking-glasses. . . . The fifteenth of April went by and still there was no sign of Léa.

The mournful monotony of Chéri's existence was tempered by several provoking incidents. There was a visit from Madame Peloux, who thought she was breathing her last when she found Chéri looking as thin as a greyhound, eyes wandering, and mouth tight shut. There was the letter from Edmée: a letter all in the same surprising tone, explaining that she would stay on at Neuilly 'until further orders', and had undertaken to pass on to Chéri 'Madame de la Berche's best regards'. . . . He thought she was laughing at him, did not know what to answer, and ended by throwing away the enigmatic screed; but he did not go to Neuilly.

April advanced, leafy, cold, bright, and scenting all Paris with tulips, bunches of hyacinths, pawlonias, and laburnums like dropping-wells of gold. Chéri buried himself all the deeper in austere seclusion. The harassed, ill-treated, angry but well-paid Vicomte Desmond was given his orders: now to protect Chéri from familiar young women and indiscreet young men; now to recruit both sections and form a troop, who ate, drank, and rushed screaming at the top of their voices between Montmartre, the restaurants in the Bois, and the cabarets on the left bank.

One night the Pal was alone in her room, smoking opium and bewailing some shocking disloyalty of La Loupiote's, when her door opened to reveal the young man, with satanic eyebrows tapering towards his temples. He begged for 'a glass of really cold water' to allay some secret ardour that had parched his beautiful lips. He showed not the slightest interest in the Pal and the woes she poured out. She pushed towards him the lacquer tray with its pipe: he would accept nothing, and took up his usual position on the mat, to share with her the semi-obscurity in silence. There he stayed till dawn, moving as little as possible, like a man who fears that the least gesture may bring back his pain. At dawn, he questioned the Pal: 'Why weren't you wearing your pearls to-day; you known, the big ones?' and politely took his leave.

Walking alone at night was becoming an unconscious habit with him. With rapid lengthy strides he would make off towards some positive but inaccessible goal. Soon after midnight he would escape from Desmond, who discovered him again only towards daybreak, asleep on his hotel bed, flat on his stomach, his head pillowed on his folded arms, in the posture of a fretful child.

'Oh, good, he's here all right,' Desmond would say with relief. 'One can never be sure with such a crackpot.'

One night, when out on a tramp, his eyes wide open in the darkness, Chéri had felt compelled to walk up the Avenue Bugeaud; for during the day he had disregarded the superstition that made him return there once every twenty-four hours. There are maniacs who cannot go to sleep without having first touched the door-knob three times; a similar obsession made him run his hand along the railings, then put his finger to the bell-push, and call out Hullo! under his breath, as if in fun, before making off in haste.

But one night, that very night, as he stood before the railings, his heart jumped almost into his mouth: there, in the court, the electric globe shone like a mauve moon above the front-door steps, the back door stood wide open shedding a glow on the paved courtyard, while, on the first floor, the bedroom lights filtered through the shutters to make a golden comb. Chéri supported himself against the nearest tree and lowered his head.

'It can't be true. As soon as I look up, it will all be dark again.'

He straightened up at the sound of a voice. Ernest, the

concierge, was shouting in the passage: 'At nine to-morrow, Marcel will help me carry up the big black trunk, Madame.'

Chéri turned round in a flash and ran as far as the Avenue du Bois. There he sat down. In front of his eyes danced the image of the electric globe he had been staring at—a dark purple ball fringed with gold, against a black group of trees in bud. He pressed his hand to his heart, and took a deep breath. Early lilac blossom scented the night air. He threw his hat away, undid the buttons of his overcoat and, leaning back on a seat, let himself go, his legs outstretched and his hands hanging feebly by his sides. A crushing yet delicious weight had just fallen upon him. 'Ah!' he whispered, 'so this is what they call happiness. I never knew.'

For a moment he gave way to self-pity and self-contempt. How many good things had he missed by leading such a pointless life—a young man with lots of money and little heart! Then he stopped thinking for a moment, or possibly for an hour. Next, he persuaded himself there was nothing in the world he wanted, not even to go and see Léa.

When he found himself shivering in the cold, and heard the blackbirds carolling the dawn, he got up and, stumbling a little but light-hearted, set off towards the Hôtel Morris without passing through the Avenue Bugeaud. He stretched himself, filled his lungs with the morning air, and overflowed with goodwill to all.

'Now,' he sighed, the devil driven out of him, 'now ... Oh now you'll see just how nice to the girl I shall be.'

Shaved, shod, and impatient—he had been up since eight— Chéri shook Desmond. Sleep gave him a swollen look, livid and quite frightful, like a drowned man. 'Desmond! Hey, Desmond! Up you get. . . . You look too hideous when you're asleep!'

The sleeper woke, sat up, and turned towards Chéri eyes the colour of clouded water. He pretended to be fuddled with sleep so that he could make a long and close examination of Chéri—Chéri dressed in blue, pathetic, superb, and pale under the lightest coat of powder.

There were still moments when Desmond felt painfully aware of the contrast between his ugly mask and Chéri's good looks. He pretended to give a long yawn. 'What's he up to now?' he wondered. 'The idiot is in far better looks than yesterday—especially his eyelashes, and what eyelashes he has . . .' He was staring at the lustrous sweep of Chéri's thick lashes and the shadow they shed on the dark pupils and bluish whites of his eyes. Desmond noticed also that, this morning, the contemptuously arched lips were moist and fresh, and that he was breathing through them as if he had just that moment finished making love.

Quickly he relegated his jealousy to the back of his mind—where he kept his personal feelings—and asked Chéri in tones of weary condescension: 'May one enquire whether you are going out at this hour of the morning, or just coming in?'

'I'm going out,' Chéri said. 'Don't worry about me. I'm off shopping. I'm going to the florist's, the jeweller's, to my mother's, to my wife's, to . . .'

'Don't forget the Papal Nuncio!'

'I know what's what,' Chéri answered. 'He shall have some imitation gold studs and a sheaf of orchids.'

It was rare for Chéri to respond to jokes: he usually accepted them in stony silence. His facetious reply proved that he was pleased with himself, and revealed this unaccustomed mood to Desmond. He studied Chéri's reflection in the looking-glass, noted the pallor of his dilated nostrils, observed that his eyes were continually on the rove, and ventured to put the most discreet of questions.

'Will you be coming back for luncheon? . . . Hey, Chéri, I'm speaking to you. Are we lunching together?'

Chéri answered by shaking his head. He whistled softly, arranging himself in front of the pier-glass so that it framed his figure exactly like the one between the two windows in Léa's room—the one which would soon frame in its heavy gold, against a sunny pink background, the reflection of his body—naked or loosely draped in silk—the magnificent picture of a young man, handsome, loved, happy, and pampered, playing with the rings and necklaces of his mistress. 'Perhaps her young man's reflection is already there, in Léa's looking-glass!' This sudden thought cut so fiercely into his exhilaration that it dazed him, and he fancied he had heard it actually spoken.

'What did you say?' he asked Desmond.

'I never said a word,' his well-trained friend said stiffly. 'It must have been someone talking outside in the courtyard.'

Chéri went out, slamming the door behind him, and returned to his own rooms. They were filled with the dim continual hubbub of the fully awakened Rue de Rivoli, and Chéri, through the open window, could see the spring foliage, the leaves stiff and transparent like thin jade knives against the sun. He closed the window and sat down on a useless little chair which stood against the wall in a dingy corner between his bed and the bathroom door.

'How can it be? . . .' he began in a low voice, and then said no more. He did not understand why it was that during the last six and a half months he had hardly given a thought to Léa's lover. *'I'm making a perfect fool of myself,'* were the actual words of the letter so piously preserved by Charlotte Peloux.

'A perfect fool?' Chéri shook his head. 'It's funny, but that's not how I see her at all. What sort of a man can she be in love with? Somebody like Patron—rather than like Desmond, of course. An oily little Argentine? Maybe. Yet all the same . . .' He smiled a simple smile. 'Apart from me, who is there she could possibly care for?'

A cloud passed over the sun and the room darkened. Chéri leaned his head against the wall. 'My Nounoune . . . My Nounoune . . . Have you betrayed me? are you beastly enough to deceive me? . . . Have you really done that?'

He tried to give a sharper edge to his suffering by a misuse of his imagination: the words and sights it presented left him more astonished than enraged. He did his best to evoke the elation of early morning delights when he was living with Léa, the solace of the prolonged and perfect silences of certain afternoons, with Léa—the delicious sleepy hours in winter spent in a warm bed in a freshly aired room, with Léa . . . ; but, all the time, in the suffused cherry-coloured afternoon light aflame behind the curtains of Léa's room, he saw in Léa's arms one lover and one lover only—Chéri. He jumped up, revived by a spontaneous act of faith. 'It's as simple as that! If I'm unable to see anyone but myself beside her, then it's because there is no one else to see.'

He seized the telephone, and was on the point of ringing her up, when he gently replaced the receiver. 'No nonsense. . . .'

He walked out into the street, erect, with shoulders squared. He went in his open motor to the jeweller's, where he became sentimental over a slender little bandeau of burning blue sapphires invisibly mounted on blue steel, 'so exactly right for Edmée's hair,' and took it away with him. He bought some stupid, rather pompous flowers. As it had only just struck eleven, he frittered away a further half-hour, drawing money from the Bank, turning over English illustrated papers at a kiosk, visiting his scent-shop and a tobacconist's that specialized in Oriental cigarettes. Finally, he got back into his motor, and sat down between his sheaf of flowers and a heap of little beribboned parcels.

'Home.'

The chauffeur swivelled round on his basket-seat.

'Monsieur? . . . What did Monsieur say? . . .'

'I said Home—Boulevard d'Inkermann. D'you require a map of Paris?'

The motor went full speed towards the Champs-Élysées. The chauffeur drove much faster than usual and his thoughts could almost be read in his back. He seemed to be brooding uneasily over the gulf which divided the flabby young man of the past months—with his 'As you like', and his 'Have a glass of something, Antonin?'—from young Monsieur Peloux, strict with the staff and mindful of the petrol.

'Young Monsieur Peloux' leaned back against the morocco leather, hat on knees, drinking in the breeze and exerting all his energy in an effort not to think. Like a coward, he closed his eyes between the Avenue Malakoff and the Porte Dauphine to avoid a passing glimpse of the Avenue Bugeaud, and he congratulated himself on his resolution.

The chauffeur sounded his horn in the Boulevard d'Inker-mann for the gate to be opened, and it sang on it hinges with a heavy musical note. The capped concierge hurried about his business, the watch-dogs barked in recognition of their re-turning master. Very much at his ease, sniffing the green smell of the newly mown lawns, Chéri entered the house and with a master's step climbed the stairs to the young woman whom he had left behind three months before, much as a sailor from

Europe leaves behind, on the other side of the world, a little savage bride.

XI

LÉA sat at her bureau, throwing away photographs from the last trunk to be unpacked. 'Heavens, how hideous people are! The women who had the nerve to give me these! And they think I'm going to put them up in a row on the mantelpiece—in plated frames or little folding-cases. Tear them all up quick, and straight into the waste-paper basket!'

She picked up the photographs again and, before throwing them away, subjected each to the closest scrutiny of which her blue eyes were capable. A postcard with a dark background of a powerful lady encased in full-length stays, doing her best to veil her hair and the lower part of her face with a wisp of tulle, in the teeth of a strong sea-breeze. 'To dearest Léa, in memory of exquisite hours spent at Guéthary. Anita.' Another photograph, stuck on the middle of a piece of cardboard with a surface like dried mud, portrayed a large and lugubrious family. They might have been a penal colony, with a dumpy, heavily painted grandmother in charge. Holding above her head a tambourine tricked out with favours, she was resting one foot on the bent knee of what looked like a robust and shifty young butcher-boy. 'That should never have seen the light of day,' Léa said decisively, crumpling the rough-cast cardboard.

She smoothed out an unmounted print, to disclose two old provincial spinsters. An eccentric, loud-voiced, and aggressive couple, they were to be found every morning on a bench somewhere along a promenade, and every evening between a glass of cassis and their needlework-frames, on which they were embroidering black pussy-cats, fat toads, or a spider. 'To our beautiful fairy! From her little friends at Le Trayas, Miquette and Riquette.'

Léa destroyed these souvenirs of her travels—and brushed a hand across her forehead. 'It's horrible. And there'll be dozens and dozens more after these, just as there were dozens before them, all much the same. There's nothing to be done about it. It's life. Maybe wherever a Léa is to be found, there at once spring from the earth a myriad creatures like Charlotte Peloux, de la Berche, and Aldonza, or old horrors who were once handsome young men, people who are . . . well, who are impossible, impossible, impossible. . . .'

She heard, so fresh was her memory, voices that had called out to her from the top of hotel steps or hailed her with a 'Hoo-hoo' from afar, across golden sands, and she lowered her head in anger like a bull.

She had returned, after an absence of six months, thinner, more flabby, less serene. Now and again a nervous twitch of the jaw jerked her chin down against her neck, and careless henna-shampooing had left too orange a glint in her hair; but her skin had been tanned to amber by sea and wind. This gave her the glowing complexion of a handsome farmer's wife, and she might have done without rouge. All the same, she would have to arrange something carefully round her neck, not to say cover it up completely; for it had shrunk and was encircled with wrinkles that had been inaccessible to sunburn.

Still seated, she dawdled over tidying away her various odds and ends, and her eyes began to glance round the room, as if some chair were missing. But what she was looking for was her old energy, the old anxiety to see at once that everything was as it should be in her comfortable home.

'Oh! That trip!' she sighed. 'How could I? How exhausting it all is!'

She frowned, once again with that irritable jerk of her chin, when she noticed the broken glass of a little picture by Chaplin which she thought perfectly lovely—the head of a young girl, all silver and rose.

'And I could put both hands through that tear in the lace curtains. . . . And that's only the beginning. . . . What a fool I was to stay away so long! And all in *his* honour! As if I couldn't just as well have nursed my grief here, in peace and comfort!'

She rose, disgruntled, and, gathering up the flounces of her tea-gown, went over to ring the bell, saying to herself, 'Get along with you, you old baggage!'

Her maid entered, under a heap of underclothes and silk stockings.

'Eleven o'clock, Rose. And my face hasn't been done yet. I'm late.'

'There's nothing to be late for. There aren't any old maids now to drag Madame off on excursions, or turn up at crack of dawn to pick every rose in the place. There's no Monsieur Roland to drive Madame mad by throwing pebbles through her window. . . .'

'Rose, there's only too much to keep us busy in the house. The proverb may well be true that three moves are as bad as a fire, but I'm quite convinced that being away from home for six months is as bad as a flood. I suppose you've noticed the hole in the curtain?'

'That's nothing. . . . Madame has not yet seen the linen-room: mouse-droppings everywhere and holes nibbled in the floor. And it's a funny thing that I left Émérancie with twenty-eight glass-cloths and I come back to find twenty-two.'

'No!'

'It's the truth—every word I say, Madame.'

They looked at each other, sharing the same indignation, both of them deeply attached to this comfortable house, muffled in carpets and silks, with its well-stocked cupboards and its shiny white basement. Léa gave her knee a determined slap.

'We'll soon change all that, my friend. If Ernest and Émérancie don't want their week's notice, they'll manage to find those six glass-cloths. And did you write to Marcel, and tell that great donkey which day to come back?'

'He's here, Madame.'

Léa dressed quickly, then opened the window and leaned out, gazing complacently at her avenue of trees in bud. No more of those fawning old maids, and no more of Monsieur Roland—the athletic young heavyweight at Cambo. . . . 'The idiot,' she sighed.

She forgave this passing acquaintance his silliness, and blamed him only for having failed to please her. In her memory—that of a healthy woman with a forgetful body—Monsieur Roland was now only a powerful animal, slightly ridiculous and, when it came to the point, so very clumsy. Léa would now have denied that, one rainy evening when the showers were falling in fragrance on the rose-geraniums,

a flood of blinding tears had served to blot out Monsieur
Roland behind the image of Chéri.

This brief encounter had left Léa unembarrassed and
unregretful. In the villa she had taken at Cambo, the 'idiot'
and his frolicking old mother would have been made just
as welcome as before. They could have gone on enjoying
the well-arranged meals, the rocking-chairs on the wooden
balcony, all the creature comforts that Léa dispensed with
such justifiable pride. But the idiot had felt sore and gone
away, leaving Léa to the attentions of a stiff, handsome officer,
greying at the temples, who aspired to marriage with 'Madame
de Lonval.'

'Our years, our fortunes, the taste we both have for
independence and society, doesn't everything show that we
were destined for each other?' murmured the colonel, who
still kept his slim waist.

She laughed, and enjoyed the company of this dry, dapper
man, who ate well and knew how to hold his liquor. He
mistook her feelings and he read into the lovely blue eyes,
and the trustful, lingering smiles of his hostess, the acceptance
he was expecting. The end of their dawning friendship was
marked by a decisive gesture on her part: one she regreted
in her heart of hearts and for which she was honest enough
to accept the blame. 'It's my own fault. One should never
treat a Colonel Ypoustègue, descendant of an ancient Basque
family, as one would treat a Monsieur Roland. I've never
given anyone such a snub. All the same, it would have been
gentlemanly, and intelligent too, if he had come back as usual
the next day in his dog-cart, to smoke his cigar, meet the two
old girls, and pull their legs.'

She failed to understand that a middle-aged man could
accept his dismissal, but not certain glances—glances ap-
praising his physique, comparing him in that respect so
unmistakably with another, unknown and invisible. Léa,
caught in his sudden kiss, had subjected him to the searching,
formidable gaze of a woman who knows exactly where to
find the tell-tale marks of age. From the dry, well-cared-for
hands, ribbed with veins and tendons, her glance rose to the
pouched chin and furrowed brows, returning cruelly to the
mouth entrapped between double lines of inverted commas.

Whereupon all the aristocratic refinement of the 'Baroness de Lonval' collapsed in an 'Oh, la la,' so insulting, so explicit, so common, that the handsome figure of Colonel Ypoustègue passed through her door for the last time.

'The last of my idylls,' Léa was thinking, as she leaned out over her window-ledge. But the weather over Paris was fine, her echoing courtyard was dapper, with its laurel trees rising ball-shaped in green tubs, and from the room behind her a breath of scented warmth came playing over the nape of her neck: all this gradually helped her to recover her good humour, and her sense of mischief. She watched the silhouettes of women passing on their way down to the Bois. 'So skirts are changing again!' Léa observed, 'and hats are higher.' She planned sessions with her dressmaker, others with her milliner; the sudden desire to look beautiful made her straighten her back. 'Beautiful? For whom? Why, for myself, of course. And then to aggravate old Ma Peloux!'

Léa had heard about Chéri's flight, but knew no more than that. While disapproving of Madame Peloux's private-detective methods, she did not scruple to listen to a young *vendeuse*, who would show her gratitude for all Léa's kindnesses by pouring gossip in her ear at a fitting, or else by sending it to her, with 'a thousand thanks for the delicious chocolates' on a huge sheet of paper embossed with the letter-head of her establishment. A postcard from Lili, forwarded to Léa at Cambo—a postcard scribbled by the dotty old harridan in a trembling hand without commas or full stops—had recounted an incomprehensible story of love and flight and a young wife kept under lock and key at Neuilly.

'It was weather like this,' Léa recalled, 'the morning I read Lili's postcard in my bath at Cambo.'

She could see the yellow bathroom, the sunlight dancing on the water and ceiling. She could hear the thin-walled villa re-echoing with a great peal of laughter—her own laughter, rather ferocious and none too spontaneous—then the cries that followed it: 'Rose! Rose!'

Breasts and shoulders out of water, dripping, robust, one magnificent arm outstretched, looking more than ever like a naiad on a fountain, she had waved the card with the tips of her wet fingers. 'Rose, Rose! Chéri . . . Monsieur Peloux has done a bunk! He's left his wife!'

'That doesn't surprise me, Madame,' Rose had said. 'The divorce will be gayer than the wedding, when the dead seemed to be burying the dead.'

All through the day Léa had given way to unseemly mirth. 'Oh! that fiendish boy. Oh! the naughty child! Just think of it!'

And she shook her head, laughing softly to herself, like a mother whose son has stayed out all night for the first time.

A bright varnished park-phaeton flashed past her gates, sparkled behind its prancing high-steppers and vanished almost without a sound on its rubber wheels.

'There goes Spéleïeff,' Léa observed, 'he's a good sort. And there goes Merguillier on his piebald: eleven o'clock. It won't be long before that dried-up old Berthellemy passes on his way to thaw out his bones on the Sentier de la Vertu. Curious how people can go on doing the same thing day after day! I could almost believe I'd never left Paris, except that Chéri isn't here. My poor Chéri! He's finished with, for the present. Night-life, women, eating at any hour, drinking too much. It's a pity. He might have turned into a decent sort, perhaps, if he'd only had pink chaps like a pork-butcher and flat feet. . . .'

She left the window, rubbing her numbed elbows, and shrugged her shoulders. 'Chéri could be saved once, but not a second time.' She polished her nails, breathed on a tarnished ring, peered closely at the disastrous red of her hair and its greying roots, and jotted down a few notes on a pad. She did everything at high speed and with less composure than usual, trying to ward off an attack of her old insidious anxiety. Familiar as this was, she denied its connexion with her grief and called it 'her moral indigestion'. She began wanting first one thing, then suddenly another—a well-sprung victoria with a quiet horse appropriate to a dowager; then a very fast motor-car; then a suite of Directoire furniture. She even thought of doing her hair differently; for twenty years she had worn it high, brushed straight off the neck. 'Rolled curls low on the neck, like Lavallière? then I should be able to cope with this year's loose-waisted dresses. With a strict diet, in fact, and my hair properly hennaed, I can hope for ten—no, let's say five years more of . . .'

With an effort she recovered her good sense, her pride, her lucidity. 'A woman like me would never have the courage to call a halt? Nonsense, my pretty, we've had a good run for our money.' She surveyed the tall figure, erect, hands on hips, smiling at her from the looking-glass. She was still Léa.

'Surely a woman like that doesn't end up in the arms of an old man? A woman like that, who's had the luck never to soil her hands or her mouth on a withered stick! Yes, there she stands, the "vampire", who needs must feed off youthful flesh.'

She conjured up the chance acquaintances and lovers of her early days; always she had escaped elderly lechers; so felt pure, and proud of thirty years devoted to radiant youths and fragile adolescents.

'And this youthful flesh of theirs certainly owes me a great debt. How many of them have me to thank for their good health, their good looks, the harmlessness of their sorrows! And then their egg-nogs when they suffered from colds, and the habit of making love unselfishly and always refreshingly! Shall I now, merely to fill my bed, provide myself with an old gentleman of . . . of . . .' She hunted about and finished up with majestic forgetfulness of her own age, 'An old gentleman of forty?'

She rubbed her long shapely hands together and turned away in disgust. 'Pooh! Farewell to all that! It's much prettier. Let's go out and buy playing-cards, good wine, bridge-scorers, knitting-needles—all the paraphernalia to fill a gaping void, all that's required to disguise that monster, an old woman.'

In place of knitting-needles she bought a number of dresses, and négligées like the gossamer clouds of dawn. A Chinese pedicure came once a week, the manicurist twice, the masseuse every day. Léa was to be seen at plays, and before the theatre at restaurants where she never thought of going in Chéri's time.

She allowed young women and their friends—as well as Kühn, her former tailor, now retired—to ask her to their box or to their table. But the young women treated her with a deference she did not appreciate; and when Kühn, at their first supper together, called her 'my dear friend,' she retorted: 'Kühn, I assure you it doesn't suit you at all to be a customer.'

She sought refuge with Patron, now a referee and boxing promoter. But Patron was married to a young person who ran a bar, a little creature as fierce and jealous as a terrier. To join the susceptible athlete, Léa went as far out as the Place d'Italie, at considerable risk to her dark sapphire-blue dress, heavy with gold embroidery, to her birds of paradise, her impressive jewels, and her new rich red-tinted coiffure. She had had enough after one sniff of the sweat, vinegar, and turpentine exuded by Patron's 'white hopes', and she left, deciding never to venture again inside that long, low, gas-hissing hall.

An unaccountable weariness followed her every attempt to get back to the bustling life of people with nothing to do.

'What can be the matter with me?'

She rubbed her ankles, a little swollen by evening, looked at her strong teeth, and gums that had hardly begun to recede; and thumped her strong ribs and healthy stomach as if sounding a cask. Yet some indefinable weight, now that the chock had been knocked from under her, was shifting within her, and dragging her down. It was the Baroness de la Berche—met by chance in a 'public bar' where she was washing down two dozen snails with cabbies' white wine—who in the end informed her of the prodigal's return to the fold, and of the dawn of a crescent honeymoon in the Boulevard d'Inkermann. Léa listened calmly to this Moral Tale; but she turned pale with emotion the following day when she recognized the blue limousine outside her gates and saw Charlotte Peloux on her way to the house.

'At last, at last! Here you are again, Léa, my beauty! . . . Lovelier than ever! Thinner than last year! take care, Léa, we mustn't get too thin at our age! So far, and no further! And yet . . . But what a treat it is to see you!'

Never had that bitter tongue sounded so sweet to Léa. She let Madame Peloux prattle on, thankful for the breathing-space afforded by this acid stream. She had settled Charlotte Peloux into a deep armchair, in the soft light of the little pink-panelled salon, as in the old days. Automatically she had herself taken the straight-backed chair, which forced her to lift her shoulders and keep up her chin, as in the old days. Between them stood the table covered by a cloth of heavy embroidery, and on it, as in the old days, the large cut-glass decanter half full of old brandy, the shimmering petal-thin goblets, iced water, and shortbread biscuits.

'My beauty, now we'll be able to see each other again in peace, in peace. You know my motto: "When in trouble, shun your friends: let them only share your luck!" All the time Chéri was playing truant, I purposely didn't show you any sign of life, you understand. Now that all's well and my children are happy again, I shout it aloud, I throw myself into your arms, and we start our pleasant existence all over again. . . .' She broke off and lit a cigarette, as clever with her pauses as an actress, '. . . without Chéri, of course.'

'Of course,' Léa acquiesced with a smile.

She was watching and listening to her old enemy in satisfied astonishment. The huge inhuman eyes, the chattering lips, the restless, tight little body—all that was facing her across the table had come simply to test her powers of resistance, to humiliate her, as in the old days, always as in the old days. But, as in the old days, Léa knew when to answer, when to be scornful, when to smile, and when to retaliate. Already that sorry burden, which had weighed so heavily the day before and the days before that, was beginning slowly to lift. The light seemed normal once more, and familiar, as it played over the curtains and suffused the little drawing-room.

'Here we are again,' Léa thought, in lighter vein. 'Two women, both a little older than a year ago, the same habits of backbiting and the same stock phrases; good-natured wariness at meals shared together; the financial papers in the morning, scandalmongering in the afternoon: all this will have to be taken up again, since it's Life, my life. The Aldonzas and the de la Berches, the Lilis, and a few homeless old gentlemen: the whole lot squeezed round a card table, with the packs jostling the brandy-glasses, and perhaps, thrown in, a pair of little woollen shoes, begun for a baby who's soon to be born. . . . We'll start all over again, since it is ordained. Let's enter on it cheerfully. After all, it's only too easy to sink back into the grooves of the old life.'

And she settled back, eyes bright and mouth relaxed, to listen to Charlotte Peloux, who was greedily expatiating upon her daughter-in-law.

'My Léa, you should know, if anyone, that what I've always longed for is peace and quiet. Well now, I've got them. Chéri's escapade, you see, was nothing more than sowing a few wild oats. Far be it from me to reproach you, Léa dear, but as you'll be the first to admit, from eighteen to twenty-five he really never had the time to lead the life of a bachelor! And now he's done it with a vengeance!'

'It's a very good thing that he did,' Léa said, without the flicker of a smile; 'it acts as a sort of guarantee to his wife for the future.'

'The very word, the very word I was hunting for!' barked Madame Peloux, beaming. 'A guarantee! And ever since that day—one long dream! And, you know, when a Peloux does come home again after being properly out on the spree, he never goes off again!'

'Is that a family tradition?' Léa asked.

But Charlotte took no notice.

'And what's more, he was very well received when he did return home. His little wife—ah, there's a little wife for you, Léa!—and I've seen a fair number of little wives in my time, you know, and I don't mind telling you I've never seen one to hold a candle to Edmée!'

'Her mother is so remarkable,' Léa said.

'Think, just think, my beauty—Chéri left her on my hands for very nearly three months! and between you and me she was very lucky to have me there.'

'That's exactly what I was thinking,' Léa said.

'And then, my dear, never a word of complaint, never a scene, never a tactless word! Nothing, nothing! She was patience itself, and sweetness ... and the face of a saint, a saint!'

'It's terrifying,' Léa said.

'And then, what d'you suppose happened when our young rascal walked in one morning, all smiles, as though he'd just come in from a stroll in the Bois? D'you suppose she allowed

herself a single comment? Not one. Far from it. Nothing.
As for him, though at heart he must have felt just a little
ashamed . . .'

'Oh, why?' Léa asked.

'Well, really! After all . . . He was welcomed with open
arms, and the whole thing was put right in their bedroom—in
two ticks—just like that—no time lost! Oh, I can assure you,
for the next hour or so there wasn't a happier woman in the
world than me.'

'Except, perhaps, Edmée,' Léa suggested.

But Madame Peloux was all exaltation, and executed a
superb soaring movement with her little arms: 'I don't know
what you can be thinking of. Personally, I was only thinking
of the happy hearth and home.'

She changed her tune, screwed up her eyes, and pouted:
'Besides, I can't see that little girl frantic with passion, or
sobbing with ecstasy. Twenty, and skinny at that. . . . Pah!
at that age they stammer and stutter. And then, between
ourselves, I think her mother's cold.'

'Aren't you being carried away by you sense of family?' Léa
said.

Charlotte Peloux expanded her eyes to show their very
depths, but absolutely nothing was to be read there.

'Certainly not, certainly not! Heredity, heredity! I'm a firm
believer in it. Look at my son, who is fantasy incarnate . . .
What? You don't know that he's fantasy incarnate?'

'It must have escaped my memory,' Léa apologized.

'Well, I have high hopes for my son's future. He'll love his
home as I love mine, he'll look after his fortune, he'll love his
children, as I loved him. . . .'

'For goodness' sake, don't paint such a depressing picture,'
Léa begged. 'What's it like, the young people's home?'

'Sinister!' shrieked Madame Peloux. 'Positively sinister.
Purple carpets. Purple! A black-and-gold bathroom. A salon
with no furniture in it, full of Chinese vases larger than me!
So, what happens is that they're always at Neuilly. Besides,
without being conceited, I must say that girl adores me.'

'Her nerves have not been upset at all?' Léa asked anxiously.

Charlotte Peloux's eyes brightened. 'No danger of that! She
plays her hand well, and we must face the fact.'

'Who d'you mean by "we"?'

'Forgive me, my beauty, pure habit. We're dealing here with what I call a brain, a real brain. You should see the way she gives orders without raising her voice, and takes Chéri's teasing, and swallows the bitterest pills as if they were lollipops. . . . I begin to wonder, I really begin to wonder, whether there is not positive danger lying ahead for my son. I'm afraid, Léa dear, I'm afraid she may prove a damper on his originality, on—'

'What? Is he being an obedient little boy?' Léa interrupted. 'Do have some more of my brandy, Charlotte, it comes from Spéleïeff and it's seventy-four years old—you could give it to a new-born babe.'

' "Obedient" is hardly the right word, but he's . . . inter—impertur—'

'Imperturbable?'

'That's the word! For instance, when he knew I was coming to see you . . .'

'Did he know, then?'

An impetuous blush leapt to Léa's cheeks, and she cursed her hot blood and the bright daylight of the little drawing-room. Madame Peloux, a benign expression in her eyes, fed on Léa's confusion.

'But of course he knew. That oughtn't to bring a blush to your cheeks, my beauty. What a child you are!'

'In the first place, how did you know I was back?'

'Oh, come, Léa, don't ask such foolish questions. You've been seen about everywhere.'

'Yes, but Chéri—did you tell him I was back?'

'No, my beauty, it was he who told me.'

'Oh, it was he who . . . That's funny.'

She heard her heart beating in her voice and dared not risk more than the shortest answers.

'He even added: "Madame Peloux, you'll oblige me by going to find out news of Nounoune." He's still so fond of you, the dear boy.'

'How nice!'

Madame Peloux, crimson in the face, seemed to abandon herself to the influence of the old brandy and talked as in a dream, wagging her head from side to side. But her russet eyes remained fixed and steely, and she kept a close watch on Léa, who was sitting bolt upright, armed against herself, waiting for the next thrust.

'It's nice, but it's quite natural. A man doesn't forget a woman like you, Léa dear. And . . . if you want to know what I really think, you've only to lift a finger and . . .'

Léa put a hand on Charlotte Peloux's arm. 'I don't want to know what you really think,' she said gently.

The corners of Madame Peloux's mouth fell: 'Oh, I can understand, I approve,' she sighed in a passionless voice. 'When one has made other arrangements for one's life, as you have . . . I haven't even had a word with you about yourself!'

'But it seems to me that you have.'

'Happy?'

'Happy.'

'Divinely happy? A lovely trip? Is *he* nice? Where's his photo?'

Léa, relieved, sharpened her smile and shook her head. 'No, no, you'll find out nothing, search where you will. Have your detectives let you down, Charlotte?'

'I rely on no detectives,' Charlotte answered. 'It's certainly not because anyone has told me . . . that you'd been through another heart-breaking desertion . . . that you'd been terribly worried, even over money. . . . No, no, you know what small attention I pay to gossip!'

'No one knows it better than me. My dear Lolotte, you can go back home without any fears on my behalf. And please reassure our friends, and tell them that I only wish they had made half what I did out of Oil shares between December and February.'

The alcoholic cloud-screen, which softened the features of Madame Peloux, lifted in a trice; a clear, sharp, throughly alert face emerged. 'You were in on Oil? I might have known it! And you never breathed a word to me.'

'You never asked me about it. . . . You were thinking only of your family, as was natural. . . .'

'Fortunately, I was thinking of Compressed Fuel at the same time.' The muted trumpet resembled a flute.

'Ah! and you never let on to me either!'

'Intrude upon love's young dream? Never! Léa, my dear,
I'm off now, but I'll be back.'

'You'll come back on Thursday, because at present, my dear
Lolotte, your Sundays at Neuilly . . . they're finished for me.
Would you like it if I started having a few people here on
Thursdays? Nobody except old friends, old Ma Aldonza, our
Reverend-Father-the-Baroness—poker for you, knitting for
me. . . .'

'Do you knit?'

'Not yet, but it will soon come. Well?'

'I jump for joy at the idea! See if I'm not jumping! And
you may be sure I won't say a word about it at home. That
bad boy would be quite capable of coming and asking for a
glass of port on one of your Thursdays. Just one more little
kiss, my beauty. . . . Heavens, how good you smell. Have you
noticed that as the skin gets less firm, the scent sinks in better
and lasts much longer? It's really very nice.'

'Be off, be off . . .' Quivering, Léa stood watching Madame
Peloux as she crossed the courtyard. 'Go on your mischievous
way! Nothing can stop you. You twist your ankle, yes—but
it never brings you down. Your chauffeur is careful not
to skid, so you'll never crash into a tree. You'll get back
safely to Neuilly, and you'll choose your moment—to-day, or
to-morrow, or one day next week—to come out with words
that should never pass your lips. You'll try and upset those
who, perhaps, are happy and at peace. The least harm you'll
do is to make them tremble a little, as you made me, for a
moment. . . .'

She was trembling at the knees, like a horse after a steep
pull, but she was not in pain. She felt overjoyed at having kept
so strict a control over herself and her words. Her looks and
her colour were enhanced by her recent encounter, and she
went on pulping her handkerchief to release her bottled-up
energy.

She could not detach her thoughts from Madame Peloux.
'We've come together again,' she said to herself, 'like two dogs
over an old slipper which both have got used to chewing. How
queer it is! That woman is my enemy, and yet it's from her I now
draw my comfort. How close are the ties that bind us!'

Thus, for a long time, she mused over her future, veering between alarm and resignation. Her nerves were relaxed, and she slept for a little. As she sat with one cheek pressed against a cushion, her dreams projected her into her fast-approaching old age. She saw day follow day with clockwork monotony, and herself beside Charlotte Peloux—their spirited rivalry helping the time to pass. In this way she would be spared, for many years, the degrading listlessness of women past their prime, who abandon first their stays, then their hair-dye, and who finally no longer bother about the quality of their underclothes. She had a foretaste of the sinful pleasures of the old—little else than a concealed aggressiveness, day-dreams of murder, and the keen recurrent hope for catastrophes that will spare only one living creature and one corner of the globe. Then she woke up, amazed to find herself in the glow of a pink twilight as roseate as the dawn.

'Ah, Chéri!' she sighed.

But it was no longer the raucous hungry cry of a year ago. She was not now in tears, nor was her body suffering and rebellious, because threatened by some sickness of the soul. Léa rose from her chair, and rubbed her cheek, embossed by the imprint of the embroidered cushion.

'My poor Chéri! It's a strange thought that the two of us—you by losing your worn old mistress, and I by losing my scandalous young lover—have each been deprived of the most honourable possession we had upon his earth!'

Two days went by after the visit of Charlotte Peloux: two grey days that passed slowly for Léa. She faced this new life with the patience of an apprentice. 'Since this is going to be my new life,' she said to herself, 'I'd better make a start.' But she set about it clumsily, altogether too conscientiously, so that it was a strain on her perseverance. On the second day, about eleven in the morning, she was seized with a desire to go for a walk through the Bois as far as the Lakes.

'I'll buy a dog,' she thought. 'He'll be a companion, and force me to walk.' And Rose had to hunt through the bottom of the summer cupboards for a pair of strong-soled brown boots and a tweed coat and skirt, smelling of alpine meadows and pine forests. Léa set off with the resolute stride proper to the wearer of heavy footwear and rough country clothes.

'Ten years ago, I should not have feared to carry a stick,' she said to herself. When still quite near the house, she heard behind her a brisk light tread, which she thought she recognized. She became unnerved, almost paralysed by a compelling fear; and before she could recover she let herself unwittingly be overtaken, and then passed, by an unknown young man. He was in a hurry, and never even glanced at her.

'I really am a fool,' she breathed in her relief.

She bought a dark carnation to pin on her jacket and started off again. But thirty yards ahead of her, looming out of the diaphanous mist above the grass verges of the Avenue, the silhouette of a man was waiting.

'This time I do recognize the cut of that coat and that way of twirling a cane.... Oh, no thank you, the last thing I want is for him to see me shod like a postman and wearing a thick jacket that makes me look stocky. If I must run into him, I'd far rather he saw me in something else ... and he never could stand me in brown, anyhow.... No, no ... I'm off home.... I ...'

At that moment the waiting man hailed an empty taxi, stepped in, and drove past Léa: he was a young man with fair hair and a small close-clipped moustache. But this time Léa did not smile or feel relief. She turned on her heel and walked back home.

'One of my off-days, Rose.... Bring me the peach-blossom tea-gown, the new one, and the big embroidered cloak. I'm stifling in these woollen things.'

'It's no good being obstinate,' Léa thought. 'Twice in succession it's turned out not to be Chéri: the third time it would have been. I know the little jokes Fate plays on one. There's nothing to be done about it. I've no fight left in me to-day, I'm feeling limp.'

She spent the rest of the day once more trying patiently to learn to be alone. After luncheon she enjoyed a cigarette and a look at the papers, and welcomed with a short-lived joy a telephone call from Baroness de la Berche, then another from Spéleïeff, her former lover, the handsome horse-coper, who had seen her in the street the previous evening and offered to sell her a spanking pair.

There followed an hour of complete and frightening silence. 'Come, come . . .' She began to walk up and down, with her hands on her hips, her arms free of the heavy gold rose-embroidered cloak, its magnificent train sweeping the floor behind her.

'Come, come. . . . Let's try to take stock. This isn't the moment to become demoralized—now that I'm no longer in love with the boy. I've been living on my own now for six months. I managed perfectly well when I was in the south. To start with, I moved about from place to place. And the people I got to know on the Riviera or in the Pyrenees did me good; I felt positively refreshed each time any of them went away. Starch poultices may not cure a burn, but they do bring relief when constantly renewed. My six months of keeping on the move reminds me of the story of that hideous Sarah Cohen, who married a monster of ugliness. 'Each time I look at him, I think that I am pretty.'

'But I knew what it was like to live alone before these last six months. What sort of life did I lead after I'd left Spéleïeff, for instance? Oh yes, I went chasing round bistros and bars with Patron, and then all of a sudden Chéri came into my life. But before Spéleïeff, there was little Lequellec: when his family dragged him away from me to lead him to the altar, his beautiful eyes were brimming with tears, poor boy. . . . After him, I was all alone for four months, I remember. The first month, I cried a great deal. Oh, no, it was for Bacciocchi I cried so much. But when I was through with my tears, there was no holding me. It was so delightful to find myself alone. Yes, but at the Bacciocchi time I was twenty-eight, and thirty after Lequellec, and in between these two, I had known . . . Well, no matter. After Spéleïeff, I became disgusted—so much money so ill spent. Whereas now, after Chéri, I'm . . . I'm fifty, and I was unwise enough to keep him for six whole years!'

She wrinkled her forehead, and looked ugly with her mouth in a sulky droop.

'It serves me right. At my age, one can't afford to keep a lover six years. Six years! He has ruined all that was left of

me. Those six years might have given me two or three quite
pleasant little happinesses, instead of one profound regret. A
liaison of six years is like following your husband out to the
colonies: when you get back again nobody recognizes you and
you've forgotten how to dress.'

To relieve the strain, she rang for Rose, and together they
went through the contents of the little cupboard where she
kept her lace. Night fell, set the lamps blossoming into light,
and called Rose back to the cares of the house.

'To-morrow,' Léa said to herself, 'I'll order the motor and
drive out to Spéléïeff's stud-farm in Normandy. I'll take old
La Berche, if she wants to come: it will remind her of the past
glories of her own carriages. And, upon my word, should the
younger Spéléïeff cast an eye in my direction, I'm not saying
I . . .'

She carefully smiled a mysterious and provocative smile,
to delude what ghosts there might be hovering round the
dressing-table or round the formidable bed, glimmering in
the shadows. But she felt entirely frigid, and full of contempt
for the pleasures other people found in love.

She dined off grilled sole and pastries, and found the
meal a recreation. She chose a dry champagne in place of
the Bordeaux, and hummed as she left the table. Eleven
o'clock caught her by surprise, still taking the measurements
of the space between the windows in her bedroom, where she
planned to replace the large looking-glasses with old painted
panels of flowers and balustrades. She yawned, scratched her
head, and rang for her maid to undress her. While Rose knelt
to take off her silk stockings, Léa reviewed her achievements
of the day already slipping into the pages of the past, and was
as pleased with her performance as if she had polished off
an imposition. Protected for the night against the dangers of
idleness, she could look forward to so many hours of sleep, so
many when she would lie awake. Under cover of night, the
restless regain the privilege of yawning aloud or sighing, of
cursing the milkman's cart, the street-cleaners, and the early
morning sparrows.

During her preparations for the night, she thought over a
number of mild projects that would never come into being.

'Aline Mesmacker has a restaurant bar and is simply coining

money. . . . Obviously, it gives her something to do, as well as being a good investment. . . . But I can't see myself sitting at a cash-desk; and if one employs a manageress, it's no longer worth while. Dora and that fat Fifi run a night-club together, Mother La Berche told me. Everybody's doing it now. And they wear stiff collars and dinner jackets, to attract a special clientèle. Fat Fifi has three children to bring up—they're her excuse. . . . Then there's Kühn, who's simply kicking his heels, and would gladly take some of my capital to start a new dressmaker's.' Naked, and brick-pink from the reflection of her Pompeian bathroom, she sprayed herself with her favourite sandalwood, and, without thinking about it, enjoyed unfolding a long silk nightgown.

'All that's so much poppycock! I know perfectly well that I dislike working. To bed with you, Madame! You'll never have any other place of business, and all your customers are gone!'

The coloured lining of the white gandoura she put on was suffused with a vague pink. She went back to her dressing-table, and combed and tugged at the hairs stiffened by dye, lifting both her arms, and thus framing her tired face. Her arms were still so beautiful, from the full deep hollow of the armpit up to the rounded wrists, that she sat gazing at them in the looking-glass.

'What lovely handles for so old a vase!'

With a careless gesture she thrust a pale tortoiseshell comb into the back of her hair, and, without much hope, picked a detective story from the shelf of a dark closet. She had no taste for fine bindings and had never lost the habit of relegating books to the bottom of a cupboard, along with cardboard boxes and empty medicine bottles.

As she stood smoothing the cool linen sheets on her huge uncovered bed, the big bell in the courtyard rang out. The full, solemn, unwonted peal jarred on the midnight hour.

'What in the world . . .?' she said out loud.

She held her breath while listening, her lips parted. A second peal sounded even louder than the first, and Léa, with an instinctive movement of self-preservation and modesty, ran to powder her face. She was about to ring for Rose when she heard the front door slam, followed by footsteps in the hall and on the stairs, and the sound of two voices mingling—her maid's and someone else's. She had no time to make up her mind: the door of her room was flung open by a ruthless hand. Chéri stood before her—his top-coat unbuttoned over evening clothes, his hat on his head—pale and angry-looking.

He leaned back against the door now shut behind him, and did not move. He looked not so much at Léa as all round the room, with the quick shifting glance of a man about to be attacked.

Léa, who that morning had trembled at the half-surmised outline of a figure in the mist, felt at first only the resentment of a woman caught at her toilet. She drew her wrap more closely about her, settled her comb, and with one foot hunted for a missing slipper. She blushed, yet by the time the high colour died down she had already recovered the semblance of calm. She raised her head and appeared taller than the young man who was leaning, all in black, against the white of the door.

'That's a nice way to come into a room,' she said in a rather loud voice. 'You might at least take your hat off and say good evening.'

'Good evening,' Chéri said in surly tones.

The sound of his voice seemed to astonish him. He looked all about less like an angry animal, and a sort of smile drifted from his eyes down to his mouth, as he repeated a gentler 'Good evening.'

He took off his hat and came forward a few steps.

'May I sit down?'

'If you like,' Léa said.

He sat down on a pouffe and saw that she remained standing.

'Are you in the middle of dressing? Aren't you going out?'

She shook her head, sat down far away from him, picked up her nail-buffer and never said a word. He lit a cigarette, and asked her permission only after it was alight.

'If you like,' Léa repeated indifferently.

He said nothing more and dropped his gaze. Noticing that his hand with the cigarette in it was shaking, he rested it on the edge of a table. Léa continued polishing her nails deliberately and from time to time cast a brief glance at Chéri's face, especially at his lowered eyelids and the dark fringe of his lashes.

'It was Ernest who opened the front door to me as usual,' Chéri said at last.

'And why shouldn't it have been Ernest? Ought I to have changed my staff because you got married?'

'No . . . I mean, I simply said that . . .'

Again silence fell, broken by Léa.

'May I know whether you intend to remain for some time, sitting on that pouffe? I don't even ask why you take the liberty of entering my house at midnight. . . .'

'You may ask me why,' he said quickly.

She shook her head. 'It doesn't interest me.'

He jumped up precipitously, sending the pouffe rolling away behind him, and bore down upon Léa. She felt him bending over her as if he were going to strike her, but she did not flinch. The thought came to her: 'What in this world is there for me to be frightened of?'

'So you don't know what brings me here! You don't want to know what brings me here!'

He tore off his coat and sent it flying on to the chaise-longue, then he crossed his arms, and shouted quite close to Léa's face, in strained but triumphant voice, 'I've come back!'

She was using a delicate pair of tweezers, and these she carefully put away before wiping her fingers. Chéri dropped into a chair, as though his strength was completely exhausted.

'Good,' Léa said. 'You've come back. That's very nice! Whose advice did you take about that?'

'My own,' Chéri said.

She got up in her turn, the better to dominate him. Her surging heartbeats had subsided, allowing her to breathe in comfort. She wanted to play her role without a mistake.

'Why didn't you ask me for my advice? I'm an old friend who knows all your clownish ways. Why did it never occur to you that your coming here might well embarrass . . . someone?'

Lowering his head, he searched every corner of the room from under his eyebrows—the closed doors, the bed, metal-girt and heaped with luxurious pillows. He found nothing exceptional, nothing new, and shrugged his shoulders.

Léa expected more than that and drove home her point. 'You understand what I mean?'

'Perfectly,' he answered. ' "Monsieur" has not come in yet? "Monsieur" is sleeping out?'

'That's none of your business, child,' she said calmly.

He bit his lip and nervously knocked off his cigarette ash into a jewel tray.

'Not in that, I keep on telling you!' Léa cried. 'How many times must I . . .?'

She broke off to reproach herself for having unconsciously adopted the tone of their old familiar quarrels. But he did not appear to have heard and went on examining one of Léa's rings—an emerald she had purchased on her recent trip.

'What's . . . what's this?' he stammered.

'That? It's an emerald.'

'I'm not blind. What I mean is, who gave it you?'

'No one you know.'

'Charming!' Chéri said bitterly.

The note in his voice was enough to restore Léa's authority, and she pressed her advantage, taking pleasure in leading him still further astray.

'Isn't it charming! I get compliments on it wherever I go. And the setting, you've seen it . . . the filigree of diamonds . . .'

'Enough!' bawled Chéri furiously, smashing his fist down on the fragile table.

A few roses shed their petals at the impact, and a china cup slithered without breaking on to the thick carpet. Léa reached for the telephone, but Chéri caught her hand in a rough grasp. 'What are you going to do with that telephone?'

'Call the police,' Léa said.

He took hold of both her arms, pretending to be up to some playful nonsense as he pushed her away from the instrument.

'Oh, go on with you, that's all right. Don't be silly! Can't I even open my mouth without your getting all melodramatic?'

She sat down and turned her back on him. He remained standing, with nothing in his hands: his parted lips were swollen, giving him the look of a sulky child; one black lock hung down over his eyebrow. Surreptitiously, Léa watched him in a looking-glass, till his reflection vanished when he sat down. In her turn, Léa was embarrassed when she felt him staring at her back, broadened by the loose folds of her gandoura. She returned to her dressing-table, smoothed her hair, rearranged her comb, and, as if for want of something better to do, began unscrewing the top of a scent-bottle. Chéri turned his head as the first whiff reached his nostrils.

'Nounoune!' he called.

She did not answer.

'Nounoune!'

'Beg my pardon,' she ordered, without turning round.

'Not likely!' he sneered.

'I can't force you. But you'll leave the house. And at once. . . .'

'I beg your pardon,' he said at once peevishly.

'Better than that.'

'I beg your pardon,' he repeated, quite low.

'That's better.'

She went over to him and ran her hand lightly over his bowed head. 'Come, tell me all about it.'

He shivered, trembling under her touch. 'What do you want me to tell you? It's not very complicated. I've come back, that's all.'

'Tell me! Come along, tell me!'

He rocked backwards and forwards on his seat, pressing his hands between his knees, and raised his head towards Léa without meeting her eyes. She watched the quivering of his nostrils, and she heard him trying to control his rapid breathing. She had only to say once more, 'Come, tell me all about it,' and give him a prod with her finger, as if to push him over. At once he cried out, 'Nounoune darling! Nounoune darling!' and threw all his weight upon her, clasping her long legs, so that they gave way under her.

Once seated, she let him slither to the floor and sprawl over her with tears, and inarticulate words, and groping fingers that caught at her lace and her pearls and hunted feverishly under her dress for the shape of her shoulder and under her hair to touch her ears.

'Nounoune darling! We're together again, my Nounoune! Oh, my Nounoune! your shoulder, and your scent, and your pearls, my Nounoune, oh, it's so stunning . . . and that little burnt taste your hair has, oh, it's . . . it's stunning. . . .'

He leaned back to breathe out this silly word with what might have been the last breath of his body: then, still on his knees, he clasped Léa in his arms, offering her a forehead shadowed under tousled hair, a trembling mouth moist with tears, and eyes bright with weeping and happiness. She was so lost in contemplating him, so perfectly oblivious of everything that was not Chéri, that she never thought of kissing him. She twined her arms round his neck and gently hugged him to her, rocking him to the rhythm of murmured words.

'My pet . . . my naughty boy . . . You're here . . . You've come back again. . . . What have you been up to now? You're so naughty . . . my pretty. . . .'

He was moaning softly, keeping his lips together and hardly speaking, as he listened to Léa. He rested his cheek on her breast and begged her to go on, if for a moment she ceased her tender lullaby. And Léa, fearful that her own tears would flow, went on with her scolding.

'Wicked monster . . . heartless little devil . . . Get along with you, you great slut!'

He looked at her in gratitude: 'That's right . . . Go on slanging me! Oh, Nounoune!'

She held him at arm's length to see him properly. 'So you love me, then?'

He lowered his eyes in childish confusion: 'Yes, Nounoune.'

A little burst of uncontrollable laughter warned Léa that she was on the verge of giving way to the most terrible joy of her life. An embrace, followed by collapse, the uncovered bed, two bodies joined together like the two living halves of an animal that has been cut through. 'No, no,' she said to herself, 'not yet, oh, not yet. . . .'

'I'm thirsty,' Chéri sighed. 'Nounoune, I'm thirsty.'

She rose quickly and put a hand on the now tepid jug of water; hardly had she hurried from the room before she was back again. Chéri, curled up in a ball, was lying with his head on the pouffe. 'Rose will bring you some lemonade,' Léa said. 'Don't stay there. Come and sit on the chaise-longue. Does the lamp hurt your eyes?'

She was trembling with delight in her imperious solicitude. She sat down at the other end of the chaise-longue and Chéri half stretched out to nestle against her.

'Perhaps now you'll tell me a little . . .'

They were interrupted by the entry of Rose. Chéri, without getting up, languidly turned his head in her direction: 'Evening, Rose.'

'Good evening, Monsieur,' Rose said discreetly.

'Rose, to-morrow at nine, I'd like—'

'Brioches and chocolate,' Rose finished for him.

Chéri shut his eyes again with a sigh of contentment. 'And that's that. . . . Rose, where am I going to dress to-morrow morning?'

'In the boudoir,' Rose answered accommodatingly. 'Only I had better take the settee out, I suppose, and put back the shaving-mirror, as it used to be?'

She sought confirmation in the eye of Léa, who was proudly displaying her spoilt child, supported by her arm as he drank.

'If you like,' Léa said. 'We'll see. You can go, Rose.'

Rose retired, and during the ensuing moment's silence nothing could be heard except the vague murmuring of the wind and the cry of a bird bewildered by the brightness of the moon.

'Chéri, are you asleep?'

He gave one of his long-drawn sighs like an exhausted retriever. 'Oh, no, Nounoune, I'm too happy to sleep.'

'Tell me, child. . . You haven't been unkind over there?'

'At home? No, Nounoune, far from it. I swear to you.'

He looked up at her, without raising his trusting head.

'Of course not, Nounoune. I left because I left. The girl's very nice. There was no fuss at all.'

'Ah!'

'I wouldn't swear that she didn't have an inkling all the same. This evening she was wearing what I call her "orphanage look", you know, pathetic dark eyes under her pretty head of hair. . . . You know how pretty her hair is?'

'Yes.'

She threw out these monosyllables in a whisper as if intent on the words of someone talking in his sleep.

'I even think,' Chéri continued, 'that she must have seen me going through the garden.'

'Oh?'

'Yes. She was on the balcony, in her white sequin dress, congealed whiteness. Oh! I don't like that dress. . . . Ever since dinner it had been making me long to cut and run.'

'No.'

'Yes it had, Nounoune, I can't say whether she saw me. The moon wasn't up. It came up while I was waiting.'

'Where were you waiting?'

Chéri waved a vague hand in the direction of the avenue. 'There. I was waiting, don't you understand. I wanted to see. I'd waited a long time.'

'But what for?'

He hastily jumped away and sat further off. He resumed his expression of primitive distrust. 'I wanted to be sure there was nobody here.'

'Oh, yes. . . . You thought that . . .'

She could not resist a scornful laugh. A lover in her house! A lover while Chéri was still living! It was grotesque. 'How stupid he is!' she thought in her enthusiasm.

'You're laughing?'

He stood up in front of her and put his hand on her forehead, forcing back her head. 'You're laughing! You're making fun of me. You're . . . Then you have a lover! There is someone!'

He leaned over her as he spoke, pushing her head back against the end of the chaise-longue. She felt the breath of an insulting mouth on her eyelids, and made no effort to be free of the hand that was crushing her hair against her forehead.

'I dare you to say you have a lover!'

She fluttered her eyelids, dazzled by the radiance of the face bearing down on her, and finally, in a toneless voice, she said: 'No, I have no lover. I . . . love you. . . .'

He relaxed his hold and began pulling off his dinner jacket and waistcoat; his tie whistled through the air and ended up round the neck of Léa's bust—up on the mantelpiece.

Meanwhile, he never moved away from her, and kept her, wedged between his knees, where she sat on the chaise-longue.

When she saw him half-naked, she asked, with a note of sadness: 'Do you really want to? . . . Do you? . . .'

He did not answer, carried away by the thought of his approaching pleasure and the consuming desire to take her again. She gave way and served her young lover like a good mistress, with devout solicitude. Nevertheless, she anticipated with a sort of terror the moment of her own undoing; she endured Chéri as she might a torture, warding him off with strengthless hands, and holding him fast between strong knees. Finally, she seized him by the arm, uttered a feeble cry, and foundered in the deep abyss, whence love emerges pale and in silence, regretful of death.

They remained enfolded in their close embrace and no words troubled the prolonged silence of their return to life. The upper part of his body had slipped down and he lay across Léa's thigh, his pendent head, with eyes closed, resting upon the sheets as if he had been stabbed to death over the body of his mistress. She, meanwhile, partly turned away from him, bore almost the full weight of this unsparing body. She breathed softly but unevenly. Her left arm ached, crushed beneath her. Chéri could feel the back of his neck growing numb. Both were waiting, concentrated and motionless, for the abating tempest of their pleasure to recede.

'He's asleep,' Léa thought. With her free hand, she was still clinging to Chéri's wrist, and she squeezed it gently. One of her knees was being crushed by a knee—how well she knew its lovely shape! About the level of her own heart she could feel the steady muffled beating of another. Chéri's favourite scent—insistent, clinging, reminding her of fat waxy flowers and exotic glades—was all pervasive. 'He is here!' she whispered, immersed in a feeling of blind security. 'He is here for ever!' her senses re-echoed. The well-ordered prudence, the happy common sense that had been her guide through life, the humiliating vagaries of her riper years and the subsequent renunciations, all beat a retreat and vanished into thin air before the presumptuous brutality of love. 'He is here!' she thought. 'He has left his own home and his pretty silly little wife to come back, to come back to me! Who can take him from me now? Now at last I'll be able to organize our existence. He doesn't always know what he wants; but I do. No doubt we shall have to go away. We shan't go into hiding, but we'll look for somewhere peaceful. For I must find time to look at him. When I was unaware I loved him, I can't ever have looked at him properly. I must find a place where there'll be room enough for his whims and my wishes. I'll do the thinking for both of us—let him do the sleeping.'

While she was painstakingly withdrawing her left arm, cramped and pricking with pins and needles, and her numbed shoulder, she glanced at Chéri's averted face and found that he was not asleep. She could see the whites of his eyes and the flutter of the little black wings of his long eyelashes.

'Why, you're not asleep!'

She felt him tremble against her, before he turned over in a single movement.

'But you're not asleep, either, Nounoune!'

He stretched a hand out to the bedside table and switched on the lamp: a flood of rosy light covered the big bed, throwing the patterns of the lace into high relief, hollowing out shadowed valleys between swelling hills in the quilted folds of the eiderdown. Chéri, stretched out at full length, surveyed the field of his victory and of his peace. Léa, leaning on one elbow beside him, stroked his beloved, long eyebrows, and swept back the rebellious locks. Lying with his hair dishevelled over his forehead, he looked as if he had been blown over by a raging wind.

The enamel clock struck. Chéri straightened himself at a bound and sat up. 'What time is it?'

'I don't know. What difference can it make to us?'

'Oh, I just asked. . . .'

He gave a short laugh, and did not immediately lie down again. Outside, the first milkcart clinked out its tinkling carillon, and he made a vague movement in the direction of the avenue. The strawberry-coloured curtains were slit through by the cold blade of dawning day. Chéri turned back to look at Léa, and stared at her with the formidable intensity of a suspicious dog or a puzzled child. An undecipherable thought appeared in the depths of his eyes; their shape, their dark wallflower hue, their harsh or languorous glint, were used only to win love, never to reveal his mind. From sheets crumpled as though by a storm, rose his naked body, broad-shouldered, slim-waisted; and his whole being breathed forth the melancholy of perfect works of art.

'Ah, you . . .' sighed the infatuated Léa.

He did not smile, accustomed as he was to accepting personal praise.

'Tell me, Nounoune. . . .'

'What, my pretty?'

He hesitated, fluttered his eyelids, and shivered. 'I'm tired . . . and then to-morrow, how will you manage about—'

Léa gave him a gentle push and pulled the naked body and drowsy head down to the pillows again.

'Don't worry. Lie down and go to sleep. Isn't Nounoune here to look after you? Don't think of anything. Sleep. You're cold, I'm sure. . . . Here, take this, it's warm. . . .'

She rolled him up in the silk and wool of a little feminine garment, retrieved from somewhere in the bed, and put out the light. In the dark, she lent him her shoulder, settled him happily against her side, and listened till his breathing was in rhythm with her own. No desires clouded her mind, but she did not wish for sleep. 'Let him do the sleeping; it's for me to do the thinking,' she repeated to herself. 'I'll contrive our flight with perfect tact and discretion; I believe in causing as little suffering and scandal as possible. . . . For the spring we shall like the south best. If there were only myself to be considered, I'd rather stay here, in peace and quiet; but there's Ma Peloux and the young Madame Peloux. . . .' The vision of a young wife in her nightgown, anxiously standing beside a window, checked Léa only long enough for her to shrug her shoulders with cold impartiality. 'I can't help that. What makes one person's happiness . . .'

The black silky head stirred on her breast, and her sleeping lover moaned in his dream. With a zealous arm, Léa shielded him against nightmares, and rocked him gently so that—without sight, without memory, without plans for the future—he might still resemble that 'naughty little boy' never born to her.

XII

HE had lain awake for some little while, taking great care
not to stir. Cheek on folded arms, he tried to guess the
time. Under a clear sky, the avenue must be vibrating with
heat too insistent for early morning, since no shadow of
a cloud passed across the lambent rose-red curtains. 'Ten
o'clock, perhaps?' He was tormented by hunger; he had
eaten little the previous evening. A year ago he would have
bounded out of bed, roughly aroused Léa from sleep by
ferocious shouts for cream-frothed chocolate and butter off
the ice.

He did not stir. He was afraid, did he move, of crumbling
away what remained to him of his rapture, the visual pleasure
he derived from the shining curtains and from the steel and
brass spirals of the bed, twinkling in the coloured aura of the
room. Last night's great happiness had dwindled, it seemed,
had melted, and sought refuge in the dancing iridescence of
a cut-glass jug.

On the landing, Rose trod the carpet with circumspect
step; a discreet besom was sweeping the courtyard; and
Chéri heard the tinkle of china coming from the pantry.
'How the morning drags on,' he said to himself. 'I'll get
up.' But he remained without moving a muscle, for, behind
him, Léa yawned and stretched her legs. He felt the touch
of a gentle hand on his back. He shut his eyes again,
and, for no good reason, his whole body began to act a
lie, feigning the limpness of sleep. He was aware of Léa
leaving the bed and of her dark silhouette between him
and the curtains, which she drew half apart. She turned
round to look at him, and with a toss of the head smiled
in his direction—in no sense a smile of triumph, but
a resolute smile, ready to accept all dangers. She was
in no hurry to leave the room, and Chéri kept watch
on her through hardly parted eyelashes. He saw her
open a railway time-table and run her fingers down the
columns; then she seemed absorbed in some calculation,
brow puckered and face upturned. Not yet powdered, a
meagre twist of hair at the back of her head, double chin,

and raddled neck, she was exposing herself rashly to the unseen observer.

She moved away from the window, and, taking her cheque-book from a drawer, wrote and tore out several cheques. Then she put a pair of white pyjamas at the foot of the bed, and silently left the room.

Alone, Chéri took several deep breaths, realizing that he had hardly dared to breathe since Léa had left the bed. He got up, put on the pyjamas, and opened a window. 'It's stifling in here,' he gasped. He had the vague uncomfortable feeling of having done something reprehensible. 'Because I pretended to be asleep? But I've watched Léa a hundred times just after she's got out of bed. Only, this time, I made the pretence of being asleep.'

The dazzling light restored the rose-pink glow of the room, and the delicate nacreous tints of the picture by Chaplin smiled down at him from the wall. Chéri bowed his head and shut his eyes, in an effort to remember the room as it had looked the night before—the mysterious colour, like the inside of a water-melon, the enchanted dome of lamp-light, and, above all, his exaltation when reeling under the intensity of his pleasures.

'You're up! The chocolate's already on its way.'

He was pleased to note that it had taken Léa only these few moments to do her hair, touch up her face, and spray herself with the familiar scent. The room seemed suddenly to be filled with the cheerful sound of her lovely voice, and with the smell of chocolate and hot toast. Chéri sat down beside the two steaming cups and was handed the thickly buttered toast by Léa. She did not suspect that he was trying to find something to say, for she knew that he was seldom talkative, especially when he was eating. She enjoyed a good breakfast, eating with the haste and preoccupied gaiety of a woman who, her trunks packed, is ready to catch her train.

'Your second piece of toast, Chéri?'

'No, thank you, Nounoune.'

'Not hungry any more?'

'Not hungry.'

With a smile, she shook her finger at him. 'You know what you're in for! You're going to swallow down two rhubarb pills!'

He wrinkled his nose, shocked. 'Listen, Nounoune. You've got a mania for fussing . . .'

'Ta ti ta ta! That's my look out. Put out your tongue. You won't show it me! Then wipe off your chocolate moustache, and let's have a quick sensible talk. Tiresome subjects can't be dealt with too quickly!'

She stretched across the table to take Chéri's hand and hold it between her own.

'You've come back. That was our fate. Do you trust yourself to me? I'll be responsible for you.'

She could not help breaking off, and closed her eyes as if hugging her victory. Chéri noticed the flush on his mistress's face.

'Oh!' she continued in a lower voice, 'When I think of all that I never gave you, all that I never said to you! When I think that I believed you merely a passing fancy, like all the others—only a little more precious than all the others! What a fool I was not to understand that you were my love, *the* love, the great love that comes only once!'

When she opened her blue eyes, they seemed to have become bluer, gaining depth in the shade of her eyelids, and her breathing was uneven.

'Oh,' Chéri prayed inwardly, 'Don't let her ask me a question, don't let her expect an answer from me now! I couldn't speak a single word.'

She gave his hand a little shake. 'Come along, let's be serious. As I was saying—we're leaving, we've already left. What will you do about *over there*? Let Charlotte arrange all the settlement details—it's much the wisest—and make her be generous, I beg of you. How will you let them know *over there*? A letter, I imagine. None too easy, but the less ink spilled, the better. We'll see about that between us. Then there's the question of your luggage. I've none of your things here any more. Such little details are far more upsetting than a major decision, but don't worry too much. . . . Will you kindly stop tearing the skin off the side of your toe all the time! That's the way to get an ingrowing toe-nail!'

Automatically, he let his foot drop to the floor. Under the weight of his sullen taciturnity, he found it a strain to focus his jaded attention on what Léa was saying. He stared at his mistress's happy, animated, imperious features, and asked himself vaguely: 'Why does she look so happy?'

His bewilderment became so obvious that Léa stopped in the middle of her monologue on their chances of buying old Berthellemy's yacht from him. 'Could anyone believe that you've not got one word of advice to give? Oh, you might still be twelve!'

Chéri, snatched from his stupor, put a hand to his forehead and looked at Léa, his eyes filled with melancholy.

'Being with you, Nounoune, is likely to keep me twelve for half a century.'

She blinked her eyes several times as if he had breathed on their lids, and let silence settle again.

'What are you trying to say?' she asked at last.

'Nothing, except what I did say, Nounoune. Nothing but the truth. And can you deny it, you, the most honest person alive?'

She decided to laugh, but her gaiety masked a terrible fear.

'But half your charm lies in your childishness, stupid! Later on it will be the secret of your eternal youth. Why complain of it? And you have the cheek to complain of it to *me!*'

'Yes, Nounoune. Do you expect me to complain to anyone but you?' and he caught hold of the hand she had taken away. 'My own Nounoune, dearest, darling Nounoune, I'm not only complaining of myself: I'm accusing you!'

She felt the grip of his firm hand. Instead of looking away, his large dark eyes with lashes gleaming clung pitifully to hers. She was determined not to tremble, yet. 'It's nothing, it's nothing,' she thought. 'It calls only for two or three sharp words and he'll become insulting, then sulky, and then I'll forgive him. . . . It's no more than that.' But she failed to find the quick rebuke which would change the expression on his face. 'Come, come, child . . . You know quite well there are certain jokes I will not tolerate.' But at the same moment she knew her voice to be sounding false and feeble. 'How badly I said that . . . bad theatre. . . .'

It was half-past ten, and the sun was now shining on the table between them. Léa's polished nails twinkled in its beams; but the light fell also on the soft flabby skin on the back of her well-shaped hands and on her wrists. This emphasized—like criss-crossings on a clay soil when heavy rain is followed by a dry spell—the complicated network of tiny concentric grooves and miniature parallelograms. Léa rubbed her hands absent-mindedly, turning her head to make Chéri look out of the window; but he persisted in his miserable hang-dog moodiness. The two hands were pretending, as if in disgrace, to toy with a loop of her belt. Brusquely he pounced upon them, kissed and kissed them again, then pressed his cheek against them, murmuring 'My Nounoune. . . . Oh, my poor Nounoune . . .'

'Let me alone,' she cried with inexplicable anger, snatching her hands away from him.

She took a moment to regain her control, frightened of her weakness, for she had been on the verge of tears. As soon as she was able, she smiled and spoke.

'So now it's me you're sorry for! Why did you accuse me a moment ago?'

'I was wrong,' he said humbly. 'For me you have been always . . .' He made a gesture to express his inability to find words worthy of her.

'*You have been?*' she underlined in a biting voice. 'That sounds like an obituary notice, my good child!'

'You see . . .' he began reproachfully.

He shook his head, and she saw only too well that she could not rouse any anger in him. She tightened all her muscles, and reined in her thoughts with the help of those few words, ever the same, and inwardly repeated again and again: 'Here he is, in front of my eyes. I've only to look to see he's still there. He's not out of reach. But is he still here, with me, really and truly?'

Her thoughts escaped from the domination of these re-peated phrases, only to sink into a great unvoiced lament. 'Oh! if only, if only I could somehow be returned to the moment when I was saying, "Your second piece of toast, Chéri!" for that moment's only just round the corner—it's not yet lost and gone for ever! Let's start again from there.

The little that's taken place since won't count—I'll wipe it out, I'll wipe it out. I'm going to talk to him as though we're back where we were a moment ago. I'm going to talk to him about our departure, our luggage.'

She did, in fact, speak, and said, 'I see . . . I see I cannot treat as a man a creature who, from sheer feebleness of character, can drive two women to distraction. Do you think that I don't understand? You like your journeys short, don't you? Yesterday at Neuilly, here today, but to-morrow! To-morrow, where? Here? No, no, my child, no need to lie. That guilty look would never take in even a woman stupider than I am, if there is one like that over there. . . .'

She threw out an arm to indicate Neuilly with so violent a gesture that she upset a cake-stand, which Chéri picked up again. Her words had sharpened her grief into anguish, an angry jealous anguish pouring forth like a young wife's outburst. The rouge on her cheek turned to the deep purple of wine-lees; a strand of her hair, crimped by the curling-tongs, wriggled down her neck like a small dry snake.

'And even the woman over there, even your wife won't be found waiting there every time you choose to come back home! A wife, my child, may not always be easy to find, but she's much easier to lose! You'll have yours kept under lock and key by Charlotte, eh? That's a marvellous idea! Oh, how I'll laugh, the day when . . .'

Chéri got up, pale and serious. 'Nounoune! . . .'

'Why Nounoune? What d'you mean, Nounoune? Do you think you're going to frighten me? You want to lead your own life, do you? Go ahead! You're bound to see some pretty scenes, with a daughter of Marie-Laure's. She may have thin arms and a flat behind, but that won't prevent her from . . .'

'I forbid you, Nounoune!'

He seized her by the arm; but she rose, vigorously shook herself free, and broke into hoarse laughter: 'Why, of course, "I forbid you to say a word against my wife!" Isn't that it?'

He walked round the table, trembling with indignation, and went straight up to her. 'No, I forbid you—d'you hear me?—I forbid you to spoil my Nounoune!' She retreated to the end of the room, babbling, 'What's that? what's that?' He followed her as though bent on chastising her. 'You heard what I said.

Is that the way for Nounoune to speak? What do you mean by such behaviour? Cheap little jibes like Madame Peloux's, is that what you go in for? To think they could come from you, Nounoune, from you. . . .'

Arrogantly he threw back his head. 'I know how Nounoune should speak. I know how she ought to think. I've had time to learn. I've not forgotten the day when you said to me, just before I married, "At least don't be cruel. Try not to make her suffer. I have the feeling that a doe is being thrown to a greyhound." Those were your words. That's really you. And the night before I married, when I ran away to come and see you, I remember you said to me . . .'

He could not go on, but all his features were bright with the memory.

'Darling, pull yourself together.' He put his hands on Léa's shoulders. 'And even last night,' he went on, 'it wasn't the first time you asked me whether I might not have hurt somebody *over there*! My Nounoune, I knew you as a fine woman, and I loved you as a fine woman, when we first started. If we have to make an end of it, must you start behaving like all the other women?'

She dimly felt the cunning behind the compliment and sat down, hiding her face in her hands.

'How hard you are, how hard,' she stammered. 'Why did you come back? . . . I was so calm on my own, getting so used to . . .'

She heard herself lying and stopped.

'Well, *I* wasn't!' Chéri said quickly. 'I came back because . . . because . . .'

He raised his arms, let them drop, and lifted them again. 'Because I couldn't go on without you, there's no point in looking for any other explanation.'

For a moment no word was spoken.

Quite overcome, she looked at this impatient young man, who with light feet and open arms, as white as a seagull, seemed poised for flight.

Chéri let his dark eyes rove all over her body.

'Oh, you can be proud of yourself,' he said suddenly. 'You can be proud of yourself for having made me—and what's more for three months—lead such a life, such a life!'

'I did?'

'Who else, if it wasn't you? If a door opened, it was
Nounoune; the telephone rang, Nounoune; a letter in the
garden postbox, perhaps Nounoune. . . . In the very wine I
drank, I looked for you, and I never found a Pommery to
equal yours. And then at nights . . . Oh, heavens above!'

He was walking up and down the carpet with rapid,
noiseless steps. 'I know now what it is to suffer for a
woman, and no mistake! After you, I know what all the
other women will be . . . dust and ashes! Oh, how well you've
poisoned me!'

She drew herself up slowly in her chair, and, letting
her body turn now this way, now that, followed Chéri's
movements. Her cheeks were dry, rather shiny, and their
fevered flush made the blue of her eyes almost intolerable.
He was walking up and down, head lowered, and he never
stopped talking.

'Imagine Neuilly with you not there, the first days after my
return! For that matter, everything—with you not there! I
almost went mad. One night, the child was ill—I no longer
remember what it was, headache, pains, something. I felt
sorry for her, but I had to leave the room; otherwise
nothing in the world could have stopped me saying, "Wait,
don't cry, I'll go and fetch Nounoune and she'll make you
well"—and you would have come, wouldn't you, Nounoune?
Great heavens, what a life it was. . . . I took on Desmond at the
Hôtel Morris, paid him well into the bargain, and sometimes
at night I would tell him stories. . . . I used to speak as if you
were unknown to him. "Old boy, there's never been a skin like
hers. . . . Take one look at that cabochon sapphire of yours,
and then hide it away for ever, because no light can turn the
blue of *her* eyes to grey!" I used to tell him how you could be
tough when you wanted to be; and that no one had ever got
the better of you, least of all me! I used to say, "That woman,
old boy, when she's wearing just the right hat"—the dark blue
one with the white wing, Nounoune, last summer's—"and
with the way she has of putting on her clothes—you can
match her against any other woman you may choose—and
she'll put every one of them in the shade!" And then that
wonderful manner you have of walking—of talking—your

smile—the erect way you hold yourself, I used to say to him—to Desmond: "Ah! A woman like Léa *is* something!" '

He snapped his fingers with proprietary pride and stopped, quite out of breath from his talking and walking. 'I never said all that to Desmond,' he thought, 'and yet I'm not telling lies. Desmond understood all right.'

He wanted to go on and glanced at Léa. She was still ready to listen. Sitting bolt upright now, she exposed to him in the full light her noble face in its disarray, the skin shining like wax where the hot tears had dried. Her cheeks and chin were pulled down by an invisible weight, and this added a look of sadness to the trembling corners of her mouth. Chéri found intact amidst this wreckage of beauty the lovely commanding nose and the eyes as blue as a blue flower.

'And so you see, Nounoune, after months of that sort of life, I come back here, and . . .' He pulled himself up, frightened by what he had nearly said.

'You come back here, and find an old woman,' Léa said calmly, in a whisper.

'Nounoune! Listen, Nounoune!'

He threw himself on his knees beside her, looking like a guilty, tongue-tied child no longer able to hide his misdemeanour.

'And you find an old woman,' Léa repeated. 'So what are you afraid of, child?'

She put her arms round his shoulders, and felt his body rigid and resistant, in sympathy with the hurt she was suffering. 'Come, cheer up, my Chéri. Don't cry, my pretty. . . . What is it you're afraid of? Of having hurt me? Far from it: I feel so grateful to you.'

He gave a sob of protestation, finding no strength to gainsay her.

She put her cheek against his tousled black hair. 'Did you say all that, did you really think all that of me? Was I really so lovely in your eyes, tell me? And so kind? At the age when a woman's life is so often over, was I really the loveliest for you, the most kind, and were you really in love with me? How grateful I am to you, my darling! The finest, did you say? . . . My poor child.'

He let himself go, while she supported him in her arms.

'Had I really been the finest, I should have made a man of you, and not thought only of the pleasures of your body, and my own happiness. The finest! Oh, no, my darling, I certainly wasn't that, since I kept you to myself. And now it's almost too late. . . .'

He seemed to be asleep in Léa's arms; but his obstinately tight-shut eyelids quivered incessantly, and with one lifeless hand he was clutching hold of her négligée and slowly tearing it.

'It's almost too late, it's almost too late. But all the same . . .' She leaned over him. 'Listen to me, my darling. Wake up, my pretty, and listen to me with your eyes open. Don't be afraid of looking at me. I am, after all, the woman you were in love with, you know, the finest woman . . .'

He opened his eyes, and his first tearful glance was already filled with a selfish, mendicant hope.

Léa turned away her head. 'His eyes . . . Oh, we must get this over quickly. . . .' She put her cheek against his forehead.

'It was I, child, it was my real self who said to you, "Don't cause unnecessary pain; spare the doe. . . ." I had quite forgotten, but luckily you remembered. You are breaking away from me very late in the day, my naughty little boy; I've been carrying you next to my heart for too long, and now you have a load of your own to carry: a young wife, perhaps a child. . . . I am to blame for everything you lack. . . . Yes, yes, my pretty, here you are, thanks to me, at twenty-five, so light-hearted, so spoilt, and at the same time so sad. . . . I'm very worried about you. You're going to suffer and make others suffer. You who have loved me. . . .'

His fingers tightened their grip on her négligée, and Léa felt the sharp nails of her 'naughty child' bite into her breast.

'You who have loved me,' she went on after a pause, 'will you be able to? . . . I don't know how to explain what I mean. . . .'

He drew back in order to listen: and she could barely restrain herself from saying, 'Put your hand back on my breast and your nails where they have left their mark; my strength abandons me as soon as your flesh is parted from mine.' Instead, she leaned over him as he knelt in front of

her, and continued: 'You have loved me, and you will regret
...'

She smiled at him, looking down into his eyes.

'What vanity, eh! ... But you will regret me! I beg of you,
when you're tempted to terrify the girl entrusted to your care
and keeping, do restrain yourself! At such moments, you
must find for yourself the wisdom and kindness you never
learned from me. I never spoke to you of the future. Forgive
me, Chéri—I've loved you as if we were both destined to die
within the same hour. Because I was born twenty-four years
before you, I was doomed, and I dragged you down with
me....'

He was listening very attentively, which made his face look
hard. She put her hand on his forehead to smooth the furrows
of anxiety.

'Can you see us, Chéri, going out to lunch together at
Armenonville! ... Can you see us inviting Monsieur and
Madame Lili! ...'

She gave a sad little laugh, and shivered.

'Oh, I'm just about as done for as that old creature....
Quick, quick, child, run off after your youth! Only a small
piece of it has been snipped off by ageing women: all the rest
is there for you and the girl who is waiting for you. You've
now had a taste of youth! It never satisfies, but one always
goes back for more. Oh, you had started to make comparisons
before last night.... And what am I up to now, doling
out all this advice and displaying the greatness of my soul!
What do I know of you two? She loves you: it's her turn to
tremble; but her misery will come from passion and not from
perverted mother-love. And you will talk to her like a master,
not capriciously, like a gigolo. Quick, quick, run off....'

She spoke in tones of hasty supplication. He listened,
standing planted before her, his chest bare, his hair temp-
estuous: and so alluring, that she had to clasp her hands to
prevent their seizing hold of him. He guessed this, perhaps,
and did not move away. For an instant they shared a lunatic
hope—do people feel like this in mid-air when falling from a
tower?—then the hope vanished.

'Go,' she said in a low voice. 'I love you. It's too late. Go
away. But go away at once. Get dressed!'

She rose and fetched him his shoes, spread out his crumpled shirt and his socks. He stood helpless, moving his fingers awkwardly as if they were numb. She had to find his braces and his tie; but she was careful not to go too close to him and offered him no further help. While he was dressing, she glanced into the courtyard several times, as if she were expecting a carriage at the door.

He looked even paler when he was dressed, and a halo of fatigue round his eyes made them seem larger.

'You don't feel ill?' she asked him. And she added timidly, lowering her eyes, 'You could always lie down for a little.' But at once she pulled herself together and came over to him, as though he were in great danger. 'No, no, you'll be better at home. Hurry, it's not yet midday; a good hot bath will soon put you to rights, and then the fresh air ... Here are your gloves. . . . Your hat? On the floor, of course. Put your coat on, there's a nip in the air. Au revoir, my Chéri, au revoir. That's right. And tell Charlotte that . . .' She closed the door behind him, and silence put an end to her vain and desperate words. She heard Chéri stumble on the staircase and she ran to the window. He was going down the front steps and then he stopped in the middle of the courtyard.

'He's coming back! He's coming back!' she cried, raising her arms.

An old woman, out of breath, repeated her movements in the long pier-glass, and Léa wondered what she could have in common with that crazy creature.

D. H. Lawrence

THE VIRGIN AND THE GIPSY

1930

DAVID HERBERT LAWRENCE (1885–1930) was born at East-wood, near Nottingham, the son of a coal-miner and of a woman who had been a schoolteacher and who had literary tastes and wrote poetry. As a child he had pneumonia, and this left him always frail; he was in danger of contracting tuberculosis, and in the end did contract it and died from it. Winning a scholarship to the local High School and then to Nottingham University College, he acquired the essential literacy that enabled him to function as a writer, and after the publication of his first novel, *The White Peacock* (1911), he gave up his teaching post and took to the life of a professional writer. In the years 1912–14 he took the opportunity to travel in Europe, spending time in Germany, France, and Italy. On his return in 1914 he married Frieda von Richthofen, the daughter of the military governor of Metz and sister of the Baron von Richthofen who was to become so famous as a fighter pilot in the conflict that was imminent; she first had to obtain a divorce from her husband, Professor Ernest Weekley of Nottingham University College, whom she left with two small daughters.

The First World War, when it came, was a profound shock to Lawrence; his physical frailty made enlistment impossible, but that Europe should tear itself to pieces in this way was an outrage to all his values, and, as if attracted by his general *malaise*, troubles began to rain on him. In 1915 he published *The Rainbow*, a book full of poetic feeling but uncomfortably frank, for those days, in its treatment of sexual relations. It was the subject of a police prosecution. Lawrence retired with Frieda to a cottage at Zennor, Cornwall, to work on *Women in Love*, but once more the police intervened; probably it was naïve of him to settle on a strategically sensitive area to live in, and he was ordered to move out. Residence in London, in Berkshire, and in Derbyshire followed. By this time Lawrence had only one wish as far as England was concerned: he wanted to leave it. In 1919 the opportunity to do so came, and the Lawrences left, never to return except on brief visits. For the eleven years that remained to him Lawrence lived in Italy, then America, where he moved by way of Ceylon and Australia, remaining in the latter country long enough to use it as the setting of a novel, *Kangaroo*. The Lawrences rented a ranch-house in Taos, New Mexico, then moved to Mexico itself, finally back to Italy. His last years were involved in intense and acrimonious controversy; *Lady Chatterley's Lover*, written in Florence in 1928, was prosecuted, the original manuscript of a volume of poems, *Pansies*, was confiscated, and an exhibition of his paintings in London was closed down by police action and a book containing facsimile reproductions of them was suppressed. In view of the kind of thing that has been getting into print since the 1960s all this is well-nigh incredible, but it is worth looking back on *Chatterley* and similar cases to remind oneself of the enormous changes in social and moral climate that can happen in thirty short years.

Lawrence's reputation has fluctuated very widely since his death in 1930. Very high claims have been made for his greatness both as prophet and artist, but there has always been an opposition party that has pointed to the nagging, abrasive note of scolding that so often intrudes. At his best he carries total conviction. As T.S. Eliot said in *After Strange Gods*, 'Against the living death of modern material civilization he spoke again and again; and even if these dead could speak, what he said is unanswerable.' Yet in that same book Eliot makes some sharply limiting comments.

The short stories are, by common consent, better than all but the finest passages of the novels; they are purer, less clotted with sermonizing; they vibrate with energy and awareness. *The Virgin and the Gipsy* (1930) is a *nouvelle* that upholds the standard set by the short stories, while it to some extent echoes the theme—and, I would say, more successfully—of that courageous but uneven and disappointing book, *Lady Chatterley's Lover*.

In the year that saw the first publication of this tale, Lawrence's tubercular condition worsened so much that he was taken to a clinic at Vence, near Nice, where he died and where his grave is marked by a mosaic showing the phoenix arising from the ashes, which he had long decided was to be his personal symbol.

I

WHEN the vicar's wife went off with a young and penniless man the scandal knew no bounds. Her two little girls were only seven and nine years old respectively. And the vicar was such a good husband. True, his hair was grey. But his moustache was dark, he was handsome, and still full of furtive passion for his unrestrained and beautiful wife.

Why did she go? Why did she burst away with such an *éclat* of revulsion, like a touch of madness?

Nobody gave any answer. Only the pious said she was a bad woman. While some of the good women kept silent. They knew.

The two little girls never knew. Wounded, they decided that it was because their mother found them negligible.

The ill wind that blows nobody any good swept away the vicarage family on its blast. Then lo and behold! the vicar, who was somewhat distinguished as an essayist and a controversialist, and whose case had aroused sympathy among the bookish men, received the living of Papplewick. The Lord had tempered the wind of misfortune with a rectorate in the north country.

The rectory was a rather ugly stone house down by the river Papple, before you come into the village. Further on, beyond where the road crosses the stream, were the big old stone cotton-mills, once driven by water. The road curved up-hill, into the bleak stone streets of the village.

The vicarage family received decided modification, upon its transference into the rectory. The vicar, now the rector, fetched up his old mother and his sister, and a brother from the city. The two little girls had a very different milieu from the old home.

The rector was now forty-seven years old; he had displayed an intense and not very dignified grief after the flight of his wife. Sympathetic ladies had stayed him from suicide. His hair was almost white, and he had a wild-eyed, tragic look. You had only to look at him, to know how dreadful it all was, and how he had been wronged.

Yet somewhere there was a false note. And some of the ladies, who had sympathised most profoundly with the vicar, secretly rather disliked the rector. There was a certain furtive self-righteousness about him, when all was said and done.

The little girls, of course, in the vague way of children, accepted the family verdict. Granny, who was over seventy and whose sight was failing, became the central figure in the house. Aunt Cissie, who was over forty, pale, pious, and gnawed by an inward worm, kept house. Uncle Fred, a stingy and grey-faced man of forty, who just lived dingily for himself, went into town every day. And the rector, of course, was the most important person, after Granny.

They called her the Mater. She was one of those physically vulgar, clever old bodies who had got her own way all her life by buttering the weaknesses of her men-folk. Very quickly she took her cue. The rector still 'loved' his delinquent wife, and would 'love her' till he died. Therefore hush! The rector's feeling was sacred. In his heart was enshrined the pure girl he had wedded and worshipped.

Out in the evil world, at the same time, there wandered a disreputable woman who had betrayed the rector and abandoned his little children. She was now yoked to a young and despicable man, who no doubt would bring her the degradation she deserved. Let this be clearly understood, and then hush! For in the pure loftiness of the rector's heart still bloomed the pure white snow-flower of his young bride. This white snow-flower did not wither. That other creature, who had gone off with that despicable young man, was none of his affair.

The Mater, who had been somewhat diminished and insignificant as a widow in a small house, now climbed into the chief arm-chair in the rectory, and planted her old bulk firmly again. She was not going to be dethroned. Astutely she gave a sigh of homage to the rector's fidelity to the pure white snow-flower, while she pretended to disapprove. In sly reverence for her son's great love, she spoke no word against that nettle which flourished in the evil world, and which had once been called Mrs Arthur Saywell. Now, thank heaven, having married again, she was no more Mrs Arthur Saywell. No woman bore the rector's name. The pure white snow-flower bloomed *in perpetuum*, without nomenclature. The family even thought of her as She-who-was-Cynthia.

All this was water on the Mater's mill. It secured her against Arthur's ever marrying again. She had him by his feeblest weakness, his skulking self-love. He had married an imperishable white snow-flower. Lucky man! He had been injured. Unhappy man! He had suffered. Ah, what a heart of love! And he had—forgiven! Yes, the white snow-flower was forgiven. He even had made provision in his will for her, when that other scoundrel—But hush! Don't even *think* too near to that horrid nettle in the rank outer world! She-who-was-Cynthia. Let the white snow-flower bloom inaccessible on the heights of the past. The present is another story.

The children were brought up in this atmosphere of cunning self-sanctification and of unmentionability. They too, saw the snow-flower on inaccessible heights. They too knew that it was throned in lone splendour aloft their lives, never to be touched.

At the same time, out of the squalid world sometimes would come a rank, evil smell of selfishness and degraded lust, the smell of that awful nettle, She-who-was-Cynthia. This nettle actually contrived at intervals, to get a little note through to the girls, her children. And at this the silver-haired Mater shook inwardly with hate. For if She-who-was-Cynthia ever came back, there wouldn't be much left of the Mater. A secret gust of hate went from the old granny to the girls, children of that foul nettle of lust, that Cynthia who had had such an affectionate contempt for the Mater.

Mingled with all this, was the children's perfectly distinct recollection of their real home, the vicarage in the south, and their glamorous but not very dependable mother, Cynthia. She had made a great glow, a flow of life, like a swift and dangerous sun in the home, forever coming and going. They always associated her presence with brightness, but also with danger; with glamour, but with fearful selfishness.

Now the glamour was gone, and the white snow-flower, like a porcelain wreath, froze on its grave. The danger of instability, the peculiarly *dangerous* sort of selfishness, like lions and tigers, was also gone. There was now a complete stability, in which one could perish safely.

But they were growing up. And as they grew, they became more definitely confused, more actively puzzled. The Mater, as she grew older, grew blinder. Somebody had to lead her about. She did not get up till towards midday. Yet blind or bed-ridden, she held the house.

Besides, she wasn't bed-ridden. Whenever the *men* were present, the Mater was in her throne. She was too cunning to court neglect. Especially as she had rivals.

Her great rival was the younger girl, Yvette. Yvette had some of the vague, careless blitheness of She-who-was-Cynthia. But this one was more docile. Granny perhaps had caught her in time. Perhaps!

The rector adored Yvette, and spoiled her with a doting fondness; as much as to say: am I not a soft-hearted, indulgent old boy! He liked to have this opinion of himself, and the Mater knew his weaknesses to a hair's breadth. She knew them, and she traded on them by turning them into decorations for him, for his character. He wanted, in his own eyes, to have a fascinating character, as women want to have fascinating dresses. And the Mater cunningly put beauty-spots over his defects and deficiencies. Her mother-love gave her the clue to his weaknesses, and she hid them for him with decorations. Whereas She-who-was-Cynthia—! But don't mention *her*, in this connexion. In her eyes, the rector was almost hump-backed and an idiot.

The funny thing was, Granny secretly hated Lucille, the elder girl, more than the pampered Yvette. Lucille, the uneasy and irritable, was more conscious of being under Granny's power, than was the spoilt and vague Yvette.

On the other hand, Aunt Cissie hated Yvette. She hated her very name. Aunt Cissie's life had been sacrificed to the Mater, and Aunt Cissie knew it, and the Mater knew she knew it. Yet as the years went on, it became a convention. The convention of Aunt Cissie's sacrifice was accepted by everybody, including the self-same Cissie. She prayed a good deal about it. Which also showed that she had her own private feelings somewhere, poor thing. She had ceased to be Cissie, she had lost her life and her sex. And now, she was creeping towards fifty, strange green flares of rage would come up in her, and at such times, she was insane.

But Granny held her in her power. And Aunt Cissie's one object in life was to look after the Mater.

Aunt Cissie's green flares of hellish hate would go up against all young things, sometimes. Poor thing, she prayed and tried to obtain forgiveness from heaven. But what had been done to her, *she* could not forgive, and the vitriol would spurt in her veins sometimes.

It was not as if the Mater were a warm, kindly soul. She wasn't. She only seemed it, cunningly. And the fact dawned gradually on the girls. Under her old-fashioned lace cap, under her silver hair, under the black silk of her stout, short, forward-bulging body, this old woman had a cunning heart, seeking for ever her own female power. And through the weakness of the unfresh, stagnant men she had bred, she kept her power, as her years rolled on, from seventy to eighty, and from eighty on the new lap, towards ninety.

For in the family there was a whole tradition of 'loyalty'; loyalty to one another, and especially to the Mater. The Mater, of course, was the pivot of the family. The family was her own extended ego. Naturally she covered it with her power. And her sons and daughters, being weak and disintegrated, naturally were loyal. Outside the family, what was there for them but danger and insult and ignominy? Had not the rector experienced it, in his marriage? So now, caution! Caution and loyalty, fronting the world! Let there be as much hate and friction *inside* the family, as you like. To the outer world, a stubborn fence of unison.

II

BUT it was not until the girls finally came home from school that they felt the full weight of Granny's dead old hand on their lives. Lucille was now nearly twenty-one, and Yvette nineteen. They had been to a good girl's school, and had had a finishing year in Lausanne, and were quite the usual thing, tall young creatures with fresh, sensitive faces and bobbed hair and young-manly, deuce-take-it manners.

'What's so awfully *boring* about Papplewick,' said Yvette, as they stood on the Channel boat watching the grey, grey cliffs of Dover draw near, 'is that there are no *men* about. Why doesn't Daddy have some good old sports for friends? As for Uncle Fred, he's the limit!'

'Oh, you never know what will turn up,' said Lucille, more philosophic.

'You jolly well know what to expect,' said Yvette. 'Choir on Sundays, and I hate mixed choirs. Boys' voices are *lovely*, when there are no women. And Sunday School and Girls' Friendly, and socials, all the dear old souls that inquire after Granny! Not a decent young fellow for miles.'

'Oh, I don't know!' said Lucille. 'There's always the Framleys. And you know Gerry Somercotes *adores* you.'

'Oh but I *hate* fellows who adore me!' cried Yvette, turning up her sensitive nose. 'They *bore* me. They hang on like lead.'

'Well what *do* you want, if you can't stand being adored? *I* think it's perfectly all right to be adored. You know you'll never marry them, so why not let them go on adoring, if it amuses them.'

'Oh but I *want* to get married,' cried Yvette.

'Well in that case, let them go on adoring you till you find one that you can *possibly* marry.'

'I never should, that way. Nothing puts me off like an adoring fellow. They *bore* me so! They make me fell beastly.'

'Oh, so they do me, if they get pressing. But at a distance, I think they're rather nice.'

'I should like to fall *violently* in love.'

'Oh, very likely! I shouldn't! I should hate it. Probably so would you, if it actually happened. After all, we've got to settle down a bit, before we know what we want.'

'But don't you *hate* going back to Papplewick?' cried Yvette, turning up her young, sensitive nose.

'No, not particularly. I suppose we shall be rather bored. I wish Daddy would get a car. I suppose we shall have to drag the old bikes out. Wouldn't you like to get up to Tansy Moor?'

'Oh, *love*, it! Though it's an awful *strain*, shoving an old push-bike up those hills.'

The ship was nearing the grey cliffs. It was summer, but a grey day. The two girls wore their coats with fur collars turned up, and little *chic* hats pulled down over their ears. Tall, slender, fresh-faced, naïve, yet confident, too confident, in their schoolgirlish arrogance, they were so terribly English. They seemed so free, and were as a matter of fact so tangled and tied up, inside themselves. They seemed so dashing and unconventional, and were really so conventional, so, as it were, shut up indoors inside themselves. They looked like bold, tall young sloops, just slipping from the harbour into the wide seas of life. And they were, as a matter of fact, two poor young rudderless lives, moving from one chain anchorage to another.

The rectory struck a chill into their hearts as they entered. It seemed ugly, and almost sordid, with the dank air of that middle-class, degenerated comfort which has ceased to be comfortable and has turned stuffy, unclean. The hard, stone house struck the girls as being unclean, they could not have said why. The shabby furniture seemed somehow sordid, nothing was fresh. Even the food at meals had that awful dreary sordidness which is so repulsive to a young thing coming from abroad. Roast beef and wet cabbage, cold mutton and mashed potatoes, sour pickles, inexcusable puddings.

Granny, who 'loved a bit of pork', also had special dishes, beef-tea and rusks, or a small savoury custard. The grey-faced Aunt Cissie ate nothing at all. She would sit at table, and take a single lonely and naked boiled potato on to her plate. She never ate meat. So she sat in sordid durance, while the meal went on, and Granny quickly slobbered her portion—lucky if she spilled nothing on her protuberant stomach. The food was not appetizing in itself: how could it be, when Aunt Cissie hated food herself, hated the fact of eating, and never could keep a maid-servant for three months? The girls ate with repulsion, Lucille bravely bearing up, Yvette's tender nose showing her disgust. Only the rector, white-haired, wiped his long grey moustache with his serviette, and cracked jokes. He too was getting heavy and inert, sitting in his study all day, never taking exercise. But he cracked sarcastic little jokes all the time, sitting there under the shelter of the Mater.

The country, with its steep hills and its deep, narrow valleys, was dark and gloomy, yet had a certain powerful strength of its own. Twenty miles away was the black industrialism of the north. Yet the village of Papplewick was comparatively lonely, almost lost, the life in it stony and dour. Everything was stone, with a hardness that was almost poetic, it was so unrelenting.

It was as the girls had known: they went back into the choir, they helped in the parish. But Yvette struck absolutely against Sunday School, the Band of Hope, the Girls' Friendlies— indeed against all those functions that were conducted by determined old maids and obstinate, stupid elderly men. She avoided church duties as much as possible, and got away from the rectory whenever she could. The Framleys, a big, untidy, jolly family up at the Grange, were an enormous stand-by. And if anybody asked her out to a meal, even if a woman in one of the workmen's houses asked her to stay to tea, she accepted at once. In fact, she was rather thrilled. She liked talking to the working men, they had often such fine, hard heads. But of course they were in another world.

So the months went by. Gerry Somercotes was still an adorer. There were others, too, sons of farmers or mill-owners. Yvette really ought to have had a good time. She was always out to parties and dances, friends came for her in their motor cars, and off she went to the city, to the afternoon dance in the chief hotel, or in the gorgeous new Palais de Danse, called the Pally.

Yet she always seemed like a creature mesmerized. She was never free to be quite jolly. Deep inside her worked an intolerable irritation, which she thought she *ought* not to feel, and which she hated feeling, thereby making it worse. She never understood at all whence it arose.

At home, she truly was irritable, and outrageously rude to Aunt Cissie. In fact, Yvette's awful temper became one of the family by-words.

Lucille, always more practical, got a job in the city as private secretary to a man who needed somebody with fluent French and shorthand. She went back and forth every day, by the same train as Uncle Fred. But she never travelled with him, and wet or fine, bicycled to the station, while he went on foot.

The two girls were both determined that what they wanted was a really jolly social life. And they resented with fury that the rectory was, for their friends, impossible. There were only four rooms downstairs: the kitchen, where lived the two discontented maid-servants: the dark dining-room: the rector's study: and the big, 'homely', dreary living-room or drawing-room. In the dining-room there was a gas fire. Only in the living-room was a good hot fire kept going. Because, of course, here Granny reigned.

In this room the family was assembled. At evening, after dinner, Uncle Fred and the rector invariably played cross-word puzzles with Granny.

'Now, Mater, are you ready? N blank blank blank blank W: A Siamese functionary.'

'Eh? Eh? M blank blank blank blank W?'

Granny was hard of hearing.

'No, Mater. Not M! N blank blank blank blank W: a Siamese functionary.'

'N blank blank blank blank W: a Chinese functionary.'

'SIAMESE.'

Eh?'

'SIAMESE! SIAM!'

'A Siamese functionary! Now what can that be?' said the old lady profoundly, folding her hands on her round stomach. Her two sons proceeded to make suggestions, at which she said Ah! Ah! The rector was amazingly clever at cross-word puzzles. But Fred had a certain technical vocabulary.

'This certainly is a hard nut to crack,' said the old lady, when they were all stuck.

Meanwhile Lucille sat in a corner with her hands over her ears, pretending to read, and Yvette irritably made drawings, or hummed loud and exasperating tunes, to add to the family concert. Aunt Cissie continually reached for a chocolate, and her jaws worked ceaselessly. She literally lived on chocolates. Sitting in the distance, she put another into her mouth, then looked again at the parish magazine. Then she lifted her head, and saw it was time to fetch Granny's cup of Horlicks.

While she was gone, in nervous exasperation Yvette would open the window. The room was never fresh, she imagined it smelt: smelt of Granny. And Granny, who was hard of hearing, heard like a weasel when she wasn't wanted to.

'Did you open the window, Yvette? I think you might remember there are older people than yourself in the room,' she said.

'It's stifling! It's unbearable! No wonder we've all of us always got colds.'

'I'm sure the room is large enough, and a good fire burning.'
The old lady gave a little shudder. 'A draught to give us all
our death.'

'Not a draught at all,' roared Yvette. 'A breath of fresh
air.'

The old lady shuddered again, and said: 'Indeed!'

The rector, in silence, marched to the window and firmly
closed it. He did not look at his daughter meanwhile. He hated
thwarting her. But she must know what's what!

The cross-word puzzles, invented by Satan himself, continued
till Granny had had her Horlicks, and was to go to bed. Then
came the ceremony of Goodnight! Everybody stood up. The girls
went to be kissed by the blind old woman, the rector gave his
arm, and Aunt Cissie followed with a candle.

But this was already nine o'clock, although Granny was really
getting old, and should have been in bed sooner. But when she
was in bed, she could not sleep, till Aunt Cissie came.

'You see,' said Granny, 'I have *never* slept alone. For fifty-four
years I never slept a night without the Pater's arm round me.
And when he was gone I tried to sleep alone. But as sure as
my eyes closed to sleep, my heart nearly jumped out of my
body, and I lay in a palpitation. Oh, you may think what
you will, but it was a fearful experience, after fifty-four years
of perfect married life! I would have prayed to be taken first,
but the Pater, well, no I don't think he would have been able
to bear up.'

So Aunt Cissie slept with Granny. And she hated it. She said
she could never sleep. And she grew greyer and greyer, and the
food in the house got worse, and Aunt Cissie had to have an
operation.

But the Mater rose as ever, towards noon, and at the midday
meal she presided from her arm-chair, with her stomach protruding; her reddish, pendulous face, that had a sort of horrible
majesty, dropping soft under the wall of her high brow, and her
blue eyes peering unseeing. Her white hair was getting scanty,
it was altogether a little indecent. But the rector jovially cracked
his jokes to her, and she pretended to disapprove. But she was
perfectly complacent, sitting in her ancient obesity, and after
meals, getting the wind from her stomach, pressing her bosom
with her hand as she 'rifted' in gross physical complacency.

What the girls minded most was that, when they brought their young friends to the house, Granny always was there, like some awful idol of old flesh, consuming all the attention. There was only the one room for everybody. And there sat the old lady, with Aunt Cissie keeping an acrid guard over her. Everybody must be presented first to Granny: she was ready to be genial, she liked company. She had to know who everybody was, where they came from, every circumstance of their lives. And then, when she was *au fait*, she could get hold of the conversation.

Nothing could be more exasperating to the girls. 'Isn't old Mrs Saywell wonderful! She takes *such* an interest in life, at nearly ninety!'

'She does take an interest in people's affairs, if that's life,' said Yvette.

Then she would immediately feel guilty. After all, it *was* wonderful to be nearly ninety, and have such a clear mind! And Granny never *actually* did anybody any harm. It was more that she was in the way. And perhaps it was rather awful to hate somebody because they were old and in the way.

Yvette immediately repented, and was nice. Granny blossomed forth into reminiscences of when she was a girl, in the little town in Buckinghamshire. She talked and talked away, and was *so* entertaining. She really *was* rather wonderful.

Then in the afternoon Lottie and Ella and Bob Framley came, with Leo Wetherell.

'Oh, come in!'—and in they all trooped to the sitting-room, where Granny, in her white cap, sat by the fire.

'Granny, this is Mr Wetherell.'

'Mr what-did-you-say? You must excuse me, I'm a little deaf!'

Granny gave her hand to the uncomfortable young man, and gazed silently at him, sightlessly.

'You are not from our parish?' she asked him.

'Dinnington!' he shouted.

'We want to go a picnic tomorrow, to Bonsall Head, in Leo's car. We can all squeeze in,' said Ella, in a low voice.

'Did you say Bonsall Head?' asked Granny.

'Yes!'

There was a blank silence.

'Did you say you were going in a car?'

'Yes! In Mr Wetherell's.'

'I hope he's a good driver. It's a very dangerous road.'

'He's a *very* good driver.'

'Not a very good driver?'

'Yes! He *is* a very good driver.'

'If you go to Bonsall Head, I think I must send a message to Lady Louth.'

Granny always dragged in this miserable Lady Louth, when there was company.

'Oh, we shan't go that way,' cried Yvette.

'Which way?' said Granny. 'You must go by Heanor.'

The whole party sat, as Bob expressed it, like stuffed ducks, fidgeting on their chairs.

Aunt Cissie came in—and then the maid with the tea. There was the eternal and everlasting piece of bought cake. Then appeared a plate of little fresh cakes. Aunt Cissie had actually sent to the baker's.

'Tea, Mater!'

The old lady gripped the arms of her chair. Everybody rose and stood, while she waded slowly across, on Aunt Cissie's arm, to her place at table.

During tea Lucille came in from town, from her job. She was simply worn out, with black marks under her eyes. She gave a cry, seeing all the company.

As soon as the noise had subsided, and the awkwardness was resumed, Granny said:

'You have never mentioned Mr Wetherell to me, have you, Lucille?'

'I don't remember,' said Lucille.

'You can't have done. The name is strange to me.'

Yvette absently grabbed another cake, from the now almost empty plate. Aunt Cissie, who was driven almost crazy by Yvette's vague and inconsiderate ways, felt the green rage fuse in her heart. She picked up her own plate, on which was the one cake she allowed herself, and said with vitriolic politeness, offering it to Yvette:

'Won't you have mine?'

'Oh thanks!' said Yvette, starting in her angry vagueness. And with an appearance of the same insouciance, she helped herself to Aunt Cissie's cake also, adding as an afterthought: 'If you're sure you don't want it.'

She now had two cakes on her plate. Lucille had gone white as a ghost, bending to her tea. Aunt Cissie sat with a green look of poisonous resignation. The awkwardness was an agony.

But Granny, bulkily enthroned and unaware, only said, in the centre of the cyclone:

'If you are motoring to Bonsall Head tomorrow, Lucille, I wish you would take a message from me to Lady Louth.'

'Oh!' said Lucille, giving a queer look across the table at the sightless old woman. Lady Louth was the King Charles' Head of the family, invariably produced by Granny for the benefit of visitors. 'Very well!'

'She was so very kind last week. She sent her chauffeur over with a Cross-word Puzzle book for me.'

'But you thanked her then,' cried Yvette.

'I should like to send her a note.'

'We can post it,' cried Lucille.

'Oh no! I should like you to take it. When Lady Louth called last time . . .'

The young ones sat like a shoal of young fishes dumbly mouthing at the surface of the water, while Granny went on about Lady Louth. Aunt Cissie, the two girls knew, was still helpless, almost unconscious in a paroxysm of rage about the cake. Perhaps, poor thing, she was praying.

It was a mercy when the friends departed. But by that time the two girls were both haggard-eyed. And it was then that Yvette, looking round, suddenly saw the stony, implacable will-to-power in the old and motherly-seeming Granny. She sat there bulging backwards in her chair, impassive, her reddish, pendulous old face rather mottled, almost unconscious, but implacable, her face like a mask that hid something stony, relentless. It was the static inertia of her unsavoury power. Yet in a minute she would open her ancient mouth to find out every detail about Leo Wetherell. For the moment she was hibernating in her oldness, her agedness. But in a minute her mouth would open, her mind would flicker awake and with her insatiable greed for life, other people's life, she would start on her quest for every detail. She was like the old toad which Yvette had watched, fascinated, as it sat on the ledge of the beehive, immediately in front of the little entrance by which the bees emerged, and which, with a demonish lightning-like snap of its pursed jaws, caught every bee as it came out to launch into the air, swallowed them one after the other, as if it could consume the whole hive-full, into its aged, bulging, purse-like wrinkledness. It had been swallowing bees as they launched into the air of spring, year after year, year after year, for generations.

But the gardener, called by Yvette, was in a rage, and killed the creature with a stone.

''Appen tha *art* good for th' snails,' he said, as he came down with the stone. 'But tha 'rt none goin' ter emp'y th' bee-'ive into thy guts.'

III

THE next day was dull and low, and the roads were awful, for it had been raining for weeks, yet the young ones set off on their trip, without taking Granny's message either. They just slipped out while she was making her slow trip upstairs after lunch. Not for anything would they have called at Lady Louth's house. That widow of a knighted doctor, a harmless person indeed, had become an obnoxity in their lives.

Six young rebels, they sat very perkily in the car as they swished through the mud. Yet they had a peaked look too. After all, they had nothing really to rebel against, any of them. They were left so very free in their movements. Their parents let them do almost entirely as they liked. There wasn't really a fetter to break, nor a prison-bar to file through, nor a bolt to shatter. The keys of their lives were in their own hands. And there they dangled inert.

It is very much easier to shatter prison bars than to open undiscovered doors to life. As the younger generation finds out somewhat to its chagrin. True, there was Granny. But poor old Granny, you couldn't actually say to her: 'Lie down and die, you old woman!' She might be an old nuisance, but she never really *did* anything. It wasn't fair to hate her.

So the young people set off on their jaunt, trying to be very full of beans. They could really do as they liked. And so, of course, there was nothing to do but sit in the car and talk a lot of criticism of other people, and silly flirty gallantry that was really rather a bore. If there had only been a few 'strict orders' to be disobeyed! But nothing: beyond the refusal to carry the message to Lady Louth, of which the rector would approve because he didn't encourage King Charles's Head either.

They sang, rather scrappily, the latest would-be comic songs, as they went through the grim villages. In the great park the deer were in groups near the road, roe deer and fallow, nestling in the gloom of the afternoon under the oaks by the road, as if for the stimulus of human company.

Yvette insisted on stopping and getting out to talk to them. The girls, in their Russian boots, tramped through the damp grass, while the deer watched them with big, unfrightened eyes. The hart trotted away mildly, holding back his head, because of the weight of the horns. But the doe, balancing her big ears, did not rise from under the tree, with her half-grown young ones, till the girls were almost in touch. Then she walked light-foot away, lifting her tail from her spotted flanks, while the young ones nimbly trotted.

'Aren't they awfully dainty and nice!' cried Yvette. 'You'd wonder they could lie so cosily in this horrid wet grass.'

'Well I suppose they've got to lie down *sometime*,' said Lucille. 'And it's *fairly* dry under the tree.' She looked at the crushed grass, where the deer had lain.

Yvette went and put her hand down, to feel how it felt.

'Yes!' she said doubtfully, 'I believe it's a bit warm.'

The deer had bunched again a few yards away, and were standing motionless in the gloom of the afternoon. Away below the slopes of grass and trees, beyond the swift river with its balustraded bridge, sat the huge ducal house, one or two chimneys smoking bluely. Behind it rose purplish woods.

The girls, pushing their fur collars up to their ears, dangling one long arm stood watching in silence, their wide Russian boots protecting them from the wet grass. The great house squatted square and creamy-grey below. The deer, in little groups, were scattered under the old trees close by. It all seemed so still, so unpretentious, and so sad.

'I wonder where the Duke is now,' said Ella.

'Not here, wherever he is,' said Lucille. 'I expect he's abroad where the sun shines.'

The motor horn called from the road, and they heard Leo's voice:

'Come on, boys! If we're going to get to the Head and down to Amberdale for tea, we'd better move.'

They crowded into the car again, with chilled feet, and set off through the park past the silent spire of the church, out through the great gates and over the bridge, on into the wide, damp, stony village of Woodlinkin, where the river ran. And thence, for a long time, they stayed in the mud and dark and dampness of the valley, often with sheer rock above them; the water brawling on one hand, the steep rock or dark trees on the other.

Till, through the darkness of overhanging trees, they began to climb, and Leo changed the gear. Slowly the car toiled up through the whitey-grey mud, into the stony village of Bolehill, that hung on the slope, round the old cross, with its steps, that stood where the road branched, on past the cottages whence came a wonderful smell of hot tea-cakes, and beyond, still upwards, under dripping trees and past broken slopes of bracken, always climbing. Until the cleft became shallower, and the trees finished, and the slopes on either side were bare, gloomy grass, with low dry-stone walls. They were emerging on to the Head.

The party had been silent for some time. On either side the road was grass, then a low stone fence, and the swelling curve of the hill-summit, traced with the low, dry stone walls. Above this, the low sky.

The car ran out, under the low, grey sky, on the naked tops.

'Shall we stay a moment?' called Leo.

'Oh yes!' cried the girls.

And they scrambled out once more, to look around. They knew the place quite well. But still, if one came to the Head, one got out to look.

The hills were like the knuckles of a hand, the dales were below, between the fingers narrow, steep, and dark. In the deeps a train was steaming, slowly pulling north: a small thing of the underworld. The noise of the engine re-echoed curiously upwards. Then came the dull, familiar sound of blasting in a quarry.

Leo, always on the go, moved quickly.

'Shall we be going?' he said. 'Do we *want* to get down to Amberdale for tea? Or shall we try somewhere nearer?'

They all voted for Amberdale, for the Marquis of Grantham.

'Well, which way shall we go back? Shall we go by Codnor and over Crosshill, or shall we go by Ashbourne?'

There was the usual dilemma. Then they finally decided on the Codnor top road. Off went the car, gallantly.

They were on the top of the world, now, on the back of the fist. It was naked, too, as the back of your fist, high under heaven, and dull, heavy green. Only it was veined with a network of old stone walls, dividing the fields, and broken here and there with ruins of old lead-mines and works. A sparse stone farm bristled with six naked sharp trees. In the distance was a patch of smoky grey stone, a hamlet. In some fields grey, dark sheep fed silently, sombrely. But there was not a sound nor a movement. It was the roof of England, stony and arid as any roof. Beyond, below, were the shires.

'"And see the coloured counties,"' said Yvette to herself. Here anyhow they were not coloured. A stream of rooks trailed out from nowhere. They had been walking, pecking, on a naked field that had been manured. The car ran on between the grass and the stone walls of the upland lane, and the young people were silent, looking out over the far network of stone fences, under the sky, looking for the curves downward that indicated a drop to one of the underneath, hidden dales.

Ahead was a light cart, driven by a man, and trudging along at the side was a woman, sturdy and elderly, with a pack on her back. The man in the cart had caught her up, and now was keeping pace.

The road was narrow. Leo sounded the horn sharply. The man on the cart looked round, but the woman on foot only trudged steadily, rapidly forward, without turning her head.

Yvette's heart gave a jump. The man on the cart was a gipsy, one of the black, loose-bodied, handsome sort. He remained seated on his cart, turning round and gazing at the occupants of the motor car, from under the brim of his cap. And his pose was loose, his gaze insolent in its indifference. He had a thin black moustache under his thin, straight nose, and a big silk handkerchief of red and yellow tied round his neck. He spoke a word to the woman. She stood a second, solid, to turn round and look at the occupants of the car, which had now drawn quite close. Leo honked the horn again, imperiously. The woman, who had a grey-and-white kerchief tied round her head, turned sharply, to keep pace with the cart, whose driver also had settled back, and was lifting the reins, moving his loose, light shoulders. But still he did not pull aside.

Leo made the horn scream, as he put the brakes on and the car slowed up near the back of the cart. The gipsy turned round at the din, laughing in his dark face under his dark-green cap, and said something which they did not hear, showing white teeth under the line of black moustache, and making a gesture with his dark, loose hand.

'Get out o' the way then!' yelled Leo.

For answer the man delicately pulled the horse to a standstill, as it curved to the side of the road. It was a good roan horse and a good, natty, dark-green cart.

Leo, in a rage, had to jam on the brake and pull up too.

'Don't the pretty young ladies want to hear their fortunes?' said the gipsy on the cart, laughing except for his dark, watchful eyes, which went from face to face, and lingered on Yvette's young, tender face.

She met his dark eyes for a second, their level search, their insolence, their complete indifference to people like Bob and Leo, and something took fire in her breast. She thought: 'He is stronger than I am! He doesn't care!'

'Oh yes! let's!' cried Lucille at once.

'Oh yes!' chorused the girls.

'I say! What about the time?' cried Leo.

'Oh bother the old time! Somebody's always dragging in time by the forelock,' cried Lucille.

'Well, if you don't mind *when* we get back, *I* don't!' said Leo heroically.

The gipsy man had been sitting loosely on the side of his cart, watching the faces. He now jumped softly down from the shaft, his knees a bit stiff. He was apparently a man something over thirty, and a beau in his way. He wore a sort of shooting-jacket, double-breasted, coming only to the hips, of dark green-and-black frieze; rather tight black trousers, black boots, and a dark-green cap; with the big yellow-and-red bandanna handkerchief round his neck. His appearance was curiously elegant, and quite expensive in its gipsy style. He was handsome, too, pressing in his chin with the old gipsy conceit, and now apparently not heeding the strangers any more, as he led his good roan horse off the road, preparing to back his cart.

The girls saw for the first time a deep recess in the side of the road, and two caravans smoking. Yvette got quickly down. They had suddenly come upon a disused quarry, cut in to the slope of the road-side, and in this sudden lair, almost like a cave, were three caravans, dismantled for the winter. There was also, deep at the back, a shelter built of boughs, as a stable for the horse. The grey, crude rock rose high above the caravans and curved round towards the road. The floor was heaped chips of stone, with grasses growing among. It was a hidden, snug winter camp.

The elderly woman with the pack had gone into one of the caravans, leaving the door open. Two children were peeping out, showing black heads. The gipsy man gave a little call, as he backed his cart into the quarry, and an elderly man came out to help him untackle.

The gipsy himself went up the steps into the newest caravan, that had its door closed. Underneath, a tied-up dog ranged forth. It was a white hound spotted liver-coloured. It gave a low growl as Leo and Bob approached.

At the same moment, a dark-faced gipsy-woman with a pink shawl or kerchief round her head and big gold earrings in her ears, came down the steps of the newest caravan, swinging her flounced, voluminous green skirt. She was handsome in a bold, dark, long-faced way, just a bit wolfish. She looked like one of the bold, loping Spanish gipsies.

'Good-morning, my ladies and gentlemen,' she said, eyeing the girls from her bold, predative eyes. She spoke with a certain foreign stiffness.

'Good afternoon!' said the girls.

'Which beautiful little lady like to hear her fortune? Give me her little hand?'

She was a tall woman, with a frightening way of reaching forward her neck like a menace. Her eyes went from face to face, very active, heartlessly searching out what she wanted. Meanwhile the man, apparently her husband, appeared at the top of the caravan steps smoking a pipe, and with a small, black-haired child in his arms. He stood on his limber legs, casually looking down on the group, as if from a distance, his long black lashes lifted from his full, conceited, impudent black eyes. There was something peculiarly transfusing in his stare. Yvette felt it, felt it in her knees. She pretended to be interested in the white-and-liver-coloured hound.

'How much do you want, if we all have our fortunes told?' Asked Lottie Framley, as the six fresh-faced young Christians hung back rather reluctantly from this pagan pariah woman.

'All of you? ladies and gentlemen, all?' said the woman shrewdly.

'I don't want mine told! You go ahead!' cried Leo.

'Neither do I,' said Bob. 'You four girls.'

'The four ladies?' said the gipsy woman, eyeing them shrewdly, after having looked at the boys. And she fixed her price. 'Each one give me a sheeling, and a little bit more for luck? a little bit!' She smiled in a way that was more wolfish than cajoling, and the force of her will was felt, heavy as iron beneath the velvet of her words.

'All right,' said Leo. 'Make it a shilling a head. Don't spin it out too long.'

'Oh, *you*!' cried Lucille at him. 'We want to hear it *all*.'

The woman took two wooden stools, from under a caravan, and placed them near the wheel. Then she took the tall, dark Lottie Framley by the hand, and bade her sit down.

'You don't care if everybody hear?' she said, looking up curiously into Lottie's face.

Lottie blushed dark with nervousness, as the gipsy woman held her hand, and stroked her palm with hard, cruel-seeming fingers.

'Oh, I don't mind,' she said.

The gipsy woman peered into the palm tracing the lines of the hand with a hard, dark forefinger. But she seemed clean.

And slowly she told the fortune, while the others, standing listening, kept on crying out: 'Oh, that's Jim Baggaley! Oh, I don't believe it! Oh, that's not true! A fair woman who lives beneath a tree! Why, whoever's that?' until Leo stopped them with a manly warning:

'Oh, hold on, girls! You give everything away.'

Lottie retired blushing and confused, and it was Ella's turn. She was much more calm and shrewd, trying to read the oracular words. Lucille kept breaking out with: 'Oh, I say!' The gipsy man at the top of the steps stood imperturbable, without any expression at all. But his bold eyes kept staring at Yvette, she could feel them on her cheek, on her neck, and she dared not look up. But Framley would sometimes look up at him, and got a level stare back from the handsome face of the male gipsy, from the dark conceited proud eyes. It was a peculiar look, in the eyes that belonged to the tribe of the humble: the pride of the pariah, the half-sneering challenge of the outcast, who sneered at law-abiding men, and went his own way. All the time, the gipsy man stood there, holding his child in his arms, looking on without being concerned.

Lucille was having her hand read—'You have been across the sea, and there you met a man—a brown-haired man—but he was too old—'

'Oh, I *say*!' cried Lucille, looking round at Yvette.

But Yvette was abstracted, agitated, hardly heeding: in one of her mesmerized states.

'You will marry in a few years—not now, but a few years —perhaps four—and you will not be rich, but you will have plenty—enough—and you will go away, a long journey.'

'With my husband, or without?' cried Lucille.

'With him—'

When it came to Yvette's turn, and the woman looked up boldly, cruelly, searching for a long time in her face, Yvette said nervously:

'I don't think I want mine told. No, I won't have mine told! No I won't, really!'

'You are afraid of something?' said the gipsy woman cruelly.

'No, it's not that—' Yvette fidgeted.

'You have some secret? You are afraid I shall say it? Come, would you like to go in the caravan, where nobody hears?'

The woman was curiously insinuating; while Yvette was always wayward, perverse. The look of perversity was on her soft, frail young face now, giving her a queer hardness.

'Yes!' she said suddenly. 'Yes! I might do that!'

'Oh, I say!' cried the others. 'Be a sport!'

'I don't think you'd *better!*' cried Lucille.

'Yes!' said Yvette, with that hard little way of hers. 'I'll do that. I'll go in the caravan.'

The gipsy woman called something to the man on the steps. He went into the caravan for a moment or two, then reappeared, and came down the steps, setting the small child on its uncertain feet, and holding it by the hand. A dandy, in his polished black boots, tight black trousers and tight dark-green jersey, he walked slowly across with the toddling child to where the elderly gipsy was giving the roan horse a feed of oats, in the bough shelter between pits of grey rock, with dry bracken upon the stone chip floor. He looked at Yvette as he passed, staring her full in the eyes, with his pariah's bold yet dishonest stare. Something hard inside her met his stare. But the surface of her body seemed to turn to water. Nevertheless, something hard in her registered the peculiar pure lines of his face, of his straight, pure nose, of his cheeks and temples. The curious dark, suave purity of all his body, outlined in the green jersey: a purity like a living sneer.

And as he loped slowly past her, on his flexible hips, it seemed to her still that he was stronger than she was. Of all the men she had ever seen, this one was the only one who was stronger than she was, in her own kind of strength, her own kind of understanding.

So, with curiosity, she followed the woman up the steps of the caravan, the skirts of her well-cut tan coat swinging and almost showing her knees, under the pale-green cloth dress. She had long, long-striding, fine legs, too slim rather than too thick, and she wore curiously-patterned pale-and-fawn stockings of fine wool, suggesting the legs of some delicate animal.

At the top of the steps she paused and turned, debonair, to the others, saying in her naïve, lordly way, so off-hand:

'I won't let her be long.'

Her grey fur collar was open, showing her soft throat and pale green dress, her little plaited tan-coloured hat came down to her ears, round her soft, fresh face. There was something soft and yet overbearing, unscrupulous, about her. She knew the gipsy man had turned to look at her. She was aware of the pure dark nape of his neck, the black hair groomed away. He watched as she entered his house.

What the gipsy told her, no one ever knew. It was a long

time to wait, the others felt. Twilight was deepening on the gloom, and it was turning raw and cold. From the chimney on the second caravan came smoke and a smell of rich food. The horse was fed, a yellow blanket strapped round him, and two gipsy men talked together in the distance, in low tones. There was a peculiar feeling of silence and secrecy in that lonely, hidden quarry.

At last the caravan door opened, and Yvette emerged, bending forward and stepping with long, witch-like slim legs down the steps. There was a stooping, witch-like silence about her as she emerged on the twilight.

'Did it seem long?' she said vaguely, not looking at anybody and keeping her own counsel hard within her soft, vague waywardness. 'I hope you weren't bored! Wouldn't tea be nice! Shall we go?'

'You get in!' said Bob. 'I'll pay.'

The gipsy-woman's full, metallic skirts of jade-green alpaca came swinging down the steps. She rose to her height, a big, triumphant-looking woman with a dark-wolf face. The pink cashmere kerchief stamped with red roses was slipping to one side over her black and crimped hair. She gazed at the young people in the twilight with bold arrogance.

Bob put two half-crowns in her hand.

'A little bit more, for luck, for your young lady's luck,' she wheedled, like a wheedling wolf. 'Another bit of silver, to bring you luck.'

'You've got a shilling for luck, that's enough,' said Bob calmly and quietly, as they moved away to the car.

'A little bit of silver! Just a little bit, for your luck in love!'

Yvette, with the sudden long, startling gestures of her long limbs, swung round as she was entering the car, and with long arm outstretched, strode and put something into the gipsy's hand, then stepped, bending her height, into the car.

'Prosperity to the beautiful young lady, and the gipsy's blessing on her,' came the suggestive, half-sneering voice of the woman.

The engine *birred!* then *birred!* again more fiercely, and started. Leo switched on the lights, and immediately the quarry with the gipsies fell back into the blackness of night.

'Good night!' called Yvette's voice, as the car started. But hers was the only voice that piped up, chirpy and impudent in its nonchalance. The headlights glared down the stone lane.

'Yvette, you've got to tell us what she said to you,' cried Lucille, in the teeth of Yvette's silent will *not* to be asked.

'Oh, nothing at *all* thrilling,' said Yvette, with false warmth. 'Just the usual old thing: a dark man who means good luck, and a fair one who means bad: and a death in the family, which if it means Granny, won't be so *very* awful: and I shall marry when I'm twenty-three, and have heaps of money and heaps of love, and two children. All sounds very nice, but it's a bit too much of a good thing, you know.'

'Oh, but why did you give her more money?'

'Oh well, I wanted to! You *have* to be a bit lordly with people like that—.'

IV

THERE was a terrific rumpus down at the rectory, on account of Yvette and the Window Fund. After the war, Aunt Cissie had set her heart on a stained glass window in the church, as a memorial for the men of the parish who had fallen. But the bulk of the fallen had been nonconformists, so the memorial took the form of an ugly little monument in front of the Wesleyan chapel.

This did not vanquish Aunt Cissie. She canvassed, she had bazaars, she made the girls get up amateur theatrical shows, for her precious window. Yvette, who quite liked the acting and showing-off part of it, took charge of the farce called *Mary in the Mirror*, and gathered in the proceeds, which were to be paid to the Window Fund when accounts were settled. Each of the girls was supposed to have a money-box for the Fund.

Aunt Cissie, feeling that the united sums must now almost suffice, suddenly called in Yvette's box. It contained fifteen shillings. There was a moment of green horror.

'Where is all the rest?'

'Oh!' said Yvette casually. 'I just borrowed it. It wasn't so awfully much.'

'What about the three pounds thirteen for *Mary in the Mirror?*' asked Aunt Cissie, as if the jaws of Hell were yawning.

'Oh quite! I just borrowed it. I can pay it back.'

Poor Aunt Cissie! The green tumour of hate burst inside her, and there was a ghastly, abnormal scene, which left Yvette shivering with fear and nervous loathing.

Even the rector was rather severe.

'If you needed money, why didn't you tell me?' he said coldly. 'Have you ever been refused anything in reason?'

'I—I thought it didn't matter,' stammered Yvette.

'And what have you done with the money?'

'I suppose I've spent it,' said Yvette, with wide distraught eyes and a peaked face.

'Spent it, on what?'

'I can't remember everything: stockings and things, and I gave some of it away.'

Poor Yvette! Her lordly airs and ways were already hitting back at her, on the reflex. The rector was angry: his face had a snarling, doggish look, a sort of sneer. He was afraid his daughter was developing some of the rank, tainted qualities of She-who-was-Cynthia.

'You *would* do the large with somebody else's money, wouldn't you?' he said, with a cold, mongrel sort of sneer, which showed what an utter unbeliever he was, at the heart. The inferiority of a heart which has no core of warm belief in it, no pride in life. He had utterly no belief in her.

Yvette went pale, and very distant. Her pride, that frail, precious flame which everybody tried to quench, recoiled like a flame blown far away, on a cold wind, as if blown out, and her face, white now and still like a snowdrop, the white snow-flower of his conceit, seemed to have no life in it, only this pure, strange abstraction.

'He has no belief in me!' she thought in her soul. 'I am really nothing to him. I am nothing, only a shameful thing. Everything is shameful, everything is shameful!'

A flame of passion or rage, while it might have overwhelmed or infuriated her, would not have degraded her as did her father's unbelief, his final attitude of a sneer against her.

He became a little afraid, in the silence of sterile thought. After all, he needed the *appearance* of love and belief and bright life, he would never dare to face the fat worm of his own unbelief, that stirred in his heart.

'What have you to say for yourself?' he asked.

She only looked at him from that senseless snowdrop face which haunted him with fear, and gave him a helpless sense of guilt. That other one, She-who-was-Cynthia, she had looked back at him with the same numb, white fear, the fear of his degrading unbelief, the worm which was his heart's core. He *knew* his heart's core was a fat, awful worm. His dread was lest anyone else should know. His anguish of hate was against anyone who knew, and recoiled.

He saw Yvette recoiling, and immediately his manner changed to the worldly old good-humoured cynic which he affected.

'Ah well!' he said. 'You have to pay it back, my girl, that's all. I will advance you the money out of your allowance. But I shall charge you four per cent a month interest. Even the devil himself must pay a percentage on his debts. Another time, if you can't trust yourself, don't handle money which isn't your own. Dishonesty isn't pretty.'

Yvette remained crushed, and deflowered and humiliated. She crept about, trailing the rays of her pride. She had a revulsion even from herself. Oh, why had she ever touched the leprous money! Her whole flesh shrank as if it were defiled. Why was that? Why, why was that?

She admitted herself wrong in having spent the money. 'Of course I shouldn't have done it. They are quite right to be angry,' she said to herself.

But where did the horrible wincing of her flesh come from? Why did she feel she had caught some physical contagion?

'Where you're so *silly*, Yvette,' Lucille lectured her: poor Lucille was in great distress—'is that you give yourself away to them all. You might *know* they'd find out. I could have raised the money for you, and saved all this bother. It's perfectly awful! But you never will think beforehand where your actions are going to land you! Fancy Aunt Cissie saying all those things to you! How *awful*! Whatever would Mamma have said, if she'd heard it?'

When things went very wrong, they thought of their mother, and despised their father and all the low brood of the Saywells. Their mother, of course, had belonged to a higher, if more dangerous and 'immoral', world. More selfish, decidedly. But with a showier gesture. More unscrupulous and more easily moved to contempt: but not so humiliating.

Yvette always considered that she got her fine, delicate flesh from her mother. The Saywells were all a bit leathery, and grubby somewhere inside. But then the Saywells never let you down. Whereas the fine She-who-was-Cynthia had let the rector down with a bang, and his little children along with him. Her little children? They could not quite forgive her.

Only dimly, after the row, Yvette began to realize the other sanctity of herself, the sanctity of her sensitive, clean flesh and blood, which the Saywells with their so-called morality succeeded in defiling. They always wanted to defile it. They were the life unbelievers. Whereas, perhaps She-who-was-Cynthia had only been a moral unbeliever.

Yvette went about dazed and peaked and confused. The rector paid in the money to Aunt Cissie, much to that lady's rage. The helpless tumour of her rage was still running. She would have liked to announce her niece's delinquency in the parish magazine. It was anguish to the destroyed woman that she could not publish the news to all the world. The selfishness! The selfishness! The selfishness!

Then the rector handed his daughter a little account with himself: her debt to him, interest thereon, the amount deducted from her small allowance. But to her credit he had placed a guinea, which was the fee he had to pay for complicity.

'As father of the culprit,' he said humorously, 'I am fined one guinea. And with that I wash the ashes out of my hair.'

He was always generous about money. But somehow, he seemed to think that by being free about money he could absolutely call himself a generous man. Whereas he used money, even generosity, as a hold over her.

But he let the affair drop entirely. He was by this time more amused than anything, to judge from appearances. He thought still he was safe.

Aunt Cissie, however, could not get over her convulsion. One night when Yvette had gone rather early, miserably, to bed, when Lucille was away at a party, and she was lying with soft, peaked limbs aching with a sort of numbness and defilement, the door softly opened, and there stood Aunt Cissie, pushing her grey-green face through the opening of the door. Yvette started up in terror.

'Liar! Thief! Selfish little beast!' hissed the maniacal face of

Aunt Cissie. 'You little hypocrite! You liar! You selfish beast! You greedy little beast!'

There was such extraordinary impersonal hatred in that grey-green mask, and those frantic words, that Yvette opened her mouth to scream with hysterics. But Aunt Cissie shut the door as suddenly as she had opened it, and disappeared. Yvette leaped from her bed and turned the key. Then she crept back, half demented with fear of the squalid abnormal, half numbed with paralysis of damaged pride. And amid it all, up came a bubble of distracted laughter. It *was* so filthily ridiculous!

Aunt Cissie's behaviour did not hurt the girl so very much. It was after all somewhat fantastic. Yet hurt she was: in her limbs, in her body, in her sex, hurt. Hurt, numbed, and half destroyed, with only her nerves vibrating and jangled. And still so young, she could not conceive what was happening.

Only she lay and wished she were a gipsy. To live in a camp, in a caravan, and never set foot in a house, not know the existence of a parish, never look at a church. Her heart was hard with repugnance against the rectory. She loathed these houses with their indoor sanitation and their bathrooms, and their extraordinary repulsiveness. She hated the rectory, and everything it implied. The whole stagnant, sewerage sort of life, where sewerage is never mentioned, but where it seems to smell from the centre to every two-legged inmate, from Granny to the servants, was foul. If gipsies had no bathrooms, at least they had no sewerage. There was fresh air. In the rectory there was *never* fresh air. And in the souls of the people, the air was stale till it stank.

Hate kindled her heart, as she lay with numbed limbs. And she thought of the words of the gipsy woman: 'There is a dark man who never lived in a house. He loves you. The other people are treading on your heart. They will tread on your heart till you think it is dead. But the dark man will blow the one spark up into fire again, good fire. You will see what good fire.'

Even as the woman was saying it, Yvette felt there was some duplicity somewhere. But she didn't mind. She hated with the cold, acrid hatred of a child the rectory interior, the sort of putridity in the life. She liked that big, swarthy, wolf-like gipsy-woman, with the big gold rings in her ears, the pink scarf over her wavy black hair, the tight bodice of brown velvet, the green, fan-like skirt. She liked her dusky, strong, relentless hands, that had pressed so firm, like wolf's paws, in Yvette's own soft palm. She liked her. She liked the danger and the covert fearlessness of her. She liked her covert, unyielding sex, that was immoral, but with a hard, defiant pride of its own. Nothing would ever get that woman under. She would despise the rectory and the rectory morality, utterly! She would strangle Granny with one hand. And she would have the same contempt for Daddy and for Uncle Fred, as men, as she would have for fat old slobbery Rover, the Newfoundland dog. A great, sardonic female contempt, for such domesticated dogs, calling themselves men.

And the gipsy man himself! Yvette quivered suddenly, as if she had seen his big, bold eyes upon her, with the naked insinuation of desire in them. The absolutely naked insinuation of desire made her lie prone and powerless in the bed as if a drug had cast her in a new, molten mould.

She never confessed to anybody that two of the ill-starred Window Fund pounds had gone to the gipsy woman. What if Daddy and Aunt Cissie knew *that*! Yvette stirred luxuriously in the bed. The thought of the gipsy had released the life of her limbs, and crystallized in her heart the hate of the rectory: so that now she felt potent, instead of impotent.

When later, Yvette told Lucille about Aunt Cissie's dramatic interlude in the bedroom doorway, Lucille was indignant.

'Oh, hang it all!' cried she. 'She might let it drop now. I should think we've heard enough about it by now! Good heavens, you'd think Aunt Cissie was a perfect bird of paradise! Daddy's dropped it, and after all, it's his business if it's anybody's. Let Aunt Cissie shut up!'

It was the very fact that the rector had dropped it, and that he again treated the vague and inconsiderate Yvette as if she were some specially-licensed being, that kept Aunt Cissie's bile flowing. The fact that Yvette really was most of the time unaware of other people's feelings, and being unaware, couldn't care about them, nearly sent Aunt Cissie mad. Why should that young creature, with a delinquent mother, go through life as a privileged being, even unaware of other people's existence, though they were under her nose?

Lucille at this time was very irritable. She seemed as if she simply went a little unbalanced, when she entered the rectory. Poor Lucille, she was so thoughtful and responsible. She did all the extra troubling, thought about doctors, medicines, servants, and all that sort of thing. She slaved conscientiously at her job all day in town, working in a room with artificial light from ten till five. And she came home to have her nerves rubbed almost to frenzy by Granny's horrible and persistent inquisitiveness and parasitic agedness.

The affair of the Window Fund had apparently blown over, but there remained a stuffy tension in the atmosphere. The weather continued bad. Lucille stayed at home on the afternoon of her half holiday, and did herself no good by it. The rector was in his study, she and Yvette were making a dress for the latter young woman, Granny was resting on the couch.

The dress was of blue silk velours, French material, and was going to be very becoming. Lucille made Yvette try it on again: she was nervously uneasy about the hang, under the arms.

'Oh bother!' cried Yvette, stretching her long, tender, childish arms, that tended to go bluish with the cold. 'Don't be so frightfully *fussy*, Lucille! It's quite all right.'

'If that's all the thanks I get, slaving my half-day away making dresses for you, I might as well do something for myself!'

'Well, Lucille! You know I never *asked* you! You know you can't bear it unless you *do* supervise,' said Yvette, with that irritating blandness of hers, as she raised her naked elbows and peered over her shoulder into the long mirror.

'Oh yes! you never *asked* me!' cried Lucille. 'As if I didn't know what you meant, when you started sighing and flouncing about.'

'I!' said Yvette, with vague surprise. 'Why, when did I start sighing and flouncing about?'

'Of course, you know you did.'

'Did I? No, I didn't know! When was it?' Yvette could put a peculiar annoyance into her mild, straying questions.

'I shan't do another thing to this frock, if you don't stand still and *stop* it,' said Lucille, in her rather sonorous, burning voice.

'You know you are most awfully nagging and irritable, Lucille,' said Yvette, standing as if on hot bricks.

'Now, Yvette!' cried Lucille, her eyes suddenly flashing in her sister's face, with wild flashes. 'Stop it at once! Why should everybody put up with your abominable and overbearing temper?'

'Well, I don't know about *my* temper,' said Yvette, writhing slowly out of the half-made frock, and slipping into her dress again.

Then, with an obstinate little look on her face, she sat down again at the table, in the gloomy afternoon, and began to sew at the blue stuff. The room was littered with blue clippings, the scissors were lying on the floor, the work-basket was spilled in chaos all over the table, and a second mirror was perched perilously on the piano.

Granny, who had been in a semi-coma, called a doze, roused herself on the big, soft couch and put her cap straight.

'I don't get much peace for my nap,' she said, slowly feeling her thin white hair, to see that it was in order. She had heard vague noises.

Aunt Cissie came in, fumbling in a bag for a chocolate.

'I never saw such a mess!' she said. 'You'd better clear some of that litter away, Yvette.'

'All right,' said Yvette. 'I will in a minute.'

'Which means never!' sneered Aunt Cissie, suddenly darting and picking up the scissors.

There was silence for a few moments, and Lucille slowly pushed her hands in her hair, as she read a book.

'You'd better clear away, Yvette,' persisted Aunt Cissie.

'I will, before tea,' replied Yvette, rising once more and pulling the blue dress over her head, flourishing her long, naked arms through the sleeveless armholes. Then she went between the mirrors, to look at herself once more.

As she did so, she sent the second mirror, that she had perched carelessly on the piano, sliding with a rattle to the floor. Luckily it did not break. But everybody started badly.

'She's smashed the mirror!' cried Aunt Cissie.

'Smashed a mirror! Which mirror! Who smashed it?' came Granny's sharp voice.

'I haven't smashed anything,' came the calm voice of Yvette. 'It's quite all right.'

'You'd better not perch it up there again,' said Lucille.

Yvette, with a little impatient shrug at all the fuss, tried making the mirror stand in another place. She was not successful.

'If one had a fire in one's own room,' she said crossly, 'one needn't have a lot of people fussing when one wants to sew.'

'Which mirror are you moving about?' asked Granny.

'One of our own that came from the vicarage,' said Yvette rudely.

'Don't break it in *this* house, wherever it came from,' said Granny.

There was a sort of family dislike for the furniture that had belonged to She-who-was-Cynthia. It was most of it shoved into the kitchen, and the servants' bedrooms.

'Oh, *I'm* not superstitious,' said Yvette, 'about mirrors or any of that sort of thing.'

'Perhaps you're not,' said Granny. 'People who never take the responsibility for their own actions usually don't care what happens.'

'After all,' said Yvette, 'I may say it's my own looking-glass, even if I did break it.'

'And I say,' said Granny, 'that there shall be no mirrors broken in *this* house, if we can help it; no matter who they belong to, or did belong to. Cissie, have I got my cap straight?'

Aunt Cissie went over and straightened the old lady. Yvette loudly and irritatingly trilled a tuneless tune.

'And now, Yvette, will you please clear away?' said Aunt Cissie.

'Oh, bother!' cried Yvette angrily. 'It's simply *awful* to live with a lot of people who are always nagging and fussing over trifles.'

'What people, may I ask?' said Aunt Cissie ominously.

Another row was imminent. Lucille looked up with a queer cast in her eyes. In the two girls, the blood of She-who-was-Cynthia was roused.

'Of course you may ask! You know quite well I mean the people in this beastly house,' said the outrageous Yvette.

'At least,' said Granny, 'we don't come of half-depraved stock.'

There was a second's electric pause. Then Lucille sprang from her low seat, with sparks flying from her.

'You shut up!' she shouted, in a blast full upon the mottled majesty of the old lady.

The old woman's breast began to heave with heaven knows what emotions. The pause this time, as after the thunderbolt, was icy.

Then Aunt Cissie, livid, sprang upon Lucille, pushing her like a fury.

'Go to your room!' she cried hoarsely. 'Go to your room!'

And she proceeded to push the white but fiery-eyed Lucille from the room. Lucille let herself be pushed, while Aunt Cissie vociferated:

'Stay in your room till you've apologized for this!—till you've apologized to the Mater for this!'

'I shan't apologize!' came the clear voice of Lucille, from the passage, while Aunt Cissie shoved her.

Aunt Cissie drove her more wildly upstairs.

Yvette stood tall and bemused in the sitting-room, with the air of offended dignity, at the same time bemused, which was so odd on her. She still was bare-armed, in the half-made blue dress. And even *she* was half-aghast at Lucille's attack on the majesty of age. But also, she was coldly indignant against Granny's aspersion of the maternal blood in their veins.

'Of course I meant no offence,' said Granny.

'Didn't you?' said Yvette coolly.

'Of course not. I only said we're not depraved, just because we happened to be superstitious about breaking mirrors.'

Yvette could hardly believe her ears. Had she heard right? Was it possible! Or was Granny, at her age, just telling a bare-faced lie?

Yvette knew that the old woman was telling a cool, bare-faced lie. But already, so quickly, Granny believed her own statement.

The rector appeared, having left time for a lull.

'What's wrong?' he asked cautiously, genially.

'Oh, nothing!' drawled Yvette. 'Lucille told Granny to shut up, when she was saying something. And Aunt Cissie drove her up to her room. *Tant de bruit pour une omelette!* Though Lucille *was* a bit over the mark, that time.'

The old lady couldn't quite catch what Yvette said.

'Lucille really will have to learn to control her nerves,' said the old woman. 'The mirror fell down, and it worried me. I said so to Yvette, and she said something about superstitions and the people in the beastly house. I told her the people in the house were not depraved, if they happened to mind when a mirror was broken. And at that Lucille flew at me and told me to shut up. It really is disgraceful how these children give way to their nerves. I know it's nothing but nerves.'

Aunt Cissie had come in during this speech. At first even she was dumb. Then it seemed to her, it was as Granny had said.

'I have forbidden her to come down until she comes to apologize to the Mater,' she said.

'I doubt if she'll apologize,' said the calm, queenly Yvette, holding her bare arms.

'And I don't want any apology,' said the old lady. 'It is merely nerves. I don't know what they'll come to, if they have nerves like that, at their age! She must take Vibrofat.—I am sure Arthur would like his tea, Cissie.'

Yvette swept her sewing together, to go upstairs. And again she trilled her tune, rather shrill and tuneless. She was trembling inwardly.

'More glad rags!' said her father to her, genially.

'More glad rags!' she reiterated sagely, as she sauntered upstairs, with her day dress over one arm. She wanted to console Lucille, and ask her how the blue stuff hung now.

At the first landing she stood as she nearly always did, to gaze through the window that looked to the road and the bridge. Like the Lady of Shalott, she seemed always to imagine that someone would come along singing *Tirra-lirra!* or something equally intelligent, by the river.

IT was nearly tea-time. The snowdrops were out by the short drive going to the gate from the side of the house, and the gardener was pottering at the round, damp flower-beds, on the wet grass that sloped to the stream. Past the gate went the whitish muddy road, crossing the stone bridge almost immediately, and winding in a curve up to the steep, clustering, stony, smoking northern village, that perched over the grim stone mills which Yvette could see ahead down the narrow valley, their tall chimneys long and erect.

The rectory was on one side the Papple, in the rather steep valley, the village was beyond and above, further down, on the other side the swift stream. At the back of the rectory the hill went up steep, with a grove of dark, bare larches, through which the road disappeared. And immediately across stream from the rectory, facing the house, the river-bank rose steep and bushy, up to the sloping, dreary meadows, that sloped up again to dark hillsides of trees, with grey rock cropping out.

But from the end of the house, Yvette could only see the road curving round past the wall with its laurel hedge, down to the bridge, then up again round the shoulder to that first hard cluster of houses in Papplewick village, beyond the dry-stone walls of the steep fields.

She always expected *something* to come down the slant of the road from Papplewick, and she always lingered at the landing window. Often a cart came, or a motor car, or a lorry with stone, or a labourer, or one of the servants. But never anybody who sang *Tirra-lirra!* by the river. The tirralirraing days seem to have gone by.

This day, however, round the corner on the white-grey road, between the grass and the low stone walls, a roan horse came stepping bravely and briskly down-hill, driven by a man in a cap, perched on the front of his light cart. The man swayed loosely to the swing of the cart, as the horse stepped down-hill, in the silent sombreness of the afternoon. At the back of the cart, long duster-brooms of reed and feather stuck out, nodding on their stalks of cane.

Yvette stood close to the window, and put the casement-cloth curtains behind her, clutching her bare upper arms with her hands.

At the foot of the slope the horse started into a brisk trot to the bridge. The cart rattled on the stone bridge, the brooms bobbed and flustered, the driver sat as if in a kind of dream, swinging along. It was like something seen in a sleep.

But as he crossed the end of the bridge, and was passing along the rectory wall, he looked up at the grim stone house that seemed to have backed away from the gate, under the hill. Yvette moved her hands quickly on her arms. And as quickly, from under the peak of his cap, he had seen her, his swarthy predative face was alert.

He pulled up suddenly at the white gate, still gazing upwards at the landing window; while Yvette, always clasping her cold and mottled arms, still gazed abstractedly down at him, from the window.

His head gave a little, quick jerk of signal, and he led his horse well aside, on to the grass. Then, limber and alert, he turned back the tarpaulin of the cart, fetched out various articles, pulled forth two or three of the long brooms of reed or turkey-feathers, covered the cart and turned towards the house, looking up at Yvette as he opened the white gate.

She nodded to him, and flew to the bathroom to put on her dress, hoping she had disguised her nod so that he wouldn't be sure she had nodded. Meanwhile she heard the hoarse deep roaring of that old fool, Rover, punctuated by the yapping of the young idiot, Trixie.

She and the housemaid arrived at the same moment at the sitting-room door.

'Was it the man selling brooms?' said Yvette to the maid. 'All right!' and she opened the door. 'Aunt Cissie, there's a man selling brooms. Shall I go?'

'What sort of a man?' said Aunt Cissie, who was sitting at tea with the rector and the Mater: the girls having been excluded for once from the meal.

'A man with a cart,' said Yvette.

'A gipsy,' said the maid.

Of course Aunt Cissie rose at once. She had to look at him.

The gipsy stood at the back door, under the steep dark bank where the larches grew. The long brooms flourished from one hand, and from the other hung various objects of shining copper and brass: a saucepan, a candlestick, plates of beaten copper. The man himself was neat and dapper, almost rakish, in his dark green cap and double-breasted green check coat. But his manner was subdued, very quiet: and at the same time proud, with a touch of condescension and aloofness.

'Anything today, lady?' he said, looking at Aunt Cissie with dark, shrewd searching eyes, but putting a very quiet tenderness into his voice.

Aunt Cissie saw how handsome he was, saw the flexible curve of his lips under the line of black moustache, and she was fluttered. The merest hint of roughness or aggression on the man's part would have made her shut the door contemptuously in his face. But he managed to insinuate such a subtle suggestion of submission into his male bearing, that she began to hesitate.

'The candlestick is lovely!' said Yvette. 'Did you make it?'

And she looked up at the man with her naïve, childlike eyes, that were as capable of double meanings as his own.

'Yes, lady!' He looked back into her eyes for a second, with that naked suggestion of desire which acted on her like a spell, and robbed her of her will. Her tender face seemed to go into a sleep.

'It's awfully nice!' she murmured vaguely.

Aunt Cissie began to bargain for the candlestick: which was a low, thick stem of copper, rising from a double bowl. With patient aloofness the man attended to her, without ever looking at Yvette, who leaned against the doorway and watched in a muse.

'How is your wife?' she asked him suddenly, when Aunt Cissie had gone indoors to show the candlestick to the rector, and ask him if he thought it was worth it.

The man looked fully at Yvette, and a scarcely discernible smile curled his lips. His eyes did not smile: the insinuation in them only hardened to a glare.

'She's all right. When are you coming that way again?' he murmured, in a low, caressive, intimate voice.

'Oh, I don't know,' said Yvette vaguely.

'You come Fridays, when I'm there,' he said.

Yvette gazed over his shoulder as if she had not heard him. Aunt Cissie returned, with the candlestick and the money to pay for it. Yvette turned nonchalant away, trilling one of her broken tunes, abandoning the whole affair with a certain rudeness.

Nevertheless, hiding this time at the landing window, she stood to watch the man go. What she wanted to know, was whether he really had any power over her. She did not intend him to see her this time.

She saw him go down to the gate, with his brooms and pans, and out to the cart. He carefully stowed away his pans and his brooms, and fixed down the tarpaulin over the cart. Then with a slow, effortless spring of his flexible loins, he was on the cart again, and touching the horse with the reins. The roan horse was away at once, the cart-wheels grinding uphill, and soon the man was gone, without looking round. Gone like a dream which was only a dream, yet which she could not shake off.

'No, he hasn't any power over me!' she said to herself: rather disappointed really, because she wanted somebody, or something, to have power over her.

She went up to reason with the pale and overwrought Lucille, scolding her for getting into a state over nothing.

'What does it *matter*,' she expostulated, 'if you told Granny to shut up! Why, everybody ought to be told to shut up, when they're being beastly. But she didn't mean it, you know. No, she didn't mean it. And she's quite sorry she said it. There's absolutely no reason to make a fuss. Come on, let's dress ourselves up and sail down to dinner like duchesses. Let's have our own back that way. Come on, Lucille!'

There was something strange and mazy, like having cobwebs over one's face, about Yvette's vague blitheness; her queer, misty side-stepping from an unpleasantness. It was cheering too. But it was like walking in one of those autumn mists, when gossamer strands blow over your face. You don't quite know where you are.

She succeeded, however, in persuading Lucille, and the girls got out their best party frocks: Lucille in green and silver, Yvette in a pale lilac colour with turquoise chenille threading. A little rouge and powder, and their best slippers, and the gardens of paradise began to blossom. Yvette hummed and looked at herself, and put on her most *dégagé* airs of one of the young marchionesses. She had an odd way of slanting her eyebrows and pursing her lips, and to all appearances detaching herself from every earthly consideration, and floating through the cloud of her own pearl-coloured reserves. It was amusing, and not quite convincing.

'Of course I am beautiful, Lucille,' she said blandly. 'And you're perfectly lovely, now you look a bit reproachful. Of course you're the most aristocratic of the two of us, with your nose! And now your eyes look reproachful, that adds an appealing look, and you're perfect, perfectly lovely. But I'm more *winning*, in a way.—Don't you agree?' She turned with arch, complicated simplicity to Lucille.

She was truly simple in what she said. It was just what she thought. But it gave no hint of the very different *feeling* that also preoccupied her: the feeling that she had been looked upon, not from the outside, but from the inside, from her secret female self. She was dressing herself up and looking her most dazzling, just to counteract the effect that the gipsy had had on her, when he had looked at her, and seen none of her pretty face and her pretty ways, but just the dark, tremulous potent secret of her virginity.

The two girls started downstairs in state when the dinner-gong rang: but they waited till they heard the voices of the men. Then they sailed down and into the sitting-room, Yvette preening herself in her vague, debonair way, always a little bit absent; and Lucille shy, ready to burst into tears.

'My goodness gracious!' exclaimed Aunt Cissie, who was still wearing her dark-brown knitted sports coat. 'What an apparition! Wherever do you think you're going?'

'We're dining with the family,' said Yvette naïvely, 'and we've put on our best gewgaws in honour of the occasion.'

The rector laughed aloud, and Uncle Fred said:

'The family feels itself highly honoured.'

Both the elderly men were quite gallant, which was what Yvette wanted.

'Come and let me feel your dresses, do!' said Granny. 'Are they your best? It *is* a shame I can't see them.'

'Tonight, Mater,' said Uncle Fred, 'we shall have to take the young ladies in to dinner, and live up to the honour. Will you go with Cissie?'

'I certainly will,' said Granny. 'Youth and beauty must come first.'

'Well, tonight, Mater!' said the rector, pleased.

And he offered his arm to Lucille, while Uncle Fred escorted Yvette.

But it was a draggled, dull meal, all the same. Lucille tried to be bright and sociable, and Yvette really was most amiable, in her vague, cobwebby way. Dimly, at the back of her mind, she was thinking: Why are we all only like mortal pieces of furniture? Why is nothing *important*?

That was her constant refrain to herself: Why is nothing important? Whether she was in church, or at a party of young people, or dancing in the hotel in the city, the same little bubble of a question rose repeatedly on her consciousness: Why is nothing important?

There were plenty of young men to make love to her: even devotedly. But with impatience she had to shake them off. Why were they so unimportant?—so irritating!

She never even thought of the gipsy. He was a perfectly negligible incident. Yet the approach of Friday loomed strangely significant. 'What are we doing on Friday?' she said to Lucille. To which Lucille replied that they were doing nothing. And Yvette was vexed.

Friday came, and in spite of herself she thought all day of the quarry off the road up high Bonsall Head. She wanted to be there. That was all she was conscious of. She wanted to be there. She had not even a dawning idea of going there. Besides, it was raining again. But as she sewed the blue dress, finishing it for the party up at Lambley Close tomorrow, she just felt that her soul was up there, at the quarry, among the caravans, with the gipsies. Like one lost, or whose soul was stolen, she was not present in her body, the shell of her body. Her intrinsic body was away at the quarry, among the caravans.

The next day, at the party, she had no idea that she was being sweet to Leo. She had no idea that she was snatching him away from the tortured Ella Framley. Not until, when she was eating her pistachio ice, he said to her:

'Why don't you and me get engaged, Yvette? I'm absolutely sure it's the right thing for us both.'

Leo was a bit common, but good-natured and well-off. Yvette quite liked him. But engaged! How perfectly silly! She felt like offering him a set of her silk underwear, to get engaged to.

'But, I thought it was Ella!' she said, in wonder.

'Well! It might ha' been, but for you. It's your doings, you know! Ever since those gipsies told your fortune, I felt it was me or nobody, for you, and you or nobody, for me.'

'Really!' said Yvette, simply lost in amazement. 'Really!'

'Didn't you feel a bit the same?' he asked.

'Really!' Yvette kept on gasping softly, like a fish.

'You felt a bit the same, didn't you?' he said.

'What? About what?' she asked, coming to.

'About me, as I feel about you.'

'Why? What? Getting engaged, you mean? I? No! Why how *could* I? I could never have dreamed of such an impossible thing.'

She spoke with her usual heedless candour, utterly unoccupied with his feelings.

'What was to prevent you?' he said, a bit nettled. 'I thought you did.'

'Did you *really now?*' she breathed in amazement, with that soft, virgin, heedless candour which made her her admirers and her enemies.

She was so completely amazed, there was nothing for him to do but twiddle his thumbs in annoyance.

The music began, and he looked at her.

'No! I won't dance any more,' she said, drawing herself up and gazing away rather loftily over the assembly, as if he did not exist. There was a touch of puzzled wonder on her brow, and her soft, dim virgin face did indeed suggest the snowdrop of her father's pathetic imagery.

'But of course *you* will dance,' she said, turning to him with young condescension. 'Do ask somebody to have this with you.'

He rose, angry, and went down the room.

She remained soft and remote in her amazement. Expect Leo to propose to her! She might as well have expected old Rover the Newfoundland dog to propose to her. Get engaged, to any man on earth? No, good heavens, nothing more ridiculous could be imagined!

It was then, in a fleeting side-thought, that she realized that the gipsy existed. Instantly, she was indignant. Him, of all things! Him! Never!

'Now why?' she asked herself, again in hushed amazement. 'Why? It's *absolutely* impossible: absolutely! So why is it?'

This was a nut to crack. She looked at the young men dancing, elbows out, hips prominent, waists elegantly in. They gave her no clue to her problem. Yet she did particularly dislike the forced elegance of the waists and the prominent hips, over which the well-tailored coats hung with such effeminate discretion.

'There is something about me which they don't see and never would see,' she said angrily to herself. And at the same time, she was relieved that they didn't and couldn't. It made life so very much simpler.

And again, since she was one of the people who are conscious in visual images, she saw the dark-green jersey rolled on the black trousers of the gipsy, his fine, quick hips, alert as eyes. They were elegant. The elegance of these dancers seems so stuffed, hips merely wadded with flesh. Leo the same, thinking himself such a fine dancer! and a fine figure of a fellow!

Then she saw the gipsy's face; the straight nose, the slender mobile lips, and the level, significant stare of the black eyes, which seemed to shoot her in some vital, undiscovered place, unerring.

She drew herself up angrily. How dared he look at her like that? So she gazed glaringly at the insipid beaux on the dancing floor. And she despised them. Just as the raggle-taggle gipsy women despise men who are not gipsies, despise their dog-like walk down the street, she found herself despising this crowd. Where among them was the subtle, lonely, insinuating challenge that could reach her?

She did not want to mate with a house-dog.

Her sensitive nose turned up, her soft brown hair fell like a soft sheath round her tender, flower-like face, as she sat musing. She seemed so virginal. At the same time, there was a touch of the tall young virgin *witch* about her, that made the house-dog men shy off. She might metamorphose into something uncanny before you knew where you were.

This made her lonely, in spite of all the courting. Perhaps the courting only made her lonelier.

Leo, who was a sort of mastiff among the house-dogs, returned after his dance, with fresh cheery-o! courage.

'You've had a little think about it, haven't you?' he said, sitting down beside her: a comfortable, well-nourished, determined sort of fellow. She did not know why it irritated her so unreasonably, when he hitched up his trousers at the knee, over his good-sized but not very distinguished legs, and lowered himself assuredly on to a chair.

'Have I?' she said vaguely. 'About what?'

'You know what about,' he said. 'Did you make up your mind?'

'Make up my mind about what?' she asked, innocently.

In her upper consciousness, she truly had forgotten.

'Oh!' said Leo, settling his trousers again. 'About me and you getting engaged, you know.' He was almost as off-hand as she.

'Oh that's *absolutely* impossible,' she said, with mild amiability, as if it were some stray question among the rest. 'Why I never even thought of it again. Oh, don't talk about that sort of nonsense! That sort of thing is *absolutely* impossible,' she reiterated like a child.

'That sort of thing is, is it?' he said, with an odd smile at her calm, distant assertion. 'Well, what sort of thing *is* possible, then? You don't want to die an old maid, do you?'

'Oh I don't mind,' she said absently.

'I do,' he said.

She turned round and looked at him in wonder.

'Why?' she said. 'Why should you mind if I was an old maid?'

'Every reason in the world,' he said looking up at her with a bold, meaningful smile, that wanted to make its meaning blatant, if not patent.

But instead of penetrating into some deep, secret place, and shooting her there, Leo's bold and patent smile only hit her on the outside of the body, like a tennis ball, and caused the same kind of sudden irritated reaction.

'I think this sort of thing is awfully silly,' she said, with minx-like spite. 'Why you're practically engaged to—to—' she pulled herself up in time—'probably half a dozen other girls. I'm not flattered by what you've said. I should hate it if anybody knew!—Hate it!—I shan't breathe a word of it, and I hope you'll have the sense not to.—There's Ella!'

And keeping her face averted from him, she sailed away like a tall, soft flower, to join poor Ella Framley.

Leo flapped his white gloves.

'Catty little bitch!' he said to himself. But he was of the mastiff type, he rather liked the kitten to fly in his face. He began definitely to single her out.

VI

THE next week it poured again with rain. And this irritated Yvette with strange anger. She had intended it should be fine. Especially she insisted it should be fine towards the weekend. Why, she did not ask herself.

Thursday, the half-holiday, came with a hard frost, and sun. Leo arrived with his car, the usual bunch. Yvette disagreeably and unaccountably refused to go.

'No thanks, I don't feel like it,' she said.

She rather enjoyed being Mary-Mary-quite-contrary.

Then she went for a walk by herself, up the frozen hills, to the Black Rocks.

The next day also came sunny and frosty. It was February, but in the north country the ground did not thaw in the sun. Yvette announced that she was going for a ride on her bicycle, and taking her lunch as she might not be back till afternoon.

She set off, not hurrying. In spite of the frost, the sun had a touch of spring. In the park, the deer were standing in the distance, in the sunlight, to be warm. One doe, white spotted, walked slowly across the motionless landscape.

Cycling, Yvette found it difficult to keep her hands warm, even when bodily she was quite hot. Only when she had to walk up the long hill, to the top, and there was no wind.

The upland was very bare and clear, like another world. She had climbed on to another level. She cycled slowly, a little afraid of taking the wrong lane, in the vast maze of stone fences. As she passed along the lane she thought was the right one, she heard a faint tapping noise, with a slight metallic resonance.

The gipsy man was seated on the ground with his back to the cart-shaft, hammering a copper bowl. He was in the sun, bare-headed, but wearing his green jersey. Three small children were moving quietly round, playing in the horse's shelter: the horse and cart were gone. An old woman, bent, with a kerchief round her head, was cooking over a fire of sticks. The only sound was the rapid, ringing tap-tap-tap of the small hammer on the dull copper.

The man looked up at once, as Yvette stepped from her bicycle, but he did not move, though he ceased hammering. A delicate, barely discernible smile of triumph was on his face. The old woman looked round, keenly, from under her dirty grey hair. The man spoke a half-audible word to her, and she turned again to her fire. He looked up at Yvette.

'How are you all getting on?' she asked politely.

'All right, eh! You sit down a minute?' He turned as he sat, and pulled a stool from under the caravan for Yvette. Then, as she wheeled her bicycle to the side of the quarry, he started hammering again, with that bird-like, rapid light stroke.

Yvette went to the fire to warm her hands.

'Is this the dinner cooking?' she asked childishly, of the old gipsy, as she spread her long tender hands, mottled red with the cold, to the embers.

'Dinner, yes!' said the old woman. 'For him! And for the children.'

She pointed with the long fork at the three black-eyed, staring children, who were staring at her from under their black fringes. But they were clean. Only the old woman was not clean. The quarry itself they had kept perfectly clean.

Yvette crouched in silence, warming her hands. The man rapidly hammered away with intervals of silence. The old hag slowly climbed the steps to the third, oldest caravan. The children began to play again, like little wild animals, quiet and busy.

'Are they your children?' asked Yvette, rising from the fire and turning to the man.

He looked her in the eyes, and nodded.

'But where's your wife?'

'She's gone out with the basket. They've all gone out, cart and all, selling things. I don't go selling things. I make them, but I don't go selling them. Not often. I don't often.'

'You make all the copper and brass things?' she said.

He nodded, and again offered her the stool. She sat down.

'You said you'd be here on Fridays,' she said. 'So I came this way, as it was so fine.'

'Very fine day!' said the gipsy, looking at her cheek, that was still a bit blanched by the cold, and the soft hair over her reddened ear, and the long, still mottled hands on her knee.

'You get cold, riding a bicycle?' he asked.

'My hands!' she said, clasping them nervously.

'You didn't wear gloves?'

'I did, but they weren't much good.'

'Cold comes through,' he said.

'Yes!' she replied.

The old woman came slowly, grotesquely down the steps of the caravan, with some enamel plates.

'The dinner cooked, eh?' he called softly.

The old woman muttered something, as she spread the plates near the fire. Two pots hung from a long iron horizontal bar, over the embers of the fire. A little pan seethed on a small iron tripod. In the sunshine, heat and vapour wavered together.

He put down his tools and the pot, and rose from the ground.

'You eat something along of us?' he asked Yvette, not looking at her.

'Oh, I brought my lunch,' said Yvette.

'You eat some stew?' he said. And again he called quietly, secretly to the old woman, who muttered in answer, as she slid the iron pot towards the end of the bar.

'Some beans, and some mutton in it,' he said.

'Oh, thanks awfully!' said Yvette. Then, suddenly taking courage, added: 'Well, yes, just a very little, if I may.'

She went across to untie her lunch from her bicycle, and he went up the steps to his own caravan. After a minute, he emerged, wiping his hands on a towel.

'You want to come up and wash your hands?' he said.

'No, I think not,' she said. 'They are clean.'

He threw away his wash-water, and set off down the road with a high brass jug, to fetch clean water from the spring that trickled into a small pool, taking a cup to dip it with.

When he returned, he set the jug and the cup by the fire, and fetched himself a short log, to sit on. The children sat on the floor, by the fire, in a cluster, eating beans and bits of meat with spoon or fingers. The man on the log ate in silence, absorbedly. The woman made coffee in the black pot on the tripod, hobbling upstairs for the cups. There was silence in the camp. Yvette sat on her stool, having taken off her hat and shaken her hair in the sun.

'How many children have you?' Yvette asked suddenly.

'Say five', he replied slowly, as he looked up into her eyes.

And again the bird of her heart sank down and seemed to die. Vaguely, as in a dream, she received from him the cup of coffee. She was aware only of his silent figure, sitting like a shadow there on the log, with an enamel cup in his hand, drinking his coffee in silence. Her will had departed from her limbs, he had power over her: his shadow was on her.

And he, as he blew his hot coffee, was aware of one thing only, the mysterious fruit of her virginity, her perfect tenderness in the body.

At length he put down his coffee-cup by the fire, then looked round at her. Her hair fell across her face, as she tried to sip from the hot cup. On her face was that tender look of sleep, which a nodding flower has when it is full out. Like a mysterious early flower, she was full out, like a snowdrop which spreads its three white wings in a flight into the waking sleep of its brief blossoming. The waking sleep of her full-opened virginity, entranced like a snowdrop in the sunshine, was upon her.

The gipsy supremely aware of her, waited for her like the substance of shadow, as shadow waits and is there.

At length his voice said, without breaking the spell:

'You want to go in my caravan now, and wash your hands?'

The childlike, sleep-waking eyes of her moment of perfect virginity looked into his, unseeing. She was only aware of the dark strange effluence of him bathing her limbs, washing her at last purely will-less. She was aware of *him*, as a dark, complete power.

'I think I might,' she said.

He rose silently, then turned to speak, in a low command, to the old woman. And then again he looked at Yvette, and putting his power over her, so that she had no burden of herself, or of action.

'Come!' he said.

She followed simply, followed the silent, secret, over-powering motion of his body in front of her. It cost her nothing. She was gone in his will.

He was at the top of the steps, and she at the foot, when she became aware of an intruding sound. She stood still, at the foot of the steps. A motor-car was coming. He stood at the top of the steps, looking round strangely. The old woman harshly called something, as with rapidly increasing sound, a car rushed near. It was passing.

Then they heard the cry of a woman's voice, and the brakes on the car. It had pulled up, just beyond the quarry.

The gipsy came down the steps, having closed the door of the caravan.

'You want to put your hat on,' he said to her.

Obediently she went to the stool by the fire, and took up her hat. He sat down by the cart-wheel, darkly, and took up his tools. The rapid tap-tap-tap of his hammer, rapid and angry now like the sound of a tiny machine-gun, broke out just as the voice of the woman was heard crying:

'May we warm our hands at the camp fire?'

She advanced, dressed in a sleek but bulky coat of sable fur. A man followed, in a blue great-coat; pulling off his fur gloves and pulling out a pipe.

'It looked so tempting,' said the woman in the coat of many dead little animals, smiling a broad, half-condescending, half-hesitant simper, around the company.

No one said a word.

She advanced to the fire, shuddering a little inside her coat, with the cold. They had been driving in an open car.

She was a very small woman, with a rather large nose: probably a Jewess. Tiny almost as a child, in that sable coat she looked much more bulky than she should, and her wide, rather resentful brown eyes of a spoilt Jewess gazed oddly out of her expensive get-up.

She crouched over the low fire, spreading her little hands, on which diamonds and emeralds glittered.

'Ugh!' she shuddered. 'Of course we ought not to have come in an open car! But my husband won't even let me say I'm cold!' She looked round at him with her large, childish, reproachful eyes, that had still the canny shrewdness of a bourgeois Jewess: a rich one, probably.

Apparently she was in love, in a Jewess's curious way, with the big, blond man. He looked back at her with his abstracted blue eyes, that seemed to have no lashes, and a small smile creased his smooth, curiously naked cheeks. The smile didn't mean anything at all.

He was a man one connects instantly with winter sports, ski-ing and skating. Athletic, unconnected with life, he slowly filled his pipe, pressing in the tobacco with long, powerful, reddened finger.

The Jewess looked at him to see if she got any response from him. Nothing at all, but that odd, blank smile. She turned again to the fire, tilting he eyebrows and looking at her small, white, spread hands.

He slipped off his heavily-lined coat, and appeared in one of the handsome, sharp-patterned knitted jerseys, in yellow and grey and black, over well-cut trousers, rather wide. Yes, they were both expensive! And he had a magnificent figure, and athletic, prominent chest. Like an experienced camper, he began building the fire together, quietly: like a soldier on campaign.

'D'you think they'd mind if we put some fir-cones on, to make a blaze?' he asked of Yvette, with a silent glance at the hammering gipsy.

'Love it, I should think,' said Yvette, in a daze, as the spell of the gipsy slowly left her, feeling stranded and blank.

The man went to the car, and returned with a little sack of cones, from which he drew a handful.

'Mind if we make a blaze?' he called to the gipsy.

'Eh?'

'Mind if we make a blaze with a few cones!'

'You go ahead!' said the gipsy.

The man began placing the cones lightly, carefully on the red embers. And soon, one by one, they caught fire, and burned likes roses of flame, with a sweet scent.

'Ah lovely! lovely!' cried the little Jewess, looking up at her man again. He looked down at her quite kindly, like the sun on ice. 'Don't you love fire? Oh, I love it!' the little Jewess cried to Yvette, across the hammering.

The hammering annoyed her. She looked round with a slight frown on her fine little brows, as if she would bid the man stop. Yvette looked round too. The gipsy was bent over his copper bowl, legs apart, head down, lithe arm lifted. Already he seemed so far from her.

The man who accompanied the little Jewess strolled over to the gipsy, and stood in silence looking down on him, holding his pipe to his mouth. Now they were two men, like two strange male dogs, having to sniff one another.

'We're on our honeymoon,' said the little Jewess, with an arch resentful look at Yvette. She spoke in a rather high, defiant voice, like some bird, a jay, or a rook, calling.

'Are you really?' said Yvette.

'Yes! Before we're married! Have you heard of Simon Fawcett?' —she named a wealthy and well-known engineer of the north country. 'Well, I'm Mrs Fawcett, and he's just divorcing me!' She looked at Yvette with curious defiance and wistfulness.

'Are you really!' said Yvette.

She understood now the look of resentment and defiance in the little Jewess's big, childlike brown eyes. She was an honest little thing, but perhaps her honesty was *too* rational. Perhaps it partly explained the notorious unscrupulousness of the well-known Simon Fawcett.

'Yes! As soon as we get the divorce I'm going to marry Major Eastwood.'

Her cards were now all on the table. She was not going to deceive anybody.

Behind her, the two men were talking briefly. She glanced round, and fixed the gipsy with her big brown eyes.

He was looking up, as if shyly, at the big fellow in the sparkling jersey, who was standing pipe in mouth, man to man, looking down.

'With the horses back of Arras,' said the gipsy in a low voice.

They were talking war. The gipsy had served with the artillery teams, in the Major's own regiment.

'Ein schöner Mensch!' said the Jewess. 'A handsome man, eh?'

For her, too, the gipsy was one of the common men, the Tommies.

'Quite handsome!' said Yvette.

'You are cycling?' asked the Jewess in a tone of surprise.

'Yes! Down to Papplewick. My father is rector of Papplewick: Mr Saywell!'

'Oh!' said the Jewess. 'I know! A clever writer! Very clever! I have read him.'

The fir-cones were all consumed already, the fire was a tall pile now of crumbling, shattering fire-roses. The sky was clouding over for afternoon. Perhaps towards evening it would snow.

The major came back, and slung himself into his coat.

'I thought I remembered his face!' he said. 'One of our grooms, A1 man with horses.'

'Look!' cried the Jewess to Yvette. 'Why don't you let us motor you down to Normanton. We live in Scoresby. We can tie the bicycle on behind.'

'I think I will,' said Yvette.

'Come!' called the Jewess to the peeping children, as the blond man wheeled away the bicycle. 'Come! Come here!' and taking out her little purse, she held out a shilling.

'Come!' she cried. 'Come and take it!'

The gipsy had laid down his work, and gone into his caravan. The old woman called hoarsely to the children from her enclosure. The two elder children came stealing forward. The Jewess gave them the two bits of silver, a shilling and a florin, which she had in her purse, and again the hoarse voice of the unseen old woman was heard.

The gipsy descended from his caravan and strolled to the fire. The Jewess searched his face with the peculiar bourgeois boldness of her race.

'You were in the war, in Major Eastwood's regiment?' she said.

'Yes, lady!'

'Imagine you both being here now!—It's going to snow.' She looked up at the sky.

'Later on,' said the man, looking at the sky.

He too had gone inaccessible. His race was very old, in its peculiar battle with established society, and had no conception of winning. Only now and then it could score.

But since the war, even the old sporting chance of scoring now and then was pretty well quenched. There was no question of yielding. The gipsy's eyes still had their bold look: but it was hardened and directed far away, the touch of insolent intimacy was gone. He had been through the war.

He looked at Yvette.

'You're going back in the motor-car?' he said.

'Yes!' she replied, with a rather mincing mannerism. 'The weather is so treacherous!'

'Treacherous weather!' he repeated, looking at the sky.

She could not tell in the least what his feelings were. In truth, she wasn't very much interested. She was rather fascinated, now, by the little Jewess, mother of two children, who was taking her wealth away from the well-known engineer and transferring it to the penniless, sporting young Major Eastwood, who must be five or six years younger than she. Rather intriguing!

The blond man returned.

'A cigarette, Charles!' cried the little Jewess, plaintively.

He took out his case, slowly, with his slow, athletic movement. Something sensitive in him made him slow, cautious, as if he had hurt himself against people. He gave a cigarette to his wife, then one to Yvette, then offered the case, quite simply, to the gipsy. The gipsy took one.

'Thank you, sir!'

And he went quietly to the fire, and stooping, lit it at the red embers. Both women watched him.

'Well, good-bye!' said the Jewess, with her old bourgeois freemasonry. 'Thank you for the warm fire.'

'Fire is everybody's,' said the gipsy.

The young child came toddling to him.

'Good-bye!' said Yvette. 'I hope it won't snow for you.'

'We don't mind a bit of snow,' said the gipsy.

'Don't you?' said Yvette. 'I should have thought you would!'

'No!' said the gipsy.

She flung her scarf royally over her shoulder, and followed the fur coat of the Jewess, which seemed to walk on little legs of its own.

VII

YVETTE was rather thrilled by the Eastwoods, as she called them. The little Jewess had only to wait three months now, for the final decree. She had boldly rented a small summer cottage by the moors up at Scoresby not far from the hills. Now it was dead winter and she and the Major lived in comparative isolation, without any maid-servant. He had already resigned his commission in the regular army, and called himself Mr Eastwood. In fact, they were already Mr and Mrs Eastwood, to the common world.

The little Jewess was thirty-six, and her two children were both over twelve years of age. The husband had agreed that she should have the custody, as soon as she was married to Eastwood.

So there they were, this queer couple, the tiny, finely-formed little Jewess with her big, resentful reproachful eyes, and her mop of carefully-barbered black curly hair, an elegant little thing in her way; and the big, pale-eyed young man, powerful and wintry, the remnant surely of some old uncanny Danish stock: living together in a small modern house near the moors and the hills and doing their own housework.

It was a funny household. The cottage was hired furnished, but the little Jewess had brought along her dearest pieces of furniture. She had an odd little taste for the rococo, strange curving cupboards inlaid with mother of pear, tortoiseshell, ebony, heaven knows what; strange tall flamboyant chairs, from Italy, with sea-green brocade: astonishing saints with wind-blown, richly-coloured carven garments and pink faces: shelves of weird old Saxe and Capo di Monte figurines: and finally, a strange assortment of astonishing pictures painted on the back of glass, done probably in the early years of the nineteenth century, or in the late eighteenth.

In this crowded and extraordinary interior she received Yvette, when the latter made a stolen visit. A whole system of stoves had been installed into the cottage, every corner was warm, almost hot. And there was the tiny rococo figurine of the Jewess herself, in a perfect little frock and an apron putting slices of ham on the dish while the great snow-bird of a major, in a white sweater and grey trousers, cut bread, mixed mustard, prepared coffee, and did all the rest. He had even made the dish of jugged hare which followed the cold meats and caviare.

The silver and the china were really valuable, part of the bride's trousseau. The Major drank beer from a silver mug, the little Jewess and Yvette had champagne in lovely glasses, the Major brought in coffee. They talked away. The little Jewess had a burning indignation against her first husband. She was intensely moral, so moral, that she was a divorcée. The Major, too, strange wintry bird, so powerful, handsome, too, in his way but pale round the eyes as if he had no eyelashes, like a bird, he, too, had a curious indignation against life, because of the false morality. That powerful, athletic chest hid a strange, snowy sort of anger. And his tenderness for the little Jewess was based on his sense of outraged justice, the abstract morality of the north blowing him, like a strange wind, into isolation.

As the afternoon drew on, they went to the kitchen, the Major pushed back his sleeves, showing his powerful athletic white arms, and carefully, deftly washed the dishes, while the women wiped. It was not for nothing his muscles were trained. Then he went round attending to the stoves of the small house, which only needed a moment or two of care each day. And after this, he brought out the small, closed car and drove Yvette home, in the rain, depositing her at the back gate, a little wicket among the larches, through which the earthen steps sloped downwards to the house.

She was really amazed by this couple.

'Really, Lucille!' she said. 'I do meet the most extraordinary people!' And she gave a detailed description.

'I think they sound rather nice!' said Lucille. 'I like the Major doing the housework, and looking so frightfully Bond-streety with it all. I should think, *when they're married*, it would be rather fun knowing them.'

'Yes!' said Yvette vaguely. 'Yes! Yes, it would!'

The very strangeness of the connexion between the tiny Jewess and that pale-eyed, athletic young officer made her think again of her gipsy, who had been utterly absent from her consciousness, but who now returned with sudden painful force.

'What is it, Lucille,' she asked, 'that brings people together? People like the Eastwoods, for instance? and Daddy and Mamma, so frightfully unsuitable?—and that gipsy woman who told my fortune, like a great horse, and the gipsy man, so fine and delicately cut? What is it?'

'I suppose it's sex, whatever that is,' said Lucille.

'Yes, what is it? It's not really anything *common*, like common sensuality, you know, Lucille. It really isn't.'

'No, I suppose not,' said Lucille. 'Anyhow I suppose it needn't be.'

'Because, you see, the *common* fellows, you know, who make a girl feel *low*: nobody cares much about them. Nobody feels any connexion with them. Yet they're supposed to be the sexual sort.'

'I suppose,' said Lucille, 'there's the low sort of sex, and there's the other sort, that isn't low. It's frightfully complicated, really! I *loathe* common fellows. And I never feel anything *sexual*'—she laid a rather disgusted stress on the word—'for fellows who aren't common. Perhaps I haven't got any sex.'

'That's just it!' said Yvette. 'Perhaps neither of us has. Perhaps we haven't really *got* any sex, to connect us with men.'

'How horrible it sounds: *connect us with men!*' cried Lucille, with revulsion. 'Wouldn't you hate to be connected with men that way? Oh, I think it's an awful pity there has to *be* sex! It would be so much better if we could still be men and women, without that sort of thing.'

Yvette pondered. Far in the background was the image of the gipsy as he had looked round at her, when she had said: 'The weather is so treacherous.' She felt rather like Peter when the cock crew, as she denied him. Or rather, she did not deny the gipsy; she didn't care about his part in the show, anyhow. It was some hidden part of herself which she denied: that part which mysteriously and unconfessedly responded to him. And it was a strange, lustrous black cock which crew in mockery of her.

'Yes!' she said vaguely. 'Yes! Sex is an awful bore, you know, Lucille. When you haven't got it, you feel you *ought* to have it, somehow. And when you've got it—or *if* you have it'—she lifted her head and wrinkled her nose disdainfully—'you hate it.'

'Oh, I don't know!' cried Lucille. 'I think I should *like* to be awfully in love with a man.'

'You think so!' said Yvette, again wrinkling her nose. 'But if you were you wouldn't.'

'How do you know?' asked Lucille.

'Well, I don't really,' said Yvette. 'But I think so! Yes, I think so!'

'Oh, it's very likely!' said Lucille disgustedly. 'And anyhow one would be sure to get out of love again, and it would be merely disgusting.'

'Yes,' said Yvette. 'It's a problem.' She hummed a little tune.

'Oh, hang it all, it's not a problem for us two yet. We're neither of us really in love, and we probably never shall be, so the problem is settled that way.'

'I'm not so sure!' said Yvette sagely. 'I'm not so sure. I believe, one day, I shall fall *awfully* in love.'

'Probably you never will,' said Lucille brutally. 'That's what most old maids are thinking all the time.'

Yvette looked at her sister from pensive but apparently in-souciant eyes.

'Is it?' she said. 'Do you really think so, Lucille? How perfectly awful for them, poor things! Why ever do they *care*?'

'Why do they?' said Lucille. 'Perhaps they don't, really.— Probably it's all because people say: *Poor old girl, she couldn't catch a man.*'

'I suppose it is!' said Yvette. 'They get to mind the beastly things people always do say about old maids. What a shame!'

'Anyhow we have a good time, and we do have lots of boys who make a fuss of us,' said Lucille.

'Yes! said Yvette. 'Yes! But I couldn't possibly marry any of them.'

'Neither could I,' said Lucille. 'But why shouldn't we? Why should we bother about marrying, when we have a perfectly good time with the boys, who are awfully good sorts, and you must say, Yvette, awfully sporting and *decent* to us.'

'Oh, they are!' said Yvette absently.

'I think it's time to think of marrying somebody,' said Lucille, 'when you feel you're *not* having a good time any more. Then marry, and just settle down.'

'Quite!' said Yvette.

But now, under all her bland, soft amiability, she was annoyed with Lucille. Suddenly she wanted to turn her back on Lucille.

Besides, look at the shadows under poor Lucille's eyes, and the wistfulness in the beautiful eyes themselves. Oh, if some awfully nice, kind, protective sort of man would but marry her! And if the sporting Lucille would let him!

Yvettte did not tell the rector or Granny about the Eastwoods. It would only have started a lot of talk which she detested. The rector wouldn't have minded, for himself, privately. But he, too, knew the necessity of keeping as clear as possible from that poisonous, many-headed serpent, the tongue of the people.

'But I don't *want* you to come if your father doesn't know,' cried the little Jewess.

'I suppose I'll have to tell him,' said Yvette. 'I'm sure he doesn't mind, really. But if he knew, he'd have to, I suppose.'

The young officer looked at her with an odd amusement, bird-like and unemotional, in his keen eyes. He, too, was by way of falling in love with Yvette. It was her peculiar virgin tenderness, and her straying, absent-minded detachment from things, which attracted him.

She was aware of what was happening, and she rather preened herself. Eastwood piqued her fancy. Such a smart young officer, awfully good class, so calm and amazing with a motor-car, and quite a champion swimmer, it was intriguing to see him quietly, calmly washing dishes, smoking his pipe, doing his job so alert and skilful. Or, with the same interested care with which he made his investigation into the mysterious inside of an automobile, concocting jugged hare in the cottage kitchen. Then going out in the icy weather and cleaning his car till it looked like a live thing, like a cat when she has licked herself. Then coming in to talk so unassumingly and responsively, if briefly, with the little Jewess. And apparently, never bored. Sitting at the window with his pipe in bad weather, silent for hours, abstracted, musing, yet with his athletic body alert in its stillness.

Yvette did not flirt with him. But she *did* like him.

'But what about your future?' she asked him.

'What about it?' he said, taking his pipe from his mouth, the unemotional point of a smile in his bird's eyes.

'A career! Doesn't every man have to carve out a career?— like some huge goose with gravy?' She gazed with odd naïveté into his eyes.

'I'm perfectly all right today, and I shall be all right tomorrow,' he said, with a cold, decided look. 'Why shouldn't my future be continuous todays and tomorrows?'

He looked at her with unmoved searching.

'Quite!' she said. 'I hate jobs, and all that side of life.' But she was thinking of the Jewess's money.

To which he did not answer. His anger was of the soft, snowy sort, which comfortably muffles the soul.

They had come to the point of talking philosophically together. The little Jewess looked a bit wan. She was curiously naïve, and not possessive in her attitude to the man. Nor was she at all catty with Yvette. Only rather wan, and dumb.

Yvette, on a sudden impulse, thought she had better clear herself.

'I think life's *awfully* difficult,' she said.

'Life is!' cried the Jewess.

'What's so beastly, is that one is supposed to *fall in love*, and get married!' said Yvette, curling up her nose.

'Don't you *want* to fall in love and get married?' cried the Jewess, with great glaring eyes of astounded reproach.

'No, not particularly!' said Yvette. 'Especially as one feels there's nothing else to do. It's an awful chicken-coop one has to run into.'

'But you don't know what love is?' cried the Jewess.

'No!' said Yvette. 'Do you?'

'I!' bawled the tiny Jewess. 'I! My goodness, don't I!' She looked with reflective gloom at Eastwood, who was smoking his pipe, the dimples of his disconnected amusement showing on his smooth, scrupulous face. He had a very fine, smooth skin, which yet did not suffer from the weather, so that his face looked naked as a baby's. But it was not a round face: it was characteristic enough, and took queer ironical dimples, like a mask which is comic but frozen.

'Do you mean to say you don't know what love is?' insisted the Jewess.

'No!' said Yvette, with insouciant candour. 'I don't believe I do! Is it awful of me, at my age?'

'Is there never any man that makes you feel quite, quite different?' said the Jewess, with another big-eyed look at Eastwood. He smoked, utterly unimplicated.

'I don't think there is,' said Yvette, 'Unless—yes!—unless it is that gipsy'—she had put her head pensively sideways.

'Which gipsy?' bawled the little Jewess.

'The one who was a Tommy and looked after horses in Major Eastwood's regiment in the war,' said Yvette coolly.

The little Jewess gazed at Yvette with great eyes of stupor.

'You're not in love with that *gipsy*!' she said.

'Well!' said Yvette. 'I don't know. He's the only one that makes me feel—different! He really is!'

'But how? How? Has he ever *said* anything to you?'

'No! No!'

'Then how? What has he done?'

'Oh, just looked at me!'

'How?'

'Well, you see, I don't know. But different! Yes, different! Different quite different from the way any man ever looked at me.'

'But *how* did he look at you?' insisted the Jewess.

'Why—as if he really, but *really, desired* me,' said Yvette, her meditative face looking like the bud of a flower.

'What a vile fellow! What *right* had he to look at you like that?' cried the indignant Jewess.

'A cat may look at a king,' calmly interposed the Major, and now his face had the smiles of a cat's face.

'You think he oughtn't to?' asked Yvette, turning to him.

'Certainly not! A gipsy fellow, with half a dozen dirty women trailing after him! Certainly not!' cried the tiny Jewess.

'I wondered!' said Yvette. 'Because it *was* rather wonderful, really! And it *was* something quite different in my life.'

'I think,' said the Major, taking his pipe from his mouth, 'that desire is the most wonderful thing in life. Anybody who can really feel it, is a king, and I envy nobody else!' He put back his pipe.

The Jewess looked at him stupefied.

'But, Charles!' she cried. 'Every common low man in Halifax feels nothing else!'

He again took his pipe from his mouth.

'That's merely appetite,' he said.

And he put back his pipe.

'You think the gipsy is the real thing?' Yvette asked him.

He lifted his shoulders.

'It's not for me to say,' he replied. 'If I were you, I should know, I shouldn't be asking other people.'

'Yes—but— ' Yvette trailed out.

'Charles! You're wrong! How *could* it be a real thing! As if she could possibly marry him and go round in a caravan!'

'I didn't say marry him,' said Charles.

'Or a love affair! Why it's monstrous! What would she think of herself!—That's not love! That's—that's prostitution!'

Charles smoked for some moments.

'That gipsy was the best man we had, with horses. Nearly died of pneumonia. I thought he *was* dead. He's a resurrected man to me. I'm a resurrected man myself, as far as that goes.' He looked at Yvette. 'I was buried for twenty hours under snow,' he said. 'And not much the worse for it, when they dug me out.'

There was a frozen pause in the conversation.

'Life's awful!' said Yvette.

'They dug me out by accident,' he said.

'Oh!— ' Yvette trailed slowly. 'It might be destiny, you know.'

To which he did not answer.

VIII

THE rector heard about Yvette's intimacy with the Eastwoods, and she was somewhat startled by the result. She had thought he wouldn't care. Verbally, in his would-be humorous fashion, he was so entirely unconventional, such a frightfully good sport. As he said himself, he was a conservative anarchist; which meant he was like a great many more people, a mere unbeliever. The anarchy extended to his humorous talk, and his secret thinking. The conservatism, based on a mongrel fear of the anarchy, controlled every action. His thoughts, secretly, were something to be scared of. Therefore, in his life, he was fanatically afraid of the unconventional.

When his conservatism and his abject sort of fear were uppermost, he always lifted his lip and bared his teeth a little, in a dog-like sneer.

'I hear your latest friends are the half-divorced Mrs Fawcett and the *maquereau* Eastwood,' he said to Yvette.

She didn't know what a *maquereau* was, but she felt the poison in the rector's fangs.

'I just know them,' she said. 'They're awfully nice, really. And they'll be married in about a month's time.'

The rector looked at her insouciant face with hatred. Somewhere inside him, he was cowed, he had been born cowed. And those who are born cowed are natural slaves, and deep instinct makes them fear with poisonous fear those who might suddenly snap the slave's collar round their necks.

It was for this reason the rector had so abjectly curled up, still so abjectly curled up before She-who-was-Cynthia: because of his slave's fear of her contempt, the contempt of a born-free nature for a base-born nature.

Yvette too had a free-born quality. She, too, one day, would know him, and clap the slave's collar of her contempt round his neck.

But should she? He would fight to the death, this time, first. The slave in him was cornered this time, like a cornered rat, and with the courage of a cornered rat.

'I suppose they're your sort!' he sneered.

'Well, they are, really,' she said, with that blithe vagueness. 'I do like them awfully. They seem so solid, you know, so honest.'

'You've got a peculiar notion of honesty!' he sneered. 'A young sponge going off with a woman older than himself, so that he can live on her money! The woman leaving her home and her children! I don't know where you get your idea of honesty. Not from me, I hope—And you seem to be very well acquainted with them, considering you say you just know them. Where did you meet them?'

'When I was out bicycling. They came along in their car, and we happened to talk. She told me at once who she was, so that I shouldn't make a mistake. She *is* honest.'

Poor Yvette was struggling to bear up.
'And how often have you seen them since?'
'Oh, I've just been over twice.'
'Over where?'
'To their cottage in Scoresby.'
He looked at her in hate, as if he could kill her. And he
backed away from her, against the window-curtains of his
study, like a rat at bay. Somewhere in his mind he was thinking
unspeakable depravities about his daughter, as he had thought
them of She-who-was-Cynthia. He was powerless against the
lowest insinuations of his own mind. And these depravities
which he attributed to the still-uncowed but frightened girl
in front of him, made him recoil, showing all his fangs in his
handsome face.
'So you just know them, do you?' he said. 'Lying is in your
blood, I see. I don't believe you get it from me.'
Yvette half averted her mute face, and thought of Granny's
bare-faced prevarication. She did not answer.
'What takes you creeping round such couples?' he sneered.
'Aren't there enough decent people in the world for you to
know? Anyone would think you were a stray dog, having to
run round indecent couples, because the decent ones wouldn't
have you. Have you got something worse than lying in your
blood?'
'What have I got worse than lying in my blood?' she asked.
A cold deadness was coming over her. Was she abnormal, one of
the semi-criminal abnormals? It made her feel cold and dead.
In his eyes, she was just brazening out the depravity that
underlay her virgin, tender, bird-like face. She-who-was-Cynthia
had been like this: a snow-flower. And he had convulsions of
sadistic horror, thinking what might be the *actual* depravity
of She-who-was-Cynthia. Even his *own* love for her, which
had been the lust-love of the born cowed, had been a
depravity, in secret, to him. So what must an illegal love
be?
'You know best yourself, what you have got,' he sneered.
'But it is something you had best curb, and quickly, if you
don't intend to finish in a criminal-lunacy asylum.'
'Why?' she said, pale and muted, numbed with frozen fear.
'Why criminal lunacy? What have I done?'

'That is between you and your Maker,' he jeered. 'I shall never ask. But certain tendencies end in criminal lunacy, unless they are curbed in time.'

'Do you mean like knowing the Eastwoods?' asked Yvette, after a pause of numb fear.

'Do I mean like nosing round such people as Mrs Fawcett, a Jewess, and ex-Major Eastwood, a man who goes off with an older woman for the sake of her money? Why, yes, I do!'

'But you *can't* say that,' cried Yvette. 'He's an awfully simple, straightforward man.'

'He is apparently one of your sort.'

'Well.—In a way, I thought he was. I thought you'd like him too,' she said simply, hardly knowing what she said.

The rector backed into the curtains, as if the girl menaced him with something fearful.

'Don't say any more,' he snarled, abject. 'Don't say any more. You've said too much, to implicate you. I don't want to learn any more horrors.'

'But what horrors?' she persisted.

The very naïveté of her unscrupulous innocence repelled him, cowed him still more.

'Say no more!' he said, in a low, hissing voice. 'But I will kill you before you shall go the way of your mother.'

She looked at him, as he stood there backed against the velvet curtains of his study, his face yellow, his eyes distraught like a rat's with fear and rage and hate, and a numb, frozen loneliness came over her. For her, too, the meaning had gone out of everything.

It was hard to break the frozen, sterile silence that ensued. At last, however, she looked at him. And in spite of herself, beyond her own knowledge, the contempt for him was in her young, clear, baffled eyes. It fell like the slave's collar over his neck, finally.

'Do you mean I mustn't know the Eastwoods?' she said.

'You can know them if you wish,' he sneered. 'But you must not expect to associate with your Granny, and your Aunt Cissie, and Lucille, if you do. I cannot have *them* contaminated. Your Granny was a faithful wife and a faithful mother, if ever one existed. She has already had one shock of shame and abomination to endure. She shall never be exposed to another.'

Yvette heard it all dimly, half hearing.

'I can send a note and say you disapprove,' she said dimly.

'You follow your own course of action. But remember, you have to choose between clean people, and reverence for your Granny's blameless old age, and people who are unclean in their minds and their bodies.'

Again there was a silence. Then she looked at him, and her face was more puzzled than anything. But somewhere at the back of her perplexity was that peculiar calm, virgin contempt of the free-born for the base-born. He, and all the Saywells, were base-born.

'All right,' she said. 'I'll write and say you disapprove.'

He did not answer. He was partly flattered, secretly triumphant, but abjectly.

'I have tried to keep this from your Granny and Aunt Cissie,' he said. 'It need not be public property, since you choose to make your friendship clandestine.'

There was a dreary silence.

'All right,' she said. 'I'll go and write.'

And she crept out of the room.

She addressed her little note to Mrs Eastwood. 'Dear Mrs Eastwood, Daddy doesn't approve of my coming to see you. So you will understand if we have to break it off. I'm awfully sorry—.' That was all.

Yet she felt a dreary blank when she had posted her letter. She was now even afraid of her own thoughts. She wanted, now, to be held against the slender, fine-shaped breast of the gipsy. She wanted him to hold her in his arms, if only for once, for once, and comfort and confirm her. She wanted to be confirmed by him, against her father, who had only a repulsive fear of her.

And at the same time she cringed and winced, so that she could hardly walk, for fear the thought was obscene, a criminal lunacy. It seemed to wound her heels as she walked, the fear. The fear, the great cold fear of the base-born, her father, everything human and swarming. Like a great bog humanity swamped her, and she sank in, weak at the knees, filled with repulsion and fear of every person she met.

She adjusted herself, however, quite rapidly to her new conception of people. She had to live. It is useless to quarrel with one's bread and butter. And to expect a great deal out of life is puerile. So, with the rapid adaptability of the post-war generation, she adjusted herself to the new facts. Her father was what he was. He would always play up to appearances. She would do the same. She, too, would play up to appearances.

So, underneath the blithe, gossamer-straying insouciance, a certain hardness formed, like rock crystallizing in her heart. She lost her illusions in the collapse of her sympathies. Outwardly, she seemed the same. Inwardly she was hard and detached, and, unknown to herself, revengeful.

Outwardly she remained the same. It was part of her game. While circumstances remained as they were, she must remain, at least in appearance, true to what was expected of her.

But the revengefulness came out in her new vision of people. Under the rector's apparently gallant handsomeness, she saw the weak, feeble nullity. And she despised him. Yet still, in a way, she liked him too. Feelings are so complicated.

It was Granny whom she came to detest with all her soul. That obese old woman, sitting there in her blindness like some great red-blotched fungus, her neck swallowed between her heaped-up shoulders and her rolling, ancient chins, so that she was neckless as a double potato, her Yvette really hated, with that pure, sheer hatred which is almost a joy. Her hate was so clear, that while she was feeling strong, she enjoyed it.

The old woman sat with her big, reddened face pressed a little back, her lace cap perched on her thin white hair, her stub nose still assertive, and her old mouth shut like a trap. This motherly old soul, her mouth gave her away. It always had been one of the compressed sort. But in her great age, it had gone like a toad's, lipless, the jaw pressing up like the lower jaw of a trap. The look Yvette most hated was the look of that lower jaw pressing relentlessly up, with an ancient prognathous thrust, so that the snub nose in turn was forced to press upwards, and the whole face was pressed a little back, beneath the big, wall-like forehead. The will, the ancient, toad-like, obscene *will* in the old woman, was fearful, once you saw it: a toad-like self-will that was godless, and less than human! It belonged to the old, enduring race of toads, or tortoises. And it made one feel that Granny would never die. She would live on like these higher reptiles, in a state of semi-coma, for ever.

Yvette dared not even suggest to her father that Granny was not perfect. He would have threatened his daughter with the lunatic asylum. That was the threat he always seemed to have up his sleeve: the lunatic asylum. Exactly as if a distaste for Granny and for that horrible house of relatives was in itself a proof of lunacy, dangerous lunacy.

Yet in one of her moods of irritable depression, she did once fling out:

'How perfectly beastly this house is! Aunt Lucy comes, and Aunt Nell and Aunt Alice, and they make a ring like a ring of crows, with Granny and Aunt Cissie, all lifting their skirts up and warming their legs at the fire, and shutting Lucille and me out. We're nothing but outsiders in this beastly house!'

Her father glanced at her curiously. But she managed to put a petulance into her speech, and a mere cross rudeness into her look, so that he could laugh, as at a childish tantrum. Somewhere, though, he knew that she coldly, venomously meant what she said, and he was wary of her.

Her life seemed now nothing but an irritable friction against the unsavoury household of the Saywells, in which she was immersed. She loathed the rectory with a loathing that consumed her life, a loathing so strong that she could not really go away from the place. While it endured, she was spell-bound to it, in revulsion.

She forgot the Eastwoods again. After all, what was the revolt of the little Jewess, compared to Granny and the Saywell bunch! A husband was never more than a semi-casual thing! But a family! an awful, smelly family that would never disperse, stuck half dead round the base of a fungoid old woman! How was one to cope with that?

She did not forget the gipsy entirely. But she had no time for him. She, who was bored almost to agony, and who had nothing at all to do, she had not time to think even, seriously, of anything. Time being, after all, only the current of the soul in its flow.

She saw the gipsy twice. Once he came to the house, with things to sell. And she, watching him from the landing window, refused to go down. He saw her, too, as he was putting his things back into his cart. But he too gave no sign. Being of a race that exists only to be harrying the outskirts of our society, for ever hostile and living only by spoil, he was too much master of himself, and too wary, to expose himself openly to the vast and gruesome clutch of our law. He had been through the war. He had been enslaved against his will, that time.

So now, he showed himself at the rectory, and slowly, quietly busied himself at his cart outside the white gate, with that air of silent and for ever-unyielding outsideness which gave him his lonely, predative grace. He knew she saw him. And she should see him unyielding, quietly hawking his copper vessels, on an old, old warpath against such as herself.

Such as herself? Perhaps he was mistaken. Her heart, in its stroke, now rang hard as his hammer upon his copper, beating against circumstances. But he struck stealthily on the outside, and she still more secretly on the inside of the establishment. She liked him. She liked the quiet, noiseless clean-cut presence of him. She liked that mysterious endurance in him, which endures in opposition, without any idea of victory. And she liked that peculiar added relentlessness, the disillusion in hostility, which belongs to after the war. Yes, if she belonged to any side, and to any clan, it was to his. Almost she could have found it in her heart to go with him, and be a pariah gipsy-woman.

But she was born inside the pale. And she liked comfort, and a certain prestige. Even as a mere rector's daughter, one did have a certain prestige. And she liked that. Also she liked to chip against the pillars of the temple, from the inside. She wanted to be safe under the temple roof. Yet she enjoyed chipping fragments off the supporting pillars. Doubtless many fragments had been whittled away from the pillars of the Philistine, before Samson pulled the temple down.

'I'm not sure one shouldn't have one's fling till one is twenty-six, and then give in, and marry!'

This was Lucille's philosophy, learned from older women. Yvette was twenty-one. It meant she had five more years in which to have this precious fling. And the fling meant, at the moment, the gipsy. The marriage, at the age of twenty-six, meant Leo or Gerry.

So, a woman could eat her cake and have her bread and butter.

Yvette, pitched in gruesome, deadlocked hostility to the Saywell household, was very old and very wise: with the agedness and the wisdom of the young, which always overleaps the agedness and the wisdom of the old, or the elderly.

The second time she met the gipsy by accident. It was March, and sunny weather, after unheard-of rains. Celandines were yellow in the hedges, and primroses among the rocks. But still there came a smell of sulphur from far-away steel-works, out of the steel-blue sky.

And yet it was spring!

Yvette was cycling slowly along by Codnor Gate, past the lime quarries, when she saw the gipsy coming away from the door of a stone cottage. His cart stood there in the road. He was returning with his brooms and copper things, to the cart.

She got down from her bicycle. As she saw him, she loved with curious tenderness the slim lines of his body in the green jersey, the turn of his silent face. She felt she knew him better than she knew anybody on earth, even Lucille, and belonged to him, in some way, for ever.

'Have you made anything new and nice?' she asked innocently, looking at his copper things.

'I don't think,' he said, glancing back at her.

The desire was still there, still curious and naked, in his eyes. But it was more remote, the boldness was diminished. There was a tiny glint, as if he might dislike her. But this dissolved again, as he saw her looking among his bits of copper and brass-work. She searched them diligently.

There was a little oval brass plate, with a queer figure like a palm-tree beaten upon it.

'I like that,' she said. 'How much is it?'

'What you like,' he said.

This made her nervous: he seemed off-hand, almost mocking.

'I'd rather you said,' she told him, looking up at him.

'You give me what you like,' he said.

'No!' she said, suddenly. 'If you won't tell me I won't have it.'

'All right,' he said. 'Two shilling.'

She found half-a-crown, and he drew from his pocket a handful of silver, from which he gave her sixpence.

'The old gipsy dreamed something about you,' he said, looking at her with curious, searching eyes.

'Did she!' cried Yvette, at once interested. 'What was it?'

'She said: Be braver in your heart, or you lose your game. She said it this way: "Be braver in your body, or your luck will leave you." And she said as well: "Listen for the voice of water." '

Yvette was very much impressed.

'And what does it mean?' she asked.

'I asked her,' he said. 'She says she don't know.'

'Tell me again what it was,' said Yvette.

' "Be braver in your body, or your luck will go." And: "Listen for the voice of water." '

He looked in silence at her soft, pondering face. Something almost like a perfume seemed to flow from her young bosom direct to him, in a grateful connexion.

'I'm to be braver in my body, and I'm to listen for the voice of water! All right!' she said. 'I don't understand, but perhaps I shall.'

She looked at him with clear eyes. Man or woman is made up of many selves. With one self, she loved this gipsy man. With many selves, she ignored him or had a distaste for him.

'You're not coming up to the Head no more?' he asked.

Again she looked at him absently.

'Perhaps I will,' she said, 'some time. Some time.'

'Spring weather!' he said, smiling faintly and glancing round at the sun. 'We're going to break camp soon, and go away.'

'When?' she said.

'Perhaps next week.'

'Where to?'

Again he made a move with his head.

'Perhaps up north,' he said.

She looked at him.

'All right!' she said. 'Perhaps I *will* come up before you go, and say good-bye to your wife and to the old woman who sent me the message.'

IX

YVETTE did not keep her promise. The few March days were lovely, and she let them slip. She had a curious reluctance, always, towards taking action, or making any real move of her own. She always wanted someone else to make a move for her, as if she did not want to play her own game of life.

She lived as usual, went out to her friends, to parties, and danced with the undiminished Leo. She wanted to go up and say good-bye to the gipsies. She wanted to. And nothing prevented her.

On the Friday afternoon especially she wanted to go. It was sunny, and the last yellow crocuses down the drive were in full blaze, wide open, the first bees rolling in them. The Papple rushed under the stone bridge, uncannily full, nearly filling the arches. There was the scent of a mezereon tree.

And she felt too lazy, too lazy, too lazy. She strayed in the garden by the river, half dreamy, expecting something. While the gleam of spring sun lasted, she would be out of doors. Indoors Granny, sitting back like some awful old prelate, in her bulk of black silk and her white lace cap, was warming her feet by the fire, and hearing everything that Aunt Nell had to say. Friday was Aunt Nell's day. She usually came for lunch, and left after an early tea. So the mother and the large, rather common daughter, who was a widow at the age of forty, sat gossiping by the fire, while Aunt Cissie prowled in and out. Friday was the rector's day for going to town: it was also the housemaid's half day.

Yvette sat on a wooden seat in the garden, only a few feet above the bank of the swollen river, which rolled a strange, uncanny mass of water. The crocuses were passing in the ornamental beds, the grass was dark green where it was mown, the laurels looked a little brighter. Aunt Cissie appeared at the top of the porch steps, and called to ask if Yvette wanted that early cup of tea. Because of the river just below, Yvette could not hear what Aunt Cissie said, but she guessed, and shook her head. An early cup of tea, indoors, when the sun actually shone? No thanks!

She was conscious of her gipsy, as she sat there musing in the sun. Her soul had the half painful, half easing knack of leaving her, and straying away to some place, to somebody that had caught her imagination. Some days she would be at the Framleys', even though she did not go near them. Some days, she was all the time in spirit with the Eastwoods. And today it was the gipsies. She was up at their encampment in the quarry. She saw the man hammering his copper, lifting his head to look at the road; and the children playing in the horse-shelter: and the women, the gipsy's wife and the strong, elderly woman, coming home with their packs, along with the elderly man. For this afternoon, she felt intensely that *that* was home for her: the gipsy camp, the fire, the stool, the man with the hammer, the old crone.

It was part of her nature, to get these fits of yearning for some place she knew; to be in a certain place; with somebody who meant home to her. This afternoon it was the gipsy camp. And the man in the green jersey made it home to her. Just to be where he was, that was to be at home. The caravans, the brats, the other women: everything was natural to her, her home, as if she had been born there. She wondered if the gipsy was aware of her: if he could see her sitting on the stool by the fire; if he would lift his head and see her as she rose, looking at him slowly and significantly, turning towards the steps of his caravan. Did he know? Did he know?

Vaguely she looked up the steep of dark larch trees north of the house, where unseen the road climbed, going towards the Head. There was nothing, and her glance strayed down again. At the foot of the slope the river turned, thrown back harshly, ominously, against the low rocks across stream, then pouring past the garden to the bridge. It was unnaturally full, and whitey-muddy, and ponderous. 'Listen for the voice of water,' she said to herself. 'No need to listen for it, if the voice means the noise!'

And again she looked at the swollen river breaking angrily as it came round the bend. Above it the black-looking kitchen garden hung, and the hard-natured fruit trees. Everything was on the tilt, facing south and south-west, for the sun. Behind, above the house and the kitchen garden hung the steep little wood of withered-seeming larches. The gardener was working in the kitchen garden, high up there, by the edge of the larch-wood.

She heard a call. It was Aunt Cissie and Aunt Nell. They

were on the drive, waving good-bye! Yvette waved back. Then Aunt Cissie, pitching her voice against the waters, called:

'I shan't be long. Don't forget Granny is alone!'

'All right!' screamed Yvette rather ineffectually.

And she sat on her bench and watched the two undignified, long-coated women walk slowly over the bridge and begin the curving climb on the opposite slope, Aunt Nell carrying a sort of suit-case in which she brought a few goods for Granny and took back vegetables or whatever the rectory garden or cupboard was yielding. Slowly the two figures diminished, on the whitish, up-curving road, labouring slowly up towards Papplewick village. Aunt Cissie was going as far as the village for something.

The sun was yellowing to decline. What a pity! Oh, what a pity the sunny day was going, and she would have to turn indoors, to those hateful rooms, and Granny! Aunt Cissie would be back directly: it was past five. And all the others would be arriving from town, rather irritable and tired, soon after six.

As she looked uneasily round, she heard, across the running water, the sharp noise of a horse and cart rattling on the road hidden in the larch trees. The gardener was looking up too. Yvette turned away again, lingering, strolling by the full river a few paces, unwilling to go in; glancing up the road to see if Aunt Cissie were coming. If she saw her, she would go indoors.

She heard somebody shouting, and looked round. Down the path through the larch trees the gipsy was bounding. The gardener, away beyond, was also running. Simultaneously she became aware of a great roar, which, before she could move, accumulated to a vast deafening snarl. The gipsy was gesticulating. She looked round, behind her.

And to her horror and amazement, round the bend of the river she saw a shaggy, tawny wave-front of water advancing like a wall of lions. The roaring sound wiped out everything. She was powerless, too amazed and wonder-struck, she wanted to see it.

Before she could think twice, it was near, a roaring cliff of water. She almost fainted with horror. She heard the scream of the gipsy, and looked up to see him bounding upon her, his black eyes starting out of his head.

'Run!' he screamed, seizing her arm.

And in the instant the first wave was washing her feet from

under her, swirling, in the insane noise, which suddenly for some reason seemed like stillness, with a devouring flood over the garden. The horrible mowing of water!

The gipsy dragged her heavily, lurching, plunging, but still keeping foot-hold both of them, towards the house. She was barely conscious: as if the flood was in her soul.

There was one grass-banked terrace of the garden, near the path round the house. The gipsy clawed his way up this terrace to the dry level of the path, dragging her after him, and sprang with her past the windows to the porch steps. Before they got there, a new great surge of water came mowing, mowing trees down even, and mowed them down too.

Yvette felt herself gone in an agonizing mill-race of icy water, whirled, with only the fearful grip of the gipsy's hand on her wrist. They were both down and gone. She felt a dull but stunning bruise somewhere.

Then he pulled her up. He was up, streaming forth water, clinging to the stem of the great wisteria that grew against the wall, crushed against the wall by the water. Her head was above water, he held her arm till it seemed dislocated: but she could not get her footing. With a ghastly sickness like a dream, she struggled and struggled, and could not get her feet. Only his hand was locked on her wrist.

He dragged her nearer till her one hand caught his leg. He nearly went down again. But the wisteria held him, and he pulled her up to him. She clawed at him, horribly; and got to her feet, he hanging on like a man torn in two, to the wisteria trunk.

The water was above her knees. The man and she looked into each other's ghastly streaming faces.

'Get to the steps!' he screamed.

It was only just round the corner: four strides! She looked at him: she could not go. His eyes glared on her like a tiger's, and he pushed her from him. She clung to the wall, and the water seemed to abate a little. Round the corner she staggered, but staggering, reeled and was pitched up against the cornice of the balustrade of the porch steps, the man after her.

They got on to the steps, when another roar was heard amid the roar, and the wall of the house shook. Up heaved the water round their legs again, but the gipsy had opened the hall door. In they poured with the water, reeling to the stairs. And as they did so, they saw the short but strange bulk of Granny emerge in the hall, away down from the dining-room door. She had her hands lifted and clawing, as the first water swirled round her legs, and her coffin-like mouth was opened in a hoarse scream.

Yvette was blind to everything but the stairs. Blind, unconscious of everything save the steps rising beyond the water, she clambered up like a wet, shuddering cat, in a state of unconsciousness. It was not till she was on the landing, dripping and shuddering till she could not stand erect, clinging to the banisters, while the house shook and the water raved below, that she was aware of the sodden gipsy, in paroxysms of coughing at the head of the stairs, his cap gone, his black hair over his eyes, peering between his washed-down hair at the sickening heave of water below, in the hall. Yvette, fainting, looked too and saw Granny bob up, like a strange float, her face purple, her blind blue eyes bolting, spume hissing from her mouth. One old purple hand clawed at a banister rail, and held for a moment, showing the glint of a wedding ring.

The gipsy, who had coughed himself free and pushed back his hair, said to that awful float-like face below:

'Not good enough! Not good enough!'

With a low thud like thunder, the house was struck again, and shuddered, and a strange cracking, rattling, spitting noise began. Up heaved the water like a sea. The hand was gone, all sign of anything was gone, but upheaving water.

Yvette turned in blind unconscious frenzy, staggering like a wet cat to the upper staircase, and climbing swiftly. It was not till she was at the door of her room that she stopped, paralysed by the sound of a sickening, tearing crash, while the house swayed.

'The house is coming down!' yelled the green-white face of the gipsy, in her face.

He glared into her crazed face.

'Where is the chimney? the back chimney?—which room? The chimney will stand—'

He glared with strange ferocity into her face, forcing her to understand. And she nodded with a strange, crazed poise, nodded quite serenely, saying:

'In here! In here! It's all right.'

They entered her room, which had a narrow fire-place. It was a back room with two windows, one on each side the great chimney-flue. The gipsy, coughing bitterly and trembling in every limb, went to the window to look out.

Below, between the house and the steep rise of the hill, was a wild mill-race of water rushing with refuse, including Rover's green dog-kennel. The gipsy coughed and coughed, and gazed down blankly. Tree after tree went down, mown by the water, which must have been ten feet deep.

Shuddering and pressing his sodden arms on his sodden breast, a look of resignation on his livid face, he turned to Yvette. A fearful tearing noise tore the house, then there was a deep, watery explosion. Something had gone down, some part of the house, the floor heaved and wavered beneath them. For some moments both were suspended, stupefied. Then he roused.

'Not good enough! Not good enough! This will stand. This here will stand. See! that chimney! like a tower. Yes! All right! All right! You take your clothes off and go to bed. You'll die of the cold.'

'It's all right! It's quite all right!' she said to him, sitting on a chair and looking up into his face with her white, insane little face, round which the hair was plastered.

'No!' he cried. 'No! Take your things off and I'll rub you with this towel. I rub myself. If the house falls then die warm. If it don't fall, then live, not die of pneumonia.'

Coughing, shuddering violently, he pulled up his jersey hem and wrestled with all his shuddering, cold-racked might, to get off his wet, tight jersey.

'Help me!' he cried, his face muffled.

She seized the edge of the jersey, obediently, and pulled with all her might. The garment came over his head, and he stood in his braces.

'Take your things off! Rub with this towel!' he commanded ferociously, the savageness of the war on him. And like a thing obsessed, he pushed himself out of his trousers, and got out of his wet, clinging shirt, emerging slim and livid, shuddering in every fibre with cold and shock.

He seized a towel, and began quickly to rub his body, his teeth chattering like plates rattling together. Yvette dimly saw it was wise. She tried to get out of her dress. He pulled the horrible wet death-gripping thing off her, then, resuming his rubbing, went to the door, tip-toeing on the wet floor.

There he stood, naked, towel in hand, petrified. He looked west, towards where the upper landing window had been, and was looking into the sunset, over an insane sea of waters, bristling with uptorn trees and refuse. The end corner of the house where the porch had been, and the stairs, had gone. The wall had fallen, leaving the floors sticking out. The stairs had gone.

Motionless, he watched the water. A cold wind blew in upon him. He clenched his rattling teeth with a great effort of will, and turned into the room again, closing the door.

Yvette, naked, shuddering so much that she was sick, was trying to wipe herself dry.

'All right!' he cried. 'All right! The water don't rise no more! All right!'

With his towel he began to rub her, himself shaking all over, but holding her gripped by the shoulder, and slowly, numbedly rubbing her tender body, even trying to rub up into some dryness the pitiful hair of her small head.

Suddenly he left off.

'Better lie in the bed,' he commanded, 'I want to rub myself.'

His teeth went snap-snap-snap-snap, in great snaps, cutting off his words. Yvette crept shaking and semi-conscious into her bed. He, making strained efforts to hold himself still and rub himself warm, went again to the north window, to look out.

The water had risen a little. The sun had gone down, and there was a reddish glow. He rubbed his hair into a black, wet tangle, then paused for breath, in a sudden access of shuddering, then looked out again, then rubbed again on his breast, and began to cough afresh, because of the water he had swallowed. His towel was red: he had hurt himself somewhere: but he felt nothing.

There was still the strange huge noise of water, and the horrible bump of things bumping against the walls. The wind was rising with sundown, cold and hard. The house shook with explosive thuds, and weird, weird frightening noises came up.

A terror creeping over his soul, he went again to the door. The wind, roaring with the waters, blew in as he opened it.

Through the awesome gap in the house he saw the world, the waters, the chaos of horrible waters, the twilight, the perfect new moon high above the sunset, a faint thing, and clouds pushing dark into the sky, on the cold, blustery wind.

Clenching his teeth again, fear mingling with resignation, or fatalism, in his soul, he went into the room and closed the door, picking up her towel to see if it were drier than his own, and less blood-stained, again rubbing his head, and going to the window.

He turned away, unable to control his spasms of shivering. Yvette had disappeared right under the bedclothes, and nothing of her was visible but a shivering mound under the white quilt. He laid his hand on this shivering mound, as if for company. It did not stop shivering.

'All right!' he said. 'All right! Water's going down!'

She suddenly uncovered her head and peered out at him from a white face. She peered into his greenish, curiously calm face, semi-conscious. His teeth were chattering unheeded, as he gazed down at her, his black eyes still full of the fire of life and a certain vagabond calm of fatalistic resignation.

'Warm me!' she moaned, with chattering teeth. 'Warm me! I shall die of shivering.'

A terrible convulsion went through her curled-up white body, enough indeed to rupture her and cause her to die.

The gipsy nodded, and took her in his arms, and held her in a clasp like a vice, to still his own shuddering. He himself was shuddering fearfully, and only semi-conscious. It was the shock.

The vice-like grip of his arms round her seemed to her the only stable point in her consciousness. It was a fearful relief to her heart, which was strained to bursting. And though his body, wrapped round her strange and lithe and powerful, like tentacles, rippled with shuddering as an electric current, still the rigid tension of the muscles that held her clenched steadied them both, and gradually the sickening violence of the shuddering, caused by shock, abated, in his body first, then in hers, and the warmth revived between them. And as it roused, their tortured semi-conscious minds became unconscious, they passed away into sleep.

X

THE sun was shining in heaven before men were able to get across the Papple with ladders. The bridge was gone. But the flood had abated, and the house, that leaned forwards as if it were making a stiff bow to the stream, stood now in mud and wreckage, with a great heap of fallen masonry and debris at the south-west corner. Awful were the gaping mouths of rooms!

Inside, there was no sign of life. But across-stream the gardener had come to reconnoitre, and the cook appeared, thrilled with curiosity. She had escaped from the back door and up through the larches to the high-road, when she saw the gipsy bound past the house: thinking he was coming to murder somebody. At the little top gate she had found his cart standing. The gardener had led the horse away to the Red Lion up at Darley, when night had fallen.

This the men from Papplewick learned when at last they got across the stream with ladders, and to the back of the house. They were nervous, fearing a collapse of the building, whose front was all undetermined and whose back was choked up. They gazed with horror at the silent shelves of the rector's rows of books, in his torn-open study; at the big brass bedstead of Granny's room, the bed so deep and comfortably made, but one brass leg of the bedstead perching tentatively over the torn void; at the wreckage of the maid's room upstairs. The housemaid and the cook wept. Then a man climbed in cautiously through a smashed kitchen window, into the jungle and morass of the ground floor. He found the body of the old woman: or at least he saw her foot, in its flat black slipper, muddily protruding from a mud-heap of debris. And he fled.

The gardener said he was sure that Miss Yvette was not in the house. He had seen her and the gipsy swept away. But the policeman insisted on a search, and the Framley boys rushing up at last, the ladders were roped together. Then the whole party set up a loud yell. But without result. No answer from within.

A ladder was up, Bob Framley climbed, smashed a window, and clambered into Aunt Cissie's room. The perfect homely familiarity of everything terrified him like ghosts. The house might go down any minute.

They had just got the ladder up to the top floor, when men came running from Darley, saying the old gipsy had been to the Red Lion for the horse and cart, leaving word that his son had seen Yvette at the top of the house. But by that time the policeman was smashing the window of Yvette's room.

Yvette, fast asleep, started from under the bedclothes with a scream, as the glass flew. She clutched the sheets round her nakedness. The policeman uttered a startled yell, which he converted into a cry of: 'Miss Yvette! Miss Yvette!'

He turned round on the ladder and shouted to the faces below:

'Miss Yvette's in bed!—in bed!'

And he perched there on the ladder, an unmarried man, clutching the window in peril, not knowing what to do.

Yvette sat up in bed, her hair in a matted tangle, and stared with wild eyes, clutching up the sheets at her naked breast. She had been so very fast asleep, that she was still not there.

The policeman, terrified at the flabby ladder, climbed into the room, saying:

'Don't be frightened, Miss! Don't you worry any more about it. You're safe now.'

And Yvette, so dazed, thought he meant the gipsy. Where was the gipsy? This was the first thing in her mind. Where was her gipsy of this world's-end night?

He was gone! He was gone! And a policeman was in the room! A policeman!

She rubbed her hand over her dazed brow.

'If you'll get dressed, Miss, we can get you down to safe ground. The house is likely to fall. I suppose there's nobody in the other rooms?'

He stepped gingerly into the passage and gazed in terror through the torn-out end of the house, and far-off saw the rector coming down in a motor-car, on the sunlit hill.

Yvette, her face gone numb and disappointed, got up quickly, closing the bedclothes, and looked at herself a moment, then opened her drawers for clothing. She dressed herself, then looked in a mirror, and saw her matted hair with horror. Yet she did not care. The gipsy was gone, anyhow.

Her own clothes lay in a sodden heap. There was a great sodden place on the carpet where his had been, and two blood-stained filthy towels. Otherwise there was no sign of him.

She was tugging at her hair when the policeman tapped at her door. She called him to come in. He saw with relief that she was dressed and in her right senses.

'We'd better get out of the house as soon as possible, Miss,' he reiterated. 'It might fall any minute.'

'Really!' said Yvette calmly. 'Is it as bad as that?'

There were great shouts. She had to go to the window. There, below, was the rector, his arms wide open, tears streaming down his face.

'I'm perfectly all right, Daddy!' she said, with the calmness of her contradictory feelings. She would keep the gipsy a secret from him. At the same time, tears ran down her face.

'Don't you cry, Miss, don't you cry! The rector's lost his mother, but he's thanking his stars to have his daughter. We all thought you were gone as well, we did that!'

'Is Granny drowned?' said Yvette.

'I'm afraid she is, poor lady!' said the policeman, with a grave face.

Yvette wept away into her hanky, which she had had to fetch from a drawer.

'Dare you go down that ladder, Miss?' said the policeman.

Yvette looked at the sagging depth of it, and said promptly to herself: 'No! Not for anything!'—But then she remembered the gipsy's saying: 'Be braver in the body.'

'Have you been in all the other rooms?' she said, in her weeping, turning to the policeman.

'Yes, Miss! But you was the only person in the house, you know, save the old lady. Cook got away in time, and Lizzie was up at her mother's. It was only you and the poor old lady we was fretting about. Do you think you dare go down that ladder?'

'Oh, yes!' said Yvette, with indifference. The gipsy was gone anyway.

And now the rector in torment watched his tall, slender daughter slowly stepping backwards down the sagging ladder, the policeman, peering heroically from the smashed window, holding the ladder's top end.

At the foot of the ladder Yvette appropriately fainted in her father's arms, and was borne away with him, in the car, by

Bob, to the Framley home. There the poor Lucille, a ghost of ghosts, wept with relief till she had hysterics, and even Aunt Cissie cried out among her tears: 'Let the old be taken and the young spared! Oh, I *can't* cry for the Mater, now Yvette is spared!'

And she wept gallons.

The flood was caused by the sudden bursting of the great reservoir, up in Papple Highdale, five miles from the rectory. It was found out later that an ancient, perhaps even a Roman mine tunnel, unsuspected, undreamed of, beneath the reservoir dam, had collapsed, undermining the whole dam. That was why the Papple had been, for that last day, so uncannily full. And then the dam had burst.

The rector and the two girls stayed on at the Framleys', till a new home could be found. Yvette did not attend Granny's funeral. She stayed in bed.

Telling her tale, she only told how the gipsy had got her inside the porch, and she had crawled to the stairs out of the water. It was known that he had escaped: the old gipsy had said so, when he fetched the horse and cart from the Red Lion.

Yvette could tell little. She was vague, confused, she seemed hardly to remember anything. But that was just like her.

It was Bob Framley who said:

'You know, I think that gipsy deserves a medal.'

The whole family suddenly was struck.

'Oh, we *ought* to thank him!' cried Lucille.

The rector himself went with Bob in the car. But the quarry was deserted. The gipsies had lifted camp and gone, no one knew whither.

And Yvette, lying in bed, moaned in her heart: Oh, I love him! I love him! I love him! The grief over him kept her prostrate. Yet practically, she too was acquiescent in the fact of his disappearance. Her young soul knew the wisdom of it.

But after Granny's funeral, she received a little letter, dated from some unknown place.

'Dear miss, I see in the paper you are all right after your ducking, as is the same with me. I hope I see you again one day, maybe at Tideswell cattle fair, or maybe we come that way again. I come that day to say good-bye! and I never said it, well, the water give no time, but I live in hopes. Your obdt. servant Joe Boswell.'

And only then she realized that he had a name.

Albert Camus

THE OUTSIDER

1942

ALBERT CAMUS (1913–60) was an Algerian, a French citizen who grew up not in metropolitan France but in the harsh, penetrating sunlight of North Africa, where, as Cyril Connolly remarked, 'There is no eighteenth century, no baroque, no renaissance, no crusades or troubadours in the past of the Barbary Coast; nothing but the Roman Empire, decaying dynasties of Turk and Moor, the French Conquest and the imposition of the laws and commerce of the Third Republic on the ruins of Islam.' He had barely reached manhood when the Second World War began, and the German occupation of France, against which he kept up a courageous struggle as a member of the Resistance, was obviously a shaping influence on his mind. Both his first two novels could be seen as conveying in symbolic form his reaction, and the French reaction generally, to this colossal historical misfortune. The first, *L'Étranger* (*The Outsider*) takes a very ordinary man who finds himself, without premeditation and almost without volition, committing a murder; he is condemned to death for it, but his attitude throughout remains detached and almost uninterested, as if it were happening to someone else whom he has never met. *La Peste* (*The Plague*), which followed in 1947, depicts on the surface a city struck by an all-invading physical sickness, but once again the overtones are of life under the Occupation.

Like all writers who become much discussed in France, Camus had a 'philosophy' on which his works are predicated, in his case *une philosophie de l'absurde*, which seems to have been a slightly less nihilistic version of the Existentialism of Sartre and his followers. He expounded these beliefs in a volume of essays published in the same year as *The Outsider*, *Le Mythe de Sisyphe* (Sisyphus, in Greek mythology, is one of those tormented in Hades, his punishment being eternally to roll uphill a rock which unfailingly rolls down again).

In 1956 Camus published *La Chute*, translated into English the following year as *The Fall*, a short, intense novel loaded with symbolism and suggestion and having as its centre an unforgettable portrayal of a man struggling to find some way of living with a crushing load of guilt and remorse, felt both as his personally and as pertaining to the entire human species. Some commentators saw in this novel signs of a turning towards Christian ideas, though the author himself denied this.

Camus, a brilliant playwright as well as novelist, was awarded the Nobel Prize in 1957. His death provided an example of the Absurd at its most corrosive; he was killed in a meaningless road accident while being given a lift to the railway station.

PART ONE

I

MOTHER died today. Or, maybe, yesterday; I can't be sure. The telegram from the Home says: *Your mother passed away. Funeral tomorrow. Deep sympathy.* Which leaves the matter doubtful; it could have been yesterday.

The Home for Aged Persons is at Marengo, some fifty miles from Algiers. With the two-o'clock bus I should get there well before nightfall. Then I can spend the night there, keeping the usual vigil beside the body, and be back here by tomorrow evening. I have fixed up with my employer for two days' leave; obviously, under the circumstances, he couldn't refuse. Still, I had an idea he looked annoyed, and I said, without thinking: 'Sorry, sir, but it's not my fault, you know.'

Afterwards it struck me I needn't have said that. I had no reason to excuse myself; it was up to him to express his sympathy and so forth. Probably he will do so the day after tomorrow, when he sees me in black. For the present, it's almost as if Mother weren't really dead. The funeral will bring it home to one, put an official seal on it, so to speak. . . .

I took the two-o'clock bus. It was a blazing hot afternoon. I'd lunched, as usual, at Céleste's restaurant. Everyone was most kind, and Céleste said to me, 'There's no one like a mother.' When I left they came with me to the door. It was something of a rush, getting away, as at the last moment I had to call in at Emmanuel's place to borrow his black tie and mourning-band. He lost his uncle a few months ago.

I had to run to catch the bus. I suppose it was my hurrying like that, what with the glare off the road and from the sky, the reek of petrol and the jolts, that made me feel so drowsy. Anyhow, I slept most of the way. When I woke I was leaning up against a soldier; he grinned, and asked me if I'd come from a long way off, and I just nodded, to cut things short. I wasn't in a mood for talking.

The Home is a little over a mile from the village. I went there on foot. I asked to be allowed to see Mother at once, but the door-porter told me I must see the Warden first. He wasn't free, and I had to wait a bit. The porter chatted with me while I waited; then he led me to the office. The Warden was a very small man, with grey hair and a Legion of Honour rosette in his buttonhole. He gave me a long look with his watery blue eyes. Then we shook hands, and he held mine so long that I began to feel embarrassed. After that he consulted a register on his table, and said:

'Madame Meursault entered the Home three years ago. She had no private means and depended entirely on you.'

I had a feeling he was blaming me for something, and started to explain. But he cut me short.

'There's no need to excuse yourself, my boy. I've looked up the record and obviously you weren't in a position to see that she was properly cared for. She needed someone to be with her all the time, and young men in jobs like yours don't get too much pay. In any case she was much happier in the Home.'

I said: 'Yes, sir; I'm sure of that.'

Then he added: 'She had good friends here, you know, old folks like herself, and one gets on better with people of one's own generation. You're much too young, you couldn't have been much of a companion to her.'

That was so. When we lived together, Mother was always watching me, but we hardly ever talked. During her first few weeks at the Home she used to cry a good deal. But that was only because she hadn't settled down. After a month or two she'd have cried if she'd been told to leave the Home. Because this, too, would have been a wrench. That was why, during the last year, I seldom went to see her. Also, it would have meant losing my Sunday—not to mention the fag of going to the bus, getting my ticket, and spending two hours on the journey, each way.

The Warden went on talking, but I didn't pay much attention. Finally he said:

'Now, I suppose you'd like to see your mother?'

I rose without replying and he led the way to the door. As we were going down the stairs he explained:

'I've had the body moved to our little mortuary—so as not to upset the other old people, you understand. Every time there's a death here, they're in a nervous state for two or three days. Which means, of course, extra work and worry for our staff.'

We crossed a courtyard where there were a number of old men, talking amongst themselves in little groups. They fell silent as we came up with them. Then, behind our backs, the chattering began again. Their voices reminded me of parakeets in a cage, only the sound wasn't quite so shrill. The Warden stopped outside the entrance of a small, low building.

'So here I leave you, Monsieur Meursault. If you want me for anything, you'll find me in my office. We propose to have the funeral tomorrow morning. That will enable you to spend the night beside your mother's coffin, as no doubt you would wish to do. Just one more thing; I gathered from your mother's friends that she wished to be buried with the rites of the Church. I've made arrangements for this; but I thought I should let you know.'

I thanked him. So far as I knew, my mother, though not a professed atheist, had never given a thought to religion in her life.

I entered the mortuary. It was a bright, spotlessly clean room, with whitewashed walls and a big skylight. The furniture consisted of some chairs and trestles. Two of the latter stood open in the centre of the room and the coffin rested on them. The lid was in place, but the screws had been given only a few turns and their nickelled heads stuck out above the wood, which was stained dark walnut. An Arab woman, a nurse I supposed, was sitting beside the bier; she was wearing a blue smock and had a rather gaudy scarf wound round her hair.

Just then the porter came up behind me. He'd evidently been running, as he was a little out of breath.

'We put the lid on, but I was told to unscrew it when you came, so that you could see her.'

While he was going up to the coffin I told him not to trouble.

'Eh? What's that?' he exclaimed. 'You don't want me to . . .?'

'No,' I said.

He put back the screwdriver in his pocket and stared at me. I realized then that I shouldn't have said 'No', and it made me rather embarrassed. After eyeing me for some moments he asked:

'Why not?' But he didn't sound reproachful; he simply wanted to know.

'Well, really I couldn't say,' I answered.

He began twiddling his white moustache; then, without looking at me, said gently:

'I understand.'

He was a pleasant-looking man, with blue eyes and ruddy cheeks. He drew up a chair for me near the coffin, and seated himself just behind. The nurse got up and moved towards the door. As she was going by the porter whispered in my ear:

'It's a tumour she has, poor thing.'

I looked at her more carefully and I noticed that she had a bandage round her head, just below her eyes. It lay quite flat across the bridge of her nose, and one saw hardly anything of her face except that strip of whiteness.

As soon as she had gone, the porter rose.

'Now I'll leave you to yourself.'

I don't know whether I made some gesture, but instead of going he halted behind my chair. The sensation of someone posted at my back made me uncomfortable. The sun was getting low and the whole room was flooded with a pleasant mellow light. Two hornets were buzzing overhead, against the skylight. I was so sleepy I could hardly keep my eyes open. Without looking round I asked the porter how long he'd been at the Home. 'Five years.' The answer came so pat that one could have thought he'd been expecting my question.

That started him off, and he became quite chatty. If anyone had told him ten years ago that he'd end his days as door-porter at a Home at Marengo, he'd never have believed it. He was sixty-four, he said, and hailed from Paris.

When he said that, I broke in without thinking, 'Ah, you don't come from here?'

I remembered then that, before taking me to the Warden, he'd told me something about Mother. He said she'd have to be buried mighty quickly because of the heat in these parts, especially down in the plain. 'At Paris they keep the body for three days, sometimes four.' After that he mentioned that he'd spent the best part of his life in Paris, and could never manage to forget it. 'Here', he said, 'things have to go with a rush, like. You've hardly time to get used to the idea that somebody's dead, before you're hauled off to the funeral.' 'That's enough,' his wife put in. 'You didn't ought to say such things to the poor young gentleman.' The old fellow blushed and began to apologize. I told him it was quite all right. As a matter of fact I found it rather interesting, what he'd been telling me; I hadn't thought of that before.

Now he went on to say that he'd entered the Home as an ordinary inmate. But he was still quite hale and hearty, so when the porter's job fell vacant, he offered to take it on.

I pointed out that, even so, he was really an inmate like the others, but he wouldn't hear of it. He was 'an official, like.' I'd been struck before that by his habit of saying 'they' or, less often, 'them old folks,' when referring to inmates no older than himself. Still, I could see his point of view. As door-porter he had a certain standing, and some authority over the rest of them.

Just then the nurse returned. Night had fallen very quickly; all of a sudden, it seemed, the sky went black above the skylight. The porter switched on the lamps, and I was almost blinded by the blaze of light.

He suggested I should go to the refectory for dinner, but I wasn't hungry. Then he proposed bringing me a mug of *café au lait*. As I am very fond of *café au lait* I said 'Thanks', and a few minutes later he came back with a tray. I drank the coffee, and then I wanted a cigarette. But I wasn't sure if I should smoke, under the circumstances—in Mother's presence. I thought it over; really it didn't seem to matter, so I offered the porter a cigarette and we both smoked.

After a while he started talking again.

'You know, your mother's friends will be coming soon, to keep vigil with you beside the body. We always have a "vigil" here, when anyone dies. I'd better go and get some chairs and a pot of black coffee.'

The glare from the white walls was making my eyes smart, and I asked him if he couldn't turn off one of the lamps. 'Nothing doing,' he said. They'd arranged the lights like

that; either one had them all on or none at all. After that
I didn't pay much more attention to him. He went away,
brought some chairs and set them out round the coffin. On
one he placed a coffee-pot and ten or a dozen cups. Then he
sat down facing me, on the far side of Mother. The nurse was
at the other end of the room, with her back to me. I couldn't
see what she was doing, but by the way her arms moved I
guessed that she was knitting. I was feeling very comfortable;
the coffee had warmed me up, and through the open door
came scents of flowers, and breaths of cool night air. I think
I dozed off for a while.

I was awakened by an odd rustling in my ears. After having
had my eyes closed, I had a feeling that the light had grown
even stronger than before. There wasn't a trace of shadow
anywhere, and every object, each curve or angle, scored its
outline on one's eyes. The old people, Mother's friends, were
coming in. I counted ten in all, gliding almost soundlessly
through the bleak white glare. None of the chairs creaked
when they sat down. Never in my life had I seen anyone so
clearly as I saw these people; not a detail of their clothes or
features escaped me. And yet I couldn't hear them, and it was
hard to believe they really existed.

Nearly all the women wore aprons, and the strings drawn
tight round their waists made their big stomachs bulge still
more. I'd never yet noticed what big paunches old women
usually have. Most of the men, however, were thin as rakes,
and they all carried sticks. What struck me most about their
faces was that one couldn't see their eyes, only a dull glow in
a sort of nest of wrinkles.

On sitting down, they looked at me, and wagged their heads
awkwardly, sucking their lips in between their toothless gums.
I couldn't decide if they were greeting me and trying to say
something, or if it was due to some infirmity of age. I inclined
to think that they were greeting me, after their fashion, but
it had a queer effect, seeing all those old fellows grouped
round the porter, solemnly eyeing me and dandling their
heads from side to side. For a moment I had an absurd
impression that they had come to sit in judgement on me.

A few minutes later one of the women started weeping. She
was in the second row and I couldn't see her face because of

another woman in front. At regular intervals she emitted a little choking sob; one had a feeling she would never stop. The others didn't seem to notice. They sat in silence, slumped in their chairs, staring at the coffin or at their walking-sticks or any other object just in front of them, and never took their eyes off it. And still the woman sobbed. I was rather surprised, as I didn't know who she was. I wanted her to stop crying, but dared not speak to her. After a while the porter bent towards her and whispered in her ear; but she merely shook her head, mumbled something I couldn't catch, and went on sobbing as steadily as before.

The porter got up and moved his chair beside mine. At first he kept silent; then, without looking at me, he explained.

'She was devoted to your mother. She says your mother was her only friend in the world, and now she's all alone.'

I had nothing to say, and the silence lasted quite a while. Presently the woman's sighs and sobs became less frequent, and, after blowing her nose and snuffling for some minutes, she, too, fell silent.

I'd ceased feeling sleepy, but I was very tired and my legs were aching badly. And now I realized that the silence of these people was telling on my nerves. The only sound was a rather queer one; it came at longish intervals, and at first I was puzzled by it. However, after listening attentively, I guessed what it was; the old men were sucking at the insides of their cheeks, and this caused the odd, wheezing noises that had mystified me. They were so much absorbed in their thoughts that they didn't know what they were up to. I even had an impression that the dead body in their midst meant nothing at all to them. But now I suspect that I was mistaken about this.

We all drink the coffee, which the porter handed round. After that, I can't remember much; somehow the night went by. I can recall only one moment; I had opened my eyes and I saw the old men sleeping hunched up on their chairs, with one exception. Resting his chin on his hands clasped round his stick, he was staring hard at me, as if he had been waiting for me to wake. Then I fell asleep again. I woke up after a bit, because the ache in my legs had developed into a sort of cramp.

There was a glimmer of dawn above the skylight. A minute

or two later one of the old men woke up and coughed repeatedly. He spat into a big check handkerchief, and each time he spat it sounded as if he was retching. This woke the others, and the porter told them it was time to make a move. They all got up at once. Their faces were ashen-grey after the long, uneasy vigil. To my surprise each of them shook hands with me, as though this night together, in which we hadn't exchanged a word, had created a kind of intimacy between us.

I was quite done in. The porter took me to his room and I tidied myself up a bit. He gave me some more white coffee, and it seemed to do me good. When I went out the sun was up and the sky mottled red above the hills between Marengo and the sea. A morning breeze was blowing and it had a pleasant salty tang. There was the promise of a very fine day. I hadn't been in the country for ages, and I caught myself thinking what an agreeable walk I might have had, if it hadn't been for Mother.

As it was, I waited in the courtyard under a plane-tree. I sniffed the smells of the cool earth and found I wasn't sleepy any more. Then I thought of the other fellows in the office. At this hour they'd be getting up, preparing to go to work; for me this was always the worst hour of the day. I went on thinking, like this, for ten minutes or so; then the sound of a bell inside the building attracted my attention. I could see movements behind the windows; then all was calm again. The sun had risen a little higher and was beginning to warm my feet. The Porter came across the yard and said the Warden wished to see me. I went to his office and he got me to sign some document. I noticed that he was in black, with pin-stripe trousers. He picked up the telephone-receiver and looked at me.

'The undertaker's men arrived some moments ago, and they will be going to the mortuary to screw down the coffin. Shall I tell them to wait, for you to have a last glimpse of your mother?'

'No,' I said.

He spoke into the receiver, lowering his voice.

'That's all right, Figeac. Tell the men to go there now.'

He then informed me that he was going to attend the

funeral, and I thanked him. Sitting down behind his desk, he crossed his short legs and leant back. Besides the nurse on duty, he told me, he and I would be the only mourners at the funeral. It was a rule of the Home that inmates shouldn't attend funerals, though there was no objection to letting some of them sit up beside the coffin, the night before.

'It's for their own sakes,' he explained, 'to spare their feelings. But in this particular instance I've given permission for an old friend of your mother to come with us. His name is Thomas Pérez.' The Warden smiled. 'It's a rather touching little story in its way. He and your mother had become almost inseparable. The other old people used to tease Pérez about having a "fiancée". "When are you going to marry her?" they'd ask. He'd turn it with a laugh. It was a standing joke, in fact. So, you can guess, he feels very badly about your mother's death. I thought I couldn't decently refuse him permission to attend the funeral. But, on our medical officer's advice, I forbade him to sit up beside the body last night.'

For some time we stayed without speaking. Then the Warden got up and went to the window. Presently he said:

'Ah, there's the padre from Marengo. He's a bit ahead of time.'

He warned me that it would take us a good three-quarters of an hour, walking to the church, which was in the village. Then we went downstairs.

The priest was waiting just outside the mortuary door. With him were two acolytes, one of whom had a censer. The priest was stooping over him, adjusting the length of the silver chain on which it hung. When he saw us he straightened up and said a few words to me, addressing me as 'My son'. Then he led the way into the mortuary.

I noticed at once that four men in black were standing behind the coffin and the screws in the lid had now been driven home. At the same moment I heard the Warden remark that the hearse had arrived, and the priest started his prayers. Then everybody made a move. Holding a strip of black cloth, the four men approached the coffin, while the priest, the boys and myself filed out. A lady I hadn't seen before was standing by the door. 'This is Monsieur Meursault,' the Warden said to her. I didn't catch her name, but I gathered she was a nursing sister attached to the Home. When I was introduced, she bowed, without the trace of a smile on her long, gaunt face. We stood aside from the doorway to let the coffin by; then, following the bearers down a corridor, we came to the front entrance, where a hearse was waiting. Oblong, glossy, varnished black all over, it vaguely reminded me of the pen-trays in the office.

Beside the hearse stood a quaintly dressed little man, whose duty it was, I understood, to supervise the funeral, as a sort of master of ceremonies. Near him, looking constrained, almost bashful, was old M. Pérez, my mother's special friend. He wore a soft felt hat with a pudding-basin crown and a very wide brim—he whisked it off the moment the coffin emerged from the doorway—trousers that concertina'd on his shoes, a black tie much too small for his high white double-collar. Under a bulbous, pimply nose, his lips were trembling. But what caught my attention most was his ears; pendulous, scarlet ears that showed up like blobs of sealing-wax on the pallor of his cheeks and were framed in wisps of silky white hair.

The undertaker's factotum shepherded us to our places, with the priest in front of the hearse, and the four men in black on each side of it. The Warden and myself came next, and, bringing up the rear, old Pérez and the nurse.

The sky was already a blaze of light, and the air stoking up rapidly. I felt the first waves of heat lapping my back, and my dark suit made things worse. I couldn't imagine why we waited so long for getting under way. Old Pérez, who had put on his hat, took it off again. I had turned slightly in his direction and was looking at him when the Warden started telling me more about him. I remember his saying that old Pérez and my mother used often to have a longish stroll together in the cool of the evening; sometimes they went as far as the village, accompanied by a nurse, of course.

I looked at the countryside, at the long lines of cypresses sloping up towards the skyline and the hills, the hot red soil dappled with vivid green, and here and there a lonely house sharply outlined against the light—and I could understand Mother's feelings. Evenings in these parts must be a sort of mournful solace. Now, in the full glare of the morning sun, with everything shimmering in the heat-haze, there was something inhuman, discouraging, about this landscape.

At last we made a move. Only then I noticed that Pérez had a slight limp. The old chap steadily lost ground as the hearse gained speed. One of the men beside it, too, fell back and drew level with me. I was surprised to see how quickly the sun was climbing up the sky, and just then it struck me that for quite a while the air had been throbbing with the hum of insects and the rustle of grass warming up. Sweat was trickling down my face. As I had no hat I tried to fan myself with my handkerchief.

The undertaker's man turned to me and said something that I didn't catch. At the same time he wiped the crown of his head with a handkerchief that he held in his left hand, while with his right he tilted up his hat. I asked him what he'd said. He pointed upwards.

'Sun's pretty bad today, ain't it?'

'Yes,' I said.

After a while he asked: 'Is it your mother we're burying?'

'Yes,' I said again.

'What was her age?'

'Well, she was getting on.' As a matter of fact I didn't know exactly how old she was.

After that he kept silent. Looking back, I saw Pérez limping along some fifty yards behind. He was swinging his big felt hat at arm's length, trying to make the pace. I also had a look at the Warden. He was walking with carefully measured steps, economizing every gesture. Beads of perspiration glistened on his forehead, but he didn't wipe them off.

I had an impression that our little procession was moving slightly faster. Wherever I looked I saw the same sun-drenched countryside, and the sky was so dazzling that I dared not raise my eyes. Presently we struck a patch of freshly tarred road. A shimmer of heat played over it and one's feet squelched at each step, leaving bright black gashes. In front, the coachman's glossy black hat looked like a lump of the same sticky substance, poised above the hearse. It gave one a queer, dreamlike impression, that bluey-white glare overhead and all this blackness round one: the sleek black of the hearse, the dull black of the men's clothes and the silvery black gashes in the road. And then there were the smells, smells of hot leather and horse-dung from the hearse, veined with whiffs of incense-smoke. What with these and the hangover from a poor night's sleep, I found my eyes and thoughts growing blurred.

I looked back again. Pérez seemed very far away now, almost hidden by the heat-haze; then, abruptly, he disappeared altogether. After puzzling over it for a bit, I guessed that he had turned off the road into the fields. Then I noticed that there was a bend of the road a little way ahead. Obviously Pérez, who knew the district well, had taken a short cut, so as to catch us up. He rejoined us soon after we were round the bend; then began to lose ground again. He took another short cut and met us again farther on; in fact this happened several times during the next half-hour. But soon I lost interest in his movements; my temples were throbbing and I could hardly drag myself along.

After that everything went with a rush; and also with such precision and matter-of-factness that I remember hardly any details. Except that when we were on the outskirts of the village the nurse said something to me. Her voice took me by surprise, it didn't match her face at all; it was musical and slightly tremulous. What she said was: 'If one goes too slowly, there's the risk of a heat-stroke. But, if one goes too fast, one perspires, and the cold air in the church gives one a chill.' I saw her point; either way one was for it.

Some other memories of the funeral have stuck in my mind. The old boy's face, for instance, when he caught us up for the last time, just outside the village. His eyes were streaming with tears, of exhaustion or distress, or both together. But because of the wrinkles they couldn't flow down. They spread out, criss-crossed, and formed a sort of glaze over the old, worn face.

And I can remember the look of the church, the villagers in the street, the red geraniums on the graves, Pérez's fainting-fit—he crumpled up like a rag doll—the tawny red earth pattering on Mother's coffin, the bits of white roots mixed up with it; then more people, voices, the wait outside a café for the bus, the rumble of the engine, and my little thrill of pleasure when we entered the first brightly lit streets of Algiers, and I pictured myself going straight to bed and sleeping twelve hours at a stretch.

II

ON waking I understood why my employer had looked rather glum when I asked for my two days off; it was a Saturday today. I hadn't thought of this at the time; it only struck me when I was getting out of bed. Obviously he had seen that it would mean my getting four days' holiday straight off, and one couldn't expect him to like that. Still, for one thing, it wasn't my fault if Mother was buried yesterday and not today; and then, again, I'd have had my Saturday and Sunday off in any case. But naturally this didn't prevent me from seeing my employer's point.

Getting up was an effort, as I'd been really exhausted by the previous day's experiences. While shaving, I wondered how to spend the morning, and decided that a swim would do me good. So I caught the tram that goes down to the harbour.

It was quite like old times; a lot of young people were in the swimming-pool, amongst them Marie Cardona who used to be a typist at the office. I was rather keen on her in those days, and I fancy she liked me too. But she was with us so short a time that nothing came of it.

While I was helping her to climb on to a raft, I let my hand stray over her breasts. Then she lay flat on the raft, while I trod water. After a moment she turned and looked at me. Her hair was over her eyes and she was laughing. I clambered up on to the raft, beside her. The air was pleasantly warm and, half jokingly, I let my head sink back upon her lap. She didn't seem to mind, so I let it stay there. I had the sky full in my eyes, all blue and gold, and I could feel Marie's stomach rising and falling gently under my head. We must have stayed a good half-hour on the raft, both of us half asleep. When the sun got too hot she dived off and I followed. I caught her up, put my arm round her waist, and we swam side by side. She was still laughing.

While we were drying ourselves on the edge of the swimming-pool she said: 'I'm browner than you.' I asked her if she'd come to the cinema with me that evening. She laughed again and said 'Yes', if I'd take her to the comic everybody was talking about, the one with Fernandel in it.

When we had dressed, she stared at my black tie and asked if I was in mourning. I explained that my mother had died. 'When?' she asked, and I said, 'Yesterday.' She made no remark, though I thought she shrank away a little. I was just going to explain to her that it wasn't my fault, but I checked myself, as I remembered having said the same thing to my employer, and realizing then it sounded rather foolish. Still, foolish or not—somehow one can't help feeling a bit guilty, I suppose, about things like that.

Anyhow, by the evening Marie had forgotten all about it. The film was funny in parts, but much of it downright stupid. She pressed her leg against mine while we were in the picture-house, and I was fondling her breast. Towards the end of the show I kissed her, but rather clumsily. Afterwards she came back with me to my place.

When I woke up Marie had gone. She'd told me her aunt expected her first thing in the morning. I remembered it was a Sunday, and that put me off; I've never cared for Sundays. So I turned my head and lazily sniffed the smell of brine that Marie's head had left on the pillow. I slept until ten. After that I stayed in bed until noon, smoking cigarettes. I decided not to lunch at Céleste's restaurant as I usually did; they'd be sure to pester me with questions, and I dislike being questioned. So I fried some eggs, and ate them off the pan. I did without bread as there wasn't any left, and I couldn't be bothered going down to buy it.

After lunch I felt at a loose end and roamed about the little flat. It suited us well enough when Mother was with me, but now I was by myself it was too large and I'd moved the dining-table into my bedroom. That was now the only room I used; it had all the furniture I needed; a brass bedstead, a dressing-table, some cane chairs whose seats had more or less caved in, a wardrobe with a tarnished mirror. The rest of the flat was never used, so I didn't trouble to look after it.

A bit later, for want of anything to do, I picked up an old newspaper that was lying on the floor and read it. There was an advertisement for Kruschen Salts and I cut it out and pasted in into an album where I keep things that amuse me in the papers. Then I washed my hands and, as a last resource, went out on to the balcony.

My bedroom overlooks the main street of our district. Though it was a fine afternoon the paving-blocks were black and glistening. What few people were about seemed in an absurd hurry. First of all there came a family going for their Sunday afternoon walk; two small boys in sailor suits, with short trousers hardly down to their knees, and looking rather uneasy in their Sunday best; then a little girl with a big pink bow and black patent-leather shoes. Behind them was their mother, an enormously fat woman in a brown silk dress, and their father, a dapper little man, whom I knew by sight. He had a straw hat, a walking-stick, and a butterfly tie. Seeing him beside his wife, I understood why people said he came of a good family and had married beneath him.

Next came a group of young fellows, the local 'bloods', with sleek oiled hair, red ties, coats cut very tight at the waist, braided pockets, and square-toed shoes. I guessed they were going to one of the big cinemas in the centre of the town. That was why they had started out so early and were hurrying to the tram-stop, laughing and talking at the top of their voices.

After they had passed the street gradually emptied. By this time all the matinées must have begun. Only a few shopkeepers and cats remained about. Above the sycamores bordering the road the sky was cloudless, but the light was soft. The tobacconist on the other side of the street brought a chair out on to the pavement in front of his door and sat astride it, resting his arms on the back. The trams which a few minutes before had been crowded were now almost empty. In the little café, Chez Pierrot, beside the tobacconist's, the waiter was sweeping up the sawdust in the empty restaurant. A typical Sunday afternoon . . .

I turned my chair round and seated myself like the tobacconist, as it was more comfortable that way. After smoking a couple of cigarettes I went back to the room, got a tablet of chocolate and returned to the window to eat it. Soon after, the sky clouded over and I thought a summer storm was coming. However, the clouds gradually lifted. All the same they had left in the street a sort of threat of rain, which made it darker. I stayed watching the sky for quite a while.

At five there was a loud clanging of trams. They were coming from the stadium in our suburb where there had been a football match. Even the back platforms were crowded and people were standing on the steps. Then another tram brought back the teams. I knew they were the players by the little suitcase each man carried. they were bawling out their team-song, 'Keep the ball rolling, boys'. One of them looked up at me and shouted, 'We licked them!' I waved my hand and called back, 'Good work!' From now on there was a steady stream of private cars.

The sky had changed again; a reddish glow was spreading up beyond the housetops. As dusk set in the street grew more crowded. People were returning from their walks, and I noticed the dapper little man with the fat wife amongst the passers-by. Children were whimpering and trailing wearily after their parents. After some minutes the local cinemas disgorged their audiences. I noticed that the young fellows coming from them were taking longer strides and gesturing more vigorously than at ordinary times; doubtless the picture they'd been seeing was of the Wild West variety. Those who had been to the picture-houses in the middle of the town came a little later, and looked more sedate, though a few were still laughing. On the whole, however, they seemed languid and exhausted. Some of them remained loitering in the street under my window. A group of girls came by, walking arm in arm. The young men under my window swerved so as to brush against them, and shouted humorous remarks, which made the girls turn their heads and giggle. I recognised them as girls from my part of the town, and two or three of them, whom I knew, looked up and waved to me.

Just then the street-lamps came on, all together, and they made the stars that were beginning to glimmer in the night sky paler still. I felt my eyes getting tired, what with the lights and all the movement I'd been watching in the street. There were little pools of brightness under the lamps, and now and then a tramcar passed, lighting up a girl's hair, or a smile, or a silver bangle.

Soon after this, as the trams became fewer and the sky showed velvety black above the trees and lamps, the street grew emptier, almost imperceptibly, until a time came when there was nobody to be seen and a cat, the first of the evening, crossed unhurrying the deserted street.

It struck me that I'd better see about some dinner. I had been leaning so long on the back of my chair, looking down, that my neck hurt when I straightened myself up. I went down, bought some bread and spaghetti, did my cooking and ate my meal standing. I'd intended to smoke another cigarette at my window, but the night had turned rather chilly and I decided against it. As I was coming back, after shutting the window, I glanced at the mirror and saw reflected in it a corner of my table with my spirit-lamp and some bits of bread beside it. I occurred to me that somehow I'd got through another Sunday, that Mother now was buried, and tomorrow I'd be going back to work as usual. Really, nothing in my life had changed.

III

I HAD a busy morning in my office. My employer was in a good humour. He even inquired if I wasn't too tired, and followed it up by asking what Mother's age was. I thought a bit, then answered, 'Round about sixty', as I didn't want to make a blunder. At which he looked relieved—why I can't imagine—and seemed to think that closed the matter.

There was a pile of bills of lading waiting on my desk and I had to go through them all. Before leaving for lunch I washed my hands. I always enjoyed doing this at midday. In the evening it was less pleasant, as the roller-towel after being used by so many people was sopping wet. I once brought this to my employer's notice. It was regrettable, he agreed—but, to his mind, a mere detail. I left the office building a little later than usual, at half past twelve, with Emmanuel, who works in the Forwarding Department. Our building overlooks the sea, and we paused for a moment on the steps to look at the shipping in the harbour. The sun was scorching hot. Just then a big truck came up, with a din of chains and backfires from the engine, and Emmanuel suggested we should try to jump it. I started to run. The truck was well away, and we had to chase it for quite a distance. What with the heat and the noise from the engine, I felt half dazed. All I was conscious of was our mad rush along the water-front, amongst cranes and winches, with dark hulls of ships alongside and masts swaying in the offing. I was the first to catch up with the truck. I took a flying jump, landed safely, and helped Emmanuel to scramble in beside me. We were both of us out of breath and the bumps of the truck on the roughly laid cobbles made things worse. Emmanuel chuckled, and panted in my ear, 'We've made it!'

By the time we reached Céleste's restaurant we were dripping with sweat. Céleste was at his usual place beside the entrance, with his apron bulging on his paunch, his white moustache well to the fore. When he saw me he was sympathetic and 'hoped I wasn't feeling too badly.' I said 'No', but I was extremely hungry. I ate very quickly and had some coffee, to finish up. Then I went to my place and took a short nap, as I'd drunk a glass of wine too many. When I woke I smoked a cigarette before getting off my bed. I was a bit late and had to run for the tram. The office was stifling, and I was kept hard at it all afternoon. So it came as a relief when we closed down and I was strolling slowly along the wharves in the coolness. The sky was green, and it was pleasant to be out of doors after the stuffy office. However, I went straight home as I had to put some potatoes on to boil.

The hall was dark and, when I was starting up the stairs, I almost bumped into old Salamano, who lived on the same floor as I. As usual, he had his dog with him. For eight years the two had been inseparable. Salamano's spaniel is an ugly brute, afflicted with some skin disease—mange, I expect; anyhow it has lost all its hair and its body is covered with brown scabs. Perhaps through living in one small room, cooped up with his dog, Salamano has come to resemble it. His towy hair has gone very thin, and he has reddish blotches on his face. And the dog has developed something of its master's queer hunched-up gait; it always has its muzzle stretched far forward and its nose to the ground. But, oddly enough, though so much alike, they detest each other.

Twice a day at eleven and six, the old fellow takes his dog for a walk, and for eight years that walk has never varied. You can see them in the rue de Lyon, the dog pulling his master along as hard as he can, till finally the old chap misses a step and nearly falls. Then he beats his dog and calls it names.

The dog cowers and lags behind, and it's his master's turn to drag him along. Presently the dog forgets, starts tugging at the leash again, gets another hiding and more abuse. Then they halt on the pavement, the pair of them, and glare at each other; the dog with terror and the man with hatred in his eyes. Every time they're out this happens. When the dog wants to stop at a lamp-post, the old boy won't let him, and drags him on, and the wretched spaniel leaves behind him a trail of little drops. But, if he does it in the room, it means another hiding.

It's been going on like this for eight years, and Céleste always says it's a 'crying shame', and something should be done about it; but really one can't be sure. When I met him in the hall, Salamano was bawling at his dog, calling him a bastard, a lousy mongrel, and so forth, and the dog was whining. I said, 'Good evening', but the old fellow took no notice and went on cursing. So I thought I'd ask him what the dog had done. Again, he didn't answer, but went on shouting, 'You bloody cur!' and the rest of it. I couldn't see very clearly, but he seemed to be fixing something on the dog's collar. I raised my voice a little. Without looking round, he mumbled in a sort of suppressed fury: 'He's always in the way, blast him!' Then he started up the stairs, but the dog tried to resist and flattened itself out on the floor, so he had to haul it up on the leash, step by step.

Just then the man who lives on my floor came in from the street. The general idea hereabouts is that he's a pimp. But if one asks him what his job is, he says he's a warehouseman. One thing's sure: he isn't popular in our street. Still he often has a word for me, and drops in sometimes for a short talk in my room, because I listen to him. As a matter of fact, I find what he says quite interesting. So, really, I've no reason for freezing him off. His name is Sintès: Raymond Sintès. He's short and thick-set, has a nose like a boxer's, and always dresses very sprucely. He, too, once said to me, referring to Salamano, that it was 'a bloody shame', and asked me if I wasn't disgusted by the way the old man served his dog. I answered: 'No.'

We went up the stairs together, Sintès and I, and when I was turning in at my door, he said:

'Look here! How about having some grub with me? I've a black-pudding and some wine.'

It struck me that this would save my having to cook my dinner, so I said, 'Thanks very much.'

He, too, has only one room, and a little kitchen without a window. I saw a pink-and-white plaster angel above his bed, and some photos of sporting champions and naked girls pinned to the opposite wall. The bed hadn't been made and the room was dirty. He began by lighting a paraffin lamp; then fumbled in his pocket and produced a rather grimy bandage which he wrapped round his right hand. I asked him what the trouble was. He told me he'd been having a rough house with a fellow who'd annoyed him.

'I'm not one who looks for trouble,' he explained, 'only I'm a bit short-tempered. That fellow said to me, challenging, like, "Come down off that tram, if you're a man," I says, "You keep quiet, I ain't done nothing to you." Then he said I hadn't any guts. Well, that settled it. I got down off the tram and I said to him, "You better keep your mouth shut, or I'll shut it for you"—"I'd like to see you try!" says he. Then I gave him one across the face and laid him out good and proper. After a bit I started to help him to get up, but all he did was to kick at me from where he lay. So I gave him one with my knee and a couple more swipes. He was bleeding like a pig when I'd done with him. I asked him if he'd had enough, and said, "Yes."'

Sintès was busy fixing his bandage while he talked, and I was sitting on the bed.

'So you see,' he said, 'it wasn't my fault; he was asking for it, wasn't he?'

I nodded, and he added:

'As a matter of fact, I rather want to ask your advice about something; it's connected with this business. You've knocked about the world a bit, and I dare say you can help me. And then I'll be your pal for life; I never forget anyone who does me a good turn.'

When I made no comment, he asked me if I'd like us to be pals. I replied that I had no objection, and that appeared to satisfy him. He got out the black-pudding, cooked it in a frying-pan, then laid the table, putting out two bottles of wine. While he was doing this he didn't speak.

We started dinner, and then he began telling me the whole story, hesitating a bit at first.

'There's a girl behind it—as usual. We slept together pretty regular. I was keeping her, as a matter of fact, and she cost me a tidy sum. That fellow I knocked down is her brother.'

Noticing that I said nothing, he added that he knew what the neighbours said about him, but it was a filthy lie. He had his principles like everybody else, and a job in a warehouse.

'Well,' he said, 'to go on with my story. . . . I found out one day that she was letting me down.' He gave her enough money to keep her going, without extravagance, though; he paid the rent of her room and twenty francs a day for food. 'Three hundred francs for rent, and six hundred for her grub, with a little present thrown in now and then, a pair of stockings or what not. Say, a thousand francs a month. But that wasn't enough for my fine lady; she was always grumbling that she couldn't make both ends meet with what I gave. So one day I says to her, "Look here, why not get a job for a few hours a day? That'd make things easier for me, too. I bought you a new frock this month, I pay your rent and give you twenty francs a day. But you go and waste your money at the café with a pack of girls. You give them coffee and sugar. And of course the money comes out of my pocket. I treat you on the square, and that's how you pay me back." But she wouldn't hear of working, though she kept on saying she couldn't make do with what I gave her. And then one day I found out she was doing the dirty on me.'

He went on to explain that he'd discovered a lottery ticket in her bag, and, when he asked where the money'd come from to buy it, she wouldn't tell him. Then, another time he'd found a pawn-ticket for two bracelets which he'd never set eyes on before.

'So I knew there was dirty work going on, and I told her I'd nothing more to do with her. But, first, I gave her a good hiding, and I told her some home-truths. I said that there was only one thing interested her and that was getting into bed with men whenever she'd the chance. And I warned her straight, "You'll be sorry one day, my girl, and wish you'd got me back. All the girls in the street, they're jealous of your luck in having me to keep you." '

He'd beaten her till the blood came. Before that he'd never beaten her. 'Well, not hard, anyhow; only affectionately, like. She'd howl a bit, and I had to shut the window. Then, of course, it ended as per usual. But this time I'm done with her. Only to my mind, I ain't punished her enough. See what I mean?'

He explained that it was about this he wanted my advice. The lamp was smoking, and he stopped pacing up and down the room, to lower the wick. I just listened, without speaking. I'd had a whole bottle of wine to myself and my head was buzzing. As I'd used up my cigarettes I was smoking Raymond's. Some late trams passed, and the last noises of the street died off with them. Raymond went on talking. What bored him was that he had 'a sort of lech on her' as he called it. But he was quite determined to teach her a lesson.

His first idea, he said, had been to take her to a hotel, and then call in the special police. He'd persuade them to put her on the register as a 'common prostitute' and that would make her wild. Then he'd looked up some friends of his in the underworld, fellows who kept tarts for what they could make out of them, but they had practically nothing to suggest. Still, as he pointed out, that sort of thing should have been right up their street; what's the good of being in that line if you don't know how to treat a girl who's let you down? When he told them that, they suggested he should 'brand' her. But that wasn't what he wanted either. It would need a lot of thinking out. . . . But, first, he'd like to ask me something. Before he asked it, though, he'd like to have my opinion of the story he'd been telling, in a general way.

I said I hadn't any, but I'd found it interesting.

Did I think she really had done the dirty on him?

I had to admit it looked like that. Then he asked me if I didn't think she should be punished, and what I'd do if I were in his shoes. I told him one could never be quite sure how to act in such cases, but I quite understood his wanting her to suffer for it.

I drank some more wine, while Raymond lit another cigarette and began explaining what he proposed to do. He wanted to write her a letter, 'a real stinker, that'll get her on the raw', and at the same time make her repent of what she'd done. Then, when she came back, he'd go to bed with her and, just when she was 'properly primed up', he'd spit in her face and throw her out of the room. I agreed it wasn't a bad plan; it would punish her all right.

But, Raymond told me, he didn't feel up to writing the kind of letter that was needed, and that was where I could help. When I didn't say anything, he asked me if I'd mind doing it right away, and I said, 'No', I'd have a shot at it.

He drank off a glass of wine and stood up. Then he pushed aside the plates and the bit of cold pudding that was left, to make room on the table. After carefully wiping the oilcloth, he got a sheet of squared paper from the drawer of his bedside table; after that, an envelope, a small red wooden penholder and a square inkpot with purple ink in it. The moment he mentioned the girl's name I knew she was a Moor.

I wrote the letter. I didn't take much trouble over it, but I wanted to satisfy Raymond, as I'd no reason not to satisfy him. Then I read out what I'd written. Puffing at his cigarette, he listened, nodding now and then. 'Read it again, please,' he said. He seemed delighted. 'That's the stuff,' he chuckled. 'I could tell you was a brainy sort, old boy, and you know what's what.'

At first I hardly noticed that 'old boy'. It came back to me when he slapped me on the shoulder and said, 'So now we're pals, ain't we?' I kept silence and he said it again. I didn't care one way or the other, but as he seemed so set on it, I nodded and said, 'Yes.'

He put the letter in the envelope and we finished off the wine. Then both of us smoked for some minutes, without speaking. The street was quite quiet, except when now and again a car passed. Finally I remarked that it was getting late, and Raymond agreed. 'Time's gone mighty fast this evening,' he added, and in a way that was true. I wanted to be in bed, only it was such an effort making a move. I must have looked tired, for Raymond told me 'one mustn't let things get one down.' At first I didn't catch his meaning. Then he explained that he had heard of my mother's death; anyhow, he said, that was something bound to happen one day or another. I appreciated that, and told him so.

When I rose Raymond shook hands very warmly, remarking that men always understood each other. After
closing the door behind me I lingered for some moments
on the landing. The whole building was quiet as the grave,
a dank, dark smell rising from the well-hole of the stairs. I
could hear nothing but the blood throbbing in my ears, and
for a while I stood listening to it. Then the dog began to moan
in old Salamano's room, and through the sleep-bound house
the little plaintive sound rose slowly, like a flower growing out
of the silence and the darkness.

IV

I HAD a busy time in the office throughout the week.
Raymond dropped in once to tell me he'd sent off the
letter. I went to the pictures twice with Emmanuel, who
doesn't always understand what's happening on the screen
and asks one to explain it. Yesterday was Saturday, and Marie
came as we'd arranged. She had a very pretty dress, with red
and white stripes, and leather sandals, and I couldn't take my
eyes off her. One could see the outline of her firm little breasts,
and her sun-tanned face was like a velvety brown flower. We
took the bus and went to a beach I know, some miles out of
Algiers. It's just a strip of sand between two rocky spurs, with
a line of rushes at the back, along the tide-line. At four o'clock
the sun wasn't too hot, but the water was pleasantly tepid, and
small, languid ripples were creeping up the sand.

Marie taught me a new game. The idea was, while one
swam, to suck in the spray off the waves and, when one's
mouth was full of foam, to lie on one's back and spout it out
against the sky. It made a sort of frothy haze that melted into
the air or fell back in a warm shower on one's cheeks. But very
soon my mouth was smarting with all the salt I'd drawn in;
then Marie came up and hugged me in the water, and pressed
her mouth to mine. Her tongue cooled my lips, and we let the
waves roll us about for a minute or two before swimming back
to the beach.

When we had finished dressing, Marie looked hard at me.
Her eyes were sparkling. I kissed her; after that neither of
us spoke for quite a while. I pressed her to my side as we

scrambled up the foreshore. Both of us were in a hurry to catch the bus, get back to my place, and tumble on to the bed. I'd left my window open and it was pleasant to feel the cool night air flowing over our sunburnt bodies.

Marie said she was free next morning so I proposed she should have lunch with me. She agreed, and I went down to buy some meat. On my way back I heard a woman's voice in Raymond's room. A little later old Salamano started grumbling at his dog and presently there was a sound of boots and paws on the wooden stairs; then 'Filthy brute! Get on, you cur!' and the two of them went out into the street. I told Marie about the old chap's habits, and it made her laugh. She was wearing one of my pyjama suits, and had the sleeves rolled up. When she laughed I wanted her again. A moment later she asked me if I loved her. I said that sort of question had no meaning, really; but I supposed I didn't. She looked sad for a bit, but when we were getting our lunch ready she brightened up and started laughing, and when she laughs I always want to kiss her. It was just then that the row started in Raymond's room.

First we heard a woman saying something in a high-pitched voice; then Raymond bawling at her, 'You let me down, you bitch! I'll learn you to let me down!' There came some thuds, then a piercing scream—it made one's blood run cold—and in a moment there was a crowd of people on the landing. Marie and I went out to see. The woman was still screaming and Raymond still knocking her about. Marie said, wasn't it horrible! I didn't answer anything. Then she asked me to go and fetch a policeman, but I told her I didn't like policemen. However, one turned up presently; the lodger on the second floor, a plumber, came up with him. When he banged on the door the noise stopped inside the room. He knocked again and, after a moment, the woman started crying, and Raymond opened the door. He had a cigarette dangling from his underlip and a rather sickly smile, 'Your name?' Raymond gave his name. 'Take that cigarette out of your mouth when you're talking to me,' the policeman said gruffly. Raymond hesitated, glanced at me, and kept the cigarette in his mouth. The policeman promptly swung his arm and gave him a good hard smack on the left cheek. The cigarette shot from his lips and dropped a yard away. Raymond made a wry face, but said nothing for a moment. Then, in a humble tone he asked if he mightn't pick up his fag.

The officer said 'Yes,' and added: 'But don't you forget next time that we don't stand for any nonsense, not from blokes like you.'

Meanwhile the girl went on sobbing and repeating: 'He hit me, the coward. He's a pimp.'

'Excuse me, officer,' Raymond put in, 'but is that in order, calling a man a pimp in the presence of witnesses?'

The policeman told him to 'shut his trap'.

Raymond then turned to the girl. 'Don't you worry, my pet. We'll meet again.'

'That's enough,' the policeman said, and told the girl to go away. Raymond was to stay in his room till summoned to the police-station. 'You ought to be ashamed of yourself,' the policeman added, 'getting so tight you can't stand steady. Why, you're shaking all over!'

'I'm not tight,' Raymond explained. 'Only when I see you standing there and looking at me, I can't help trembling. That's only natural.'

Then he closed his door, and we all went away. Marie and I finished getting our lunch ready. But she hadn't any appetite, and I ate nearly all. She left at one, and then I had a nap.

Towards three there was a knock at my door and Raymond came in. He sat down on the edge of my bed and for a minute or two said nothing. I asked him how it had gone off. He said it had all gone quite smoothly at first, as per programme; only then she'd slapped his face and he'd seen red, and started thrashing her. As for what happened after that, he needn't tell me, as I was there.

'Well,' I said, 'you taught her a lesson all right, and that's what you wanted, isn't it?'

He agreed, and pointed out that whatever the police did, that wouldn't change the fact she'd had her punishment. As for the police, he knew exactly how to handle them. But he'd like to know if I'd expected him to return the blow when the policeman hit him.

I told him I hadn't expected anything whatsoever and, anyhow, I had no use for the police. Raymond seemed pleased and asked if I'd like to come out for a stroll with him. I got up from the bed and started brushing my hair. Then Raymond said that what he really wanted was for me to act as his witness. I told him I had no objection; only I didn't know what he expected me to say.

'It's quite simple,' he replied. 'You've only got to tell them that the girl had let me down.'

So I agreed to be his witness.

We went out together and Raymond stood me a brandy in a café. Then we had a game of billiards; it was a close game and I lost by only a few points. After that he proposed going to a brothel, but I refused; I didn't feel like it. As we were walking slowly back he told me how pleased he was at having paid out his mistress so satisfactorily. He made himself extremely amiable to me and I quite enjoyed our walk. When we were nearly home I saw old Salamano on the doorstep; he seemed very excited. I noticed that his dog wasn't with him. He was turning like a teetotum, looking in all directions, and sometimes peering into the darkness of the hall with his little bloodshot eyes. Then he'd mutter something to himself and start gazing up and down the street again.

Raymond asked him what was wrong, but he didn't answer at once. Then I heard him grunt, 'The bastard! The filthy cur!' When I asked him where his dog was, he scowled at me and snapped out, 'Gone!' A moment later, all of a sudden, he launched out into it.

'I'd taken him to the Parade Ground as usual. There was a fair on, and one could hardly move for the crowd. I stopped at one of the booths to look at the Handcuff King. When I turned to go, the dog was gone. I'd been meaning to get a smaller collar, but I never thought the brute could slip it and get away like that.'

Raymond assured him the dog would find its way home, and told him stories of dogs that had travelled miles and miles to get back to their masters. But this seemed to make the old fellow even more worried than before.

'Don't you understand, they'll do away with him; the police, I mean. It's not likely anyone will take him in and look after him; with all those scabs he puts everybody off.'

I told him that there was a pound at the police station, where stray dogs are taken. His dog was certain to be there, and he could get it back on payment of a small charge. He asked me how much the charge was, but there I couldn't help him. Then he flew into a rage again.

'Is it likely I'd give money for a tyke like that? No bloody fear! They can kill him for all I care.' And he went on calling his dog the usual names.

Raymond gave a laugh and turned into the hall. I followed him upstairs and we parted on the landing. A minute or two later I heard Salamano's footsteps and a knock on my door.

When I opened it, he halted for a moment in the doorway.

'Excuse me . . . I hope I'm not disturbing you.'

I asked him in, but he shook his head. He was staring at his toe-caps, and the gnarled old hands were trembling. Without meeting my eyes, he started talking.

'They won't really take him from me, will they, Monsieur Meursault? Surely they wouldn't do a thing like that. If they do—I don't know what will become of me.'

I told him that, so far as I knew, they kept stray dogs in the pound for three days, waiting for their owners to call for them. After that they disposed of the dogs as they thought fit.

He stared at me in silence for a moment, then said, 'Good evening.' After that I heard him pacing up and down his room for quite a while. Then his bed creaked. Through the wall there came to me a little wheezing sound, and I guessed that he was weeping. For some reason, I don't know what, I began thinking of Mother. But I had to get up early next day; so as I wasn't feeling hungry, I did without supper, and went straight to bed.

V

RAYMOND rang me up at the office. He said that a friend of his—to whom he'd spoken about me—invited me to spend next Sunday at his little seaside bungalow just outside Algiers. I told him I'd have been delighted; only I had promised to spend Sunday with a girl. Raymond promptly replied that she could come, too. In fact, his friend's wife would be very pleased not to be the only woman in a party of men.

I'd have liked to hang up at once, as my employer doesn't approve of one's using the office phone for private calls. But Raymond asked me to hold on; he had something else to tell me, and that was why he'd rung me up, though he could have waited till the evening to pass on the invitation.

'It's like this,' he said. 'I've been shadowed all the morning by some Arabs. One of them's the brother of that girl I had the row with. If you see him hanging round the house when you came back, pass me the word.'

I promised to do so.

Just then, my employer sent for me. For a moment I felt uneasy as I expected he was going to tell me to stick to my work and not to waste time chattering with friends over the phone. However, it was nothing of the kind. He wanted to discuss a project he had in view, though so far he'd come to no decision. It was to open a branch at Paris, so as to be able to deal with the big companies on the spot, without postal delays, and he wanted to know if I'd like a post there.

'You're a young man,' he said, 'and I'm pretty sure you'd enjoy living in Paris. And, of course, you could travel about France for some months in the year.'

I told him I was quite prepared to go; but really I didn't care much one way or the other.

He then asked if a 'change of life', as he called it, didn't appeal to me, and I answered that one never changed one's real life; anyhow one life was as good as another and my present one suited me quite well.

At this he looked rather hurt, and told me that I always shilly-shallied, and that I lacked ambition—a grave defect, to his mind, when one was in business.

I returned to my work. I'd have preferred not to vex him, but I saw no reason for 'changing my life'. By and large it wasn't an unpleasant one. As a student I'd had plenty of ambition of the kind he meant. But, when I had to drop my studies, I very soon realized all that was pretty futile.

Marie came that evening and asked me if I'd marry her. I said I didn't mind; if she was keen on it, we'd get married.

Then she asked me again if I loved her, I replied, much as before, that her question meant nothing or next to nothing—but I supposed I didn't.

'If that's how you feel,' she said, 'why marry me?'

I explained that it had no importance really but, if it would give her pleasure, we could get married right away. I pointed out that anyhow the suggestion came from her; as for me, I'd merely said 'Yes.'

Then she remarked that marriage was a serious matter.

To which I answered: 'No.'

She kept silent after that, staring at me in a curious way. Then she asked:

'Suppose another girl had asked you to marry her—I mean, a girl you liked in the same way as you like me—would you have said "Yes" to her, too?'

'Naturally.'

Then she said she wondered if she really loved me or not. I, of course, couldn't enlighten her as to that. And, after another silence, she murmured something about my being 'a queer fellow'. 'And I dare say that's why I love you,' she added. 'But maybe that's why one day I'll come to hate you.'

To which I had nothing to say, so I said nothing.

She thought for a bit, then started smiling, and, taking my arm, repeated that she was in earnest; she really wanted to marry me.

'All right,' I answered. 'We'll get married whenever you like.' I then mentioned the proposal made by my employer and Marie said she'd love to go to Paris.

When I told her I'd lived in Paris for a while, she asked me what it was like.

'A dingy sort of town, to my mind. Masses of pigeons and dark courtyards. And the people have washed-out, white faces.'

Then we went for a walk all the way across the town by the main streets. The women were good-lookers, and I asked Marie if she, too, noticed this. She said 'Yes' and that she saw what I meant. After that we said nothing for some minutes. However, as I didn't want her to leave me, I suggested we should dine together at Céleste's. She'd have loved to dine with me, she said, only she was booked up for the evening. We were near my place, and I said, '*Au revoir*, then.'

She looked me in the eyes.

'Don't you want to know what I'm doing this evening?'

I did want to know, but I hadn't through of asking her, and I guessed she was making a grievance of it. I must have looked embarrassed, for suddenly she started laughing and bent towards me, pouting her lips for a kiss.

I went by myself to Céleste's. When I had just started my dinner an odd-looking little woman came in and asked if she might sit at my table. Of course she might. She had a chubby face like a ripe apple, bright eyes, and moved in a curiously jerky way as if she were on wires. After taking off her close-fitting jacket she sat down and started studying the bill of fare with a sort of rapt attention. Then she called Céleste and gave her order, very fast but quite distinctly; one didn't lose a word. While waiting for the *hors d'oeuvre* she opened her bag, took out a slip of paper and a pencil, and added up the bill in advance. Diving into her bag again, she produced a purse and took from it the exact sum plus a small tip, and placed it on the cloth in front of her.

Just then the waiter brought the *hors d'oeuvre*, which she proceeded to wolf down voraciously. While waiting for the next course, she produced another pencil, this time a blue one, from her bag, and the radio magazine for the coming week, and started making ticks against almost all the items of the daily programmes. There were a dozen pages in the magazine and she continued studying them closely throughout the meal. When I'd finished mine she was still ticking off items with the same meticulous attention. Then she rose, put on her jacket again with the same abrupt, robot-like gestures, and walked briskly out of the restaurant.

Having nothing better to do, I followed her for a short distance. Keeping on the kerb of the pavement, she walked straight ahead, never swerving or looking back, and it was extraordinary how fast she covered the ground, considering her smallness. In fact, the pace was too much for me, and I soon lost sight of her and turned back homewards. For a moment the 'little robot' (as I thought of her) had much impressed me, but I soon forgot about her.

As I was turning in at my door I ran into old Salamano. I asked him into my room, and he informed me that his dog was definitely lost. He'd been to the pound to inquire, but it wasn't there, and the staff told him it had probably been run over. When he asked them whether it was any use inquiring about it at the police station, they said the police had more important things to attend to than keeping records of stray dogs run over in the streets. I suggested he should get another dog, but, reasonably enough, he pointed out that he'd become used to this one, and it wouldn't be the same thing.

I was seated on my bed, with my legs up, and Salamano on a chair beside the table, facing me, his hands spread on his knees. He had kept on his battered felt hat and was mumbling away behind his draggled yellowish moustache. I found him rather boring, but I had nothing to do and didn't feel sleepy. So, to keep the conversation going, I asked some questions about his dog—how long he had had it and so forth. He told me he had got it soon after his wife's death. He'd married rather late in life. When a young man, he'd wanted to go on the stage; during his military service he'd often played in the regimental theatricals and acted rather well, so everybody said. However, finally, he had taken a job in the railway, and he didn't regret it, as now he had a small pension. He and his wife had never hit it off very well, but they'd got used to each other, and when she died he felt lonely. One of his mates on the railway whose bitch had just had pups, had offered him one, and he had taken it, as a companion. He'd had to feed it from the bottle at first. But, as a dog's life is shorter than a man's they'd so to speak grown old together.

'He was a cantankerous brute,' Salamano said. 'Now and then we had some proper set-tos, he and I. But he was a good tyke all the same.'

I said he looked well bred, and that evidently pleased the old man.

'Ah, but you should have seen him before his illness!' he said. 'He had a wonderful coat; in fact, that was his best point really. I tried hard to cure him; every mortal night after he got that skin disease I rubbed an ointment in. But his real trouble was old age, and there's no curing that.'

Just then I yawned, and the old chap said he'd better make a move. I told him he could stay, and that I was sorry about what had happened to his dog. He thanked me, and mentioned that my mother had been fond of his dog. He referred to her as 'your poor mother', and was afraid I must be feeling her death terribly. When I said nothing he added hastily and with a rather embarrassed air that some of the people in the street said nasty things about me because I'd sent my mother to the Home. But he, of course, knew better; he knew how devoted to my mother I had always been.

I answered—why, I still don't know—that is surprised me to learn I'd produced such a bad impression. As I couldn't afford to keep her here, it seemed the obvious thing to do, to send her to a Home. 'In any case,' I added, 'for years she'd never had a word to say to me, and I could see she was moping, with no one to talk to.'

'Yes,' he said 'and at a Home one makes friends, anyhow.'

He got up, saying it was high time for him to be in bed, and added that life was going to be a bit of a problem for him, under the new conditions. For the first time since I'd known him he held out his hand to me—rather shyly, I thought—and I could feel the scales on his skin. Just as he was going out of the door, he turned and, smiling a little, said:

'Let's hope the dogs won't bark again tonight. I always think it's mine I hear. . . .'

VI

IT was an effort waking up that Sunday morning; Marie had to jog my shoulders and shout my name. As we wanted to get into the water early, we didn't trouble about breakfast. My head was aching slightly and my first cigarette had a bitter taste. Marie told me I looked like a mourner at a funeral, and I certainly did feel very limp. She was wearing a white dress and had her hair loose. I told her she looked quite ravishing like that, and she laughed happily.

On our way out we banged on Raymond's door, and he shouted that he'd be with us in a jiffy. We went down to the street and, because of my being rather under the weather and our having kept the blind down in my room, the glare of the morning sun hit me in the eyes like a clenched fist.

Marie, however, was almost dancing with delight, and kept repeating, 'What a heavenly day!' After a few minutes I was feeling better, and noticed that I was hungry. I mentioned this to Marie but she paid no attention. She was carrying an oilcloth bag in which she had stowed our bathing kit and towel. Presently we heard Raymond shutting his door. He was wearing blue trousers, a short-sleeved white shirt, and a straw hat. I noticed that his forearms were rather hairy, but the skin was very white beneath. The straw hat made Marie giggle. Personally, I was rather put off by his get-up. He seemed in high spirits and was whistling as he came down the stairs. He greeted me with, 'Hullo, old boy!' and addressed Marie as 'Mademoiselle'.

On the previous evening we had visited the police station, where I gave evidence for Raymond—about the girl's having been false to him. So they let him off with a warning. They didn't check my statement.

After some talk on the doorstep we decided to take the bus. The beach was within easy walking distance, but the sooner we got there the better. Just as we were starting for the bus stop, Raymond plucked my sleeve and told me to look across the street. I saw some Arabs lounging against the tobacconist's window. They were staring at us silently, in the special way these people have—as if we were blocks of stone or dead trees. Raymond whispered that the second Arab from the left was 'his man', and I thought he looked rather worried. However, he assured me that all that was ancient history. Marie, who hadn't followed his remarks, asked, 'What is it?'

I explained that those Arabs across the way had a grudge against Raymond. She insisted on our going at once. Then Raymond laughed, and squared his shoulders. The young lady was quite right, he said. There was no point in hanging about here. Half-way to the bus stop he glanced back over his shoulder and said the Arabs weren't following. I, too, looked back. They were exactly as before, gazing in the same vague way at the spot where we had been.

When we were in the bus, Raymond, who now seemed quite at ease, kept making jokes to amuse Marie. I could see he was attracted by her, but she had hardly a word for him. Now and again she would catch my eye and smile.

We alighted just outside Algiers. The beach is not far from the bus stop; one has only to cross a patch of high land, a sort of plateau, which overlooks the sea and shelves down steeply to the sands. The ground here was covered with yellowish pebbles and wild lilies that showed snow-white against the blue of the sky, which had already the hard metallic glint it gets on very hot days. Marie amused herself swishing her bag against the flowers and sending the petals showering in all directions. Then we walked between two rows of little houses with wooden balconies and green or white palings. Some of them were half-hidden in clumps of tamarisks; others rose naked from the stony plateau. Before we came to the end of it, the sea was in full view; it lay smooth as a mirror, and in the distance a big headland jutted out over its black reflection. Through the still air came the faint buzz of a motor-engine and we saw a fishing-boat very far out, gliding almost imperceptibly across the dazzling smoothness.

Marie picked some rock-irises. Going down the steep path leading to the sea, we saw some bathers already on the sands.

Raymond's friend owned a small wooden bungalow at the near end of the beach. Its back rested against the cliff-side, while the front stood on piles, which the water was already lapping. Raymond introduced us to his friend, whose name was Masson. He was tall, broad-shouldered and thick-set; his wife was a plump, cheerful little woman, who spoke with a Paris accent.

Masson promptly told us to make ourselves at home. He had gone out fishing, he said, first thing in the morning, and there would be fried fish for lunch. I congratulated him on his little bungalow, and he said he always spent his week-ends and holidays here. 'With the missus, needless to say,' he added. I glanced at her, and noticed that she and Marie seemed to be getting on well together; laughing and chattering away. For the first time, perhaps, I seriously considered the possibility of my marrying her.

Masson wanted to have a swim at once, but his wife and Raymond were disinclined to move. So only the three of us, Marie, Masson, and myself, went down to the beach. Marie promptly plunged in, but Masson and I waited for a bit. He was rather slow of speech and had, I noticed, a habit of saying 'and what's more' between his phrases—even when the second added nothing really to the first. Talking of Marie, he said: 'She's an awfully pretty girl, and, what's more, charming.'

But I soon ceased paying attention to this trick of his; I was basking in the sunlight which, I noticed, was making me feel much better. The sand was beginning to stoke up under-foot and, though I was eager for a dip, I postponed it for a minute or two more. At last I said to Masson: 'Shall we go in now?' and plunged. Masson walked in gingerly and only began to swim when he was out of his depth. He swam hand over hand and made slow headway, so I left him behind and caught up Marie. The water was cold and I felt all the better for it. We swam a long way out, Marie and I side by side, and it was pleasant feeling how our movements matched, hers and mine, and how we were both in the same mood, enjoying every moment.

Once we were out in the open, we lay on our backs and, as I gazed up at the sky, I could feel the sun drawing up the film of salt water on my lips and cheeks. We saw Masson swim back to the beach and slump down on the sand under the sun. In the distance he looked enormous, like a stranded whale. Then Marie proposed that we should swim tandem. She went ahead and I put my arms round her waist from behind, and while she drew me forward with her arm-strokes, I kicked out behind to help us on.

That sound of little splashes had been in my ears for so long that I began to feel I'd had enough of it. So I let go of Marie and swam back at an easy pace, taking long, deep breaths. When I made the beach I stretched myself belly-downwards beside Masson, resting my face on the sand. I told him 'it was fine' here and he agreed. Presently Marie came back. I raised my head to watch her approach. She was glistening with brine and holding her hair back. Then she lay down beside me and what with the combined warmth of our bodies and the sun, I felt myself dropping off to sleep.

After a while Marie tugged my arm and said Masson had gone to his place; it must be nearly lunch-time. I rose at once, as I was feeling hungry, but Marie told me I hadn't kissed her once since the early morning. That was so—though I'd wanted to, several times. 'Let's go into the water again,' she said, and we ran into the sea and lay flat amongst the ripples for a moment. Then we swam a few strokes and when we were almost out of our depth she flung her arms round me and hugged me. I felt her legs twining round mine, and my senses tingled.

When we got back, Masson was on the steps of his bungalow, shouting to us to come. I told him I was ravenously hungry, and he promptly turned to his wife and said he'd taken quite a fancy to me. The bread was excellent, and I had my full share of the fish. Then came some steak and chips. None of us spoke while eating. Masson drank a lot of wine and kept refilling my glass the moment it was empty. By the time coffee was handed round I was feeling slightly muzzy, and I started smoking one cigarette after another. Masson, Raymond, and I discussed a plan of spending the whole of August on the beach together, sharing expenses.

Suddenly Marie exclaimed: 'I say! Do you know the time? It's only half past eleven!'

We were all surprised at that, and Masson remarked that we'd had a very early lunch, but really lunch was a movable feast, one had it when one felt like it.

This set Marie laughing. I don't know why. I suspect she'd drunk a bit too much.

Then Masson asked if I'd like to come with him for a stroll on the beach.

'My wife always has a nap after lunch,' he said. 'Personally I find it doesn't agree with me; what I need is a short walk. I'm always telling her it's much better for the health. But of course she's entitled to her own opinion.'

Marie proposed to stay and help with the washing-up. Mme Masson smiled and said that, in that case, the first thing was to get the men out of the way. So we went out together, the three of us.

The light was almost vertical and the glare from the water seared one's eyes. The beach was quite deserted now. One could hear a faint tinkle of knives and forks and crockery in the shacks and bungalows lining the foreshore. Heat was welling up from the rocks and one could hardly breathe.

At first Raymond and Masson talked of things and people I didn't know. I gathered that they'd been acquainted for some time and had even lived together for a while. We went down to the water's edge and walked along it; now and then a longer wave wetted our canvas shoes. I wasn't thinking of anything, as all that sunlight beating down on my bare head made me feel half asleep.

Just then Raymond said something to Masson that I didn't quite catch. But at the same moment I noticed two Arabs in blue dungarees a long way down the beach, coming in our direction. I gave Raymond a look and he nodded, saying, 'That's him.' We walked steadily on. Masson wondered how they'd managed to track us here. My impression was that they had seen us taking the bus and noticed Marie's oilcloth bathing-bag; but I didn't say anything.

Though the Arabs walked quite slowly they were much nearer already. We didn't change our pace, but Raymond said:

'Listen! If there's a rough house, you, Masson, take on the second one. I'll tackle the fellow who's after me. And you, Meursault, stand by to help if another one comes up, and lay him out.'

I said, 'Right', and Masson put his hands in his pockets.

The sand was hot as fire and I could have sworn it was glowing red. The distance between us and the Arabs was steadily decreasing. When we were only a few steps away the Arabs halted. Masson and I slowed down, while Raymond went straight up to his man. I couldn't hear what he said, but I saw the native lowering his head, as if to butt him in the chest. Raymond lashed out promptly and shouted to Masson to come. Masson went up to the man he had been marking and struck him twice with all his might. The fellow fell flat into the water and stayed there some seconds with bubbles coming up to the surface round his head. Meanwhile Raymond had been slogging the other man, whose face was streaming with blood. He glanced at me over his shoulder and shouted:

'Just you watch! I ain't finished with him yet!'

'Look out!' I cried. 'He's got a knife.'

I spoke too late. The man had gashed Raymond's arm and his mouth as well.

Masson sprang forward. The other Arab got up from the water and placed himself behind the fellow with the knife. We didn't dare to move. The two natives backed away slowly, keeping us at bay with the knife and never taking their eyes off us. When they were at a safe distance they swung round and took to their heels. We stood stock still, with the sunlight beating down on us. Blood was dripping from Raymond's wounded arm, which he was squeezing hard above the elbow.

Masson remarked that there was a doctor who always spent his Sundays here, and Raymond said: 'Good. Let's go to him at once.' He could hardly get the words out as the blood from his other wound made bubbles in his mouth.

We each gave him an arm and helped him back to the bungalow. Once we were there he told us the wounds weren't so very deep and he could walk to where the doctor was. Marie had gone quite pale, and Mme Masson was in tears.

Masson and Raymond went off to the doctor's while I was left behind at the bungalow to explain matters to the women. I didn't much relish the task and soon dried up and started smoking, staring at the sea.

Raymond came back at about half past one, accompanied by Masson. He had his arm bandaged and a strip of sticking-plaster on the corner of his mouth. The doctor assured him it was nothing serious, but he was looking very glum. Masson tried to make him laugh, but without success.

Presently Raymond said he was going for a stroll on the beach. I asked him where he proposed to go and he mumbled something about 'wanting to take the air'. We—Masson and I—then said we'd go with him, but he flew into a rage and told us to mind our own business. Masson said we mustn't insist, seeing the state he was in. However, when he went out, I followed him.

It was like a furnace outside, with the sunlight splintering into flakes of fire on the sand and sea. We walked for quite a while, and I had an idea that Raymond had a definite idea where he was going; but probably I was mistaken about this.

At the end of the beach we came to a small stream that had cut a channel in the sand, after coming out from behind a biggish rock. There we found our two Arabs again, lying on the sand in their blue dungarees. They looked harmless enough, as if they didn't bear any malice, and neither made any move when we approached. The man who had slashed Raymond stared at him without speaking. The other man was blowing down a little reed and extracting from it three notes of the scale, which he played over and over again, while he watched us from the corner of an eye.

For a while nobody moved; it was all sunlight and silence except for the tinkle of the stream and those three little lonely sounds. Then Raymond put his hand to his revolver-pocket, but the Arabs still didn't move. I noticed that the man playing on the reed had his big toes splayed out almost at right angles to his feet.

Still keeping his eyes on his man, Raymond said to me: 'Shall I plug him one?'

I thought quickly. If I told him not to, considering the mood he was in, he might very well fly into a temper and use his gun. So I said the first thing that came into my head.

'He hasn't spoken to you yet. It would be a low-down trick to shoot him like that, in cold blood.'

Again, for some moments one heard nothing but the tinkle of the stream and the flute-notes weaving through the hot, still air.

'Well,' Raymond said at last, 'if that's how you feel, I'd better say something insulting, and if he answers back I'll loose off.'

'Right,' I said. 'Only, if he doesn't get out his knife you've no business to fire.'

Raymond was beginning to fidget. The Arab with the reed went on playing, and both of them watched all our movements.

'Listen,' I said to Raymond. 'You take on the fellow on the right, and give me your revolver. If the other one starts making trouble or gets out his knife, I'll shoot.'

The sun glinted on Raymond's revolver as he handed it to me. But nobody made a move yet; it was just as if everything had closed in on us so that we couldn't stir. We could only watch each other, never lowering our eyes; the whole world seemed to have come to a standstill on this little strip of sand between the sunlight and the sea, the twofold silence of the reed and stream. And just then it crossed my mind that one might fire, or not fire—and it would come to absolutely the same thing.

Then, all of a sudden, the Arabs vanished; they'd slipped like lizards under cover of the rock. So Raymond and I turned and walked back. He seemed happier, and began talking about the bus to catch for our return.

When we reached the bungalow Raymond promptly went up the wooden steps, but I halted on the bottom one. The light seemed thudding in my head and I couldn't face the effort needed to go up the steps and make myself amiable to the women. But the heat was so great that it was just as bad staying where I was, under that flood of blinding light falling from the sky. To stay, or to make a move—it came to much the same. After a moment I returned to the beach, and started walking.

There was the same red glare as far as the eye could reach, and small waves were lapping the hot sand in little, flurried gasps. As I slowly walked towards the boulders at the end of the beach I could feel my temples swelling under the impact of the light. It pressed itself upon me, trying to check my progress. And each time I felt a hot blast strike my forehead, I gritted my teeth, I clenched my fists in my trouser-pockets and keyed up every nerve to fend off the sun and the dark befuddlement it was pouring into me. Whenever a blade of vivid light shot upwards from a bit of shell or broken glass lying on the sand, my jaws set hard. I wasn't going to be beaten, and I walked steadily on.

The small black hump of rock came into view far down the beach. It was rimmed by a dazzling sheen of light and feathery spray, but I was thinking of the cold, clear stream behind it, and longing to hear again the tinkle of running water. Anything to be rid of the glare, the sight of women in tears, the strain and effort—and to retrieve the pool of shadow by the rock and its cool silence!

But when I came nearer I saw that Raymond's Arab had returned. He was by himself this time, lying on his back, his hands behind his head, his face shaded by the rock while the sun beat on the rest of his body. One could see his dungarees steaming in the heat. I was rather taken aback; my impression had been that the incident was closed, and I hadn't given a thought to it on my way here.

On seeing me the Arab raised himself a little, and his hand went to his pocket. Naturally, I gripped Raymond's revolver in the pocket of my coat. Then the Arab let himself sink back again, but without taking his hand from his pocket. I was some distance off, at least ten yards, and most of the time I saw him as a blurred dark form wobbling in the heat-haze. Sometimes, however, I had glimpses of his eyes glowing between the half-closed lids. The sound of the waves was even lazier, feebler, than at noon. But the light hadn't changed; it was pounding fiercely as ever on the long stretch of sand that ended at the rock. For two hours the sun seemed to have made no progress; becalmed in a sea of molten steel. Far out on the horizon a steamer was passing; I could just make out from the corner of an eye the small black moving patch, while I kept my gaze fixed on the Arab.

It struck me that all I had to do was to turn, walk away, and think no more about it. But the whole beach, pulsing with heat, was pressing on my back. I took some steps towards the stream. The Arab didn't move. After all, there was still some distance between us. Perhaps because of the shadow on his face, he seemed to be grinning at me.

I waited. The heat was beginning to scorch my cheeks, beads of sweat were gathering in my eyebrows. It was just the same sort of heat as at my mother's funeral, and I had the same disagreeable sensations—especially in my forehead, where all the veins seemed to be bursting through the skin. I couldn't stand it any longer, and took another step forward. I knew it was a fool thing to do; I shouldn't get out of the sun by moving on a yard or so. But I took that step, just one step, forward. And then the Arab drew his knife and held it up towards me, athwart the sunlight.

A shaft of light shot upwards from the steel, and I felt as if a long, thin blade transfixed my forehead. At the same moment all the sweat that had accumulated in my eyebrows splashed down on my eyelids, covering them with a warm film of moisture. Beneath a veil of brine and tears my eyes were blinded: I was conscious only of the cymbals of the sun clashing on my skull, and, less distinctly, of the keen blade of light flashing up from the knife, scarring my eyelashes, and gouging into my eyeballs.

Then everything began to reel before my eyes, a fiery gust came from the sea, while the sky cracked in two, from end to end, and a great sheet of flame poured down through the rift. Every nerve in my body was a steel spring, and my grip closed on the revolver. The trigger gave, and the smooth underbelly of the butt jogged my palm. And so, with that crisp, whip-crack sound, it all began. I shook off my sweat and the clinging veil of light. I knew I'd shattered the balance of the day, the spacious calm of this beach on which I had been happy. But I fired four shots more into the inert body, on which they left no visible trace. And each successive shot was another loud, fateful rap on the door of my undoing.

PART TWO

I

I WAS questioned several times immediately after my arrest. But they were all formal examinations, as to my identity and so forth. At the first of these, which took place at the police station, nobody seemed to take much interest in the case. However, when I was brought before the examining magistrate a week later, I noticed that he eyed me with distinct curiosity. Like the others, he began by asking my name, address and occupation, the date and place of my birth. Then he inquired if I had chosen a lawyer to defend me. I answered 'No,' I hadn't thought about it and asked him if it was really necessary for me to have one. 'Why do you ask that?' he replied. I replied that I regarded my case as very simple. He smiled. 'Well, it may seem so to you. But we've got to abide by the law, and, if you don't engage a lawyer, the Court will have to appoint one for you.'

It struck me as an excellent arrangement that the authorities should see to details of this kind, and I told him so. He nodded, and agreed that the Code was all that could be desired.

At first I didn't take him quite seriously. The room in which he interviewed me was much like an ordinary sitting-room, with curtained windows and a single lamp standing on the desk. Its light fell on the armchair in which he'd had me sit, while his own face stayed in shadow.

I had read descriptions of such scenes in books, and at first it all seemed like a game. After our conversation, however, I had a good look at him. He was a tall man with clean-cut features, deep-set blue eyes, a big grey moustache and abundant, almost snow-white hair, and he gave me the impression of being highly intelligent and, on the whole, likeable enough. There was only one thing that put one off: his mouth had now and then a rather ugly twist; but it seemed to be only a sort of nervous *tic*. When leaving, I very nearly held out my hand and said 'Good-bye'; just in time I remembered that I'd killed a man.

Next day a lawyer came to my cell; a small, plump, youngish man with sleek black hair. In spite of the heat—I was in my shirt-sleeves—he was wearing a dark suit, stiff collar, and a rather showy tie, with broad black and white stripes. After depositing his brief-case on my bed, he introduced himself, and added that he'd perused the record of my case with the utmost care. His opinion was that it would need cautious handling, but there was every prospect of my getting off, provided I followed his advice. I thanked him, and he said: 'Good. Now let's get down to it.'

Sitting on the bed, he said that they'd been making investigations into my private life. They had learnt that my mother died recently in a Home. Inquiries had been conducted at Marengo and the police informed that I'd shown 'great callousness' at my mother's funeral.

'You must understand,' the lawyer said, 'that I don't relish having to question you about such a matter. But it has much importance and, unless I find some way of answering the charge of "callousness", I shall be handicapped in conducting your defence. And that is where you, and only you, can help me.'

He went on to ask me if I had felt grief on that 'sad occasion'. The question struck me as an odd one; personally I'd have been much embarrassed by having to ask anyone a thing like that.

I answered that in recent years I'd rather lost the habit of noting my feelings, and hardly knew what to answer. I could truthfully say I'd been quite fond of Mother—but really that didn't mean much. All normal people, I added, as an afterthought, had more or less desired the death of those they loved, at some time or another.

Here the lawyer interrupted me, looking greatly perturbed.

'You must promise me not to say anything of that sort at the trial, or to the examining magistrate.'

I promised, to satisfy him; but I explained that my physical condition at any given moment often influenced my feelings. For instance, on the day I attended Mother's funeral, I was fagged out and only half awake. So really I hardly took stock of what was happening. Anyhow I could assure him of one thing: that I'd rather Mother hadn't died.

The lawyer, however, looked displeased. 'That's not enough,' he said curtly.

After considering for a bit he asked me if he could say that on that day I had kept my feelings under control.

'No,' I said. 'That wouldn't be true.'

He gave me a queer look, as if I slightly revolted him; then informed me, in an almost hostile tone, that in any case the Head of the Home and some of the staff would be cited as witnesses.

'And that might do you a very nasty turn,' he concluded.

When I suggested that Mother's death had no connexion with the charge against me he merely replied that this remark showed I'd never had any dealings with the Law.

Soon after this he left, looking quite vexed. I wished he had stayed longer and I could have explained that I desired his sympathy, not for him to make a better job of my defence but, if I might put it so, spontaneously. I could see that I got on his nerves; he couldn't make me out and, naturally enough, this irritated him. Once or twice I had a mind to assure him that I was just like everybody else; quite an ordinary person. But really that would have served no great purpose, and I let it go—out of laziness as much as anything else.

Later in the day I was taken again to the examining magistrate's office. It was two in the afternoon and, this time, the room was flooded with light—there was only a thin curtain on the window—and extremely hot.

After inviting me to sit down, the magistrate informed me in a very polite tone that, 'owing to unforeseen circumstances', my lawyer was unable to be present. I should be quite entitled, he added, to reserve my answers to his questions until my lawyer could attend.

To this I replied that I could answer for myself. He pressed a bell-push on his desk and young clerk came in and seated himself just behind me. Then we—I and the magistrate—settled back in our chairs and the examination began. He led off by remarking that I had the reputation of being a taciturn, rather self-centred person, and he'd like to know what I had to say to that. I answered:

'Well, I rarely have anything much to say. So naturally I keep my mouth shut.'

He smiled as on the previous occasion, and agreed that that was the best of reasons. 'In any case,' he added, 'it has little or no importance.'

After a short silence he suddenly leant forward, looked me in the eyes and said, raising his voice a little:

'What really interests me is—you!'

I wasn't quite clear what he meant, so I made no comment.

'There are several things,' he continued, 'that puzzle me, about your crime. I feel sure that you will help me to understand them.'

When I replied that really it was quite simple, he asked me to give him an account of what I'd done that day. As a matter of fact I had already told him at our first interview—in a summary sort of way, of course—about Raymond, the beach, our swim, the fight, then the beach again, and the five shots I'd fired. But I went over it all again, and after each phrase he nodded. 'Quite so, quite so.' When I described the body lying on the sand, he nodded more emphatically, and said 'Good!'

Personally I was tired of repeating the same story; I felt as if I'd never talked so much in all my life before.

After another silence he stood up and said he'd like to help me; I interested him and, with God's help, he would do something for me in my trouble. But, first, he must put a few more questions.

He began by asking bluntly if I'd loved my mother.

'Yes,' I replied, 'like everybody else.' The clerk behind me, who had been typing away at a steady pace, must just then have hit the wrong keys, as I heard him pushing the carriage back and crossing something out.

Next, without any apparent logical connexion, the magistrate sprang another question.

'Why did you fire five consecutive shots?'

I thought for a bit; then explained that they weren't quite consecutive. I fired one at first, and the other four after a short interval.

'Why did you pause between the first and second shot?'

I seemed to see it hovering again before my eyes, the red glow of the beach, and to feel that fiery breath on my cheeks—and, this time, I made no answer.

During the silence which followed, the magistrate kept fidgeting, running his fingers through his hair, half rising, then sitting down again. Finally, planting his elbows on the desk, he bent towards me with a queer expression.

'But why, *why* did you go on firing at a prostrate man?'

Again I found nothing to reply.

The magistrate drew his hand across his forehead and repeated in a slightly different tone:

'I ask you "*Why?*" I insist on your telling me.'

I still kept silent.

Suddenly he rose, walked to a file cabinet standing against the opposite wall, pulled a drawer open, and took from it a silver crucifix, which he was waving as he came back to the desk.

'Do you know who this is?' His voice had changed completely; it was vibrant with emotion.

'Of course I do,' I answered.

That seemed to start him off; he began speaking at a great pace. He told me he believed in God, and that even the worst of sinners could obtain forgiveness of Him. But first he must repent, and become like a little child, with a simple, trustful heart, open to conviction. He was leaning right across the table brandishing his crucifix before my eyes.

As a matter of fact I had great difficulty in following his remarks as, for one thing, the office was so stifling hot and big flies were buzzing round and settling on my cheeks; also because he rather alarmed me. Of course I realized it was absurd to feel like this, considering that, after all, it was I who was the criminal. However, as he continued talking, I did my best to understand, and I gathered that there was only one point in my confession that badly needed clearing up—the fact that I'd waited before firing a second time. All the rest was, so to speak, quite in order; but this completely baffled him.

I started to tell him that he was wrong in insisting on this; the point was of quite minor importance. But, before I could get the words out, he had drawn himself up to his full height, and was asking me very earnestly if I believed in God. When I said 'No', he plumped down into his chair indignantly.

That was unthinkable, he said; all men believe in God, even those who reject Him. Of this he was absolutely sure; if ever he came to doubt it, his life would lose all meaning. 'Do you wish', he asked indignantly, 'my life to have no meaning?' Really I couldn't see how my wishes came into it, and I told him as much.

While I was talking, he thrust the crucifix again just under my nose and shouted: 'I, anyhow, am a Christian. And I pray Him to forgive you for your sins. My poor young man, how can you not believe that He suffered for your sake?'

I noticed that his manner seemed genuinely solicitous when he said, 'My poor young man'—but I was beginning to have enough of it. The room was growing steadily hotter.

As I usually do when I want to get rid of someone whose conversation bores me, I pretended to agree. At which, rather to my surprise, his face lit up.

'You see! You see! Now won't you own that you believe and put your trust in Him?'

I must have shaken my head again, for he sank back in his chair looking limp and dejected.

For some moments there was a silence during which the typewriter, which had been clicking away all the time we talked, caught up with the last remark. Then he gazed at me intently and rather sadly.

'Never in all my experience have I known a soul so case-hardened as yours,' he said in a low tone. 'All the criminals who have come before me until now wept when they saw this symbol of our Lord's sufferings.'

I was on the point of replying that was precisely because they *were* criminals. But then I realized that I, too, came under that description. Somehow it was an idea to which I never could get reconciled.

To indicate, presumably, that the interview was over, the magistrate stood up. In the same weary tone he asked me a last question: Did I regret what I had done?

After thinking a bit, I said that what I felt was less regret than a kind of vexation—I couldn't find a better word for it. But he didn't seem to understand. This was as far as things went at that day's interview.

I came before the magistrate many times more, but on these occasions my lawyer always accompanied me. The examinations were confined to asking me to amplify my previous statements. Or else the magistrate and my lawyer discussed technicalities. At such times they took very little notice of me and, in any case, the tone of the examinations changed as time went on. The magistrate seemed to have lost interest in me, and to have come to some sort of decision about my case. He never mentioned God again or displayed any of the religious fervour I had found so embarrassing at our first interview. The result was that our relations became more cordial. After a few questions, followed by an exchange of remarks with my lawyer, the magistrate closed the interview. My case was 'taking its course,' as he put it. Sometimes, too, the conversation was of a general order and the magistrate and lawyer encouraged me to join in it. I began to breathe more freely. Neither of the two men, at these times, showed the least hostility towards me, and everything went so smoothly, so amiably, that I had an absurd impression of being 'one of the family'. I can honestly say that during the eleven months these examinations lasted I got so used to them that I was almost surprised at having ever enjoyed anything better than those rare moments when the magistrate, after escorting me to the door of the office, would pat my shoulder and say in a friendly tone: 'Well, Mr Antichrist, that's all for the present!' After which I was made over to my warders.

II

THERE are some things of which I've never cared to talk. And, a few days after I'd been sent to prison, I decided that this phase of my life was one of them. However, as time went by, I came to feel that this aversion had no real substance. In point of fact, during those first few days I was hardly conscious of being in prison; I had always a vague hope that something would turn up, some agreeable surprise.

The change came soon after Marie's first and only visit. From the day when I got her letter telling me they wouldn't let her come to see me any more, because she wasn't my wife—it was from that day I realized that this cell was my last home, a dead end, as one says.

On the day of my arrest they put me in a biggish room with several other prisoners, mostly Arabs. They grinned when they saw me enter, and asked me what I'd done. I told them I'd killed an Arab, and they kept mum for a while. But presently night began to fall, and one of them explained to me how to lay out my sleeping-mat. By rolling up one end one makes a sort of bolster. All night I felt bugs crawling over my face.

Some days later I was put by myself in a cell, where I slept on a plank bed hinged to the wall. The only other furniture was a latrine bucket and a tin basin. The prison stands on rising ground, and through my little window I had glimpses of the sea. One day when I was hanging on the bars, straining my eyes towards the sunlight playing on the waves, a warder entered and said I had a visitor. I thought it must be Marie, and so it was.

To go to the Visitors' Room, I was taken along a corridor, then up a flight of steps, then along another corridor. It was a very large room, lit by a big bow-window, and divided into three compartments by high iron grilles running transversely.

Between the two grilles there was a gap of some thirty feet, a sort of no-man's-land between the prisoners and their friends. I was led to a point exactly opposite Marie, who was wearing her striped dress. On my side of the rails were about a dozen other prisoners, Arabs for the most part. On Marie's side were mostly Moorish women. She was wedged between a small old woman with tight-set lips, and a fat matron, without a hat, who was talking shrilly and gesticulated all the time. Because of the distance between the visitors and prisoners I found I, too, had to raise my voice.

When I came into the room the babel of voices echoing on the bare walls, and the sunlight streaming in, flooding everything in a harsh white glare, made me feel quite dizzy. After the relative darkness and the silence of my cell it took me some moments to get used to these conditions. After a bit, however, I came to see each face quite clearly, lit up as if a spotlight played on it.

I noticed a prison official seated at each end of the no-man's-land between the grilles. The native prisoners and their relations on the other side were squatting opposite each other. They didn't raise their voices and, in spite of the din, managed to converse almost in whispers. This murmur of voices coming from below made a sort of accompaniment to the conversations going on above their heads. I took stock of all this very quickly, and moved a step forward towards Marie. She was pressing her brown, sun-tanned face to the bars and smiling as hard as she could. I thought she was looking very pretty, but somehow couldn't bring myself to tell her so.

'Well?' she asked, pitching her voice very high. 'What about it? Are you all right, have your everything you want?'

'Oh, yes. I've everything I want.'

We were silent for some moments; Marie went on smiling. The fat woman was bawling at the prisoner beside me, her husband presumably, a tall, fair, pleasant-looking man.

'Jeanne refused to have him,' she yelled.—'That's just too bad,' the man replied.—'Yes, and I told her you'd take him back the moment you get out; but she wouldn't hear of it.'

Marie shouted across the gap that Raymond sent me his best wishes, and I said, 'Thanks.' But my voice was drowned by my neighbour's asking, 'if he was quite fit'. The fat woman gave a laugh. 'Fit? I should say he is! The picture of health.'

Meanwhile the prisoner on my left, a youngster with thin, girlish hands, never said a word. His eyes, I noticed were fixed on the little old woman opposite him, and she returned his gaze with a sort of hungry passion. But I had to stop looking at them as Marie was shouting to me that we mustn't lose hope.

'Certainly not,' I answered. My gaze fell on her shoulders and I had a sudden longing to squeeze them, through the thin dress. Its silky texture fascinated me, and I had a feeling that the hope she spoke of centred on it somehow. I imagine something of the same sort was in Marie's mind, for she went on smiling, looking straight at me.

'It'll all come right, you'll see, and then we shall get married.'

All I could see of her now was the white flash of her teeth, and the little puckers round her eyes. I answered: 'Do you really think so?' but chiefly because I felt it up to me to answer something.

She started talking very fast in the same high-pitched voice.

'Yes, you'll be acquitted, and we'll go bathing again, Sundays.'

The woman beside Marie was still yelling away, telling her husband that she'd left a basket for him in the prison office. She gave a list of the things she'd brought and told him to mind and check them carefully, as some had cost quite a lot. The youngster on my other side and his mother were still gazing mournfully at each other, and the murmur of the Arabs droned on below us. The light outside seemed to be surging up against the window, seeping through, and smearing the faces of the people facing it with a coat of yellow oil.

I began to feel slightly squeamish, and wished I could leave. The strident voice beside me was jarring on my ears. But, on the other hand, I wanted to have the most I could of Marie's company. I've no idea how much time passed. I remember Marie's describing to me her work, with that set smile always on her face. There wasn't a moment's let-up in the noise—shouts, conversations, and always that muttering undertone. The only oasis of silence was made by the young fellow and the old dame gazing into each other's eyes.

Then, one by one, the Arabs were led away; almost everyone fell silent when the first one left. The little old woman pressed herself against the bars and at the same moment a warder tapped her son's shoulder. He called '*Au revoir*, Mother,' and, slipping her hand between the bars, she gave him a small, slow wave with it.

No sooner was she gone than a man, hat in hand, took her place. A prisoner was led up to the empty place beside me, and the two started a brisk exchange of remarks—not loud, however, as the room had become relatively quiet. Someone came and called away the man on my right and his wife shouted at him—she didn't seem to realize it was no longer necessary to shout—'Now, mind you look after yourself, dear, and don't do anything rash!'

My turn came next. Marie threw me a kiss. I looked back as I walked away. She hadn't moved; her face was still pressed to the rails, her lips still parted in that tense, twisted smile.

Soon after this I had a letter from her. And it was then that the things I've never liked to talk about began. Not that they were particularly terrible; I've no wish to exaggerate and I suffered less than others. Still, there was one thing in those early days that was really irksome: my habit of thinking like a free man. For instance, I would suddenly be seized with a desire to go down to the beach for a swim. And merely to have imagined the sound of ripples at my feet, and then the smooth feel of the water on my body as I struck out, and the wonderful sensation of relief it gave, brought home still more cruelly the narrowness of my cell.

Still, that phase lasted a few months only. Afterwards, I had prisoner's thoughts. I waited for the daily walk in the courtyard, or a visit from my lawyer. As for the rest of the time, I managed quite well, really. I've often thought that had I been compelled to live in the trunk of a dead tree, with nothing to do but gaze up at the patch of sky just overhead, I'd have got used to it by degrees. I'd have learnt to watch for the passing of birds or drifting clouds, as I had come to watch for my lawyer's odd neckties, or,

in another world, to wait patiently till Sunday for a spell of
love-making with Marie. Well, here anyhow, I wasn't penned
in a hollow tree-trunk. There were others in the world worse
off than I was. I remembered it had been one of Mother's pet
ideas—she was always voicing it—that in the long run one gets
used to anything.

Usually, however, I didn't think things out so far. Those
first months were trying, of course; but the very effort I had
to make helped me through them. For instance, I was plagued
by the desire for a woman—which was natural enough,
considering my age. I never thought of Marie especially. I
was obsessed by thoughts of this woman or that, of all the ones
I'd had, all the circumstances under which I'd loved them; so
much so that the cell grew crowded with their faces, ghosts of
my old passions. That unsettled me, no doubt; but, at least, it
served to kill time.

I gradually became quite friendly with the chief gaoler, who
went the rounds with the kitchen-hands at meal-times. It was
he who brought up the subject of women. 'That's what the
men here grumble about most,' he told me. I said I felt like
that myself. 'There's something unfair about it,' I added, 'like
hitting a man when he's down.'—'But that's the whole point
of it,' he said; 'that's why you fellows are kept in prison.'—'I
don't follow.'—'Liberty,' he said, 'means that. You're being
deprived of your liberty.' It had never before struck me in
that light, but I saw his point. 'That's true,' I said. 'Otherwise
it wouldn't be a punishment.' The gaoler nodded. 'Yes, you're
different, you can use your brains. The others can't. Still,
those fellows find a way out; they do it by themselves.' With
which remark the gaoler left my cell. Next day I did like the
others.

The lack of cigarettes, too, was a trial. When I was brought
to the prison, they took away my belt, my shoe-laces, and the
contents of my pockets, including my cigarettes. Once I had
been given a cell to myself I asked to be given back anyhow
the cigarettes. Smoking was forbidden, they informed me.
That, perhaps, was what got me down the most; in fact, I
suffered really badly during the first few days. I even tore
off splinters from my plank bed and sucked them. All day
long I felt faint and bilious. It passed my understanding why

I shouldn't be allowed even to smoke; it could have done no one any harm. Later on, I understood the idea behind it; this privation, too, was part of my punishment. But, by the time I understood, I'd lost the craving, so it had ceased to be a punishment.

Except for these privations, I wasn't too unhappy. Yet again, the whole problem was: how to kill time. After a while, however, once I'd learnt the trick of remembering things, I never had a moment's boredom. Sometimes I would exercise my memory on my bedroom, and, starting from a corner, make the round, noting every object I saw on the way. At first it was over in a minute or two. But each time I repeated the experience, it took a little longer. I made a point of visualizing every piece of furniture, and each article upon or in it, and then every detail of each article, and finally the details of the details, so to speak: a tiny dent or incrustation, or a chipped edge, and the exact grain and colour of the woodwork. At the same time I forced myself to keep my inventory in mind from start to finish, in the right order and omitting no item. With the result that, after a few weeks, I could spend hours merely in listing the objects in my bedroom. I found that the more I thought, the more details, half-forgotten or malobserved, floated up from my memory. There seemed no end to them.

So I learned that even after a single day's experience of the outside world a man could easily live a hundred years in prison. He'd have laid up enough memories never to be bored. Obviously, in one way, this was a compensation.

Then there was sleep. To begin with, I slept badly at night and never in the day. But gradually my nights became better and I managed to doze off in the daytime as well. In fact, during the last months, I must have slept sixteen or eighteen hours out of the twenty-four. So there remained only six hours to fill—with meals, relieving nature, my memories . . . and the story of the Czech.

One day, when inspecting my straw mattress, I found a bit of newspaper stuck to its underside. The paper was yellow with age, almost transparent, but one could still make out the letter-print. It was the story of a crime. The first part was missing, but one gathered that its scene was some village in Czechoslovakia. One of the villagers had left his home to try his luck abroad. After twenty-five years, having made a fortune, he returned to his country with his wife and child. Meanwhile his mother and sister had been running a small hotel in the village where he was born. He decided to give them a surprise and, leaving his wife and child in another inn, he went to stay at his mother's place, booking a room under an assumed name. His mother and sister completely failed to recognize him. At dinner that evening he showed them a large sum of money he had on him, and in the course of the night they slaughtered him with a hammer. After taking the money they flung the body into the river. Next morning his wife came and, without thinking, betrayed the guest's identity. His mother hanged herself. His sister threw herself into a well. I must have read that story thousands of times. In one way it sounded most unlikely; in another, it was plausible enough. Anyhow, to my mind, the man was asking for trouble; one shouldn't play fool tricks of that sort.

So, what with long bouts of sleep, my memories, readings of that scrap of newspaper, the tides of light and darkness, the days slipped by. I'd read, of course, that in gaol one ends up by losing track of time. But this had never meant anything definite to me. I hadn't grasped how days could be at once long and short. Long, no doubt, as periods to live through, but so distended that they ended up by overlapping on each other. In fact I never thought of days as such; only the words 'yesterday' and 'tomorrow' still kept some meaning.

When, one morning the warder informed me I'd now been six months in gaol, I believed him—but the words conveyed nothing to my mind. To me it seemed like one and the same day that had been going on since I'd been in my cell, and that I'd been doing the same thing all the time.

After the gaoler left me I shined up my tin pannikin and studied my face in it. My expression was terribly serious, I thought, even when I tried to smile. I held the pannikin at different angles, but always my face had the same mournful, tense expression.

The sun was setting and it was the hour of which I'd rather not speak—'the nameless hour', I called it—when evening sounds were creeping up from all the floors of the prison in a sort of stealthy procession. I went to the barred window and in the last rays looked once again at my reflected face. It was as serious as before; and that wasn't surprising, as just then I was feeling serious. But, at the same time, I heard something that I hadn't heard for months. It was the sound of a voice; my own voice, there was no mistaking it. And I recognized it as the voice that for many a day of late had been buzzing in my ears. So I knew that all this time I'd been talking to myself.

And something I'd been told came back to me; a remark made by the nurse at Mother's funeral. No, there was no way out, and no one can imagine what the evenings are like in prison.

III

ON the whole I can't say that those months passed slowly; another summer was on its way almost before I realized the first was over. And I knew that with the first really hot days something new was in store for me. My case was down for the last Sessions of the Assize Court, and that Sessions was due to end some time in June.

The day on which my trial started was one of brilliant sunshine. My lawyer assured me the case would take only two or three days. 'From what I hear,' he added, 'the Court will despatch your case as quickly as possible, as it isn't the most important one on the Cause List. There's a case of parricide immediately after, which will take them some time.'

They came for me at half past seven in the morning and I was conveyed to the Law Courts in the prison van. The two policemen led me into a small room that smelt of darkness. We sat near a door through which came sounds of voices, shouts, chairs scraping on the floor; a vague hubbub which reminded me of one of those small town 'socials' when, after the concert's over, the hall is cleared for dancing.

One of my policemen told me the judges hadn't arrived yet, and offered me a cigarette, which I declined. After a bit he asked me if I was feeling nervous. I said 'No', and that the prospect of witnessing a trial rather interested me; I'd never had occasion to attend one before.

'Maybe,' the other policeman said. 'But after an hour or two one's had enough of it.'

After a while a small electric bell purred in the room. They unfastened my handcuffs, opened the door, and led me to the prisoner's dock.

There was a great crowd in the courtroom. Though the venetian blinds were down, light was filtering through the chinks, and the air was stifling hot already. The windows had been kept shut. I sat down, and the police officers took their stand on each side of my chair.

It was then that I noticed a row of faces opposite me. These people were staring hard at me, and I guessed they were the jury. But somehow I didn't see them as individuals. I felt as one does just after boarding a tram and one's conscious of all the people on the opposite seat staring at one in the hope of finding something in one's appearance to amuse them. Of course I knew this was an absurd comparison; what these people were looking for in me wasn't anything to laugh at, but signs of criminality. Still, the difference wasn't so very great, and, anyhow, that's the idea I got.

What with the crowd and the stuffiness of the air I was feeling a bit dizzy. I ran my eyes round the courtroom but couldn't recognize any of the faces. At first I could hardly believe that all these people had come on my account. It was such a new experience, being a focus of interest; in the ordinary way no one ever paid much attention to me. 'What a crush!' I remarked to the policeman on my left, and he explained that the newspapers were responsible for it. He pointed to a group of men at a table just below the jury-box. There they are!'—'Who?' I asked, and he replied, 'The Press.' One of them, he added, was an old friend of his.

A moment later the man he'd mentioned looked our way and, coming to the dock, shook hands warmly with the policeman. The journalist was an elderly man with a rather grim expression, but his manner was quite pleasant. Just then, I noticed that almost all the people in the courtroom were greeting each other, exchanging remarks and forming groups—behaving, in fact, as in a club where the company of others of one's own tastes and standing makes one feel at ease. That, no doubt, explained the odd impression I had of being *de trop* here, a sort of gate-crasher.

However, the journalist addressed me quite amiably, and said he hoped all would go well for me. I thanked him, and he added with a smile:

'You know, we've been featuring you a bit. We're always rather short of copy in the summer, and there's been precious little to write about except your case and the one that's coming on after it. I expect you've heard about it; it's a case of parricide.'

He drew my attention to one of the group at the Press table, a plump, small man with huge black-rimmed glasses, who made one think of an over-fed weasel.

'That chap's the special correspondent of one of the Paris dailies. As a matter of fact he didn't come on your account. He was sent for the parricide case, but they've asked him to cover yours as well.'

It was on the tip of my tongue to say, 'that was very kind of them,' but then I thought it would sound silly. With a friendly wave of his hand he left us, and for some minutes nothing happened.

Then, accompanied by some colleagues, my lawyer bustled in, in his gown. He went up to the Press table and shook hands with the journalists. They remained laughing and chatting together, all seemingly very much at home here, until a bell rang shrilly and everyone went to his place. My lawyer came up to me, shook hands, and advised me to answer all the questions as briefly as possible, not to volunteer information, and to rely on him to see me through.

I heard a chair scrape on my left, and a tall, thin man wearing pince-nez settled the folds of his red gown as he took his seat. The public prosecutor, I gathered. A clerk of the court announced that Their Honours were entering and at the same moment two big electric fans started buzzing overhead. Three judges, two in black and the third in scarlet, with brief-cases under their arms, entered and walked briskly to the bench, which was several feet above the level of the courtroom floor. The man in scarlet took the central, high-backed chair, placed his cap of office on the table, ran a

handkerchief over his small bald crown, and announced that
the hearing would now begin.

The journalists had their fountain-pens ready; they all wore
the same expression of slightly ironical indifference, with the
exception of one, a much younger man than his colleagues,
in grey flannels with a blue tie, who, leaving his pen on
the table, was gazing hard at me. He had a plain, rather
chunky face; what held my attention was his eyes, very pale,
clear eyes, riveted on me, though not betraying any definite
emotion. For a moment I had an odd impression, as if I were
being scrutinized by myself. That—and the fact that I was
unfamiliar with court procedure—may explain why I didn't
follow very well the opening phases: the drawing of lots for
the jury, the various questions put by the presiding judge to
the prosecutor, the foreman of the jury and my counsel (each
time he spoke all the jurymen's heads swung round together
towards the bench), the hurried reading of the charge-sheet,
in the course of which I recognized some familiar names of
people and places, then some supplementary questions put to
my lawyer.

Next, the judge announced that the court would call over
the witness-list. Some of the names read out by the clerk
rather surprised me. From amongst the crowd, which until
now I had seen as a mere blur of faces, rose, one after the
other, Raymond, Masson, Salamano, the door-keeper from
the Home, old Pérez, and Marie, who gave me a little nervous
wave of her hand before following the others out by a side
door. I was thinking how strange it was I hadn't noticed any of
them before when I heard the last name called, that of Céleste.
As he rose, I noticed beside him the quaint little woman with a
mannish coat and brisk, decided air, who had shared my table
at the restaurant. She had her eyes fixed on me, I noticed.
But I hadn't time to wonder about her; the judge had started
speaking again.

He said that the trial proper was about to begin, and he
need hardly say that he expected the public to refrain from
any demonstration whatsoever. He explained that he was
there to supervise the proceedings, as a sort of umpire, and
he would take a scrupulously impartial view of the case. The
verdict of the jury would be interpreted by him in a spirit of

justice. Finally, at the least sign of a disturbance he would have the court cleared.

The day was stoking up. Some of the public were fanning themselves with newspapers, and there was a constant rustle of crumpled paper. On a sign from the presiding judge the clerk of the court brought three fans of plaited straw, which the three judges promptly put in action.

My examination began at once. The judge questioned me quite calmly and even, I thought, with a hint of cordiality. For the *n*th time I was asked to give particulars of my identity and, though heartily sick of this formality, I realized that it was natural enough; after all, it would be a shocking thing for the court to be trying the wrong man.

The judge then launched into an account of what I'd done, stopping every two or three sentences to ask me, 'Is that correct?' To which I always replied, 'Yes, sir,' as my lawyer had advised me. It was a long business, as the judge lingered on each detail. Meanwhile the journalists scribbled busily away. But I was sometimes conscious of the eyes of the youngest fixed on me; also those of the queer little robot woman. The jurymen, however, were all gazing at the red-robed judge, and I was again reminded of the row of passengers on one side of a tram. Presently he gave a slight cough, turned some pages of his file, and, still fanning his face, addressed me gravely.

He now proposed, he said, to touch on certain matters which, on a superficial view, might seem foreign to the case, but actually were highly relevant. I guessed that he was going to talk about Mother, and at the same moment realized how odious I would find this. His first question was: Why had I sent my mother to an Institution? I replied that the reason was simple; I hadn't enough money to see that she was properly looked after at home. Then he asked if the parting hadn't caused me distress. I explained that neither Mother nor I expected much of one another—or, for that matter, of anybody else; so both of us had got used to the new conditions easily enough. The judge then said that he had no wish to press the point, and asked the Prosecutor if he could think of any more questions that should be put to me at this stage.

The prosecutor, who had his back half turned to me, said, without looking in my direction, that, subject to His Honour's approval, he would like to know if I'd gone back to the stream with the intention of killing the Arab. I said 'No.' In that case, why had I taken a revolver with me, and why go back precisely to that spot? I said it was a matter of pure chance. The prosecutor then observed in a nasty tone: 'Very good. That will be all for the present.'

I couldn't quite follow what came next. Anyhow, after some palavering between the Bench, the prosecutor and my counsel, the presiding judge announced that the court would now rise; there was an adjournment till the afternoon, when evidence would be taken.

Almost before I knew what was happening, I was rushed out to the prison van, which drove me back, and I was given my midday meal. After a short time, just enough for me to realize how tired I was feeling, they came for me. I was back in the same room, confronting the same faces, and the whole thing started again. But the heat had meanwhile much increased, and by some miracle fans had been procured for everyone; the jury, my lawyer, the prosecutor, and some of the pressmen, too. The young man and the robot woman were still at their places. But they were not fanning themselves and, as before, they never took their eyes off me.

I wiped the sweat from my face, but I was barely conscious of where or who I was until I heard the Warden of the Home called to the witness-box. When asked if my mother had complained about my conduct, he said 'Yes,' but that didn't mean much; almost all the inmates of the Home had grievances against their relatives. The judge asked him to be more explicit; did she reproach me with having sent her to the Home, and he said 'Yes' again. But this time he didn't qualify his answer.

To another question he replied that on the day of the funeral he was somewhat surprised by my calmness. Asked to explain what he meant by 'My calmness', the Warden lowered his eyes and stared at his shoes for a moment. Then he explained that I hadn't wanted to see Mother's body, or shed a single tear, and that I'd left immediately the funeral ended, without lingering at her grave. Another thing had surprised him. One of the undertaker's men told him that I didn't know my mother's age. There was a short silence; then the judge asked him if he might take it that he was referring to the prisoner in the dock. The Warden seemed puzzled by this, and the judge explained: 'It's a formal question. I am bound to put it.'

The prosecutor was then asked if he had any questions to put, and he answered loudly: 'Certainly not! I have all I want.' His tone and the look of triumph on his face, as he glanced at me, were so marked that I felt as I hadn't felt for ages. I had a foolish desire to burst into tears. For the first time I'd realized how all these people loathed me.

After asking the jury and my lawyer if they had any questions, the judge heard the door-keeper's evidence. On stepping into the box the man threw a glance at me, then looked away. Replying to questions, he said that I'd declined to see Mother's body, I'd smoked cigarettes and slept, and drunk *café au lait*. It was then I felt a sort of wave of indignation spreading through the courtroom, and for the first time I understood that I was guilty. They got the door-keeper to repeat what he had said about the coffee and my smoking. The prosecutor turned to me again, with a gloating look in his eyes. My counsel asked the door-keeper if he, too, hadn't smoked. But the prosecutor took strong exception to this. 'I'd like to know', he cried indignantly, 'who is on trial in this court. Or does my friend think that by aspersing a witness for the prosecution he will shake the evidence, the abundant and cogent evidence, against his client?' None the less, the judge told the door-keeper to answer the question.

The old fellow fidgeted a bit. Then, 'Well, I know I didn't ought to have done it,' he mumbled, 'but I did take a fag from the young gentleman when he offered it—just out of politeness.'

The judge asked me if I had any comment to make. 'None,' I said, 'except that the witness is quite right. It's true I offered him a cigarette.'

The door-keeper looked at me with surprise and a sort of gratitude. Then, after humming and hawing for a bit, he volunteered the statement that it was he who'd suggested I should have some coffee.

My lawyer was exultant. 'The jury will appreciate', he said, 'the importance of this admission.'

The prosecutor, however, was promptly on his feet again. 'Quite so,' he boomed above our heads. 'The jury will appreciate it. And they will draw the conclusion that, though a third party might inadvertently offer him a cup of coffee, the prisoner, in common decency, should have refused it, if only out of respect for the dead body of the poor woman who had brought him into the world.'

After which the door-keeper went back to his seat.

When Thomas Pérez was called, a court officer had to help him to the box. Pérez stated that, though he had been a great friend of my mother, he had met me once only, on the day of the funeral. Asked how I had behaved that day, he said:

'Well, I was most upset, you know. Far too much upset to notice things. My grief sort of blinded me, I think. It had been a great shock, my dear friend's death; in fact I fainted during the funeral. So I didn't hardly notice the young gentlemen at all.'

The prosecutor asked him to tell the court if he'd seen me weep. And when Pérez answered 'No,' added emphatically: 'I trust the jury will take note of this reply.'

My lawyer rose at once, and asked Pérez in a tone that seemed to me needlessly aggressive:

'Now think well, my man! Can you swear you saw he didn't shed a tear?'

Pérez answered, 'No.'

At this some people tittered and my lawyer, pushing back one sleeve of his gown, said sternly:

'That is typical of the way this case is being conducted. No attempt is being made to elicit the true facts.'

The prosecutor ignored this remark; he was making dabs with his pencil on the cover of his brief, seemingly quite indifferent.

There was a break of five minutes, during which my lawyer told me the case was going very well indeed. Then Céleste was called. He was announced as a witness for the defence. The defence meant me.

Now and again Céleste threw me a glance; he kept squeezing his panama hat between his hands as he gave evidence.

He was in his best suit, the one he wore when sometimes of a Sunday he went with me to the races. But evidently he hadn't been able to get his collar on; the top of his shirt, I noticed, was secured only by a brass stud. Asked if I was one of his customers, he said, 'Yes, and a friend as well.' Asked to state his opinion of me, he said that I was 'all right' and, when told to explain what he meant by that, he replied that everyone knew what that meant. 'Was I a secretive sort of man?'—'No,' he answered, 'I shouldn't call him that. But he isn't one to waste his breath, like a lot of folks.'

The prosecutor asked him if I always settled my monthly bill at his restaurant when he presented it. Céleste laughed. 'Oh, he paid on the nail all right. But the bills were just details, like, between him and me.' Then he was asked to say what he thought about the crime. He placed his hands on the rail of the box and one could see he had a speech all ready.

'To my mind it was just an accident, or a stroke of bad luck, if you prefer. And a thing like that takes you off your guard.'

He wanted to continue, but the judge cut him short. 'Quite so. That's all, thank you.'

For a bit Céleste seemed flabbergasted; then he explained that he hadn't finished what he wanted to say. They told him to continue, but to make it brief.

He only repeated that it was 'just an accident.'

'That's as it may be,' the judge observed. 'But what we are here for is to try such accidents, according to law. You can stand down.'

Céleste turned and gazed at me. His eyes were moist and his lips trembling. It was exactly as if he'd said: 'Well, I've done my best for you, old chap. I'm afraid it hasn't helped much. I'm sorry.'

I didn't say anything, or make any movement, but for the first time in my life I wanted to kiss a man.

The judge repeated his order to stand down and Céleste returned to his place amongst the crowd. During the rest of the hearing he remained there, leaning forward, elbows on knees and his panama between his hands, not missing a word of the proceedings.

It was Marie's turn next. She had a hat on, and still looked quite pretty, though I much preferred her with her hair free. From where I was I had glimpses of the soft curves of her breasts, and her underlip had the little pout that always fascinated me. She appeared very nervous.

The first question was: How long had she known me? Since the time when she was in our office, she replied. Then the judge asked her what were the relations between us, and she said she was my girl friend. Answering another question, she admitted promising to marry me. The prosecutor, who had been studying a document in front of him, asked her rather sharply when our 'liaison' had begun. She gave the date. He then observed with a would-be casual air that apparently she meant the day following my mother's funeral. After letting this sink in he remarked in a slightly ironic tone that obviously this was a 'delicate topic' and he could enter into the young lady's feelings, but—and here his voice grew sterner—his duty obliged him to waive considerations of delicacy.

After making this announcement he asked Marie to give a full account of our doings on the day when I had 'intercourse' with her for the first time. Marie wouldn't answer at first, but the prosecutor insisted, and then she told him that we had met at the baths, gone together to the pictures, and then to my place. He then informed the court that, as a result of certain statements made by Marie at the proceedings before the magistrate, he had studied the cinema programmes of that date, and turning to Marie asked her to name the film that we had gone to see. In a very low voice she said it was a picture with Fernandel in it. By the time she had finished, the courtroom was so still you could have heard a pin drop.

Looking very grave, the prosecutor drew himself up to his full height and, pointing at me, said in such a tone that I could have sworn he was genuinely moved:

'Gentlemen of the jury, I would have you note that on the next day after his mother's funeral that man was visiting the swimming-pool, starting a liaison with a girl, and going to see a comic film. That is all I wish to say.'

When he sat down there was the same dead silence. Then all of a sudden Marie burst into tears. He'd got it all wrong, she said; it wasn't a bit like that really, he'd bullied her into saying the opposite of what she meant. She knew me very well, and she was sure, I hadn't done anything really wrong—and so on. At a sign from the presiding judge, one of the court officers led her away, and the hearing continued.

Hardly anyone seemed to listen to Masson, the next witness. He stated that I was a respectable young fellow; 'and what's more, a very decent chap.' Nor did they pay any more attention to Salamano, when he told them how kind I'd always been to his dog, or when, in answer to a question about my mother and myself, he said that really Mother and I had very little in common and that explained why I'd fixed up for her to enter the Home. 'You've got to understand,' he added. 'You've got to understand.' But no one seemed to understand. He was told to stand down.

Raymond was the next, and last, witness. He gave me a little wave of his hand and led off by saying I was innocent. The judge rebuked him.

'You are here to give evidence, not your views on the case, and you must confine yourself to answering the questions put you.'

He was then asked to make clear his relations with the deceased, and Raymond took this opportunity of explaining that it was he, not I, against whom the dead man had a grudge, because he, Raymond, had beaten up his sister. The judge asked him if the deceased had no reason to dislike me, too. Raymond told him that my presence on the beach that morning was a pure coincidence.

'How comes it then,' the prosecutor inquired, 'that the letter which led up to this tragedy was the prisoner's work?'

Raymond replied that this, too, was due to mere chance.

To which the prosecutor retorted that in this case 'chance' or 'mere coincidence' seemed to play a remarkably large part. Was it by chance that I hadn't intervened when Raymond assaulted his mistress? Did this convenient term 'chance' account for my having vouched for Raymond at the police station and having made, on that occasion, statements extravagantly favourable to him? In conclusion, he asked Raymond to state what were his means of livelihood.

On his describing himself as a warehouseman, the prosecutor informed the jury it was common knowledge that the witness lived on the immoral earnings of women. I, he said, was this man's intimate friend and associate; in fact, the whole background of the crime was of the most squalid description. And what made it even more odious was the personality of the prisoner, an inhuman monster wholly without moral sense.

Raymond began to expostulate, and my lawyer, too, protested. They were told that the prosecutor must be allowed to finish his remarks.

'I have nearly done,' he said; then turned to Raymond. 'Was the prisoner your friend?'

'Certainly. We were the best of pals, as they say.'

The prosecutor then put me the same question. I looked hard at Raymond, and he did not turn away.

Then, 'Yes', I answered.

The prosecutor turned towards the jury.

'Not only did the man before you in the dock indulge in the most shameful orgies on the day following his mother's funeral. He killed a man cold-bloodedly, in pursuance of some sordid vendetta in the underworld of prostitutes and pimps. That, gentlemen of the jury, is the type of man the prisoner is.'

No sooner had he sat down than my lawyer, out of all patience, raised his arms so high that his sleeves fell back, showing the full length of his starched shirtcuffs.

'Is my client on trial for having buried his mother, or for killing a man?' he asked.

There were some titters in court. But then the prosecutor sprang to his feet, and, draping his gown round him, said he was amazed at his friend's ingenuousness in failing to see that between these two elements of the case there was a vital link. They hung together psychologically, if he might put it so. 'In short,' he concluded, speaking with great vehemence, 'I accuse the prisoner of behaving at his mother's funeral in a way that showed he was already a criminal at heart.'

These words seemed to make much effect on the jury and public. My lawyer merely shrugged his shoulders and wiped the sweat from his forehead. But obviously he was rattled, and I had a feeling things weren't going well for me.

Soon after this incident the court rose. As I was being taken from the courthouse to the prison van, I was conscious for a few brief moments of the once familiar feel of a summer evening out of doors. And, sitting in the darkness of my moving cell, I recognized, echoing in my tired brain, all the characteristic sounds of a town I'd loved, and of a certain hour of the day which I had always particularly enjoyed. The shouts of newspaper-boys in the already languid air, the last calls of birds in the public garden, the cries of sandwich-vendors, the screech of trams at the steep corners of the upper town, and that faint rustling overhead as darkness sifted down upon the harbour—all these sounds made my return to prison like a blind man's journey along a route whose every inch he knows by heart.

Yes, this was the evening hour when—how long ago it seemed!—I always felt so well content with life. Then, what awaited me was a night of easy, dreamless sleep. This was the same hour, but with a difference; I was returning to a cell and what awaited me was a night haunted by forebodings of the coming day. And so I learnt that familiar paths traced in the dusk of summer evenings may lead as well to prison as to innocent, carefree sleep.

IV

IT is always interesting, even in the prisoner's dock, to hear oneself being talked about. And certainly in the speeches of my lawyer and the prosecuting counsel a great deal was said about me; more, in fact, about me personally than about my crime.

Really there wasn't any very great difference between the two speeches. Counsel for the defence raised his arms to heaven and pleaded Guilty, but with extenuating circumstances. The prosecutor made similar gestures; he agreed that I was guilty, but denied extenuating circumstances.

One thing about this phase of the trial was rather irksome. Quite often, interested as I was in what they had to say, I was tempted to put in a word, myself. But my lawyer had advised me not to. 'You won't do your case any good by talking,' he had warned me. In fact there seemed to be a conspiracy to exclude me from the proceedings; I wasn't to have any say and my fate was to be decided out of hand.

It was quite an effort at times for me to refrain from cutting them all short, and saying: 'But, damn it all, who's on trial in this court, I'd like to know? It's a serious matter for a man, being accused of murder. And I've something really important to tell you.'

However, on second thoughts, I found I had nothing to say. In any case, I must admit that hearing oneself talked about loses its interest very soon. The prosecutor's speech, especially, began to bore me before he was half-way through it. The only things that really caught my attention were occasional phrases, his gestures, and some elaborate tirades—but these were isolated patches.

What he was aiming at, I gathered, was to show that my crime was premeditated. I remember his saying at one moment, 'I can prove this, gentlemen of the jury, to the hilt. First, you have the facts of the crime, which are as clear as daylight. And then you have what I may call the night side of this case, the dark workings of a criminal mentality.'

He began by summing up the facts, from my mother's death onwards. He stressed my heartlessness, my inability to state Mother's age, my visit to the bathing-pool where I met Marie, our matinée at the pictures where a Fernandel film was showing, and finally my return with Marie to my rooms. I didn't quite follow his remarks at first as he kept on mentioning 'the prisoner's mistress', whereas for me she was just 'Marie'. Then he came to the subject of Raymond. It seemed to me that his way of treating the facts showed a certain shrewdness. All he said sounded quite plausible. I'd written the letter in collusion with Raymond so as to entice his mistress to his room and subject her to ill-treatment by a man 'of more than dubious reputation'. Then, on the beach, I'd provoked a brawl with Raymond's enemies, in the course of which Raymond was wounded. I'd asked him for his revolver and gone back myself with the intention of using it. Then I'd shot the Arab. After the first shot I waited. Then, 'to be certain of making a good job of it', I fired four more shots deliberately, point blank and in cold blood, at my victim.

'That is my case,' he said. 'I have described to you the series of events which led this man to kill the deceased, fully aware of what he was doing. I emphasize this point. We are not concerned with an act of homicide committed on a sudden impulse which might serve as extenuation. I ask you to note, gentlemen of the jury, that the prisoner is an educated man. You will have observed the way in which he answered my questions; he is intelligent and he knows the value of words. And I repeat that it is quite impossible to assume that, when he committed the crime, he was unaware what he was doing.'

I noticed that he laid stress on my 'intelligence'. It puzzled me rather why what would count as a good point in an ordinary person should be used against an accused man as an overwhelming proof of his guilt. While thinking this over, I missed what he said next, until I heard him exclaim indignantly: 'And has he uttered a word of regret for his most odious crime? Not one word, gentlemen. Not once in the course of these proceedings did this man show the least contrition.'

Turning towards the dock, he pointed a finger at me, and went on in the same strain. I really couldn't understand why he harped on this point so much. Of course I had to own that he was right; I didn't feel much regret for what I'd done. Still, to my mind he overdid it, and I'd have liked to have a chance of explaining to him, in a quite friendly, almost affectionate way, that I have never been able really to regret anything in all my life. I've always been far too much absorbed in the present moment, or the immediate future, to think back. Of course, in the position into which I had been forced, there was no question of my speaking to anyone in that tone. I hadn't the right to show any friendly feeling or possess good intentions. And I tried to follow what came next, as the prosecutor was now considering what he called my 'soul'.

He said he'd studied it closely—and had found a blank, 'literally nothing, gentlemen of the jury'. Really, he said, I had no soul, there was nothing human about me, not one of those moral qualities which normal men possess had any place in my mentality. 'No doubt', he added, 'we should not reproach him with this. We cannot blame a man for lacking what it was never in his power to acquire. But in a criminal court the wholly passive ideal of tolerance must give place to a sterner, loftier ideal, that of Justice. Especially when this lack of every decent instinct is such as that of the man before you, a menace to society.' He proceeded to discuss my conduct towards my mother, repeating what he had said in the course of the hearing. But he spoke at much greater length of my crime; at such length, indeed, that I lost the thread and was conscious only of the steadily increasing heat.

A moment came when the prosecutor paused and, after a short silence, said in a low, vibrant voice: 'This same court, gentlemen, will be called on to try tomorrow that most odious of crimes, the murder of a father by his son.' To his mind, such a crime was almost unimaginable. But, he ventured to hope, Justice would be meted out without faltering. And yet, he made bold to say, the horror that even the crime of parricide inspired in him paled beside the loathing inspired by my callousness.

'This man, who is morally guilty of his mother's death, is no less unfit to have a place in the community than that other man who did to death the father who begat him. And, indeed, the one crime led on to the other; the first of these two criminals, the man in the dock, set a precedent, if I may put it so, and authorized the second crime. Yes, gentlemen, I am convinced'—here he raised his voice a tone—'that you will not find I am exaggerating the case against the prisoner when I say that he is also guilty of the murder to be tried tomorrow in this court. And I look to you for a verdict accordingly.'

The prosecutor paused again, to wipe the sweat off his face. He then explained that his duty was a painful one, but he would do it without flinching. 'This man has, I repeat, no place in a community whose basic principles he flouts without compunction. Nor, heartless as he is, has he any claim to mercy. I ask you to impose the extreme penalty of the law; and I ask it without a qualm. In the course of a long career, in which it has often been my duty to ask for a capital sentence, never have I felt that painful duty weigh so little on my mind as in the present case. In demanding a verdict of murder without extenuating circumstances, I am following not only the dictates of my conscience and a sacred obligation, but also those of the natural and righteous indignation I feel at the sight of a criminal devoid of the least spark of human feeling.'

When the prosecutor sat down there was a longish silence. Personally I was quite overcome by the heat and my amazement at what I had been hearing. The presiding judge gave a short cough, and asked me in a very low tone if I had anything to say. I rose, and as I felt in the mood to speak, I said the first thing that crossed my mind: that I'd had no intention of killing the Arab. The judge replied that this statement would be taken into consideration by the court. Meanwhile he would be glad to hear, before my counsel addressed the court, what were the motives of my crime. So far, he must admit, he hadn't fully understood the grounds of my defence.

I tried to explain that it was because of the sun, but I spoke too quickly and ran my words into each other. I was only too conscious that it sounded nonsensical, and, in fact, I heard people tittering.

My lawyer shrugged his shoulders. Then he was directed to address the court, in his turn. But all he did was to point out the lateness of the hour and to ask for an adjournment till the following afternoon. To this the judge agreed.

When I was brought back next day, the electric fans were still churning up the heavy air and the jurymen playing their gaudy little fans in a sort of steady rhythm. The speech for the defence seemed to me interminable. At one moment, however, I pricked up my ears; it was when I heard him saying: 'It is true I killed a man.' He went on in the same strain, saying 'I' when he referred to me. It seemed so queer that I bent towards the policeman on my right and asked him to explain. He told me to shut up; then, after a moment, whispered: 'They all do that.' It seemed to me that the idea behind it was still further to exclude me from the case, to put me off the map, so to speak, by substituting the lawyer for myself. Anyway, it hardly mattered; I already felt worlds away from this courtroom and its tedious 'proceedings'.

My lawyer, in any case, struck me as feeble to the point of being ridiculous. He hurried through his plea of provocation, and then he, too, started in about my 'soul'. But I had an impression that he had much less talent than the prosecutor.

'I, too,' he said, 'have closely studied this man's soul; but, unlike my learned friend for the prosecution, I have found something there. Indeed, I may say that I have read the prisoner's mind like an open book.' What he had read there was that I was an excellent young fellow, a steady, conscientious worker who did his best by his employer; that I was popular with everyone and sympathetic in others' troubles. According to him I was a dutiful son, who had supported his mother as long as he was able. After anxious consideration I had reached the conclusion that, by entering a Home, the old lady would have comforts that my means didn't permit me to provide for her. 'I am astounded, gentlemen,' he added, 'by the attitude taken up by my learned friend in referring to this Home. Surely if proof be needed of the excellence of such institutions, we need only remember that they are promoted and financed by a Government department.' I noticed that he made no reference to the funeral, and this seemed to me a serious omission. But, what with his long-windedness, the endless days and hours they had been discussing my 'soul', and the rest of it, I found that my mind had gone blurred; everything was dissolving into a greyish, watery haze.

Only one incident stands out; towards the end, while my counsel rambled on, I heard the tin trumpet of an ice-cream vendor in the street, a small, shrill sound cutting across the flow of words. And then a rush of memories went through my mind—memories of a life which was mine no longer and had once provided me with the surest, humblest pleasures: warm smells of summer, my favourite streets, the sky at evening, Marie's dresses and her laugh. The futility of what was happening here seemed to take me by the throat, I felt like vomiting, and I had only one idea: to get it over, to go back to my cell, and sleep . . . and sleep.

Dimly I heard my counsel making his last appeal.

'Gentlemen of the jury, surely you will not send to his death a decent, hard-working young man, because for one tragic moment he lost his self-control? Is he not sufficiently punished by the lifelong remorse that is to be his lot? I confidently await your verdict, the only verdict possible—that of homicide with extenuating circumstances.'

The court rose and the lawyer sat down, looking thoroughly exhausted. Some of his colleagues came to him and shook his hand. 'You put up a magnificent show, old chap,' I heard one of them say. Another lawyer even called me to witness: 'Fine, wasn't it?' I agreed, but insincerely; I was far too tired to judge if it had been 'fine' or otherwise.

Meanwhile the day was ending and the heat becoming less intense. By some vague sounds that reached me from the street I knew that the cool of the evening had set in. We all sat on, waiting. And what we all were waiting for really concerned nobody but me. I looked round the courtroom. It was exactly as it had been on the first day. I met the eyes of the journalist in grey and the robot woman. This reminded me that not once during the whole hearing had I tried to catch Marie's eye. It wasn't that I'd forgotten her; only I was too preoccupied. I saw her now, seated between Céleste and Raymond. She gave me a little wave of her hand, as if to say, 'At last!' She was smiling, but I could tell that she was rather anxious. But my heart seemed turned to stone, and I couldn't even return her smile.

The judges came back to their seats. Someone read out to the jury, very rapidly, a string of questions. I caught a word here and there. 'Murder of malice aforethought . . . Provocation . . . Extenuating circumstances.' The jury went out, and I was taken to the little room where I had already waited. My lawyer came to see me; he was very talkative and showed more cordiality and confidence than ever before. He assured me that all would go well and I'd get off with a few years' imprisonment or transportation. I asked him what were the chances of getting the sentence quashed. He said there was no chance of that. He had not raised any point of law, as this was apt to prejudice the jury. And it was difficult to get a judgement quashed except on technical grounds. I saw his point, and agreed. Looking at the matter dispassionately, I shared his view. Otherwise there would be no end to litigation. 'In any case,' the lawyer said, 'you can appeal in the ordinary way. But I'm convinced the verdict will be favourable.'

We waited for quite a while, a good three-quarters of an hour, I should say. Then a bell rang. My lawyer left me, saying:

'The foreman of the jury will read out the answers. You will be called on after that to hear the judgement.'

Some doors banged. I heard people hurrying down flights of steps, but couldn't tell whether they were near by or distant. Then I heard a voice droning away in the courtroom.

When the bell rang again and I stepped back into the dock, the silence of the courtroom closed in round me and, with the silence, came a queer sensation when I noticed that, for the first time, the young journalist kept his eyes averted. I didn't look in Marie's direction. In fact, I had no time to look as the presiding judge had already started pronouncing a rigmarole to the effect that 'in the name of the French People' I was to be decapitated in some public place.

It seemed to me then that I could interpret the look on the faces of those present; it was one of almost respectful sympathy. The policemen, too, handled me very gently. The lawyer placed his hand on my wrist. I had stopped thinking altogether. I heard the judge's voice asking if I had anything more to say. After thinking for a moment, I answered, 'No.' Then the policemen led me out.

V

I HAVE just refused, for the third time, to see the prison chaplain. I have nothing to say to him, don't feel like talking—and shall be seeing him quite soon enough, anyway. The only thing that interests me now is the problem of circumventing the machine, learning if the inevitable admits a loophole.

They have moved me to another cell. In this one, lying on my back, I can see the sky, and there is nothing else to see. All my time is spent in watching the slowly changing colours of the sky, as day moves on to night. I put my hands behind my head, gaze up, and wait.

This problem of a loophole obsesses me; I am always wondering if there have been cases of condemned prisoners escaping from the implacable machinery of justice at the last moment, breaking through the police cordon, vanishing in the nick of time before the guillotine falls. Often and often I blame myself for not having given more attention to accounts of public executions. One should always take an interest in such matters. There's never any knowing what one may come to. Like everyone else I'd read descriptions of executions in the papers. But technical books dealing with this subject must certainly exist; only I'd never felt sufficiently interested to

look them up. And in these books I might have found escape
stories. Surely they'd have told me that in one case anyhow the
wheels had stopped; that once, if only once, in that inexorable
march of events, chance or luck had played a happy part.
Just once! In a way I think that single instance would have
satisfied me. My emotion would have done the rest. The
papers often talk of 'a debt owed to society'—a debt which,
according to them, must be paid by the offender. But talk
of that sort doesn't touch the imagination. No, the one thing
that counted for me was the possibility of making a dash for
it and defeating their blood-thirsty rite; of a mad stampede
to freedom that would anyhow give me a moment's hope, the
gambler's last throw. Naturally all that 'hope' could come to
was to be knocked down at the corner of a street or picked
off by a bullet in my back. But, all things considered, even
this luxury was forbidden me; I was caught in the rat-trap
irrevocably.

Try as I might, I couldn't stomach this brutal certitude. For
really, when one came to think of it, there was a disproportion
between the judgement on which it was based and the
unalterable sequence of events starting from the moment
when that judgement was delivered. The fact that the verdict
was read out at 8 p.m. rather than at 5, the fact that it might
have been quite different, that it was given by men who change
their underclothes, and was credited to so vague an entity as
the 'French People'—for that matter, why not to the Chinese
or the German People?—all these facts seemed to deprive
the court's decision of much of its gravity. Yet I could but
recognize that, from the moment the verdict was given, its
effects became as cogent, as tangible, as, for example, this wall
against which I was lying, pressing my back to it.

When such thoughts crossed my mind, I remembered a
story Mother used to tell me about my father. I never set eyes
on him. Perhaps the only things I really knew about him were
what Mother had told me. One of these was that he'd gone to
see a murderer executed. The mere thought of it turned his
stomach. But he'd seen it through and, on coming home, was
violently sick. At the time I found my father's conduct rather
disgusting. But now I understood; it was so natural. How had
I failed to recognize that nothing was more important than an

execution; that, viewed from one angle, it's the only thing that can genuinely interest a man? And I decided that, if ever I got out of gaol, I'd attend every execution that took place. I was unwise, no doubt, even to consider this possibility. For, the moment I'd pictured myself in freedom, standing behind a double rank of policemen—on the right side of the line, so to speak—the mere thought of being an onlooker who comes to see the show, and can go home and vomit afterwards, flooded my mind with a wild, absurd exultation. It was a stupid thing to let my imagination run away with me like that; a moment later I had a shivering fit and had to wrap myself closely in my blanket. But my teeth went on chattering; nothing would stop them.

Still, obviously, one can't be sensible all the time. Another equally ridiculous fancy of mine was to frame new laws, altering the penalties. What was wanted, to my mind, was to give the criminal a chance, if only a dog's chance; say, one chance in a thousand. There might be some drug, or combination of drugs, which would kill the patient (I thought of him as 'the patient') nine hundred and ninety times in a thousand. That he should know this was, of course, essential. For after taking much thought, calmly, I came to the conclusion that what was wrong about the guillotine was that the condemned man had no chance at all, absolutely none. In fact, the patient's death had been ordained irrevocably. It was a foregone conclusion. If by some fluke the knife didn't do its job, they started again. So it came to this, that—against the grain, no doubt—the condemned man had to hope the apparatus was in good working order! This, I thought, was a flaw in the system; and, on the face of it, my view was sound enough. On the other hand, I had to admit it proved the efficiency of the system. It came to this: the man under sentence was obliged to collaborate mentally, it was in his interest that all should go off without a hitch.

Another thing I had to recognize was that, until now, I'd had wrong ideas on the subject. For some reason I'd always supposed that one had to go up steps and climb on to a scaffold to be guillotined. Probably that was because of the 1789 Revolution; I mean, what I'd learnt about it at school, and the pictures I had seen. Then one morning I remembered a photograph the newspapers had featured on the occasion of the execution of a famous criminal. Actually the apparatus stood on the ground; there was nothing very impressive about it, and it was much narrower than I'd imagined. It struck me as rather odd that picture had escaped my memory until now. What had struck me at the time was the neat appearance of the guillotine; its shining surfaces and finish reminded one of some laboratory instrument. One always has exaggerated ideas about what one doesn't know. Now I had to admit it seemed a very simple process, getting guillotined; the machine is on the same level as the man, and he walks towards it as one steps forward to meet somebody one knows. In a sense, that, too, was disappointing. The business of climbing a scaffold, leaving the world below one, so to speak, gave something for a man's imagination to get hold of. But, as it was, the machine dominated everything; they killed you discreetly, with a hint of shame and much efficiency.

There were two other things about which I was always thinking: the dawn, and my appeal. However, I did my best to keep my mind off these thoughts. I lay down, looked up at the sky, and forced myself to study it. When the light began to turn green I knew that night was coming. Another thing I did to deflect the course of my thoughts was to listen to my heart. I couldn't imagine that this faint throbbing, which had been with me for so long, would ever cease. Imagination has never been one of my strong points. Still, I tried to picture a moment when the beating of my heart no longer echoed in my head. But in vain. The dawn and my appeal were still there. And I ended by believing it was a silly thing to try to force one's thoughts out of their natural groove.

They always came for one at dawn; that much I knew. So really all my nights were spent in waiting for that dawn. I have never liked being taken by surprise. When something happens to me I want to be ready for it. That's why I got into the habit of sleeping off and on in the daytime and watching through the night for the first hint of daybreak in the dark dome above. The worst period of the night was that vague hour when, I knew, they usually came; once it was after midnight I waited, listening intently. Never before had my ears perceived so many noises, such tiny sounds. Still, I must say I was lucky in one respect; never during any of those periods did I hear footsteps. Mother used to say that however miserable one is, there's always something to be thankful for. And each morning, when the sky brightened and light began to flood my cell, I agreed with her. Because I might just as well have heard footsteps, and felt my heart shattered into bits. Even though the faintest rustle sent me hurrying to the door and, pressing an ear to the rough, cold wood, I listened so intently that I could hear my breathing, quick and hoarse like a dog's panting—even so there was an end; my heart hadn't split, and I knew I had another twenty-four hours' respite.

Then all day there was my appeal to think about. I made the most of this idea, studying my effects so as to squeeze out the maximum of consolation. Thus I always began by assuming the worst; my appeal was dismissed. That meant, of course, I was to die. Sooner than others, obviously. 'But', I reminded myself, 'it's common knowledge that life isn't worth living anyhow.' And, on a wide view, I could see that it makes little difference whether one dies at the age of thirty or three-score and ten—since, in either case, other men and women will continue living, the world will go on as before. Also, whether I died now or forty years hence, this business of dying had to be got through, inevitably. Still, somehow this line of thought wasn't as consoling as it should have been; the idea of all those years of life in hand was a galling reminder! However, I could argue myself out of it, by picturing what would have been my feelings when my term was up, and death had cornered me. Once one's up against it, the precise manner of one's death has obviously small importance. Therefore—but it was hard not to lose the thread of the argument leading up to that 'therefore'—I should be prepared to face the dismissal of my appeal.

At this stage, but only at this stage, I had, so to speak, the *right*, and accordingly I gave myself leave, to consider the other alternative; that my appeal was successful. And then the trouble was to calm down that sudden rush of joy racing through my body and even bringing tears to my eyes. But it was up to me to bring my nerves to heel and steady my mind; for, even in considering this possibility, I had to keep some order in my thoughts, so as to make my consolations, as regards the first alternative, more plausible. When I'd succeeded, I had earned a good hour's peace of mind; and that, anyhow, was something.

It was at one of these moments that I refused once again to see the chaplain. I was lying down and could mark the summer evening coming on by a soft golden glow spreading across the sky. I had just turned down my appeal, and felt my blood circulating with slow, steady throbs. No, I didn't want to see the chaplain. . . . Then I did something I hadn't done for quite a while; I fell to thinking about Marie. She hadn't written for ages; probably, I surmised, she had grown tired of being the mistress of a man sentenced to death. Or she might be ill, or dead. After all, such things happen. How could I have known about it, since, apart from our two bodies, separated now, there was no link between us, nothing to remind us of each other? Supposing she were dead, her memory would mean nothing; I couldn't feel an interest in a dead girl. This seemed to me quite normal; just as I realized people would soon forget me once I was dead. I couldn't even say that this was hard to stomach; really, there's no idea to which one doesn't get acclimatized in time.

My thoughts had reached this point when the chaplain walked in, unannounced. I couldn't help giving a start on seeing him. He noticed this evidently, as he promptly told me not to be alarmed. I reminded him that usually his visits were at another hour, and for a pretty grim occasion. This, he replied, was just a friendly visit; it had no concern with my appeal, about which he knew nothing. Then he sat down on my bed, asking me to sit beside him. I refused—not because I had anything against him; he seemed a mild, amiable man.

He remained quite still at first, his arms resting on his knees, his eyes fixed on his hands. They were slender but sinewy hands, which made me think of two nimble little animals. Then he gently rubbed them together. He stayed so long in the same position that for a while I almost forgot he was there.

All of a sudden he jerked his head up and looked me in the eyes.

'Why', he asked, 'don't you let me come to see you?'

I explained that I didn't believe in God.

'Are you really so sure of that?'

I said I saw no point in troubling my head about the matter; whether I believed or didn't was, to my mind, a question of so little importance.

He then leant back against the wall, laying his hands flat on his thighs. Almost without seeming to address me, he remarked that he'd often noticed one fancies one is quite sure about something, when in point of fact one isn't. When I said nothing he looked at me again, and asked:

'Don't you agree?'

I said that seemed quite possible. But, though I mightn't be so sure about what interested me. I was absolutely sure about what didn't interest me. And the question he had raised didn't interest me at all.

He looked away and, without altering his posture, asked if it was because I felt utterly desperate that I spoke like this. I explained that it wasn't despair I felt, but fear—which was natural enough.

'In that case,' he said firmly, 'God can help you. All the men I've seen in your position turned to Him in their time of trouble.'

Obviously, I replied, they were at liberty to do so, if they felt like it. I however, didn't want to be helped, and I hadn't time to work up interest for something that didn't interest me.

He fluttered his hands fretfully; then, sitting up, smoothed out his cassock. When this was done he began talking again, addressing me as 'my friend'. It wasn't because I'd been condemned to death, he said, that he spoke to me in this way. In his opinion every man on the earth was under sentence of death.

There, I interrupted him; that wasn't the same thing, I pointed out, and, what's more, could be no consolation.

He nodded. 'Maybe. Still, if you don't die soon, you'll die one day. And then the same question will arise. How will you face that terrible, final hour?'

I replied that I'd face it exactly as I was facing it now.

Thereat he stood up, and looked me straight in the eyes. It was a trick I knew well. I used to amuse myself trying it on Emmanuel and Céleste and nine times out of ten they'd look away uncomfortably. I could see the chaplain was an old hand at it, as his gaze never faltered. And his voice was quite steady when he said: 'Have you no hope at all? Do you really think that when you die you die outright, and nothing remains?'

I said: 'Yes.'

He dropped his eyes and sat down again. He was truly sorry for me, he said. It must make life unbearable for a man, to think as I did.

The priest was beginning to bore me, and, resting a shoulder on the wall, just beneath the little skylight, I looked away. Though I didn't trouble much to follow what he said, I gathered he was questioning me again. Presently his tone became agitated, urgent, and, as I realized that he was genuinely distressed, I began to pay more attention.

He said he felt convinced my appeal would succeed, but I was saddled with a load of guilt, of which I must get rid. In his view man's justice was a vain thing; only God's justice mattered. I pointed out that the former had condemned me. Yes, he agreed, but it hadn't absolved me from my sin. I told him that I wasn't conscious of any 'sin'; all I knew was that I'd been guilty of a criminal offence. Well, I was paying the penalty of that offence, and no one had the right to expect anything more of me.

Just then he got up again, and it struck me that if he wanted to move in this tiny cell, almost the only choice lay between standing up and sitting down. I was staring at the floor. He took a single step towards me, and halted, as if he didn't dare to come nearer. Then he looked up through the bars at the sky.

'You're mistaken, my son,' he said gravely. 'There's more that might be required of you. And perhaps it *will* be required of you.'

'What do you mean?'

'You might be asked to see . . .'

'To see what?'

Slowly the priest gazed round my cell, and I was struck by the sadness of his voice when he spoke again.

'These stone walls, I know it only too well, are steeped in human suffering. I've never been able to look at them without a shudder. And yet—believe me, I am speaking from the depths of my heart—I *know* that even the wretchedest among you have sometimes seen, taking form upon that greyness, a divine face. It's that face you are asked to see.'

This roused me a little. I informed him that I'd been staring at those walls for months; there was nobody, nothing in the world, I knew better than I knew them. And once upon a time, perhaps, I used to try to see a face. But it was a sun-gold face, glowing with desire—Marie's face. I had no luck; I'd never seen it, and now I'd given up trying. Indeed I'd never seen anything 'taking form', as he called it, against those grey walls.

The chaplain gazed at me mournfully. I now had my back to the wall and light was flowing over my forehead. He muttered some words I didn't catch; then abruptly asked if he might kiss me. I said, 'No.' Then he turned, came up to the wall, and slowly drew his hand along it.

'Do you really love these earthly things so very much?' he asked in a low voice.

I made no reply.

For quite a while he kept his eyes averted. His presence was getting more and more irksome, and I was on the point of telling him to go, and leave me in peace, when all of a sudden he swung round on me, and burst out passionately:

'No! No! I refuse to believe it. I'm sure you've often wished there was an after-life.'

Of course I had, I told him. Everybody has that wish at times. But that had no more importance than wishing to be rich, or to swim very fast, or to have a better-shaped mouth. It was in the same order of things. I was going on in the same vein, when he cut in with a question. How did I picture my life after the grave?

I fairly bawled out at him: 'A life in which I can remember this life on earth. That's all I want of it.' And in the same breath I told him I'd had enough of his company.

But, apparently, he had more to say on the subject of God. I went close up to him and made a last attempt to explain that I'd very little time left, and I wasn't going to waste it on God.

Then he tried to change the subject by asking me why I hadn't once addressed him as 'Father', seeing that he was a priest. That irritated me still more, and I told him he wasn't my father; quite the contrary, he was on the others' side.

'No, no, my son,' he said, laying his hand on my shoulder. 'I'm on *your* side, though you don't realize it—because your heart is hardened. But I shall pray for you.'

Then, I don't know how it was, but something seemed to break inside me, and I started yelling at the top of my voice. I hurled insults at him, I told him not to waste his rotten prayers on me; it was better to burn than to disappear. I'd taken him by the neckband of his cassock, and, in a sort of ecstasy of joy and rage, I poured out on him all the thoughts that had been simmering in my brain. He seemed so cocksure, you see. And yet none of his certainties was worth one strand of a woman's hair. Living as he did, like a corpse, he couldn't even be sure of being alive. It might look as if my hands were empty. Actually, I was sure of myself, sure about everything, far surer than he; sure of my present life and of the death that was coming. That, no doubt, was all I had; but at least that certainty was something I could get my teeth into—just as it had got its teeth into me. I'd been right, I was still right, I was always right. I'd passed my life in a certain way, and I might have passed it in a different way, if I'd felt like it. I'd acted thus, and I hadn't acted otherwise; I hadn't done *x*, whereas I had done *y* or *z*. And what did that mean? That, all the time, I'd been waiting for this present moment, for that dawn, tomorrow's or another day's, which was to justify me. Nothing, nothing had the least importance, and I knew quite well why. He, too, knew why. From the dark horizon of my future a sort of slow, persistent breeze had been blowing towards me, all my life long, from the years that were to come. And on its way that breeze had levelled out all the ideas that people tried to foist on me in the equally unreal years I then was living through. What difference could they make to me, the death of others, or a mother's love, or his God; or the way one decides to live, the fate one thinks one chooses, since one and the same fate was bound to 'choose' not only me but thousands of millions of privileged people who, like him, called themselves my brothers. Surely, surely he must see that? Every man alive was privileged; there was only one class of men, the privileged class. All alike would be condemned to die one day; his turn, too, would come like the others'. And what difference could it make if, after being charged with murder, he were executed because he didn't weep at his mother's funeral, since it all came to the same thing in the end? The same thing for Salamano's wife and for Salamano's dog. That little robot woman was as 'guilty' as the girl from Paris who had married Masson, or as Marie, who wanted me to marry her. What did it matter if Raymond was as much my pal as Céleste, who was a far worthier man? What did it matter if at this very moment Marie was kissing a new boy friend? As a condemned man himself, couldn't he grasp what I meant by that dark wind blowing from my future? . . .

I had been shouting so much that I'd lost my breath, and just then the warders rushed in and started trying to release the chaplain from my grip. One of them made as if to strike me. The chaplain quietened them down, and gazed at me for a moment without speaking. I could see tears in his eyes. Then he turned and left the cell.

Once he'd gone, I felt calm again. But all this excitement had exhausted me and I dropped heavily on to my sleeping-plank. I must have had a longish sleep, for, when I woke, the stars were shining down on my face. Sounds of the country-side came faintly in, and the cool night air, veined with smells of earth and salt, fanned my cheeks. The marvellous peace of the sleepbound summer night flooded through me like a tide. Then, just on the edge of daybreak, I heard a steamer's siren. People were starting on a voyage to a world which had ceased to concern me, for ever. Almost for the first time in many months I thought of my mother. And now, it seemed to me, I understood why at her life's end she had taken on a 'fiancé'; why she'd played at making a fresh start. There, too, in that Home where lives were flickering out, the dusk came as a mournful solace. With death so near, Mother must have felt like someone on the brink of freedom, ready to start life all over again. No one, no one in the world had any right to weep for her. And I, too, felt ready to start life over again. It was as if that great rush of anger had washed me clean, emptied me of hope, and, gazing up at the dark sky spangled with its signs and stars, for the first time, the first, I laid my heart open to the benign indifference of the universe. To feel it so like myself, indeed so brotherly, made me realize that I'd been happy, and that I was happy still. For all to be accomplished, for me to feel less lonely, all that remained was to hope that on the day of my execution there should be a huge crowd of specta-tors and that they should greet me with howls of execration.

Carson McCullers

THE MEMBER OF
THE WEDDING

1946

MODERN life with its relentless drive towards standardization has ironed out differences between nations; to go from one country, even from one continent, to another is to remain within much the same world of plastics and canned music and convenience foods and interchangeable people. Differences between the regions within one country are naturally disappearing at an even faster rate. The Southern States of America, up to about fifty years ago, were culturally very different from the Northern; two centuries ago they must have felt like an entirely different civilization, and in the 1860s they were politically and culturally distinct to the point of feeling justified in going to war against each other.

All regions of America have had their own writers who express their way of life with a particular understanding and intimacy, but the South in particular had a fully-fledged literature of its own, different in tone, timbre, and preoccupations from those of the North or West. This remained true until the 1940s and was as evident in poetry as in prose; a poem like Allen Tate's 'Ode to the Confederate Dead' is as removed in its rhetorical openness as in its subject-matter from anything that could have come from a New England poet like Robert Frost. In the novels of William Faulkner, Erskine Caldwell, and Eudora Welty, the plays of Tennessee Williams, the Southern quality is equally evident.

Nowadays the South, no longer predominantly agrarian, seems virtually indistinguishable from the North. The climate is different, but everything else is the same, with every graceful old Southern city surrounded by a ring of suburbs that duplicate the suburbs of every Middle-Western city, and Birmingham, Alabama, marinated in the same pop culture as Birmingham, England. Inevitably, then, the Southern tradition in American literature has closed down. Perhaps its last fully developed representative was Carson McCullers (1917–67), a mistress of the short, intensely felt and lyrically written novel. She achieved immediate fame with her first book, *The Heart is a Lonely Hunter* (1940) and consolidated it with *Reflections in a Golden Eye* (1941) and then *The Member of the Wedding* (1946), which she herself turned into a long-running and award-winning play. *The Ballad of the Sad Café* (1951) collects her shorter fiction.

For Elizabeth Ames

PART ONE

IT HAPPENED that green and crazy summer when Frankie
was twelve years old. This was the summer when for a long
time she had not been a member. She belonged to no club and
was a member of nothing in the world. Frankie had become
an unjoined person who hung around in doorways, and she
was afraid. In June the trees were bright dizzy green, but later
the leaves darkened, and the town turned black and shrunken
under the glare of the sun. At first Frankie walked around doing
one thing and another. The sidewalks of the town were gray in
the early morning and at night, but the noon sun put a glaze on
them, so that the cement burned and glittered like glass. The
sidewalks finally became too hot for Frankie's feet, and also
she got herself in trouble. She was in so much secret trouble
that she thought it was better to stay at home—and at home
there was only Berenice Sadie Brown and John Henry West.
The three of them sat at the kitchen table, saying the same
things over and over, so that by August the words began to
rhyme with each other and sound strange. The world seemed
to die each afternoon and nothing moved any longer. At last the
summer was like a green sick dream, or like a silent crazy jungle
under glass. And then, on the last Friday of August, all this was
changed: it was so sudden that Frankie puzzled the whole blank
afternoon, and still she did not understand.

'It is so very queer,' she said. 'The way it all just happened.'

'Happened? Happened?' said Berenice.

John Henry listened and watched them quietly.

'I have never been so puzzled.'

'But puzzled about what?'

'The whole thing,' Frankie said.

And Berenice remarked: 'I believe the sun has fried your
brains.'

'Me too,' John Henry whispered.

Frankie herself almost admitted maybe so. It was four o'clock
in the afternoon and the kitchen was square and gray and
quiet. Frankie sat at the table with her eyes half closed, and
she thought about a wedding. She saw a silent church, a
strange snow slanting down against the colored windows.
The groom in this wedding was her brother, and there was

a brightness where his face should be. The bride was there in a long white train, and the bride also was faceless. There was something about this wedding that gave Frankie a feeling she could not name.

'Look here at me,' said Berenice. 'You jealous?'

'Jealous?'

'Jealous because your brother going to be married?'

'No,' said Frankie. 'I just never saw any two people like them. When they walked in the house today it was so queer.'

'You jealous,' said Berenice. 'Go and behold yourself in the mirror. I can see from the color in your eye.'

There was a watery kitchen mirror hanging above the sink. Frankie looked, but her eyes were gray as they always were. This summer she was grown so tall that she was almost a big freak, and her shoulders were narrow, her legs too long. She wore a pair of blue track shorts, a B.V.D. undervest, and she was barefooted. Her hair had been cut like a boy's, but it had not been cut for a long time and was now not even parted. The reflection in the glass was warped and crooked, but Frankie knew well what she looked like; she drew up her left shoulder and turned her head aside.

'Oh,' she said. 'They were the two prettiest people I ever saw. I just can't understand how it happened.'

'But what, Foolish?' said Berenice. 'Your brother come home with the girl he means to marry and took dinner today with you and your Daddy. They intend to marry at her home in Winter Hill this coming Sunday. You and your Daddy are going to the wedding. And that is the A and the Z of the matter. So whatever ails you?'

'I don't know,' said Frankie. 'I bet they have a good time every minute of the day.'

'Less us have a good time,' John Henry said.

'Us have a good time?' Frankie asked. 'Us?'

The three of them sat at the table again and Berenice dealt the cards for three-handed bridge. Berenice had been the cook since Frankie could remember. She was very black and broad-shouldered and short. She always said that she was thirty-five years old, but she had been saying that at least three years. Her hair was parted, plaited, and greased close to the skull, and she had a flat and quiet face. There was only one thing wrong about Berenice—her left eye was bright blue glass. It stared out fixed and wild from her quiet, colored face, and why she had wanted a blue eye nobody human would ever know. Her right eye was dark and sad. Berenice dealt slowly, licking her thumb when the sweaty cards stuck together. John Henry watched each card as it was being dealt. His chest was white and wet and naked, and he wore around his neck a tiny lead donkey tied by a string. He was blood kin to Frankie, first cousin, and all summer he would eat dinner and spend the day with her, or eat supper and spend the night; and she could not make him go home. He was small to be six years old, but he had the largest knees that Frankie had ever seen, and on one of them there was always a scab or a bandage where he had fallen down and skinned himself. John Henry had a little screwed white face and he wore tiny gold-rimmed glasses. He watched all of the cards very carefully, because he was in debt; he owed Berenice more than five million dollars.

'I bid one heart,' said Berenice.

'A spade,' said Frankie.

'I want to bid spades,' said John Henry. 'That's what I was going to bid.'

'Well, that's your tough luck. I bid them first.'

'Oh, you fool jackass!' he said. 'It's not fair!'

'Hush quarreling,' said Berenice. 'To tell the truth, I don't think either one of you got such a grand hand to fight over the bid about. I bid two hearts.'

'I don't give a durn about it,' Frankie said. 'It is immaterial with me.'

As a matter of fact this was so: she played bridge that afternoon like John Henry, just putting down any card that suddenly occurred to her. They sat together in the kitchen, and the kitchen was a sad and ugly room. John Henry had covered the walls with queer, child drawings, as far up as his arm would reach. This gave the kitchen a crazy look, like that of a room in the crazy-house. And now the old kitchen made Frankie sick. The name for what had happened to her Frankie did not know, but she could feel her squeezed heart beating against the table edge.

'The world is certainy a small place,' she said.

'What makes you say that?'

'I mean sudden,' said Frankie. 'The world is certainy a sudden place.'

'Well, I don't know,' said Berenice. 'Sometimes sudden and sometimes slow.'

Frankie's eyes were half closed, and to her own ears her voice sounded ragged, far away:

'To me it is sudden.'

For only yesterday Frankie had never thought seriously about a wedding. She knew that her only brother, Jarvis, was to be married. He had become engaged to a girl in Winter Hill just before he went to Alaska. Jarvis was a corporal in the army and he had spent almost two years in Alaska. Frankie had not seen her brother for a long, long time, and his face had become masked and changing, like a face seen under water. But Alaska! Frankie had dreamed of it constantly, and especially this summer it was very real. She saw the snow and frozen sea and ice glaciers. Esquimau igloos and polar bears and the beautiful Northern lights. When Jarvis had first gone to Alaska, she had sent him a box of homemade fudge, packing it carefully and wrapping each piece separately in waxed paper. It had thrilled her to think that her fudge would be eaten in Alaska, and she had a vision of her brother passing it around to furry Esquimaux. Three months later, a thank-you letter had come from Jarvis with a five-dollar bill enclosed. For a while she mailed candy almost every week, sometimes divinity instead of fudge, but Jarvis did not send her another bill, except at Christmas time. Sometimes his short letters to her father disturbed her a little. For instance, this summer he mentioned once that he had been in swimming and that the mosquitoes were something fierce. This letter jarred upon her dream, but after a few days of bewilderment, she returned to her frozen seas and snow. When Jarvis had come back from Alaska, he had gone straight to Winter Hill. The bride was named Janice Evans and the plans for the wedding were like this: her brother had wired that he and the bride were coming this Friday to spend the day, then on the following Sunday there was to be the wedding at Winter Hill. Frankie and her father were going to the wedding, traveling nearly a hundred miles to Winter Hill, and Frankie had already packed a suitcase. She looked forward to the time her brother and the bride should come, but she did not picture them to herself, and did not think about the wedding. So on the day before the visit she only commented to Berenice:

'I think it's a curious coincidence that Jarvis would get to go to Alaska and that the very bride he picked to marry would come from a place called Winter Hill. Winter Hill,' she repeated slowly, her eyes closed, and the name blended with dreams of Alaska and cold snow. 'I wish tomorrow was Sunday instead of Friday. I wish I had already left town.'

'Sunday will come,' said Berenice.

'I doubt it,' said Frankie. 'I've been ready to leave this town so long. I wish I didn't have to come back here after the wedding. I wish I was going somewhere for good. I wish I had a hundred dollars and could just light out and never see this town again.'

'It seems to me you wish for a lot of things,' said Berenice.

'I wish I was somebody else except me.'

So the afternoon before it happened was like the other August afternoons. Frankie had hung around the kitchen, then toward dark she had gone out into the yard. The scuppernong arbor behind the house was purple and dark in the twilight. She walked slowly. John Henry West was sitting beneath the August arbor in a wicker chair, his legs crossed and his hands in his pockets.

'What are you doing?' she asked.

'I'm thinking.'

'About what?'

He did not answer.

Frankie was too tall this summer to walk beneath the arbor as she had always done before. Other twelve-year-old people could still walk around inside, give shows, and have a good time. Even small grown ladies could walk underneath the arbor. And already Frankie was too big; this year she had to hang around and pick from the edges like the grown people. She stared into the tangle of dark vines, and there was the smell of crushed scuppernongs and dust. Standing beside the arbor, with dark coming on, Frankie was afraid. She did not know what caused this fear, but she was afraid.

'I tell you what,' she said. 'Suppose you eat supper and spend the night with me.'

John Henry took his dollar watch from his pocket and looked at it as though the time would decide whether or not he would come, but it was too dark under the arbor for him to read the numbers.

'Go on home and tell Aunt Pet. I'll meet you in the kitchen.'

'All right.'

She was afraid. The evening sky was pale and empty and the light from the kitchen window made a yellow square reflection in the darkening yard. She remembered that when she was a little girl she believed that three ghosts were living in the coal house, and one of the ghosts wore a silver ring.

She ran up the back steps and said: 'I just now invited John Henry to eat supper and spend the night with me.'

Berenice was kneading a lump of biscuit dough, and she dropped it on the flour-dusted table. 'I thought you were sick and tired of him.'

'I am sick and tired of him,' said Frankie. 'But it seemed to me he looked scared.'

'Scared of what?'

Frankie shook her head. 'Maybe I mean lonesome,' she said finally.

'Well, I'll save him a scrap of dough.'

After the darkening yard the kitchen was hot and bright and queer. The walls of the kitchen bothered Frankie—the queer drawings of Christmas trees, airplanes, freak soldiers, flowers. John Henry had started the first pictures one long afternoon in June, and having already ruined the wall, he went on and drew whenever he wished. Sometimes Frankie had drawn also. At first her father had been furious about the walls, but later he said for them to draw all the pictures out of their systems, and he would have the kitchen painted in the fall. But as the summer lasted, and would not end, the walls had begun to bother Frankie. That evening the kitchen looked strange to her, and she was afraid.

She stood in the doorway and said: 'I just thought I might as well invite him.'

So at dark John Henry came to the back door with a little week-end bag. He was dressed in his white recital suit and had put on shoes and socks. There was a dagger buckled to his belt. John Henry had seen snow. Although he was only six years old, he had gone to Birmingham last winter, and there he had seen snow. Frankie had never seen snow.

'I'll take the week-end bag,' said Frankie. 'You can start right in making a biscuit man.'

'O.K.'

John Henry did not play with the dough; he worked on the biscuit man as though it were a very serious business. Now and then he stopped off, settled his glasses with his little hand, and studied what he had done. He was like a tiny watchmaker, and he drew up a chair and knelt on it so that he could get directly over the work. When Berenice gave him some raisins, he did not stick them all around as any other human child would do; he used only two for the eyes; but immediately he realized they were too large—so he divided one raisin carefully and put in eyes, two specks for the nose, and a little grinning raisin mouth. When he had finished, he wiped his hands on the seat of his shorts, and there was a little biscuit man with separate fingers, a hat on, and even walking stick. John Henry had worked so hard that the dough was now gray and wet. But it was a perfect little biscuit man, and, as a matter of fact, it reminded Frankie of John Henry himself.

'I better entertain you now,' she said.

They ate supper at the kitchen table with Berenice, since her father had telephoned that he was working late at his jewelry store. When Berenice brought the biscuit man from the oven, they saw that it looked exactly like any biscuit man ever made by a child—it had swelled so that all the work of John Henry had been cooked out, the fingers were run together, and the walking stick resembled a sort of tail. But John Henry just looked at it through his glasses, wiped it with his napkin, and buttered the left foot.

It was a dark, hot August night. The radio in the dining room was playing a mixture of many stations: a war voice crossed with the gabble of an advertiser, and underneath there was the sleazy music of a sweet band. The radio had stayed on all the summer long, so finally it was a sound that as a rule they did not notice. Sometimes, when the noise became so loud that they could not hear their own ears, Frankie would turn it down a little. Otherwise, music and voices came and went and crossed and twisted with each other, and by August they did not listen any more.

'What do you want to do?' asked Frankie. 'Would you like for me to read to you out of Hans Brinker or would you rather do something else?'

'I rather do something else,' he said.

'What?'

'Less play out.'

'I don't want to,' Frankie said.

'There's a big crowd going to play out tonight.'

'You got ears,' Frankie said. 'You heard me.'

John Henry stood with his big knees locked, then finally he said: 'I think I better go home.'

'Why, you haven't spent the night! You can't eat supper and just go on off like that.'

'I know it,' he said quietly. Along with the radio they could hear the voices of the children playing in the night. 'But less go out, Frankie. They sound like they having a mighty good time.'

'No they're not,' she said. 'Just a lot of ugly silly children. Running and hollering and running and hollering. Nothing to it. We'll go upstairs and unpack your week-end bag.'

Frankie's room was an elevated sleeping porch which had been built onto the house, with a stairway leading up from the kitchen. The room was furnished with an iron bed, a bureau, and a desk. Also Frankie had a motor which could be turned on and off; the motor could sharpen knives, and, if they were long enough, it could be used for filing down your fingernails. Against the wall was the suitcase packed and ready for the trip to Winter Hill. On the desk there was a very old typewriter, and Frankie sat down before it, trying to think of any letters she could write: but there was nobody for her to write to, as every possible letter had already been answered, and answered even several times. So she covered the typewriter with a raincoat and pushed it aside.

'Honestly,' John Henry said, 'don't you think I better go home?'

'No,' she answered, without looking around at him. 'You sit there in the corner and play with the motor.'

Before Frankie there were now two objects—a lavender

seashell and a glass globe with snow inside that could be shaken into a snowstorm. When she held the seashell to her ear, she could hear the warm wash of the Gulf of Mexico, and think of a green palm island far away. And she could hold the snow globe to her narrowed eyes and watch the whirling white flakes fall until they blinded her. She dreamed of Alaska. She walked up a cold white hill and looked on a snowy wasteland far below. She watched the sun make colors in the ice, and heard dream voices, saw dream things. And everywhere there was the cold white gentle snow.

'Look,' John Henry said, and he was staring out of the window. 'I think those big girls are having a party in their clubhouse.'

'Hush!' Frankie screamed suddenly. 'Don't mention those crooks to me.'

There was in the neighborhood a clubhouse, and Frankie was not a member. The members of the club were girls who were thirteen and fourteen and even fifteen years old. They had parties with boys on Saturday night. Frankie knew all of the club members, and until this summer she had been like a younger member of their crowd, but now they had this club and she was not a member. They had said she was too young and mean. On Saturday night she could hear the terrible music and see from far away their light. Sometimes she went around to the alley behind the clubhouse and stood near a honeysuckle fence. She stood in the alley and watched and listened. They were very long, those parties.

'Maybe they will change their mind and invite you,' John Henry said.

'The son-of-a-bitches.'

Frankie sniffled and wiped her nose in the crook of her arm. She sat down on the edge of the bed, her shoulders slumped and her elbows resting on her knees. 'I think they have been spreading it all over town that I smell bad,' she said. 'When I had those boils and that black bitter smelling ointment, old Helen Fletcher asked what was that funny smell I had. Oh, I could shoot every one of them with a pistol.'

She heard John Henry walking up to the bed, and then she felt his hand patting her neck with tiny little pats. 'I don't think you smell so bad,' he said. 'You smell sweet.'

'The son-of-a-bitches,' she said again. 'And there was something else. They were talking nasty lies about married people. When I think of Aunt Pet and Uncle Ustace. And my own father! The nasty lies! I don't know what kind of fool they take me for.'

'I can smell you the minute you walk in the house without even looking to see if it is you. Like a hundred flowers.'

'I don't care,' she said. 'I just don't care.'

'Like a thousand flowers,' said John Henry, and still he was patting his sticky hand on the back of her bent neck.

Frankie sat up, licked the tears from around her mouth, and wiped off her face with her shirttail. She sat still, her nose widened, smelling herself. Then she went to her suitcase and took out a bottle of Sweet Serenade. She rubbed some on the top of her head and poured some more down inside the neck of her shirt.

'Want some on you?'

John Henry was squatting beside the open suitcase and he gave a little shiver when she poured the perfume over him. He wanted to meddle in her traveling suitcase and look carefully at everything she owned. But Frankie only wanted him to get a general impression, and not count and know just what she had and what she did not have. So she strapped the suitcase and pushed it back against the wall.

'Boy!' she said. 'I bet I use more perfume than anybody in this town.'

The house was quiet except for the low rumble of the radio in the dining room downstairs. Long ago her father had come home and Berenice had closed the back door and gone away. There was no longer the sound of children's voices in the summer night.

'I guess we ought to have a good time,' said Frankie.

But there was nothing to do. John Henry stood, his knees locked and his hands clasped behind his back, in the middle of the room. There were moths at the window—pale green moths and yellow moths that fluttered and spread their wings against the screen.

'Those beautiful butterflies,' he said. 'They are trying to get in.'

Frankie watched the soft moths tremble and press against the window screen. The moths came every evening when the lamp on her desk was lighted. They came from out of the August night and fluttered and clung against the screen.

'To me it is the irony of fate,' she said. 'The way they come here. Those moths could fly anywhere. Yet they keep hanging around the windows of this house.'

John Henry touched the gold rim of his glasses to settle them on his nose and Frankie studied his flat little freckled face.

'Take off those glasses,' she said suddenly.

John Henry took them off and blew on them. She looked through the glasses and the room was loose and crooked. Then she pushed back her chair and stared at John Henry. There were two damp white circles around his eyes.

'I bet you don't need those glasses,' she said. She put her hand down on the typewriter. 'What is this?'

'The typewriter,' he said.

Frankie picked up the shell. 'And this?'

'The shell from the Bay.'

'What is that little thing crawling there on the floor?'

'Where?' he asked, looking around him.

'That little thing crawling along near your feet.'

'Oh,' he said. He squatted down. 'Why, it's an ant. I wonder how it got up here.'

Frankie tilted back in her chair and crossed her bare feet on her desk. 'If I were you I'd just throw those glasses away,' she said. 'You can see good as anybody.'

John Henry did not answer.

'They don't look becoming.'

She handed the folded glasses to John Henry and he wiped them with his pink flannel glasses rag. He put them back on and did not answer.

'O.K.' she said. 'Suit yourself. I was only telling you for your own good.'

They went to bed. They undressed with their backs turned to each other and then Frankie switched off the motor and the light. John Henry knelt down to say his prayers and he prayed for a long time, not saying the words aloud. Then he lay down beside her.

'Good night,' she said.

'Good night.'

Frankie stared up into the dark. 'You know it is still hard for me to realize that the world turns around at the rate of about a thousand miles an hour.'

'I know it,' he said.

'And to understand why it is that when you jump up in the air you don't come down in Fairview or Selma or somewhere fifty miles away.'

John Henry turned over and made a sleepy sound.

'Or Winter Hill,' she said. 'I wish I was starting for Winter Hill right now.'

Already John Henry was asleep. She heard him breathe in the darkness, and now she had what she had wanted so many nights that summer; there was somebody sleeping in the bed with her. She lay in the dark and listened to him breathe, then after a while she raised herself on her elbow. He lay freckled and small in the moonlight, his chest white and naked, and one foot hanging from the edge of the bed. Carefully she put her hand on his stomach and moved closer; it felt as though a little clock was ticking inside him and he smelled of sweat and Sweet Serenade. He smelled like a sour little rose. Frankie leaned down and licked him behind the ear. Then she breathed deeply, settled herself with her chin on his sharp damp shoulder, and closed her eyes: for now, with somebody sleeping in the dark with her, she was not so much afraid.

The sun woke them early the next morning, the white August sun. Frankie could not make John Henry go home. He saw the ham Berenice was cooking, and that the special company dinner was going to be good. Frankie's father read the paper in the living room, then went downtown to wind the watches at his jewelry store.

'If that brother of mine don't bring me a present from Alaska, I will be seriously mad,' said Frankie.

'Me too,' agreed John Henry.

And what were they doing that August morning when her brother and the bride came home? They were sitting in the arbor shade and talking about Christmas. The glare was hard and bright, the sun-drunk bluejays screamed and murdered among themselves. They talked, and their voices tired down into a little tune and they said the same things over and over.

They just drowsed in the dark shade of the arbor, and Frankie was a person who had never thought about a wedding. That was the way they were that August morning when her brother and the bride walked in the house.

'Oh, Jesus!' Frankie said. The cards on the table were greasy and the late sun slanted across the yard. 'The world is certainy a sudden place.'

'Well, stop commenting about it,' said Berenice. 'You don't have your mind on the game.'

Frankie, however, had some of her mind on the game. She played the queen of spades, which were trumps, and John Henry threw off a little two of diamonds. She looked at him. He was staring at the back of her hand as though what he wanted and needed was angled eyesight that could cut around corners and read people's cards.

'You got a spade,' said Frankie.

John Henry put his donkey necklace in his mouth and looked away.

'Cheater,' she said.

'Go on and play your spade,' said Berenice.

Then he argued: 'It was hid behind the other card.'

'Cheater.'

But still he would not play. He sat there sad and holding up the game.

'Make haste,' said Berenice.

'I can't,' he said finally. 'It's a jack. The only spade I got is a jack. I don't want to play my jack down under Frankie's queen. I'm not going to do it either.'

Frankie threw her cards down on the table. 'See!' she said to Berenice. 'He don't even follow the first beginning laws! He is a child! It is hopeless! Hopeless! Hopeless!'

'Maybe so,' said Berenice.

'Oh,' Frankie said, 'I am sick unto death.'

She sat with her bare feet on the rungs of the chair, her eyes closed, and her chest against the table edge. The red greasy cards were messed together on the table, and the sight of them made Frankie sick. They had played cards after dinner every single afternoon; if you would eat those old cards, they would taste like a combination of all the dinners of that August, together with a sweaty-handed nasty taste. Frankie swept the cards from the table. The wedding was bright and beautiful as snow and the heart in her was mashed. She got up from the table.

'It is a known truth that gray-eyed people are jealous.'

'I told you I wasn't jealous,' Frankie said, and she was walking fast around the room. 'I couldn't be jealous of one of them without being jealous of them both. I sociate the two of them together.'

'Well, I were jealous when my foster brother married,' said Berenice. 'I admit that when John married Clorina I sent a warning I would tear the ears off her head. But you see I didn't. Clorina got ears like anybody else. And now I love her.'

'J A,' said Frankie. 'Janice and Jarvis. Isn't that the strangest thing?'

'What?'

'J A,' she said. 'Both their names begin with J A.'

'And? What about it?'

Frankie walked round and round the kitchen table. 'If only my name was Jane,' she said. 'Jane or Jasmine.'

'I don't follow your frame of mind,' said Berenice.

'Jarvis and Janice and Jasmine. See?'

'No,' said Berenice. 'By the way, I heard this morning on the radio that the French people are chasing the Germans out of Paris.'

'Paris,' Frankie repeated in a hollow tone. 'I wonder if it is against the law to change your name. Or to add to it.'

'Naturally. It is against the law.'

'Well, I don't care,' she said. 'F. Jasmine Addams.'

On the staircase leading to her room there was a doll, and John Henry brought it to the table and sat rocking it in his arms. 'You serious when you gave me this,' he said. He pulled up the doll's dress and fingered the real panties and body-waist. 'I will name her Belle.'

Frankie stared at the doll for a minute. 'I don't know what went on in Jarvis's mind when he brought me that doll. Imagine bringing me a doll! And Janice tried to explain that she had pictured me as a little girl. I had counted on Jarvis bringing me something from Alaska.'

'Your face when you unwrapped the package was a study,' said Berenice.

It was a large doll with red hair and china eyes that opened and closed, and yellow eyelashes. John Henry held her in a lying-down position, so that the eyes were shut, and he was now trying to open them by pulling up the eyelashes.

'Don't do that! It makes me nervous. In fact, take that doll somewhere out of my sight.'

John Henry took it to the back porch where he could pick it up when he went home.

'Her name is Lily Belle,' he said.

The clock ticked very slowly on the shelf above the stove, and it was only quarter to six. The glare outside the window was still hard and yellow and bright. In the back yard the shade beneath the arbor was black and solid. Nothing moved. From somewhere far away came the sound of whistling, and it was a grieving August song that did not end. The minutes were very long.

Frankie went again to the kitchen mirror and stared at her own face. 'The big mistake I made was to get this close crew-cut. For the wedding I ought to have long bright yellow hair. Don't you think so?'

She stood before the mirror and she was afraid. It was the summer of fear, for Frankie, and there was one fear that could be figured in arithmetic with paper and a pencil at the table. This August she was twelve and five-sixths years old. She was five feet five and three-quarter inches tall, and she wore a number seven shoe. In the past year she had grown four inches, or at least that was what she judged. Already the hateful little summer children hollered to her: 'Is it cold up there?' And the comments of grown people made Frankie shrivel on her heels. If she reached her height on her eighteenth birthday, she had five and one-sixth growing years ahead of her. Therefore, according to mathematics and unless she could somehow stop herself, she would grow to be over nine feet tall. And what would be a lady who is over nine feet high? She would be a Freak.

In the early autumn of every year the Chattahoochee Exposition came to town. For a whole October week the fair went on down at the fair grounds. There was the Ferris Wheel, the Flying Jinney, the Palace of Mirrors—and there, too, was the House of the Freaks. The House of the Freaks was a long pavilion which was lined on the inside with a row of booths. It cost a quarter to go into the general tent, and you could look at each Freak in his booth. Then there were special private exhibitions farther back in the tent which cost a dime apiece. Frankie had seen all of the members of the Freak House last October:

> The Giant
> The Fat Lady
> The Midget
> The Wild Nigger
> The Pin Head
> The Alligator Boy
> The Half-Man Half-Woman

The Giant was more than eight feet high, with huge loose hands and a hang-jaw face. The Fat Lady sat in a chair, and the fat on her was like loose-powdered dough which she kept slapping and working with her hands—next was the squeezed Midget who minced around in little trick evening clothes. The Wild Nigger came from a savage island. He squatted in his booth among the dusty bones and palm leaves and he ate raw living rats. The fair gave a free admission to his show to all who brought rats of the right size, and so children carried them down in strong sacks and shoe boxes. The Wild Nigger knocked the rat's head over his squatted knee and ripped off the fur and crunched and gobbled and flashed his greedy Wild Nigger eyes. Some said that he was not a genuine Wild Nigger, but a crazy colored man from Selma. Anyway, Frankie did not like to watch him very long. She pushed through the crowd to the Pin Head booth, where John Henry had stood all afternoon. The little Pin Head skipped and giggled and sassed around, with a shrunken head no larger than an orange, which was shaved except for one lock tied with a pink bow at the top. The last booth was always very crowded, for it was the booth of the Half-Man Half-Woman, a morphidite and a miracle of science. This Freak was divided completely in half—the left side was a man and the right side a woman. The costume on the left was a leopard skin and on the right side a brassiere and a sprangled skirt. Half the face was dark-bearded and the other half bright glazed with paint. Both eyes were strange. Frankie had wandered around the tent and looked at every booth. She

was afraid of all the Freaks, for it seemed to her that they had
looked at her in a secret way and tried to connect their eyes
with hers, as though to say: we know you. She was afraid of
their long Freak eyes. And all the year she had remembered
them, until this day.

'I doubt if they ever get married or go to a wedding,' she
said. 'Those Freaks.'

'What freaks you talking about?' asked Berenice.

'At the fair,' said Frankie. 'The ones we saw there last
October.'

'Oh, those folks.'

'I wonder if they make a big salary,' she said.

And Berenice answered: 'How would I know?'

John Henry held out an imaginary skirt and, touching his
finger to the top of his big head, he skipped and danced like
the Pin Head around the kitchen table.

Then he said: 'She was the cutest little girl I ever saw. I never
saw anything so cute in my whole life. Did you, Frankie?'

'No,' she said. 'I didn't think she was cute.'

'Me and you both,' said Berenice.

'Shoo!' John Henry argued. 'She was, too.'

'If you want my candy opinion,' said Berenice, 'that whole
crowd of folks down yonder at the fair just give me the creeps.
Ever last one of them.'

Frankie watched Berenice through the mirror, and finally
she asked in a slow voice. 'Do *I* give you the creeps?'

'You?' asked Berenice.

'Do you think I will grow into a Freak?' Frankie whispered.

'You?' said Berenice again. 'Why, certainly not, I trust Jesus.'

Frankie felt better. She looked sidewise at herself in the
mirror. The clock ticked six slow times, and then she said:
'Well, do you think I will be pretty?'

'Maybe. If you file down them horns a inch or two.'

Frankie stood with her weight resting on her left leg, and
she slowly shuffled the ball of her right foot on the floor. She
felt a splinter go beneath the skin. 'Seriously,' she said.

'I think when you fill out you will do very well. If you
behave.'

'But by Sunday,' Frankie said. 'I want to do something to
improve myself before the wedding.'

'Get clean for a change. Scrub your elbows and fix yourself nice. You will do very well.'

Frankie looked for a last time at herself in the mirror, and then she turned away. She thought about her brother and the bride, and there was a tightness in her that would not break.

'I don't know what to do. I just wish I would die.'

'Well, die then!' said Berenice.

And: 'Die,' John Henry echoed in a whisper.

The world stopped.

'Go home,' said Frankie to John Henry.

He stood with his big knees locked, his dirty little hand on the edge of the white table, and he did not move.

'You heard me,' Frankie said. She made a terrible face at him and grabbed the frying pan that hung above the stove. She chased him three times around the table, then up through the front hall and out of the door. She locked the front door and called again: 'Go home.'

'Now what makes you act like that?' asked Berenice. 'You are too mean to live.'

Frankie opened the door to the stairway that led up to her room, and sat down on one of the lower steps. The kitchen was silent and crazy and sad.

'I know it,' she said. 'I intend to sit still by myself and think over everything for a while.'

This was the summer when Frankie was sick and tired of being Frankie. She hated herself, and had become a loafer and a big no-good who hung around the summer kitchen: dirty and greedy and mean and sad. Besides being too mean to live, she was a criminal. If the Law knew about her, she could be tried in the courthouse and locked up in the jail. Yet Frankie had not always been a criminal and a big no-good. Until the April of that year, and all the years of her life before, she had been like other people. She belonged to a club and was in the seventh grade at school. She worked for her father on Saturday morning and went to the show every Saturday afternoon. She was not the kind of person ever to think of being afraid. At night she slept in the bed with her father, but not because she was scared of the dark.

Then the spring of that year had been a long queer season. Things began to change and Frankie did not understand this change. After the plain gray winter the March winds banged on the windowpanes, and clouds were shirred and white on the blue sky. April that year came sudden and still, and the green of the trees was a wild bright green. The pale wistarias bloomed all over town, and silently the blossoms shattered. There was something about the green trees and the flowers of April that made Frankie sad. She did not know why she was sad, but because of this peculiar sadness, she began to realize she ought to leave the town. She read the war news and thought about the world and packed her suitcase to go away; but she did not know where she should go.

It was the year when Frankie thought about the world. And she did not see it as a round school globe, with the countries neat and different-colored. She thought of the world as huge and cracked and loose and turning a thousand miles an hour. The geography book at school was out of date; the countries of the world had changed. Frankie read the war news in the paper, but there were so many foreign places, and the war was happening so fast, that sometimes she did not understand. It was the summer when Patton was chasing the Germans across France. And they were fighting, too, in Russia and Saipan. She saw the battles, and the soldiers. But there were too many different battles, and she could not see in her mind the millions and millions of soldiers all at once. She saw one Russian soldier, dark and frozen with a frozen gun, in Russian snow. The single Japs with slanted eyes on a jungle island gliding among green vines. Europe and the people hung in trees and the battleships on the blue oceans. Four-motor planes and burning cities and a soldier in a steel war helmet, laughing. Sometimes these pictures of the war, the world, whirled in her mind and she was dizzy. A long time ago she had predicted that it would take two months to win the whole war, but now she did not know. She wanted to be a boy and go to the war as a Marine. She thought about flying aeroplanes and winning gold medals for bravery. But she could not join the war, and this made her sometimes feel restless and blue. She decided to donate blood to the Red Cross; she wanted to donate a quart a week and her blood would be in the veins of Australians and Fighting French and Chinese, all over the whole world, and it would be as though she were close kin to all of these people. She could hear the army doctors saying that the blood of Frankie Addams was the reddest and the strongest blood that they had ever known. And she could picture ahead, in the years after the war, meeting the soldiers who had her blood, and they would say that they owed their life to her; and they would not call her Frankie—they would call her Addams. But this plan for donating her blood to the war did not come true. The Red Cross would not take her blood. She was too young. Frankie felt mad with the Red Cross, and left out of everything. The war and the world were too fast and big and strange. To think about the world for very long made her afraid. She was not afraid of Germans or bombs or Japanese. She was afraid because in the war they would not include her, and because the world seemed somehow separate from herself.

So she knew she ought to leave the town and go to some place far away. For the late spring, that year, was lazy and too sweet. The long afternoons flowered and lasted and the green sweetness sickened her. The town began to hurt Frankie. Sad and terrible happenings had never made Frankie cry, but this season many things made Frankie suddenly wish to cry. Very early in the morning she would sometimes go out into the yard and stand for a long time looking at the sunrise sky. And it was as though a question came into her heart, and the sky did not answer. Things she had never noticed much before began to hurt her: home lights watched from the evening sidewalks, an unknown voice from an alley. She would stare at the lights and listen to the voice, and something inside her stiffened and waited. But the lights would darken, the voice fall silent, and though she waited, that was all. She was afraid of these things that made her suddenly wonder who she was, and what she was going to be in the world, and why she was standing at that minute, seeing a light, or listening, or staring up into the sky: alone. She was afraid, and there was a queer tightness in her chest.

One night in April, when she and her father were going to bed, he looked at her and said, all of a sudden: 'Who is this great big long-legged twelve-year-old blunderbuss who still wants to sleep with her old Papa.' And she was too big to sleep with her father any more. She had to sleep in her upstairs room alone. She began to have a grudge against her father and they looked at each other in a slant-eyed way. She did not like to stay at home.

She went around town, and the things she saw and heard seemed to be left somehow unfinished, and there was the tightness in her that would not break. She would hurry to do something, but what she did was always wrong. She would call her best friend, Evelyn Owen, who owned a football suit and a Spanish shawl, and one would dress in the football suit and the other in the Spanish shawl and they would go down to the ten-cent store together. But that was a wrong thing and not what Frankie wanted. Or after the pale spring twilights, with the smell of dust and flowers sweet and bitter in the air, evenings of lighted windows and the long drawn calls at supper time, when the chimney swifts had gathered and whirled above the town and flown off somewhere to their home together, leaving the sky empty and wide; after the long twilights of this season, when Frankie had walked around the sidewalks of the town, a jazz sadness quivered her nerves and her heart stiffened and almost stopped.

Because she could not break this tightness gathering within her, she would hurry to do something. She would go home and put the coal scuttle on her head, like a crazy person's hat, and walk around the kitchen table. She would do anything that suddenly occurred to her—but whatever she did was always wrong, and not at all what she had wanted. Then, having done these wrong and silly things, she would stand, sickened and empty, in the kitchen door and say:

'I just wish I could tear down this whole town.'

'Well, tear it down, then. But quit hanging around here with that gloomy face. Do something.'

And finally the troubles started.

She did things and she got herself in trouble. She broke the law. And having once become a criminal, she broke the law again, and then again. She took the pistol from her father's bureau drawer and carried it all over town and shot up the cartridges in a vacant lot. She changed into a robber and stole a three-way knife from the Sears and Roebuck Store. One Saturday afternoon in May she committed a secret and unknown sin. In the MacKeans' garage, with Barney MacKean, they committed a queer sin, and how bad it was she did not know. The sin made a shriveling sickness in her stomach, and she dreaded the eyes of everyone. She hated Barney and wanted to kill him. Sometimes alone in the bed at night she planned to shoot him with the pistol or throw a knife between his eyes.

Her best friend, Evelyn Owen, moved away to Florida, and Frankie did not play with anybody any more. The long and flowering spring was over and the summer in the town was ugly and lonesome and very hot. Every day she wanted more and more to leave the town: to light out for South America or Hollywood or New York City. But although she packed her suitcase many times, she could never decide to which of these places she ought to go, or how she would get there by herself.

So she stayed home and hung around the kitchen, and the summer did not end. By dog days she was five feet five and three-quarter inches tall, a great big greedy loafer who was too mean to live. She was afraid, but not as she had been before. There was only the fear of Barney, her father, and the Law. But even these fears were finally gone; after a long time the sin in the MacKeans' garage became far from her and was remembered only in her dreams. And she would not think of her father or the Law. She stuck close in the kitchen with John Henry and Berenice. She did not think about the war, the world. Nothing hurt her any longer; she did not care. She never stood alone in the back yard in order to stare up at the sky. She paid no attention to sounds and summer voices, and did not walk the streets of town at night. She would not let things make her sad and she would not care. She ate and wrote shows and practiced throwing knives against the side of the garage and played bridge at the kitchen table. Each day was like the day before, except that it was longer, and nothing hurt her any more.

So that Sunday when it happened, when her brother and the bride came to the house, Frankie knew that everything was changed; but why this was so, and what would happen to her next, she did not know. And though she tried to talk with Berenice, Berenice did not know either.

'It gives me this kind of a pain,' she said, 'to think about them.'

'Well, don't,' said Berenice. 'You done nothing but think and carry on about them all this afternoon.'

Frankie sat on the bottom step of the stairs to her room, staring into the kitchen. But although it gave her a kind of a pain, she had to think about the wedding. She remembered the way her brother and the bride had looked when she walked into the living room, that morning at eleven o'clock. There had been in the house a sudden silence, for Jarvis had turned off the radio when they came in ; after the long summer, when the radio had gone on day and night, so that no one heard it any more, the curious silence had startled Frankie. She stood in the doorway, coming from the hall, and the first sight of her brother and the bride had shocked her heart. Together they made in her this feeling that she could not name. But it was like the feelings of the spring, only more sudden and more sharp. There was the same tightness and in the same queer way she was afraid. Frankie thought until her mind was dizzy and her foot had gone to sleep.

Then she asked Berenice: 'How old were you when you married your first husband?'

While Frankie was thinking, Berenice had changed into her Sunday clothes, and now she sat reading a magazine. She was waiting for the people who were due to meet her at six o'clock, Honey and T. T. Williams; the three of them were going to eat supper at the New Metropolitan Tea Room and sashay together around the town. As Berenice read, she moved her lips to shape each word. Her dark eye looked up as Frankie spoke, but, since Berenice did not raise her head, the blue glass eye seemed to go on reading the magazine. This two-sighted expression bothered Frankie.

'I were thirteen years old,' said Berenice.

'What made you get married so young for?'

'Because I wanted to,' said Berenice. 'I were thirteen years old and I haven't growed a inch since.'

Berenice was very short, and Frankie looked hard at her and asked: 'Does marrying really stop your growth?'

'It certainly do,' said Berenice.

'I didn't know that,' Frankie said.

had been married four different times. Her first
was Ludie Freeman, a brickmason, and the favorite
one of the four; he gave Berenice her fox fur, and
once they had gone to Cincinnati and seen snow. Berenice and
Ludie Freeman had seen a whole winter of Northern snow.
They loved each other and were married for nine years, until
the November he was sick and died. The other three husbands
were all bad, each one worse than the one before, and it made
Frankie blue just to hear about them. The first was a sorry
old liquor-drinker. The next went crazy on Berenice: he did
crazy things, had eating dreams in the night and swallowed a
corner of the sheet; and what with one thing and another he
distracted Berenice so much that finally she had to quit him.
The last husband was terrible. He gouged out Berenice's eye
and stole her furniture away from her. She had to call the Law
on him.

'Did you marry with a veil every time?' asked Frankie.

'Two times with a veil,' said Berenice.

Frankie could not keep still. She walked around the kitchen,
although there was a splinter in her right foot and she was
limping, her thumbs hooked in the belt of her shorts and her
undershirt clinging and wet.

Finally she opened the drawer of the kitchen table and
selected a long sharp butcher knife. Then she sat down and
rested the ankle of her sore foot on her left knee. The sole of
her foot was long and narrow, pitted with ragged whitish scars,
as every summer Frankie stepped on many nails; Frankie had
the toughest feet in town. She could slice off waxy yellow rinds
from the bottoms of her feet, and it did not hurt her very much,
although it would hurt other people. But she did not chisel for
the splinter immediately—she just sat there, her ankle on her
knee and the knife in her right hand, looking across the table
at Berenice.

'Tell me,' she said. 'Tell me exactly how it was.'

'You know!' said Berenice. 'You seen them.'

'But tell me,' Frankie said.

'I will discuss it for the last time,' said Berenice. 'Your brother
and the bride come late this morning and you and John Henry
hurried in from the back yard to see them. Then next thing
I realize you busted back through the kitchen and run up to

your room. You came down with your organdie dress on and lipstick a inch thick from one ear to the next. Then you all just sat around up in the living room. It was hot. Jarvis had brought Mr. Addams a bottle of whiskey and they had liquor drinks and you and John Henry had lemonade. Then after dinner your brother and the bride took the three-o'clock train back to Winter Hill. The wedding will be this coming Sunday. And that is all. Now, is you satisfied?'

'I am so disappointed they couldn't stay longer—at least spend the night. After Jarvis being away so long. But I guess they want to be together as long as they can. Jarvis said he had some army papers to fill out at Winter Hill.' She took a deep breath. 'I wonder where they will go after the wedding.'

'On their honeymoon. Your brother will have a few days' leave.'

'I wonder where that honeymoon will be.'

'Well, I'm sure I don't know.'

'Tell me,' Frankie said again. 'Exactly what did they look like?'

'Look like?' said Berenice. 'Why, they looked natural. Your brother is a good-looking blond white boy. And the girl is kind of brunette and small and pretty. They make a nice white couple. You seen them, Foolish.'

Frankie closed her eyes, and, though she did not see them as a picture, she could feel them leaving her. She could feel the two of them together on the train, riding and riding away from her. They were them, and leaving her, and she was her, and sitting left all by herself there at the kitchen table. But a part of her was with them, and she could feel this part of her own self going away, and farther away; farther and farther, so that a drawn-out sickness came in her, going away and farther away, so that the kitchen Frankie was an old hull left there at the table.

'It is so queer,' she said.

She bent over the sole of her foot, and there was something wet, like tears or sweat drops on her face; she sniffled and began to cut for the splinter.

'Don't that hurt you none?' asked Berenice.

Frankie shook her head and did not answer. Then after a moment she said: 'Have you ever seen any people that afterward you remembered more like a feeling than a picture?'

'How you mean?'

'I mean this,' said Frankie slowly. 'I saw them O.K. Janice had on a green dress and green high-heel dainty shoes. Her hair was done up in a knot. Dark hair and a little piece of it was loose. Jarvis sat by her on the sofa. He had on his brown uniform and he was sunburned and very clean. They were the two prettiest people I ever saw. Yet it was like I couldn't see all of them I wanted to see. My brains couldn't gather together quick enough and take it all in. And then they were gone. You see what I mean?'

'You hurting yourself,' said Berenice. 'What you need is a needle.'

'I don't care anything about my old feet,' Frankie said.

It was only half-past six, and the minutes of the afternoon were like bright mirrors. From outside there was no longer the sound of whistling and in the kitchen nothing moved. Frankie sat facing the door that opened onto the back porch. There was a square cat-hole cut in a corner of the back door, and near-by a saucer of lavender sour milk. In the beginning of dog days Frankie's cat had gone away. And the season of dog days is like this: it is the time at the end of the summer when as a rule nothing can happen—but if a change does come about, that change remains until dog days are over. Things that are done are not undone and a mistake once made is not corrected.

That August Berenice scratched a mosquito bite under her right arm and it became a sore: that sore would never heal until dog days were over. Two little families of August gnats picked out the corners of John Henry's eyes to settle down in, and though he often shook himself and blinked, those gnats were there to stay. Then Charles disappeared. Frankie did not see him leave the house and walk away, but on the fourteenth of August, when she called him to his supper, he did not come, and he was gone. She looked for him everywhere and sent John Henry wailing out his name through all the streets of town. But it was the season of dog days and Charles did not come back again. Every afternoon Frankie said exactly the same words to Berenice, and the answers of Berenice were always the same. So that now the words were like an ugly little tune they sang by heart.

'If only I just knew where he has gone.'

'Quit worrying yourself about that old alley cat. I done told you he ain't coming back.'

'Charles is not alley. He is almost pure Persian.'

'Persian as I is,' Berenice would say. 'You seen the last of that old tom cat. He gone off to hunt a friend.'

'To hunt a friend?'

'Why, certainy. He roamed off to find himself a lady-friend.'

'You really think so?'

'Naturally.'

'Well, why don't he bring his friend home with him. He ought to know I would be only too glad to have a whole family of cats.'

'You seen the last of that old alley cat.'

'If only I just knew where he is gone.'

And so each gloomy afternoon their voices sawed against each other, saying the same words, which finally reminded Frankie of a raggedy rhyme said by two crazies. She would end by telling Berenice: 'It looks to me like everything has just walked off and left me.' And she would put her head down on the table and feel afraid.

But this afternoon Frankie suddenly changed all this. An idea came to her, and she put down the knife and got up from the table.

'I know what I ought to do,' she suddenly said. 'Listen.'

'I can hear.'

'I ought to notify the police force. They will find Charles.'

'I wouldn't do that,' said Berenice.

Frankie went to the hall telephone and explained to the Law about her cat. 'He is almost pure Persian,' she said. 'But with short hair. A very lovely color of gray and with a little white spot on his throat. He answers to the name of *Charles*, but if he don't answer to that, he might come if you call *Charlina*. My name is Miss F. Jasmine Addams and the address is 124 Grove Street.'

Berenice was giggling when she came back, a soft high giggle. 'Whew! They going to send around here and tie you up and drag you off to Milledgeville. Them fat blue police chasing tomcats around alleys and hollering: *Oh Charles, Oh come here, Charlina!* Sweet Jesus!'

'Aw, shut up,' Frankie said.

Berenice was sitting at the table; she had stopped giggling and her dark eye roved in a teasing way as she sloshed coffee into a white china saucer to cool.

'At the same time,' she said, 'I can't see how it is such a wise idea to trifle around with the Law. No matter for what reason.'

'I'm not trifling with the Law.'

'You just now set there and spelled them out your name and your house number. Where they can lay hold of you if ever they take the notion.'

'Well, let them!' said Frankie angrily. 'I don't care! I don't care!' And suddenly she did not care if anybody knew she was a criminal or not. 'Let them come get me for all I care.'

'I was just teasing you,' said Berenice. 'The trouble with you is that you don't have no sense of humor any more.'

'Maybe I'd be better off in jail.'

Frankie walked around the table and she could feel them going away. The train was traveling to the North. Mile after mile they went away, farther and farther away from the town, and as they traveled to the North, a coolness came into the air and dark was falling like the evening dark of wintertime. The train was winding up into the hills, the whistle wailing in a winter tone, and mile after mile they went away. They passed among themselves a box of bought store candy, with chocolates set in dainty, pleated shells, and watched the winter miles pass by the window. Now they had gone a long, long way from town and soon would be in Winter Hill.

'Sit down,' said Berenice. 'You make me nervous.'

Suddenly Frankie began to laugh. She wiped her face with the back of her hand and went back to the table. 'Did you hear what Jarvis said?'

'What?'

Frankie laughed and laughed.

'They were talking about whether to vote for C. P. Mac-Donald. And Jarvis said: *Why, I wouldn't vote for that scoundrel if he was running to be the dog-catcher.* I never heard anything so witty in my life.'

Berenice did not laugh. Her dark eye glanced down in a corner, quickly saw the joke, and then looked back at Frankie. Berenice wore her pink crepe dress and her hat with the pink

heart that beats in your head when you have fever. Frankie was dizzy, and she picked up the knife from the kitchen table.

'You better quit!'

Berenice stopped very suddenly. The kitchen was suddenly shrunken and quiet.

'You lay down that knife.'

'Make me.'

She steadied the end of the handle against her palm and bent the blade slowly. The knife was limber, sharp, and long.

'Lay it down, DEVIL!'

But Frankie stood up and took careful aim. Her eyes were narrowed and the feel of the knife made her hands stop trembling.

'Just throw it!' said Berenice. 'You just!'

All the house was very quiet. The empty house seemed to be waiting. And then there was the knife whistle in the air and the sound the blade made when it struck. The knife hit the middle of the stairway door and shivered there. She watched the knife until it did not shiver any longer.

'I am the best knife-thrower in this town,' she said.

Berenice, who stood behind her, did not speak.

'If they would have a contest I would win.'

Frankie pulled the knife from the door and laid it on the kitchen table. Then she spat on her palm and rubbed her hands together.

Berenice said finally: 'Frances Addams, you going to do that once too often.'

'I never miss outside of a few inches.'

'You know what your father said about knife-throwing in this house.'

'I warned you to quit picking with me.'

'You are not fit to live in a house,' said Berenice.

'I won't be living in this one much longer. I'm going to run away from home.'

'And a good riddance to a big old bad rubbage,' said Berenice.

'You wait and see. I'm leaving town.'

'And where you think you are going?'

Frankie looked at all the corners of the room, and then said, 'I don't know.'

'I do,' said Berenice. 'You going crazy. That's where you going.'

'No,' said Frankie. She stood very still, looking around the queerly pictured wall, and then she closed her eyes. 'I'm going to Winter Hill. I'm going to the wedding. And I swear to Jesus by my two eyes I'm never coming back here any more.'

She had not been sure that she would throw the knife until it struck and shivered on the stairway door. And she had not known that she would say these words until already they were spoken. The swear was like the sudden knife; she felt it strike in her and tremble. Then when the words were quiet, she said again:

'After the wedding I'm not coming back.'

Berenice pushed back the damp bangs of Frankie's hair and finally she asked: 'Sugar? You serious?'

'Of course!' said Frankie. 'Do you think I would stand here and swear that swear and tell a story? Sometimes, Berenice, I think it takes you longer to realize a fact than it does anybody who ever lived.'

'But,' said Berenice, 'you say you don't know where you're going. You going, but you don't know where. That don't make no sense to me.'

Frankie stood looking up and down the four walls of the room. She thought of the world, and it was fast and loose and turning, faster and looser and bigger than ever it had been before. The pictures of the War sprang out and clashed together in her mind. She saw bright flowered islands and a land by a northern sea with the gray waves on the shore. Bombed eyes and the shuffle of soldiers' feet. Tanks and a plane, wing broken, burning and downward-falling in a desert sky. The world was cracked by the loud battles and turning a thousand miles a minute. The names of places spun in Frankie's mind: China, Peachville, New Zealand, Paris, Cincinnati, Rome. She thought of the huge and turning world until her legs began to tremble and there was sweat on the palms of her hands. But still she did not know where she should go. Finally she stopped looking around the four kitchen walls and said to Berenice:

'I feel just exactly like somebody has peeled all the skin off me. I wish I had some cold good chocolate ice cream.'

Berenice had her hands on Frankie's shoulders and was shaking her head and staring with the live eye narrowed into Frankie's face.

'But every word I told you was the solemn truth,' she said. 'I'm not coming back here after the wedding.'

There was a sound, and when they turned they saw that Honey and T. T. Williams were standing in the doorway. Honey, though he was her foster brother, did not resemble Berenice—and it was almost as though he came from some foreign country, like Cuba or Mexico. He was light-skinned, almost lavender in color, with quiet narrow eyes like oil, and a limber body. Behind the two of them stood T. T. Williams, and he was very big and black; he was gray-haired, older even than Berenice, and he wore a church suit with a red badge in the buttonhole. T. T. Williams was a beau of Berenice, a well-off colored man who owned a colored restaurant. Honey was a sick, loose person. The army would not include him, and he had shoveled in a gravel pit until he broke one of his insides and could not do heavy work any more. They stood, the three of them, dark and grouped together in the door.

'What you all creep up like that for?' asked Berenice. 'I didn't even hear you.'

'You and Frankie too busy discussing something,' said T. T.

'I am ready to go,' said Berenice. 'I been ready. But do you wish a small little quickie before we start?'

T. T. Williams looked at Frankie and shuffled his feet. He was very proper, and he liked to please everybody, and he always wanted to do the right thing.

'Frankie ain't no tattle-tale,' said Berenice. 'Is you?'

Frankie would not even answer such a question. Honey wore a dark red rayon slack suit and she said: 'That sure is a cute suit you got on, Honey. Where did you get it?'

Honey could talk like a white school-teacher; his lavender lips could move as quick and light as butterflies. But he only answered with a colored word, a dark sound from the throat that can mean anything. 'Ahhnnh,' he said.

The glasses were before them on the table, and the hair-straightening bottle that held gin, but they did not drink. Berenice said something about Paris and Frankie had the extra feeling that they were waiting for her to leave. She stood in the door and looked at them. She did not want to go away.

'You wish water in yours, T. T.?' asked Berenice.

They were together around the table and Frankie stood extra in the door alone. 'So long, you all,' she said.

''Bye, Sugar,' said Berenice. 'You forget all that foolishness we was discussing. And if Mr. Addams don't come home by dark, you go on over to the Wests. Go play with John Henry.'

'Since when have I been scared of the dark?' said Frankie. 'So long.'

'So long,' they said.

She closed the door, but behind her she could hear their voices. With her head against the kitchen door she could hear the murmuring dark sounds that rose and fell in a gentle way. Ayee—ayee. And then Honey spoke above the idle wash of voices and he asked: 'What was it between you and Frankie when we come in the house?' She waited, her ear pressed close against the door, to hear what Berenice would say. And finally the words were: 'Just foolishness. Frankie was carrying on with foolishness.' She listened until at last she heard them go away.

The empty house was darkening. She and her father were alone at night, as Berenice went to her own home directly after supper. Once they had rented the front bedroom. It was the year after her grandmother died, when Frankie was nine. They rented the front bedroom to Mr. and Mrs. Marlowe. The only thing Frankie remembered about them was the remark said at the last, that they were common people. Yet for the season they were there, Frankie was fascinated by Mr. and Mrs. Marlowe and the front room. She loved to go in when they were away and carefully, lightly meddle with their things—with Mrs. Marlowe's atomizer which skeeted perfume, the gray-pink powder puff, the wooden shoe-trees of Mr. Marlowe. They left mysteriously after an afternoon that Frankie did not understand. It was a summer Sunday and the hall door of the Marlowes' room was open. She could see only a portion of the room, part of the dresser and only the footpiece of the bed with Mrs. Marlowe's corset on it. But there was a sound in the quiet room she could not place, and when she stepped over the threshold she was startled by a sight that, after a single glance, sent her running to the kitchen, crying: Mr. Marlowe is having a fit! Berenice had hurried through the hall, but when she looked into the front room, she merely bunched her lips and banged the door. And evidently told her father, for that evening he said the Marlowes would have to leave. Frankie had tried to question Berenice and find out what was the matter. But Berenice had only said that they were common people and added that with a certain party in the house they ought at least to know enough to shut a door. Though Frankie knew she was the certain party, still she did not understand. What kind of a fit was it? she asked. But Berenice would only answer: Baby, just a common fit. And Frankie knew from the voice's tones that there was more to it than she was told. Later she only remembered the Marlowes as common people, and being common they owned common things—so that long after she had ceased to think about the Marlowes or fits, remembering merely the name and the fact that once they had rented the front bedroom, she associated common people with gray-pink powder puffs and perfume atomizers. The front bedroom had not been rented since.

Frankie went to the hall hatrack and put on one of her father's hats. She looked at her dark ugly mug in the mirror. The conversation about the wedding had somehow been wrong. The questions she had asked that afternoon had all been the wrong questions, and Berenice had answered her with jokes. She could not name the feeling in her, and she stood there until dark shadows made her think of ghosts.

Frankie went out to the street before the house and looked up into the sky. She stood staring with her fist on her hip and her mouth open. The sky was lavender and slowly darkening. She heard in the neighborhood the sound of evening voices and noticed the light fresh smell of watered grass. This was the time of the early evening when, since the kitchen was too hot, she would go for a little while outdoors. She practiced knife-throwing, or sat before the cold-drink store in the front yard. Or she would go around to the back yard, and there

the arbor was cool and dark. She wrote shows, although she
had outgrown all of her costumes, and was too big to act in
them beneath the arbor; this summer she had written very
cold shows—shows about Esquimaux and frozen explorers.
Then when night had come she would go again back in the
house.

But this evening Frankie did not have her mind on knives
or cold-drink stores or shows. Nor did she want to stand there
staring up into the sky; for her heart asked the old questions,
and in the old way of the spring she was afraid.

She felt she needed to think about something ugly and plain,
so she turned from the evening sky and stared at her own house.
Frankie lived in the ugliest house in town, but now she knew
that she would not be living there much longer. The house
was empty, dark. Frankie turned and walked to the end of
the block, and around the corner, and down the sidewalk to
the Wests'. John Henry was leaning against the banisters of
his front porch, with a lighted window behind him, so that
he looked like a little black paper doll on a piece of yellow
paper.

'Hey,' she said. 'I wonder when that Papa of mine is coming
home from town.'

John Henry did not answer.

'I don't want to go back in that dark old ugly house all by
myself.'

She stood on the sidewalk, looking at John Henry, and the
smart political remark came back to her. She hooked her thumb
in the pockets of her pants and asked: 'If you were going to vote
in an election, who would you vote for?'

John Henry's voice was bright and high in the summer night.
'I don't know,' he said.

'For instance, would you cast your vote for C. P. MacDonald
to be mayor of this town?'

John Henry did not answer.

'Would you?'

But she could not get him to talk. There were times when
John Henry would not answer anything you said to him. So
she had to remark without an argument behind her, and all
by herself like that it did not sound so very smart: 'Why, I
wouldn't vote for him if he was running to be dog-catcher.'

The darkening town was very quiet. For a long time now her brother and the bride had been at Winter Hill. They had left the town a hundred miles behind them, and now were in a city far away. They were them and in Winter Hill, together, while she was her and in the same old town all by herself. The long hundred miles did not make her sadder and make her feel more far away than the knowing that they were them and both together and she was only her and parted from them, by herself. And as she sickened with this feeling a thought and explanation suddenly came to her, so that she knew and almost said aloud: *They are the we of me.* Yesterday, and all the twelve years of her life, she had only been Frankie. She was an *I* person who had to walk around and do things by herself. All other people had a *we* to claim, all other except her. When Berenice said *we*, she meant Honey and Big Mama, her lodge, or her church. The *we* of her father was the store. All members of clubs have a *we* to belong to and talk about. The soldiers in the army can say *we*, and even the criminals on chain-gangs. But the old Frankie had had no *we* to claim, unless it would be the terrible summer *we* of her and John Henry and Berenice—and that was the last *we* in the world she wanted. Now all this was suddenly over with and changed. There was her brother and the bride, and it was as though when first she saw them something she had known inside of her: *They are the we of me.* And that was why it made her feel so queer, for them to be away in Winter Hill while she was left all by herself; the hull of the old Frankie left there in the town alone.

'Why are you all bent over like that?' John Henry called.

'I think I have a kind of pain,' said Frankie. 'I must have ate something.'

John Henry was still standing on the banisters, holding to the post.

'Listen,' she said finally. 'Suppose you come on over and eat supper and spend the night with me.'

'I can't,' he answered.

'Why?'

John Henry walked across the banisters, holding out his arms for balance, so that he was like a little blackbird against the yellow window light. He did not answer until he safely reached the other post.

'Just because.'

'Because why?'

He did not say anything, and so she added: 'I thought maybe me and you could put up my Indian tepee and sleep out in the back yard. And have a good time.'

Still John Henry did not speak.

'We're blood first cousins. I entertain you all the time. I've given you so many presents.'

Quietly, lightly, John Henry walked back across the banisters and then stood looking out at her with his arm around the post again.

'Sure enough,' she called. 'Why can't you come?'

At last he said. 'Because, Frankie, I don't want to.'

'Fool jackass!' she screamed. 'I only asked you because I thought you looked so ugly and so lonesome.'

Lightly John Henry jumped down from the banisters. And his voice as he called back to her was a clear child's voice.

'Why, I'm not a bit lonesome.'

Frankie rubbed the wet palms of her hands along the sides of her shorts and said in her mind: Now turn around and take yourself on home. But in spite of this order, she was somehow unable to turn around and go. It was not yet night. Houses along the street were dark, lights showed in windows. Darkness had gathered in the thick-leaved trees and shapes in the distance were ragged and gray. But the night was not yet in the sky.

'I think something is wrong,' she said. 'It is too quiet. I have a peculiar warning in my bones. I bet you a hundred dollars it's going to storm.'

John Henry watched her from behind the banister.

'A terrible terrible dog day storm. Or maybe even a cyclone.'

Frankie stood waiting for the night. And just at that moment a horn began to play. Somewhere in the town, not far away, a horn began a blues tune. The tune was grieving and low. It was the sad horn of some colored boy, but who he was she did not know. Frankie stood stiff, her head bent and her eyes closed, listening. There was something about the tune that brought back to her all of the spring: flowers, the eyes of strangers, rain.

The tune was low and dark and sad. Then all at once, as Frankie listened, the horn danced into a wild jazz spangle that zigzagged upward with sassy nigger trickiness. At the end of the jazz spangle the music rattled thin and far away. Then the tune returned to the first blues song, and it was like the telling of that long season of trouble. She stood there on the dark sidewalk and the drawn tightness of her heart made her knees lock and her throat feel stiffened. Then, without warning, the thing happened that at first Frankie could not believe. Just at the time when the tune should be laid, the music finished, the horn broke off. All of a sudden the horn stopped playing. For a moment Frankie could not take it in, she felt so lost.

She whispered finally to John Henry West: 'He has stopped to bang the spit out of his horn. In a second he will finish.'

But the music did not come again. The tune was left broken, unfinished. And the drawn tightness she could no longer stand. She felt she must do something wild and sudden that never had been done before. She hit herself on the head with her fist, but that did not help any at all. And she began to talk aloud, although at first she paid no attention to her own words and did not know in advance what she would say.

'I told Berenice that I was leaving town for good and she did not believe me. Sometimes I honestly think she is the biggest fool that ever drew breath.' She complained aloud, and her voice was fringed and sharp like the edge of a saw. She talked and did not know from one word to the next what she would say. She listened to her own voice, but the words she heard did not make much sense. 'You try to impress something on a big fool like that and it's just like talking to a block of cement. I kept on telling and telling and telling her. I told her I had to leave this town for good because it is inevitable.'

She was not talking to John Henry. She did not see him any more. He had moved from the lighted window; but he was still listening from the porch, and after a little while he asked her:

'Where?'

Frankie did not answer. She was suddenly very still and quiet. For a new feeling had come to her. The sudden feeling was that she knew deep in her where she would go. She knew, and in another minute the name of the place would come to her. Frankie bit the knuckles of her fist and waited: but she did not hunt for the name of the place and did not think about the turning world. She saw in her mind her brother and the bride, and the heart in her was squeezed so hard that Frankie almost felt it break.

John Henry was asking in his high child voice: 'You want me to eat supper and sleep in the tepee with you?'

She answered: 'No.'

'You just a little while ago invited me!'

But she could not argue with John Henry West or answer anything he said. For it was just at that moment that Frankie understood. She knew who she was and how she was going into the world. Her squeezed heart suddenly opened and divided. Her heart divided like two wings. And when she spoke her voice was sure.

'I know where I'm going,' she said.

He asked her: 'Where?'

'I'm going to Winter Hill,' she said. 'I'm going to the wedding.'

She waited, to give him a chance to say: 'I already knew that, anyhow.' Then finally she spoke the sudden truth aloud.

'I'm going with them. After the wedding at Winter Hill, I'm going off with the two of them to whatever place that they will ever go. I'm going with them.'

He did not answer.

'I love the two of them so much. We'll go to every place together. It's like I've known it all my life, that I belong to be with them. I love the two of them so much.'

And having said this, she did not need to wonder and puzzle any more. She opened her eyes, and it was night. The lavender sky had at last grown dark and there was slanted starlight and twisted shade. Her heart had divided like two wings and she had never seen a night so beautiful.

Frankie stood looking into the sky. For when the old question came to her—the who she was and what she would be in the world, and why she was standing there that minute—when the old question came to her, she did not feel hurt and unanswered. At last she knew just who she was and understood where she was going. She loved her brother and the bride and she was a member of the wedding. The three of them would go into the world and they would always be together. And finally, after the scared spring and the crazy summer, she was no more afraid.

PART TWO

I

THE DAY before the wedding was not like any day that F. Jasmine had ever known. It was the Saturday she went into the town, and suddenly, after the closed blank summer, the town opened before her and in a new way she belonged. Because of the wedding, F. Jasmine felt connected with all she saw, and it was as a sudden member that on this Saturday she went around the town. She walked the streets entitled as a queen and mingled everywhere. It was the day when, from the beginning, the world seemed no longer separate from herself and when all at once she felt included. Therefore, many things began to happen—nothing that came about surprised F. Jasmine and, until the last at least, all was natural in a magic way.

At the country house of an uncle of John Henry, Uncle Charles, she had seen old blindered mules going round and round in the same circle, grinding juice from the sugar cane for syrup. In the sameness of her tracks that summer, the old Frankie had somehow resembled that country mule; in town she browsed around the counters of the ten-cent store, or sat on the front row of the Palace show, or hung around her father's store, or stood on street corners watching soldiers. Now this morning was altogether different. She went into places she had never dreamed of entering until that day. For one thing, F. Jasmine went to a hotel—it was not the finest hotel in the town, or even the next to the finest, but nevertheless it was a hotel and F. Jasmine was there. Furthermore, she was there with a soldier, and that, too, was an unforeseen event, as she had never in her life laid eyes on him until that day. Only yesterday, if the old Frankie had glimpsed a box-like vision of this scene, as a view seen through a wizard's periscope, she would have bunched her mouth with unbelief. But it was a morning when many things occurred, and a curious fact about this day was a twisted sense of the astonishing; the unexpected did not make her wonder, and only the long known, the familiar, struck her with a strange surprise.

The day began when she waked up at dawn, and it was as though her brother and the bride had, in the night, slept on the bottom of her heart, so that the first instant she recognized the wedding. Next, and immediately, she thought about the town. Now that she was leaving home she felt in a curious way as though on this last day the town called to her and was now waiting. The windows of her room were cool dawn-blue. The old cock at the MacKeans' was crowing. Quickly she got up and turned on the bed-lamp and the motor.

It was the old Frankie of yesterday who had been puzzled, but F. Jasmine did not wonder any more; already she felt familiar with the wedding for a long, long time. The black dividing night has something to do with this. In the twelve years before, whenever a sudden change had come about there was a certain doubt during the time when it was happening; but after sleeping through a night, and on the very next day, the change did not seem so sudden after all. Two summers past, when she had traveled with the Wests to Port Saint Peter on the bay, the first sea evening with the scalloped gray ocean and empty sand was to her like a foreign place, and she had gone around with slanted eyes and put her hands on things in doubt. But after the first night, as soon as she awoke next day, it was as though she had known Port Saint Peter all her life. Now it was likewise with the wedding. No longer questioning, she turned to other things.

She sat at her desk wearing only the blue-and-white striped trousers of her pajamas which were rolled up above the knees, vibrating her right foot on the ball of her bare foot, and considering all that she must do on this last day. Some of these things she could name to herself, but there were other things that could not be counted on her fingers or made into a list with words. To start with, she decided to make herself some visiting cards with _Miss F. Jasmine Addams, Esq._, engraved with squinted letters on a tiny card. So she put on her green visor eyeshade, cut up some cardboard, and fitted ink pens behind both ears. But her mind was restless and zigzagged to other things, and soon she began to get ready for town. She dressed carefully that morning in her most grown and best, the pink organdie, and put on lipstick and Sweet Serenade.

Her father, a very early riser, was stirring in the kitchen when she went downstairs.

'Good morning, Papa.'

Her father was Royal Quincy Addams and he owned a jewelry store just off the main street of the town. He answered her with a kind of grunt, for he was a grown person who liked to drink three cups of coffee before he started conversation for the day; he deserved a little peace and quiet before he put his nose down to the grindstone. F. Jasmine had heard him bungling about his room when once she waked up to drink water in the night, and his face was pale as cheese this morning, his eyes had a pink and ragged look. It was a morning when he despised a saucer because his cup would rattle against it and not fit, so he put his cup down on the table or stove top until brown circles were left all over everywhere and flies settled in quiet rings. There was some sugar spilt on the floor, and each time his step made a gritty sound his face shivered. This morning he wore a pair of saggy-kneed gray trousers and a blue shirt unfastened at the collar and with the tie loose. Since June she had had this secret grudge against him that almost she did not admit—since the night he had asked who was the great big blunderbuss, who still wanted to sleep with her old Papa—but now she had this grudge no longer. All of a sudden it seemed to F. Jasmine that she saw her father for the first time, and she did not see him only as he was at that one minute, but pictures of the old days swirled in her mind and crossed each other. Remembrance, changing and fast, made F. Jasmine stop very still and stand with her head cocked, watching him both in the actual room and from somewhere inside her. But there were things that must be said, and when she spoke her voice was not unnatural.

'Papa, I think I ought to tell you now. I'm not coming back here after the wedding.'

He had ears to hear with, loose large ears with lavender rims, but he did not listen. He was a widowman, for her mother had died the very day that she was born—and, as a widowman, set in his ways. Sometimes, especially in the early morning, he did not listen to things she said or new suggestions. So she sharpened her voice and chiseled the words into his head.

'I have to buy a wedding dress and some wedding shoes and a pair of pink, sheer stockings.'

He heard and, after a consideration, gave her a permission nod. The grits boiled slowly with blue gluey bubbles, and as she set the table, she watched him and remembered. There were the winter mornings with frost flowers on the windowpanes and the roaring stove and the look of his brown crusty hand as he leaned over her shoulder to help with a hard part of the last-minute arithmetic that she was working at the table, his voice explaining. Blue long spring evenings, she saw also, and her father on the dark front porch with his feet propped on the banisters, drinking the frosted bottles of beer he had sent her to bring home from Finny's Place. She saw him bent over the workbench down at the store, dipping a tiny spring in gasoline, or whistling and peering with his round jeweler's glass into a watch. Remembrances came sudden and swirled, each colored with its own season, and for the first time she looked back on all the twelve years of her life and thought of them from a distance as a whole.

'Papa,' she said, 'I will write you letters.'

Now he walked the dawn-stale kitchen like a person who has lost something, but has forgotten what it is that he has lost. Watching him, the old grudge was forgotten, and she felt sorry. He would miss her in the house all by himself when she was gone. He would be lonesome. She wanted to speak some sorry words and love her father, but just at that moment he cleared his throat in the special way he used when he was going to lay down the law to her and said:

'Will you please tell me what has become of the monkey-wrench and screw-driver that were in my tool chest on the back porch?'

'The monkey-wrench and screw-driver——' F. Jasmine stood with her shoulders hunched, her left foot drawn up to the calf of the right leg. 'I borrowed them, Papa.'

'Where are they now?'

F. Jasmine considered. 'Over at the Wests'.'

'Now pay attention and listen to me,' her father said, holding the spoon that had been stirring the grits, and shaking it to mark the words. 'If you don't have the sense and judgment to leave things alone——' He stared at her in a long and threatening way, and finished: 'You'll have to be taught. From now on you walk the chalkline. Or you'll have to be taught.' He sniffed suddenly. 'Is that toast burning?'

It was still early in the morning when F. Jasmine left the house that day. The soft gray of the dawn had lightened and the sky was the wet pale blue of a watercolor sky just painted and not yet dried. There was a freshness in the bright air and cool dew on the burnt brown grass. From a back yard down the street, F. Jasmine could hear children's voices. She heard the calling voices of the neighborhood children who were trying to dig a swimming pool. They were all sizes and ages, members of nothing, and in the summers before, the old Frankie had been like leader or president of the swimming-pool diggers in that part of town—but now that she was twelve years old, she knew in advance that, though they would work and dig in various yards, not doubting to the very last the cool clear swimming pool of water, it would all end in a big wide ditch of shallow mud.

Now, as F. Jasmine crossed her yard, she saw in her mind's eye the swarming children and heard from down the street their chanting cries—and this morning, for the first time in her life, she heard a sweetness in these sounds, and she was touched. And, strange to say, her own home yard which she had hated touched her a little too; she felt she had not seen it for a long time. There, under the elm tree was her old cold-drink store, a light packing case that could be dragged around according to the shade, with a sign reading, DEW DROP INN. It was the time of morning when, the lemonade in a bucket underneath the store, she used to settle herself with her bare feet on the counter and the Mexican hat tilted down over her face—her eyes closed, smelling the strong smell of sun-warmed straw, waiting. And sometimes there would be customers, and she would send John Henry to the A. & P. to buy some candy, but other times the Tempter Satan got the best of her and she drank up all the stock instead. But now this morning the store looked very small and staggered, and she knew that she would never run it any more. F. Jasmine thought of the whole idea as something over and done with that had happened long ago. A sudden plan came to her: after tomorrow, when she was with Janice and Jarvis, in the

far place where they would be, she would look back on the old
days and—But this was a plan F. Jasmine did not finish, for, as
the names lingered in her mind, the gladness of the wedding
rose up inside her and, although the day was an August day,
she shivered.

The main street, too, seemed to F. Jasmine like a street
returned to after many years, although she had walked up
and down it only Wednesday. There were the same brick
stores, about four blocks of them, the big white bank, and in
the distance the many-windowed cotton mill. The wide street
was divided by a narrow aisle of grass on either side of which
the cars drove slowly in a browsing way. The glittering gray
sidewalks and passing people, the striped awning over the
stores, all was the same—yet, as she walked the street that
morning, she felt free as a traveler who had never seen the
town before.

And that was not all; she had no sooner walked down the left
side of the main street and up again on the right sidewalk, when
she realized a further happening. It had to do with various
people, some known to her and others strangers, she met
and passed along the street. An old colored man, stiff and
proud on his rattling wagon seat, drove a sad blindered mule
down toward the Saturday market. F. Jasmine looked at him,
he looked at her, and to the outward appearance that was all.
But in that glance, F. Jasmine felt between his eyes and her
own eyes a new unnameable connection, as though they were
known to each other—and there even came an instant vision
of his home field and country roads and quiet dark pine trees
as the wagon rattled past her on the paved town street. And
she wanted him to know her, too—about the wedding.

Now the same thing happened again and again on those
four blocks: with a lady going into MacDougal's store, with
a small man waiting for the bus before the big First National
Bank, with a friend of her father's called Tut Ryan. It was a
feeling impossible to explain in words—and later when she
tried to tell of it at home Berenice raised up her eyebrows and
dragged the word in a mocking way: Connection? Connection?
But nevertheless it was there, this feeling—a connection close
as answers to calls. Furthermore, on the sidewalk before the
First National Bank she found a dime and any other day that

would have been a grand surprise, but now this morning she only paused to shine the dime on her dress front and put it in her pink pocketbook. Under the fresh blue early sky the feeling as she walked along was one of newly risen lightness, power, entitlement.

It was in a place called the Blue Moon that she first told about the wedding, and she came to the Blue Moon in a roundabout way, as it was not on the main street, but on the street called Front Avenue which bordered the river. She was in this neighborhood because she had heard the organ of the monkey and the monkey-man and had set out immediately to find them. She had not seen the monkey and the monkey-man through the whole summer and it seemed a sign to her that she should run across them on this last day in town. She had not seen them for so long that sometimes she thought the pair of them might even be dead. They did not go around the streets in wintertime, for the cold wind made them sick; they went South in October to Florida and came back to the town in warm late spring.

They, the monkey and the monkey-man, wandered to other towns also—but the old Frankie would come across them on various shaded streets through all the summers she could remember, except this one. He was a darling little monkey, and the monkey-man was nice also; the old Frankie had always loved them, and now she was dying to tell her plans and let them know about the wedding. So, when she first heard the broken-sounding, faint organ, she went at once in search of it, and the music seemed to come from near the river on Front Avenue. So she turned from the main street and hurried down the side street, but just before she reached Front Avenue the organ stopped, and when she gazed up and down the avenue she could not see the monkey or the monkey-man and all was silent and they were nowhere in sight. They had stopped, maybe, in a doorway or a shop—so F. Jasmine walked slowly with a watchful air.

Front Avenue was a street that had always drawn her, although it had the sorriest, smallest stores in town. On the left side of the street there were warehouses, and in between were glimpses of brown river and green trees. On the right side there was a place with a sign reading Prophylactic Military, the business of which had often puzzled her, then other various places: a smelly fish shop with the shocked eyes of a single fish staring from some crushed ice in the window, a pawnshop, a second-hand clothing store with out-of-style garments hanging from the narrow entrance and a row of broken shoes lined up on the sidewalk outside. Then finally there was the place called the Blue Moon. The street itself was cobbled with brick and angry-looking in the glare, and along the gutter she passed some eggshells and rotten lemon peels. It was not a fine street, but nevertheless the old Frankie had liked to come here now and then at certain times.

The street was quiet in the mornings and on the week-day afternoons. But toward evening, or on holidays, the street would fill with the soldiers who came from the camp nine miles away. They seemed to prefer Front Avenue to almost any other street, and sometimes the pavement resembled a flowing river of brown soldiers. They came to town on holidays and went around in glad, loud gangs together, or walked the sidewalks with grown girls. And the old Frankie had always watched them with a jealous heart; they came from all over the whole country and were soon going all over the world. They went around in gangs together, those lasting twilights of the summertime—while the old Frankie dressed in her khaki shorts and Mexican hat, watched from a distance by herself. Noises and weathers of distant places seemed to hover about them in the air. She imagined the many cities that these soldiers came from, and thought of the countries where they would go—while she was stuck there in the town forever. And stealing jealousy sickened her heart. But now this morning her heart was occupied with one intention: to tell of the wedding and her plans. So, after walking down the burning pavement, hunting for the monkey and the monkey-man, she came to the Blue Moon and it occurred to her that maybe they were there.

The Blue Moon was a place at the end of Front Avenue, and often the old Frankie had stood out on the sidewalk with her palms and nose pressed flat against the screen door, watching all that went on there. Customers, most of them soldiers, sat at the boothed tables, or stood at the counter having drinks, or crowded around the juke-box. Here sometimes there were sudden commotions. Late one afternoon when she passed the Blue Moon, she heard wild angry voices and a sound like a bottle being thrown, and as she stood there a policeman came out on the sidewalk pushing and jerking a torn-looking man with wobbly legs. The man was crying, shouting; there was blood on his ripped shirt and dirty tears dripped down his face. It was an April afternoon of rainbow showers, and by and by the Black Maria screamed down the street, and the poor, arrested criminal was thrown into the prisoners' cage and carried off down to the jail. The old Frankie knew the Blue Moon well, although she had never been inside. There was no written law to keep her out, no lock and chain on the screen door. But she had known in an unworded way that it was a forbidden place to children. The Blue Moon was a place for holiday soldiers and the grown and free. The old Frankie had known she had no valid right to enter there, so she had only hung around the edges and never once had she gone inside. But now this morning before the wedding all of this was changed. The old laws she had known before meant nothing to F. Jasmine, and without a second thought she left the street and went inside.

There in the Blue Moon was the red-headed soldier who was to weave in such an unexpected way through all that day before the wedding. F. Jasmine, however, did not notice him at first; she looked for the monkey-man, but he was not there. Aside from the soldier the only other person in the room was the Blue Moon owner, a Portuguese, who stood behind the counter. This was the person F. Jasmine picked to be the first to hear about the wedding, and he was chosen simply because he was the one most likely and near.

After the fresh brightness of the street, the Blue Moon seemed dark. Blue neon lights burned over the dim mirror behind the counter, tinting the faces in the place pale green, and an electric fan turned slowly so that the room was scalloped with warm stale waves of breeze. At that early morning hour the place was very quiet. There were booth tables across the room, all empty. At the back of the Blue Moon a lighted wooden stairway led up to the second floor. The place smelled of dead beer and morning coffee. F. Jasmine ordered coffee from the owner behind the counter, and after he had brought it to her, he sat down on a stool across from her. He was a sad, pale man with a very flat face. He wore a long white apron and, hunched on the stool with his feet on the rungs, he was reading a romance magazine. The telling of the wedding gathered inside her, and when it was so ready she could no longer resist, she hunted in her mind a good opening remark—something grown and offhand, to start between them the conversation. She said in a voice that trembled a little: 'It certainly has been an unseasonable summer, hasn't it?'

The Portuguese at first did not seem to hear her and went on reading the romance magazine. So she repeated her remark, and when his eyes were turned to hers and his attention caught, she went on in a higher voice: 'Tomorrow this brother of mine and his bride are marrying at Winter Hill.' She went straight to the story, as a circus dog breaks through the paper hoop, and as she talked, her voice became clearer, more definite, and sure. She told her plans in a way that made them sound completely settled, and not in the least open to question. The Portuguese listened with his head cocked to one side, his dark eyes ringed with ash-gray circles, and now and then he wiped his damp veined dead-white hands on his stained apron. She told about the wedding and her plans and he did not dispute with her or doubt.

It is far easier, it came to her as she remembered Berenice, to convince strangers of the coming to pass of dearest wants than those in your own home kitchen. The thrill of speaking certain words—Jarvis and Janice, wedding and Winter Hill—was such that F. Jasmine, when she had finished, wanted to start all over again. The Portuguese took from behind his ear a cigarette which he tapped on the counter but did not light. In the unnatural neon glow his face looked startled, and when she had finished he did not speak. With the telling of the wedding still sounding inside her, as the last chord of a guitar murmurs a long time after the strings are struck, F. Jasmine turned toward the entrance and the framed blazing street beyond the door: dark people passed along the sidewalk and footsteps echoed in the Blue Moon.

'It gives me a funny feeling,' she said. 'After living in this town all my whole life, to know that after tomorrow I'll never be back here any more.'

It was then she noticed him for the first time, the soldier who at the very end would twist so strangely that last, long day. Later, on thinking back, she tried to recall some warning hint of future craziness—but at the time he looked to her like any other soldier standing at a counter drinking beer. He was not tall, nor short, nor fat, nor thin—except for the red hair there was nothing at all unusual about him. He was one of the thousands of soldiers who came to the town from the camp near-by. But as she looked into this soldier's eyes, in the dim light of the Blue Moon, she realized that she gazed at him in a new way.

That morning, for the first time, F. Jasmine was not jealous. He might have come from New York or California—but she did not envy him. He might be on his way to England or India—she was not jealous. In the restless spring and crazy summer, she had watched the soldiers with a sickened heart, for they were the ones who came and went, while she was stuck there in the town forever. But now, on this day before the wedding, all this was changed; her eyes as she looked into the soldier's eyes were clear of jealousy and want. Not only did she feel that unexplainable connection she was to feel between herself and other total strangers of that day, there was another sense of recognition: it seemed to F. Jasmine they exchanged the special look of friendly, free travelers who meet for a moment at some stop along the way. The look was long. And with the lifting of the jealous weight, F. Jasmine felt at peace. It was quiet in the Blue Moon, and the telling of the wedding seemed still to murmur in the room. After this long gaze of fellow travelers, it was the soldier who finally turned his face away.

'Yes,' said F. Jasmine, after a moment and to no one in particular, 'it gives me a mighty funny feeling. In a way it's like I ought to do all the things I would have done if I was staying in the town forever. Instead of this one day. So I guess I better get a move on. Adios.' She spoke the last word to the Portuguese, and at the same time her hand reached automatically to lift the Mexican hat she had worn all summer until that day, but, finding nothing, the gesture withered and her hand felt shamed. Quickly she scratched her head, and with a last glance at the soldier, left the Blue Moon.

It was the morning different from all other mornings she had ever known because of several reasons. First, of course, there was the telling of the wedding. Once, and a long time ago, the old Frankie had liked to go around the town playing a game. She had walked all around—through the north side of town with the grass-lawned houses and the sad mills section and colored Sugarville—wearing her Mexican hat and the high-laced boots and a cowboy rope tied round her waist, she had gone around pretending to be Mexican. Me no speak English—Adios Buenos Noches—abla pokie peekie poo, she had jabbered in mock Mexican. Sometimes a little crowd of children gathered and the old Frankie would swell up with pride and trickery—but when the game was over, and she was home, there would come over her a cheated discontent. Now this morning reminded her of those old days of the Mexican game. She went to the same places, and the people, mostly strangers to her, were the same. But this morning she was not trying to trick people and pretend; far from it, she wanted only to be recognized for her true self. It was a need so strong, this want to be known and recognized, that F. Jasmine forgot the wild hard glare and choking dust and miles (it must have been at least five miles) of wandering all over town.

A second fact about that day was the forgotten music that sprang suddenly into her mind—snatches of orchestra minuets, march tunes and waltzes, and the jazz horn of Honey Brown—so that her feet in the patent-leather shoes stepped always according to a tune. A last difference about that morning was the way her world seemed layered in three different parts, all the twelve years of the old Frankie, the present day itself, and the future ahead when the J A three of them would be together in all the many distant places.

As she walked along, it seemed as though the ghost of the old Frankie, dirty and hungry-eyed, trudged silently along not far from her, and the thought of the future, after the wedding, was constant as the very sky. That day alone seemed equally important as both the long past and the bright future—as a hinge is important to a swinging door. And since it was the day when past and future mingled, F. Jasmine did not wonder that it was strange and long. So these were the main reasons why F. Jasmine felt, in an unworded way, that this was a morning different from all mornings she had ever known. And of all these facts and feelings the strongest of all was the need to be known for her true self and recognized.

Along the shaded sidewalks on the north side of the town, near the main street, she passed a row of lace-curtained boarding houses with empty chairs behind the banisters until she came upon a lady sweeping her front porch. To this lady, after the opening remark about the weather, F. Jasmine told her plans and, as with the Portuguese in the Blue Moon café and all the other people she was to meet that day, the telling of the wedding had an end and a beginning, a shape like a song.

First, just at the moment she commenced, a sudden hush came in her heart; then, as the names were named and the plan unfolded, there was a wild rising lightness and at the end content. The lady meanwhile leaned on the broom, listening. Behind her there was a dark open hall, with a bare stairway, and to the left a table for letters, and from this dark hall came the strong hot smell of cooking turnip greens. The strong waves of smell and the dark hall seemed to mingle with F. Jasmine's joy, and when she looked into the lady's eyes, she loved her, though she did not even know her name.

The lady neither argued nor accused. She did not say anything. Until at the very end, just as F. Jasmine turned to go, she said: 'Well, I declare.' But already F. Jasmine, a quick gay band tune marching her feet, was hurrying on her way again.

In a neighborhood of shaded summer lawns she turned down a side street and met some men mending the road. The sharp smell of melted tar and hot gravel and the loud tractor filled the air with noisy excitement. It was the tractor-man F. Jasmine chose to hear her plans—running beside him, her head thrown back to watch his sunburned face, she had to cup her hands around her mouth to make her voice heard. Even so it was uncertain if he understood, for when she stopped, he laughed and yelled back to her something she could not quite catch. Here, among the racket and excitement, was the place F. Jasmine saw the ghost of the old Frankie plainest of all—hovering close to the commotion, chewing a great big lump of tar, hanging around at noon to watch the lunch-pails being opened. There was a fine big motorcycle parked near the street-menders, and before going on F. Jasmine looked at it admiringly, then spat on the broad leather seat and shined it carefully with her fist. She was in a very nice neighborhood near the edge of town, a place of new brick houses with flower-bordered sidewalks and cars parked in paved driveways; but the finer the neighborhood, the fewer people are about, so F. Jasmine turned back toward the center of the town. The sun burned like an iron lid on her head and her slip was stuck wet to her chest, and even the organdie dress was wet and clinging in spots also. The march tune had softened to a dreaming song on a violin that slowed her footsteps to a wander. To this kind of music she crossed to the opposite side of the town, beyond the main street and the mill, to the gray crooked streets of the mill section, where, among the choking dust and sad gray rotten shacks, there were more listeners to tell about the wedding.

(From time to time, as she went around, a little conversation buzzed on the bottom of her mind. It was the voice of Berenice when later she would know about this morning. And you just roamed around, the voice said, taking up with total strangers! I never heard of such a thing in all my life! So the Berenice voice sounded, heard but unnoticed like the buzzing of a fly.)

From the sad alleys and crooked streets of the mill section she crossed the unseen line dividing Sugarville from the white people's town. Here were the same two-room shacks and rotted privies, as in the mill section, but round thick chinaberry trees cast solid shade and often cool ferns grew in pots upon the porches. This was a part of town well known to her, and as she walked along she found herself remembering these familiar lanes in long-past times and other weathers—the ice-pale mornings in the wintertime when even the orange fires under the black iron pots of wash-women seemed to be shivering, the windy autumn nights.

Meanwhile, the glare was dizzy bright and she met and talked to many people, some known to her by sight and name, some strangers. The plans about the wedding stiffened and fixed with each new telling and finally came unchangeable. By eleven-thirty she was very tired, and even the tunes dragged with exhaustion; the need to be recognized for her true self was for the time being satisfied. So she went back to the place

from which she started—to the main street where the glittering
sidewalks were baked and half-deserted in the white glare.

Always she went by her father's store whenever she came
to town. Her father's store was on the same block as the Blue
Moon, but two doors from the main street and in a much
better location. It was a narrow store with precious jewels in
velvet boxes placed in the window. Beyond the window was her
father's workbench, and when you walked along the sidewalk
you could see her father working there, his head bent over the
tiny watches, and his big brown hands hovered as carefully as
butterflies. You could see her father like a public person in the
town, well known to all by sight and name. But her father was
not proud and did not even look up at those who stopped and
gazed at him. This morning, however, he was not at his bench,
but behind the counter rolling down his shirt-sleeves as though
making ready to put on his coat and go outside.

The long glass showcase was bright with jewels and watches
and silverware and the store smelled of watch-fixing kerosene.
Her father wiped the sweat from his long upper lip with his
forefinger and rubbed his nose in a troubled way.

'Where in the world have you been all morning? Berenice
has called here twice trying to locate you.'

'I've been all over the whole town,' she said.

But he did not listen. 'I'm going around to your Aunt Pet's,'
he said. 'She's had a sad piece of news today.'

'What sad piece of news?' F. Jasmine asked.

'Uncle Charles is dead.'

Uncle Charles was the great-uncle of John Henry West, but
though she and John Henry were first cousins, Uncle Charles
was not blood kin to her. He lived twenty-one miles out on the
Renfroe Road in a shaded wooden country house surrounded
by red cotton fields. An old, old man, he had been sick a long
time; it was said he had one foot in the grave—and he always
wore bedroom slippers. Now he was dead. But that had nothing
to do with the wedding and so F. Jasmine only said: 'Poor Uncle
Charles. That certainy is a pity.'

Her father went back behind the gray sour velvet curtain that
divided the store into two parts, the larger public part in front
and behind a small dusty private part. Behind the curtain was
the water cooler, some shelves of boxes, and the big iron safe

where diamond rings were locked away from robbers in the night. F. Jasmine heard her Papa moving around back there, and she settled herself carefully at the workbench before the front window. A watch, already taken apart, was laid out on the green blotter.

There was a strong streak of watchmaker's blood in her and always the old Frankie had loved to sit at her father's bench. She would put on her father's glasses with the jeweler's loupe attached and, scowling busily, dip them in gasoline. She worked with the lathe, too. Sometimes a little crowd of sidewalk lazies would collect to watch her from the street and she would imagine how they said: 'Frankie Addams works for her father and makes fifteen dollars a week. She fixes the hardest watches in the store and goes to the Woodmen of the World Club with her father. Look at her. She is a credit to the family and a big credit to the whole town.' So she would imagine these conversations, as she scowled with a busy expression at a watch. But now today she looked down at the watch spread out on the blotter, and did not put on the jeweler's loupe. There was something more she ought to say about the death of Uncle Charles.

When her father returned to the front of the store, she said: 'At one time Uncle Charles was one of the leading citizens. It will be a loss to the whole county.'

The words did not seem to impress her father. 'You had better go on home. Berenice has been phoning to locate you.'

'Well, remember you said I could get a wedding dress. And stockings and shoes.'

'Charge them at MacDougal's.'

'I don't see why we always have to trade at MacDougal's just because it's a local store,' she grumbled as she went out of the door. 'Where I am going there will be stores a hundred times bigger than MacDougal's.'

The clock in the tower of the First Baptist Church clanged twelve, the mill whistle wailed. There was a drowsing quietness about the street, and even the very cars, parked slantwise with their noses toward the center aisle of grass, were like exhausted cars that have all gone to sleep. The few people out at the noon hour kept close beneath the blunt shade of the awnings. The sun took the color from the sky and the brick stores seemed shrunken, dark, beneath the glare—one building had an overhanging cornice at the top which, from a distance, gave it the queer look of a brick building that has begun to melt. In this noon quietness, she heard again the organ of the monkey-man, the sound that always magnetized her footsteps so that she automatically went toward it. This time she would find them and tell them good-bye.

As F. Jasmine hurried down the street, she saw the two of them in her mind's eye—and wondered if they would remember her. The old Frankie had always loved the monkey and the monkey-man. They resembled each other—they both had an anxious, questioning expression, as though they wondered every minute if what they did was wrong. The monkey, in fact, was nearly always wrong; after he danced to the organ tune, he was supposed to take off his darling little cap and pass it around to the audience, but likely as not he would get mixed up and bow and reach out his cap to the monkey-man, and not the audience. And the monkey-man would plead with him, and finally begin to chatter and fuss. When he would make as if to slap the monkey, the monkey would cringe down and chatter also—and they would look at each other with the same scared exasperation, their wrinkled faces very sad. After watching them a long time, the old Frankie, fascinated, began to take on the same expression as she followed them around. And now F. Jasmine was eager to see them.

She could hear the broken-sounding organ plainly, although they were not on the main street, but up farther and probably just around the corner of the next block. So F. Jasmine hurried toward them. As she neared the corner, she heard other sounds that puzzled her curiosity so that she listened and stopped. Above the music of the organ there was the sound of a man's voice quarreling and the excited higher fussing of the monkey-man. She could hear the monkey chattering also. Then suddenly the organ stopped and the two different voices were loud and mad. F. Jasmine had reached the corner, and it was the corner by the Sears and Roebuck store; she passed the store slowly, then turned and faced a curious sight.

It was a narrow street that went downhill toward Front Avenue, blinding bright in the wild glare. There on the sidewalk was the monkey, the monkey-man, and a soldier holding out a whole fistful of dollar bills—it looked at the first glance like a hundred dollars. The soldier looked angry, and the monkey-man was pale and excited also. Their voices were quarreling and F. Jasmine gathered that the soldier was trying to buy the monkey. The monkey himself was crouched and shivering down on the sidewalk close to the brick wall of the Sears and Roebuck store. In spite of the hot day, he had on his little red coat with silver buttons and his little face, scared and desperate, had the look of someone who is just about to sneeze. Shivering and pitiful, he kept bowing at nobody and offering his cap into the air. He knew the furious voices were about him and he felt blamed.

F. Jasmine was standing near-by, trying to take in the commotion, listening and still. Then suddenly the soldier grabbed at the monkey's chain, but the monkey screamed, and before she knew what it was all about, the monkey had skittered up her leg and body and was huddled on her shoulder with his little monkey hands around her head. It happened in a flash, and she was so shocked she could not move. The voices stopped and, except for the monkey's jibbered scream, the street was silent. The soldier stood slack-jawed, surprised, still holding out the handful of dollar bills.

The monkey-man was the first to recover; he spoke to the monkey in a gentle voice, and in another second the monkey sprang from off her shoulder and landed on the organ which the monkey-man was carrying on his back. The two of them went away. They quickly hurried around the corner and at the last second, just as they turned, they both looked back with the same expression—reproaching and sly. F. Jasmine leaned against the brick wall, and she still felt the monkey on her shoulder and smelt his dusty, sour smell; she shivered. The soldier muttered until the pair of them were out of sight, and F. Jasmine noticed then that he was red-haired and the same soldier who had been in the Blue Moon. He stuffed the bills in his side pocket.

'He certainy is a darling monkey,' F. Jasmine said. 'But it gave me a mighty funny feeling to have him run up me like that.'

The soldier seemed to realize her for the first time. The

look on his face changed slowly, and the angry expression went away. He was looking at F. Jasmine from the top of her head, down the organdie best dress, and to the black pumps she was wearing.

'I guess you must have wanted the monkey a whole lot,' she said. 'I've always wanted a monkey, too.'

'What?' he asked. Then he remarked in a muffled voice, as if his tongue were made of felt or a very thick piece of blotting paper, 'Which way are we going?' the soldier said. 'Are you going my way or am I going yours?'

F. Jasmine had not expected this. The soldier was joining with her like a traveler who meets another traveler in a tourist town. For a second, it occurred to her that she had heard this remark before, perhaps in a picture show—that furthermore it was a set remark requiring a set answer. Not knowing the ready-made reply, she answered carefully.

'Which way are you going?'

'Hook on,' he said, sticking out his elbow.

They walked down the side street, on their shrunken noontime shadows. The soldier was the only person during that day who spoke first to F. Jasmine and invited her to join with him. But, when she began to tell about the wedding, something seemed lacking. Perhaps it was because she had already told her plans to so many people all over town that now she could rest satisfied. Or perhaps it was because she felt the soldier was not really listening. He looked at the pink organdie dress from the corner of his eye, and there was a half-smile on his mouth. F. Jasmine could not match her steps to his, although she tried, for his legs seemed loosely fastened to his body so that he walked in a rambling way.

'What state do you come from, if I may ask?' she said politely.

In that second that passed before his answer there was time for her skimming mind to picture Hollywood, New York, and Maine. The soldier answered: 'Arkansas.'

Now of all the forty-eight states in the Union, Arkansas was one of the very few that had never especially appealed to her—but her imagination, balked, immediately turned the opposite way so that she asked:

'Do you have any idea where you will be going?'

'Just banging around,' the soldier said. 'I'm out loose on a three-day pass.'

He had mistaken the meaning of her question, for she had asked it to him as a soldier liable to be sent to any foreign country in the world, but, before she could explain what she had meant, he said:

'There's a kind of hotel around the corner I'm staying at.' Then, still looking at the pleated collar of her dress, he added: 'It seems like I've seen you somewhere before. Do you ever go dancing at the Idle Hour?'

They walked down Front Avenue, and now the street was beginning to have the air of Saturday afternoon. A lady was drying her yellow hair in the window of the second floor above the fish store, and she called down to two soldiers who passed along the street. A street preacher, a known town character, was preaching on a corner to a group of warehouse colored boys and scraggly children. But F. Jasmine did not have her mind on what was going on around her. The soldier's mention of dancing and the Idle Hour touched like a story-tale wand upon her mind. She realized for the first time that she was walking with a soldier, with one of the groups of loud, glad gangs that roamed around the streets together or walked with the grown girls. They danced at the Idle Hour and had a good time, while the old Frankie was asleep. And she had never danced with anybody, excepting Evelyn Owen, and had never put foot in the Idle Hour.

And now F. Jasmine walked with a soldier who in his mind included her in such unknown pleasures. But she was not altogether proud. There was an uneasy doubt that she could no quite place or name. The noon air was thick and sticky as hot syrup, and there was the stifling smell of the dye-rooms from the cotton mill. She heard the organ-grinder sounding faintly from the main street.

The soldier stopped: 'This is the hotel,' he said.

They were before the Blue Moon and F. Jasmine was surprised to hear it spoken of as a hotel, as she had thought it was only a café. When the soldier held the screen door open for her, she noticed that he swayed a little. Her eyes saw blinding red, then black, after the glare, and it took them a minute to get used to the blue light. She followed the soldier to one of the booths on the right.

'Care for a beer,' he said, not in an asking voice, but as though he took her reply for granted.

F. Jasmine did not enjoy the taste of beer; once or twice she had sneaked swallows from her father's glass and it was sour. But the soldier had not left her any choice. 'I would be delighted,' she said. 'Thank you.'

Never had she been in a hotel, although she had often thought about them and written about them in her shows. Her father had stayed in hotels several times, and once, from Montgomery, he had brought her two little tiny cakes of hotel soap which she had saved. She looked around the Blue Moon with new curiosity. All of a sudden she felt very proper. On seating herself at the booth table, she carefully smoothed down her dress, as she did when at a party or in church, so as not to sit the pleats out of the skirt. She sat up straight and on her face there was a proper expression. But the Blue Moon still seemed to her more like a kind of café than a real hotel. She did not see the sad, pale Portuguese, and a laughing fat lady with a golden tooth poured beer for the soldier at the counter. The stairway at the back led probably to the hotel rooms upstairs, and the steps were lighted by a blue neon bulb and covered with a runner of linoleum. A sassy chorus on the radio was singing an advertisement: Denteen Chewing Gum! Denteen Chewing Gum! Denteen! The beery air reminded her of a room where a rat has died behind a wall. The soldier walked back to the booth, carrying two glasses of the beer; he licked some foam that had spilled over his hand and wiped the hand on his trousers seat. When he was settled in the booth, F. Jasmine said, in a voice that was absolutely new to her—a high voice spoken through the nose, dainty and dignified:

'Don't you think it is mighty exciting? Here we are sitting here at this table and in a month from now there's no telling where on earth we'll be. Maybe tomorrow the army will send you to Alaska like they sent my brother. Or to France or Africa or Burma. And I don't have any idea where I will be. I'd like for us to go to Alaska for a while, and then go somewhere else. They say that Paris has been liberated. In my opinion the war will be over next month.'

The soldier raised his glass, and threw back his head to gulp the beer. F. Jasmine took a few swallows also, although it tasted nasty to her. Today she did not see the world as loose and cracked and turning a thousand miles an hour, so that the spinning views of war and distant lands made her mind dizzy. The world had never been so close to her. Sitting across from the soldier at that booth in the Blue Moon, she suddenly saw the three of them—herself, her brother, and the bride—walking beneath a cold Alaskan sky, along the sea where green ice waves lay frozen and folded on the shore; they climbed a sunny glacier shot through with pale cold colors and a rope tied the three of them together, and friends from another glacier called in Alaskan their J A names. She saw them next in Africa where, with a crowd of sheeted Arabs, they galloped on camels in the sandy wind. Burma was jungle-dark, and she had seen pictures in *Life* magazine. Because of the wedding, these distant lands, the world seemed altogether possible and near: as close to Winter Hill as Winter Hill was to the town. It was the actual present, in fact, that seemed to F. Jasmine a little bit unreal.

'Yes, it's mighty exciting,' she said again.

The soldier, his beer finished, wiped his wet mouth with the back of his freckled hand. His face, although not fat, seemed swollen, and it was glossy in the neon light. He had a thousand little freckles, and the only thing that seemed to her pretty was his bright, red curly hair. His eyes were blue, set close together, and the whites were raw. He was staring at her with a peculiar expression, not as one traveler gazes at another, but as a person who shares a secret scheme. For several minutes he did not talk. Then, when at last he spoke, the words did not make sense to her and she did not understand. It seemed to her the soldier said:

'Who is a cute dish?'

There were no dishes on the table and she had the uneasy feeling he had begun to talk a kind of double-talk. She tried to turn the conversation.

'I told you my brother is a Member of the Armed Forces.'

But the soldier did not seem to listen. 'I could of sworn I'd run into you some place before.'

The doubt in F. Jasmine deepened. She realized now that the soldier thought she was much older than she was, but her

pleasure in this was somehow uncertain. To make conversation
she remarked:

'Some people are not partial to red hair. But to me it's my
favorite color.' She added, remembering her brother and
the bride. 'Except dark brown and yellow. I always think it's a
pity for the Lord to waste curly hair on boys. When so many
girls are going around with hair as straight as pokers.'

The soldier leaned over the booth table and, still staring at
her, he began to walk his fingers, the second and third fingers
of both hands, across the table toward her. The fingers were
dirty, with rinds of black beneath the nails. F. Jasmine had the
sense that something strange was going to happen, when just
at that moment there was a sudden racket and commotion and
three or four soldiers shoved each other into the hotel. There
was a babble of voices and the screen door banged. The soldier's
fingers stopped walking across the table and, when he glanced
at the other soldiers, the peculiar expression was scattered from
his eyes.

'That certainy is a darling little monkey,' she said.

'What monkey?'

The doubt deepened to the feeling that something was
wrong. 'Why, the monkey you tried to buy a few minutes
ago. What's the matter with you?'

Something was wrong and the soldier put his fists up to his
head. His body limpened and he leaned back in the seat of
the booth, as though collapsed. 'Oh, that monkey!' he said in
his slurred voice. 'The walk in the sun after all those beers.
I was slamming around all night.' He sighed, and his hands
were open loose upon the table. 'I guess maybe I'm just about
beat.'

For the first time F. Jasmine began to wonder what she was
doing there and if she ought not to take herself on home. The
other soldiers had crowded around a table near the stairway,
and the lady with the golden tooth was busy behind the counter.
F. Jasmine had finished her beer and a lace of creamy foam
lined the inside of the empty glass. The hot, close smell in the
hotel suddenly made her feel a little queer.

'I have to go home now. Thank you for treating me.'

She got up from the booth, but the soldier reached out
toward her and caught a piece of her dress. 'Hey!' he said.

'Don't just walk off like that. Let's fix up something for this evening. How bout a date for nine o'clock?'

'A date?' F. Jasmine felt as though her head was big and loose. The beer made her legs feel peculiar, too, almost as though she had four legs to manage instead of two. On any other day than this it would have seemed almost impossible that anyone, much less a soldier, would have invited her to a date. The very word, *date*, was a grown word used by older girls. But here again there was a blight upon her pleasure. If he knew she was not yet thirteen, he would never have invited her, or probably never joined with her at all. There was a troubled sense, a light uneasiness. 'I don't know—'

'Sure,' he urged. 'Suppose we link up here at nine o'clock. We can go to the Idle Hour or something. That suit you all right? Here at nine o'clock.'

'O.K.' she said finally. 'I will be delighted.'

Again she was on the burning sidewalks, where passing walkers looked dark and shrunken in the angry glare. It took her a little while to come back to the wedding feeling of that morning, for the half-hour in the hotel had slightly distracted her frame of mind. But it did not take her very long, and by the time she reached the main street, the wedding feeling was recovered. She met a little girl, two grades below her at the school, and stopped her on the street to tell her her plans. She told her also that a soldier had invited her to have a date, and now she told it in a bragging tone. The girl went with her to buy the wedding clothes, which took an hour and meant the trying-on of more than a dozen beautiful dresses.

But the main thing that brought back the wedding frame of mind was an accident that occurred on the way home. It was a mysterious trick of sight and the imagination. She was walking home when all at once there was a shock in her as though a thrown knife struck and shivered in her chest. F. Jasmine stopped dead in her tracks, one foot still raised, and at first she could not take it in just what had happened. There was something sideways and behind her that had flashed across the very corner edge of her left eye; she had half-seen something, a dark double shape, in the alley she had just that moment passed. And because of this half-seen object, the quick flash in the corner of her eye, there had sprung up in her the sudden picture of her brother and the bride. Ragged and bright as lightning she saw the two of them as they had been when, for a moment, they stood together before the living-room mantelpiece, his arm around her shoulders. So strong was this picture that F. Jasmine felt suddenly that Jarvis and Janice were there behind her in the alley, and she had caught a glimpse of them—although she knew, and well enough, that they were in Winter Hill, almost a hundred miles away.

F. Jasmine lowered her raised foot to the pavement and slowly turned to look around. The alley lay between two grocery stores: a narrow alley, dark in the glare. She did not look at it directly, for somehow it was as though she was almost afraid. Her eyes stole slowly down the brick wall and she glimpsed again the dark double shapes. And what was there? F. Jasmine was stunned. There in the alley were only two colored boys, one taller than the other and with his arm resting on the shorter boy's shoulder. That was all—but something about the angle or the way they stood, or the pose of their shapes, had reflected the sudden picture of her brother and the bride that had so shocked her. And with this vision of them plain and exact the morning ended, and she was home by two o'clock.

II

THE afternoon was like the center of the cake that Berenice had baked last Monday, a cake which failed. The old Frankie had been glad the cake had failed, not out of spite, but because she loved these fallen cakes the best. She enjoyed the damp, gummy richness near the center, and did not understand why grown people thought such cakes a failure. It was a loaf cake, that last Monday, with the edges risen light and high and the middle moist and altogether fallen—after the bright, high morning the afternoon was dense and solid as the center of that cake. And because it was the last of all the afternoons, F. Jasmine found an unfamiliar sweetness in the known old kitchen ways and tones. At two o'clock, when she came in, Berenice was pressing clothes. John Henry sat at the table blowing soapbubbles with a spool, and he gave her a long, green, secret look.

'Where in the world have you been?' asked Berenice.

'We know something you don't know,' John Henry said. 'Do you know what?'

'What?'

'Berenice and me are going to the wedding.'

F. Jasmine was taking off her organdie dress, and his words startled her.

'Uncle Charles is dead.'

'I heard that, but——'

'Yes,' said Berenice. 'The poor old soul passed on this morning. They're taking the body to the family graveyard in Opelika. And John Henry is to stay with us for several days.'

Now that she knew the death of Uncle Charles would in a sense affect the wedding, she made room for it in her thoughts. While Berenice finished pressing clothes, F. Jasmine sat in her petticoat on the stairs leading up to her room; she closed her eyes. Uncle Charles lived in a shady wooden house out in the country, and he was too old to eat corn on the cob. In June of this summer he took sick, and ever since he had been critical. He lay in the bed, shrunken and brown and very old. He complained that the pictures were hung crooked on the wall, and they took down all the framed pictures—it was not that. He complained that his bed was placed in a wrong corner, and so they moved the bed—it was not that. Then his voice failed, and when he tried to talk, it was as though his throat had filled with glue, and they could not understand the words. One Sunday the Wests had gone out to see him and taken Frankie with them; she had tiptoed to the open door of the back bedroom. He looked like an old man carved in brown wood and covered with a sheet. Only his eyes had moved, and they were like blue jelly, and she had felt they might come out from the sockets and roll like blue wet jelly down his stiff face. She had stood in the doorway staring at him—then tiptoed away, afraid. They finally made out that he complained the sun shone the wrong way through the window, but that was not the thing that hurt him so. And it was death.

F. Jasmine opened her eyes and stretched herself.

'It is a terrible thing to be dead!' she said.

'Well,' said Berenice. 'The old man suffered a lot and he had lived up his span. The Lord appointed the time for him.'

'I know. But at the same time it seems mighty queer that he would have to die the very day before the wedding. And why on earth do you and John Henry have to go tagging to the wedding? Seems to me like you would just stay home.'

'Frankie Addams,' said Berenice, and she suddenly put her arms akimbo, 'you are the most selfish human being that ever breathed. We all been cooped up in this kitchen and——'

'Don't call me Frankie!' she said. 'I don't wish to have to remind you any more.'

It was the time of early afternoon when in the old days a sweet band would be playing. Now with the radio turned off, the kitchen was solemn and silent and there were sounds from far away. A colored voice called from the sidewalk calling the names of vegetables in a dark slurred tone, a long unwinding hollering in which there were no words. Somewhere, near in the neighborhood, there was the sound of a hammer and each stroke left a round echo.

'You would be mighty surprised if you knew whereall I've been today. I was all over this whole town. I saw the monkey and the monkey-man. There was this soldier who was trying to buy the monkey and holding a hundred dollars in his hand. Have you ever seen anybody try to buy a monkey on the street?'

'No. Was he drunk?'

'Drunk?' F. Jasmine said.

'Oh,' said John Henry. 'The monkey and the monkey-man!'

Berenice's question had disturbed F. Jasmine, and she took a minute to consider. 'I don't think he was drunk. People don't get drunk in broad daylight.' She had meant to tell Berenice about the soldier, but now she hesitated. 'All the same there was something——' Her voice trailed at the end, and she watched a rainbow soapbubble floating in silence across the room. Here in the kitchen, barefooted and wearing only her petticoat, it was hard to realize and judge the soldier. About the promise for that evening she felt double-minded. The indecision bothered her, and so she changed the subject. 'I hope you washed and ironed everything good of mine today. I have to take them to Winter Hill.'

'What for?' said Berenice. 'You only going to be there just one day.'

'You heard me,' F. Jasmine said. 'I told you I wasn't coming back here after the wedding.'

'Fool's hill. You have a whole lot less of sense than I was giving you credit for. What makes you think they want to take you along with them? Two is company and three is a crowd. And that is the main thing about a wedding. Two is company and three is a crowd.'

F. Jasmine always found it hard to argue with a known saying. She loved to use them in her shows and in her conversation, but they were very hard to argue with, and so she said:

'You wait and see.'

'Remember back to the time of the flood? Remember Noah and the ark?'

'And what has that got to do with it?' she asked.

'Remember the way he admitted them creatures.'

'Oh, hush up your big old mouth,' she said.

'Two by two,' said Berenice. 'He admitted them creatures two by two.'

The argument that afternoon was, from the beginning to the end, about the wedding. Berenice refused to follow F. Jasmine's frame of mind. From the first it was as though she tried to catch F. Jasmine by the collar, like the Law catches a no-good in the wrong, and jerk her back where she had started—back to the sad and crazy summer that now seemed to F. Jasmine like a time remembered from long ago. But F. Jasmine was stubborn and not to be caught. Berenice had flaws to find in all of her ideas, and from the first word to the last she did her terrible, level best to try and deny the wedding. But F. Jasmine would not let it be denied.

'Look,' F. Jasmine said, and she picked up the pink organdie dress that she had just taken off. 'Remember when I bought this dress the collar had teeny little pleats. But you have been ironing the collar like it was supposed to be ruffled. Now we got to set those little pleats like they ought to be.'

'And who is going to do it?' said Berenice. She picked up the dress and judged the collar. 'I got more to do with my time and trouble.'

'Well, it's got to be done,' F. Jasmine argued. 'It's the way the collar is supposed to be. And besides, I might be wearing it out somewhere this evening.'

'And where, pray tell me?' said Berenice. 'Answer the question I asked when you came in. Where in the world have you been all morning?'

It was exactly as F. Jasmine had known it would be—the way Berenice refused to understand. And, since it was more a matter of feelings than of words or facts, she found it difficult to explain. When she spoke of connections, Berenice gave her a long, uncomprehending stare—and, when she went on to the Blue Moon and the many people, the broad, flat nose of Berenice widened and she shook her head. F. Jasmine did not mention the soldier; although she was on the verge of speaking of him several times, something warned her not to.

When she had finished, Berenice said:

'Frankie, I honestly believe you have turned crazy on us. Walking around all over town and telling total strangers this big tale. You know in your soul this mania of yours is pure foolishness.'

'You wait and see,' F. Jasmine said. 'They will take me.'

'And if they don't?'

F. Jasmine picked up the shoe box with the silver slippers and the wrapped box with the wedding dress. 'These are my wedding clothes. I'll show them to you later.'

'And if they don't?'

F. Jasmine had already started up the stairs, but she stopped and turned back toward the kitchen. The room was silent.

'If they don't, I will kill myself,' she said. 'But they will.'

'Kill yourself how?' asked Berenice.

'I will shoot myself in the side of the head with a pistol.'

'Which pistol?'

'The pistol that Papa keeps under his handkerchiefs along with Mother's picture in the right-hand bureau drawer.'

Berenice did not answer for a minute and her face was a puzzle. 'You heard what Mr. Addams told you about playing with that pistol. Go on upstairs now. Dinner will be ready in a little while.'

It was a late dinner, this last meal that the three of them would ever eat together at the kitchen table. On Saturdays they were not regular about the times of meals, and they began the dinner at four o'clock, when already the August sun was slanting long and stale across the yard. It was the time of afternoon when the bars of sunlight crossed the back yard like the bars of a bright strange jail. The two fig trees were green and flat, the arbor sun-crossed and casting solid shade. The sun in the afternoon did not slant through the back windows of the house, so that the kitchen was gray. The three of them began their dinner at four o'clock, and the dinner lasted until twilight. There was hopping-john cooked with the ham bone, and as they ate they began to talk of love. It was a subject F. Jasmine had never talked about in all her life. In the first place, she had never believed in love and had never put any of it in her shows. But this afternoon when Berenice began this conversation, F. Jasmine did not stop up both her ears, but as she quietly ate the peas and rice and pot-liquor she listened.

'I have heard of many a queer thing,' said Berenice. 'I have knew mens to fall in love with girls so ugly that you wonder if their eyes is straight. I have seen some of the most peculiar weddings anybody could conjecture. Once I knew a boy with his whole face burned off so that——'

'Who?' asked John Henry.

Berenice swallowed a piece of cornbread and wiped her mouth with the back of her hand. 'I have knew womens to love veritable Satans and thank Jesus when they put their split hooves over the threshold. I have knew boys to take it into their heads to fall in love with other boys. You know Lily Mae Jenkins?'

F. Jasmine thought a minute, and then answered: 'I'm not sure.'

'Well, you either know him or you don't know him. He prisses around with a pink satin blouse and one arm akimbo. Now this Lily Mae fell in love with a man name Juney Jones. A man, mind you. And Lily Mae turned into a girl. He changed his nature and his sex and turned into a girl.'

'Honest?' F. Jasmine asked. 'Did he really?'

'He did,' said Berenice. 'To all intents and purposes.'

F. Jasmine scratched behind her ear and said: 'It's funny I can't think who you are talking about. I used to think I knew so many people.'

'Well, you don't need to know Lily Mae Jenkins. You can live without knowing him.'

'Anyway, I don't believe you,' F. Jasmine said.

'Well, I ain't arguing with you,' said Berenice. 'What was it we was speaking about?'

'About peculiar things.'

'Oh, yes.'

They stopped off a few minutes to get on with the dinner. F. Jasmine ate with her elbows on the table and her bare heels hooked on the rungs of the chair. She and Berenice sat opposite each other, and John Henry faced the window. Now hopping-john was F. Jasmine's very favorite food. She had always warned them to wave a plate of rice and peas before her nose when she was in her coffin, to make certain there was no mistake; for if a breath of life was left in her, she would sit up and eat, but if she smelled the hopping-john, and did not stir, then they could just nail down the coffin and be certain she was truly dead. Now Berenice had chosen for her death-test a piece of fried fresh-water trout, and for John Henry it was divinity fudge. But though F. Jasmine loved the hopping-john the very best, the others also liked it well enough, and all three of them enjoyed the dinner that day: the ham knuckle, the hopping-john, cornbread, hot baked sweet potatoes, and the buttermilk. And as they ate, they carried on the conversation.

'Yes, as I was just now telling you,' said Berenice. 'I have seen many a peculiar thing in my day. But one thing I never knew and never heard tell about. No siree, I never did.'

Berenice stopped talking and sat there shaking her head, waiting for them to question her. But F. Jasmine would not speak. And it was John Henry who raised his curious face from his plate and asked: 'What, Berenice?'

'No,' said Berenice. 'I never before in all my days heard of anybody falling in love with a wedding. I have knew many peculiar things, but I never heard of that before.'

F. Jasmine grumbled something.

'So I have been thinking it over and have come to a conclusion.'

'How?' John Henry suddenly asked. 'How did that boy change into a girl?'

Berenice glanced at him and straightened the napkin tied around his neck. 'It was just one of them things, Candy Lamb. I don't know.'

'Don't listen at her,' F. Jasmine said.

'So I have been thinking it over in my mind and come to this conclusion. What you ought to begin thinking about is a beau.'

'What?' F. Jasmine asked.

'You heard me,' said Berenice. 'A beau. A nice little white boy beau.'

F. Jasmine put down her fork and sat with her head turned to one side. 'I don't want any beau. What would I do with one?'

'Do, Foolish?' asked Berenice. 'Why, make him treat you to the picture show. For one thing.'

F. Jasmine pulled the bangs of her hair down over her forehead and slid her feet across the rung of the chair.

'Now you belong to change from being so rough and greedy and big,' said Berenice. 'You ought to fix yourself up nice in your dresses. And speak sweetly and act sly.'

F. Jasmine said in a low voice: 'I'm not rough and greedy any more. I already changed that way.'

'Well, excellent,' said Berenice. 'Now catch you a beau.'

F. Jasmine wanted to tell Berenice about the soldier, the hotel, and the invitation for the evening date. But something checked her, and she hinted around the edges of the subject: 'What kind of a beau? Do you mean something like——' F. Jasmine paused, for at home in the kitchen that last afternoon, the soldier seemed unreal.

'Now that I cannot advise,' said Berenice. 'You got to decide for yourself.'

'Something like a soldier who would maybe take me dancing at the Idle Hour?' She did not look at Berenice.

'Who is talking about soldiers and dancing? I'm talking about a nice little white boy beau your own age. How about that little old Barney?'

'Barney MacKean?'

'Why, certainy. He would do very well to begin with. You could make out with him until somebody else comes along. He would do.'

'That mean nasty Barney!' The garage had been dark, with thin needling sunlight coming through the cracks of the closed door, and with the smell of dust. But she did not let herself remember the unknown sin that he had showed her, that later made her want to throw a knife between his eyes. Instead, she shook herself hard and began mashing peas and rice together on her plate. 'You are the biggest crazy in this town.'

'The crazy calls the sane the crazy.'

So they began to eat again, all except John Henry. F. Jasmine was busy slicing open cornbread and spreading it with butter and mashing her hopping-john and drinking milk. Berenice ate more slowly, peeling off bits of ham from the knuckle in a dainty way. John Henry looked from one of them to the other, and after listening to their talk he had stopped eating to think for a little while. Then after a minute he asked:

'How many of them did you catch? Them beaus.'

'How many?' said Berenice. 'Lamb, how many hairs is in these plaits? You talking to Berenice Sadie Brown.'

So Berenice was started, and her voice went on and on. And when she had begun this way, on a long and serious subject, the words flowed one into the other and her voice began to sing. In the gray of the kitchen on summer afternoons the tone of her voice was golden and quiet, and you could listen to the color and the singing of her voice and not follow the words. F. Jasmine let the long tones linger and spin inside her ears, but her mind did not stamp the voice with sense or sentences. She sat there listening at the table, and now and then she thought of a fact that all her life had seemed to her most curious: Berenice always spoke of herself as though she was somebody very beautiful. Almost on this one subject, Berenice was really not in her right mind. F. Jasmine listened to the voice and stared at Berenice across the table: the dark face with the wild blue eye, the eleven greased plaits that fitted her head like a skull-cap, the wide flat nose that quivered as she spoke. And whatever else Berenice might be, she was not beautiful. It seemed to her she ought to give Berenice advice. So she said at the next pause:

'I think you ought to quit worrying about beaus and be content with T. T. I bet you are forty years old. It is time for you to settle down.'

Berenice bunched up her lips and stared at F. Jasmine with the dark live eye. 'Wisemouth,' she said. 'How do you know so much? I got as much right as anybody else to continue to have a good time so long as I can. And as far as that goes, I'm not so old as some peoples would try and make out. I can still ministrate. And I got many a long year ahead of me before I resign myself to a corner.'

'Well, I didn't mean go into a corner,' F. Jasmine said.

'I heard what you meant,' said Berenice.

John Henry had been watching and listening, and there was a little crust of pot-liquor around his mouth. A big blue lazy fly was hovering around him and trying to light on his sticky face, so that from time to time John Henry waved his hand to shoo the fly away.

'Did they all treat you to the picture show?' he asked. 'All those beaus.'

'To the show, or to one thing or another,' she answered.

'You mean you never pay your own way?' John Henry asked.

'That's what I'm telling you,' said Berenice. 'Not when I go out with a beau. Now if I was to go somewhere with a crowd of womens, I would have to pay my way. But I'm not the kind of person to go around with crowds of womens.'

'When you all took the trip to Fairview——' F. Jasmine said—for one Sunday that last spring there had been a colored pilot who took up colored people in his aeroplane. 'Who paid the way?'

'Now let me see,' said Berenice. 'Honey and Clorina took care of their expense, except I loaned Honey one dollar and forty cents. Cape Clyde paid his own way. And T. T. paid for himself and for me.'

'Then T. T. treated you to the aeroplane ride?'

'That's what I'm telling you. He paid the bus tickets to and from Fairview and the aeroplane ride and the refreshments. The complete trip. Why, naturally he paid the way. How else do you think I could afford to fly around in an aeroplane? Me making six dollars a week.'

'I didn't realize that,' F. Jasmine admitted finally. 'I wonder where T. T. got all of his money.'

'Earned it,' said Berenice. 'John Henry, wipe off your mouth.'

So they rested at the table, for the way they ate their meals, this summer, was in rounds: they would eat awhile and then let the food have a chance to spread out and settle inside their stomachs, and a little later they would start in again. F. Jasmine crossed her knife and fork on her empty plate, and began to question Berenice about a matter that had bothered her.

'Tell me. Is it just us who call this hopping-john? Or is it known by that name through all the country. It seems a strange name somehow.'

'Well, I have heard it called various things,' said Berenice.

'What?'

'Well, I have heard it called peas and rice. Or rice and peas and pot-liquor. Or hopping-john. You can vary and take your pick.'

'But I'm not talking about this town,' F. Jasmine said. I mean in other places. I mean through all the world. I wonder what the French call it.'

'Oh,' said Berenice. 'Well, you ask me a question I cannot answer.'

'Merci à la parlez,' F. Jasmine said.

They sat at the table and did not speak. F. Jasmine was tilted back in her chair, her head turned toward the window and the sun-crossed empty yard. The town was silent and the kitchen was silent except for the clock. F. Jasmine could not feel the world go round, and nothing moved.

'Now a funny thing has happened to me,' F. Jasmine began. 'I don't hardly know how to tell just what I mean. It was one of those strange things you can't exactly explain.'

'What, Frankie?' John Henry asked.

F. Jasmine turned from the window, but before she could speak again there was the sound. In the silence of the kitchen they heard the tone shaft quietly across the room, then again the same note was repeated. A piano scale slanted across the August afternoon. A chord was struck. Then in a dreaming way a chain of chords climbed slowly upward like a flight of castle stairs: but just at the end, when the eighth chord should have sounded and the scale made complete, there was a stop. This next to the last chord was repeated. The seventh chord, which seems to echo all of the unfinished scale, struck and insisted again and again. And finally there was a silence. F. Jasmine and John Henry and Berenice looked at each other. Somewhere in the neighborhood an August piano was being tuned.

'Jesus!' said Berenice. 'I seriously believe this will be the last straw.'

John Henry shivered. 'Me too,' he said.

F. Jasmine sat perfectly still before the table crowded with plates and dinner dishes. The gray of the kitchen was a stale gray and the room was too flat and too square. After the silence another note was sounded, and then repeated an octave higher. F. Jasmine raised her eyes each time the tone climbed higher, as though she watched the note move from one part of the kitchen to another; at the highest point her eyes had reached a ceiling corner, then, when a long scale slid downward, her head turned slowly as her eyes crossed from the ceiling corner to the floor corner at the opposite side of the room. The bottom bass note was struck six times, and F. Jasmine was left staring at an old pair of bedroom slippers and an empty beer bottle which were in that corner of the room. Finally she shut her eyes, and shook herself, and got up from the table.

'It makes me sad,' F. Jasmine said. 'And jittery too.' She began to walk around the room. 'They tell me that when they want to punish them over in Milledgeville, they tie them up and make them listen to piano-tuning.' She walked three times around the table. 'There's something I want to ask you. Suppose you ran into somebody who seemed to you terribly peculiar, but you didn't know the reason why.'

'In what ways peculiar?'

F. Jasmine thought of the soldier, but she could not further explain. 'Say you might meet somebody you think he almost might be a *drunk*, but you're not sure about anything. And he wanted you to join with him and go to a big party or dance. What would you do?'

'Well, on the face of it, I don't know. It would depend on how I feel. I might go with him to the big party and meet up with somebody that suited me better.' The live eye of Berenice suddenly narrowed, and she looked hard at F. Jasmine. 'But why do you ask that?'

The quietness in the room stretched out until F. Jasmine could hear the drip-drop from the faucet of the sink. She was trying to frame a way to tell Berenice about the soldier. Then all at once the telephone rang. F. Jasmine jumped up and, turning over her empty milk glass, dashed to the hall—but John Henry, who was nearer, reached the telephone first. He knelt on the telephone chair and smiled into the mouthpiece before he said hello. Then he kept on saying hello until F. Jasmine took the receiver from him and repeated the hellos at least two dozen times before she finally hung up.

'Anything like that makes me so mad,' she said when they had gone back to the kitchen. 'Or when the express truck stops before the door and the man peers at our number and then takes the box somewhere else. I look on those things as a kind of sign.' She raked her fingers through her crew-cut blond hair. 'You know I'm really going to get my fortune told before I leave home in the morning. It's something I've been meaning to do for a long time.'

Berenice said: 'Changing the subject, when are you going to show me the new dress? I'm anxious to see what you selected.'

So F. Jasmine went up to get the dress. Her room was what was known as a hotbox; the heat from the rest of the house rose up to her room and stayed there. In the afternoon the air seemed to make a buzzing sound, so it was a good idea to keep the motor running. F. Jasmine turned on the motor and opened the closet door. Until this day before the wedding she had always kept her six costumes hung in a row on coat-hangers, and she just threw her ordinary clothes up on the shelf or kicked them into a corner. But when she had come home this afternoon, she had changed this: the costumes were thrown up on the shelf and the wedding dress hung alone in the closet on a coat-hanger. The silver slippers were placed carefully on the floor beneath the dress with the toes pointed north, toward Winter Hill. For some reason F. Jasmine tiptoed around the room as she began to dress.

'Shut your eyes!' she called. 'Don't watch me coming down the stairs. Don't open your eyes until I tell you.'

It was as though the four walls of the kitchen watched her, and the skillet hanging on the wall was a watching round black eye. The piano-tuning was for a minute silent. Berenice sat with her head bowed, as though she was in church. And John Henry had his head bowed also, but he was peeking. F. Jasmine stood at the foot of the stairs and placed her left hand on her hip.

'Oh, how pretty!' John Henry said.

Berenice raised her head, and when she saw F. Jasmine her face was a study. The dark eye looked from the silver hair ribbon to the soles of the silver slippers. She said nothing.

'Now tell me your honest opinion,' F. Jasmine said.

But Berenice looked at the orange satin evening dress and shook her head and did not comment. At first she shook her head with short little turns, but the longer she stared, the longer these shakes became, until at the last shake F. Jasmine heard her neck crack.

'What's the matter?' F. Jasmine asked.

'I thought you was going to get a pink dress.'

'But when I got in the store I changed my mind. What is wrong with this dress? Don't you like it, Berenice?'

'No,' said Berenice. 'It don't do.'

'What do you mean? It don't do.'

'Exactly that. It just don't do.'

F. Jasmine turned to look in the mirror, and she still thought the dress was beautiful. But Berenice had a sour and stubborn look on her face, an expression like that of an old long-eared mule, and F. Jasmine could not understand.

'But I don't see what you mean,' she complained. 'What is wrong?'

Berenice folded her arms over her chest and said: 'Well, if you don't see it I can't explain it to you. Look there at your head, to begin with.'

F. Jasmine looked at her head in the mirror.

'You had all your hair shaved off like a convict, and now you tie a silver ribbon around this head without any hair. It just looks peculiar.'

'Oh, but I'm washing my hair tonight and going to try to curl it,' F. Jasmine said.

'And look at them elbows,' Berenice continued. 'Here you got on this grown woman's evening dress. Orange satin. And that brown crust on your elbows. The two things just don't mix.'

F. Jasmine hunched her shoulders and covered her rusty elbows with her hands.

Berenice gave her head another quick wide shake, then bunched her lips in judgment. 'Take it back down to the store.'

'But I can't!' said F. Jasmine. 'It's bargain basement. They don't take back.'

Berenice always had two mottoes. One was the known saying that you can't make a silk purse out of a sow's ear. And the other was the motto that you have to cut your suit according to the cloth, and make the best of what you have. So F. Jasmine was not certain if it was the last of these mottoes that made Berenice change her mind, or if she really began to improve her feelings about the dress. Anyway, Berenice stared for several seconds with her head to one side, and finally said:

'Come here. We'll make it fit better at the waist and see what we can do.'

'I think you're just not accustomed to seeing anybody dressed up,' F. Jasmine said.

'I'm not accustomed to human Christmas trees in August.'

So Berenice took off the sash and patted and pulled the dress in various places. F. Jasmine stood stiff like a hatrack and let her work with the dress. John Henry had got up from his chair and was watching, with the napkin still tied around his neck.

'Frankie's dress looks like a Christmas tree,' he said.

'Two-faced Judas!' F. Jasmine said. 'You just now said it was pretty. Old double-faced Judas!'

The piano tuned. Whose piano it was F. Jasmine did not know, but the sound of the tuning was solemn and insistent in the kitchen, and it came from somewhere not so far away. The piano-tuner would sometimes fling out a rattling little tune, and then he would go back to one note. And repeat. And bang the same note in a solemn and crazy way. And repeat. And bang. The name of the piano-tuner in the town was Mr. Schwarzenbaum. The sound was enough to shiver the gizzards of musicians and make all listeners feel queer.

'It almost makes me wonder if he does that just to torment us,' F. Jasmine said.

But Berenice said no: 'They tune pianos the same way in Cincinnati and the world over. It is just the way they do it. Less turn on the radio in the dining room and drown him out.'

F. Jasmine shook her head. 'No,' she said. 'I can't explain why. But I don't want to have that radio turned on again. It reminds me too much of this summer.'

'Step back a little now,' said Berenice.

She had pinned the waist higher and done one thing and another to the dress. F. Jasmine looked in the mirror over the sink. She could only see herself from the chest up, so after admiring this top part of herself, she stood on a chair

and looked at the middle section. Then she began to clear
away a corner of the table so she could climb up and see in
the mirror the silver shoes, but Berenice prevented her.

'Don't you honestly think it is pretty?' F. Jasmine said. 'I think
so. Seriously, Berenice. Give me your candy opinion.'

But Berenice rared up and spoke in an accusing voice: 'I
never knew somebody so unreasonable! You ask me my candy
opinion, and I give it to you. Then you ask me again, and I give
it to you. But what you want is not my honest opinion, but my
good opinion on something I know is wrong. Now what kind
of way is that to act?'

'All right,' F. Jasmine said. 'I only want to look good.'

'Well, you look very well,' said Berenice. 'Pretty is as pretty
does. You look well enough for anybody's wedding. Excepting
your own. And then, pray Jesus, we will be in a position to do
better. What I have to do now is get John Henry a fresh suit
and figure about the outfit I'm going to wear myself.'

'Uncle Charles is dead,' John Henry said. 'And we are going
to the wedding.'

'Yes, Baby,' said Berenice. And from the sudden dreaming
quietness of her, F. Jasmine felt that Berenice was carried back
to all the other dead people she knew. The dead were walking
in her heart, and she was remembering back to Ludie Freeman
and the long-gone time of Cincinnati and the snow.

F. Jasmine thought back to the other seven dead people
she knew. Her mother had died the very day that she was
born, so she could not count her. There was a picture of her
mother in the right-hand drawer of her father's bureau: and
the face looked timid and sorry, shut up with the cold folded
handkerchiefs in the drawer. Then there was her grandmother
who had died when Frankie was nine years old, and F. Jasmine
remembered her very well—but with crooked little pictures
that were sunken far back in her mind. A soldier from that
town called William Boyd had been killed that year in Italy, and
she had known him both by sight and name. Mrs. Selway, two
blocks away, had died; and F. Jasmine had watched the funeral
from the sidewalk, but she was not invited. The solemn grown
men stood around out on the front porch and it had rained,
there was a gray silk ribbon on the door. She knew Lon Baker,
and he was dead also. Lon Baker was a colored boy and he

was murdered in the alley out behind her father's store. On an April afternoon his throat was slashed with a razor blade, and all the alley people disappeared in back doorways, and later it was said his cut throat opened like a crazy shivering mouth that spoke ghost words into the April sun. Lon Baker was dead and Frankie knew him. She knew, but only in a chancing kind of way, Mr. Pitkin at Brawer's Shoe Shop, Miss Birdie Grimes, and a man who had climbed poles for the telephone company: all dead.

'Do you think very frequently about Ludie?' F. Jasmine asked.

'You know I do,' said Berenice. 'I think about the years when me and Ludie was together, and about all the bad times I seen since. Ludie would never have let me be lonesome so that I took up with all kinds of no-good men. Me and Ludie,' she said. 'Ludie and me.'

F. Jasmine sat vibrating her leg and thinking of Ludie and Cincinnati. Of all the dead people out of the world, Ludie Freeman was the one F. Jasmine knew the best, although she had never laid eyes on him, and was not even born when he had died. She knew Ludie and the city of Cincinnati, and the winter when Ludie and Berenice had gone together to the North and seen the snow. A thousand times they had talked of all these things, and it was a conversation that Berenice talked slowly, making each sentence like a song. And the old Frankie used to ask and question about Cincinnati. What exactly they would eat in Cincinnati and how wide would be the Cincinnati streets? And in a chanting kind of voice they talked about the Cincinnati fish, the parlor in the Cincinnati house on Myrtle Street, the Cincinnati picture shows. And Ludie Freeman was a brickmason, making a grand and a regular salary, and he was the man of all her husbands that Berenice had loved.

'Sometimes I almost wish I had never knew Ludie at all,' said Berenice. 'It spoils you too much. It leaves you too lonesome afterward. When you walk home in the evening on the way from work, it makes a little lonesome quinch come in you. And you take up with too many sorry men to try to get over the feeling.'

'I know it,' F. Jasmine said. 'But T. T. Williams is not sorry.'

'I wasn't referring to T. T. He and me is just good friends.'

'Don't you think you will marry him?' F. Jasmine asked.

'Well, T. T. is a fine upstanding colored gentleman,' said Berenice. 'You never hear tell of T. T. raring around like a lot of other mens. If I was to marry T. T., I could get out of this kitchen and stand behind the cash register at the restaurant and pat my foot. Furthermore, I respect T. T. sincerely. He has walked in a state of grace all of his life.'

'Well, when are you going to marry him?' she asked. 'He is crazy about you.'

Berenice said: 'I ain't going to marry him.'

'But you just now was saying—' said F. Jasmine.

'I was saying how sincerely I respect T. T. and sincerely regard him.'

'Well, then—?' F. Jasmine said.

'I respect and regard him highly,' said Berenice. Her dark eye was quiet and sober and her flat nose widened as she spoke. 'But he don't make me shiver none.'

After a moment F. Jasmine said: 'To think about the wedding makes me shiver.'

'Well, it's a pity,' said Berenice.

'It makes me shiver, too, to think about how many dead people I already know. Seven in all,' she said. 'And now Uncle Charles.'

F. Jasmine put her fingers in her ears and closed her eyes, but it was not death. She could feel the heat from the stove and smell the dinner. She could feel a rumble in her stomach and the beating of her heart. And the dead feel nothing, hear nothing, see nothing: only black.

'It would be terrible to be dead,' she said, and in the wedding dress she began to walk around the room.

There was a rubber ball on the shelf, and she threw it against the hall door and caught it on the rebound.

'Put that down,' said Berenice. 'Go take off the dress before you dirty it. Go do something. Go turn on the radio.'

'I told you I don't want that radio on.'

And she was walking around the room, and Berenice had said to go do something, but she did not know what to do. She walked in the wedding dress, with her hand on her hip. The silver slippers had squeezed her feet so that the toes felt swollen and mashed like ten big sore cauliflowers.

'But I advise you to keep the radio on when you come back,' F. Jasmine said suddenly. 'Some day very likely you will hear us speaking over the radio.'

'What's that?'

'I say very likely we might be asked to speak over the radio some day.'

'Speak about what, pray tell me,' said Berenice.

'I don't know exactly what about,' F. Jasmine said. 'But probably some eye-witness account about something. We will be asked to speak.'

'I don't follow you,' said Berenice. 'What are we going to eye-witness? And who will ask us to speak?'

F. Jasmine whirled around and, putting both fists on her hips, she set herself in a staring position. 'Did you think I meant you and John Henry and me? Why, I have never heard of anything so funny in my whole life.'

John Henry's voice was high and excited. 'What, Frankie? Who is speaking on the radio?'

'When I said *we*, you thought I meant you and me and John Henry West. To speak over the world radio. I have never heard of anything so funny since I was born.'

John Henry had climbed up to kneel on the seat of his chair and the blue veins showed in his forehead and you could see the strained chords of his neck. 'Who?' he hollered. 'What?'

'Ha ha ha!' she said, and then she burst out laughing; she went banging around the room and hitting things with her fist. 'Ho ho ho!'

And John Henry wailed and F. Jasmine banged around the kitchen in the wedding dress and Berenice got up from the table and raised her right hand for peace. Then suddenly they all stopped at once. F. Jasmine stood absolutely still before the window, and John Henry hurried to the window also and watched on tiptoe with his hands to the sill. Berenice turned her head to see what had happened. And at that moment the piano was quiet.

'Oh!' F. Jasmine whispered.

Four girls were crossing the back yard. They were girls of fourteen and fifteen years old, and they were the club members. First came Helen Fletcher, and then the others walking slowly in single file. They had cut across from the

O'Neils' back yard and were passing slowly before the arbor. The long gold sun slanted down on them and made their skin look golden also, and they were dressed in clean, fresh dresses. When they had passed the arbor, their single shadows stretched out long and gangling across the yard. Soon they would be gone. F. Jasmine stood motionless. In the old days that summer she would have waited in the hope that they might call her and tell her she had been elected to the club—and only at the very last, when it was plain that they were only passing, she would have shouted in angry loudness that they were not to cut across her yard. But now she watched them quietly, without jealousy. At the last there came an urge to call out to them about the wedding, but before the words could be formed and spoken, the club of girls was gone. There was only the arbor and the spinning sun.

'Now I wonder—' F. Jasmine said finally. But Berenice cut her short:

'Nothing, Curiosity,' she said. 'Curiosity, nothing.'

When they began the second round of that last dinner, it was past five o'clock, and nearing twilight. It was the time of afternoon when in the old days, sitting with the red cards at the table, they would sometimes begin to criticize the Creator. They would judge the work of God, and mention the ways how they would improve the world. And Holy Lord God John Henry's voice would rise up happy and high and strange, and his world was a mixture of delicious and freak, and he did not think in global terms: the sudden long arm that could stretch from here to California, chocolate dirt and rains of lemonade, the extra eye seeing a thousand miles, a hinged tail that could be let down as a kind of prop to sit on when you wished to rest, the candy flowers.

But the world of the Holy Lord God Berenice Sadie Brown was a different world, and it was round and just and reasonable. First, there would be no separate colored people in the world, but all human beings would be light brown color with blue eyes and black hair. There would be no colored people and no white people to make the colored people feel cheap and sorry all through their lives. No colored people, but all human men and ladies and children as one loving family on the earth.

And when Berenice spoke of this first principle her voice was a strong deep song that soared and sang in beautiful dark tones leaving an echo in the corners of the room that trembled for a long time until silence.

No war, said Berenice. No stiff corpses hanging from the Europe trees and no Jews murdered anywhere. No war, and the young boys leaving home in army suits, and no wild cruel Germans and Japanese. No war in the whole world, but peace in all countries everywhere. Also, no starving. To begin with, the real Lord God had made free air and free rain and free dirt for the benefit of all. There would be free food for every human mouth, free meals and two pounds of fatback a week, and after that each able-bodied person would work for whatever else he wished to eat or own. No killed Jews and no hurt colored people. No war and no hunger in the world. And, finally, Ludie Freeman would be alive.

The world of Berenice was a round world, and the old Frankie would listen to the strong deep singing voice, and she would agree with Berenice. But the old Frankie's world was the best of the three worlds. She agreed with Berenice about the main laws of her creation, but she added many things: an aeroplane and a motorcycle to each person, a world club with certificates and badges, and a better law of gravity. She did not completely agree with Berenice about the war; and sometimes she said she would have one War Island in the world where those who wanted to could go, and fight or donate blood, and she might go for a while as a WAC in the Air Corps. She also changed the seasons, leaving out summer altogether, and adding much snow. She planned it so that people could instantly change back and forth from boys to girls, whichever way they felt like and wanted. But Berenice would argue with her about this, insisting that the law of human sex was exactly right just as it was and could in no way be improved. And then John Henry West would very likely add his two cents' worth about this time, and think that people ought to be half boy and half girl, and when the old Frankie threatened to take him to the Fair and sell him to the Freak Pavilion, he would only close his eyes and smile.

So the three of them would sit there at the kitchen table and criticize the Creator and the work of God. Sometimes their voices crossed and the three worlds twisted. The Holy Lord God John Henry West. The Holy Lord God Berenice Sadie Brown. The Holy Lord God Frankie Addams. The Worlds at the end of the long stale afternoons.

But this was a different day. They were not loafing or playing cards, but still eating dinner. F. Jasmine had taken off the wedding dress and was barefooted and comfortable in her petticoat once more. The brown gravy of the peas had stiffened, the food was neither hot nor cold, and the butter had melted. They started in on second helpings, passing the dishes back and forth among themselves, and they did not talk of the ordinary subjects that usually they thought about this time of the afternoon. Instead, there began a strange conversation, and it came about in this way:

'Frankie,' said Berenice, 'Awhile back you started to say something. And we veered off from the subject. It was about something unnatural, I think.'

'Oh, yes,' F. Jasmine said. 'I was going to tell you about something peculiar that happened to me today that I don't hardly realize. Now I don't exactly know how to explain just what I mean.'

F. Jasmine broke open a sweet potato and tilted back in her chair. She began to try to tell Berenice what had happened when she had been walking home and suddenly seen something from the tail of her eye, and when she turned to look, it was the two colored boys back at the end of the alley. As she talked, F. Jasmine stopped now and then to pull her lower lip and study just for the right words to tell of a feeling that she had never heard named before. Occasionally she glanced at Berenice, to see if she was following her, and a remarkable look was breaking on Berenice's face: the glass blue eye was bright and astonished, as always, and at first her dark eye was astonished also; then a queer and conniving look changed her expression, and from time to time she turned her head with short little jerks, as though to listen from different earpoints and make sure that what she heard was true.

Before F. Jasmine finished, Berenice had pushed back her plate and reached into her bosom for her cigarettes. She smoked home-rolled cigarettes, but she carried them in a Chesterfield package, so that from the outward appearance she was smoking store Chesterfields. She twisted off a ragged fringe of loose tobacco and raised back her head when she held the match, so that the flame would not go up her nose. A blue layer of smoke hung over the three of them at the table. Berenice held the cigarette between her thumb and forefinger; her hand had been drawn and stiffened by a winter rheumatism so that the last two fingers could not be straightened out. She sat listening and smoking, and when F. Jasmine had finished, there was long pause, then Berenice leaned forward and asked suddenly:

'Listen at me! Can you see through them bones in my forehead? Have you, Frankie Addams, been reading my mind?'

F. Jasmine did not know what to answer.

'This is one of the queerest things I ever heard of,' Berenice went on. 'I cannot get over it.'

'What I mean—' F. Jasmine started again.

'I know what you mean,' said Berenice. 'Right here in this very corner of the eye.' She pointed to the red-webbed outside corner of the dark eye. 'You suddenly catch something there. And this cold shiver run all the way down you. And you whirl around. And then you stand facing Jesus knows what. But not Ludie and not who you want. And for a minute you feel like you been dropped down a well.'

'Yes,' F. Jasmine said. 'That is it.'

'Well, this is mighty remarkable,' said Berenice. 'This is a thing been happening to me all my life. Yet just now is the first time I ever heard it put into words.'

F. Jasmine covered her nose and her mouth with her hand, so that it would not be noticed that she was pleased about being so remarkable, and her eyes were closed in a modest way.

'Yes, that is the way when you are in love,' said Berenice. 'Invariably. A thing known and not spoken.'

So that was how the queer conversation began at quarter to six on the last afternoon. It was the first time ever they had talked about love, with F. Jasmine included in the conversation as a person who understood and had worth-while opinions. The old Frankie had laughed at love, maintained it was a big fake, and did not believe in it. She never put any of it in her shows, and never went to love shows at the Palace. The old

Frankie had always gone to the Saturday matinee, when the shows were crook shows, war shows, or cowboy shows. And who was it who had caused the confusion at the Palace that last May, when the movie had run an old show on Saturday called *Camille?* The old Frankie. She had been in her seat on the second row and she stamped and put two fingers in her mouth and began to whistle. And the other half-fare people in the first three rows began to whistle and stamp also, and the longer the love picture lasted, the louder they became. So that finally the manager came down with a flashlight and rooted the whole crowd of them out of their seats and marched them up the aisle and left them standing on the sidewalk: done out of their dimes, and disgusted.

The old Frankie had never admitted love. Yet here F. Jasmine was sitting at the table with her knees crossed, and now and then she patted her bare foot on the floor in an accustomed way, and nodded at what Berenice was saying. Furthermore, when she reached out quietly toward the Chesterfield package beside the saucer of melted butter, Berenice did not slap her hand away, and F. Jasmine took herself a cigarette. She and Berenice were two grown people smoking at the dinner table. And John Henry West had his big child head hunched close to his shoulder, watching and listening to all that went on.

'Now I will tell you a story,' said Berenice. 'And it is to be a warning to you. You hear me, John Henry? You hear me, Frankie?'

'Yes,' John Henry whispered. He pointed with his gray little forefinger. 'Frankie is smoking.'

Berenice sat up straight, her shoulders square, and her dark twisted hands folded before her on the table. She raised her chin and drew in her breath in the way of a singer who is beginning a song. The piano tuned and insisted, but when Berenice began to speak, her dark gold voice rang in the kitchen and they did not listen to the piano notes. But to start this warning Berenice began with the old same story that they had heard many times before. The story of her and Ludie Freeman. A long time ago.

'Now I am here to tell you I was happy. There was no human woman in all the world more happy that I was in them days,' she said. 'And that includes everybody. You listening to me, John Henry? It includes all queens and millionaires and first ladies of the land. And I mean it includes people of all color. You hear me, Frankie? No human woman in all the world was happier than Berenice Sadie Brown.'

She had started with the old story of Ludie. And it began an afternoon in late October almost twenty years ago. The story started at the place where first they met each other, in front of Camp Campbell's Filling Station outside of the city limits of the town. It was the time of the year when the leaves were turning and the countryside was smoky and autumn gray and gold. And the story went on from that first meeting to the wedding at the Welcome Ascension Church in Sugarville. And then on through the years with the two of them together. The house with the brick front steps and the glass windows on the corner of Barrow Street. The Christmas of the fox fur, and the June of the fish fry thrown for twenty-eight invited relatives and guests. The years with Berenice cooking dinner and sewing Ludie's suits and shirts on the machine and the two of them always having a good time. And the nine months they lived up North, in the city of Cincinnati, where there was snow. Then Sugarville again, and days merging one into another, and the weeks, the months, the years together. And the pair of them always had a good time, yet it was not so much the happenings she mentioned as the way she told about these happenings that made F. Jasmine understand.

Berenice spoke in an unwinding kind of voice, and she had said that she was happier than a queen. As she told the story, it seemed to F. Jasmine that Berenice resembled a strange queen, if a queen can be colored and sitting at a kitchen table. She unwound the story of her and Ludie like a colored queen unwinding a bolt of cloth of gold—and at the end, when the story was over, her expression was always the same: the dark eye staring straight ahead, her flat nose widened and trembling, her mouth finished and sad and quiet. As a rule, when the story was over, they would sit for a moment and then suddenly get busy doing something in a hurry: start a hand of cards, or make milk-shakes, or just stir around the kitchen with no particular purpose. But this afternoon they did not move or speak for a long time after Berenice had finished, until finally F. Jasmine asked:

'What exactly did Ludie die of?'

'It was something similar to pneumonia,' said Berenice. 'November the year 1931.'

'The very year and the very month I was born,' F. Jasmine said.

'The coldest November I ever seen. Every morning there was frost and puddles were crusted with ice. The sunshine was pale yellow like it is in wintertime. Sounds carried far away, and I remember a hound dog that used to howl toward sundown. I kept a fire in the hearth going day and night, and in the evening when I walk around the room there was this shaking shadow following alongside of me on the wall. And everything I seen come to me as a kind of sign.'

'I think it is a kind of sign I was born the same year and the same month he died,' F. Jasmine said. 'Only the dates are different.'

'And then it was a Thursday toward six o'clock in the afternoon. About this time of day. Only November. I remember I went to the passage and opened the front door. We were living that year at 233 Prince Street. Dark was coming on, the old hound was howling far away. And I go back in the room and lay down on Ludie's bed. I lay myself down over Ludie with my arms spread out and my face on his face. And I pray that the Lord would contage my strength to him. And I ask the Lord let it be anybody, but not let it be Ludie. And I lay there and pray for a long time. Until night.'

'How?' John Henry asked. It was a question that did not mean anything, but he repeated it in a higher, wailing voice: 'How, Berenice?'

'That night he died,' she said. She spoke in a sharp tone, as though they had disputed with her. 'I tell you he died. Ludie! Ludie Freeman! Ludie Maxwell Freeman died!'

She was finished, and they sat there at the table. Nobody moved. John Henry stared at Berenice, and the fly that had been hovering above him lighted on the left rim of his glasses; the fly walked slowly across the left lens, and over the nosepiece, and across the right lens. It was only when the fly had flown away that John Henry blinked and waved his hand.

'One thing,' F. Jasmine said finally. 'There is Uncle Charles laying there dead right now. Yet somehow I can't cry. I know I ought to feel sad. Yet I feel sadder about Ludie than I do about Uncle Charles. Although I never laid eyes on Ludie. And I knew Uncle Charles all my life and he was blood kin to blood kin of mine. Maybe it's because I was born so soon after Ludie died.'

'Maybe so,' said Berenice.

It seemed to F. Jasmine that they might just sit there the rest of the afternoon, without moving or speaking, when suddenly she remembered something.

'You were starting out to tell a different story,' she said. 'It was some kind of warning.'

Berenice looked puzzled for a moment, then she jerked her head up and said: 'Oh, yes! I was going to tell you how this thing we was talking about applies to me. And what happened with them other husbands. Now you perk your ears.'

But the story of the other three husbands was an old story also. As Berenice began to talk, F. Jasmine went to the refrigerator and brought back to the table some sweetened condensed milk to pour on crackers as a dessert. At first she did not listen very carefully.

'It was the April of the following year that I went one Sunday to the Forks Falls Church. And you ask what I was doing out there and I tell you. I was visiting that Jackson branch of my foster cousins who live out there and we had gone to their church. So there I was praying in this church where the congregation was strangers to me. I had my forehead down on the top of the pew in front of me, and my eyes were open—not gazing around in secret, mind you, but just open. When suddenly this shiver run all the way through me. I had caught sight of something from the corner of my eye. And I looked slowly to the left. And guess what I seen there? There on the pew, just six inches from my eye, was this *thumb*.'

'What thumb?' F. Jasmine asked.

'Now I'm telling you,' said Berenice. 'To understand this, you have to know that there was only one little portion of Ludie Freeman which was not pretty. Every other part about him was handsome and pretty as anyone would ever wish. All except his right thumb, which had been mashed in a hinge. This one thumb had a mashed chewed appearance that was not pretty. You understand?'

'You mean you suddenly saw Ludie's thumb when you were praying?'

'I mean I seen *this* thumb. And as I kneel there a shiver run from my head to my heels. I just kneel there staring at this thumb, and before I looked any further, to find out whose thumb it might be, I begun to pray in earnest. I prayed out loud: Lord, manifest! Lord, manifest!'

'And did He?' F. Jasmine asked. 'Manifest?'

Berenice turned aside and made a sound like spitting. 'Manifest, my foot!' she said. 'You know who that thumb belonged to?'

'Who?'

'Why Jamie Beale,' said Berenice. 'That big old no-good Jamie Beale. It was the first time I ever laid eyes on him.'

'Is that why you married him?' F. Jasmine asked, for Jamie Beale was the name of the sorry old liquor-drinker, who was the second husband. 'Because he had a mashed thumb like Ludie's?'

'Jesus knows,' said Berenice. 'I don't. I felt drawn to him on account of the thumb. And then one thing led to another. First thing I knew I had married him.'

'Well, I think that was silly,' F. Jasmine said. 'To marry him just because of that thumb.'

'Me too,' said Berenice. 'I'm not trying to dispute with you. I'm just telling you what happened. And the very same thing occurred in the case of Henry Johnson.'

Henry Johnson was the third husband, the one who had gone crazy on Berenice. He was all right for three weeks after they had married, but then he went crazy, and he behaved in such a crazy way that finally she had to quit him.

'You mean to sit there and tell me Henry Johnson had one of those mashed thumbs too?'

'No,' said Berenice. 'It was not the thumb that time. It was the coat.'

F. Jasmine and John Henry looked at each other, for what she was saying did not seem to make much sense. But Berenice's dark eye was sober and certain, and she nodded to them in a definite way.

'To understand this, you have to know what happened after Ludie died. He had a policy due to pay off two hundred and fifty dollars. I won't go into the whole business, but what happened was that I was cheated by them policy people out of fifty dollars. And in two days I had to scour around and raise the fifty dollars to make out for the funeral. Because I couldn't let Ludie be put away cheap. I pawned everything I could lay hands on. And I sold my coat and Ludie's coat. To that second-hand clothing store on Front Avenue.'

'Oh!' F. Jasmine said. 'Then you mean Henry Johnson bought Ludie's coat and you married him because of it.'

'Not exactly,' said Berenice. 'I was walking down that street alongside of the City Hall one evening when I suddenly seen this shape before me. Now the shape of this boy ahead of me was so similar to Ludie through the shoulders and the back of the head that I almost dropped dead there on the sidewalk. I followed and run behind him. It was Henry Johnson, and that was the first time I ever saw him also, since he lived in the country and didn't come much into town. But he had chanced to buy Ludie's coat and he was built on the same shape as Ludie. And from the back view it looked like he was Ludie's ghost or Ludie's twin. But how I married him I don't exactly know, for to begin with it was clear that he did not have his share of sense. But you let a boy hang around and you get fond of him. Anyway, that's how I married Henry Johnson.'

'People certainy do curious things.'

'You telling me,' said Berenice. She glanced at F. Jasmine, who was pouring a slow ribbon of condensed milk over a soda cracker, to finish her dinner with a sweet sandwich.

'I swear, Frankie! I believe you got a tateworm. I am perfectly serious. Your father looks over them big grocery bills and he naturally suspicions that I carry things off.'

'You do,' F. Jasmine said. 'Sometimes.'

'He reads over them grocery bills and he complains to me, Berenice, what in the name of holy creation did we do with six cans of condensed milk and forty-leven dozen eggs and eight boxes of marshmallows in one week. And I have to admit to him: Frankie eat them. I have to say to him: Mr. Addams, you

think you feeding something human back here in your kitchen.
That's what you think. I have to say to him: Yes, you imagine it
is something human.'

'After today I'm not going to be greedy any more,' F. Jasmine
said. 'But I don't understand the point of what you was telling.
I don't see how that about Jamie Beale and Henry Johnson
applies to me.'

'It applies to everybody and it is a warning.'

'But how?'

'Why, don't you see what I was doing?' asked Berenice. 'I
loved Ludie and he was the first man I loved. Therefore, I
had to go and copy myself forever afterward. What I did was
to marry off little pieces of Ludie whenever I come across them.
It was just my misfortune they all turned out to be the wrong
pieces. My intention was to repeat me and Ludie. Now don't
you see?'

'I see what you're driving at,' F. Jasmine said. 'But I don't
see how it is a warning applied to me.'

'Then do I have to tell you?' asked Berenice.

F. Jasmine did not nod or answer, for she felt that Berenice
had laid a trap for her, and was going to make remarks
she did not want to hear. Berenice stopped to light herself
another cigarette and two blue slow scrolls of smoke came
from her nostrils and lazed above the dirty dishes on the
table. Mr. Schwarzenbaum was playing an arpeggio. F. Jasmine
waited and it seemed a long time.

'You and that wedding at Winter Hill,' Berenice said finally.
'That is what I am warning about. I can see right through them
two gray eyes of yours like they was glass. And what I see is the
saddest piece of foolishness I ever knew.'

'Gray eyes is glass,' John Henry whispered.

But F. Jasmine would not let herself be seen through and
outstared; she hardened and tensed her eyes and did not look
away from Berenice.

'I see what you have in your mind. Don't think I don't. You
see something unheard of at Winter Hill tomorrow, and you
right in the center. You think you going to march down the
center of the aisle right in between your brother and the bride.
You think you going to break into that wedding, and then Jesus
knows what else.'

'No,' F. Jasmine said. 'I don't see myself walking down the center of the aisle between them.'

'I see through them eyes,' said Berenice. 'Don't argue with me.'

John Henry said again, but softer: 'Gray eyes is glass.'

'But what I'm warning is this,' said Berenice. 'If you start out falling in love with some unheard-of thing like that, what is going to happen to you? If you take a mania like this, it won't be the last time and of that you can be sure. So what will become of you? Will you be trying to break into weddings the rest of your days? And what kind of life would that be?'

'It makes me sick to listen at people who don't have any sense,' F. Jasmine said, and she put her two fingers in her ears, but she did not push in the fingers very tight and she could still hear Berenice.

'You just laying yourself this fancy trap to catch yourself in trouble,' Berenice went on. 'And you know it. You been through the B section of the seventh grade and you are already twelve years old.'

F. Jasmine did not speak of the wedding, but her argument passed over it, and she said: 'They will take me. You wait and see.'

'And when they don't?'

'I told you,' F. Jasmine said. 'I will shoot myself with Papa's pistol. But they will take me. And we're never coming back to this part of the country again.'

'Well, I been trying to reason seriously,' said Berenice. 'But I see it is no use. You determined to suffer.'

'Who said I was going to suffer?' F. Jasmine said.

'I know you,' said Berenice. 'You will suffer.'

'You are just jealous,' F. Jasmine said. 'You are just trying to deprive me of all the pleasure of leaving town. And kill the joy of it.'

'I am just trying to head this off,' said Berenice. 'But I see it is no use.'

John Henry whispered for the last time: 'Gray eyes is glass.'

It was past six o'clock, and the slow old afternoon began slowly to die. F. Jasmine took her fingers from her ears and breathed a long tired sigh. When she had sighed, John Henry sighed also, and Berenice concluded with the longest sigh of all. Mr. Schwarzenbaum had played a ragged little waltz; but the piano was not yet tuned to suit him, and he began to harp and insist on another note. Again he played the scale up until the seventh note, and again he stuck there and did not finish. F. Jasmine was no longer watching the music with her eyes; but John Henry was watching, and when the piano stuck on the last note F. Jasmine could see him harden his behind and sit there stiff in the chair, his eyes raised, waiting.

'It is that last note,' F. Jasmine said. 'If you start with A and go on up to G, there is a curious thing that seems to make the difference between G and A all the difference in the world. Twice as much difference as between any other two notes in the scale. Yet they are side by side there on the piano just as close together as the other notes. Do ray mee fa sol la tee. Tee. Tee. Tee. It could drive you wild.'

John Henry was grinning with his snaggle teeth and giggling softly. 'Tee-tee,' he said, and he pulled at Berenice's sleeve. 'Did you hear what Frankie said? Tee-tee.'

'Shut your trap,' F. Jasmine said. 'Quit always being so evil-minded.' She got up from the table, but she did not know where to go. 'You didn't say anything about Willis Rhodes. Did he have a mashed thumb or a coat or something?'

'Lord!' said Berenice, and her voice was so sudden and shocked that F. Jasmine turned and went back to the table. 'Now that is a story would make the hair rise on your head. You mean to say I never told you about what happened with me and Willis Rhodes?'

'No,' F. Jasmine said. Willis Rhodes was the last and the worst of the four husbands, and he was so terrible that Berenice had had to call the Law on him. 'What?'

'Well, imagine this!' said Berenice. 'Imagine a cold bitter January night. And me laying all by myself in the big parlor bed. Alone in the house, because everybody else had gone for the Saturday night to Forks Falls. Me, mind you, who hates to sleep in a empty old bed all by myself and is nervous in a house alone. Past twelve o'clock on this cold bitter January night. Can you remember wintertime, John Henry?'

John Henry nodded.

'Now imagine this!' said Berenice again. She had begun stacking the dishes so that three dirty plates were piled before her on the table. Her dark eye circled around the table, roping in F. Jasmine and John Henry as her audience. F. Jasmine leaned forward, her mouth open and her hands holding the table edge. John Henry shivered down in his chair and he watched Berenice through his glasses without batting his eyes. Berenice had started in a low and creepy voice, then suddenly she stopped and sat there looking at the two of them.

'So what?' F. Jasmine urged, leaning closer across the table. 'What happened?'

But Berenice did not speak. She looked from one of them to the other, and shook her head slowly. Then when she spoke again her voice was completely changed, and she said: 'Why, I wish you would look yonder. I wish you would look.'

F. Jasmine glanced quickly behind her, but there was only the stove, the wall, the empty stair.

'What?' she asked. 'What happened?'

'I wish you would look,' Berenice repeated. 'Them two little pitchers and them four big ears.' She got up suddenly from the table. 'Come on, less wash the dishes. Then we going to make some cup cakes to take tomorrow on the trip.'

There was nothing F. Jasmine could do to show Berenice how she felt. After a long time, when the table before her was already cleared and Berenice stood washing dishes at the sink, she only said:

'If it's anything I mortally despise it's a person who starts out to tell something and works up people's interest and then stops.'

'I admit it,' said Berenice. 'And I am sorry. But it was just one of them things I suddenly realize I couldn't tell you and John Henry.'

John Henry was skipping an scuttling back and forth across the kitchen, from the stairway to the back porch door. 'Cup cakes!' he sang. 'Cup cakes! Cup cakes!'

'You could have sent him out of the room,' F. Jasmine said. 'And told me. But don't think I care. I don't care a particle what happened. I just wish Willis Rhodes had come in about that time and slit your throat.'

'That is a ugly way to talk,' said Berenice. 'Especially since I got a surprise for you. Go out on the back porch and look in the wicker basket covered with a newspaper.'

F. Jasmine got up, but grudgingly, and she walked in a crippled way to the back porch. Then she stood in the doorway holding the pink organdie dress. Contrary to all that Berenice had maintained, the collar was pleated with tiny little pleats, as it was meant to be. She must have done it before dinner when F. Jasmine was upstairs.

'Well, this is mighty nice of you,' she said. 'I appreciate it.'

She would have liked for her expression to be split into two parts, so that one eye stared at Berenice in an accusing way, and the other eye thanked her with a grateful look. But the human face does not divide like this, and the two expressions canceled out each other.

'Cheer up,' said Berenice. 'Who can tell what will happen? You might dress up in that fresh pink dress tomorrow and meet the cutest little white boy in Winter Hill you ever seen. It's just on such trips as these that you run into beaus.'

'But that's not what I'm talking about,' F. Jasmine said. Then, after a while, still leaning against the doorway, she added: 'Somehow we got off on the wrong kind of conversation.'

The twilight was white, and it lasted for a long while. Time in August could be divided into four parts: morning, afternoon, twilight, and dark. At twilight the sky became a curious blue-green which soon faded to white. The air was soft gray, and the arbor and trees were slowly darkening. It was the hour when sparrows gathered and whirled above the rooftops of the town, and when in the darkened elms along the street there was the August sound of the cicadas. Noises at twilight had a blurred sound, and they lingered: the slam of a screen door down the street, voices of children, the whir of a lawnmower from a yard somewhere. F. Jasmine brought in the evening newspaper, and dark was coming in the kitchen. The corners in the room at first were dark, then the drawings on the wall faded. The three of them watched the dark come on in silence.

'The army is now in Paris.'

'That's good.'

They were quiet awhile and then F. Jasmine said: 'I have a lot of things to do. I ought to start out now.'

But although she stood ready in the doorway, she did not

go. On this last evening, the last time with the three of them together in the kitchen, she felt there was some final thing she ought to say or do before she went away. For many months she had been ready to leave this kitchen, never to return again; but now that the time had come, she stood there with her head and shoulder leaning against the door jamb, somehow unready. It was the darkening hour when the remarks they made had a sad and beautiful sound, although there would be nothing sad or beautiful about the meanings of the words.

F. Jasmine said quietly: 'I intend to take two baths tonight. One long soaking bath and scrub with a brush. I'm going to try to scrape this brown crust off my elbows. Then let out the dirty water and take a second bath.'

'That's a good idea,' said Berenice. 'I will be glad to see you clean.'

'I will take another bath,' John Henry said. His voice was thin and sad; she could not see him in the darkening room, since he stood in the corner by the stove. At seven Berenice had bathed him and dressed him in his shorts again. She heard him shuffle carefully across the room, for after the bath he had put on Berenice's hat and was trying to walk in Berenice's high-heeled shoes. Again he asked a question which by itself meant nothing. 'Why?' he asked.

'Why what, Baby?' said Berenice.

He did not answer, and it was F. Jasmine who finally said: 'Why is it against the law to change your name?'

Berenice sat in a chair against the pale white light of the window. She held the newspaper open before her, and her head was twisted down and to one side as she strained to see what was printed there. When F. Jasmine spoke, she folded the paper and put it away on the table.

'You can figure that out,' she said. 'Just because. Think of the confusion.'

'I don't see why,' F. Jasmine said.

'What is that on your neck?' said Berenice. 'I thought it was a head you carried on that neck. Just think. Suppose I would suddenly up and call myself Mrs. Eleanor Roosevelt. And you would begin naming yourself Joe Louis. And John Henry would try to pass off as Henry Ford. Now what kind of confusion do you think that would cause?'

'Don't talk childish,' F. Jasmine said. 'That is not the kind of changing I mean. I mean from a name that doesn't suit you to a name you prefer. Like I changed from Frankie to F. Jasmine.'

'But still it would be a confusion,' Berenice insisted. 'Suppose we all suddenly change to entirely different names. Nobody would ever know who anybody was talking about. The whole world would go crazy.'

'I don't see——'

'Because things accumulate around your name,' said Berenice. 'You have a name and one thing after another happens to you, and you behave in various ways and do things, so that soon the name begins to have a meaning. Things have accumulated around the name. If it is bad and you have a bad reputation, then you just can't jump out of your name and escape like that. And if it is good and you have a good reputation, then you should be content and satisfied.'

'But what had accumulated around my old name?' F. Jasmine asked. Then, when Berenice did not reply at once, F. Jasmine answered her own question. 'Nothing! See? My name just didn't mean anything.'

'Well, that's not exactly so,' said Berenice. 'People think of Frankie Addams and it brings to the mind that Frankie is finished with the B section of the seventh grade. And Frankie found the golden egg at the Baptist Easter Hunt. And Frankie lives on Grove Street and——'

'But those things are nothing,' F. Jasmine said. 'See? They're not worth while. Nothing ever happened to me.'

'But it will,' said Berenice. 'Things will happen.'

'What?' F. Jasmine asked.

Berenice sighed and reached for the Chesterfield package inside her bosom. 'You pin me down like that and I can't tell you truthfully. If I could I would be a wizard. I wouldn't be sitting here in this kitchen right now, but making a fine living on Wall Street as a wizard. All I can say is that things will happen. Just what, I don't know.'

'By the way,' F. Jasmine said after a while. 'I thought I would go around to your house and see Big Mama. I don't believe in those fortunes, or anything like that, but I thought I might as well.'

'Suit yourself. However, I don't think it is necessary.'

'I suppose I ought to leave now,' F. Jasmine said.

But still she waited in the darkening door and did not go away. The sounds of the summer twilight crossed within the silence of the kitchen. Mr. Schwarzenbaum had finished tuning the piano, and for the past quarter of an hour he had been playing little pieces. He played music memorized by note, and he was a nervous spry old man who reminded F. Jasmine of a silver spider. His music was spry and stiff also, and he played faint jerking waltzes and nervous lullabies. Farther down the block a solemn radio announced something they could not hear. In the O'Neils' back yard, next door, children were calling and swatting a ball. The sounds of evening canceled out each other, and they were faded in the darkening twilight air. The kitchen itself was very quiet.

'Listen,' F. Jasmine said. 'What I've been trying to say is this. Doesn't it strike you as strange that I am I, and you are you? I am F. Jasmine Addams. And you are Berenice Sadie Brown. And we can look at each other, and touch each other, and stay together year in and year out in the same room. Yet always I am I, and you are you. And I can't ever be anything else but me, and you can't ever be anything else but you. Have you ever thought of that? And does it seem to you strange?'

Berenice had been rocking slightly in the chair. She was not sitting in a rocking chair, but she had been tilting back in the straight chair, then letting the front legs hit the floor with little taps, her dark stiff hand held to the table edge for balance. She stopped rocking herself when F. Jasmine spoke. And finally she said: 'I have thought of it occasionally.'

It was the hour when the shapes in the kitchen darkened and voices bloomed. They spoke softly and their voices bloomed like flowers—if sounds can be like flowers and voices bloom. F. Jasmine stood with her hands clasped behind her head, facing the darkening room. She had the feeling that unknown words were in her throat, and she was ready to speak them. Strange words were flowering in her throat and now was the time for her to name them.

'This,' she said. 'I see a green tree. And to me it is green. And you would call the tree green also. And we would agree on this. But is the color you see as green the same color I see as green? Or say we both call a color black. But how do we know that what you see as black is the same color I see as black?'

Berenice said after a moment: 'Those things we just cannot prove.'

F. Jasmine scraped her head against the door, and put her hand up to her throat. Her voice shattered and died. 'That's not what I meant to say, anyway.'

The smoke of Berenice's cigarette lay bitter and warm and stagnant in the room. John Henry shuffled in the high-heeled shoes from the stove to the table and back again. A rat rattled behind the wall.

'This is what I mean,' F. Jasmine said. 'You are walking down a street and you meet somebody. Anybody. And you look at each other. And you are you. And he is him. Yet when you look at each other, the eyes make a connection. Then you go off one way. And he goes off another way. You go off into different parts of town, and maybe you never see each other again. Not in your whole life. Do you see what I mean?'

'Not exactly,' said Berenice.

'I'm talking about this town,' F. Jasmine said in a higher voice. 'There are all these people here I don't even know by sight or name. And we pass alongside each other and don't have any connection. And they don't know me and I don't know them. And now I'm leaving town and there are all these people I will never know.'

'But who do you want to know?' asked Berenice.

F. Jasmine answered: 'Everybody. In the world. Everybody in the world.'

'Why, I wish you would listen to that,' said Berenice. 'How about people like Willis Rhodes? How about them Germans? Them Japanese?'

F. Jasmine knocked her head against the door jamb and looked up at the dark ceiling. Her voice broke, and again she said: 'That's not what I mean. That's not what I'm talking about.'

'Well, what *is* you talking about?' asked Berenice.

F. Jasmine shook her head, almost as though she did not know. Her heart was dark and silent, and from her heart the unknown words flowered and bloomed and she waited to name them. From next door there was the evening sound of children's baseball and the long call: Batteruup! Batteruup! Then the hollow pock of a ball and the clatter of a thrown bat and running footsteps and wild voices. The window was a rectangle of pale clear light and a child ran across the yard and under the dark arbor after the ball. The child was quick as a shadow and F. Jasmine did not see his face—his white shirttails flapped loose behind him like queer wings. Beyond the window the twilight was lasting and pale and still.

'Less play out, Frankie,' John Henry whispered. 'They sound like they having a mighty good time.'

'No,' F. Jasmine said. 'You go.'

Berenice stirred in her chair and said: 'I suppose we could turn on the light.'

But they did not turn on the light. F. Jasmine felt the unsaid words stick in her throat and a choked sickness made her groan and knock her head against the door jamb. Finally she said again in a high ragged voice:

'This:'

Berenice waited, and when she did not speak again, she asked: 'What on earth is wrong with you?'

F. Jasmine could not speak the unknown words, so after a minute she knocked her head a last time on the door and then began to walk around the kitchen table. She walked in a stiff-legged delicate way, as she felt sick, and did not wish to joggle the different foods that she had eaten and mix them up inside her stomach. She began to talk in a high fast voice, but they were the wrong words, and not what she had meant to say.

'Boyoman! Manoboy!' she said. 'When we leave Winter Hill we're going to more places than you ever thought about or even knew existed. Just where we will go first I don't know, and it don't matter. Because after we go to that place we're going on to another. We mean to keep moving, the three of us. Here today and gone tomorrow. Alaska, China, Iceland, South America. Traveling on trains. Letting her rip on motorcycles. Flying around all over the world in aeroplanes. Here today and gone tomorrow. All over the world. It's the damn truth. Boyoman!'

F. Jasmine jerked open the drawer of the table and fumbled inside for the butcher knife. She did not need the butcher knife, but she wanted something to grasp in her hand and wave about as she hurried around the table.

'And talking of things happening,' she said. 'Things will happen so fast we won't hardly have time to realize them. Captain Jarvis Addams sinks twelve Jap battleships and decorated by the President. Miss F. Jasmine Addams breaks all records. Mrs. Janice Addams elected Miss United Nations in beauty contest. One thing after another happening so fast we don't hardly notice them.'

'Hold still, Fool,' said Berenice. 'And lay down that knife.'

'And we will meet them. Everybody. We will just walk up to people and know them right away. We will be walking down a dark road and see a lighted house and knock on the door and strangers will rush to meet us and say: Come in! Come in! We will know decorated aviators and New York people and movie stars. We will have thousands of friends, thousands and thousands and thousands of friends. We will belong to so many clubs that we can't even keep track of all of them. We will be members of the whole world. Boyoman! Manoboy!'

Berenice had a very strong long right arm, and when F. Jasmine passed her the next time as she was running around the table, this arm reached out and snatched her by the petticoat so quickly that she was caught up with a jerk that made her bones crack and her teeth rattle.

'*Is* you gone raving wild?' she asked. The long arm pulled F. Jasmine closer and wrapped around her waist. 'You sweating like a mule. Lean down and let me feel your forehead. Is you got a fever?'

F. Jasmine pulled one of Berenice's plaits and pretended she was going to saw it off with the knife.

'You trembling,' said Berenice. 'I truly believe you took a fever walking around in that sun today. Baby, you sure you ain't sick?'

'Sick?' asked F. Jasmine. 'Who, me?'

'Set here in my lap,' said Berenice. 'And rest a minute.'

F. Jasmine put the knife on the table and settled down on Berenice's lap. She leaned back and put her face against Berenice's neck; her face was sweaty and Berenice's neck was sweaty also, and they both smelled salty and sour and sharp. Her right leg was flung across Berenice's knee, and it was trembling—but when she steadied her toes on the floor, her leg did not tremble any more. John Henry shuffled toward them in the high-heeled shoes and crowded up jealous and close to Berenice. He put his arm around Berenice's head and held on to her ear. Then after a moment he tried to push F. Jasmine out of her lap, and he pinched F. Jasmine with a mean and tiny little pinch.

'Leave Frankie alone,' said Berenice. 'She ain't bothered you.'

He made a fretting sound: 'I'm sick.'

'Now no, you ain't. Be quiet and don't grudge your cousin a little bit of love.'

'Old mean bossy Frankie,' he complained in a high sad voice.

'What she doing so mean right now? She just laying here wore out.'

F. Jasmine rolled her head and rested her face against Berenice's shoulder. She could feel Berenice's soft big ninnas against her back, and her soft wide stomach, her warm solid legs. She had been breathing very fast, but after a minute her breath slowed down so that she breathed in time with Berenice; the two of them were close together as one body, and Berenice's stiffened hands were clasped around F. Jasmine's chest. Their backs were to the window, and before them the kitchen was now almost dark. It was Berenice who finally sighed and started the conclusion of the last queer conversation.

'I think I have a vague idea what you were driving at,' she said. 'We all of us somehow caught. We born this way or that way and we don't know why. But we caught anyhow. I born Berenice. You born Frankie. John Henry born John Henry. And maybe we wants to widen and bust free. But no matter what we do we still caught. Me is me and you is you and he is he. We each one of us somehow caught all by ourself. Is that what you was trying to say?'

'I don't know,' F. Jasmine said. 'But I don't want to be caught.'

'Me neither,' said Berenice. 'Don't none of us. I'm caught worse than you is.'

F. Jasmine understood why she had said this, and it was John Henry who asked in his child voice: 'Why?'

'Because I am black,' said Berenice. 'Because I am colored. Everybody is caught one way or another. But they done drawn completely extra bounds around all colored people. They done squeezed us off in one corner by ourself. So we caught that firstway I was telling you, as all human beings is caught. And we caught as colored people also. Sometimes a boy like Honey feel like he just can't breathe no more. He feel like he got to break something or break himself. Sometimes it just about more that we can stand.'

'I know it,' F. Jasmine said. 'I wish Honey could do something.'

'He just feels desperate like.'

'Yes,' F. Jasmine said. 'Sometimes I feel like I want to break something, too. I feel like I wish I could just tear down the whole town.'

'So I have heard you mention,' said Berenice. 'But that won't help none. The point is that we all caught. And we try in one way or another to widen ourself free. For instance, me and Ludie. When I was with Ludie, I didn't feel so caught. But then Ludie died. We go around trying one thing or another, but we caught anyhow.'

The conversation made F. Jasmine almost afraid. She lay there close to Berenice and they were breathing very slowly. She could not see John Henry, but she could feel him; he had climbed up on the back rungs of the chair and was hugging Berenice's head. He was holding her ears, for in a moment Berenice said: 'Candy, don't wrench my ears like that. Me and Frankie ain't going to float up through the ceiling and leave you.'

Water dropped slowly in the kitchen sink and the rat was knocking behind the wall.

'I believe I realize what you were saying,' F. Jasmine said. 'Yet at the same time you almost might use the word loose instead of caught. Although they are two opposite words. I mean you walk around and you see all the people. And to me they look loose.'

'Wild, you mean?'

'Oh, no!' she said. 'I mean you don't see what joins them up together. You don't know where they all came from, or where they're going to. For instance, what made anybody ever come to this town in the first place? Where did all these people come from and what are they going to do? Think of all those soldiers.'

'They were born,' said Berenice. 'And they going to die.'

F. Jasmine's voice was thin and high. 'I know,' she said. 'But what is it all about? People loose and at the same time caught. Caught and loose. All these people and you don't know what joins them up. There's bound to be some sort of reason and connection. Yet somehow I can't seem to name it. I don't know.'

'If you did you would be God,' said Berenice. 'Didn't you know that?'

'Maybe so.'

'We just know so much. Then beyond that we don't know no more.'

'But I wish I did.' Her back was cramped and she stirred and stretched herself on Berenice's lap, her long legs sprawling out beneath the kitchen table. 'Anyway, after we leave Winter Hill I won't have to worry about things any more.'

'You don't have to now. Nobody requires you to solve the riddles of the world.' Berenice took a deep meaning breath and said: 'Frankie, you got the sharpest set of human bones I ever felt.'

This was a strong hint for F. Jasmine to stand up. She would turn on the light, then take one of the cup cakes from the stove, and go out to finish her business in the town. But for a moment longer she lay there with her face pressed close to Berenice's shoulder. The sounds of the summer evening were mingled and long-drawn.

'I never did say just what I was talking about,' she said finally. 'But there's this. I wonder if you have ever thought about this. Here we are—right now. This very minute. Now. But while we're talking right now, this minute is passing. And it will never come again. Never in all the world. When it is gone it is gone. No power on earth could bring it back again. It is gone. Have you ever thought about that?'

Berenice did not answer, and the kitchen was now dark. The three of them sat silent, close together, and they could feel and hear each other's breaths. Then suddenly it started, though why and how they did not know; the three of them began to cry. They started at exactly the same moment, in the way that often on these summer evenings they would suddenly start a song. Often in the dark, that August, they would all at once begin to sing a Christmas carol, or a song like the Slitbelly Blues. Sometimes they knew in advance that they would sing, and they would agree on the tune among themselves.

Or again, they would disagree and start off on three different songs at once, until at last the tunes began to merge and they sang a special music that the three of them made up together. John Henry sang in a high wailing voice, and no matter what he named his tune, it sounded always just the same: one high trembling note that hung like a musical ceiling over the rest of the song. Berenice's voice was dark and definite and deep, and she rapped the offbeats with her heel. The old Frankie sang up and down the middle space between John Henry and Berenice, so that their three voices were joined, and the parts of the song were woven together.

Often they would sing like this and their tunes were sweet and queer in the August kitchen after it was dark. But never before had they suddenly begun to cry; and though their reasons were three different reasons, yet they started at the same instant as though they had agreed together. John Henry was crying because he was jealous, though later he tried to say he cried because of the rat behind the wall. Berenice was crying because of their talk about colored people, or because of Ludie, or perhaps because F. Jasmine's bones were really sharp. F. Jasmine did not know why she cried, but the reason she named was the crew-cut and the fact that her elbows were so rusty. They cried in the dark for about a minute. Then they stopped as suddenly as they had begun. The unaccustomed sound had quieted the rat behind the wall.

'Get up from there,' said Berenice. They stood around the kitchen table and F. Jasmine turned on the light. Berenice scratched her head and sniffled a little. 'We certainy is a gloomy crowd. Now I wonder what started that.'

The light was sudden and sharp after the darkness. F. Jasmine ran the faucet of the sink and put her head beneath the stream of water. And Berenice wiped off her face with a dishrag and patted her plaits before the mirror. John Henry stood like a little old woman dwarf, wearing the pink hat with

the plume, and the high-heel shoes. The walls of the kitchen
were crazy drawn and very bright. The three of them blinked
at each other in the light as though they were three strangers
or three ghosts. Then the front door opened and F. Jasmine
heard her father trudging slowly down the hall. Already the
moths were at the window, flattening their wings against the
screen, and the final kitchen afternoon was over at last.

III

EARLY that evening F. Jasmine passed before the jail; she was
on her way to Sugarville to have her fortune told and, though
the jail was not directly on the way, she had wanted to have
one final look at it before she left the town forever. For the jail
had scared and haunted her that spring and summer. It was an
old brick jail, three stories high, and surrounded by a cyclone
fence topped with barbed wire. Inside were thieves, robbers,
and murderers. The criminals were caged in stone cells with
iron bars before the windows, and though they might beat on
the stone walls or wrench at the iron bars, they could never
get out. They wore striped jail clothes and ate cold peas with
cockroaches cooked in them and cold cornbread.

F. Jasmine knew some people who had been locked up in
jail, all of them colored—a boy called Cape, and a friend
of Berenice who was accused by the white lady she worked
for of stealing a sweater and a pair of shoes. When you were
arrested, the Black Maria screamed to your house and a crowd
of policemen burst in the door to haul you off down to the
jail. After she took the three-bladed knife from the Sears
and Roebuck Store, the jail had drawn the old Frankie—and
sometimes on those late spring afternoons she would come to
the street across from the jail, a place known as Jail-Widow's
Walk, and stare for a long time. Often some criminals would
be hanging to the bars; it seemed to her that their eyes, like the
long eyes of the Freaks at the fair, had called to her as though
to say: We know you. Occasionally, on Saturday afternoon,
there would be wild yells and singing and hollering from the
big cell known as the Bull Pen. But now this evening the jail
was quiet—but from a lighted cell there was one criminal, or
rather the outline of his head and his two fists around the bars.

The brick jail was gloomy dark, although the yard and some cells were lighted.

'What are you locked up for?' John Henry called. He stood at a little distance from F. Jasmine and he was wearing the jonquil dress, as F. Jasmine had given him all the costumes. She had not wished to take him with her; but he had pleaded and pleaded, and finally followed at a distance, anyway. When the criminal did not answer, he called again in a thin, high voice. 'Are you going to be hung?'

'Hush up!' F. Jasmine said. The jail did not frighten her this evening, for this time tomorrow she would be far away. She gave the jail a last glance and then walked on. 'How would you like for somebody to holler something like that to you if you were in jail?'

It was past eight o'clock when she reached Sugarville. The evening was dusty and lavender. Doors of the crowded houses on either side were open, and from some parlors there was the quavered flutter of oil lamps, lighting up the front-room beds and decorated mantelpieces. Voices sounded slurred and from a distance came the jazz of a piano and horn. Children played in alleyways, leaving whorled footsteps in the dust. The people were dressed for Saturday night, and on a corner she passed a group of jesting colored boys and girls in shining evening dresses. There was a party air about the street that reminded her that she, also, could go that very evening to a date at the Blue Moon. She spoke to people on the street and felt again the unexplainable connection between her eyes and other eyes. Mixed with the bitter dust, and smells of privies and suppertime, the smell of a clematis vine threaded the evening air. The house where Berenice lived was on the corner of Chinaberry Street—a two-room house with a tiny front yard bordered by shards and bottle-caps. A bench on the front porch helds pots of cool, dark ferns. The door was only partly open and F. Jasmine could see the gold-gray flutters of the lamplight inside.

'You stay out here,' she said to John Henry.

There was the murmuring of a strong, cracked voice behind the door, and when F. Jasmine knocked, the voice was quiet a second and then asked:

'Who that? Who is it?'

'Me,' she said, for if she answered her true name, Big Mama would not recognize it. 'Frankie.'

The room was close, although the wooden shutter stood open, and there was the smell of sickness and fish. The crowded parlor was neat. One bed stood against the right wall, and on the opposite side of the room were a sewing machine and a pump organ. Over the hearth hung a photograph of Ludie Freeman; the mantelpiece was decorated with fancy calendars, fair prizes, souvenirs. Big Mama lay in the bed against the wall next to the door, so that in the daytime she could look out through the front window onto the ferny porch and street outside. She was an old colored woman, shriveled and with bones like broomsticks; on the left side of her face and neck the skin was the color of tallow, so that part of her face was almost white and the rest copper-colored. The old Frankie used to think that Big Mama was slowly turning to a white person, but Berenice had said it was a skin disease that sometimes happened to colored people. Big Mama had done fancy washing and fluted curtains until the year the misery had stiffened her back so that she took to bed. But she had not lost any faculties; instead, she suddenly found second-sight. The old Frankie had always thought she was uncanny, and when she was a little girl Big Mama was connected in her mind with the three ghosts who lived inside the coalhouse. And even now, a child no longer, she still had an eerie feeling about Big Mama. She was lying on three feather pillows, the covers of which were bordered with crochet, and over her bony legs there was a many-colored quilt. The parlor table with the lamp was pulled up close beside the bed so that she could reach the objects on it: a dream-book, a white saucer, a workbasket, a jellyglass of water, a Bible, and other things. Big Mama had been talking to herself before F. Jasmine came in, as she had the constant habit of telling herself just who she was and what she was doing and what she intended to do as she lay there in the bed. There were three mirrors on the walls which reflected the wavelike light from the lamp that fluttered gold-gray in the room and cast giant shadows; the lampwick needed trimming. Someone was walking in the back room.

'I came to get my fortune told,' F. Jasmine said.

While Big Mama talked to herself when alone, she could be

very silent at other times. She stared at F. Jasmine for several seconds before she answered: 'Very well. Draw up that stool before the organ.'

F. Jasmine brought the stool close to the bed, and leaning forward, stretched out her palm. But Big Mama did not take her palm. She examined F. Jasmine's face, then spat the wad of snuff into a chamberpot which she pulled from underneath the bed, and finally put on her glasses. She waited so long that it occurred to F. Jasmine that she was trying to read her mind, and his made her uneasy. The walking in the back room stopped and there was no sound in the house.

'Cast back your mind and remember,' she said finally. 'Tell me the revelation of your last dream.'

F. Jasmine tried to cast back her mind, but she did not dream often. Then finally she remembered a dream she had had that summer: 'I dreamed there was a door,' she said. 'I was just looking at it and while I watched, it began slowly to open. And it made me feel funny and I woke up.'

'Was there a hand in the dream?'

F. Jasmine thought. 'I don't think so.'

'Was there a cockroach on that door?'

'Why—I don't think so.'

'It signifies as follows.' Big Mama slowly closed and opened her eyes. 'There going be a change in your life.'

Next she took F. Jasmine's palm and studied it for quite a while. 'I see here where you going to marry a boy with blue eyes and light hair. You will live to be your threescore and ten, but you must act careful about water. I see here a red-clay ditch and a bale of cotton.'

F. Jasmine thought to herself that there was nothing to it, only a pure waste of money and time. 'What does that signify?'

But suddenly the old woman raised her head and the cords of her neck stiffened as she called: 'You, Satan!'

She was looking at the wall between the parlor and the kitchen, and F. Jasmine turned to look over her shoulder also.

'Yessum,' a voice replied from the back room, and it sounded like Honey.

'How many times is I got to tell you to take them big feets off the kitchen table!'

'Yessum.' Honey said again. His voice was meek as Moses, and F. Jasmine could hear him put his feet down on the floor.

'Your nose is going to grow into that book, Honey Brown. Put it down and finish up your supper.'

F. Jasmine shivered. Had Big Mama looked clear through the wall and seen Honey reading with his feet up on the table? Could those eyes pierce through a pure plank wall? It seemed as though it would behoove her to listen carefully to every word.

'I see here a sum of money. A sum of money. And I see a wedding.' F. Jasmine's outstretched hand trembled a little. 'That!' she said. 'Tell me about that!'

'The wedding or the money?'

'The wedding.'

The lamplight made an enormous shadow of them on the bare boards of the wall. 'It's the wedding of a near relation. And I foresee a trip ahead.'

'A trip?' she asked. 'What kind of a trip? A long trip?'

Big Mama's hands were crooked, spotted with freckly pale blots, and the palms were like melted pink birthday candles. 'A short trip,' she said.

'But how—?' F. Jasmine began.

'I see a going and a coming back. A departure and a return.'

There was nothing to it, for surely Berenice had told her about the trip to Winter Hill and the wedding. But if she could see straight through a wall—'Are you sure?'

'Well—' This time the old cracked voice was not so certain. 'I see a departure and a return, but it may not be for *now*. I can't guarantee. For at the same time I see roads, trains, and a sum of money.'

'Oh!' F. Jasmine said.

There was the sound of footsteps, and Honey Camden Brown stood on the threshold between the kitchen and the parlor. He wore tonight a yellow shirt with a bow tie, for he was usually a natty dresser—but his dark eyes were sad, and his long face still as stone. F. Jasmine knew what Big Mama had said about Honey Brown. She said he was a boy God had not finished. The Creator had withdrawn His hand from him too soon. God had not finished him, and so he had to go around doing one thing and then another to finish himself up. When she had first heard this remark, the old Frankie did not understand the hidden meaning. Such a remark put her in mind of a peculiar half-boy—one arm, one leg, half a face—a half-person hopping in the gloomy summer sun around the corners of the town. But later she understood it a little better. Honey played the horn, and had been first in his studies at the colored high school. He ordered a French book from Atlanta and learned himself some French. At the same time he would suddenly run hog-wild all over Sugarville and tear around for several days, until his friends would bring him home more dead than living. His lips could move as light as butterflies and he could talk as well as any human she had ever heard—but other times he would answer with a colored jumble that even his own family could not follow. The Creator, Big Mama said, had withdrawn His hand from him too soon, so that he was left eternally unsatisfied. Now he stood there leaning against the door jamb, bony and limp, and although the sweat showed on his face he somehow looked cold.

'Do you wish anything before I go?' he asked.

There was something about Honey that evening that struck F. Jasmine; it was as though, on looking into his sad, still eyes, she felt she had something to say to him. His skin in the lamplight was the color of dark wistaria and the lips were quiet and blue.

'Did Berenice tell you about the wedding?' F. Jasmine asked. But, for once, it was not about the wedding that she felt she had to speak.

'Aaannh,' he answered.

'There's nothing I wish now. T. T. is due here in a minute to visit with me for a while and meet up with Berenice. Where you off to, boy?'

'I'm going over to Forks Falls.'

'Well, Mr. Up and Sudden, when you done decide that?'

Honey stood leaning against the door jamb, stubborn and quiet.

'Why can't you act like everybody else?' Big Mama said.

'I'll just stay over through Sunday and come back Monday morning.'

The feeling that she had something to say to Honey Brown

still troubled F. Jasmine. She said to Big Mama: 'You were telling me about the wedding.'

'Yes.' She was not looking at F. Jasmine's palm, but at the organdie dress and the silk hose and the new silver slippers. 'I told you you would marry a light-haired boy with blue eyes. Later on.'

'But that's not what I'm talking about. I mean the other wedding. And the trip and what you saw about the roads and trains.'

'Exactly,' said Big Mama, but F. Jasmine had the feeling she was no longer paying much mind to her, although she looked again at her palm. 'I foresee a trip with a departure and a return and later a sum of money, roads and trains. Your lucky number is six, although thirteen is sometimes lucky for you too.'

F. Jasmine wanted to protest and argue, but how could you argue with a fortune-teller? She wanted at least to understand the fortune better, for the trip with the return did not fit in with the foreseeing of roads and trains.

But as she was about to question further, there were footsteps on the front porch, a door knock, and T. T. came into the parlor. He was very proper, scraping his feet, and bringing Big Mama a carton of ice cream. Berenice had said he did not make her shiver, and it was true he was nobody's pretty man; his stomach was like a watermelon underneath his vest and there were rolls of fat on the back of his neck. He brought in with him the stir of company that she had always loved and envied about this two-room house. Always it had seemed to the old Frankie, when she could come here hunting Berenice, that there would be many people in the room—the family, various cousins, friends. In the wintertime they would sit by the hearth around the draughty, shivering fire and talk with woven voices. On clear autumn nights they were always the first to have sugar cane and Berenice would hack the joints of the slick, purple cane and they would throw the chewed, twisted pieces, marked with their teethprints, on a newspaper spread upon the floor. The lamplight gave the room a special look, a special smell.

Now, with the coming of T. T., there was the old sense of company and commotion. The fortune was evidently over, and F. Jasmine put a dime in the white china saucer on the parlor table—for, although there was no fixed price, the future-anxious folks who came to Big Mama usually paid what they felt due.

'I declare I never did see anybody grow like you do, Frankie,' Big Mama remarked. 'What you ought to do is tie a brickbat to your head.' F. Jasmine shriveled on her heels, her knees bent slightly, and her shoulders hunched. 'That's a sweet dress you got on. And them silver shoes! And silk stockings! You look like a regular grown girl.'

F. Jasmine and Honey left the house at the same time, and she was still fretted by the feeling that she had something to say to him. John Henry, who had been waiting in the lane, rushed toward them, but Honey did not pick him up and swing him around as he sometimes did. There was a cold sadness about Honey this evening. The moonlight was white.

'What are you going to do in Forks Falls?'

'Just mess around.'

'Do you put any faith in those fortunes?' When Honey did not answer, she went on: 'You remember when she hollered back to you to take your feet off the table. Gave me a shock. How did she know your feet were on the table?'

'The mirror,' Honey said. 'She has a mirror by the door so she can see what goes on in the kitchen.'

'Oh,' she said. 'I never have believed in fortunes.'

John Henry was holding Honey's hand and looking up into his face. 'What are horsepowers?'

F. Jasmine felt the power of the wedding; it was as though, on this last evening, she ought to order and advise. There was something she ought to tell Honey, a warning or some wise advice. And as she fumbled in her mind, an idea came to her. It was so new, so unexpected, that she stopped walking and stood absolutely still.

'I know what you ought to do. You ought to go to Cuba or Mexico.'

Honey had walked on a few steps farther, but when she spoke he stopped also. John Henry was midway between them, and as he looked from one to the other, his face in the white moonlight had a mysterious expression.

'Sure enough. I'm perfectly serious. It don't do you any good to mess around between Fork Falls and this town. I've seen a whole lot of pictures of Cubans and Mexicans. They have a good time.' She paused. 'This is what I'm trying to discuss. I don't think you will ever be happy in this town. I think you ought to go to Cuba. You are so light-skinned and you even have a kind of Cuban expression. You could go there and change into a Cuban. You could learn to speak the foreign language and none of those Cubans would ever know you are a colored boy. Don't you see what I mean?'

Honey was still as a dark statue, and as silent.

'What?' John Henry asked again. 'What do they look like—them horsepowers?'

With a jerk Honey turned and went on down the lane. 'It is fantastic.'

'No, it is not!' Pleased that Honey had used the word fantastic to her, she said it quietly to herself before she went on to insist. 'It's not a particle fantastic. You mark my words. It's the best thing you can do.'

But Honey only laughed and turned off at the next alley. 'So long.'

The streets in the middle of the town reminded F. Jasmine of a carnival fair. There was the same air of holiday freedom; and, as in the early morning, she felt herself a part of everything, included and gay. On a Main Street corner a man was selling mechanical mice, and an armless beggar, with a tin cup in his lap, sat cross-legged on the sidewalk, watching. She had never seen Front Avenue at night before, for in the evening she was supposed to play in the neighborhood close to home. The warehouses across the street were black, but the square mill at the far end of the avenue was lighted in all its many windows and there was a faint mill humming and the smell of dyeing vats. Most of the businesses were open, and the neon signs made a mingling of varied lights that gave to the avenue a watery look. There were soldiers on corners, and other soldiers strolling along with grown date girls. The sounds were slurred late-summer sounds—footsteps, laughter, and above the shuffled noises, the voices of someone calling from an upper story down into the summer street. The buildings smelled of sunbaked brick and the sidewalk was warm beneath the soles of her new silver shoes. F. Jasmine stopped on the corner across from the Blue Moon. It seemed a long time since that morning when she had joined up with the soldier;

the long kitchen afternoon had come between, and the soldier had somehow faded. The date, that afternoon, had seemed so very far away. And now that it was almost nine o'clock, she hesitated. She had the unexplainable feeling that there was a mistake.

'Where are we going?' John Henry asked. 'I think it's high time we went home.'

His voice startled her, as she had almost forgotten him. He stood there with his knees locked, big-eyed and drabbled in the old tarletan costume. 'I have business in town. You go home.' He stared up at her and took the bubble gum he had been chewing from his mouth—he tried to park the gum behind his ear, but sweat had made his ear too slippery, so finally he put the gum back in his mouth again. 'You know the way home as well as I do. So do what I tell you.' For a wonder, John Henry minded her; but, as she watched him going away from her down the crowded street, she felt a hollow sorriness—he looked so babyish and pitiful in the costume.

The change from the street to the inside of the Blue Moon was like the change that comes on leaving the open fairway and entering a booth. Blue lights and moving faces, noise. The counter and tables were crowded with soldiers, and men, and bright-faced ladies. The soldier she had promised to meet was playing the slot machine in a far corner, putting in nickel after nickel, but winning none.

'Oh, it's you,' he said when he noticed her standing at his elbow. For a second his eyes had the blank look of eyes that are peering back into the brain to recollect—but only for a second. 'I was scared you had stood me up.' After putting in a final nickel, he banged the slot machine with his fist. 'Let's find a place.'

They sat at a table between the counter and the slot machine, and, although by the clock the time was not long, it seemed to F. Jasmine endless. Not that the soldier was not nice to her. He was nice, but their two conversations would not join together, and underneath there was a layer of queerness she could not place and understand. The soldier had washed, and his swollen face, his ears and hands, were clean; his red hair was darkened from wetting and ridged with a comb. He said he had slept that afternoon. He was gay and his talk was sassy. But although she liked gay people and sassy talk, she could not think of any answers. It was again as though the soldier talked a kind of double-talk that, try as she would, she could not follow—yet it was not so much the actual remarks as the tone underneath she failed to understand.

The soldier brought two drinks to the table; after a swallow F. Jasmine suspected there was liquor in them and, although a child no longer, she was shocked. It was a sin and against the law for people under eighteen to drink real liquor, and she pushed the glass away. The soldier was both nice and gay, but after he had had two other drinks she wondered if he could be drunk. To make conversation she remarked that her brother had been swimming in Alaska, but this did not seem to impress him very much. Nor would he talk about the war, nor foreign countries and the world. To his joking remarks she could never find replies that fitted, although she tried. Like a nightmare pupil in a recital who has to play a duet to a piece she does not know, F. Jasmine did her best to catch the tune and follow. But soon she broke down and grinned until her mouth felt wooden. The blue lights in the crowded room, the smoke and noisy commotion, confused her also.

'You're a funny kind of girl,' the soldier said finally.

'Patton,' she said. 'I bet he will win the war in two weeks.'

The soldier was quiet now and his face had a heavy look. His eyes gazed at her with the same strange expression she had noticed that day at noon, a look she had never seen on anyone before and could not place. After a while he said, and his voice was softened, blurred:

'What did you say your name is, Beautiful?'

F. Jasmine did not know whether or not to like the way he called her, and she spoke her name in a proper voice.

'Well, Jasmine, how bout going on upstairs?' His tone was asking, but when she did not answer at once, he stood up from the table. 'I've got a room here.'

'Why, I thought we were going to the Idle Hour. Or dancing or something.'

'What's the rush?' he said. 'The band don't hardly tune up until eleven o'clock.'

F. Jasmine did not want to go upstairs, but she did not know how to refuse. It was like going into a fair booth, or fair ride,

that once having entered you cannot leave until the exhibition
or the ride is finished. Now it was the same with this soldier,
this date. She could not leave until it ended. The soldier was
waiting at the foot of the stairs and, unable to refuse, she
followed after him. They went up two flights, and then along
a narrow hall that smelled of wee-wee and linoleum. But every
footstep F. Jasmine took, she felt somehow was wrong.

'This sure is a funny hotel,' she said.

It was the silence in the hotel room that warned and
frightened her, a silence she noticed as soon as the door
was closed. In the light of the bare electric bulb that hung
down from the ceiling, the room looked hard and very ugly.
The flaked iron bed had been slept in and a suitcase of
jumbled soldier's clothes lay open in the middle of the floor.
On the light oak bureau there was a glass pitcher full of
water and a half-eaten package of cinnamon rolls covered
with blue-white icing and fat flies. The screenless window
was open and the sleazy voile curtains had been tied at the
top in a knot together to let in air. There was a lavatory in
the corner and, cupping his hands, the soldier dashed cold
water to his face—the soap was only a bar of ordinary soap,
already used, and over the lavatory a sign read: STRICTLY
WASHING. Although the soldier's footsteps sounded, and
the water made a trickling noise, the sense of silence somehow
remained.

F. Jasmine went to the window which overlooked a narrow
alley and a brick wall; a rickety fire-escape led to the ground
and light shafted from the two lower stories. Outside there
was the August evening sounds of voices and a radio, and in
the room there were sounds also—so how could the silence be
explained? The soldier sat on the bed, and now she was seeing
him altogether as a single person, not as a member of the loud
free gangs who for a season roamed the streets of town and
then went out into the world together. In the silent room he
seemed to her unjoined and ugly. She could not see him any
more in Burma, Africa, or Iceland, or even for that matter in
Arkansas. She saw him only as he sat there in the room. His
light blue eyes, set close together, were staring at her with the
peculiar look—with a filmed softness, like eyes that have been
washed with milk.

The silence in the room was like that silence in the kitchen when, on a drowsy afternoon, the ticking of the clock would stop—and there would steal over her a mysterious uneasiness that lasted until she realized what was wrong. A few times before she had known such silence—once in the Sears and Roebuck store the moment before she suddenly became a thief, and again that April afternoon in the MacKeans' garage. It was the forewarning hush that comes before an unknown trouble, a silence caused, not by lack of sounds, but by a waiting, a suspense. The soldier did not take those strange eyes from her and she was scared.

'Come on, Jasmine,' he said, in an unnatural voice, broken and low, as he reached out his hand, palm upward, toward her. 'Let's quit this stalling.'

The next minute was like a minute in the fair Crazy-House, or real Milledgeville. Already F. Jasmine had started for the door, for she could no longer stand the silence. But as she passed the soldier, he grasped her skirt and, limpened by fright, she was pulled down beside him on the bed. The next minute happened, but it was too crazy to be realized. She felt his arms around her and smelled his sweaty shirt. He was not rough, but it was crazier that if he had been rough—and in a second she was paralyzed by horror. She could not push away, but she bit down with all her might upon what must have been the crazy soldier's tongue—so that he screamed out and she was free. Then he was coming toward her with an amazed pained face, and her hand reached the glass pitcher and brought it down upon his head. He swayed a second, then slowly his legs began to crumple, and slowly he sank sprawling to the floor. The sound was hollow like the hammer on a coconut, and with it the silence was broken at last. He lay there still, with the amazed expression on his freckled face that was now pale, and a froth of blood showed on his mouth. But his head was not broken, or even cracked, and whether he was dead or not she did not know.

The silence was over, and it was like those kitchen times when, after the first uncanny moments, she realized the reason for her uneasiness and knew that the ticking of the clock had stopped—but now there was no clock to shake and hold for a minute to her ear before she wound it, feeling relieved. There

slanted across her mind twisted remembrances of a common
fit in the front room, basement remarks, and nasty Barney;
but she did not let these separate glimpses fall together, and
the word she repeated was 'crazy.' There was water on the walls
which had been slung out from the pitcher and the soldier had
a broken look in the strewn room. F. Jasmine told herself: Get
out! and after first starting toward the door, she turned and
climbed out on the fire-escape and quickly reached the alley
ground.

She ran like a chased person fleeing from the crazy-house at
Milledgeville, looking neither to the right nor left, and when
she reached the corner of her own home block, she was glad to
see John Henry West. He was out looking for bats around the
street light, and the familiar sight of him calmed her a little.

'Uncle Royal has been calling you,' he said. 'What makes you
shake like that for, Frankie?'

'I just now brained a crazy man,' she told him when she could
get her breath. 'I brained him and I don't know if he is dead.
He was a crazy man.'

John Henry stared without surprise. 'How did he act like?'
And when she did not answer all at once, he went on: 'Did
he crawl on the ground and moan and slobber?' For that was
what the old Frankie had done one day to try to fool Berenice
and create some excitement. Berenice had not been fooled.
'Did he?'

'No,' F. Jasmine said. 'He—' But as she looked into those
cold, child eyes she knew that she could not explain. John
Henry would not understand, and his green eyes gave her
a funny feeling. Sometimes his mind was like the pictures
he drew with crayons on tablet paper. The other day he had
drawn such a one and showed it to her. It was a picture of a
telephone man on a telephone pole. The telephone man was
leaning against his safety belt, and the picture was complete
down to his climbing shoes. It was a careful picture, but after
she had looked at it uneasiness had lingered in her mind. She
looked at the picture again until she realized what was wrong.
The telephone man was drawn in side-view profile, yet this
profile had two eyes—one eye just above the nose bridge and
another drawn just below. And it was no hurried mistake; both
eyes had careful lashes, pupils, and lids. Those two eyes drawn

in a side-view face gave her a funny feeling. But reason with John Henry, argue with him? You might as well argue with cement. Why did he do it? Why? Because it was a telephone man. What? Because he was climbing the pole. It was impossible to understand his point of view. And he did not understand her either.

'Forget what I just now told you,' she said. But after saying it, she realized that was the worst remark she could have said, for he would be sure not to forget. So she took him by the shoulders and shook him slightly. 'Swear you won't tell. Swear this: If I tell I hope God will sew up my mouth and sew down my eyes and cut off my ears with the scissors.'

But John Henry would not swear; he only hunched his big head down near his shoulders and answered, very quietly: 'Shoo.'

She tried again. 'If you tell anybody I might be put in jail and we couldn't go to the wedding.'

'I ain't going to tell,' John Henry said. Sometimes he could be trusted, and other times not. 'I'm not a tattletale.'

Once inside the house, F. Jasmine locked the front door before she went into the living room. Her father was reading the evening paper, in his sock feet, on the sofa. F. Jasmine was glad to have her father between her and the front door. She was afraid of the Black Maria and listened anxiously.

'I wish we were going to the wedding right this minute,' she said. 'I think that would be the best thing to do.'

She went back to the icebox and ate six tablespoons of sweetened condensed milk, and the disgust in her mouth began to go away. The waiting made her feel restless. She gathered up the library books, and stacked them on the living-room table. On one of them, a book from the grown sections which she had not read, she wrote in the front with pencil: *If you want to read something that will shock you, turn to page 66.* On page 66 she wrote: *Electricity. Ha! Ha!* By and by her anxiousness was eased; close to her father she felt less afraid.

'These books belong to go back to the library.'

Her father, who was forty-one, looked at the clock: 'It's time for everybody under forty-one to get to bed. Quick, march, and without any argument. We have to be up at five o'clock.'

F. Jasmine stood in the doorway, unable to leave. 'Papa,' she said, after a minute, 'if somebody hits somebody with a glass pitcher and he falls out cold, do you think he is dead?'

She had to repeat the question, feeling a bitter grudge against him because he did not take her seriously, so that her questions must be asked twice.

'Why, come to think about it, I never hit anybody with a pitcher,' he said. 'Did you?'

F. Jasmine knew he asked this as a joke, so she only said as she went away: 'I'll never be so glad to get to any place in all my life as Winter Hill tomorrow. I will be so thankful when the wedding is over and we have gone away. I will be so thankful.'

Upstairs she and John Henry undressed, and after the motor and the light were off, they lay down on the bed together—although she said she could not sleep a wink. But nevertheless she closed her eyes, and when she opened them again a voice was calling and the room was early gray.

PART THREE

SHE SAID: 'Farewell, old ugly house,' as, wearing a dotted Swiss dress and carrying the suitcase, she passed through the hall at quarter to six. The wedding dress was in the suitcase, ready to be put on when she reached Winter Hill. At that still hour the sky was the dim silver of a mirror, and beneath it the gray town looked, not like a real town, but like an exact reflection of itself, and to this unreal town she also said farewell. The bus left the station at ten past six—and she sat proud, like an accustomed traveler, apart from her father, John Henry, and Berenice. But after a while a serious doubt came in her, which even the answers of the bus-driver could not quite satisfy. They were supposed to be traveling north, but it seemed to her rather that the bus was going south instead. The sky turned burning pale and the day blazed. They passed the fields of windlesss corn that had a blue look in the glare, red-furrowed cotton land, stretches of black pine woods. And mile by mile the countryside became more southern. The towns they passed—New City, Leeville, Cheehaw—each town seemed smaller that the one before, until at nine o'clock they reached the ugliest place of all, where they changed buses, called Flowering Branch. Despite its name there were no flowers and no branch—only a solitary country store, with a sad old shredded circus poster on the clapboard wall and a chinaberry tree beneath which stood an empty wagon and a sleeping mule. There they waited for the bus to Sweet Well, and, still doubting anxiously, Frances did not despise the box of lunch that had so shamed her at the first, because it made them look like family people who do not travel very much. The bus left at ten o'clock, and they were in Sweet Well by eleven. The next hours were unexplainable. The wedding was like a dream, for all that came about occurred in a world beyond her power; from the moment when, sedate and proper, she shook hands with the grown people until the time, the wrecked wedding over, when she watched the car with the two of them driving away from her, and, flinging herself down in the sizzling dust, she cried out for the last time: 'Take me! Take me!'—from the beginning to the end the wedding was unmanaged as a nightmare. By mid-afternoon it was all finished and the return bus left at four o'clock.

'The show is over and the monkey's dead,' John Henry quoted, as he settled himself in the next to the last bus seat beside her father. 'Now we go home and go to bed.'

Frances wanted the whole world to die. She sat on the back seat, between the window and Berenice, and, though she was no longer sobbing, the tears were like two little brooks, and also her nose ran water. Her shoulders were hunched over her swollen heart and she no longer wore the wedding dress. She was sitting next to Berenice, back with the colored people, and when she thought of it she used the mean word she had never used before, nigger—for now she hated everyone and wanted only to spite and shame. For John Henry West the wedding had only been a great big show, and he had enjoyed her misery at the end as he had enjoyed the angel cake. She mortally despised him, dressed in his best white suit, now stained with strawberry ice cream. Berenice she hated also, for to her it had only meant a pleasure trip to Winter Hill. Her father, who had said that he would attend to her when they got home, she would like to kill. She was against every single person, even strangers in the crowded bus, though she only saw them blurred by tears—and she wished the bus would fall in a river or run into a train. Herself she hated the worst of all, and she wanted the whole world to die.

'Cheer up,' said Berenice. 'Wipe your face and blow your nose and things will look better by and by.'

Berenice had a blue party handkerchief, to match her blue best dress and blue kid shoes—and this she offered to Frances, although it was made of fine georgette and not, of course, due to be blown on. She would not notice it. In the seat between them there were three wet handkerchiefs of her father's, and Berenice began to dry the tears with one, but Frances did not move or budge.

'They put old Frankie out of the wedding.' John Henry's big head bobbed over the back of his seat, smiling and snaggled-toothed. Her father cleared his throat and said: 'That's sufficient, John Henry. Leave Frankie alone.' And Berenice added: 'Sit down in that seat now and behave.'

The bus rode for a long time, and now direction made no difference to her; she did not care. From the beginning the wedding had been queer like the card games in the kitchen the first week last June. In those bridge games they played and played for many days, but nobody ever drew a good hand, the cards were all sorry, and no high bids made—until finally Berenice suspicioned, saying: 'Less us get busy and count these old cards.' And they got busy and counted the old cards, and it turned out the jacks and the queens were missing. John Henry at last admitted that he had cut out the jacks and then the queens to keep them company and, after hiding the clipped scraps in the stove, had secretly taken the pictures home. So the fault of the card game was discovered. But how could the failure of the wedding be explained?

The wedding was all wrong, although she could not point out single faults. The house was a neat brick house out near the limits of the small, baked town, and when she first put foot inside, it was as though her eyeballs had been slightly stirred; there were mixed impressions of pink roses, the smell of floor wax, mints and nuts in silver trays. Everybody was lovely to her. Mrs. Williams wore a lace dress, and she asked F. Jasmine two times what grade she was in at school. But she asked, also, if she would like to play out on the swing before the wedding, in the tone grown people use when speaking to a child. Mr. Williams was nice to her, too. He was a sallow man with folds in his cheeks and the skin beneath his eyes was the grain and color of an old apple core. Mr. Williams also asked her what grade she was in at school; in fact, that was the main question asked her at the wedding.

She wanted to speak to her brother and the bride, to talk to them and tell them of her plans, the three of them alone together. But they were never once alone; Jarvis was out checking the car someone was lending for the honeymoon, while Janice dressed in the front bedroom among a crowd of beautiful grown girls. She wandered from one to the other of them, unable to explain. And once Janice put her arms around her, and said she was so glad to have a little sister—and when Janice kissed her, F. Jasmine felt an aching in her throat and could not speak. Jarvis, when she went to find him in the yard, lifted her up in a rough-house way and said: 'Frankie the lankie the alaga fankie, the tee-legged toe-legged bow-legged Frankie.' And he gave her a dollar.

She stood in the corner of the bride's room, wanting to say: I love the two of you so much and you are the we of me. Please take me with you from the wedding, for we belong to be together. Or even if she could have said: May I trouble you to step into the next room, as I have something to reveal to you and Jarvis? And get the three of them in a room alone together and somehow manage to explain. If only she had written it down on the typewriter in advance, so that she could hand it to them and they would read! But this she had not thought to do, and her tongue was heavy in her mouth and dumb. She could only speak in a voice that shook a little—to ask where was the veil?

'I can feel in the atmosphere a storm is brewing,' said Berenice. 'These two crooked joints can always tell.'

There was no veil except a little veil that came down from the wedding hat, and nobody was wearing fancy clothes. The bride was wearing a daytime suit. The only mercy of it was that she had not worn her wedding dress on the bus, as she had first intended, and found it out in time. She stood in a corner of the bride's room until the piano played the first notes of the wedding march. They were all lovely to her at

Winter Hill, except that they called her Frankie and treated
her too young. It was so unlike what she had expected, and,
as in those June card games, there was, from first to last, the
sense of something terribly gone wrong.

'Perk up,' said Berenice. 'I'm planning a big surprise for
you. I'm just sitting here planning. Don't you want to know
what it is?'

Frances did not answer even by a glance. The wedding was
like a dream outside her power, or like a show unmanaged by
her in which she was supposed to have no part. The living room
was crowded with Winter Hill company, and the bride and her
brother stood before the mantelpiece at the end of the room.
And seeing them again together was more like singing feeling
than a picture that her dizzied eyes could truly see. She watched
them with her heart, but all the time she was only thinking: I
have not told them and they don't know. And knowing this
was heavy as a swallowed stone. And afterward, during the
kissing of the bride, refreshments served in the dining room,
the stir and party bustle—she hovered close to the two of
them, but words would not come. They are not going to take
me, she was thinking, and this was the one thought she could
not bear.

When Mr. Williams brought their bags, she hastened after
with her own suitcase. The rest was like some nightmare show
in which a wild girl in the audience breaks onto the stage to
take upon herself an unplanned part that was never written
or meant to be. You are the we of me, her heart was saying,
but she could only say aloud: 'Take me!' And they pleaded and
begged with her, but she was already in the car. At the last she
clung to the steering wheel until her father and somebody else
had hauled and dragged her from the car, and even then she
could only cry in the dust of the empty road: 'Take me! Take
me!' But there was only the wedding company to hear, for the
bride and her brother had driven away.

Berenice said: 'School will begin now in only three more
weeks. And you'll go into the A section of the seventh grade
and meet a lot of nice new children and make another bosom
friend like that Evelyn Owen you were so wild about.'

The kind tone Frances could not stand. 'I never meant to
go with them!' she said. 'It was all just a joke. They said they

were going to invite me to a visit when they get settled, but I wouldn't go. Not for a million dollars.'

'We know all about that,' said Berenice. 'Now listen to my surprise I've planned. Soon as you get settled in school and have a chance to make these friends, I think it would be a good idea to have a party. A lovely bridge party in the living room, with potato salad and those little olive sandwiches your Aunt Pet had for a club meeting you were so carried away about—the round-shaped kind with the tiny round hole in the middle and the olive showing. A lovely bridge party with delicious refreshments. How would you like that?'

The baby promises rasped her nerves. Her cheap heart hurt, and she pressed her crossed arms over it and rocked a little. 'It was a framed game. The cards were stacked. It was a frame-up all around.'

'We can have that bridge party going on in the living room. And out in the back yard we can have another party at the same time. A costume party with hot dogs. One party dainty and the other one rough. With prizes for the highest bridge score and the funniest costume. How does that strike you?'

Frances refused to look at Berenice or answer.

'You could call up the society editor of the *Evening Journal* and have the party written up in the paper. And that would make the fourth time your name has been published in the paper.'

It would, but a thing like that no longer mattered to her. Once, when her bike ran into an automobile, the paper had called her Fankie Addams. *Fankie!* But now she did not care.

'Don't be so blue,' said Berenice. 'This is not doomsday.'

'Frankie, don't cry,' John Henry said. 'We will go home and put up the tepee and have a good time.'

She could not stop crying and the sobbing had a strangled sound. 'Oh, hush up your mouth!'

'Listen to me. Tell me what you would like and I'll try to do it if it's in my power.'

'All I would like,' said Frances, after a minute, 'all I wish in the world, is for no human being ever to speak to me so long as I live.'

And Berenice said, finally: 'Well. Then bawl, then, Misery.'

They did not talk the rest of the way back to the town.

Her father slept with a handkerchief over his nose and eyes, snoring a little. John Henry West lay in her father's lap and slept also. The other passengers were drowsy quiet and the bus rocked like a cradle and made a softly roaring sound. Outside the afternoon shimmered and now and then there was a buzzard lazily balanced against the blazing pale sky. They passed red empty crossroads with deep red gulches on either side, and rotten gray shacks set in the lonesome cotton fields. Only the dark pine trees looked cool—and the low blue hills when seen from miles away. Frances watched from the window with a stiff sick face and for four hours did not say a word. They were entering the town, and a change came. The sky lowered and turned a purple-gray against which the trees were a poison green. There was a jellied stillness in the air and then the mutter of the first thunder. A wind came through the treetops with a sound like rushing water, forewarning storm.

'I told you so,' said Berenice, and she was not speaking of the wedding. 'I could feel the misery in these joints. After a good storm we will all feel much better.'

The rain did not come, and there was only a feeling of expectation in the air. The wind was hot. Frances smiled a little at Berenice's words, but it was a scorning smile that hurt.

'You think it's all over,' she said, 'but that only shows how little you know.'

They thought it was finished, but she would show them. The wedding had not included her, but she would still go into the world. Where she was going she did not know; however, she was leaving town that night. If she could not go in the way she had planned, safe with her brother and the bride, she would go, anyway. Even if she had to commit every crime. For the first time since the night before she thought about the soldier—but only in a glancing way, for her mind was busy with hasty plans. There was a train that passed through the town at two o'clock, and she would take it; the train went north in a general way, probably to Chicago or New York. If the train went to Chicago, she would go on to Hollywood and write shows or get a job as a movie starlet—or, if worse came to worse, even act in comedies. If the train went to New York, she would dress like a boy and give a false name and a false age and join the Marines. Meanwhile, she had to wait until her father was asleep, and she could still hear him moving in the kitchen. She sat at the typewriter and wrote a letter.

Dear Father:

This is a farewell letter until I write you from a different place. I told you I was going to leave town because it is inevitable. I cannot stand this existance any longer because my life has become a burden. I am taking the pistol because who can tell when it might come in handy and I will send back the money to you at the very first opportunaty. Tell Berenice not to worry. The whole thing is a irony of fate and it is inevitable. Later I will write. Please Papa do not try to capture me.

Sincerely yours,
Frances Addams

The green-and-white moths were nervous at the window screen and the night outside was queer. The hot wind had stopped and the air was so still that it seemed solid and there was a weight against you when you moved. The thunder grumbled low occasionally. Frances sat motionless before the typewriter, wearing the dotted Swiss dress, and the strapped suitcase was beside the door. After a while the light in the kitchen was turned off and her father called from the foot of the stairs: 'Good night, Picklepriss. Good night, John Henry.'

Frances waited a long time. John Henry was sleeping across the foot of the bed, still dressed and with his shoes on, and his mouth was open and one ear of his glasses frame had come loose. After waiting as long as she could stand it, she took the suitcase and tiptoed very quietly down the stairs. It was dark down there, dark in her father's room, dark through the house. She stood on the threshold of her father's room and he was snoring softly. The hardest time was the few minutes she stood there, listening.

The rest was easy. Her father was a widow-man, set in his ways, and at night he folded his pants over a straight chair and left his wallet, watch, and glasses on the right-hand side of the bureau. She moved very quietly in the darkness and laid hand on the wallet almost immediately. She was careful opening the bureau drawer, stopping to listen each time there was a scraping sound. The pistol felt heavy and cool in her hot hand. It was easy except for the loudness of beating heart and for an accident that happened just as she crept from the room. She stumbled over a waste-paper basket and the snoring stopped. Her father stirred, muttered. She held her breath—then finally, after a minute, the snoring went on again.

She put the letter on the table and tiptoed to the back porch. But there was one thing she had not counted on—John Henry began to call.

'Frankie!' The high child voice seemed to carry through all the rooms of the night house. 'Where are you?'

'Hush,' she whispered. 'Go back to sleep.'

She had left the light on in her room, and he stood in the stairway door and looked down into the dark kitchen. 'What are you doing down there in the dark?'

'Hush!' she said again in a loud whisper. 'I'll be there by the time you get to sleep.'

She waited a few minutes after John Henry had gone, then groped to the back door, unlocked it, and stepped outside. But, though she was very quiet, he must have heard her. 'Wait, Frankie!' he wailed. 'I'm coming.'

The child wailing had waked her father, and she knew it before she reached the corner of the house. The night was dark and heavy, and as she ran, she heard her father calling her. Behind the corner of the house she looked and saw the kitchen light go on; the bulb swung back and forth, making a swinging gold reflection on the arbor and the dark yard. He will read the letter now, she thought, and chase and try to capture me. But after she had run a few blocks, the suitcase bumping against her legs and sometimes nearly tripping her, she remembered that her father would have to put on pants and a shirt—for he would not chase her through the streets dressed only in pajama bottoms. She stopped for a second to look behind. No one was there. At the first street light she put down the suitcase and, taking the wallet from the front pocket of her dress, opened it with shaking hands. Inside there was three dollars and fifteen cents. She would have to hop a box car, or something.

All at once, alone there in the night-empty street, she realized she did not know how. It is easy to talk about hopping a freight train, but how did bums and people really do it? She was three blocks from the station and she walked toward it slowly. The station was closed and she went round it and stared at the platform, long and empty under the pale lights, with the Chiclet machines against the station wall and scraps of chewing-gum paper and candy wrappings on the platform. The train tracks gleamed silver and exact and some freight cars were off on a siding in the distance, but they were not hooked to any engine. The train would not come until two o'clock, and would she be able to hop a car, as she had read about, and get away? There was a red lantern a little way down the tracks, and against this colored light she saw a railroad man come walking slowly. She could not hang around like that until two o'clock—but as she left the station, one shoulder dragged down by the weight of the bag, she did not know where she should go.

The streets were lonesome and idle with Sunday night. The red-and-green neon lights in the signboards mixed with the street lights to make a pale hot haze above the town, but the sky was starless, black. A man in a tilted hat took out his cigarette and turned to stare at her as she passed by. She could not wander around the town like this, for by this time her father would be chasing her. In the alley behind Finny's Place she sat down on the suitcase, and only then she realized that the pistol was still in her left hand. She had been going around with the pistol held right in her hand, and she felt that she had lost her mind. She had said that she would shoot herself if the bride and her brother would not take her. She pointed the pistol at the side of her head and held it there a minute or two. If she squeezed down on the trigger she would be dead—and deadness was blackness, nothing but pure terrible blackness that went on and on and never ended until the end of all the world. When she lowered the pistol, she told herself that at the last minute she had changed her mind. The pistol she put in her suitcase.

The alley was black and smelled of garbage cans, and it was in this alley where Lon Baker had his throat slashed that spring afternoon so that his neck was like a bloody mouth that gibbered in the sun. It was here Lon Baker had been killed. And had she killed the soldier, when she brained his head with the water pitcher? She was scared in the dark alley and her mind felt splintered. If only there was someone with her! If only she could hunt down Honey Brown and they could go away together! But Honey had gone to Forks Falls and would not be back until tomorrow. Or if she could find the monkey and the monkey-man and join with them to run away! There was a scuttling noise, and she jerked with terror. A cat had leaped up on a garbage can, and in the darkness she could see its outline against the light at the end of the alley. She whispered: 'Charles!' and then, 'Charlina.' But it was not her Persian cat, and when she stumbled toward the can it sprang away.

She could stand the black sour alley no longer and, carrying the suitcase toward the light at the end, she stood close to the sidewalk, but still inside the shadow of a wall. If there was only somebody to tell her what to do and where to go and how to get there! The fortune of Big Mama had turned out true—about the sort of trip and a departure and a return, and even the cotton bales, for the bus had passed a truck of them on the way back from Winter Hill. And there was the sum of money in her father's wallet, so that already she had lived up all the fortune Big Mama had foreseen. Should she go down to the house in Sugarville and say that she had used up the whole future, and what was she now to do?

Beyond the shadow of the alley the gloomy street was like a street that waited, with the winking neon Coco-Cola sigh on the next corner, and a lady walking back and forth beneath a street light as though expecting someone. A car, a long closed car that maybe was a Packard, came slowly down the street, and the way it cruised close to the curb reminded her of a gangster's car, so that she shrank back closer to the wall. Then, on the opposite sidewalk, two people passed, and a feeling like a sudden flame sprang up inside her, and for less than a second it seemed that her brother and the bride had come for her and were now *there*. But the feeling blew out instantly and she was just watching a stranger couple passing down the street. There was a hollow in her chest, but at the bottom of this emptiness a heavy weight pressed down and bruised her stomach, so that she felt sick. She told herself she ought to get busy and pick up her feet and go away. But she still stood there, her eyes closed, and her head against the warm brick wall.

When she left the alley, it was a long time after midnight and she had reached the point where any sudden idea seemed a good idea. She had seized on first one notion and then another. To hitch-hike to Forks Falls and track down Honey, or to wire Evelyn Owen to meet her in Atlanta, or even to go back to the house and get John Henry, so that at least there would be somebody with her and she would not have to go into the world alone. But there was some objection to each of these ideas.

Then, all at once, from the tangle of turning impossibilities, she thought of the soldier; and this time the thought was not a glancing one—it lingered, stuck, and did not go away. She wondered if she ought to go to the Blue Moon and find if she had killed the soldier, before she left the town forever. The idea, once seized on, seemed to her good, and she started for Front Avenue. If she had not killed the soldier, then when she found him what could she say? How the next thought occurred to her she did not know, but suddenly it seemed she might as well ask the soldier to marry with her, and then the two of them could go away. Before he had gone crazy, he had been a little nice. And because it was a new and sudden idea, it also seemed reasonable. She remembered a part of the fortune she had forgotten, that she would marry a light-haired person with blue eyes, and the fact that the soldier had light red hair and blue eyes were like a proof that this was the right thing to do.

She hurried faster. The night before was like a time that had happened so long ago that the soldier was unraveled in her memory. But she recalled the silence in the hotel room; and all at once a fit in a front room, the silence, the nasty talk behind the garage—these separate recollections fell together in the darkness of her mind, as shafting searchlights meet in the night sky upon an aeroplane, so that in a flash there came in her an understanding. There was a feeling of cold surprise; she stopped a minute, then went on toward the Blue Moon. The stores were dark and closed, the pawn-shop window locked with criss-crossed steel against night robbers, and the only lights were those from the open wooden stairs of buildings and the greenish splash of brightness from the Blue Moon. There was a sound of quarreling voices from an upper story, and the footsteps of two men, far down the street, walking away. She was no longer thinking of the soldier; the discovery of the moment before had scattered him from her mind. There was only knowing that she must find somebody, anybody, that she could join with to go away. For now she admitted she was too scared to go into the world alone.

She did not leave the town that night, for the Law caught her in the Blue Moon. Officer Wylie was there when she walked in, although she did not see him until she was settled at the window table with the suitcase on the floor beside her. The juke-box sounded a sleazy blues and the Portuguese owner stood with his eyes closed, playing up and down the wooden counter in time to the sad juke tune. There were only a few people in a corner booth and the blue light gave the place a look of being undersea. She did not see the Law until he was standing beside the table, and when she looked up at him, her startled heart quivered a little and then stopped still.

'You're Royal Addams's daughter,' the Law said, and her head admitted with a nod. 'I'll phone in to headquarters to say you're found. Just stay right here.'

The Law went back to the telephone booth. He was calling the Black Maria to haul her off down to the jail, but she did not care. Very likely she had killed that soldier, and they had been following clues and hunting her all over town. Or the Law maybe had found out about the three-way knife she had stolen from the Sears and Roebuck Store. It was not plain just what she was captured for, and the crimes of the long spring and summer merged together as one guilt which she had lost the power to understand. It was as though the things that she had done, the sins committed, had all been done by someone else—a stranger a long time ago. She sat very still, her legs wrapped tight around each other, and her hands clasped in her lap. The Law was a long time at the telephone, and, staring straight ahead of her, she watched two people leave a booth and, leaning close against each other, start to dance. A soldier banged the screen door and walked through the café, and only the distant stranger in her recognized him; when he had climbed up the stairs, she only thought slowly and with no feeling that a curly red head such as that one was like cement. Then her mind went back to thoughts of jail and cold peas and cold cornbread and iron-barred cells. The Law came back from the telephone and sat down across from her and said:

'How did you happen to come in here?'

The Law was big in his blue policeman's suit and, once arrested, it was a bad policy to lie or trifle. He had a heavy face, with a squatty forehead and unmatched ears—one ear was larger than the other one, and had a torn look. When he questioned her, he did not look into her face, but at some point just above her head.

'What am I doing in here?' she repeated. For all at once she had forgotten, and she told the truth when she said finally, 'I don't know.'

The voice of the Law seemed to come from a distance like a question asked through a long corridor. 'Where were you headed for?'

The world was now so far away that Frances could no longer think of it. She did not see the earth as in the old days, cracked and loose and turning a thousand miles an hour; the earth was enormous and still and flat. Between herself and all the places there was a space like an enormous canyon she could not hope to bridge or cross. The plans for the movies or the Marines were only child plans that would never work, and she was careful when she answered. She named the littlest, ugliest place she knew, for to run away there could not be considered so very wrong.

'Flowering Branch.'

'Your father phoned headquarters you had left a letter that you were running away. We located him at the bus station and he'll be here in a minute to take you home.'

It was her father who had sicked the Law on her, and she would not be carried to the jail. In a way she was sorry. It was better to be in a jail where you could bang the walls than in a jail you could not see. The world was too far away, and there was no way any more that she could be included. She was back to the fear of the summertime, the old feelings that the world was separate from herself—and the failed wedding had quickened the fear to terror. There had been a time, only yesterday, when she felt that every person that she saw was somehow connected with herself and there was between the two of them an instant recognition. Frances watched the Portuguese who still played a mock piano on the counter to the juke-box tune. He swayed as he played and his fingers skittered up and down the counter, so that a man at the far end protected his glass with his hand. When the tune was over, the Portuguese folded his arms upon his chest; Frances narrowed and tensed her eyes to will him to look at her. He had been the first person she had told the day before about the wedding, but as he gave an owner's look around the place, his glance passed by her in a casual way and there was in those eyes no feeling of connection. She turned to the others in the room, and it was the same with all of them and they were strangers. In the blue light she felt queer as a person drowning. At last she was staring at the Law and finally he looked into her eyes. He looked at her with eyes as china as a doll's, and in them there was only the reflection of her own lost face.

The screen door slammed and the Law said: 'Here's your Daddy come to take you home.'

Frances was never once to speak about the wedding. Weathers had turned and it was in another season. There were the changes and Frances was now thirteen. She was in the kitchen with Berenice on the day before they moved, the last afternoon that Berenice would be with them; for when it had been decided that she and her father would share with Aunt Pet and Uncle Ustace a house out in the new suburb of town, Berenice had given quit notice and said that she might as well marry T. T. It was the end of an afternoon in late November, and in the east the sky was the color of a winter geranium.

Frances had come back to the kitchen, for the other rooms were hollow since the van had taken the furniture away. There were only the two beds in the downstairs bedrooms and the kitchen furniture, and they were to be moved tomorrow. It was the first time in a long while that Frances had spent an afternoon back in the kitchen, alone with Berenice. It was not the same kitchen of the summer that now seemed so long ago. The pencil pictures had disappeared beneath a coat of calcimine, and new linoleum covered the splintery floor. Even the table had been moved, pushed back against the wall, since now there was nobody to take meals with Berenice.

The kitchen, done over and almost modern, had nothing that would bring to mind John Henry West. But nevertheless there were times when Frances felt his presence there, solemn and hovering and ghost-gray. And at those times there would come a hush—a hush quivered by voiceless words. A similar hush would come, also, when Honey was mentioned or brought to mind, for Honey was out on the road now with a sentence of eight years. Now the hush came that late November afternoon as Frances was making the sandwiches, cutting them into fancy shapes and taking great pains—for Mary Littlejohn was coming at five o'clock. Frances glanced at Berenice, who was sitting idle in a chair, wearing an old raveled sweater, her limp arms hanging at her sides. In her lap there was the thin little pinched fox fur that Ludie had given her many years ago. The fur was sticky and the sharp little face foxwise and sad. The fire from the red stove brushed the room with flickers of light and changing shadows.

'I am just mad about Michelangelo,' she said.

Mary was coming at five o'clock to take dinner, spend the night, and ride in the van to the new house tomorrow. Mary collected pictures of great masters and pasted them in an art book. They read poets like Tennyson together; and Mary was going to be a great painter and Frances a great poet—or else the foremost authority on radar. Mr. Littlejohn had been connected with a tractor company and before the war the Littlejohns had lived abroad. When Frances was sixteen and Mary eighteen, they were going around the world together. Frances placed the sandwiches on a plate, along with eight chocolates and some salted nuts; this was to be a midnight feast, to be eaten in the bed at twelve o'clock.

'I told you we're going to travel around the world together.'

'Mary Littlejohn,' said Berenice, in a tinged voice. 'Mary Littlejohn.'

Berenice could not appreciate Michelangelo or poetry, let alone Mary Littlejohn. There had at first been words between them on the subject. Berenice had spoken of Mary as being lumpy and marshmallow-white, and Frances had defended fiercely. Mary had long braids that she could very nearly sit on, braids of a woven mixture of corn-yellow and brown, fastened at the ends with rubber bands and, on occasions, ribbons. She had brown eyes with yellow eyelashes, and her dimpled hands tapered at the fingers to little pink blobs of flesh, as Mary bit her nails. The Littlejohns were Catholics, and even on this

point Berenice was all of a sudden narrow-minded, saying that
Roman Catholics worshiped Graven Images and wanted the
Pope to rule the world. But for Frances this difference was
a final touch of strangeness, silent terror, that completed the
wonder of her love.

'There's no use our discussing a certain party. You could
not possibly ever understand her. It's just not in you.' She had
said that once before to Berenice, and from the sudden faded
stillness in her eye she knew that the words had hurt. And
now she repeated them, angered because of the tinged way
Berenice had said the name, but once the words were spoken
she was sorry. 'Anyhow, I consider it the greatest honor of
my existence that Mary has picked me out to be her one most
intimate friend. Me! Of all people!'

'Have I ever said anything against her?' said Berenice. 'All
I said was it makes me nervous to watch her just sitting there
sucking them pigtails.'

'Braids!'

A flock of strong-winged arrowed geese flew over the yard,
and Frances went to the window. There had been frost
that morning, silvering the brown grass and the roofs of
neighbors' houses, and even the thinned leaves of the rusty
arbor. When she turned back to the kitchen, the hush was in
the room again. Berenice sat hunched with her elbow on her
knee, and her forehead resting in her hand, staring with one
mottled eye at the coal scuttle.

The changes had come about at the same time, during
the middle of October. Frances had met Mary at a raffle
two weeks before. It was the time when countless white and
yellow butterflies danced among the last fall flowers; the time,
too, of the Fair. First, it was Honey. Made crazy one night by
a marihuana cigarette, by something called smoke or snow,
he broke into the drugstore of the white man who had been
selling them to him, desperate for more. He was locked in
the jail, awaiting trial, and Berenice rushed back and forth,
canvassing money, seeing a lawyer, and trying to get admission
to the jail. She came in on the third day, worn out, and with
the red curdled glare already in the eye. A headache, she said
she had, and John Henry West put his head down on the table
and said he had a headache, also. But nobody paid any mind

to him, thinking he copied Berenice. 'Run along,' she said, 'for I don't have the patience to fool with you.' Those were the last words spoken to him in the kitchen, and later Berenice recalled them as judgment on her from the Lord. John Henry had meningitis and after ten days he was dead. Until it was all over, Frances had never believed for a serious minute that he could die. It was the time of golden weather and Shasta daisies and the butterflies. The air was chilled, and day after day the sky was a clear green-blue, but filled with light, the color of a shallow wave.

Frances was never allowed to visit John Henry, but Berenice helped the trained nurse every day. She would come in toward dark, and the things that she said in her cracked voice seemed to make John Henry West unreal. 'I don't see why he has to suffer so,' Berenice would say: and the word *suffer* was one she could not associate with John Henry, a word she shrank from as before an unknown hollow darkness of the heart.

It was the time of the Fair and a big banner arched the main street and for six days and nights the Fair went on down at the fairground. Frances went twice, both times with Mary, and they rode on nearly everything, but did not enter the Freak Pavilion, as Mrs. Littlejohn said it was morbid to gaze at Freaks. Frances bought John Henry a walking stick and sent him the rug she had won at Lotto. But Berenice remarked that he was beyond all this, and the words were eerie and unreal. As the bright days followed one upon the other, the words of Berenice became so terrible that she would listen in a spell of horror, but a part of her could not believe. John Henry had been screaming for three days and his eyeballs were walled up in a corner, stuck and blind. He lay there finally with his head drawn back in a buckled way, and he had lost the strength to scream. He died the Tuesday after the Fair was gone, a golden morning of the most butterflies, the clearest sky.

Meanwhile Berenice had got a lawyer and had seen Honey at the jail. 'I don't know what I've done,' she kept saying. 'Honey in this fix and now John Henry.' Still, there was some part of Frances that did not even yet believe. But on the day he was to be taken to the family graveyard in Opelika, the same place where they had buried Uncle Charles, she saw the coffin, and then she knew. He came to her once or twice in nightmare dreams, like an escaped child dummy from the window of a department store, the wax legs moving stiffly only at joints, and the wax face wizened and faintly painted, coming toward her until terror snatched her awake. But the dreams came only once or twice, and the daytime now was filled with radar, school, and Mary Littlejohn. She remembered John Henry more as he used to be, and it was seldom now that she felt his presence—solemn, hovering, and ghost-gray. Only occasionally at twilight time or when the special hush would come into the room.

'I was by the store about school and Papa had a letter from Jarvis. He is in Luxembourg,' said Frances. 'Luxembourg. Don't you think that's a lovely name?'

Berenice roused herself. 'Well, Baby—it brings to my mind soapy water. But it's a kind of pretty name.'

'There is a basement in the new house. And a laundry room.' She added, after a minute, 'We will most likely pass through Luxembourg when we go around the world together.'

Frances turned back to the window. It was almost five o'clock and the geranium glow had faded from the sky. The last pale colors were crushed and cold on the horizon. Dark, when it came, would come on quickly, as it does in winter-time. 'I am simply mad about——' But the sentence was left unfinished for the hush was shattered when, with an instant shock of happiness, she heard the ringing of the bell.